REPUBLIC COMMANDO™

By Karen Traviss

CITY OF PEARL
CROSSING THE LINE
THE WORLD BEFORE

Star Wars: Republic Commando: Hard Contact
Star Wars: Republic Commando: Triple Zero

REPUBLIC COMMANDO™

HARD CONTACT
TRIPLE ZERO

KAREN TRAVISS

This is a work of fiction. Names, places, and incidents either are products of the authors' imagination or are used fictitiously.

Printing History: LucasBooks/Del Rey paperback, November 2004.

Printing History: LucasBooks/Del Rey paperback, March 2006.

First SFBC Science Fiction printing: May 2006.

Published by arrangement with:
The Random House Publishing Group
A division of Random House, Inc.
1745 Broadway
New York, NY 10019

Visit The SFBC at http://www.sfbc.com
Visit Del Rey at http://www.randomhouse.com/delrey/
Visit the official Star Wars website at http://www.starwars.com

ISBN-10: 0-7394-6686-0
ISBN-13: 978-0-7394-6686-5

Printed in the United States of America.

CONTENTS

Star Wars Novels Timeline . . . vi

HARD CONTACT . . . 1

TRIPLE ZERO . . . 243

"Omega Squad: Targets" . . . 583

Glossary . . . 605

THE STAR WARS NOVELS TIMELINE

33 YEARS BEFORE *STAR WARS: A New Hope*

Darth Maul: Saboteur*

32.5 *YEARS BEFORE STAR WARS: A New Hope*

Cloak of Deception
Darth Maul: Shadow Hunter

32 *YEARS BEFORE STAR WARS: A New Hope*

***STAR WARS:* EPISODE I**
THE PHANTOM MENACE

29 *YEARS BEFORE STAR WARS: A New Hope*

Rogue Planet

27 *YEARS BEFORE STAR WARS: A New Hope*

Outbound Flight

22.5 *YEARS BEFORE STAR WARS: A New Hope*

The Approaching Storm

22 *YEARS BEFORE STAR WARS: A New Hope*

***STAR WARS:* EPISODE II**
ATTACK OF THE CLONES

Republic Commando: Hard Contact

21.5 *YEARS BEFORE STAR WARS: A New Hope*

Shatterpoint

21 *YEARS BEFORE STAR WARS: A New Hope*

The Cestus Deception
The Hive*

Republic Commando: Triple Zero

20 *YEARS BEFORE STAR WARS: A New Hope*

MedStar I: Battle Surgeons
MedStar II: Jedi Healer

19.5 *YEARS BEFORE STAR WARS: A New Hope*

Jedi Trial
Yoda: Dark Rendezvous

19 *YEARS BEFORE STAR WARS: A New Hope*

Labyrinth of Evil

***STAR WARS:* EPISODE III**
REVENGE OF THE SITH

Dark Lord: The Rise of Darth Vader

10-0 *YEARS BEFORE STAR WARS: A New Hope*

The Han Solo Trilogy:
The Paradise Snare
The Hutt Gambit
Rebel Dawn

5-2 *YEARS BEFORE STAR WARS: A New Hope*

The Adventures of Lando Calrissian

The Han Solo Adventures

STAR WARS: A New Hope YEAR 0

***STAR WARS:* EPISODE IV**
A NEW HOPE

0-3 *YEARS AFTER STAR WARS: A New Hope*

Tales from the Mos Eisley Cantina
Galaxies: The Ruins of Dantooine
Splinter of the Mind's Eye

3 *YEARS AFTER STAR WARS: A New Hope*

***STAR WARS:* EPISODE V**
THE EMPIRE STRIKES BACK

Tales of the Bounty Hunters

3.5 *YEARS AFTER STAR WARS: A New Hope*

Shadows of the Empire

4 *YEARS AFTER STAR WARS: A New Hope*

***STAR WARS:* EPISODE VI**
RETURN OF THE JEDI

Tales from Jabba's Palace
Tales from the Empire
Tales from the New Republic

The Bounty Hunter Wars:
The Mandalorian Armor
Slave Ship
Hard Merchandise

The Truce at Bakura

*An ebook novella

6.5-7.5 YEARS AFTER *STAR WARS: A New Hope*

X-Wing:

Rogue Squadron
Wedge's Gamble
The Krytos Trap
The Bacta War
Wraith Squadron
Iron Fist
Solo Command

8 *YEARS AFTER STAR WARS: A New Hope*

The Courtship of Princess Leia
A Forest Apart*
Tatooine Ghost

9 *YEARS AFTER STAR WARS: A New Hope*

The Thrawn Trilogy:

Heir to the Empire
Dark Force Rising
The Last Command

X-Wing: Isard's Revenge

11 *YEARS AFTER STAR WARS: A New Hope*

The Jedi Academy Trilogy:

Jedi Search
Dark Apprentice
Champions of the Force

I, Jedi

12-13 *YEARS AFTER STAR WARS: A New Hope*

Children of the Jedi
Darksaber
Planet of Twilight
X-Wing: Starfighters of Adumar

14 *YEARS AFTER STAR WARS: A New Hope*

The Crystal Star

16-17 *YEARS AFTER STAR WARS: A New Hope*

The Black Fleet Crisis Trilogy:

Before the Storm
Shield of Lies
Tyrant's Test

17 *YEARS AFTER STAR WARS: A New Hope*

The New Rebellion

18 *YEARS AFTER STAR WARS: A New Hope*

The Corellian Trilogy:

Ambush at Corellia
Assault at Selonia
Showdown at Centerpoint

19 *YEARS AFTER STAR WARS: A New Hope*

The Hand of Thrawn Duology:

Specter of the Past
Vision of the Future

22 *YEARS AFTER STAR WARS: A New Hope*

Fool's Bargain*
Survivor's Quest

25 YEARS AFTER *STAR WARS: A New Hope*

The New Jedi Order:

Vector Prime
Dark Tide I: Onslaught
Dark Tide II: Ruin
Agents of Chaos I: Hero's Trial
Agents of Chaos II: Jedi Eclipse
Balance Point
Recovery*
Edge of Victory I: Conquest
Edge of Victory II: Rebirth
Star by Star
Dark Journey
Enemy Lines I: Rebel Dream
Enemy Lines II: Rebel Stand
Traitor
Destiny's Way
Ylesia*
Force Heretic I: Remnant
Force Heretic II: Refugee
Force Heretic III: Reunion
The Final Prophecy
The Unifying Force

35 *YEARS AFTER STAR WARS: A New Hope*

The Dark Nest Trilogy:

The Joiner King
The Unseen Queen
The Swarm War

40 YEARS AFTER *STAR WARS: A New Hope*

Legacy of the Force:

Betrayal
Bloodlines
Tempest

STAR WARS®
REPUBLIC COMMANDO
HARD CONTACT

ACKNOWLEDGEMENTS

Long ago, in a cinema far away, a film critic watched and reviewed a brand-new movie called *Star Wars.* If she'd known she was going to end up writing this book, she'd have taken more notes . . . so my thanks go to editors Shelly Shapiro (Del Rey), Keith Clayton (Del Rey), and Sue Rostoni (Lucasfilm) for their wise advice; to the many *Star Wars* fans who made me welcome in their world; and especially to Ryan Kaufman at LucasArts—*Star Wars* oracle, polymath, wit, and all-around good bloke, who gave generously of his time and knowledge, and never ran out of patience when I asked for the umpteenth time, "Yes, but does the armor have to be white?" It was the best of times, folks. Thanks.

PROLOGUE

Okay, this is how it happened.

It's pitch black below and we're fast-roping into the crevasse, *too* fast: I can feel the impact in my back teeth when I land. I'm first down and I flood the chamber with my helmet spot-lamp.

There's a triple-sealed blast door between us and the Geonosians and I haven't got time to calculate the charge needed to blow it. A lot, then. *P for plenty,* like I was taught. Stick the thermal tape around the edges and push in the detonator. Easier said than done: the alloy door's covered with crud.

Delta Squad's CO gets on the helmet comlink. "You having a party down there, Theta?"

"Can't rush an artist . . ."

"You want to tell that to the spider droids?"

"Patience, Delta." *Come on, come on. Stick to the metal, will you?* "Nearly there."

"A *lot* of spider droids . . ."

"I hear you, Delta."

"In your own time. No pressure. None at all . . ."

"Clear!"

We flatten ourselves against the cavern walls. It's all white light and painful noise and flying dust for a fraction of a second. When we can see again, the doors are blown inward, ripped apart, billowing smoke. "Delta Squad—clear to enter. *Take take take.*"

"I thought you'd never ask." Delta Squad hits the ground and they're straight in, firing, while we stand back and cover their six. It's a warren of tunnels down here. If we're not careful, something could jump us from any direction.

My helmet's supposed to protect against high decibels, but war is noisy. *Really* noisy. I can't hear my helmet comlink through the *omph-omph-omph* of the Geonosians' sonic rounds and our own blasterfire. I can hear anti-armor going off, too. *Fierfek,* I can feel it through my boots.

Movement catches my eye up ahead, and then it's gone. I'm looking up through the DC-17's scope, checking that it was just my imagination, and Taler gestures toward another of the five tunnels facing us.

"Darman, take that E-Web and hold this position." He beckons Vin and Jay and they move almost back-to-back toward the mouth of the tunnel, checking to all sides.

And then I look up, overhead.

There's more Geonosians around than we thought. A *lot* more. I take down two above me and then more come out of the tunnel to the left so I open fire with the repeating blaster, nice and early, because if I let them get too close the blast will fry me as well.

Even so, it's knocking me back like a trip-hammer.

"Taler, Darman here, over." I can't see him. I can't see any of them, but I can hear rapid fire. "Taler, Darman here, you receiving me, over?"

Not so much silence as an absence of a familiar voice. Then a few fragmented, crackling shouts of ". . . down! Man down here!"

Who? Who's down? "Taler? Vin? Jay? You receiving, over?"

I've lost contact with my squad.

It's the last time I see them.

1

SCRAMBLE LINE ENCRYPTED

STAND BY STAND BY

GEONOSIS FORWARD CONTROL TO FLEET SUPPORT, ORD MANTELL.

PREPARE TO RECEIVE CASEVAC TRANSPORT. MED TRIAGE TEAM ESTIMATE SERIOUS INJURIES, TWELVE THOUSAND, REPEAT TWELVE THOUSAND. WALKING WOUNDED EIGHT THOUSAND, REPEAT EIGHT THOUSAND. ETA TEN HOURS. LOGISTICS PRIORITY FOR BACTA TANK SUPPORT TEAMS.

PREP FOR SEVENTY-TWO THOUSAND COMBAT-FIT TROOPS, REPEAT SEVENTY-TWO THOUSAND, PENDING REDEPLOYMENT. PRIORITY WEAPONS SUPPORT FOR COMMANDO UNITS.

THAT IS ALL. OUT.

Republic assault ship *Implacable:* inbound for extraction from Geonosis. Stand by.

Republic Commando 1136 studied every face in line waiting to board the gunships.

Some were helmeted, and some were not, but—one way or another—they all had his face. And they were all strangers.

"Move it," the loadmaster shouted, gesturing side-to-side with one outstretched arm. "Come on, shift it, people—fast as you can." The gunships dropped down in clouds of dust and troopers embarked, some turning to pull comrades inboard so the ships could lift again quickly. There was no reason to scramble for it. They'd done it a thousand times in training; extraction from a real battle was what they'd prepared for. This wasn't a retreat. They'd grabbed their first victory.

The gunships' downdraft kicked the red Geonosian soil into the air. RC-1136—Darman—took off his helmet and ran his gauntlet carefully across the pale gray dome, wiping away the dust and noting a few scrapes and burn marks.

The loadmaster turned to him. He was one of the very, very few outsiders whom Darman had ever seen working with the Grand Army, a short, wrinkled Duros with a temper to match. "Are you embarking or what?"

Darman continued wiping his helmet. "I'm waiting for my mates," he said.

"You shift your shiny silver backside *now,*" the loadmaster said irritably. "I got a schedule."

Darman carefully brought up his knuckle plate just under the loadmasters's chin, and held it there. He didn't need to eject the vibroblade and he didn't need to say a word. He'd made his point.

"Well, whenever you're ready, sir," the Duros said, stepping back to chivy clone troopers instead. It wasn't a great idea to upset a commando, especially not one coming down from the adrenaline high of combat.

But there was still no sign of the rest of his squad. Darman knew that there was no point in waiting any longer. They hadn't called in. Maybe they had comlink failures. Maybe they had made it onto another gunship.

It was the first time in his artificially short life that Darman hadn't been able to reach out and touch the men he had been raised with.

He waited half a standard hour more anyway, until the gunships became less frequent and the lines of troopers became shorter. Eventually there was nobody standing on the desert plain but him, the Duros loadmaster, and half a dozen clone troopers. It was the last lift of the day.

"You better come now, sir," the loadmaster said. "There's nobody unaccounted for. Nobody alive, anyway."

Darman looked around the horizon one last time, still feeling as if he were turning his back on someone reaching out to him.

"I'm coming," he said, and brought up the rear of the line. As the gunship lifted, he watched the swirling dust, dwindling rock formations, and scattered shrinking patches of scrub until Geonosis became a blur of dull red.

He could still search the *Implacable.* It wasn't over yet.

The gunship slipped into the *Implacable*'s giant docking bay, and Darman looked down into the cavern, onto a sea of white armor and orderly movement. The first thing that struck him when the gunship killed its thrusters and locked down on its pad was how *quiet* everyone seemed.

In the crowded bay full of troopers, the air stank of sweat and stale fear and the throat-rasping smell of discharged blaster rifles. But it was so silent that if Darman hadn't seen the evidence of exhausted and injured men, he'd have believed that nothing significant had happened in the last thirty hours.

The deck vibrated under the soles of his boots. He was still staring down at them, studying the random patterns of Geonosian dust that clung to them, when an identical pair came into view.

"Number?" said a voice that was also his own. The commander swept him with a tally sensor: he didn't need Darman to tell him his number, or anything else for that matter, because the sensors in the enhanced Katarn armor reported his status silently, electronically. *No significant injury.* The triage team on Geonosis had waved him past, concentrating on the injured, ignoring both those too badly hurt to help and those who could help themselves. "Are you listening to me? Come on. Talk to me, son."

"I'm okay, sir," he said. "Sir, RC-one-one-three-six. I'm not in shock. I'm fine." He paused. Nobody else was going to call him by his squad nickname—*Darman*—again. They were all dead, he knew it. Jay, Vin, Taler. *He just knew.* "Sir, any news of RC-one-one-three-five—"

"No," said the commander, who had obviously heard similar questions every time he stopped to check. He gestured with the small bar in his hand. "If they're not in casevac or listed on this sweep, then they didn't make it."

It was stupid to ask. Darman should have known better. Clone troopers—and especially Republic commandos—just got on with the job. That was their sole purpose. And they were *lucky,* their training sergeant had told them; outside, in the ordinary world, every being from every species in the galaxy fretted about their purpose in life, searching for meaning. A clone didn't need to. Clones *knew.* They had been perfected for their role, and doubt need never trouble them.

Darman had never known what doubt was until now. No amount of training had prepared him for *this.* He found a space against a bulkhead and sat down.

A clone trooper settled down next to him, squeezing into the gap and briefly clunking a shoulder plate against his. They glanced at each other. Darman rarely had any contact with the other clones: commandos trained apart from everyone, including ARC troopers.

The trooper's armor was white, lighter, less resistant; commandos enjoyed upgraded protection. And Darman displayed no rank colors.

But they both knew exactly who and what they were.

"Nice Deece," the trooper said enviously. He was looking at the DC-17: troopers were issued the heavier, lower-spec rifle, the DC-15. "Ion pulse blaster, RPG anti-armor, *and* sniper?"

"Yeah." Every item of his kit was manufactured to a higher spec. A trooper's life was less valuable than a commando's. It was the way things were, and Darman had never questioned it—not for long, anyway. "Full house."

"Tidy." The trooper nodded approval. "Job done, eh?"

"Yeah," Darman said quietly. "Job done."

The trooper didn't say anything else. Maybe he was wary of conversation with commandos. Darman knew what troopers thought about him and his kind. *They don't train like us and they don't fight like us. They don't even talk like us.* A bunch of prima donnas.

Darman didn't think he was arrogant. It was just that he could do every job a soldier could be called upon to do, and then some: siege assault, counterinsurgency, hostage extraction, demolitions, assassination, surveillance, and every kind of infantry activity on any terrain and in any environment, at any time. He *knew* he could, because he'd *done* it. He'd done it in training, first with simunition and then with live rounds. He'd done it with his squad, the three brothers with whom he'd spent every moment of his conscious life. They'd competed against other squads, thousands just like them, but not like them, because they were squad brothers, and that was *special.*

He had never been taught how to live apart from the squad, though. Now he would learn the hardest way of all.

Darman had absolute confidence that he was one of the best special ops soldiers ever created. He was undistracted by the everyday concerns of raising a family and making a living, things that his instructors said he was lucky never to know.

But now he was alone. Very, very alone. It was very distracting indeed.

He considered this for a long time in silence. Surviving when the rest of your squad had been killed was no cause for pride. It felt instead like something his training sergeant had described as *shame.* That was what you felt when you lost a battle, apparently.

But they had won. It was their first battle, and they had *won.*

The landing ramp of the *Implacable* eased down, and the bright sunlight of Ord Mantell streamed in. Darman replaced his helmet without thinking and stood in an orderly line, waiting to disembark and be reassigned. He was going to be chilled down, kept in suspended animation until duty called again.

So this was the aftermath of victory. He wondered how much worse defeat might feel.

Imbraani, Qiilura: 40 light-years from Ord Mantell, Tingel Arm

The field of barq flowed from silver to ruby as the wind from the southwest bent the ripening grain in waves. It could have been a perfect late-summer day; instead it was turning into one of the worst days of Etain Tur-Mukan's life.

Etain had run and run and she had nothing left in her. She flung herself flat between the furrows, not caring where she fell. Etain held her breath as something stinking and wet squelched under her.

The pursuing Weequay couldn't hear her above the wind, she knew, but she held her breath anyway.

"Hey girlie!" His boots crunched closer. He was panting. "Where you go? Don't be shy."

Don't breathe.

"I got bottle of urrqal. You want to have party?" He had a remarkably large vocabulary for a Weequay, all of it centered on his baser needs. "I *fun* when you get to know me."

I should have waited for it to get dark. I could influence his mind, try to make him leave.

But she hadn't. And she couldn't, try as she might to concentrate. She was too full of adrenaline and uncontrolled panic.

"Come on, you scrag-end, where are you? I find you . . ."

He sounded as if he was kicking his way through the crop, and getting closer. If she got up and ran for it, she was dead. If she stayed where she was, he'd find her—eventually. He wasn't going to get bored, and he wasn't going to give up.

"Girlie . . ."

The Weequay's voice was close, to her right, about twenty meters away. She sipped a strangled breath and clamped her lips shut again, lungs aching, eyes streaming with the effort.

"Girlie . . ." Closer. He was going to step right on her. "Girleeeeee . . ."

She knew what he'd do when he found her. If she was lucky, he'd kill her afterward.

"Gir—"

The Weequay was interrupted by a loud, wet *thwack.* He let out a grunt and then there was a second *thwack*—shorter, sharper, harder. Etain heard a squeal of pain.

"How many times have I got to tell you, *di'kut*?" It was a different voice, human, with an hard edge of authority. *Thwack.* "Don't—waste—my—time." Another *thwack:* another squeal. Etain kept her face pressed in the dirt. "You get drunk *one* more time, you go chasing females *one* more time, and I'm going to slit you from here to—*here.*"

The Weequay shrieked. It was the sort of incoherent animal sound that beings made when pain overwhelmed them. Etain had heard too much of that sound in her short time on Qiilura. Then there was silence.

She hadn't heard the voice before, but she didn't need to. She knew exactly who it belonged to.

Etain strained to listen, half expecting a heavy boot to suddenly stamp on her back, but all she could hear was the swish and crunch of two pairs of feet wading through the crop. Away from her. She caught snatches of the fading conversation as the wind took it: the Weequay was still being berated.

". . . more important . . ."

What was?

". . . later, but right now, *di'kut,* I need you to . . . okay? Or I'll cut . . ."

Etain waited. Eventually all she could hear was the breath of the wind, the rustling grain, and the occasional fluting call of a ground-eel seeking a mate. She allowed herself to breathe normally again, but still she waited, facedown in ripe manure, until dusk started to fall. She had to move *now.* The gdans would be out hunting, combing the fields in packs. On top of that, the smell that hadn't bothered her while she was gripped by terror was starting to really bother her now.

She eased herself up on her elbows, then her knees, and looked around.

Why did they have to manure barq so late in the season anyway? She fumbled in the pockets of her cloak for a cloth. Now if only she could find a stream, she could clean herself up. She pulled a handful of stalks, crushed them into a ball, and tried to scrape off the worst of the dung and debris stuck to her.

"That's a pretty expensive crop to be using for *that,*" a voice said.

Etain gulped in a breath and spun around to find a local in a grubby smock scowling at her. He looked thin, worn out, and annoyed; he was holding a threshing tool. "Do you know how much that stuff's worth?"

"I'm sorry," she said. Sliding her hand carefully inside her cloak, she felt for the familiar cylinder. She hadn't wanted the Weequay to know that she was a Jedi, but if this farmer was considering turning her in for a few loaves or a bottle of urrqal, she'd need her lightsaber handy. "It was your barq or my life, I'm afraid."

The farmer stared at the crushed stalks and the scattered bead-like grains, tight-lipped. Yes, barq fetched a huge price in the restaurants of Coruscant: it was a luxury, and the people who grew it for export couldn't afford it. That didn't seem to bother the Neimoidians who controlled the trade. It never did.

"I'll pay for the damage," Etain said, her hand still inside the cloak.

"What were they after you for?" the farmer asked, ignoring her offer.

"The usual," she said.

"Oh-ah, you're not that good looking."

"Charming."

"I know who you are."

Oh no. Her grip closed. "You do?"

"I reckon."

A little more food for his family. A few hours' drunken oblivion, courtesy of urrqal. That was all she was to him. He made as if to step closer and she drew her arm clear of her cloak, because she was fed up with running and she didn't like the look of that threshing tool.

Vzzzzzmmmm.

"Oh, great," the farmer sighed, eyeing the shaft of pure blue light. "Not one of you lot. That's all we need."

"Yes," she said, and held the lightsaber steady in front of her face. Her stomach had knotted, but she kept her voice under control. "I am Padawan Etain Tur-Mukan. You can try to turn me in, if you want to test my skill, but I'd prefer that you help me instead. Your call, sir."

The farmer stared at the lightsaber as if he was trying to work out a price for it. "Didn't help your Master much, that thing, did it?"

"Master Fulier was unfortunate. *And* betrayed." She lowered the lightsaber but didn't cut the beam. "Are you going to help me?"

"We're going to have Ghez Hokan's thugs all over us if I—"

"I think they're busy," Etain said.

"What do you want from us?"

"Shelter, for the moment."

The farmer sucked his teeth thoughtfully. "Okay. Come on, Padawan—"

"Get used to calling me Etain, please." She thumbed off the lightsaber: the light died with a *ffumm* sound, and she slipped the hilt back inside her cloak. "Just to be on the safe side."

Etain trailed after him, trying not to smell herself, but it was hard, nauseatingly hard. Even a scent-hunting gdan wouldn't recognize her as a human. It was getting dark now, and the farmer kept glancing over his shoulder at her.

"Oh-ah." He shook his head, engaged in some internal conversation. "I'm Birhan, and this is my land. And I thought you lot were supposed to be able to use some sort of mind control tricks."

"How do you know I haven't?" Etain lied.

"Oh-ah," he said, and nothing more.

She wasn't going to volunteer the obvious if he hadn't spotted it for himself. A disappointment to her Master, she was clearly not the best of the bunch. She struggled with the Force and she grappled with self-discipline, and she was here because she and Master Fulier happened to be nearby when a job needed doing. Fulier never could resist a challenge and long odds, and it looked as if he'd paid the price. They hadn't found his body yet, but there had been no word from him, either.

Yes, Etain was a Padawan, technically speaking.

She just happened to be one who was a breath away from building permadomes in refugee camps. She reasoned that part of a Jedi's skill was the simple use of psychology. And if Birhan wanted to think the Force was strong in her, and that there was a lot more behind the external shell of a gawky, plain girl covered in stinking dung, then that was fine by her.

It would keep her alive a little longer while she worked out what to do next.

Fleet Support, Ord Mantell, barrack block 5 Epsilon

It was a waste, a rotten waste.

RC-1309 busied himself maintaining his boots. He cleaned out the clamps, blowing the red dust clear with a squirt of air from the pressure gun. He rinsed the liners and shook them dry. There was no point being idle while he was waiting to be chilled down.

"Sergeant?"

He looked up. The commando who had walked in placed his survival pack, armor, and black bodysuit on the bunk opposite and stared back. His readout panel identified him as RC-8015.

"I'm Fi," he said, and held out his hand for shaking. "So you lost your squad, too."

"Niner," RC-1309 said without taking the proffered hand. "So, *ner vod*—my brother—you're the sole survivor?"

"Yes."

"Did you hold back while your brothers pressed on? Or were you just lucky?"

Fi stood there with his hands on his hips, identical to Niner in every way except that he was . . . *different.* He spoke a little differently. He smelled subtly different. He moved his hands . . . not like Niner's squad did, not at all.

"I did my job," Fi said carefully. "And I'd rather be with them than here . . . *ner vod.*"

Niner considered him for a while, and went back to cleaning his boots. Fi put his kit in the locker beside the bunks, then swung himself up into the top rack in one smooth motion. He folded his arms under his head very precisely and lay staring up at the bulkhead as if he were meditating.

If he had been Sev, Niner would have known exactly what he was doing, even without looking. But Sev was gone.

Clone troopers lost brothers in training. So did commandos. But troopers were socialized with whole sections, platoons, companies, even regiments, and that meant that even after the inevitable deaths and removals during live exercises, there were still plenty of people around you whom you knew well. Commandos worked solely with each other.

Niner had lost everyone he had grown up with, and so had Fi.

He'd lost a brother before—Two-Eight—on exercise. The three survivors had welcomed the replacement, although they had always felt he was slightly *different*—a little distant—as if he had never quite believed he'd been accepted.

But they performed to expected levels of excellence together—and as long as they did, their Kaminoan technicians and motley band of alien instructors didn't seem to care how they felt about it.

But the commandos cared. They just kept it to themselves.

"It was a waste," Niner said.

"What was?" Fi said.

"Deploying us in an operation like Geonosis. It was an infantry job. Not special ops."

"That sounds like criticism of—"

"I'm just making the point that we couldn't perform to maximum effectiveness."

"Understood. Maybe when we're revived we'll be able to do what we're really trained for."

Niner wanted to say that he missed his squad, but that wasn't something to confide in a stranger. He inspected his boots and was satisfied. Then he stood up and spread his bodysuit flat on the mattress and checked it for vacuum integrity with the sweep-sensor in his glove. It was a ritual so ingrained in him that he hardly thought about it: maintain boots, suit, and armor plates, recalibrate helmet systems, check heads-up display, strip down and reassemble DC-17, empty and repack survival pack. *Done.* It took him twenty-six minutes and twenty seconds, give or take two seconds. Well-maintained kit was often the difference between life and death. So was two seconds.

He closed the top of his pack with a *clack* and secured the seal. Then he checked the catches that held the separate ordnance pack to see that they were moving freely. That mattered when he needed to jettison explosive materials fast. When he glanced up, Fi was propped on one elbow, looking down at him from the bunk.

"Dry rations go on the *fifth* layer," he said.

Niner always packed them farther down, between his spare rappelling line and his hygiene kit. "In *your* squad, maybe," he said, and carried on.

Fi took the hint and rolled over on his back again, no doubt to meditate on how differently things might be done in the future.

After a while he started singing very quietly, almost under his breath: *Kom'rk tsad droten troch nyn ures adenn, Dha Werda Verda a'den tratu.* They were the wrath of the warrior's shadow and the gauntlet of the Republic; Niner knew the song. It was a traditional Mandalorian war chant, designed to boost the morale of normal men who needed a bit of psyching up before a fight. The words had been altered a little to have meaning for the armies of clone warriors.

We don't need all that, Niner thought. *We were born to fight, nothing else.*

But he found himself joining in anyway. It was a comfort. He placed his kit in the locker, rolled onto his bunk, and matched note and beat perfectly with Fi, two identical voices in the deserted barrack room.

Niner would have traded every remaining moment of his life for a chance to rerun the previous day's engagement. He would have held Sev and DD back; he would have sent O-Four west with the E-Web cannon.

But he hadn't.

Gra'tua cuun hett su dralshy'a. Our vengeance burns brighter still.

Fi's voice trailed off into silence the merest fraction of a section before Niner's. He heard him swallow hard.

"I was up there with them, Sarge," he said quietly. "I didn't hang back. Not at all."

Niner closed his eyes. He regretted hinting that Fi might have done anything less.

"I know, brother," he said. "I know."

2

Clone personnel have free will, even if they do follow orders. If they couldn't think for themselves, we'd be better off with droids—and they're a lot cheaper, too. They have to be able to respond to situations we can't imagine. Will that change them in ways we can't predict? Perhaps. But they have to be mentally equipped to win wars. Now thaw those men out. They have a job to do.

—Jedi Master Arligan Zey, intelligence officer

Secure briefing room, Fleet Support, Ord Mantell, three standard months after Geonosis

Fleet Support Base hadn't been built to accommodate tens of thousands of troops, and it showed. The briefing room was a cold store, and it still smelled of food and spices. Darman could see the loading rails that spanned the ceiling, but he kept his focus on the holoscreen in front of him.

It didn't feel so bad to be revived after stasis. He was still a commando. They hadn't reconditioned him. That meant—that meant he'd performed to expected standards at Geonosis. *He'd done well.* He felt positive.

But his helmet felt different. There was a lot more data on the HUD, the heads-up display. He flicked between modes for a while, controlling each command with rapid blinks, noting the extra systems and hardware that had been installed since Geonosis.

Sitting to his left was his new sergeant, who preferred to be called Niner when superior officers weren't around, and RC-8015, nicknamed Fi. They, too, were the sole survivors of their squads. At least they knew what he was going through.

There was a fourth makeshift seat in the row—a blue alloy packing crate—and it was unoccupied. Jedi Master Arligan Zey, hands clasped behind his back, paced up and down in front of the screen, cloak flapping, breaking the holoprojection each time. Another Jedi, who had not been identified, was splitting his attention between Zey and the three helmeted commandos sitting absolutely still on the row of crates.

The reflective surfaces of the spray-clean alloy walls enabled Darman to discreetly observe an unusual alien—one he had never seen before. He had been trained to take in every detail of his surroundings, although it was very difficult not to notice the creature.

The alien was about a meter and a half long, and it was slinking around the walls, sniffing. Black-furred and glossy, it prowled on long delicate legs, thrusting a narrow muzzle into crevices and exhaling sharply each time it did. Earlier, Darman had heard Zey address it as Valaqil: he also said it was a Gurlanin, a shapeshifter.

Darman had heard about shapeshifters in training, but this wasn't a Clawdite. He was watching its reflection in his right-field peripheral vision when the door swung open and another commando entered, helmet tucked rigidly under his right arm, and saluted smartly.

"RC-three-two-two-two, sir," he said. "Apologies for keeping you, sir. The medics didn't want to discharge me."

No wonder: there was a stripe of raw flesh across his face that started just under his right eye, ran clean across his mouth, and finally ended at the left side of his jaw. He certainly didn't look like any of the other clones now. Darman wondered what level of persuasion it had taken to get the medical staff to skip a course of bacta.

"Are you fit, soldier?" Zey said.

"Fit to fight, sir." He sat down next to Darman and assumed the same ramrod posture, glancing at him briefly in acknowledgment. So this was their fourth man. They were a squad again—numerically, anyway. *Omega Squad.*

The other Jedi was staring at the newcomer with an expression of barely concealed astonishment. Zey seemed to notice and nudged his colleague. "Padawan Jusik is new to clone armies, as are we all." That was understandable: Darman had never seen Jedi before the Battle of Geonosis, and he was equally fascinated. "You'll excuse his curiosity."

Zey gestured at the holoscreen.

"This is your objective, gentlemen—Qiilura." He glanced at his datapad, reading intently. "This data has been obtained from high-altitude reconnaissance, so it has its limitations."

Zey went on, "Qiilura is technically neutral. Unfortunately, its neutral status is likely due to end very soon."

He had referred to them as *gentlemen.* Maybe Zey didn't know what to call commandos. It was still early days for all of them.

The image on the screen began as a blue-and-white disc, zooming in to views of chains of islands, deep river inlets, and rolling plains peppered with patches of woodland and gameboard fields. It looked pleasant and peaceful, and hence utterly alien to Darman, whose entire life beyond Tipoca City had been spent on battlefields, real or virtual.

"You're looking at farming communities, almost all of them located *here* in this region because it's the most fertile land," Zey said. "They produce barq, kushayan, and fifty percent of the luxury foodstuffs and beverages in the galaxy. There's also gem mining. The population is nevertheless living at subsistence level, and there is no government other than the law of commerce and profit—Neimoidian traders effectively own the planet, or at least the productive areas that are of use to them. They enforce their stewardship through a militia controlled by Ghez Hokan—a Mandalorian so unpleasantly violent that he was actually asked to leave the Death Squad for enjoying his work too much."

Jusik looked up from his datapad. He appeared to be following the presentation. "Scum," he said. "One of our sources calls them scum, indicating . . . a very disagreeable group of people."

Zey paused for breath as if to ensure that the last snippet of information had made its point. "Given how thinly stretched our resources are, we are unfortunately unable to justify intervening to deal with any injustice on Qiilura at this time. But we have excellent intelligence that indicates a significant military asset located there."

Darman was listening, and still watching the Gurlanin peripherally. It had moved around the room to sit upright beside Jusik, with its front paws neatly clasped before its chest. He was also observing Jusik. The Padawan still appeared riveted by the commandos. Darman was careful not to stare—even though any eye movement was disguised by his helmet—because Jedi knew things without having to see. His instructors had told him so. Jedi were omniscient, omnipotent, and to be obeyed at all times.

Darman hung on Zey's every word.

"Qiilura isn't on the main lane, so to speak," Zey said. "Ideal for hiding, if that's your intention. And there *are* things hidden there. We need you to apprehend one, and destroy the other—a Separatist scientist, Ovolot Qail Uthan, and her most recent project, a nanovirus. We have reason to believe both are at a research facility on Qiilura."

Zey paused, and Jusik filled the space. "We have a Jedi there, Master Kast Fulier, but we haven't heard from him or his Padawan in some weeks."

Zey picked up again. "And let me assure you that we've been searching diligently for them. We have a location for our targets, but no plans of the buildings. The lack of plans will make your retrieval and sabotage task more challenging, as will the communications situation. Questions?"

Niner raised a gloved hand from his lap. "Sir, what is the comm situation, exactly?"

"Neimoidians."

"Not quite with you, sir."

Zey looked blank for a moment, and then his face lit up with revelation. "The Neimoidians own and control all the infrastructure—the native population scarcely have pits for refreshers, but their overlords enjoy the finest comlink net and air traffic control that credits can buy. They like to ensure that nobody does business without their knowledge. So they monitor everything, and very little intelligence comes out—you'll have to avoid using the long-range comlink. Do you understand me, soldier?"

"Sir, yes *sir,* General Zey."

There was a pause, a long pause, and Zey looked along the row of three helmets and a damaged face as if waiting for something. The Jedi had said he hadn't worked with clones before; maybe he was expecting a dialogue. He stopped at Darman. The potential embarrassment to the Master prompted Darman to fill the silent void.

It was an obvious question to ask, really.

"What's the nature of the nanovirus, sir?"

Zey's head moved back just a fraction. "An intelligent and significant question," he said.

"Thank you, sir."

"The answer, then, should be of great interest to you personally. It appears to be specifically aimed at clone personnel."

The sleek black Gurlanin drew itself up to a greater height. "They fear you, and with good reason," it said in a deep, liquid voice. "So they wish to kill, as all ignorant beings do when they encounter something they fear and misunderstand."

It continued elongating and now appeared to be standing. It had changed shape.

"Yes," Zey said slowly, dragging the word into two syllables, and he looked away from the spectacle of molecular rearrangement. "At this time you still have an advantage—the Separatists almost certainly aren't aware of your potential as clone commandos. They have no idea what you can achieve, and perhaps we have no idea, either. But you have been created for excellence, and trained to realize that potential by the most experienced instructors in the galaxy. We have very high expectations." Zey slipped his hands into his cloak, head lowered slightly. "If you happen to find Master Fulier safe, we would be relieved, but Uthan and the facility are your main priorities. Do you understand everything I have said?"

"Yes sir." Darman nodded once and so did the others, but it wasn't quite a synchronized movement. *We'll get it right,* he thought. *A couple of days' training, that'll sort it. Train hard, fight easy.*

"I'll leave you to my Padawan, then," Zey said, and swept out, pausing briefly at the door to look back at the commandos, tilting his head as if he was either amazed or amused.

Jusik swallowed hard. The Gurlanin flowed from a column back into a four-limbed thing, and moved to sit beside RC-3222, gazing up at him. The commando didn't react.

"Ahhh," it sighed. It had a voice like running water. "My, that's indeed Fett's face. Fascinating."

Jusik gestured to the exit. "I'm your armorer," he said. "Weapons and data. Follow me and I'll show you what you'll have at your disposal."

The commandos rose as one—more or less—and followed him through the door and down a passage still strewn with victualing containers. The place smelled of stewed nerf even through Darman's filtration mask. The Gurlanin flowed before them, now a sinuous predator, now a trotting quadruped, shifting shape as it went.

Jusik stopped at a door at the end of the passage and turned to them."I wonder if I could ask the rest of you to remove your helmets."

Nobody asked why, and they all obeyed, even though it wasn't phrased as the unequivocal order they were expecting. The helmet seals made faint *ssss* sounds as they opened.

"Oh," Jusik said, and stared for a second. Then he opened the door and they stepped into a makeshift armory.

It was a cache of treasures. There were upgrades and bolt-ons that Darman knew might fit his existing kit, and ordnance that he didn't recognize but looked like Republic issue, and there were . . . *exotics.* Weapons he recalled from his database as belonging to a dozen different species—and quite a few that he couldn't place at all—were laid out neatly on trestle tables. It was inviting, almost as inviting as a meal.

"That all looks rather *useful,* sir," Niner said.

"Delta Squad has been collecting a few things here and there," Jusik said. The commandos were focused on the weaponry, but Darman was also noting Jusik's behavior with growing interest. The Padawan stood back to let the men get a closer look at the armaments but he was watching them carefully. "You're nothing like droids at all, are you?"

"No sir," Fi said. "We're flesh and blood. Bred to be the best."

"Like Advanced Recon Commandos?"

"Not quite ARCs, sir. Not like clone troopers, either. We don't work alone and we don't work in formations. We just look the same."

"This is your unit of four, then? A squad?" He seemed to be recalling a hurried lesson. "Almost like a family?"

Niner cut in. "It is now, sir." He picked up a portable missile launcher that looked slightly different from the standard-issue plex. "Light. *Very* light."

"Merr-Sonn prototype," Jusik said. "Novel alloy, heavier payloads, extra range. It has a microrepulsorlift stabilizing unit, but they haven't resolved all the more challenging technical issues yet. So consider it shoulder-launching." He peered at 3222's face. "Is that painful?"

"Not too bad, sir," the commando said. But the wound had to hurt like fire. The abraded skin was still weeping. "I'll see to it later."

It didn't seem to be the answer Jusik was expecting, judging by the slight *uh* sound he made. Maybe he thought clones didn't feel pain, like droids. "Do you have names? I don't mean numbers. *Names.*"

Now, that was a very private thing. You kept your name to yourself, your squad, and your training sergeant. Darman was embarrassed for him.

"My squad called me Atin," the wounded commando said.

Niner glanced at Fi but said nothing. *Atin* was Mandalorian for "stubborn."

Jusik held up two reels of line that looked like matte ribbon, one black, one white. He took a ribbon of each color, twisted two short lengths together, and held up the braid in one hand and a bead-sized detonator in the other. "One meter is the equivalent yield of a thermal detonator, but it's directional. Ideal for making a frame charge. But be cautious with the quantity if you want to enter a building, rather than destroy it completely. You have some special implosion ordnance for that purpose."

"Any useful hand-thrown stuff?" Darman asked. "Stun grenades?"

"We have a few Geonosian sonic detonators, and a box of EMPs for anti-droid use."

"That'll do me fine. I'll take the lot."

Niner was watching Darman intently. "You're obviously our demolitions man," he said. Then the sergeant turned back to the Padawan. "We've been thoroughly trained, sir. You can have complete confidence in us."

That was true, Darman thought. They had been *very* thoroughly trained, day in, day out, for ten years, and the only time they weren't training was when they were sleeping. Even if they were untested as a special forces unit—apart from playing infantry three months ago—Darman had no doubt that they would perform to expected standards. He was happy to have the demolition role. He was proud of his skill in what was delicately known as rapid entry.

"What do you think happened to Master Fulier, sir?" Darman asked. He wouldn't normally have posed unnecessary questions, but Arligan Zey had seemed to approve of his curiosity, and Darman was conditioned to do whatever Jedi generals wished.

Jusik opened a case of Kamino saberdarts and held it out as if offering a tray of uj cakes. "Valaqil believes he was betrayed by a native," he said. "They've been known to do anything to earn food or a few credits."

Darman wondered how a Jedi could be taken by anything less than an army. He'd seen them fight at Geonosis. His warfare was a science; theirs appeared to be an art. "Didn't he have his lightsaber?"

"He did," the Gurlanin said. "But Master Fulier has, or had, some *discipline* issues."

Darman—a soldier able to withstand every privation in the field, and whose greatest fear was to wither from age rather than die in combat—felt inexplicably uncomfortable at the idea of a Jedi having failings.

"Master Fulier was—is a courageous Jedi," Jusik said, almost losing his composed manner for a moment. "He is simply passionate about justice."

Niner defused the moment. Darman felt reassured by his effortless authority. "Sir, how long have we got to plan the mission and attempt a few dry runs?" he said.

"Eight standard hours," Jusik replied, almost apologetic. "Because that's how long the journey to Qiilura will take. You're embarking now."

Etain emptied her bag on the straw mattress in the drying barn.

Despite appearances, this was the guest suite. Livestock wasn't allowed in the barn at this time of year because animals had a tendency to eat the barq grain, and that was an awfully expensive way to fatten merlies for the table. The animals were allowed in the main house, and in the winter they even slept there, partly to keep the place warm and partly to protect them from prowling gdans.

The house had smelled like it, too. Nothing of the merlies—not even their body heat or their pungent odor—was ever wasted. "Keeps them bugs away," Birhan had told her. "It's a *good* stink."

Etain knelt beside the mattress and tried to think her way out of her predicament. Master Fulier was probably dead: if he weren't, he would have returned for her. He was—had been—brilliant, magnificently skilled when he was focused on being so. But he was also impatient, and inclined not to walk away from matters that weren't his concern, and those were two factors that didn't mix well with a covert mission.

He'd decided one of Hokan's thugs needed to learn a lesson in how to respect the local population. All it took was for one of the Mandalorian's lieutenants to offer the same locals more than the price of a bottle of urrqal to say where and when Fulier was in town.

Town. That was a joke.

Imbraani wasn't Coruscant, not at all. The only infrastructure in the rambling collection of farmsteads was devoted to what it took to grow, harvest, and export its cash crops, and to the comfort of its commercial overlords. Etain had grown up in a world where you could travel at will and send messages easily, and neither of those taken-for-granted facilities was readily available here.

Etain needed one of two things right now: to get passage off Qiilura, or to get a data transmission out in her stead. She still had a mission to complete, if only to justify Master Fulier's sacrifice. She took a small sphere from the scattering of possessions on the mattress and opened it in two halves like a shef'na fruit.

A holochart blossomed into three dimensions in her cupped hands, then another, then another. She had layouts of half a dozen Neimoidian and Separatist buildings in the surrounding region, because Fulier hadn't been the only one who was careless. After a few bottles of urrqal, the local construction workers dropped their guard.

Etain was neither a natural warrior nor a great charmer, but she was aware of her talent for spotting opportunities. It made up for a lot.

She wasn't sure if her Master's fate was tied in to the holoschematics, or if he'd been seen as a direct threat to Uthan. She suspected Ghez Hokan might even have done something simply because he didn't much care for Jedi. *Play warriors,* he called them. He despised anyone who didn't fight with hard metal or their fists. Mandalorians were tough; but Hokan operated at a totally different level of brutality. Etain had realized that the moment she and Fulier had walked through what was left of a four-house village that must have displeased him in some way.

She would never erase those images from her mind. She meditated hard twice a day. It still wasn't helping. Settling down on her knees, she tried again, slowing her breathing, calming her heart.

The gravel outside the barn crunched.

Etain picked up her lightsaber from the mattress as she stuffed the holochart sphere in her tunic. Her thumb hovered over the controls set in the hilt. She should have sensed someone coming, but she had allowed her fatigue and despair to get the better of her. *I didn't check for another exit,* she thought. *Stupid, stupid, stupid. I might have to use this . . .*

As the plank door swung open, she flicked the button and the blue light pierced the dusty air. The merlie that wandered in didn't appear impressed. Nor did the small elderly woman who followed it.

"You're jumpy," she said. She had a covered tray in her hands and something bundled under one arm. The merlie nuzzled Etain's knees, seeking attention. They were distressingly intelligent animals, nearly a meter high at the shoulder and covered with long brown ringlets of wool; their round, green eyes were too disturbingly human for Etain's peace of mind. "Here's your dinner."

"Thank you," Etain said, watching as the woman put the tray down on the mattress and placed the bundle of brown fabric beside it.

"Quite a job getting that dung off your cloak," the woman said, eyeing the lightsaber the way Birhan had. "Still a bit damp. But clean."

"Thank you," Etain repeated. She turned off the blade and peeled the cloth back from the tray. Two rough clay plates held a couple of thin-breads and a mush of stew, on top of which whole barq grains were visible. She could smell their cloying musky scent.

That quantity of barq was a week's earnings for these people.

"You shouldn't have gone to that trouble for me," Etain said, embarrassed.

"You're a guest," the woman said. "Besides, once I'd scraped the dung off, shame to waste the grains stuck to it, eh? Oh-ah."

Etain's stomach rolled but she kept a steady expression. Coruscant's food hygiene regulations certainly didn't apply here.

"Very kind of you," she said, and forced a smile.

"They're coming, you know," the woman said.

"I'll be ready," Etain lied, and indicated the lightsaber.

"No, not them Hokan thugs. Not them at all."

Etain wondered whether to press her, but decided against it for the time being. She had no idea who she'd be asking for answers.

The woman sighed and shooed the merlie out the door with impatient hands. "They're coming, all right," she said, and smiled, closing the door behind her.

3

CLASSIFIED, HIGHEST: ENCRYPTION ONLY

You're the best in your field—the best soldiers, tacticians, sappers, communicators, survival experts. I picked you personally because I want you to train the best commandos in the galaxy. You'll have everything you need, whatever you want, except one thing—home. This is a top-secret project. You'll not tell anyone where you're going and you'll not leave Kamino, ever. As far as your friends and family are concerned, you're already dead.

—Jango Fett, recruiting his handpicked commando instructors, the Cuy'vul Dar—in the Mandalorian tongue, "those who no longer exist"

The Neimoidians had a taste for elaborate and wholly inappropriate grandeur, and Ghez Hokan despised them for it.

Lik Ankkit's huge villa was set on top of a hill overlooking a kushayan plantation—a foolish choice given the prevailing winds, but it seemed to satisfy the Neimoidian's need to show he was boss. The location might have made sense from a military perspective, but—as Ankkit was a bean-counting coward like all of his kind—he didn't need defensibility, either.

No, the Neimoidian was a *di'kut.* A complete and utter *di'kut.*

Hokan ran up the hedge-flanked steps of the veranda spanning the entire front of the building, headdress tucked under one arm, his shatter gun, knives, and rope-spike provocatively visible in his belt.

He wasn't rushing to see his paymaster, oh no. He was just in a hurry to get the meeting over with. He ignored the servants and minions and swept into Ankkit's spacious office with its panoramic view of the countryside. Qiilura's commercial overlord was watering pots of flowers on the windowsill. He paused to flick one with his fingertip, and it sprayed a powerful, sickly scent into the air. He inhaled with parted lips.

"I do wish you would knock, Hokan," Ankkit said without turning around. "It's really most discourteous."

"You summoned me," Hokan said flatly.

"Merely checking on the progress of your conversations with the Jedi."

"Had there been any, I would have called you."

"You haven't killed him, have you? Do tell me you haven't. I need to know if his activities will affect market prices."

"I'm not an amateur."

"But one has to do the best with the staff one has, yes?"

"I do my own dirty work, thanks. No, he isn't talking. He's rather . . . resistant for a Jedi."

If Ankkit had had a nose, he would have been looking down it at Hokan. Hokan controlled an impulsive urge to cut this glorified shopkeeper, this *grocer,* down to size. For all his height, the Neimoidian was soft and weak, his only strength contained within his bank account. He blinked with passionless, liquid red eyes. Hokan almost—*almost*—reached for his rope-spike.

"Jedi do not visit worlds like this to take the therapeutic waters, Hokan. Have you confirmed that he has an associate?"

"He's a Jedi Master. He was seen with a Padawan."

"Not a very discreet Jedi Master, it seems."

Fulier couldn't have been good at calculating odds or he'd never have started on Gar-Ul in the tavern. But at least he was prepared to stand up for himself, despite all that soft mystical nonsense he spouted. Hokan admired guts, even if he rarely tolerated them. They were always in short supply.

"We'll find the Padawan, and we'll find out what intelligence Fulier has, if any."

"Make sure you do. I have a lucrative contract resting on this."

Hokan had become practiced at controlling his urge to lash out, but he saw no reason to subject his mouth to the same discipline. "If I succeed, it'll be because I take pride in my work."

"You need the credits."

"For the time being. But one day, Ankkit, I won't need you at all."

Ankkit gathered his robes a little closer and drew himself up to his full height, which had no effect on Hokan at all.

"You must learn to accept your reduced station in the galactic order, Hokan," Ankkit said. "This is no longer the hierarchy of brute force in which your warrior ancestors thrived. Today we need to be soldiers of intellect and commerce, and no amount of strutting around in that museum-piece uniform will revive your . . . *glorious* past. Alas, even the great Jango Fett succumbed to a Jedi in the end."

News traveled fast. Fett was a source of pride among the remaining handful of Mandalorians in diaspora. Even if he fought for money, he was the *best.* Ankkit must have known perfectly well how much that comment would sting.

Hokan was determined that the Neimoidian would see no evidence on his face to prove it. He'd certainly tried to keep that out of his mind when he was interrogating Fulier, much as he wanted to blame all Jedi for the humiliation of a cultural hero. He had to be clear why he was smashing the Jedi's bones. Revenge was unprofessional.

He took a careful breath. "Do you keep gdans as pets, Ankkit? I hear some offworlders do try."

"Gdans? No. Filthy little creatures. Most savage."

"But if you did keep one, and didn't feed it well, would you be surprised if it bit you?"

"I suppose not."

"Then feed me well."

Hokan turned and walked out without being dismissed, deliberately unbidden, and deliberately fast so that Ankkit couldn't have the last word. He replaced his helmet and ran down the steps of the ludicrously extravagant villa.

He didn't care if Ankkit rented the whole planet out to Separatist scientists. They weren't honorable enough to fight with real weapons, either: they got bugs to do their work for them. It was a disgrace. It was *unnatural.*

Hokan felt in his blood-red jacket for the Jedi's weapon. It didn't look like much at all. And it was surprisingly easy to activate, even though he suspected that fully mastering it might be another matter. A humming blue shaft of light, vivid as day, shot out from the hilt. Hokan swept it scythe-style along a neatly clipped tarmul hedge, cutting its height in half.

The lightsaber wasn't bad for a soft Jedi weapon.

Hokan suspected the lightsaber looked at odds with his traditional Mandalorian helmet and its distinctive T-shaped eye slit. But a warrior had to adapt.

And Fulier had questions to answer.

Docking Bay D-768, Fleet Support Air Station, Ord Mantell

The Nar Shaddaa agri-utility crop sprayer on the pad looked as if only its rust was holding it together. It was, to use Jusik's uncharacteristically colorful description, an old clunker.

And—somehow—it was taking them to Qiilura. It wouldn't attract much attention flying over farming country, unless, of course, it broke up in flight. This didn't seem out of the question.

"Well, they don't build them like that anymore," Fi said.

"That's because not even the Hutt Aviation Authority would certify this Narsh dirt-crate airworthy," Niner said, straining to prevent his pack from bending him over backward. He was laden with nearly double the twenty-five-kilo weight he was used to carrying, along with a powered emergency chute. Niner had never actually come across the HAA, but he'd absorbed every scrap of intel read, seen, or heard in his life. "Anyway, all it has to do is get us down there."

"It's making a noble sacrifice," Jusik said, suddenly right behind them. He smiled and murmured *dirt-crate* to himself as if it amused him. Niner wondered for a moment if he'd broken protocol by using the phrase. "Are you certain you can do this? I could ask Master Zey if he would allow me to accompany you."

Niner wanted to laugh, but you didn't laugh at a Jedi, especially one who seemed to care what happened to you. "We lost too many officers at Geonosis, sir. They can't grow you to order."

The Padawan lowered his eyes for a second. "It's considerate of you to think of me as an officer, Sergeant."

"You're a commander now, sir. We won't let you down. There's nobody better prepared for this than us."

"This is your first special operation, isn't it?"

"Yes sir."

"Doesn't that worry you?"

"No sir. Not at all. The six P's, sir. Proper Planning Prevents Pi . . . *Inadequate* Performance, sir."

Jusik appeared to be counting and then raised his eyebrows. "This is *real,* Sergeant."

Ah. For all their skills and wisdom, there were still some things that even Jedi didn't know. Niner hesitated to lecture Jusik.

Real. Oh yes, Niner knew what *real* was, all right.

Padawan Bardan Jusik had certainly never seen the Killing House on Kamino. He'd never stormed the building, with its twisting corridors and innumerable flights of stairs; he didn't know how many commandos died in training when the rounds were live and the terrorists—or whoever the directing staff were being that day—aimed to kill, and frequently did.

He also had no idea what it was like spending four days lying prone in a scrape in the undergrowth on observation, rifle ready, urinating where you lay because you couldn't move and give away your position. He had no idea how you learned to judge the amount of charge required for rapid entry to a building the hard way, because if you didn't get it just right, in a hurry and under fire, it could blow your head clean off. Two-Eight had learned that way.

Jusik didn't know just how far and how long you could carry a wounded comrade when you had to. He probably didn't even know how to perform an emergency field tracheotomy with a vibroblade and a clean length of fuel line.

It wasn't Jusik's fault. He had far bigger issues to worry about. There was no reason for a Jedi commander to concern himself with the details of a clone commando's life. But Niner thought he probably would, and he admired the Padawan all the more for that.

"We'll be fine, sir," Niner said. "The training is quite realistic."

Inside the shabby Narsh vessel, the tanks had been stripped out, and the bulkheads lined with securing straps and stealth sheeting that would render the ship's cargo invisible to any probe or scan.

Niner realized that four men would be pretty cramped in there with packs and weapons. A couple of BlasTech E-Web repeating blasters were already stowed, and, at Atin's request, two Trandoshan LJ-50 concussion rifles.

Atin's livid face wound was looking less alarming now, but he'd always have a scar: the bacta spray could fix plenty if you used it soon enough, but it couldn't reverse scarring. He pulled himself through the open hatch with an APC array blaster in one hand and his DC-17 strapped across his chest, just about keeping his balance under the weight of his pack. Darman, acting as loadmaster, gave him a helpful leg up and eyed the blaster.

"Got a thing for Trandoshan technology?" Darman asked.

"This'll deal with shields better than our E-Web," Atin replied.

"And the LJ-fifty is a nice backup when we take out the facility. Just in case. Republic doesn't make all the best gear."

Niner wondered if Atin ever talked about anything but kits. His squad must have been a miserable bunch, with a miserable instructor. Clones might have looked utterly standardized to outsiders, but every squad was altered slightly by the cumulative effects of its experiences, including the influences of the individual trainers. Every commando battalion had its own nonclone instructor, and seemed to take on some of his—or her—unique characteristics and vocabulary.

We learn, Niner thought. *We learn fast, and unfortunately we learn everything. Like* dirt-crate.

Every squad developed its own dynamics, as well. It was part of their hardwired human biology. Put four men in a group, and soon you'd have a pecking order defined by the roles and foibles that accompanied them. Niner knew his, and he thought he knew Fi's, and he was pretty sure he knew where Darman was heading. But Atin wasn't sliding into place just yet.

Fi had a Geonosian force pike. He hefted it and smiled.

"Where'd you get that?" Atin asked, suddenly interested.

"Souvenir of Geonosis," Fi said, and winked. "Seemed a shame to waste it." He flipped it over in his hand and twirled it, arm outstretched, missing Atin by a calculated handspan. He didn't react. "You wouldn't even need to use the power setting, would you? This thing's *heavy.*" He brought it down in a slicing movement. "*Wallop.* That'll make their eyes water."

"I don't think I need any souvenirs of Geonosis," Atin said. His tone was distinctly frosty. "Indelibly etched, you might say."

"Hey—"

Niner cut in. "Chat later," he said. "Shift it, people."

Niner already knew he would have his work cut out with Atin and wondered if anything would trigger his natural urge to be one of the squad. He also wondered about his apparent negativity. *He'll shake down, sooner or later. He'll have to.*

Backing up to a convenient ledge on the port bulkhead, Niner unclipped his backpack. Forty-five kilos lighter, he eased between Fi and Atin, and peered into the cockpit.

An R5 droid was at the controls. The unit was still fueling up the vessel from a droid bowser, burbling and whistling to itself. Niner leaned across to plug his datapad into the console to confirm the flight plan and synchronize it with the vessel's actual path.

The R5 didn't take any notice. It would fly the route it was given.

Improvising, thinking on his feet, making the most of the resources at hand, were all part of operating as a commando. But so was acquiring adequate intelligence. What they had wasn't enough to plan a mission, and that meant they would either have to acquire it in the field, or fail. Niner didn't want to fail Padawan Jusik. He ejected his datapad and edged back to the hatch, trying not to clip Fi or Atin.

"Comm silence from the time you take off," Jusik said, leaning through the open hatch. "The assault ship the *Majestic* is diverting to Qiilura, and will remain on station a parsec from the planet until she receives your request for extraction. Then gunships will be at your transmitted location within the hour."

Niner almost asked just how long the *Majestic* might wait, but he feared it would look as if he doubted his squad's competence. He knew the answer: the ship would wait until Uthan was taken, even if that was several commando missions down the line. It wasn't waiting for *them.*

"We won't keep the *Majestic* waiting," Niner said.

"Anything else you need?"

Niner shook his head. "No, Commander."

Darman stood to one side of the ramp, like an honor guard, waiting for the Jedi to leave.

"Very well," Jusik said, looking hesitant, as if he wanted to walk away but thought better of it. "I hope to debrief you on your return."

Niner took that literally, although Jusik was looking at him as if it meant something else. It made sense for the Padawan commander to process whatever intel they might gain. Jusik turned and walked away, and Darman jumped inside. The hatch closed with a slight shudder, sending fine fragments of rusting metal to the deck.

It only has to land, Niner thought.

He switched on the holoprojection in his datapad and studied the three-dimensional flight path over fields, lakes, and forest. It was part real image, part simulation. Projected onto an existing chart, they were looking at an area thirty klicks north of a small town called Imbraani.

A single-story building with shabby sheet-metal roofing—ringed by an incongruously well-cut expanse of grass—nestled in a plantation of kuvara trees. Some of the image was blurred, but it was the best resolution that a surveillance remote could manage at that distance above the planet. Specks—people—wandered around an encircling path.

"It's the *capture alive* bit that complicates matters," Darman said, gazing at the image over Niner's shoulder. "Or else we could just bomb it back into Hutt space."

"That's why they created us," Niner said. "For the complicated jobs."

He closed his eyes for a few moments to visualize the insertion: he saw it from takeoff to landing, smooth and planned, every detail, or as many details as their incomplete intel could furnish and his own experience of a hundred exercises could confirm.

In this detached state, something occurred to him. He pictured Jusik's face and his awkward, nervous shrugs. He realized what the Padawan had meant when he said he was hoping to debrief them personally on their return.

He meant *Good luck.* He wanted them to survive.

Niner, who had known for as long as he could remember that he was a soldier bred to die, found that intriguing.

Gdans were about thirty centimeters long, fully grown, and it took a whole pack of them to bring down even a merlie calf. But at night—when they emerged from their warrens and hunted—the farmers locked their doors and stayed clear of the fields.

It wasn't so much their teeth that the locals feared. It was the deadly bacteria the animals carried; a minor scratch or a bite was almost always fatal. And Master Fulier had used their entire supply of bacta spray in administering first aid to villagers, so Etain was as housebound at night as any of her hosts.

She could hear the little predators outside, squabbling and scrabbling. She sat cross-legged on the mattress and chewed on the thinbreads, almost hungry enough to gulp down the stew, but not *that* hungry. *A few bacteria are good for your immune system,* she thought. *You've probably eaten worse without knowing.*

But she *knew* this time.

Leaving the bowl where it stood, she rolled the holochart sphere over and over in her palms, running through all the possibilities for getting the information to the Jedi Council. Stow away in a transport—possible. Transmit the data from ground? No, all transmissions were tightly controlled by the Neimoidians; any other message traffic from Qiilura to Coruscant would draw instant attention. There was always the possibility of finding the right droid courier, but that was a long shot, and it might take so much time as to be useless.

Perhaps she'd have to do the job herself.

Lightsabers were superb weapons, but right now she needed an army. The realization that she had beaten the odds to obtain valuable information but was now unable to get it to those who needed it almost crushed her.

"I'm not done yet," she said aloud. But she feared that she was, at least for the night. Her eyelids felt heavy and she braced her elbows on her knees, letting her head rest in her hands.

A good night's sleep. She might have a better idea in the morning. Her eyes closed. Images of Coruscant, her clan practicing passing a ball by thought alone, a nice hot bath, food she trusted to be clean . . .

Then, suddenly, every fiber in her body leapt at once. Heart pounding, Etain thought at first that she'd had one of those half dreams of falling that sometimes came when she was dozing off. But now she was fully awake and knew that she hadn't.

Something had changed. Something in the Force had been altered, and forever. She jumped to her feet, suddenly clear what it was; she needed no training or education to understand it. Every instinct coded in her genes cried out.

Something—*someone*—was gone from the Force.

"Master," she said.

She had *suspected* he was dead. Now she knew he was, and she knew it had happened right then. It was impossible not to wonder how and where, but she knew enough about the Neimoidians' hired muscle and their techniques to guess.

Ignoring the ever-present gdans, she went to the barn door and swung it open. It was an act of helplessness. There was nothing she could do, now or ever.

Something rustled in the grass. It was a solitary something, and it sounded larger than a gdan. She noticed for the first time that the constant snuffling and squabbling of the gdan packs had stopped. They'd gone.

Etain felt for her lightsaber, just in case.

Loud squawking and a flurry of wings made her start. A disturbed flock of leatherbacks rose into the air and scattered in the darkness, trailing sparks of light from their scales. Through the Force, she detected only small creatures with simple desires, and a male merlie wandering along the fence, armed with such fearsome tusks that not even gdans would risk approaching him.

She looked up at the night sky. It appeared unchanging, constant: but she knew it never was.

They're coming.

She thought she heard the old woman's voice. Putting it down to grief and lack of sleep, Etain stumbled back inside and barred the door.

* * *

It was just another crop sprayer hired to dress the fields after the barq harvest, laden with bug killers and soil enhancers and piloted by a droid. At least, that was what the Narsh crate's transponder had told the Qiilura traffic controller, and judging by the absence of a missile up the tailpipe, he had believed it.

Darman was still exploring the enhancements to his helmet and suit. "I used to think I wore this armor," he said. "Now I think it's wearing me."

"Yeah, they spent some credits upgrading this since last time," Fi said. "Wow. Walking weapons system, eh?"

"Two hundred klicks," Atin said, without looking up from his datapad. He'd propped his helmet beside him with the tactical beam pointed up to provide some light in the closed bay. Darman couldn't hear him over the noise of the vessel's atmosphere engines, but he could lip-read easily enough. "Let's hope everything works."

It was helmets on at one hundred klicks. The squad was prepared both for a controlled landing and an early bailout and free fall if they were picked up by Separatist ground units. Darman hoped their luck would hold. They were landing heavy, with more kits than they'd ever used in training, and they'd have to hit the drop zone accurately to avoid an impossible trek across country. Accurate, if they had to jump for it, meant high-altitude low-opening procedure. They could drift for fifty klicks if they opted for the safer, slower high-opening technique.

Darman didn't relish being defenseless in the air for that long.

Niner was studying his datapad, balancing it on his right thigh. A three-dimensional shimmering holo of their flight path played out a handspan above it. He glanced up at Darman and gave him a silent thumbs-up: *On course and on target.* Darman returned the gesture.

There was an art to loading up for a mission when carrying the firepower of a small army among four men. Darman had loaded his pack to capacity. The rest of his weapons and ordnance was in a second shockproof container that stood knee-high. The bowcaster—he loved that weapon—was strapped across his chest plate with jury-rigged webbing, to leave his hands free for the DC-17. He had an assortment of detonators, kept safely separate from the charges and other ordnance in the lower section. He was now so heavy even without the extra equipment that he had to bounce to get upright from a sitting position. He rehearsed standing a few times. It was tough. Fortunately, the squad would be inserted close to the target. He didn't have to haul it far.

"One hundred klicks," Atin said. He switched off his spot-lamp. "Helmets."

The compartment was suddenly dark, and there was a collective hiss of helmet seals purging and reengaging. They could only talk to each other at very short range now: on Qiilura, anything more than ten meters risked detection. The only visible light was the faint blue glow from the heads-up display in their visors, a group of ghostly disembodied T-shapes in the gloom, and the shimmering landscape playing out from Niner's datapad. His head was tilted down slightly, watching the actual position of the utility vessel in the simulated landscape.

The sprayer started to lose height, exactly on course. In a matter of minutes, they would be—

Bang.

A shudder ran through the airframe, and then there was no engine noise at all.

For a second Darman thought they'd been hit by anti-aircraft fire. Niner was on his feet instantly, moving forward to the cockpit, accidentally whacking Atin with his pack as he turned. Darman, without conscious decision, grabbed the emergency hatch handle and prepared to activate it for a bailout.

Darman could see the droid clicking and flashing, apparently engaged in a dialogue of some kind with the vessel. The ship wasn't listening.

"AA, Sarge?"

"Birdstrike," Niner said, deceptively quiet. "Atmos engine's fried."

"Can the R5 glide this thing down?"

"It's trying."

The deck tilted, and Darman grabbed at the bulkhead to stay upright. "No, that isn't gliding. That's crashing."

"Bang out," Niner said. "Bang out now."

The Narsh dirt-crate hadn't let them down. It had just succumbed to being in the wrong airspace at the wrong time, and met the local avian species the hard way. Now they were plummeting toward the kind of landing not even the latest Katarn armor could help them survive.

Darman blew the hatch, and the inrush of air sent dirt and debris whirling through the cargo bay. The door fell away through the opening. It was pitch black outside, a challenge for a free-faller even with night vision. Darman was starting to experience serious doubt for the second time in his life. He wondered if he was becoming one of those despised creatures that his training sergeant had called *cowards.*

"Go go *go,*" Niner shouted. Fi and Atin eased through the hatch and stepped out. *Don't try to jump, just let yourself fall.* Darman stood back to make way for Niner: he wanted to salvage as much kit as he could. They needed the repeating blasters. He grabbed some of the dismantled sections.

"Now," Niner said. "You first."

"We need the kit." Darman thrust two sections at him. "Take these. I'll—"

"I said *jump.*"

Darman wasn't a rash man. None of them were. They took calculated risks, though, and he calculated that Niner wouldn't leave him. His sergeant was standing at the open hatch, arm held out imperiously, a clear sign to get on with it and *jump.* No, Darman had made up his mind. He lunged forward and shoulder-charged Niner out of the hatch, grabbing the door frame just in time to stop from plunging after him. It was clear from the stream of expletives that Niner was not expecting this, nor was he happy about it. The extra pack jerked out after him on its tether. Darman heard one last profanity and then Niner was out of range.

Darman grabbed a strap and peered down, but he couldn't see his sergeant falling, and that probably meant nobody else could, either. He now had a minute, more or less, to salvage what he could and get out before the utility hit the ground.

He switched on his helmet lamp. He couldn't afford the time to listen to the rushing wind and the complete absence of reassuring engine noise, but he heard it anyway. He dropped the bowcaster and began lashing the blaster sections together with a line. It was a shame. He loved the bowcaster, but they needed those cannons more.

Knotting lines was hard enough with gloves on, but was even harder when you were seconds from crashing. Darman fumbled a knot. He cursed. He looped the line again and this time it held. He let out a sob of relief, dropped the weapon, and dragged the kit down to the hatch. Nobody could hear him at this range, and he didn't care what the droid thought.

Then he stepped out into black void. The wind took him.

There was no rushing landscape beneath him yet to take his attention from the heads-up display. He was free-falling at nearly two hundred kilometers an hour, trailing sections of heavy, heavy cannon. He maneuvered into tracking position, pack square across his back, rifle tight into his side, the remainder of his kit on the container that rested on the backs of his legs. When he deployed the canopy at eight hundred meters, he would release the container. And he'd use the powered-descent option, because that might save him from the unsupported, potentially lethal weight of cannon that was falling with him.

Yes, he knew exactly what he was doing. And yes, he was scared.

He'd never jumped with so much unsecured load in training.

The canopy deployed, and it felt like he'd slammed into a wall. The power pack kicked in, heating up the air around him. He could steer now. He counted down fifteen seconds.

Something flared into brilliant white flame beneath him, off to his right—the Narsh vessel crashing some thirty klicks short of the target zone.

Darman realized he had thought nothing of leaving the R5 on board the stricken utility. It was expendable.

And that was how he was seen, he supposed. It was surprisingly easy to think that way.

He could see the ground now. His night vision could pick out the tops of trees, right beneath.

No, no, no.

He tried to miss. He failed.

He hit something very, very hard in the air. Then he hit the ground and didn't feel anything at all.

4

This is the true art of genetic selection and manipulation. A human is naturally a learning creature, but it is also violent, selfish, lustful, and undisciplined. So we must walk the knife-edge between suppressing the factors that lead to disobedience and destroying that prized capacity for applying intelligence and aggression.

—Hali Ke, senior research geneticist of Kamino

Niner was hauling in his canopy when the explosion jerked him upright. A column of white roiling fire shot into the night sky above the tops of the trees. He knew it was hot and bright because his helmet visor's filter kicked in to stop it from overwhelming his night vision.

Even though he knew it was coming, his heart sank. Darman probably hadn't made it. He'd disobeyed his order. He hadn't jumped when he told him to.

So maybe you've lost a brother. Maybe not. Either way, you'll lose two more if you don't get your act together fast.

Niner triangulated the position of the blast and then went on bundling up the free-fall canopy, cutting away the lengths of cord before burying it. With a breaking strength of five hundred kilos, the cord was bound to come in handy. He wound each length in a figure-eight around his thumb and smallest finger and slipped the skeins into a belt pouch, then went in search of his extra pack.

It hadn't fallen far from him. The low-opening technique worked well if you needed accuracy. Niner found the pack at the edge of a field, covered in small dark-furred animals that seemed fascinated by it and were gnawing at the soft padding strip on one side. He flashed his spot-lamp to scatter them, but they stared back up the beam, burst into angry chatter, and then turned toward him.

It was unnerving, nothing more. Their little teeth snapped impotently on his armor. He stood still, assessing them, his data bank scrolling in front of his eyes and telling him that they were gdans, and that they weren't logged as a hostile alien species. All the nonhuman life Niner had ever seen for real, other than Kaminoans and various instructors, had been on Geonosis and through a blaster sight. He was utterly dependent on the intelligence loaded into his database—that, or finding things out for himself.

All but one of the gdans gave him up as inedible within a minute and disappeared into the waist-high crop. The remaining creature worried away at his left boot, a tribute to its tenacity, if not its intelligence. Those boots were specced to withstand every assault from hard vacuum to acid and molten metal. The little animal clearly believed in aiming high.

Darman would have found it fascinating, he was sure. It was a pity to lose him. He had all the makings of a good comrade.

"Come on," Niner said, nudging the animal with the butt of his blaster rifle. "I've got to get to work. Shove off."

The gdan, teeth locked around a clamp, looked up and met his eyes, or at least it seemed like it. It could only have really seen a faint blue light. Then it let go and trotted back toward the field, pausing once to stare back at him before disappearing into a hole in the ground with all the ease of a diver.

Niner took out his datapad and calculated his position. There was no GPS he could lock in to without the Neimoidians detecting him, but he could at least use dead reckoning based on the sprayer's last position, matching features on the landscape to his chart. It was old-fashioned soldiering. He liked it. He had to be able to do the business when the tech wasn't there, even if that meant using nothing but a Trandoshan blade.

If you stab someone in the heart, they can still run. I once saw a man run a hundred meters like that, screaming as well. Go for the neck, like this. Sergeant Skirata had taught them a lot about knives. *Put a bit of weight behind it, son.*

Still, tech had its place. A speeder bike would have been handy, although they hadn't thought they'd need them. The insert was supposed to be five klicks from the target.

Never mind, he thought. *It would make me look pretty conspicuous out here anyway.* The kit would slow him on his way to the pre-agreed rendezvous point, but he'd get there. If Fi and Atin had landed safely, they'd be heading for RV Alpha, too.

He started tabbing, trying to make ten klicks an hour, avoiding tracks and open ground. In the end he had to drag the extra pack behind him on straps like a sled. Tactical advance into battle—*tabbing,* as Skirata called it—meant walking at six to ten klicks an hour with a twenty-five-kilo pack. "But that's for *ordinary men,*" the instructor would say, as if nonclones were subhuman. "You are clone commandos. You will *do* better because you *are* better."

Niner was lugging nearly three times that load now. He didn't feel better at all right then. He decided to add a portable repulsorlift to his new list of kits to request upon return.

Qiilura's moon was in its new phase, and he was grateful for that. In his light gray armor, he would have stood out like a beacon. *Hadn't the top brass thought of that, either?* He stifled the uncharacteristically critical opinion about his superiors and decided there had to be something he didn't know but they did. He had his orders.

Even so, he diverted to a narrow river shown on the holochart and stopped long enough to smear mud over his armor and kit. There was no point chancing his luck.

At four hundred meters from RV point Alpha, he slowed down, and not because he was struggling under the weight. A silent approach was necessary. He hid the pack he was dragging deep in the undergrowth and recorded its location to collect later. Fi and Atin might have been tracked. They might not have made it at all. There was always the possibility of ambush. No, he definitely wasn't taking chances.

For the last two hundred meters, he got down in the grass and crawled.

But they were there, and alone.

Niner found himself staring up into the beam from Fi's helmet and he knew that the infrared targeting was centered at the point between his filtration mask and the top of his chest plate. It was a vulnerable point, provided one got close enough and used the right caliber rounds. Not many hostiles could get that close, of course.

"You gave me a start, Sarge," Fi said, holding his blaster clear and looking him over. He killed the light and indicated his chest plate. "Great minds, eh?"

Fi's armor was no longer pristine, either. Niner wasn't sure what he'd smeared over it, but it disrupted his outline well enough. The thought had obviously occurred to all of them. Atin was daubed with something dark and matte as well.

"Shape, shine, shadow, silhouette, smell, sound, and movement," Niner said, repeating the rules of basic camouflage. If it hadn't been for Darman's absence, he would have found the situation funny. He tried. "Shame they couldn't find something beginning with S to complete the set."

"I could," Atin said. "Any contact from Darman?"

They were forty kilometers from the point where Niner had landed. "I saw the blast. He was last off."

"You saw him jump, then."

"No. He was grabbing as much kit and ordnance as he could salvage." Niner felt he needed to explain. "He shoved me out the hatch first. I shouldn't have let that happen. But I didn't abandon him."

Atin shrugged. "So what have we got, then?"

"We've got a brother missing."

"I meant by way of resources. He had most of the demolition ordnance."

"I know you meant that, and I don't want to hear it." If he could feel concern—even sorrow—for Darman, then why couldn't Atin? But it was no time to start a fight. They had to stick together now. A four-man mission with three men: their chances of succeeding had plummeted already. "We're a squad now. Get used to it."

Fi interrupted. He seemed to have a knack for defusing situations. "All our kit's intact, anyway. We can still put quite a dent in them if we have to."

And what did they have to put a dent in, exactly? They had high-altitude drone recces of the target building, but no idea yet if the walls were just plastered blocks or if they were lined with shock-absorbing alloy plates. There could be just the thirty or so guards seen walking the perimeter, or hundreds more holed up in underground barracks. Without better intelligence, they had no way of knowing just how much kit was enough for the job.

It was a case of adding P for plenty, just to be sure. Niner liked to be sure.

"How much time are we going to spend looking for him?" Atin asked. "They know they've got company now. It wasn't exactly a silent insert."

"SOPs," Niner said. *Standard operating procedures:* that was how things should be done; how commandos expected them to be done. "We get to each RV point for the time we agreed upon, and if he doesn't show we'll go to the position of the blast and see what's left. *Then* we'll decide if we're going to consider him MIA or not."

"You'd want us to search if it was you missing," Fi said to Atin. "He can't call in. Not at this range. Too risky."

"I wouldn't expect you to compromise the mission for me," Atin said, distinctly acid.

"He's alone, for fierfek's sake. *Alone.*"

"Just shut it, will you?" Niner said. The good thing about ultra-short-range comlinks was that you could stand around and have a blazing argument inside those helmets, and nobody outside could hear you. "Finding him isn't only the right thing to do, it's the sensible thing to do. Locate him and we find his kit. Okay?"

"Yes Sarge," Fi said.

"Got it," Atin said. "But there has to be a point where we consider him dead."

"Without a body, that'll be when Geonosis freezes over," Niner said, still angry and not knowing why. "Until then, we're going to sweat our guts out to find him, provided it doesn't blow the mission. Now let's see if we can sling this kit between some poles or something. We'll never keep this pace up for tens of kilometers unless we find a better way of transporting it."

Niner set his helmet comlink to receive long-range anyway. There was no harm in listening. If Darman was out there, Niner wasn't planning on abandoning him.

The clearing hadn't been there yesterday.

Etain picked her way through flattened kuvara saplings and into a circle of blackened stubble, following Birhan's steps. The air smelled of smoke and roasted barq.

He was swearing fluently. She didn't know much Qiiluran, but she knew a curse when she heard one.

"This is your lot again," Birhan said. He surveyed the field, hands to his brow to block out the sun breaking over the horizon. Now that it was daylight, they could see the extent of the damage from last night's explosion. "What am I going to do? What's going to happen to our contract?"

It wasn't phrased like a question. The Neimoidians weren't known to be sympathetic about the host of natural disasters constantly threatening the farming communities' precarious existence. But this was no natural disaster.

The blast area spanned around five hundred meters, and the crater at the center was twelve, maybe fifteen meters wide. Etain didn't know how deep it was, but a Trandoshan and an Ubese were standing at the edge of it, peering down, blasters in hand, looking as if they were searching in the soil. They didn't take the slightest notice of her or Birhan. She must have looked suitably starved and dowdy, rough enough to pass for a farm girl.

It was probably too late to convince them the crater was caused by a meteor fragment. But at this point Etain didn't know any more than they did.

"Why do you think it's *my lot*?" she asked.

"Obvious," Birhan said sourly. "I seen loads of speeders and freighters and sprayers come down hard. They don't leave craters. They falls apart and burns, yes, but they *don't* blow up half the countryside. This is off-planet. It's *soldiers*." He kicked around some of the charred and blackened stalks. "Can't you have your fight on someone else's planet? Don't you think I got enough problems?"

She wondered for a moment if he was considering turning her in to Hokan's men for a few credits to make up for the loss of the precious barq. She was already an extra mouth to feed at a time when money he was counting on had just gone up in a fireball with much of his crop. It was time to find somewhere else to hide, and some other plan for getting that information off Qiilura.

Etain was still considering the scorched land when the Ubese and the Trandoshan jerked upright and turned to jog away toward the dirt track beside the field. The Ubese had one hand pressed to the side of his helmet as if he was listening to something: a comlink, probably. Whatever the summons had been, it had been urgent enough to get them running. It also confirmed that this wasn't just a Narsh sprayer making an all-too-frequent crash landing.

Etain waited a moment longer, then walked forward to peer into the pit to see what had so engrossed them.

It had been a monstrous blast. The sides of the blackened crater were blown almost smooth, and there was debris everywhere. It was an enormous blast area for a small craft.

She left Birhan and walked around inspecting the ground as Hokan's men had done, not sure what she was seeking. She was almost at the kuvara orchard before she saw it.

The early sunlight caught a scraped metal edge of something embedded in the ground, rammed deep by the explosion. Etain crouched down, as casually as she could, and worked the soil loose from it with her fingers. It took her a few minutes to expose enough to understand the shape, and a few more to work out why the scorched colors were so familiar. It was distorted, the metal frozen in a moment of being torn apart by enormous force, but she was pretty sure she'd seen one intact before.

It was a plate from an R5 astromech droid—a plate with Republic markings.

They're coming.

Whoever they were, she hoped they'd made it alive.

Darman knew it was risky moving around by day, and the fact that his right leg seemed to scream every time he put his weight on it didn't help matters.

He'd spent two painful hours scooping out a shallow depression in a thicket about a hundred meters from what passed for a road. Roots and stones had slowed him down. So had the pounding he'd taken hitting the canopies of trees during his landing. But he'd dug in now, and he lay under a lattice of branches and leaves on his belly, watching the road, sometimes through his rifle sight, sometimes with the electrobinocular panel that flipped down in his visor.

At least the little animals that had swarmed over him in the night had disappeared. He'd given up trying to fend them off. They had explored his armor for a while and then moved on to watch him from distance. Now that it was daylight, there were no more glittering eyes staring out from the undergrowth.

He still wasn't sure of his position, either. There was no GPS network he could use without being picked up. He needed to get out and about and do a recce if he was going to have any chance of aligning landscape features with the holochart.

He knew he was facing north: the arc of small stones around a thin branch he'd stuck in the soil charted the sun's progress, and gave him his east–west line. If his datapad had calculated speed and distance correctly, he was between forty and fifty klicks northeast of the first RV point. He'd never cover that distance on foot in time, not with the extra kit and not with his leg in this state. If he dragged the pack, he'd draw a neat *follow-me* line through the vegetation.

Darman eased himself over on his back, removed his leg plates, and unsealed his undersuit at the knee. It felt as if he'd torn a muscle or a tendon above the joint. He soaked the makeshift bandage with bacta again and replaced the legging and plates before rolling back into position.

It was high time he ate something, but he decided that he could wait a little longer.

He checked the dirt road through the crosswires of the DC-17's electromag scope. The first time he had worn the helmet with the built-in display shimmering before his eyes, he had been overwhelmed and disoriented by the flurry of symbols in his field of vision. The rifle scope made it seem even more chaotic. Lights, lights, lights: it was like looking from the windows of Tipoca City at night with the lamps and reflective surfaces of the refectory behind you—so many competing images that you couldn't focus on what lay beyond the stormproof glass.

But in time—that time being the short, desperate morning when the whole of Kilo and Delta squads first wore the HUD display while using live ordnance—he got used to it. Those who didn't get used to it fast didn't return from the exercise. He learned to see, and yet not see. He was constantly aware of all the status displays that told him when his weapons were charging, and if his suit was compromised, and what was happening around him.

Now he was focused solely on looking down a clear tunnel framed by interlocking segments of soothing blue, with a highlighted area to show when he had an optimum firing solution for his target. The information on range, environment, and the score of other options was still there. He could take them in without consciously seeing them. He saw only his target.

A faint rumbling sound made him stiffen. Voices: they were approaching from his right. Then they stopped.

He waited. Eventually the voices started again and two Weequays came into his field of view, too slowly for his liking. They were looking at the road's shoulders with unusual diligence. One stopped suddenly and peered at the ground, apparently excited, if his arm gestures were any indication.

Then he looked up and started walking almost directly toward Darman's position. He took out a blaster pistol.

He can't possibly see me, Darman thought. *I've done this by the book. No reflection, no movement, no smells, nothing.*

But the Weequay kept coming, right into the bushes. He stopped about ten meters from Darman and was casting around as if he'd followed something and lost the trail. Then he moved forward again.

Darman had almost stopped breathing. His helmet masked all sound, but it certainly didn't feel that way. The Weequay was so close now that Darman could smell his distinctive sweat and see the detailed tooling on his sidearm—a KYD-21 with a hadrium barrel—and that there was a vibroblade in his other hand. Right at that moment Darman couldn't even swallow.

It's okay to be scared.

The Weequay stepped sideways, looking at waist height as if browsing for discs on a library shelf.

It's okay to be scared as long as you . . .

The Weequay was right on him now, squatting over his position. Darman felt boots depress branches that were touching his back, and then the creature looked down and said something that sounded like *gah.*

. . . as long as you use it.

Darman brought his fist up hard under the Weequay's jaw, ramming his own vibroblade up into the throat and twisting his fist off to one side to sever blood vessels. He supported the deadweight of the impaled Weequay on one arm, until it stopped moving. Then Darman lowered his arm, shaking with the effort, and let the body roll to the ground as quietly as he could.

"What you find?" the other Weequay yelled. "Gar-Ul? Gar?"

No answer. *Well, here we go.* Darman aimed his DC-17 and waited.

The second Weequay began running in a straight line toward the bushes, and that was a stupid thing for him to do when he had no idea what had happened to his comrade. They'd been lording it over farmers for too long; they were sloppy. He also made the mistake of pulling out his blaster.

Darman had a clear head shot and he took it almost without thinking. The Weequay dropped, cleanly and silently, and lay crumpled, with wisps of smoke rising from his head.

"Oh, clever," Darman sighed, as much to hear the reassurance of his own voice as anything. Now he'd have to break cover and retrieve the body. He couldn't leave it there like a calling card. He waited a few minutes, listening, and then eased himself onto his injured leg to limp out into open ground.

He dragged the Weequay into the bushes, noting the smell of cooked meat. Now he could see what the first Weequay had been following: a broad path of tiny animal footprints. The curious gdans had given him away. He limped out again, checking carefully, and obliterated the drag marks with a branch.

Waste not, want not. The Weequays wouldn't be needing the blasters or vibroblades now. Darman, pulse slowing to normal, searched the bodies for anything else of use, pocketing data cards and valuables. He didn't feel that he was a thief; he had no personal possessions that weren't the Grand Army's property, and he felt no need to acquire any. But there was a chance the cards contained information that would help him achieve his objective, and the beads and coins would come in handy if he needed to buy or bribe something or someone.

He found a suitable spot to hide the bodies. He didn't have time to bury them, but was suddenly aware of movement in the undergrowth, animal movement, and gradually small heads appeared, sniffing the air.

"You again, eh?" Darman said, although the gdans couldn't possibly hear him beyond the helmet. "Way past your bedtime." They edged forward and then swarmed across the Weequay with the shattered head, taking tiny bites as they settled on him in a dark-furred blanket of snapping motion.

Darman wouldn't have to worry about burying anyone.

The faintest of liquid sounds made him look around at the other Weequay. Darman had his rifle aimed instantly. The Weequay wasn't dead, not quite. For some reason, that upset Darman more than he could have ever imagined.

He'd killed plenty of times at Geonosis, smashing droids with grenade launchers and cannons at a distance, hyped up on fear and the instinct to live. *Survive to fight.*

But this was different. It wasn't distant, and the debris of the kill wasn't metal. The Weequay's blood had dried in a stream down his glove and right forearm plate. And he hadn't managed a clean kill. It was *wrong.*

They had drilled him to kill, and kill, and kill, but nobody had thought to teach him what he was supposed to feel afterward. He did feel something, and he wasn't certain what it was.

He'd think about it later.

Aiming his rifle, he corrected his mistake before the small army of carnivores could move on to their next meal.

5

Think of yourselves as a hand. Each of you is a finger, and without the others you're useless. Alone, a finger can't grasp, or control, or form a fist. You are nothing on your own, and everything together.
—Commando instructor Sergeant Kal Skirata

Darman moved on fast, up a tree-covered slope a kilometer south. He planned on spending the rest of the daylight hours in a carefully constructed hide at the highest vantage point he could find, slightly below the skyline.

He concentrated on making a crude net out of the canopy cords he had salvaged. The activity kept him occupied and alert. He hadn't slept in nearly forty standard hours; fatigue made you more careless and dangerously unfocused than alcohol. When he had finished tying the cord into squares, he wove grass, leaves, and twigs into the knots. On inspection, he decided it was a pretty good camouflage net.

He also continued observation. Qiilura was *astonishing.* It was alive and different, a riot of scent and color and texture and sounds. Now that his initial pounding fear had subsided into a general edginess, he began to take it all in.

It was the little living noises that concerned him most. Around him, creatures crawled, flew, and buzzed. Occasionally things squealed and fell silent. Twice now he'd heard something larger prowling in the bushes.

Apart from the brief intensity of Geonosis, Darman's only environmental experience had been the elegant but enclosed stilt cities of

Kamino, and the endless churning seas around them. The cleanly efficient classrooms and barracks where he had spent ten years turning from instant child to perfect soldier were unremarkable, designed to get a job done. His training in desert and mountain and jungle had been entirely artificial, holoprojection, simulation.

The red desert plains of Geonosis had been far more arid and starkly magnificent than his instructors' imaginations; and now Qiilura's fields and woods held so much more than three-dimensional charts could offer.

It was still open country, though—a terrain that made it hard for him to move around unnoticed.

Concentrate, he told himself. *Gather intel. Make the most of your enforced idleness.*

Lunch would have been welcome about now. A *decent* lunch. He chewed on a concentrated dry ration cube and reminded himself that his constant hunger wasn't real. He was just *tired.* He had consumed the correct amount of nutrients for his needs, and if he gave in to eating more, he would run out of supplies. There was exactly enough for a week's operations in his pack and two days' worth in his emergency belt. The belt was the only thing he would grab, apart from his rifle, if he ever had to make a last-ditch run for it without his forty-kilo pack.

Beneath him, farm transports passed along a narrow track, all heading in the same direction, carrying square tanks with security seals on the hatches. *Barq*. Darman had never tasted it, but he could smell it even from here. The nauseatingly musky, almost fungal scent took the edge off his appetite for a while. If he had his holochart aligned correctly, the transports were all heading for the regional depot at Teklet. He twisted the image this way and that in his hands and held it up to map onto the actual landscape.

Yes, he was sure enough now where he was. He was ten klicks east of the small town called Imbraani, about forty klicks northeast of RV point Beta and forty klicks almost due east of RV point Gamma. They'd picked RV points along the flight path because the Separatists would expect dispersal, not a retracing of their steps. Between RVs Alpha and Beta was a stretch of woodland, ideal for moving undetected by day. If the rest of his squad had landed safely and were on schedule, they would be making their way to Beta.

Things could be looking up again. All he had to do was get to RV Gamma and wait for his squad. And if they hadn't made it, then he'd need to rethink the mission.

The idea produced a feeling of desolation. *You are nothing on your own, and everything together.* He'd been raised to think, function, even breathe as one of a group of four. He could do nothing else.

But ARCs always operate alone, don't they?

He pondered that, fighting off drowsiness. Leaves rustled suddenly behind him, and he turned to scan with the infrared filter of his visor. He caught a blur of moving animal. It fled. His database said there were no large predators on Qiilura, so whatever it was could be no more troublesome than the gdans—not as long as he was wearing his armor, anyway.

Darman waited motionless for a few moments, but the animal was gone. He turned back and refocused on the road and the surrounding fields, struggling to stay awake. *Lay off the stims.* No, he wasn't going to touch his medpac for a quick boost. Not yet. He'd save his limited supply for later, for when things got really tough, as he knew they would.

Then something changed in his field of vision. The frozen tableau had come to life. He flipped down the binoc filter for a closer look, and what he saw made him snap it back and gaze through the sniperscope of his rifle.

A thin wisp of smoke rose from a group of wooden buildings. It was quickly becoming a pall. It wasn't the smoke of domestic fires; he could see flames, flaring tongues of yellow and red. The structures—barns, judging by their construction—were on fire. A group of people in drab clothing was scrambling around, trying to drag objects clear of the flames, uncoordinated, panicking. Another group—Ubese, Trandoshan, mainly Weequay—was stopping them, standing in a line around the barn.

One of the farmers broke the line and disappeared into a building. He didn't come out again, not as long as Darman watched.

Nothing in his training corresponded to what he was witnessing. There was not a memory, a pattern, a maneuver, or a lesson that flashed in his mind and told him how this should be played out. Civilian situations were outside his experience. Nor were these citizens of the Republic: they weren't *anyone's* citizens.

His training taught him not to be distracted by outside issues, however compelling.

But there was still some urge in him that said *Do something.* What? His mission, his reason for staying alive, was to rejoin his squad and thwart the nanovirus project. Breaking cover to aid civilians cut across all of that.

The Separatists—or whoever controlled this band of assorted thugs—knew he was here.

It didn't take a genius to work it out. The sprayer had exploded on landing, detonating any demolition ordnance that Darman hadn't been able to cram into his packs. The Weequay patrol hadn't called in when their masters had expected. Now the humans—farmers—were being punished and threatened, and it was all to do with him. The Separatists were looking for him.

Escape and evasion procedure.

No, not yet. Darman inhaled and leveled his rifle carefully, picking out an Ubese in the crosswires. Then he lined up the rest of the group, one at a time. Eight hostiles, forty rounds: he knew he could slot every one, first time.

He held his breath, forefinger resting on the trigger.

Just a touch.

How many more targets were there that he couldn't see? He'd give away his position.

This isn't your business.

He exhaled and relaxed his grip on the rifle, sliding his forefinger in front of the trigger guard. What would happen to his mission if they caught him?

In the next two minutes, reluctant to move, he targeted each Ubese, Weequay, and Trandoshan several times, but didn't squeeze the trigger. He wanted to more than he could have imagined. It wasn't the hard-drilled trained response of a sniper, but a helpless, impotent anger whose origin he couldn't begin to identify.

Don't reveal your position. Don't fire unless you can take out the target. Keep firing until the target is down and stays down.

And then there were times when a soldier just had to take a chance.

They could be Republic citizens, one day.

They could be allies now.

Darman wasn't tired anymore, or even hungry. His pulse was pounding loud in his ears and he could feel the constriction in his throat muscles, the fundamental human reflex to flee or fight. Fleeing wasn't an option. He could only fight.

He targeted the first Weequay, a clean head shot, and squeezed the trigger. The creature dropped, and for a moment his comrades stared at the body, unsure of what had happened. Darman had nothing against Weequays. It was only coincidence that this was the third one he'd killed in a few hours.

And, suddenly unfrozen, the band of thugs all turned to stare in the direction of the shot, drawing their weapons.

The first bolt hit the bushes to Darman's left; the second went three meters over his head. They'd worked out where he was, all right. Darman snapped on the DC-17's grenade attachment and watched through the scope as the civilians scattered. The grenade sent a shower of soil and shattered wood into the air, along with four of the eight militia.

He'd certainly pinpointed his position now.

When he sprang to his feet and began the run down the slope, the four remaining enemy stood and stared for a couple of seconds. He had no idea why, but they were transfixed long enough for him to gain the advantage. A couple of plasma bolts hit him, but his armor simply took it like a punch in the chest and he ran on, laying down a hail of particle rounds. The bolts came toward him like horizontal luminous rain. One Trandoshan turned and ran; Darman took him down with a bolt in the back that blew him a few meters farther as he fell.

Then the white-hot rain stopped and he was running over bodies. Darman slowed and pulled up, suddenly deafened by the sound of his own panting breath.

Maybe they'd managed to report his presence via their comlinks in time, and maybe they hadn't. The information wouldn't have been much use on its own anyway. He ran from barn to barn, checking for more hostiles, walking through the flames unscathed because his armor and bodysuit could easily withstand the heat of a wood fire. Even with the visor, he couldn't see much through the thick smoke, and he moved quickly outside again. He glanced at his arm; smoke curled off the soot-blackened plates.

Then he almost walked straight into a youth in a farmer's smock, staring at him. The boy bolted.

Darman couldn't find any more of Hokan's troops. He came to the last barn and booted the door open. His spot-lamp illuminated the dim interior and picked out four terrified human faces—two men, a woman, and the boy he'd just seen—huddling in a corner next to a threshing machine. His automatic response was to train the rifle on them until he was sure they weren't hostiles. *Not every soldier wears a uniform.* But his instincts said these were just terrified civilians.

He was still trailing smoke from his armor. He realized how frightening he looked.

A thin, wavering wail began. He thought it was the woman, but it seemed to be coming from one of the men, a man just as old as Sergeant Skirata who was staring at him in horror. Darman had never seen civilians that close, and he'd never seen anyone that scared.

"I'm not going to hurt you," he said. "Is this your farm?"

Silence, except for that noise the man was making; he couldn't understand it. He'd rescued them from their attackers, hadn't he? What was there to fear?

"How many troops has Hokan got? Can you tell me?"

The woman found her voice, but it was shaky. "What are you?"

"I'm a soldier of the Republic. I need information, ma'am."

"You're not him?"

"Who?"

"Hokan."

"No. Do you know where he is?"

She pointed south in the direction of Imbraani. "They're down at the farm the Kirmay clan used to own before Hokan sold them to Trandoshans. About fifty, maybe sixty of them. What are you going to do to us?"

"Nothing, ma'am. Nothing at all."

It didn't seem to be the answer they were expecting. The woman didn't move.

"He brought them here looking for him," said the man who wasn't whining, pointing at Darman. "We've got nothing to thank him for. Tell him to—"

"Shut up," the woman said, glaring at the man. She turned back to Darman. "We won't say a word. We won't say we saw you. Just go. Get out. We don't want your help."

Darman was totally unprepared for the reaction. He'd been taught many things, but none of his accelerated learning had mentioned anything about *ungrateful civilians, rescues thereof.* He backed away and checked outside the barn door before darting from barn to bush to fence and up the slope to where he'd left his kit. It was time to move on. He was leaving a trail behind him now, a trail of engagements and bodies. He wondered if he'd see *civvies,* as Skirata called them, in quite the same benign way in the future.

He checked the chrono readout in his visor. It had been only minutes since he had run down the slope, firing. It always felt like hours, hours when he couldn't see anything but the target in front of him. *Don't worry,* Skirata had said. *It's your forebrain shutting down, just a fear reflex. You're bred from sociopathic stock. You'll fight just fine. You'll carry on fighting when normal men have turned into basket cases.*

Darman was never sure if that was good or not, but it was what he was, and he was fine with that. He loaded his extra pack on his back and began working his way to the RV point. Maybe he shouldn't have expended so many rounds. Maybe he should have just left the farmers to their fate. He'd never know.

Then it struck him why both the militia and the civilians had frozen when they first spotted him. The helmet. The armor. *He looked like a Mandalorian warrior.*

Everyone must be terrified of Ghez Hokan. The similarity would either work to his advantage or get him killed.

"Down!" Atin yelled.

Niner flung himself flat and heard Fi grunt as he did the same, the air knocked from his lungs.

An airspeeder flew overhead with a deceptively gentle hum. Atin, squatting in the cover of a fallen tree, followed it with his rifle scope.

"Two up, camo and custom armament," he said. "Somehow I don't think the locals drive those. Not with mounted cannons, anyway."

The hum of engines faded. Niner struggled to his feet and regained his balance, wishing for the speeder bikes and an absence of armor. The squad was too heavily laden and the armor wasn't designed for blending into the landscape, although it was the difference between life and death in hostile territory: protection against blasterfire, nerve agents, and even hard vacuum. And when they got to their target it would come into its own. The armor was designed for FIBUA ops, fighting in built-up areas and inside buildings, urban warfare of the kind the galaxy now had plenty to offer. For now, they'd just have to make the best of the scenic part of the mission.

He was tired. They all were. Not even the animal panic brought on by the risk of discovery could shake that off. They needed to sleep.

Niner checked his datapad. They were still ten klicks from RV Beta and it was midday. It was much easier to move by night, so he wanted to press on and make the RV point by midafternoon, then lie up until nightfall. If Darman had made it—and maybe he hadn't, but Niner's mind was made up—they would wait for him.

"He's back," Atin said. "Everyone down."

The quiet drone of engines interrupted Niner's calculations. The airspeeder was heading south toward them again. They froze, mud-smeared, invisible from that altitude—or so they hoped.

It wasn't entirely training that produced the reaction.

Aerial surveillance was especially threatening. Niner recalled the Kaminoan KE-8 Enforcer craft cruising above the training grounds of Tipoca City, ready to pluck out and discipline any defective clone who didn't conform. They were equipped with electroshock devices.

He'd seen a KE-8 in action, just once. After that he worked extra hard to conform.

"He's on a square search," Atin said. He was turning into an excellent point man; for some reason he was slightly more attuned to his surroundings than Fi or even Niner himself. "He must be working out from the center."

"Center of what, though?" Fi asked.

Niner forgot his fatigue. *You never leave your mates behind.* "If he hasn't seen us, he's seen Darman."

"Or what's left of him."

"Shut it, Atin. What's your problem?"

"I've been Darman," Atin said.

He said nothing more. Niner didn't think it was a good time to ask for an explanation. The engines were overhead. Then the sound faded a little and dropped in pitch, but soon resumed full volume.

"He's circling," Atin said.

"Fierfek," Niner said, and all three men reached for their anti-armor grenade attachments at the same time. "What's he seen?"

"Maybe nothing," Fi said. "Maybe us."

They fell silent. The airspeeder was indeed circling. It had also dropped lower and was now about level with the tops of the trees. Niner could see its twin cannons. His helmet wasn't telling him it had locked on, but that didn't mean it hadn't. You could never count on tech.

Best piece of gear is the eyeball. It was the first piece of advice Skirata had ever given him. Accelerated learning was fine, but anything direct from the mouths of men who had fought real engagements left a bigger impression.

Niner leveled his rifle and peered through the scope, trusting to BlasTech Industries that the sight really wasn't reflective. He'd find out the hard way if it was.

He could see the sun glinting off the human pilot's goggles. The gunner was a droid. He wondered if they felt vulnerable without any armored canopy, heads conveniently skylined for a shot. He suspected that anyone looking down from that height with a cannon or two didn't feel vulnerable at all.

The fuselage banked above him and turned slowly, rising well above the trees as if the pilot was trying to get a visual fix again. It wasn't coincidence. Niner kept the DC-17 trained on the central propulsion unit.

Then a red flashing symbol went off in his visor.

The thing had a lock on him.

He squeezed the trigger. The white-hot blast kicked his visor into blackness for an instant, and the detonation was so close that the shock wave hit him like a body blow.

He scrambled to his feet and ran. How he ran with more than fifty kilos of deadweight on his back he would never know, but adrenaline could do remarkable things. His instinct was to get clear before debris rained down on him. Armor and bodysuits could withstand a lot, but the human instinct buried deep inside him screamed *get clear.*

When he stopped he had covered a hundred meters even in the tangled undergrowth of the coppice. He was panting like a mott and the suit was struggling to cool him down.

Behind him, a fire burned, with smaller flames scattered around it like seedlings around a tree. He turned to look for Fi and Atin. His first thought was that he had brought the speeder crashing down on them.

"Did you have to?"

Fi was right next to him. He hadn't heard him above the noise of his own breathing.

"He got a lock on me," Niner said, feeling relieved, and then oddly guilty, but not sure why.

"I know. I saw your Deece go up and I thought I'd better get moving or I'd be wearing a speedie."

"Atin?"

"Can't hear him."

That didn't mean anything. The close-range comm setting was only ten meters; Atin could be anywhere. Niner didn't know him well enough yet to guess his movements, and it had been enough of a close shave for him not to spend much time contemplating the issue. Now he was worried that he—the sergeant, the man they looked to for leadership—had run for it without thinking of them, and that they knew it.

"This is going to make a nice marker," Fi said, staring up at the climbing smoke. It would be visible for a long, long way.

"What did you expect me to do? Lie there and take a cannon round?"

"No, Sarge. I thought you'd manage a double tap, though." He laughed. "Better make sure nobody survived."

It was a remote chance, but speeders could be surprisingly robust. Niner and Fi walked back through the smoke, rifles ready. Droid parts were scattered across the scene of devastation, one scuttle-shaped faceplate staring up at the pall of smoke as if in surprise.

"They don't bounce much, then," Fi said, and moved it with his boot. "Atin—Fi here. You there, over?"

Silence. Fi put his left gauntlet against his ear. Niner wondered if he'd now lost two men in as many days.

"Atin here, over."

Atin stepped out of the smoke, dragging his extra pack and a scorched hunk of metal that trailed a few wires and plugs. It looked like the speeder's onboard computer. "The pilot didn't bounce either," he said. "Here, help me get this strapped on again."

It took both Fi and Niner to lift the pack and reattach it to his armor. A few days earlier, either one of them could have managed it single-handed. *We're too exhausted to be safe,* Niner thought. *Time we got out of here and got some rest.*

"I might be able to get something from this," Atin said, indicating the charred metal box in one hand. It was the first time Niner had heard him sound remotely cheerful. Atin seemed to relate to kits better than he did to people. "Worth a try."

Niner took over the point position and they struggled into denser cover. He glanced back and hoped the flames would burn themselves out; they didn't have a hope of outrunning a full-scale forest fire. But maybe that was the least of their problems. And if Darman was alive and anywhere near, he'd see their handiwork, and Niner hoped he'd recognize it as such.

The squad had now left a couple of telltale marks of combat on the sleepy rural landscape. Whether it wanted it or not, Qiilura was involved in the war.

"You're a *di'kut,*" Hokan said.

He took off his helmet. His face was centimeters from the Ubese's, and he wanted it to look him in the eye. As a species they weren't prone to trembling, but this one was doing a fine job of being an exception.

"*What* are you?" he whispered.

"A *di'kut,* sir."

"You've made me look like a *di'kut,* too. I don't like that."

Hokan had assembled his entire senior staff in the room. He reminded himself that the room was in fact a disused merlie-shearing shed, and that his lieutenants were the twenty least stupid individuals selected from the criminal detritus that had washed down society's sewer to Qiilura. It disappointed him that the Neimoidians would spend so much on secure communications and so little on personnel.

A few credits more and he could have bought the small army he needed.

The Ubese—Cailshh—was standing absolutely still in the middle of the room as Hokan circled. It might have been a female, because you never could tell with Ubese, but Hokan suspected it was male. He hadn't wanted to hire Ubese. They could be unpredictable, even sly. But very few mercenaries wanted to work on Qiilura and those who did were simply unemployable anywhere else, almost always because of a criminal record even a Hutt would balk at. And here he was, paying them what he could because Ankkit wouldn't fork out for proper support.

Hokan despaired. And when he despaired of professional standards, he suspected extreme coaching was necessary to refocus the team.

"So you torched another farm," he said.

"It was a warning, sir. In case they got ideas. You know. Hiding people they shouldn't."

"No, that's not how it works." Hokan propped his backside against the edge of the table and stared into the anonymous masked face, arms folded. He didn't like people whose eyes he couldn't see. "You warn them first. If they break the rules, *then* you punish them. If you punish them before they break the rules, they have nothing to lose, and they hate you, and they will seek revenge, and so will their offspring."

"Yes sir."

"Do you understand that?" Hokan looked around at the assembled staff, and spread his arms in invitation to join the coaching session. "Does everyone understand that?"

There were some grunts.

"Does everyone *understand that*?" Hokan snarled. "What do we say when an officer asks you a question?"

"Yes . . . sir!" It was almost a chorus.

"Good," Hokan said quietly.

He stood up again. Then he took out Fulier's lightsaber, activated the beam, and sliced it through the Ubese's neck, sending the head flying—bloodless, quiet, and clean.

There was sudden and absolute silence. The staff had been quiet before, but they'd been making the marginal noises of people forced to endure a boring lesson. Now there was not the slightest swallow, cough, or sigh. Nobody breathed.

He peered down at the body and then at the legs of his dark gray uniform trousers. Perfectly clean: no blood. He rather liked this lightsaber now. He sat back on the edge of the desk.

"That," Hokan said, "was *punishment* for Cailshh. It's a *warning* for the rest of you. Now, is the difference clear? It's very important."

"Yes sir." Fewer voices joined in this time, and they wavered.

"Then go and find our visitors. And you, Mukit. Clear up this mess. You're Ubese. You understand the proper way to dispose of the remains."

The group began filing out, and Mukit edged over to the neatly sundered body of Cailshh. Hokan caught the arm of his senior Weequay lieutenant as he tried to slip through the door.

"Guta-Nay, where's your brother and his friend?" he asked. "They haven't shown up for two meals, and they haven't signed off shift."

"Don't know, sir."

"Are they making a few credits on the side with that Trandoshan? A bit of freelance slaving?"

"Sir—"

"I need to know. To work out if anything . . . unusual might have happened to them."

Guta-Nay, no doubt recalling what Hokan had done to him when he chased that farm girl, moved his lips soundlessly. Then his voice managed to surface above his fear. "I never seen, sir, not at all, not since yesterday. I swear."

"I chose you as my right-hand . . . *man* because you could very nearly express yourself in several syllables."

"Sir."

"That makes you an intellectual among your kind. Don't make me doubt my judgment."

"Not seen him, sir, honest. Never."

"Then get out on the route they were patrolling and see what you can find." Hokan reached across his desk and took out the electroshocker. It was only an agricultural instrument for herding, but it worked fine on most nonanimal species. Guta-Nay eyed it cautiously. "This is why I disapprove of undisciplined acts like thieving and drinking. When I need to be certain of someone's whereabouts, I can't be. When I need resources, they're already committed. When I need competence, my staff is . . . distracted." He pushed the shocker up into the Weequay's armpit. "There is a Republic presence here. We don't know the size of the force, but we do have a speeder down and a large black crater at Imbraani. The more data I have, the more I can assess the size of the threat and deal with it. Understood?"

"Yes sir."

Hokan lowered the shocker and the Weequay shot out the door, his enthusiasm for his career refreshed. Hokan prided himself on motivational skills.

It's started, he thought. He shut himself in his room and switched on all the comlink screens. *They're coming to take Qiilura.*

Hokan had some idea of what kind of deal Ankkit had with the Separatists. There had been a significant amount of construction work carried out to convert a grain store into the kind of building that had triple-sealed doors, and the type of walls that could be sterilized with extreme heat. Then he'd had to try to make credible bodyguards out of the rabble he employed because important Separatist scientists came and went, and the Neimoidians saw conspiracy everywhere they looked. They weren't always wrong about that.

Then the Jedi came to Imbraani, and it all fell into place, as neatly as the arrival of the Republic forces now on the planet. There was a military target here.

I'm my father's son, though. I'm a warrior. Hokan wondered if all cultures separated from their heritage were unable to move on, doomed to relive old glories. *I'd rather be fighting a worthy opponent than terrorizing farmers who haven't got the guts to stand up for themselves.*

Fighting soldiers also commanded a higher fee, of course. And the greater the fee, the quicker he would be off this planet and heading . . . somewhere.

There was no longer a home for him, and few of his kind left. But things could change. Yes, they very well might one day.

Hokan leaned back in the chair and let the chatter of comlinks wash over him.

6

You want to know how clones tell each other apart? Who cares? They're here to fight, not to socialize.
—Sergeant Kal Skirata

"Get out," Birhan yelled. "Get out and don't come back! You've brought all this on us. Go on, clear off."

The farmer shied a clod of dirt at Etain, and she sidestepped it. It broke into dust behind her. The old woman—who wasn't Birhan's wife, she'd discovered—came up from behind and grabbed his arm.

"Don't be a fool," she said. "If we take care of the Jedi, then they'll take care of us when the Republic comes."

Birhan was still staring at Etain as if he was debating whether to go and grab his pitchfork. "Republic my rump," he said. "Them's no different to Neimies when it comes to it. We'll still be bottom of the pile whoever runs the show."

Etain stood with her arms folded, wondering how the old woman, Jinart, had managed to attach herself to Birhan's sprawling family. She was an appalling cook and couldn't have been much help with heavy farm labor. Etain imagined she earned her keep spinning merlie wool like the rest of the elderly Qiilurans she'd met.

But right now, Etain doubted even Jinart's powers of persuasion. She decided to try her own again.

"Birhan, you want me to stay," she said carefully, concentrating as Master Fulier had taught her. "You want to cooperate with me."

"I rotten well *don't* want to cooperate with you, missy," he said. "And say *please.*"

She'd never quite mastered Jedi persuasion when under stress. Unfortunately, that was always the time when she needed it.

Jinart nudged Birhan roughly, no mean feat for such a short woman. "If them Jedi have landed, fool, then she'll bring them around here to sort you out," she said. "This is no time to make new enemies. And if they haven't—well, it'll all blow over and then you'll have someone who can make things grow. That's right, innit, girl? Jedi can make crops grow?"

Etain watched the display of rustic logic with growing respect. "We can harness the Force to nurture plants, yes."

That was all too true: she had heard the stories of Padawans joining the agri corps when they didn't perform well during training. That was all she needed—life on a backwater planet, talking to fields of grain. It wasn't just the intelligence data she had hidden in her cloak that made her want to get off the planet as fast as she could. Agriculture spelled failure. She didn't need further reminding of her inadequacy.

"Yah," Birhan spat, and trudged off, muttering profanities.

"We all get nervous when Hokan's thugs start burning down farms," Jinart said. She took Etain's arm and steered her back to the barn that had become her home. No, it wasn't home. There could never be *home* for her. *No loves, no attachments, no commitments except the Force.* Well, at least it wouldn't be hard to tear herself away from here. "And killing farmers, of course."

"So why aren't *you* nervous?" Etain asked.

"You're a cautious child."

"I have a dead Master. It encourages you somewhat."

"I have a broader view of life," Jinart said, not at all like a wool-spinning old woman. "Now you keep yourself safe and don't go wandering about."

Etain was developing a Neimoidian level of paranoia and wondered if even her own instincts were deceiving her. She had at least always been able to sense another's emotions and condition. "So they know where to find me?" she said quietly, testing.

Jinart stiffened visibly. "Depends on who *they* might be," she said, wafting the pungent scent of merlie as she walked. "I don't care for urrqal much, and at my time of life there's little left to covet."

"You said they were coming."

"I did indeed."

"I have no patience for riddles."

"Then you should have, and you should also be reassured, because they're here and they'll help you. But you also need to help them."

Etain's mind raced ahead. Her stomach knotted. No, she was falling for carnival fortune-teller's tricks. She was adding her own knowledge and senses to vague generalities and seeing meaning where there was none. Of course Jinart knew strangers had arrived. The whole of Imbraani had known about Master Fulier, and it was very hard *not* to know something had happened when vessels crash-landed on your farm, and when every hiding hole in the area was being searched by Hokan's militia. For some reason or another, Jinart was playing a guessing game.

"When you specify something, I'll take you seriously," Etain said.

"You should be less suspicious," Jinart said slowly, "and you should look at what you think you see much more carefully."

Etain opened the barn door and the scent of straw and barq tumbled out, almost solid. She felt suddenly calmer, and even hopeful. She had no idea why. Perhaps Jinart was naturally reassuring, as comforting as a grandmother, despite all her odd talk.

Etain couldn't actually remember a grandmother, or any of her biological family, of course. *Family* wasn't familiar or soothing because she had grown up in a commune of Jedi novices, educated and raised and cared for by her own kind, and by that she never meant *human.*

But family, even from what she had seen briefly of squabbling farmers' clans, suddenly seemed desirable. It was difficult to be alone right then.

"I wish I had time to educate you in survival," Jinart said. "That task will have to fall to someone else. Be ready to come with me when it gets dark."

Jinart was becoming much more articulate. She was more than she appeared to be. Etain decided to trust the old woman because she was the nearest she had to an ally.

She still had her lightsaber, after all.

Darman came to the edge of the wood and found himself facing an open field the size of Kamino's oceans.

It seemed like it, anyway. He couldn't see the boundary on either side of him, just straight across where the trees began again. The rows of grain—steel gray, shining, sighing in the wind—were only waist-high. He was thirty klicks east of RV Gamma, desperate to reach it and get some sleep while waiting for the rest of the squad.

Following the cover of the hedge—wherever that might take him—would cost him a lot of time. He opted to take the direct route. He removed one of the three micro-remotes from his belt pack and activated it. The tiny viewing device was about the size of a pygmy hummer, small enough to grasp in his palm, and he set it to scout the area for five kilometers around him. He didn't like using them unless he absolutely had to. On a planet like this, their shiny metallic coating was hardly geared toward stealth. They also had a tendency to go missing. And because they recorded as well as transmitted, they were one of the last things he wanted to let fall into the enemy's hands.

But he wasn't exactly invisible, either. He glanced down at his filthy armor, streaked with dried mud, wet green moss, and far, far worse, and knew he was still a big plastoid-alloy industrial object in a gentle organic environment.

He lowered himself onto all fours, adjusting his balance carefully so the packs sat squarely down the length of his back. His knee still hurt. Crawling through a field wasn't going to help it. *The sooner you get there, the sooner you rest.*

The remote soared vertically into the air, playing back a rapidly shrinking view of the field, then the wider landscape of farmland and woods, all within Darman's visor display. There were no buildings as far as he could see. That didn't necessarily mean the area was deserted.

Crawling with his packs generated a lot of heat, but the bodysuit regulated it obediently. The armor system had more pluses than disadvantages. He didn't have to worry about wildlife waiting to bite, sting, poison, infect, or otherwise ruin his entire day.

But it was slow going. He had to loop wide if he was going to avoid the little town, Imbraani. In fact, the whole day had been one of slow progress, although the only timetable he could latch on to now was that of his comrades, and how long it would take them to make RV Gamma. Then they'd move on if he didn't show by the appointed time. After that—well, after that they were off the chart, so to speak. It would be a matter of regrouping and gathering enough intel to take the target.

Darman suspected it would take longer than a few days. A *lot* longer. He had started making notes of what local flora and fauna might be edible, and the positions of springs and watercourses that hadn't shown up on the high-altitude recce. He wondered if the gdans made decent eating. He reckoned it might not be worth trying.

Every so often he paused to kneel and sip some water from his bottle. His stomach's fantasies were no longer of sizzling nerf strips but of sweet, filling, sticky, amber uj cake. It was a rare treat. His training sergeant had allowed his squad—his original squad—to try it, breaking the Kaminoan rules on feeding clones carefully balanced nutritional mixes. "You're still just boys," he'd told them. "Fill yer boots." And they had. *Good old Kal.*

The flavor was still achingly vivid in Darman's mind. He wondered what other normal civilian indulgences he might enjoy if he had access to them.

He slapped the thought down hard. His discipline was his self-esteem. He was a professional.

He still thought about that uj cake, though.

"Come on, get moving," he said, very tired of the absence of comrades' voices and seeking comfort in his own. He would be his commanding officer, just to stay sharp. "Shift it."

The remote continued to relay predictable images of bucolic peace, neat patchworks of fields punctuated by the wild tangled woods, reminders of an unsettled and untamed world. There were no giant harvester droids out yet. At one point, he thought he saw a dark form moving through the field some way to his left, but when he focused on it there was simply a gap opened by the wind.

Then there was a sudden patch of darkness in his visor.

Darman stopped dead. The thing had malfunctioned. But the image returned, glowing, red, and wet, and he realized he was looking into the digestive tract of a living creature.

Something had swallowed the remote.

A few moments later a large bird, slowly flapping four wings, sailed overhead and cast an alarming shadow before him. He glanced up. It was probably the same kind that had been sucked into the Narsh sprayer's atmos engine.

"I hope it gives you gutache, you scumbag," he said, and waited for it to dwindle to a black speck before moving on.

It took more than half an hour to reach the other side of the field, and he still had twenty-five klicks to go to the RV point. He'd decided to go north of the town, although he shouldn't have risked moving by day at all. *Get there early. Wait for them, just in case they decide I'm dead and they don't hang about.* He eased into the bushes, scattering small creatures that he could hear but not see, and considered taking off his packs just for a moment's relief.

But he knew that would make it much harder to move when he slotted them back into place again. Exhausted, he fumbled in his belt for a ration cube and chewed, willing the nutrients to hit his bloodstream as fast as they could, before he slumped into sleep and didn't get up again. Lights danced in front of his eyes. Fatigue was giving him a heads-up display of its own.

The last of the cube dissolved in his mouth. "Come on, soldier, haul it up," he said. Playing mind games could keep him going. The trick was to remember where the game ended and then snap back to reality. Right then he decided to let his commander-self shout him into action.

"Sir!" he said, and sprang up from a kneeling position in one move. He tottered slightly when his knees locked out, but he stayed upright and leaned against a tree. He made a mental note that he needed to keep better hydrated.

It was so dark in the wood that his night vision kicked in from time to time, superimposing ghostly green images on the trunks and branches. He'd grown used to the range of animal sounds, and the occasional whisper of leaves or snap of twigs blended into the pattern of what his brain was cataloging as NFQ—normal for Qiilura. From time to time a slightly abnormal snap or rustle would make him drop to a squat and turn, rifle ready; but he was clear.

He followed the river on his holochart for part of the way, although it was actually more of a stream. The faint trickle of liquid over rocks was reassuring in the way that the sound of water could be, and after an hour he came upon a break in the tree canopy that allowed sunlight to filter down on the stream in slanted shafts. Brilliantly colored insects circled and danced above the surface.

Darman had never seen anything quite like it. Yes, he knew all about geological formations and what they foretold for soldiers: sources of water, treacherous scree, risk of landslide, caverns to shelter in, high ground for defense, passes to block. Accelerated learning packaged the natural world for him and explained how he could use it to military advantage.

But nobody told him it looked so . . . *nice.* He had no words for it. Like the uj cake, it was a glimpse of another world that wasn't his.

Sit down and rest. You're too tired. You'll start making fatal mistakes.

It was weakness talking. He shook his head rapidly to clear it. *No stims, no, not yet.* He had to press on. The insects kept up a constant circuit of the stream like recce aircraft, circling, seeking.

You're hours ahead. Stop. No sleep makes you careless. You can't afford to be careless.

It did sound like common sense. It wasn't the game-voice, his imaginary commander, giving him orders: it felt deep within him, instinct. And it was right. He was making slower and slower progress and he had to concentrate on putting one foot in front of the other.

He stopped and unclipped one pack, then the other. It was a good enough place to camp. He filled his water bottle and hauled a few half-decayed logs into place to build a defensive sanger, just as Sergeant Kal had taught them. It was only a low defensive circle of rocks—or whatever came to hand—but it made a difference on a battlefield when you couldn't dig in. He sat in the walled hollow he had created, staring at the water.

Then he cracked the seal on his helmet and breathed unfiltered air for the first time in many hours.

It smelled complex. It wasn't the air-conditioning of Tipoca City and it wasn't the dry dead air of Geonosis. It was alive. Darman released all the gription panels on his armor and stacked the plates inside the circle of the sanger, set his helmet to detect movement, and left it on the makeshift wall. Then he peeled off his bodysuit section by section and rinsed it in the flowing water.

The day was surprisingly warm; he'd had no way of telling what it felt like while he was sealed in the suit, just the ambient environment data on his display.

But the water was shockingly cold when he stepped in. He washed quickly, sat in the pool of sunlight to dry off, and then replaced the panels of bodysuit. They'd dried a lot more quickly than he had.

Before he let himself nod off he put his armor back on. There was no sense in getting used to the pleasant sensation of not wearing it. It was drilled so thoroughly into him that he was surprised he'd thought otherwise even for a second: in enemy territory, you slept in full kit with your blaster ready. He cradled his rifle in his arms, leaned back on his pack, and watched the insects dancing on the sunlit water.

They were hypnotically beautiful. Their wings were electric blues and bright vermilion and they wove a figure-eight. Then, one by one, they dropped down and floated on the surface, drifting with the current, still wonderfully vivid, but now apparently dead.

Darman reacted. *Airborne toxin.* He shut his eyes tight, puffed out the air in his lungs, and snapped his helmet back into place, drawing breath again only when the seal was secure and his filtration mask could take over. But there was no data on his visor to indicate a contaminant. The air was still clean.

He leaned out and scooped up a couple of the insects caught in an eddy. One kicked a leg a few times and then was still. When he looked up, there were none left flying. It seemed sad. What bothered him more was that it seemed inexplicable.

Curious, he fumbled for an empty ration cube container and dropped the insects into it to consider them later. Then he closed his eyes and tried to doze, rifle ready.

But sleep eluded him. His helmet detected movement and woke him every few minutes at the intrusion of small creatures no threat to him. Once or twice it picked up a gdan, and he opened his eyes to see glittering points of reflected light staring back at him.

The system picked up something larger once, but it wasn't as large as any humanoid in his database, and kept its distance before disappearing.

Get some sleep. You're going to need it, son.

Darman wasn't sure if it was his own voice or that of his imaginary commander. Either way, it was an order he was only too willing to obey.

Ghez Hokan never took kindly to being summoned, but Ovolot Qail Uthan had the gift of being charming about it. She *invited* him to meet her in the research complex. She even sent one of her staff with a speeder to collect him from his offices.

Hokan appreciated the gesture. The woman understood how to use power and influence. The Neimoidian grocer had yet to learn.

Uthan was not particularly pretty but she did have the knack of dressing well—in plain dark robes—and carrying herself like an empress. That balanced the scales. What Hokan liked most about her was that while she seemed to know that feminine charm wouldn't override his common sense, she never dropped her seductively reasonable facade. She was a professional, and mutual respect went a long way with him. The fact that she was a scientist with subtle political skills impressed him further still. He could almost forgive the unnatural act of fighting without real weapons.

The decaying exterior of farm buildings gave way to reinforced alloy doors and lengthy corridors with what appeared to be emergency bulkheads. Hokan carried his helmet under one arm, unwilling to leave it—or his weapons—with the servant. The wizened man looked local. The locals were all thieves.

"Expecting some grain silo fires, then?" he said, and prodded the recessed blast bulkheads with his forefinger.

Uthan laughed a low, tinkling laugh that he knew could just as easily switch to a commanding voice and freeze a parade ground of troops. "I'm grateful you could make the time to see me, General Hokan," she said. "Under normal circumstances, I would never bypass someone with whom I had a contract and speak directly to his . . . subcontractor. It's very rude, don't you think? But I'm a little concerned."

Ah, Ankkit wasn't part of this conversation. Hokan began to understand. And she was laying on the flattery with a trowel. "I'm merely Hokan, a citizen. Let me address your concerns . . . madam?" He felt suddenly foolish. He had no idea what to call her. "Mistress Uthan?"

"*Doctor* will be fine, thank you."

"How can I reassure you, then, Doctor?"

She steered him into a side room and indicated three shimmering beige brocade upholstered chairs, clearly imported from Coruscant. He hesitated to sit on such a conspicuously decadent seat, but he did because he would not stand before her like a servant. Uthan took the chair nearest him.

"You have some idea of the importance of the work I carry out here, I think."

"Not in any detail. Viruses. From the building specification, anyway." He'd policed the construction crews, who were also all thieves. "Hazardous materials."

If Uthan was surprised, she gave no indication whatsoever. "Exactly," she said. "And I confess I'm somewhat disturbed by the events of recent days. Lik Ankkit assures me my security is guaranteed, but I would really welcome your assessment of the situation." Her tone hardened just a fraction: still syrup, but now with gritty, sharp crystals in it. "Is this project under any threat? And can you maintain its security?"

Hokan didn't hesitate. "Yes, I believe your facility is vulnerable." He was a master of his trade. He saw no reason to lose his reputation over a restriction not of his making. "And no, I can't guarantee anything with the level and quality of staff that I have."

Uthan sat back with controlled slowness. "Last matter first. Do you not have the resources to employ them? Ankkit's contract is quite generous."

"That generosity has not filtered down to my operation."

"Ah. Perhaps we should shorten the supply chain in the interests of efficiency."

"I have no opinion on that. Ankkit's welcome to his cut as long as I have the tools to do the job."

"That wasn't quite the cut I had in mind for Lik Ankkit." She smiled. There was no warmth in it. "And you believe the recent incursions are related to this facility?"

"Circumstantial evidence. Yes." Hokan returned the smile and suspected his was a few degrees cooler. If she'd do this to Ankkit, she'd do it to him. "It's a big planet. Why the Imbraani region? Why send Jedi agents?"

"Have you located any forces?"

"No. I've identified at least two points of hard contact and one downed vessel, though."

"Hard contact?"

"Situations when soldiers actually engage each other." Not that his rabble of mercenaries rated the distinction of *soldiers.* "I can't gauge numbers."

"If I were to arrange for you to have command of Separatist droids and their officers from our nearby garrison, would that make your task easier?"

"I take no sides. I won't lie to you and pretend to support your cause."

"You have military experience, of course. There's no disgrace in being a mercenary."

"I'm Mandalorian. It's in my soul as well as part of my education. No, there's no shame in it as long as you give of your best."

Uthan suddenly melted into what seemed to be a thoroughly genuine and sympathetic half smile. "I think I should share something with you. It might be distressing." There were still hard edges in her unctuous tone. "The Republic has created an army of cloned troops. *Millions.* They have been bred to fight and serve Jedi generals without question, altered to be their willing servants. They have had no normal life and they age very rapidly—if they survive being wasted in foolish battles. Do you know whose genetic material was used to create these unfortunate slaves?"

"No, I don't." Hokan was never embarrassed to admit ignorance. That was for small men. "Tell me."

"Jango Fett."

"What?"

"Yes. The finest Mandalorian warrior of his day has been used to churn out cannon fodder for the aggrandizement of the Jedi."

If she had spat in his face, he couldn't have been more appalled. He knew she was aware of what would enrage him; she used the emotional term *warrior,* not *bounty hunter.* She knew how much the revelation would offend his cultural pride. But she was right to tell him. It was a matter of honor, and more than his own. He would not see his heritage used in this travesty of honest war.

"I'd take the contract even if you didn't pay me," he said.

Uthan seemed to relax. "We can give you up to a hundred droids to start with. Ask if you need more. It's a small garrison because we didn't want to attract attention, but now that we have that attention anyway we can reinforce if necessary. What about your existing militia?"

"I think layoff notices might be in order. Perhaps your troops might start by helping me with the administration of that."

Uthan blinked for a second, and Hokan realized she had taken longer than usual to understand what he meant. She'd grasped the meaning: *I can be as ruthless as you.* She'd think twice before undermining him as she was undermining Ankkit.

"That might be a sensible start," she said.

Hokan stood up and held his helmet in both hands. He had always been proud of that tradition, proud that it hadn't changed in thousands of years except for a technical enhancement here and there. What really mattered was what lay under Mandalorian armor—a warrior's heart.

"Would you like to know what virus we're developing here, Major Hokan?" Uthan asked.

So he had a real rank now, not the flatteringly extravagant *General.* "Do I need to?"

"I think so. You see, it's specifically for the clones."

"Let me see. To make them proper men again?"

"Nothing can do that. This is to kill them."

Hokan replaced his helmet carefully.

"The kindest solution," he said, and meant it.

7

Bal kote, darasuum kote,
Jorso'ran kando a tome.
Sa kyr'am Nau tracyn kad, Vode an.

(And glory, eternal glory,
We shall bear its weight together.
Forged like the saber in the fires of death,
Brothers all.)
—Traditional Mandalorian war chant

It would have been much, much easier to fight in a different environment.

Niner decided that when he got back to base he'd ask to amend the training manual on nonurban warfare, to reflect the fact that SOPs for temperate rural terrain were definitely *not* interchangeable with jungle tactics.

It was the fields. There was too much open ground between areas of cover. Niner had been sitting in the fork of a tree for so long that one buttock was numb and the other was catching up fast. And still the group of militia was sprawled in the grass at the edge of a recently mown field, passing around bottles of urrqal.

Niner didn't stir under his camouflage of leaves. It was nearly autumn, so it was a trick they wouldn't be able to rely on much longer, as almost all the woodland was deciduous. They planned to pull out long before then.

"Anything happening, Sarge?" Fi's voice was a whisper in his helmet, even though the sound wouldn't carry. It was a smart habit, just in case. If one precaution was good, two was better. "Still swigging?"

"Yeah. We could always wait until they die of liver failure. Save the ammo."

"You okay?"

"My bladder's a bit full, but fine otherwise."

"Atin's shredding that speedie's onboard computer."

"I hope he's doing it quietly."

"He's moved into the wood a bit. He reckons he's downloaded some high-res charts, but the rest are probably fried. He's on the encryption files now."

"As long as he's happy."

Fi made a stifled snort of laughter. "Yeah, he's happy."

I've been Darman. Niner still had no idea what Atin had meant by that. He'd remember to ask him at a more appropriate moment. All he wanted right then was for Hokan's men to get up and move on so they could cross over to RV Beta, just four klicks ahead. It would have been easy to pick them off from here, but that would leave a nice pile of calling cards and the squad had left too many already. Niner wanted to avoid all the hard contact that he could.

They have to run out of urrqal soon.

And they can't be taking Ghez Hokan very seriously.

Niner was watching the group through his rifle scope, wondering why there was a preponderance of Weequays, when they all looked up, but not at him. They were looking to his right.

"Five more targets approaching," Fi said.

Niner tracked right very gently. "Got 'em."

They didn't look like militia. There was an Umbaran, very smart in a pale gray uniform that matched his skin, and four battle droids marching behind him. Some of the militia boys got to their feet. One of them, reclining on the ground, held his bottle out in offering, muttering something about curing rust.

The only words of conversation that Niner could pick up from the Umbaran were ". . . Hokan asks . . . any contact . . ." The breeze took the rest. *They've got reinforcements,* he thought. *They look like a different problem altogether.*

And they were, but not for him this time. The reinforcement droids raised their integral blasters without warning and simply opened fire into the group of militia. They fired a few bolts in an orderly manner and then waited, looking down at their victims as if checking. The Umbaran—commissioned officer or sergeant?—

stepped forward and fired another blast at close range into a Weequay. Apparently satisfied that their job was done, they gathered up the group's assortment of blasters and sidearms, searched the bodies for something—ID, Niner suspected—and marched calmly away, back down their approach route.

Niner heard Fi exhale at the same time he did.

"Well," Fi said. "You can empty your bladder now, I suppose."

Niner slid down from the fork of the tree, and his leg buckled under him. He removed the plates and rubbed his thigh to get the circulation going. "What do you reckon that was all about, then?"

"Hokan doesn't like them drinking on duty?"

Atin appeared, a jumble of circuitry and wires in one hand. "Looks like the tinnies have shown up to take over. But why shoot them?"

"Tinnies?" Fi said.

"What did your squad call them?"

"Droids."

Niner nudged Fi. "General Zey said Hokan was violent and unpredictable. He executes his own people in cold blood. Let's remember that."

They gathered up their kits and this time it was the turn of Atin and Niner to carry the load they'd rigged underslung on a pole. Fi walked ahead on point.

"I haven't fired a shot yet," he said.

"On this sort of mission, the fewer the better," Atin said.

Niner took it as a sign that Atin was joining in. His tone wasn't as defensive. Regular people said they couldn't tell the difference between one clone and another, did they? That was what came of spending too much time looking at faces and not enough wondering what shaped people and went on inside their heads.

"Save 'em for later," Niner said. "I think we're going to need every single round."

I must be out of my mind.

Etain watched the ramshackle farmhouse buildings through a gap in the barn's planked walls. The roofs were outlined against the deepening turquoise of the dusk sky: two lamps stood by the porch of the main building to keep the gdans away from the path to the outside refresher. There were so many of the little predators nesting around the farm that one of their warrens had subsided, leaving a gaping hole in the farmyard that was now filling up every time it rained. Birhan wasn't big on maintenance.

That did make some tasks easier, though. Satisfied that nobody was approaching, she went back to working boards loose from the barn's frame at the rear of the building. There was no other exit if she were ambushed, so she was making one.

She concentrated on the boards, fixing their shape and position in her mind. Then she visualized them separating and moving aside, creating a gap. *Move,* she thought. *Just part, swing aside* . . . and the boards did indeed move. She rehearsed shifting them with the Force a few times, letting them fall back into place quietly.

Yes, she could use the Force. When she felt confident and controlled, she could master everything Fulier had taught her; but those days could be few and far between. She wrestled with a temper unbefitting a Jedi. She watched those with serene acceptance of the Force and envied their certainty. She wondered why Jedi blood had bothered to manifest itself in someone who was so fallible.

Etain hoped she could manage to use the Force to do something more momentous than moving planks if the situation demanded it. She was certain that the next few days would test her beyond her limits.

Jinart arrived just after it grew completely dark. Despite watching intently through the crack in the wall, lightsaber ready, Etain didn't see her approach, or even hear her until the door swung open.

But she *felt* her. And she wondered why she hadn't felt her before.

"Ready, girl?" Jinart asked. She was wrapped in a filthy shawl that seemed about to walk of its own accord. It was a pretty convincing disguise.

"Why didn't you tell me?" Etain asked.

"Tell you what?" Jinart asked.

"I might be less than the ideal Padawan, but I can always sense another Jedi. I want to know why."

"You're wrong. I'm not that at all. But we *are* serving the same cause."

Jinart cast around and picked up the remnants of a loaf that Etain hadn't finished. She shoved it under her shawl.

"That wasn't an explanation," Etain said, and followed her out the door. There were no gdans to be seen. If this woman was strong in the Force and not a Jedi, she had to know why. "I need to know what you are."

"No, you don't."

"How do I know you're not someone who has turned to the dark side?"

Jinart stopped abruptly and spun around, suddenly faster and more upright than an old woman should have been. "I can choose when I am detected and *not* detected. And given your competence, I'm the one who's most at risk. Now, *silence.*"

It wasn't quite the answer Etain was expecting. She felt the same authority as she had in the presence of Fulier, except that he exhibited peaks and troughs of the Force, while Jinart projected an infinite steadiness.

She was *certainty*. Etain envied certainty.

Jinart led her into the woodland that skirted Imbraani to the east. She was keeping up a punishing pace, and Etain decided not to ask any more questions for the time being. At various points along the way, Jinart deviated: "Mind the warrens," she said, and Etain sidestepped holes and depressions that told her colonies of gdans had been busy beneath the ground.

They finally paused half an hour later, having covered an arc that brought them north to the edge of the Braan River. As rivers went, it was more of a large stream. Jinart stood still, apparently looking at the water but not appearing to focus. Then she jerked her head around and stared west, taking a deep breath and exhaling slowly.

"Walk upstream," she said. "Follow the riverbank and keep your wits about you. Your soldier is still there, and he needs those plans."

"A soldier. *One?*"

"That's what I said. Come on. He won't be there much longer."

"Not a group, then. Not even a few."

"Correct. There are others, but they're a little way from here. Now go."

"What makes you think I have plans?"

"If you hadn't, I wouldn't be risking myself to direct you toward your contact," Jinart said. "I have other work to do now. When you find your soldier, I'll try to persuade Birhan to take him in for a while. He'll need somewhere to hide. Get on with it. He won't hang around."

Etain watched Jinart start away toward the town, looking back just once. The Padawan slipped out her lightsaber and tried to get a sense of what might lie west along the riverbank, and when she glanced back again Jinart was nowhere to be seen. She was aware of the scrabbling of small clawed feet around her. Whatever influence had kept the gdans at bay while Jinart was with her was gone. She kicked out occasionally and hoped her boots were thick enough.

If she went back to the farm, nothing would have changed and she would be no nearer to delivering the information. She had no choice but to go on.

The bank was overgrown in places and she stepped into the river, knowing it would be shallow. The knowledge didn't make it any more pleasant to wade in sodden boots. But it was a reliable route, and it kept the gdans from trying their luck with her.

They were wary of Jinart. Etain wondered why the Force didn't deter them from stalking her as well. It was more confirmation, if she ever needed it, that she really wasn't much of a Jedi when it came to utilizing the Force. She had to concentrate. She had to find that single-minded sense of both purpose and acceptance that had so long eluded her.

Although Etain had clearly not yet come close to mastering control of the Force, she could see and feel beyond the immediate world. She could feel the nocturnal creatures around her; she even felt the little silver weed-eels parting to avoid her before they brushed her boots on the way downstream.

Then she became aware of something she wasn't expecting to encounter in the wilds of the Imbraani woods.

A child.

She could feel a child nearby. There was something unusual about the child, but it was definitely a youngster, and there was a feeling of loss about it. She couldn't imagine any of the townspeople letting a child out at night with gdans about.

Ignore it. This isn't your problem now.

But it was a child. It wasn't afraid. It was anxious, but not *scared* as any sensible child should have been, wandering around alone at night.

Suddenly there was something touching her forehead. She put out her hand instinctively as if shooing away an insect, but there was nothing there. And still she felt something right between her brows.

It dipped briefly to her chest, exactly on her sternum, and back up to her forehead. Then she was suddenly blinded by a light of painful intensity that shot out of the darkness and overwhelmed her.

She had nothing to lose. She drew her lightsaber, prepared to die on her feet if nothing else. She didn't need to see her opponent.

There was a slight *ah* sound. The light snapped off. She could still sense a child right in front of her.

"Sorry, ma'am," a man's voice said. "I didn't recognize you."

And still she detected only a child, so close that it had to be next to the man. For some reason she couldn't sense him in the Force at all.

Red ghost-images of the light still blinded her. She held her lightsaber steady. When her vision cleared, she knew exactly who she was staring at, and she also knew Jinart had betrayed her.

She'd probably betrayed Fulier, too.

Etain could see the distinctive full-face Mandalorian helmet of Ghez Hokan.

The sinister T-shaped slit told her all she needed to know. She raised the lightsaber. Both his hands were resting on his rifle. Perhaps the child—the unseen child—had been a lure, a distraction projected by Jinart.

"Ma'am? Put the weapon down, ma'am—"

"Hokan, this is for Master Fulier," she hissed, and swung at him.

Hokan leapt back with astonishing reflexes. She didn't recognize his voice: it was younger, almost accentless. He didn't even raise his rifle. The monster was playing with her. She spun on the ball of her foot and very nearly took his arm off. Sudden rage constricted her throat. She slashed again but found only air.

"Ma'am, please don't make me disarm you."

"Try it," she said. She beckoned him forward with one hand, lightsaber steady in the other. "You want this? Try me."

He launched himself at her, hitting her square in the chest and knocking her backward into the river. *The child was still there.* Where? How? And then Hokan was on top of her, holding her under the water with one hand, and she dropped the lightsaber. She fought and choked and thought she was going to drown and she had no idea why she couldn't fight off an ordinary man with both her fists. She should have been able to muster more physical strength than this human.

He hauled her up out of the water one-handed and dumped her on the riverbank flat on her back, holding both her arms down.

"Ma'am, steady now—"

But she wasn't finished yet. With an animal grunt she drove her knee up hard between his thighs, as hard as she could, and when she was frightened and desperate and angry that was very hard indeed. She hadn't known it until now.

Etain gasped as her knee went *crack.* It hurt. But it didn't seem to hurt him.

"Ma'am, with respect, please *shut up.* You're going to get us both killed." The sinister mask loomed over her. "I'm not Hokan. I'm *not him.* If you just calm down I'll show you." He loosened his grip slightly and she almost struggled free. Now his tone was bewildered. "Ma'am, stop this, please. I'm going to let go and you're going to listen to me explain who I am."

Her breath was coming in gasps and she coughed water. The ever-present child so disoriented her that she stopped trying to dislodge him and let him struggle to his feet.

Etain could see him—it—clearly now. She could see well in the darkness, better than a normal human. She was staring at a huge droid-like creature clad in pale gray armor plates with no face and no markings. And it had a blaster rifle. It—he—held out a hand as if to pull her to her feet.

Well, it wasn't Ghez Hokan. That was all she could tell. She took his armored hand and got to her feet.

"What in creation's name are you?" she managed to ask.

"Ma'am, my apologies. I didn't recognize you at first. This is entirely my fault for failing to identify myself correctly." He touched black-gloved fingers briefly to his temple, and she noticed the knuckle plate on the back of the gauntlets. "Commando of the Grand Army CC-one-one-three-six, ma'am. I await your orders, General."

"General?" Voices coming from things that appeared to have no lips reminded her too much of droids.

He tilted his head slightly. "My apologies. I didn't see the braid . . . Commander."

"And what's the Grand Army?"

"The Republic's army, ma'am. Sorry. I should have realized that you've been out of contact with Coruscant for a while now, and . . ."

"Since when did we acquire a Grand Army?"

"About ten years ago." He gestured to the bushes along the bank. "Shall we discuss this somewhere less public? You're presenting something of a target to anyone with a night scope. I think even the local militia can manage one of those between them."

"I dropped my lightsaber in the river."

"Let me get it, ma'am," he said. He stepped into the shallow water, and the light on his helmet flicked on. He bent down and fumbled in the illuminated water, then stood up with the hilt in his hand. "Please don't use it on me again, will you?"

Etain raked her soaking hair back from her face with chilled fingers. She took the lightsaber carefully. "I don't think I'd have much luck anyway. Look, why are you calling me *Commander*?"

"Ma'am, Jedi are all officers now. You *are* a Jedi, aren't you?"

"Hard to believe, isn't it?"

"No offense, ma'am—"

"I'd ask the same question if I were you." *Commander. Commander?* "I'm Padawan Etain Tur-Mukan. Master Kast Fulier is dead. It seems you're the soldier I have to help." She looked up at him. "What's your name?"

"Ma'am, Commando CC—"

"Your name. Your *real* name."

He hesitated. "Darman," he said, sounding as if he were embarrassed by it. "We need to get out of here. They're looking for me."

"They won't have much trouble finding you in *that* outfit," she said sarcastically.

"The dirt's rinsed off." He stood silent for a moment. "Do you have orders for me, ma'am? I have to make RV point Gamma and find the rest of my squad. "

He was talking army gibberish. "When do you have to do that? Now?"

He paused. "Within twelve standard hours."

"Then we've got time. I have plans to show you. Come back with me and let's work out what we have to do next." She took the lightsaber from him and gestured with both arms. "I'll help you carry what I can."

"It's heavy, ma'am."

"I'm a Jedi. I might not be a very competent Jedi, but I *am* physically strong. Even if you did take me down."

"A bit of training will fix that, ma'am," he said, and he eased off that terrible Mandalorian helmet with a faint *pop* of its seal. "You're a commander."

He was a young man, probably in his early twenties, with close-cropped black hair and dark eyes. And despite the hard planes of his face he had a trusting and innocent expression that was so full of confidence that it surprised her. He wasn't just confident in himself; he exuded confidence in *her*. "You're probably just a bit rusty, ma'am. We'll get you back on form in no time."

"Are you *on form,* Darman?" He had overpowered her. It wasn't supposed to be like that. "How good are you?"

"I'm a commando, ma'am. Bred to be the best. Bred to serve *you.*"

He wasn't joking. "How old are you, Darman?"

He didn't even blink. She could see the hard muscle in his neck. There wasn't even a hint of fat on his face. He looked extremely fit indeed, upright, a model soldier.

"I'm ten years old, ma'am," Darman said.

Droids didn't drink or chase women, and they had no interest in making money on the side. They weren't real warriors, soldiers with pride and honor, but at least Ghez Hokan could trust that they wouldn't be found lying in the gutter with an empty bottle the next morning.

And they did look truly magnificent when they marched.

They were marching now, along the wide gravel path that led up to Lik Ankkit's villa. Hokan walked beside them, then behind them, moving position because he was so fascinated by the absolute precision of their steps, and the complete unvarying conformity of their height and profile. They looked like bricks in a perfect wall, a wall that could never be breached.

Machines could be made to be identical, and that was good. But it was anathema to do that to men—especially Mandalorian men.

The Umbaran lieutenant raised his arm and brought the droid platoon to a halt ten meters from the veranda steps. Lik Ankkit was already standing on the top stair, gazing down at them in his fancy headdress and that *di'kutla* robe like the weak, decadent grocer he was.

Hokan walked forward, helmet under his arm, and nodded politely.

"Good morning, Hokan," Ankkit said. "I see you've finally made some friends."

"I'd like to introduce you to them," Hokan said. "Because you're going to be seeing a great deal of each other." He turned to the lieutenant. "Proceed, Cuvin."

The Umbaran saluted. "Platoon—advance."

It was all vulgar theatrics, but Hokan had waited a long time for this. It was also necessary. He had to billet some troops near Uthan's facility for rapid deployment. They would be little use in the base thirty kilometers away.

Ankkit stepped forward as the droids reached the steps. "This is an outrage," he said. "The Trade Federation will not tolerate—"

The Neimoidian stood aside just as the first rank of paired droids reached the intricately inlaid kuvara door, with its marquetry image of entwined vines.

Hokan wasn't expecting a display of heroics, and he didn't get one. "It's very good of you to allow me to billet my troops here," he said. "A noble use of all that wasted space. The Separatists are grateful for the personal sacrifice you've made to ensure the security of Doctor Uthan's project."

Ankkit walked down the steps as fast as his towering headdress and long robe would allow. Even by Neimoidian standards of anxiety, he looked terribly upset. He *shook.* He stood almost a head taller than Hokan even without the headdress, which was rustling as if some creature had landed in it and was struggling to escape. "I have a *contract* with Doctor Uthan and her government."

"And you failed to honor the clause that guaranteed adequate resourcing for security. Doctor Uthan's notice of penalty should be on its way to your office."

"I do not take kindly to betrayal."

"That's no way to address a commissioned officer of the Separatist forces."

"An *officer*?"

"Field commission." Hokan smiled because he was genuinely happy. "I have no need of you now, Ankkit. Just be grateful you're alive. By the way, Doctor Uthan's government has paid a bonus directly to the Trade Federation to ensure I'm allowed to work unhindered. Enemy troops have landed, and this region is now under martial law."

Ankkit's slit of a mouth was clamped tight in anger. At least he wasn't pleading for his life. Hokan would have had to kill him if he had begged. He couldn't bear whining.

"And I suppose that means you, Hokan," Ankkit said.

"*Major* Hokan, please. If you see any of my former employees wandering around, don't shelter them, will you? Some of them have failed to show up to collect their severance payment. I'd like to handle their outplacement package personally."

"You're the paradigm of efficient management for us all," Ankkit said.

Hokan enjoyed the moment of revenge, then put it aside as the distracting bauble that it was. Ankkit was no threat now; you couldn't bribe droids. The Umbaran and Aqualish officers now knew what happened to negligent soldiers because they'd carried out his execution orders. Hokan was careful to ensure that everyone was clear on what happened if they left his employment under a cloud.

"And where do *I* live?" Ankkit asked.

"Oh, plenty of room here," Hokan replied. There was a loud crash, followed by the tinkle of fragile glass hitting a hard floor. Droids could be so careless. "I'm sure you won't get in their way."

He touched his fingers to his helmet and strode off.

There were still a few of his former troops missing. One was his Weequay lieutenant Guta-Nay. He wanted to locate him very badly, as he needed to demonstrate to the new officers that he would happily do his own disciplinary work. It was an image he wanted planted in their heads should Ankkit ever attempt to bribe *them*.

He walked down the path to the waiting speeder bike. A farmer had found scraps of circuitry on his land and wanted to know if it was worth a bottle of urrqal to reveal the location.

Hokan set off to visit him personally, to show that the information was worth more than that. It was worth a farmer's life.

RV point Beta should have been a coppice at the top of a shallow escarpment west of Imbraani. When Niner got within visual range of it, there were no trees to be found.

"Coordinates are right, or else this visor is up the creek," Atin said, tilting his head one way, then the other. "No, position's accurate. Confirm no trees, though. Shall I deploy a remote to recce?"

"No," Niner said. "Let's save them for ordnance. Too conspicuous out here. We'll have to lay up as close as we can and rely on eyeballing Darman if he shows. Where's the nearest cover?"

"About one klick east."

"That'll have to do."

Atin looped back, keeping within the trees and retracing their steps to ensure they weren't being tracked. His armor was now caked with moss, and Niner was glad he wasn't downwind of him. Whatever he'd crawled through smelled authentically rural. Fi and Niner tabbed on, carrying the extra kits between them, an assortment of entry equipment including three dynamic hammers, a hydraulic ram, and a ratchet attachment for the *really* difficult doors. They had transferred all the explosive ordnance to their backpacks. If they made hard contact and had to drop the load and hurry out, Niner didn't fancy being left with a hydraulic ram and ration packs for self-defense. A pile of grenades was far more useful.

"Logging," Fi said quietly.

"What?"

"The missing coppice. It's coming up on autumn. They've been out cutting trees for winter since the recce was done."

"That's the problem with intel," Niner said. "Goes stale really fast."

"Not like exercises."

"No. It's not. This is going to be invaluable for training updates when we get back."

Fi sounded as if he had sighed. That was the funny thing about helmet comlinks. One got used to listening to every nuance of breath and tone and even the different ways his brothers swallowed. They couldn't see each other's facial expressions, and had to listen for them. It was probably like being blind. Niner had never known any blind people, but he had heard of a batch of clones whose eyesight wasn't 20/20 disappearing after their first exercise. Kaminoans were obsessive about quality control.

He might have been bred for selfless obedience, but he wasn't stupid. The Kaminoan technicians were the only things that truly terrified him, and what he felt when he obeyed their instructions was different than the feelings he had when a Jedi gave him orders. He wondered if Fi and Atin felt the same way.

"You don't think we're going to make it, do you, Fi?"

"I'm not afraid to die. Not in combat, anyway."

"I didn't say you were."

"It's just . . ."

"Ten-meter range, son. No Kaminoans listening."

"It's just so inefficient. You said it yourself. You said it was a waste."

"That was Geonosis."

"They spend so much time and trouble making us perfect and then they don't give us what we need to do the job. You remember what Sergeant Kal used to say?"

"He used to swear a lot, I remember that."

"No, he used to get upset when he'd had a few drinks and say that he could make us better soldiers if we had time to go out and live. *Data-rich, experience-poor.* That's what he used to say."

"He used to slur the words quite a bit, too. And he didn't like clones."

"That was all bluster. And you know it."

Yes, Kal Skirata said awful things about clones, but it never sounded as if he meant them, not to the clones, anyway. He got uj cake from home, no easy feat on secret, sealed Kamino, and shared it with the commando squads he was responsible for training. He called them his Dead Men, his Wet Droids, all kinds of abusive things. But if you caught him off duty in his cabin, he would sometimes fight back tears and make you eat some delicacy smuggled in for him, or encourage you to read one of his illicit texts that wasn't on the accelerated training curriculum. They were often stories of soldiers who could have done many other things, but chose to fight. Sergeant Kal was especially eager for his Wet Droids to read stuff about a culture called Mandalorian. He admired Jango Fett. "This is who you really are," he'd say. "Be proud, however much these ugly gray freaks treat you like cattle."

No, he didn't like Kaminoans much, did Kal Skirata.

Once he signed up with the Kaminoans, he said, they never let him go home again. But he'd told Niner that he didn't want to. He couldn't leave his boys now, not since he *knew*. "Brief," he'd say, gesturing with a glass of colorless alcohol, "is never glorious."

Niner was determined to work out what Kal Skirata had come to understand, and why it upset him so much.

"Nobody has all the answers," Niner said. "The trouble with getting used to being powerful is that you can forget the small details that'll bring you down."

Fi made that *ffff* sound as if he was about to start laughing. "I know who you're quoting."

Niner didn't even realize he'd said it. It was Sergeant Kal all right. He'd even started using the word *son*.

He missed him.

Then the comlink warning light in his HUD interrupted his thoughts. *Medium range.* What was Atin—

"Contact, five hundred meters, dead on your six." Atin's voice cut through. "Droids. Ten, one humanoid—confirm ten tinnies, one wet, looks like an officer." There was a loud blast behind them. "Correction—hard contact."

Niner knew this by rote and Fi didn't even exchange words with him. They dropped the kits and darted back the way they had come, rifles up, safetys off, and when they got within fifty meters of Atin's location they dropped into the prone position to aim.

Atin was pinned down at the foot of a tree. There was one droid slumped on its side with wisps of smoke rising from it, but the others were formed up, laying down covering fire while two advanced in short sprints, zigzagging. Atin was managing to get off the occasional shot. If they'd wanted him dead, they probably had the blaster power to do it.

They wanted Atin alive.

"I can see the wet," Fi said. He was to Niner's left, staring down the sniperscope. "Aqualish captain, in fact."

"Okay. Take him when you're ready."

Niner snapped on his grenade launcher and aimed at the line of droids. They were spread, maybe forty meters end-to-end. It might take two rounds to knock them out if they didn't scatter. Droids were great on battlefields. But they weren't made for smart stuff, and if their officer was down . . .

Crack.

The air expanded instantly with the release of heat and energy. That was what gave plasma bolts their satisfying sound. The Aqualish fell backward, chest plate shattered, and lumps that looked like clods of wet soil but weren't flew from him and dropped. The droids stopped for a fraction of a second, then carried on their course as if that was the best idea they had.

Fi scrambled away from his position and rolled.

No, they really weren't good at close-quarters combat, at least not without direction from a wet. But there were always a lot of them, and they could return fire as well as any organic life-form. Three of the seven remaining droids turned their attention to the direction of Fi's bolt.

The bushes where Fi had been firing exploded in flame. Niner perceived that it was all happening slowly—at heartbeat pace—but it wasn't, not at all. He aimed and fired, once, twice. The twin explosions almost merged into one. Soil and grass and metal fragments rained down around him. At close range, droids were almost as dangerous when you hit them as when they hit you: they were their own shrapnel.

The firing stopped. Smoke drifted from at least five impact points. Niner could see nothing moving.

"One tinnie intact but immobile," Fi said.

"Got it," Niner said. He fired again, just in case.

"Looks sorted out there," Fi said. He lowered his rifle. "Atin? You okay?"

"Nothing missing that I can't bolt back on."

"You're a laugh a minute," Niner said, and started to ease up on one arm. It was amazing how he could forget the weight of his pack for the few moments it took to save his life. "Now, how did they—"

"Down!" Atin yelled.

A bolt flew a meter above Niner's head and he dropped back on his belly. It sounded like two shots. Then there was silence.

"*Now* it's sorted," Atin said. "Someone help me get up, please?"

When Niner managed to get into a kneeling position he could see a thoroughly shattered pile of droid, a bit closer to him than the line. It had been two shots he'd heard: one had been aimed at him and one had come from Atin, to make sure there wasn't a second.

"Coming, brother," Niner said.

Atin's mud-smeared chest plate was a different color now, matte black with streaks radiating from the center. "I can't breathe properly," he said, utterly matter-of-fact, in the way badly injured men often were. He gulped in a breath. "My chest hurts."

Fi propped him up against the trunk of a tree and took his helmet off. There was no blood coming from his mouth: he was bone white, and his raw scar looked dramatic, but he wasn't bleeding out. His pupils looked okay: he wasn't in shock. Fi released the gription on his chest plate and eased the armor off.

The bodysuit was intact.

"Sure it's just your chest?" Fi asked. He didn't have a tally scan to check Atin's status. You didn't start removing armor or embedded objects until you knew what you were dealing with. Sometimes that was all that was holding a man together. Atin nodded. Fi peeled away the section of suit starting at the collar.

"Phwoar," Fi said. "That's going to be a monster of a bruise." There was a livid patch from his sternum to halfway down his chest. "You collecting distinguishing features or something?"

"Hit me square on," Atin said, panting. "Not a regular round. Armor works though, eh?"

Fi took his helmet off and listened to Atin's breathing with his ear pressed to his chest.

"Ow."

"Shut up and breathe."

Atin took shallow breaths, wincing. Fi straightened up and nodded. "Can't hear any pneumothorax," he said. "But let's keep an eye on him. The air trapped inside can build up. Might be fractured ribs, might just be a bad bruise." He took out a canister of bacta and sprayed the rapidly developing bruise. Atin lifted his arms slightly as if testing them.

Fi sealed the bodysuit and armor back in place.

"I'll take your pack," Niner said, and unclipped it. It was the least he could do. "I think we can skip RV Beta now. Let's leave some souvenirs around there so Darman can spot them if he shows up. You never know if more tinnies will follow. They're not original thinkers."

They probably had a few minutes, even if any of the droids had managed to call in to base. Fi sprinted off through the trees with a few pieces of debris to leave them at the RV point. Niner searched the remains of the Aqualish officer and took everything that looked like a key, a data medium, or proof of ID. Then he dragged Atin's pack behind him on a webbing strap, heading for the place they'd left the entry equipment.

It was going to be a tough slog to RV Gamma, at least until Atin could carry his pack again.

The whole engagement had lasted five minutes and eight seconds, first shot to last, including running time. He had no idea if it had been one second or half an hour. Funny thing, time perception under fire. Niner's boots crunched over droid shrapnel and he wondered how long a firefight felt to a droid.

"Is that how they see us?" Niner asked. "Ordinary people, that is. Like droids?"

"No," Atin said. "We don't have any scrap value." He laughed and stopped short with a small gasp. It must have hurt him. "I'm going to slow you down."

"Don't go gallant on me. You're coming the rest of the way because I'm not lugging all that kit around with Fi. I want a break sometime."

"Okay."

"And thanks. I owe you."

"No. You don't."

"Thanks anyway. Want to explain why you've been Darman?"

Atin was holding his rifle carefully, a handspan clear of his chest. "I've been the last man left standing in two squads now."

"Oh." Silence. Niner prompted: "Want to tell me how?"

"First squad tried to rescue me on a live range exercise. I didn't need rescuing. Not that badly, anyway."

"Ah." Niner felt instantly appalled at himself for thinking Atin didn't care what happened to Darman. He was just caring too much. "My training sergeant said there was something called survivor's guilt. He also said that in those cases, having you survive was what your squad wanted."

"They bred a lot of stuff out of us. Why not that as well?"

Niner stopped dragging Atin's pack and slung his rifle over his shoulder. He lifted the pack and was glad to carry it.

"If they had, I might not be here now," he said, and knew Darman would be waiting for them tomorrow.

Ghez Hokan surveyed the scrap heap that had been a functioning droid platoon a few hours earlier. Whatever had hit them had hit fast and hard. And—judging by the precisely placed sniper shot and the blast pattern of only two grenades—they had been taken out by experts.

It might have been one man or it might have been a platoon. You typically couldn't ambush battle droids like that with a handful of men, but that depended entirely on who the men were. It was a shame the captain hadn't called back with a sitrep as instructed: if he hadn't been killed, Hokan would have had him shot for disobeying operational procedure. He studied the droid escort lined up neatly by the speeder bikes and wondered if they felt anything when they saw dismantled comrades.

"There's no sign of a camp, sir." Lieutenant Cuvin came jogging back from the woods opposite the clearing. It was curious to see the Umbaran's deathly pallor tinged pink by the exertion. "Some broken branches at knee height and crushed grass from troops firing prone, but I honestly can't tell how many men we're dealing with."

"You can't tell much, can you, Lieutenant?" Hokan said.

"Sir, I'll check again." He was white-faced now, white even for an Umbaran.

"Sir! Sir!" Second Lieutenant Hurati was enthusiastic, no doubt keen to be elevated to Cuvin's rank. He *sprinted* to his commander, an attitude Hokan appreciated. "I've found the most extraordinary thing."

"I'm glad one of you has found something. What is it?"

"A pile of droid parts, sir."

"And this is extraordinary because . . . ?"

"No, sir, they're some way from here and they're sort of *arranged,* sir."

Hokan strode off for the speeder. "Show me."

The trees had been cut down a few days earlier because there was already klol fungus growing on them in a pale-pink mesh. One broad stump—the flattest one, almost like an altar—supported the remains of a droid.

The torn pieces of its trunk were laid flat. The arms were neatly arranged on one side of the thorax and the legs on the other. Part of the faceplate was propped up as if looking skyward.

"That's how the droid pilot was left, too, sir." Hurati *was* a good man. He'd obviously studied the report the militia had filed, however appallingly inadequate its presentation had been. "I think it's a sign."

It was a long way to move a dead droid from a battle. There were no drag marks leading to the stump. It was a heavy load to carry on foot; they might even have a transport, although he could see no signs that a repulsorlift had passed over the ground. Hokan stared at the ritually arranged debris and tried to think who would want to send the Separatists a message—and what it might mean.

"It's a trophy," Hokan said. "They're taunting us. They're showing how easy this is for them."

That made him angry. He was Mandalorian. Being an easy enemy wasn't his way. "A curfew, Hurati. Declare a permanent curfew on all powered vehicles until further notice. Anything moving under power is either ours or the enemy. We can track all friendly transports." He paused. "You have made sure all our vehicles have their own transponders, haven't you?"

“Yes sir.”

“Why the delay, then?”

“It’s—it’s harvest, sir. How will the farmers get their produce to Teklet for shipping?”

“I imagine they have handcarts,” Hokan said. He swung his leg over the speeder’s saddle. “Ankkit will have to find an alternative means of conveyance for his crops.”

Hokan pondered on the carefully arranged droid debris all the way back to his new headquarters in Ankkit’s villa. He feared that moving into that vulgar Hutt bordello of a house would make him soft and decadent, too, so he set up his office in an outbuilding. He didn’t care for fancy drapery and useless ornaments. It just happened to be convenient for the research facility, and close to his troops.

So who had the Republic sent to target Uthan’s project? They were clearly bold men; first they made sport of an aerial patrol, now a droid platoon and its captain. They seemed to be choosing their targets casually. The clone army must have been terribly important to the Republic’s strategy for these troops to land like this. Where were the conventional armies? Where were the Jedi generals? When would they come?

This was a new kind of war. He could feel it.

He hated not knowing who was out there, preparing to fight him. If he hadn’t known the man was dead, he would have sworn it was Jango Fett himself.

8

You know what makes you especially effective? It's not just that you're genetically superior and intensively trained. And it's not just because you obey orders without question. It's because you're all prepared to shoot to kill, every time. Only one percent of civilians are prepared to kill, and less than a quarter of ordinary human soldiers, even under fire.

—Sergeant Kal Skirata, from his opening lecture to commandos on military psychology

The droid fired a volley of bolts at the sealed alloy doors until they glowed red. And still nothing happened.

"Stop!"

The droid appeared not to hear.

Dr. Ovolot Qail Uthan ran down the flight of steps, red and black strands of hair streaming out behind her. She was wearing a voluminous dark blue nightgown; it looked as expensive as her day wear. Hokan saluted her politely and went on watching the droid's progress.

"Have you gone mad?" Uthan whispered fiercely. She didn't strike Hokan as the sort of woman who would need to raise her voice to make her point. "There's a *biohazard* behind that door."

"I know," Hokan said. "Just testing. It's all holding up well indeed. Excellent safety bulkheads."

Uthan took a discreet but deep breath and glanced briefly at the backs of her hands. "This facility has been built and tested to the highest containment standards, Major. You needn't worry."

"But I do, Doctor." He watched the droid patiently wasting bolt after bolt on the door for a while. It paused to swap power packs. *"Stop."*

It stopped. Hokan took out the lightsaber he had taken from Kast Fulier and ran its pure blue light down the seam between the two doors. Smoke curled up from the surface, but no breach appeared. It would take even a Jedi a long time to cut through this plating.

"Forgive my insistence, but could this not wait until the morning?" Uthan asked. "I'm working around the chrono as it is to weaponize this agent. I even sleep here. I would prefer to be doing that right now."

"My apologies, Doctor, but we might not have the luxury of time."

"What's time got to do with it?"

"I think I need to relocate you."

Uthan had a way of lowering her head slightly, then straightening up as if she were a krayt dragon. It was most impressive. "This is a high-risk biohazard facility. It can't be relocated like some *tent.*"

"I appreciate the inconvenience involved. I still believe it would be safer if you were to pack up your materials and staff and move elsewhere."

"Why? You have the security situation under control."

"I have it more under control than I did, that's true, but enemy troops have landed. I don't know their numbers, and I don't know what matériel and armaments they have at their disposal. All I know—all I think I know—is that this is what they've come for."

"This is a fortress. You have a hundred droids at your disposal. Let them come. You can repel them."

"All fortresses can be breached in time. I could give you a list of circumstances under which someone who's very resourceful could get past these doors, but I want you to trust my judgment and accept what I say. Let's move you and your work to somewhere less obvious until I have a more accurate assessment of the threat."

Uthan looked completely impassive, staring slightly past Hokan as if she was calculating something.

"I can remove the biomaterials and my staff," she said at last. "The equipment can be replaced if needed. I won't be able to continue working without a safe laboratory environment, of course, but if you believe the project is at risk, then idle time is a better option than wasting three months' work."

What a splendidly sensible woman she was, almost Mandalorian in her discipline and dedication. Hokan ushered the droid out. "How long?" he asked.

"Six hours, perhaps."

"Is this material that dangerous?"

She tilted her head slightly. "Only if you're a clone. If you're not, it might simply make you unwell."

"It must be strange to fight with weapons you can't see."

"War is about technology," she said.

Hokan smiled politely and walked back out into the courtyard to stand in the dim light from the doorway. There was the first hint of chill on the night air; winter was coming, and the landscape would be much easier to patrol when the leaves had fallen. When the snows came, it would be even easier. But he suspected that this conflict was going to be a rapid one. Intelligence reports were starting to come in that the Republic was now fighting on hundreds of different fronts. *Hundreds.*

Their new army would have to be millions strong to achieve that dispersal. So they were all clones. *Sad travesties of the great Jango Fett.*

Well, he knew one thing. The Republic wouldn't be sending clones to deal with this particular problem. They had to know the Separatists already had the one weapon that could stop them in their tracks. And this kind of operation was beyond the capacity of the docile infantry clones Uthan had described. This was not a game of numbers.

Hokan replaced his helmet and started visualizing the research facility as a trap. So they wanted to come and take a look, did they? He'd make them welcome.

"Droids, form up. Two ranks across this entrance."

The droids moved as one, even in the darkness, and Hokan again admired their precision. Now they were a road sign pointing the way to the target, confirming what the Republic thought it knew. But they'd be wrong. They'd be sending their best men to a decoy.

War is about technology.

"No," Hokan said aloud. The droids snapped to attention. "War isn't even about firepower." He tapped his temple. "It's about applying your brains." Then he touched his chest. "And it's about courage."

He didn't expect the droids to understand that. Clones probably didn't understand it, either.

The straw stank of something awful, but Darman was too exhausted to care. It looked like it might be soft enough to sink into. That was good enough for him.

But first he walked around the walls of the barn and checked for an exit if he needed one in an emergency. There were several loose boards in one wall that would do fine. The rickety building looked as if he could actually punch an escape hole through any fragile plank he chose.

Reassured, he dropped everything he was carrying and tried to sit on the bales, but it turned into more of an uncontrolled slump. He didn't even take his helmet off. He sat back and let out a breath.

The Padawan commander leaned over him. "Are you all right, Darman?" She held her hand out, palm down over him, as if she was going to touch him but didn't.

"I'm fit to fight, Commander." He started to sit up, and she held her hand in a slightly different gesture that clearly meant *Stay where you are.*

"I didn't ask that," she said. "I can feel you're in some distress. Tell me."

It was an order. It came from a Jedi. "I injured my leg when I landed. Apart from that I'm just tired and a bit hungry." *Bit hungry?* He was ravenous. "Nothing at all, Commander."

"Landed?"

"I free-fell from a vessel."

"With all that equipment?"

"Yes ma'am."

"You astound me." He couldn't tell if that was good or bad. "Two things, though. Please don't call me *Padawan* or *Commander*—I don't want to be recognized as a Jedi. And I'd rather be called Etain than *ma'am.*" She paused, no doubt thinking of some other failure on his part. "And please take your helmet off. It's rather disturbing."

So far Darman had met three Jedi and they all seemed to find him distracting in some way, with or without his helmet. All his life he had been taught that he and his brothers were created for the Jedi, to help them fight their enemies; he'd expected some recognition of that bond, or at least an expression of satisfaction. He removed his helmet and sat feeling confused, torn between the absolute clarity of his military expertise, and the confusion of dealing with the civilian world he had been thrust into for the first time.

The Padawan—no, *Etain,* she'd made her orders clear—took a small sphere out of her cloak and opened it in both hands. Layer after layer of holographic images spilled out of it, stacking neatly like plates.

"Plans," she said. Her voice had changed completely. She radiated relief. "Plans of all the Separatist and Neimoidian buildings in this region. Floor plans, utility layouts, wiring diagrams, drainage, ducts, specifics on materials used—every detail of how the contractors built them. This is what you need, isn't it? What you are looking for?"

Darman wasn't tired anymore. He reached out and broke the beam of the projection, flipping a plan vertically so he could read it. He looked through them all and heard himself let out an involuntary breath.

Etain was right. It was nearly every bit of intelligence they needed, apart from more fluid details such as personnel numbers and routines. With these plans they knew how to cut power to the buildings, where to insert nerve agents into air ducts or water supplies, and exactly what they would see and where they would have to go when they gained entry. The plans showed the construction of walls, doors, bulkheads, and windows, so they knew precisely what size of charge or type of ram would be needed to breach them. This was a set of clear instructions for achieving their objective.

But Etain didn't seem to know that objective. "What are you going to do with this?" she asked.

"We've come to abduct Ovolot Qail Uthan and destroy her research facility," Darman said. "She's developing a nanovirus intended to kill clones."

Etain leaned closer. "Clones?"

"I'm a clone. The whole Grand Army is composed of clones, millions of us, all commanded by Jedi generals."

Her face was a study in blank surprise. It was also fascinating in a way he couldn't define. He had never seen a human female this close, this *real.* He was astonished by the dappling of small brown dots across the bridge of her nose and her cheeks, and the different strands of colors in her long, unkempt hair—light browns, golds, even reds. And she was as thin as the locals. He could see blue veins in the backs of her hands, and she smelled different from anyone he'd ever shared space with. He wasn't sure if she was pretty or downright ugly. He just knew she was utterly alien and utterly fascinating, as alien as a gdan or a Gurlanin. It was almost stopping him from concentrating on the job.

"All like you?" she said at last, blinking rapidly. She seemed unsettled by his scrutiny. "What have I said?"

"No ma'am—sorry, *Etain.* I'm a commando. We're trained differently. Some people say . . . that we're *eccentric.* I realize you haven't received much by way of intelligence."

"All I knew—all my Master would tell me—was that Uthan was here and that the plans were critical to the Republic's safety. Clones didn't come into the conversation." She was staring at him just as Jusik had. "There's an old woman who told me you were coming, but she didn't tell me much else. How many of there are you on Qiilura now?"

"Four."

"*Four?* You said there were millions of you! What use is four going to be?"

"We're commandos. Special forces. You understand that term?"

"Obviously not. How are four ten-year-olds going to storm Uthan's complex?"

It took him a few moments to realize she was being sarcastic. "We fight differently."

"You're going to have to be very different indeed, Darman." She looked absolutely crushed, as if he'd let her down simply by showing up. "Are you really ten years old?"

"Yes. Our growth is accelerated."

"How can we possibly train competent soldiers in that time?"

"It's very intensive training." He was finding it hard not to say *ma'am* each time. "They created us from the best genetic stock. From Jango Fett."

Etain raised her eyebrows, but said nothing else. Then she stood up, reached for a basket balanced on a low beam, and handed it to him. It was full of odd round items that smelled edible, but he thought he'd check anyway.

"Is this food?"

"Yes. The local bread and some sort of steamed cake. Nothing exciting, but it'll fill you up."

Darman bit into a lump that yielded slightly in his fingers. It was glorious. It was strongly flavored and chewy and among the most satisfying meals he had ever eaten: not quite on the scale of uj cake, but so far from the odorless, tasteless, textureless field rations that it might well have been.

Etain watched him carefully. "You *must* be starving."

"It's wonderful."

"That doesn't say much for army food."

Darman reached into his belt and pulled out a dry ration cube. "Try this."

She sniffed it and bit into it. The expression of vague disbelief on her face changed slowly into one of revulsion. "It's appalling. There's nothing in it."

"It's the perfect nutritional profile for our requirements. It has no smell, so the enemy can't detect it, and no fiber, so we excrete minimal waste products that would enable us to be tracked, and—"

"I get the idea. Is that how they treat you? Like farm animals?"

"We don't go hungry."

"What do you like doing?"

He really didn't know what answer she was after. "I'm a good shot. I like the DC-seventeen—"

"I meant in your free time. Do you get free time?"

"We study."

"No family, of course," she said.

"Yes, I've got squad brothers."

"I meant—" She checked herself. "No, I understand." She pushed the basket of bread closer to him. "My life hasn't been that much different from yours, except the food was better. Go on. You can finish the whole lot if you want."

And he did. He tried not to watch while Etain wrung water from her robe and shook out her boots. She made him feel uncomfortable but he didn't know why, apart from the fact that she wasn't quite the Jedi commander he had been so thoroughly trained to expect.

The only females he could recall were Kaminoan medical technicians whose quietly impersonal tones intimidated him more than a yelling drill sergeant. And his platoon had once experienced an unpleasantly memorable lecture in encryption techniques from a female Sullustan.

He feared females. Now he feared his Jedi officer and was also agitated by her in a way that he didn't even have a word for. It didn't feel *acceptable.*

"We need to move on," he said. "I have to make the RV point. I've been out of comm contact with my squad for nearly two days, and I don't even know if they're alive."

"This gets worse by the second," she said wearily. "First we have four. Now we might be down to one."

"Two. Unless you have other duties."

"You've seen me fight."

"You're a Jedi. A commander."

"That's a title, not an assessment of my ability. I'm not exactly the best of the best."

"You must be. I know what Jedi can do. Nobody can defeat you as long as you have the Force."

She gave him a very odd smile and picked up the holochart sphere. She seemed to be struggling to find her thread again. She swallowed a few times. "Show me where your RV point is—that's right, isn't it? RV? Show me where it is on this chart."

Darman took out his datapad and linked his mission charts with the image projected from the sphere. He pointed to the coordinates.

"It's here," he said. "Before we set out on exercises or missions, we agree where we'll meet up if anything goes wrong. We had to bail out when our transport crashed, so we're scattered, and the procedure is that we go to an RV point for a set time window."

He zoomed in on the area northwest of Imbraani. Etain tilted her head to follow.

"What's this?" she asked.

"Primary target. Uthan's facility."

"No, it's not."

"Intel said—"

"No, that's the Separatist base. Their garrison." Her eyes darted back and forth, scanning the chart. She pointed. "*This* group of buildings is the facility. You can see. Look." She superimposed the floor plans of the facility with the layout of the farm buildings and shrank the image to fit. They lined up perfectly.

Darman's stomach knotted. "My squad will be heading for the Separatists, then."

"We'd better make sure we intercept them," Etain said. "Or they'll run smack-bang into a hundred droids."

Darman was suddenly on his feet in one move, even before he'd realized that he'd heard someone coming.

"I don't think so," a woman's voice said. "Because the droids are all heading for Imbraani."

Darman's sidearm was out of his belt and aimed before Etain could even turn her head.

9

There is something very touching about them. They look like soldiers; they fight like soldiers; and sometimes they even talk like soldiers. They have all the finest qualities of the fighting man. But behind that is nothing—
no love, no family, no happy memory that comes from having truly lived. When I see one of these men killed, I weep more for him than for any ordinary soldier who has lived a full and normal life.
—Jedi General Ki-Adi-Mundi

Darman had flattened Jinart's face against the wall and put his blaster to her head in the time it took Etain to jump to her feet.

"Steady there, boy," Jinart said quietly. "I mean you no harm."

He had her pinned securely. The expression on his earnest face was entirely benign, so far divorced from the potential violence he was ready to mete out that Etain shuddered.

"Let her go, Darman," she said. "She's a fellow Jedi."

Darman stood back instantly and let Jinart go.

"I'm not a Jedi, I tell you," Jinart said irritably. She looked up into Darman's face. "So you'd shoot an old woman, would you?"

"Yes ma'am," Darman said. Etain stared, horrified. "Threats come in all guises. Not all soldiers are young males, and not all soldiers wear uniforms."

Etain waited for Jinart to aim a kick at his groin, but the old woman broke into a satisfied grin. "There's a sensible boy," she said. "You'll do well. Trust this one, Etain. He's very good at his job." She peered at the blaster, still firmly in his grip. "DC-seventeen, I see."

"There are *four* of them," Etain said, expecting Jinart to react with the same disappointment she had.

"I know." The woman handed Etain a bundle of rags. "A complete squad of clone commandos. Here, dry clothing. Nothing chic, but at least it's clean. Yes, I know all about them. I've been tracking the other three."

"They're okay?" Darman was all anxiety again, still emitting that same sense of *child* that Etain found hard to bear. "I've got to rejoin them. Where are they?"

"Heading north."

"To RV Gamma."

"Whatever you say, lad. You've all led me on something of a dance. You're a challenge to track."

"That's how they trained us, ma'am."

"I know."

Jinart was still staring at Darman's face. "You really *are* a perfect copy of Fett, aren't you? In his prime, of course." Her voice had become lower, with less of the hoarse cracking typical of the very old, and Etain wondered if this was the moment at which she would reveal that she was a Sith. The Padawan slid her hand slowly into her sodden cloak.

Jinart suddenly became black as Coruscant marble, and then devoid of texture and hair and fabric and wrinkles, as if she were wax poured into a crude mold. Her form began flowing.

Darman's incongruously innocent face broke into something like a familiar smile. Etain was ready this time. She was focused; she visualized the lightsaber as part of her arm. She was prepared to fight.

"You're the Gurlanin," Darman said. "We weren't told you were on this mission. How did you manage that?"

"I'm not Valaqil," said a soothing liquid voice. "I'm his consort." Jinart, now a four-legged, black-furred creature, sat up on her haunches and seemed to simply extend upward like a column of molten metal. "Girl, you do look surprised."

Etain couldn't argue with that. Even if you'd encountered the full diversity of nonhuman species—and she certainly had, even within her own Jedi clan—seeing a shapeshifter metamorphose before your eyes was mesmerizing. On top of that, even this naïve clone soldier knew what this creature was. She didn't.

"You're quite a revelation, Jinart. But why can I sense something about you that feels like the Force?"

"We're telepaths," the Gurlanin said.

"Oh . . ."

"No, I'm not delving into your mind. It doesn't work like that. We communicate only with each other."

"But I heard your voice that night, in my mind."

"I was standing near you, actually. Not in any shape you'd notice, of course."

"And me, ma'am?" Darman asked, seeming totally absorbed by the conversation.

"Yes, I told you to get some sleep. I make a convincing fallen tree, don't I?" Jinart flowed and changed and reassembled herself into the epitome of a crone again. "I know, stereotypical, but effective. Old women are invisible. Like you, Darman, we go where others won't and do what others can't. The communications network here is totally controlled by the Trade Federation, and in practice that means a single relay and monitoring ground station at Teklet. And while my kind cannot transmit details over interstellar distances, we *can* communicate broad ideas and notions to each other. My consort and I are your comlink. Not perfect, but better than silence."

The Gurlanin made a liquid sound like water boiling. "I've spent the last two days running myself ragged to gather this intelligence, and it's as much for this young man as it is for you. Ghez Hokan now has command of the armed forces here, such as they are, and he's no fool—he realizes Republic troops are here for Uthan's box of tricks. Darman, he's tracking your comrades."

"We're pretty good at evasion."

"Yes, but they do tend to leave bodies and parts behind them. He admits he doesn't know how many of you there are, and that troubles him."

"You're privy to his concerns, then?" Etain said. She trusted nobody now. She still didn't know who had betrayed Master Fulier, and until she did she would keep an open and cautious mind. Although her Master hadn't told her about the clones, he must have known if he had discovered Uthan's activities. But he hadn't trusted her. For all his kind words, when it came down to it he simply confirmed—even from the grave—that she was not fit to become a Jedi Knight.

"I know Hokan's concerns because I can make a very convincing old man as well as an excellent grandmother," Jinart said. The reply made no sense. "I'll catch up with Darman's comrades and try to direct them to somewhere safe. They have no reliable *intel,* as you call it, a finite amount of ordnance, and no advantage of surprise any longer. Hokan knows what you have come to do and he has enough firepower and droids to stop you. That makes your mission next to impossible without some change of plan or intervention."

Darman considered her carefully. Jinart's news hadn't dented that tangible confidence: Etain saw not a flicker on his face. "It could be worse. I quite liked the sound of a single transmitter."

"Might I also add that the locals will turn you in for one chance to get disgustingly drunk."

Darman looked at Etain. She squirmed. "Out of ideas, soldier?" she asked.

"I await your orders, Commander."

It was the final straw. Weeks of fear, hunger, and fatigue on top of years of doubt and disillusion suddenly brought Etain's fragile edifice crashing down. She had done all she could do, and there was nothing left in her to give.

"Stop it, stop calling me *Commander.*" She felt her nails dig into her palms. "I am *not* your blasted commander. I haven't a clue what to do next. You're on your own, Darman. *You're* the soldier. *You* come up with a plan."

Jinart said nothing. Etain felt her face burn. She had lost all dignity. A lifetime of careful training in the art of control and contemplation had come to nothing.

Darman changed before her eyes. He transformed not in the physical sense that the Gurlanin had, but the change was just as startling because the sense of the child that Etain detected so clearly simply evaporated. Its place was taken by calm resignation and something else, a rather forlorn feeling. She couldn't pin it down.

"Yes ma'am," he said. "I'll do that right away."

Jinart jerked her head in the direction of the door. "Get some air, Darman—I need to talk to *Commander* Tur-Mukan."

Darman hesitated for a moment and then slipped outside. Jinart rounded on Etain.

"Listen to me, girl," she whispered, all harsh sibilants. Droplets of fine saliva glittered briefly in the dim light. "That soldier may think a Jedi's every word is a divine pronouncement, but I don't. You'd better sharpen up *fast.* The commandos and I are all that stands between maintaining some kind of order in the galaxy and its fragmentation, because if the clone army can be wiped out, then the Separatists will *win.*

"You can either help us or stand aside, but you will *not* be an obstacle, and that's what you are if you can't lead those men. They've been bred to obey Jedi without question. Sadly, in this case that means *you.*"

Etain was used to feeling worthless. There was no lower place that Jinart could cast her. "I didn't ask for that responsibility."

"And neither did Darman." Jinart flashed back into a mass of seething black sinews for a terrifying second. "That's the nature of duty. It calls and you give your all. He will. So will his comrades, every single one of them. They need you to help them do their job."

"I'm still learning how."

"Then learn fast. If those soldiers weren't conditioned to obey you I'd consider cutting you down now and have done with it. My kind have nothing to thank Jedi for, nothing at all. But we share a common enemy, and I want to see Valaqil again. Think yourself lucky."

Jinart swept out. Etain sank down on her knees in the hay and wondered how she had come to this. The barn door creaked open slowly, and Darman peered around.

"Don't mind me," she said.

"You okay, ma'am?" He winced visibly. "Apologies. *Etain.*"

"You probably think I'm useless as well, don't you?"

"I came up with a plan, as you ordered."

"Bred for diplomacy, too, eh?"

"If Hokan has set the facility as a decoy, then we need him to think that we believe it's still the genuine target. So we split—"

"I'll take that as a yes."

Darman lapsed into silence.

"I'm sorry," she said. "Carry on."

He knelt down, facing her, and swept the floor clear with his hand, creating a clear space on which to demonstrate something. He reached for some crusts of bread and a lump of insect-eaten wood.

"What do you think I am?" he asked quietly.

"From what Jinart says, a clone soldier bred to obey." She watched him break the wood and the crusts into separate chunks and place them in a row like game pieces. "No choice."

"But I do have a choice," he said. "A choice in how I interpret your orders. I'm intelligent. I've seen Jedi fight, so I know what you're capable of. Once you're exposed to situations that call on your skills, you'll be the same."

He was all contradictions. She wondered for a moment if he wasn't a clone soldier at all but another Gurlanin playing spiteful games with her. But she could feel a combination of quiet desperation and . . . faith. Yes, *faith.*

He was the only person in many years who had shown any degree of confidence in her, and the first since Master Fulier who had shown her real kindness.

"Very well," she said. "This is your overriding order. Whatever happens, you are to intervene if anything I do or say compromises your mission. No, don't look at me like that." She held up her hand to stifle the protest she could see forming on his lips. "Think of me as a commander in training. You must train me. That might mean showing me the correct way to do things, or even saving me from my own lack of . . . experience." She could hardly bring herself to say it. "And . . . and that's an order."

He almost smiled. "This is why I have confidence in obeying a Jedi commander. Your wisdom is unequaled."

Etain had to think about that for a few seconds. If Jinart had said it, she would have seethed. Darman meant it. And perhaps he meant it in a number of ways.

Yes, he was intelligent and subtle, not a droid at all. How did a ten-year-old get that way? Disturbed, she concentrated on the comfort of believing that he had seen things that she never had, and so knew best. "Go on," she said. "You had a plan."

RV Gamma, laying-up point, nightfall

"How do you feel now?" Niner asked.

Atin moved his arms, bent at the elbow in a swimming motion, testing his pectoral muscles. "Nearly good as new. No breathing problems, either. No, just a hard smack on the plate."

Fi's disembodied voice spoke up in their helmet comlinks. He was tucked under a bush on the edge of the ridge, keeping watch on the track below. "I'm such a good field medic. Wait till you see me do a tracheotomy."

"I'll pass if that's all right with you," Atin said, easing off his helmet. "Dinner?"

"What do you prefer," Niner asked. "Dry rats, dry rats, or maybe dry rats?"

"Let's go with the dry rats for a change." Yes, Atin was definitely feeling better, and not just physically. "Who used to say that, then?"

"Uh?"

"The dry rations thing."

"Oh. Skirata. Our old instructor sergeant."

Atin took a bite out of the white cube and washed it down with a gulp of water from his bottle. "He never trained us. Heard a lot about him."

"Trained Fi and Darman, too. Our squads were all in the same battalion."

"We had Walon Vau."

"That explains where you get your cheery outlook."

"Sergeant Vau taught us the importance of planning for the worst scenario," Atin said, all loyalty. "And maximizing your tech. *Being hard is good, being hard with superior tech is better.*"

"I'll bet."

"I'd heard everyone loved Skirata, though. Even if he was a bad-tempered drunk."

Niner had never been drunk and he didn't even know what alcohol tasted like. "He cared what happened to us. He *was* one of us, pretty much. Not just there because he couldn't cope with not being in the army anymore, or had to disappear. No, he was a good man." Niner would have given a great deal to have seen Skirata come limping through the trees right then, demanding to know what they were doing lounging around like a bunch of Kaminoan nahra artists. "No idea where he is now, not since we left Kamino. Best covert ops and sabotage man ever."

"You'd know, of course."

"We'll all know soon. I'm relying on what he taught us to get this mission completed."

Niner ate the perfectly balanced, sensibly designed, and utterly tasteless cube, and sat silently, still waiting for Darman. They couldn't even trap something and cook it: the smell of roasting meat and the light of the fire would betray their position.

With Fi on watch, he could shut his eyes and sleep for a couple of hours. He put his helmet back on, partly to be ready to move fast if they had enemy contact, and partly to keep the temperature up in his suit. It was getting chilly. He allowed himself one comfort that he didn't really need, *for morale.*

You scare me. You just absorb everything I tell you. Don't you ever forget?

"No, Sarge," Niner said.

He had no idea how long he'd been asleep. He woke with a start at the sound of Fi's voice.

"Possible contact, due east, range forty klicks. Looks like it's centered on Imbraani."

Even through the visor, it wasn't clear exactly what Fi had spotted, but Niner could see it now, too. A glow marked the horizon like a false sunrise. It was constant, the gentlest graduation from amber to deep red: it wasn't an explosion.

Niner switched between visor modes, main spectrum to infrared to full spectrum, and then back again. The glow was hot, too. The infrared long-range picked it up.

"I reckon that's one big fire coming," Fi said.

They waited, watching: Niner could hear Atin a few meters away, gathering up equipment and assembling it, ready to pull out. With the binocs on full distance, they could see that the fire was being eclipsed in places by billows of smoke. Eventually, Atin joined them, and all three observed the distant blaze in silence.

"They're not burning crop stubble at night," Fi said. "They haven't even finished harvesting that stinking barq stuff yet. They've found something."

"I know."

"Either they've found Darman, and they're teaching the locals not to shelter the enemy, or they haven't found Darman and they're trying to flush him out."

Niner thought it was relatively good news. "But it means he made the landing," he said. "So we wait here right up to the last second, and maybe a little longer just to be sure."

Atin laid the kits down again. He was too professional and disciplined to slam it on the ground, but Niner picked up on the slight sag of his shoulders. "And if he doesn't show by then?" he asked, with a level tone that suggested he didn't want to show dissent any longer. "Next plan?"

"We take another look at the whole area from Teklet to Imbraani," Niner said. "We start from scratch."

"This isn't to scale," Darman said. He scraped marks in the loose soil on the exposed dirt floor of the barn and placed pieces of stale bread carefully on the crude chart. "This is the river. These three crusts are RVs Alpha, Beta, and Gamma." He snapped the wood into more pieces and placed them. "This is the droid base . . . and this is Uthan's lab."

Etain held out her cupped hand. He dropped two chunks of wood into it. "This is Lik Ankkit's residence," she said. "He's the Neimoidian overlord, for want of a better word. He runs the agricultural produce export business, and that near enough makes him an emperor here."

"Okay. What else have we got?"

Etain crumbled her remaining lump of wood into smaller pieces and scattered them carefully in patches. "Imbraani itself, and Teklet, which is the spaceport, and its storage and distribution depot."

"And *this* was the last known position for my squad."

Etain stared at the worm-eaten wood and the moldy crusts that might help them save the Grand Army from destruction. "Why are we scraping maps in the dirt when we've got perfectly good holocharts?"

"That's what Sergeant Skirata used to do," Darman said. "He didn't like holos. Too transparent. He also thought that feeling the texture of dirt focused your mind."

"And you don't need any technology to do it."

"He was a great believer in intuition."

Darman drew his blaster and turned suddenly. The barn door opened. He relaxed and dropped his arm to his side. Jinart held more drab fabric bundled in her arms. "You have to go," she said breathlessly. "Take a look out there to the east. They're burning the fields to flush you out and deny you cover. There's somewhere you can lie low, but you have to pass for farmers—that's not going to be easy for you, lad. You're too big and well fed."

Etain didn't rise to the bait. She knew she'd fit in fine with the undernourished, shabby locals.

"I have to take my kit," Darman said. "I can lay up somewhere with it if I have to."

"Can't you leave any of it?"

"Not if we're going to blow up that facility. I've got all the implosion ordnance to deal with the nanovirus, as well as the E-Web cannon. We need it."

"Then take a cart. There's a curfew on powered vehicles." Jinart tossed one of the bundles to Darman. "And get out of that armor. You couldn't be more conspicuous if you were wearing a wedding gown."

"We can try to make RV Gamma."

"No, go to the first safe house you can find. I'll reach your squad and let them know, then I'll return to you."

There was an assortment of barrows and handcarts stored in the barn, all in various states of disrepair. They'd attract no attention: the network of dirt roads was well traveled by people trying to get their quota of barq and other crops to Teklet on foot or with merlie-carts.

Loading the sections of the blaster cannon on the sturdiest barrow they could find made Etain realize just how heavy a burden Darman had carried. When she tried to heave one of the gray packs into the cart, it nearly wrenched her shoulder from the socket, so she decided to enlist a little assistance from the Force. She hadn't expected it to be so heavy. She wasn't the only one with deceptive physical strength.

"This is all weapons?" she asked.

"Pretty much."

"Not enough to take a hundred droids, though."

"Depends how you use it," Darman said.

Etain wondered if he looked more conspicuous out of his sinister gray armor than in it. The armor had made him look much bigger, but even without it he was so solidly built that it was obvious he'd spent his life training for strength, eating adequate protein. Subsistence farmers didn't have that distinctive slope from neck to shoulder formed by overdeveloped trapezius muscles. Even the youngsters bore the marks of constant exposure to the elements; Darman simply looked strikingly healthy and unburned by the sun. He didn't even have callused hands.

And then there was that ramrod parade-ground posture. He looked exactly like the elite soldier he was. He would never pass for a local. Etain hoped the farmers would be more terrified of him than they were of Hokan.

The night horizon was amber like the urban skies of Coruscant, but it was flame, not the light of a million lamps, that caused the reflection from the clouds. It looked like rain might follow; they could cover the cart with a tarpaulin and not cause any curiosity. Layers of barq stalk, sacks of barq grain, and strips of dried kushayan buried Darman's "kit," as he kept calling it. His language swung from slang and generality to highly educated subtlety, from *kit*—his catchall noun for any artifact—to DC-17s and DC-15s and a whole slew of numbers and acronyms that left Etain befuddled.

"Look at that," Darman said, assessing the skyline. "That flame front must be four klicks, at least."

"That's a million or more credits' worth of barq going up in smoke. The farmers are going to be furious. The Neimoidians are going to be even angrier."

"So will Birhan," Jinart said. "That's a fair whack of his barq you're using for camouflage, girl. Get going." The Gurlanin took Darman's datapad and inserted a mem-stick. "These are all the relatively safe homes I could chart. Don't advertise your identity, either of you. Even if the master of the house you call on knows who you are, do him the favor of not compromising him by admitting it."

Etain had covered her distinctive Jedi cloak with an Imbraani ankle-length tunic. Jinart indicated her hair. "And that," she said.

"The braid, too?"

"Unless you want to advertise what you are."

Etain hesitated. She had once heard someone say they could never remove their betrothal ring, not until they died. Her Padawan's braid felt equally permanent, as if her soul was woven in with it, and that removing it after so long—even temporarily—would rend the fabric of the universe and underscore her belief that she was not Jedi material. But it had to be done. She unfastened the single thin braid and combed the strands of wavy hair loose with her fingers.

She felt less like a Jedi than ever, and not even remotely close to a commander.

"I imagine you never thought a Jedi commander would run away from a fight," she said to Darman as they made their carefully unhurried way up the track.

"Not running away," Darman said. "This is E and E. Escape and evasion."

"Sounds like running to me."

"Tactical withdrawal to regroup."

"You're a very positive man." The child was almost completely absent now. She could mainly sense focus and purpose. He shamed her without intention. "I'm sorry that I lost my composure earlier."

"Only in private. Not under fire, Commander."

"I said not to call me that."

"Where we can be overheard, I'll obey your order." He paused. "Everyone loses it now and then."

"I'm not supposed to."

"If you don't crack sometimes, how do you know how far you can go?"

It was a good point. For some reason he was far more reassuring than Master Fulier had ever been. Fulier, when not getting caught up in putting the galaxy right, was all effortless brilliance. Darman was expert at his craft, too, but there was a sense of hard-won skill, and there was no randomness or mystery to that.

She liked him for being so pragmatic. It crossed her mind that she might be saving clone soldiers from death by biological agent so they could die from blaster and cannon round. It was a horrible thought.

She didn't like having to kill, not even by another's actions. It was going to make life as a commander exceptionally hard.

The droids advanced along the edge of the wood with flamethrowers borrowed from the same farmer whose fields they were burning. Ghez Hokan and his lieutenants Cuvin and Hurati stood in the path of the blaze, staring back at it from three hundred meters.

"We'll have to burn a great deal of land to deny all cover to the enemy, sir," Cuvin said.

"That isn't the point," Hurati said. "This is as much to create the impression of protecting the facility as it is to flush out troops."

"Correct," Hokan said. "There's no point alienating the natives, and I can't afford to compensate them all for lost production. This is sufficient. We'll use droids on the remaining boundaries."

Cuvin seemed undeterred. "May I suggest we use hunting strills? We could bring in a pack with their handlers in two days. The Trade Federation won't welcome the disruption to the barq harvest, and a shortage of the delicacy will be noticed by some very influential people."

"I don't care," Hokan said. "The same influential people will be even more inconvenienced by the arrival of millions of Republic clones on their homeworlds."

Hokan was in full Mandalorian battle armor now, not so much for protection as to convey a message to his officers. Sometimes he had to indulge in a little theater. He knew that the glow of the flames illuminating his traditional warrior's armor made a fine spectacle, calculated to impress and overawe. He was at war. He didn't have to prostitute his martial skills as an assassin or bodyguard for weak and wealthy cowards any longer.

Cuvin was right about the strills, though. It didn't mean he wouldn't have to deal with his dissent, but finding the Republic troops wouldn't be easy.

"How many do you estimate now, Hurati?" he asked.

Hurati flicked a holochart into life and a fly-through image shimmered in the dark. "Vessel downed *here,* confirmed Republic R5 military droid." He pointed. "Remains of two Weequay militia found here, here, and here—but gdans had dismembered and dragged the cadavers over a five-klick range, so the exact location of the kill is estimated. The airspeeder was brought down *here.* The speeder circuitry was found dismantled *here,* but as it was at the entrance to gdan burrows, there's no telling where they might have found it to start with. The engagement with the droid patrol was *here,* because we deployed the patrol based on that finding."

"That's pretty much all in a five-klick corridor spanning forty klicks. Looks obvious to me that they're heading for Teklet, probably to take the port before targeting the facility."

"It would look that way, sir."

"Numbers?"

"I would have said no more than ten, sir. We have reports from farmers who've found evidence of movement across their land.

They're very protective of their crops, so they notice these subtle signs—unlike droids, sir."

"And what does that suggest, then?"

"Multiple tracks crossing an area forty klicks by thirty klicks, sir. Expertly done, too—the locals thought it might be wildlife, but these tracks are not random. I'd say we're being decoyed."

Ten troops. Ten—pathfinders, special forces, saboteurs? Were they preparing the ground for more troops, or were they tasked to complete the mission on their own? Hokan wished he had a few Mandalorian mercenaries, not droids and career officers. He kept his concern well hidden behind his full-face helmet. He also wished he had more airspeeders; he'd never needed more than one to police farms, and it would take days to have any shipped to Qiilura. "Farmers can be pretty cooperative, can't they?"

"Remarkably so, ever since that one found the circuitry, sir."

Hokan turned and started walking back toward the research facility that was now empty but lavishly and conspicuously guarded. He beckoned Hurati to follow him. Cuvin started to follow, too, but Hokan held up his hand to motion him to stay put.

"Lieutenant," he said quietly. "Any sign of my former employee, Guta-Nay?"

"Not yet, sir. Patrols have been briefed."

"Good, and keep an eye on Cuvin for me, won't you? I don't think he's going to make captain."

Hurati paused, but briefly. "Understood, sir."

It was amazing what the unspoken promise of an extra rank insignia could do. Hokan wondered what had happened to the code of conduct.

So there were perhaps ten commandos operating in the region. Hunting them down would be enormously time-consuming. Barring luck, Hokan would never catch them, not with droids and these young academy theorists. Sooner or later, the enemy would need to resupply; sooner or later, they would show themselves.

The Republic was playing decoy games with him, and he with them. It was looking better all the time. They didn't appear to be adopting their usual tactic of landing infantry in force. It was a game of wits, and if need arose he could sit tight and force the Republic to come to him.

If he wanted to bring the Republic close enough to shoot, then he might need an even more compelling bait.

Dr. Uthan would understand. She was a pragmatic woman.

* * *

Fi was getting edgy. It wasn't like him. Niner had only known him a matter of days, but you made quick judgments on small detail if you were a clone commando, especially among your own.

He didn't sleep when Niner relieved him on watch, and after fifteen minutes Fi came forward to the observation position and settled down beside him. The fires seemed to have stopped; the glow was still visible, but it was static. It had probably reached one of the streams and was burning itself out.

"They know we're here anyway," Fi said. Niner needed no telepathy to know he was worrying about Darman. "We could try the comlink at longer range."

"They'd get a fix on positions."

"They'd have to get lucky."

"And we only have to be unlucky once."

"Okay. Sorry, Sarge."

He lapsed back into silence. Niner adjusted his infrared filter to remove the distracting light of the fire. Suddenly, it was abnormally silent, and that meant the gdans had stopped their incessant prowling, which was *not good.*

Niner looked down his rifle scope one-handed to get a narrower focus on the bushes in front of him. As he panned across 180 degrees, he caught sight of little paired reflections, the alert eyes of gdans huddled in uncharacteristic stillness to avoid something.

Movement. His scope flashed blue in one quadrant, warning him. Maybe whatever it was could see infrared. He killed the targeting, switching to image intensification and the Mark One Ear'ole, as Skirata called it. *You got eyes and ears, son, good ones. Don't rely on the tech too much.* Something was coming, something slow, stealthy, smaller than a man, more sly than a droid.

Niner put his hand on Fi's shoulder—*Stay down*—not daring to speak, even on comlink.

It was ten meters away, coming straight at them, making no attempt to stalk. Maybe it didn't know what they were. It was going to get a surprise, then.

Niner flicked on his tactical spot-lamp, and the blinding beam caught a shining black shape. He cut the beam immediately, muscles relaxing. The creature was so flat to the ground now that it looked as if it were flowing water. It was only when it was right in front of them that it sat up and became Valaqil.

"I thought I'd let you see me coming, given your armaments," said a voice that wasn't Valaqil's but was equally liquid and hypnotic. "I make it a rule never to startle a humanoid with a rifle."

"Just as well that we've seen a Gurlanin before," Fi said, and touched his glove to his helmet politely.

"I didn't seem to surprise your colleague, either. I've come to brief you. I'm Jinart. Please don't call me *ma'am* every two seconds like Darman does."

Niner wanted to ask a hundred questions about Darman, but the Gurlanin had used the present tense and so he was *alive.* Niner was glad he had his helmet in place. Displays of emotion weren't professional, not to outsiders, anyway.

"You're heading for the wrong target," Jinart said. "You're on a course for the Separatist base. Normally you'd be knocking on the door of a barracks with a hundred droids inside, but they've moved half of them to defend the research facility and patrol the area. Neither Uthan nor her nanovirus is at the actual facility any longer."

"So it's all going just great," Fi said cheerfully.

"Your targets are at a villa just outside Imbraani, despite what evidence you might see of the facility being defended. It's a trap."

"What's Darman doing?" Niner asked.

"He has your special ordnance and detailed plans of your targets. I've sent him into hiding with the Jedi."

"General Fulier? We thought—"

"You thought right. He's dead. The Jedi is his Padawan, Tur-Mukan. Don't get your hopes up. She isn't commander material—not yet, perhaps never. For the time being, this is still your war."

"We weren't planning on a frontal assault, not without infantry," Niner said. "Now that we've lost the advantage of surprise, we're going to have to get it back again."

"You do have one element—Ghez Hokan has no accurate idea how few of you there are. I've made sure there are many, many obvious signs of movement through the woods and fields."

"You've been busy."

"I can do a good impersonation of a small army, or at least its movement." Jinart glanced at Atin and Fi as if checking them. Maybe she was working out how she would mimic the form of a commando. "Not thinking of shooting and eating any merlies, are you?"

"Why?"

"That armor isn't looking such a tight fit on you as it should."

Fi nodded. "She's right. Expending about thirty percent more calories than planned, Sarge. They didn't calculate for us carrying kits overland."

"You'll exhaust your rations soon," Jinart said. "Merlies are delicious. Just *never* shoot one, please. If necessary, I could hunt them and leave them for you."

"Why?"

"The one you shoot might be me."

It was one more angle they hadn't covered on exercises. Not even Kal Skirata had dealt with Gurlanins, it seemed, or if he had he hadn't mentioned it. Niner liked them. He wondered what world they came from. It was bound to be a fascinating one.

"Where will you head now?" Jinart asked. "I need to let Darman know where you are."

"I'd have said RV Gamma, but that's going the wrong way, from what you've told us."

"I can give you the location of a suitable area nearer Imbraani, and when I return to Darman I will give him the same coordinates."

Atin cut in. "They mine gems here, right?"

"Zeka quartz and various green silicates, mainly, yes."

"Picks and shovels or mechanized?"

"Mechanized."

"They'll have explosives for blasting, then. And remote detonators with nice, safe, long-range settings."

Gurlanins chuckled just like a human. She might have been amused. On the other hand, she might have been thinking Atin was a madman. But Niner liked the direction that Atin's inventive mind was taking.

"Get your holocharts," Jinart said. "Let me give you a virtual guide to the gem industry of the Imbraani region."

10

NOTICE TO QIILURAN CITIZENS

Anyone found with Republic personnel on their land will have that property confiscated and will forfeit their freedom. They, their family, and anyone employed by them in any capacity will be delivered to the Trandoshan representative at Teklet for enslavement. Anyone actively aiding or sheltering Republic personnel will face the death penalty. A reward is offered for anyone providing information leading to the capture of Republic personnel or deserters from the former militia or the Separatist armed forces, in particular Lieutenant Guta-Nay or Lieutentant Pir Cuvin.

—By order of Major Ghez Hokan,
commanding officer, Teklet Garrison

A thin, cold drizzle started falling almost as soon as the sun came up. It felt like Kamino; it felt like home, and that was at once both reassuring and unpleasant.

The moisture beaded on Darman's cloak, and he shook it off. Merlie wool was full of natural oils that made it feel unpleasantly clammy next to the skin. He longed to get back into the black bodysuit, and not only because of its ballistic properties.

Etain was pushing the rear of the cart. Darman was pulling it, walking between its twin shafts. There were times on the rutted track when she had the worst of it, but—as she kept telling him—Jedi could summon the Force.

"I could help," he said.

"I can manage." Her voice sounded like she was straining it through her teeth. "If this is lightweight kit, I'd rather not see the regular variety."

"I meant I could help with martial skills. If you want to train with your lightsaber."

"I'd probably end up slicing off something you'd miss later."

No, she wasn't what he was expecting at all. They walked on, trying hard to look downtrodden and rural, which wasn't so much of a challenge when you were hungry, wet, and tired. The dirt road was deserted: at this time of year there should have been visible activity at first light. Ahead of them was the first safe house, a single-story hut topped by a mixture of straw thatch and rusting metal plates.

"I'll knock," Etain said. "They'll probably run for their lives if they see you first."

Darman took it as a sensible observation rather than an insult. He pulled his cloak up across his mouth and pushed the cart out of sight behind the hut, looking around slowly and carefully as if he were casually taking in the countryside. There were no windows at the rear, just a simple door and a well-worn path in the grass leading to a pit with an interesting aroma and a plank across it. It wasn't an ideal location for an ambush, but he wasn't taking chances. Stopping in the open like this made you vulnerable.

He didn't like it at all. He wished he could feign invisibility like Sergeant Skirata, a short, wiry, nondescript little man who could pass completely unnoticed, until he decided to stop and fight. And Skirata could fight in a lot of ways that weren't in the training manual. Darman recalled all of them.

He pressed his elbow into his side to reassure himself that his rifle was within easy reach. Then he slipped his hand under his cloak and felt for one of the probes in his belt.

When he reached the front again, Etain was still rapping on the doorpost. There was no response. She stood back and seemed to be looking at the door as if willing it to open.

"They're gone," she said. "I can't sense anyone."

Darman straightened up and walked casually toward the rear of the house. "Let me check the regular way."

He beckoned her to follow. Once around the back, he took a probe and slid the flat sensor strip carefully under the gap beneath the back door. The readout on the section that he was holding said there were no traces of explosive or pathogen. If the place was booby-trapped, it would be very low tech. It was time for a hands-on check. He pressed on the door with his left hand, rifle in his right.

"It's empty," Etain whispered.

"Can you sense a tripwire that'll send a row of metal spikes swinging into you?" he asked.

"Point taken."

The door swung slowly open. Nothing. Darman took a remote from his belt and sent it inside, picking up low-light images from the interior. There was no movement. The room appeared clear. He let the door swing back, recalled the remote, and stood with his back to the entrance for one final check around him.

"I go in, look again, then you follow me if you hear me say *in, in, in,* okay?" he said, almost under his breath. He didn't meet her eyes. "Lightsaber ready, too."

As soon as he was inside, he pulled his rifle, stood hard up in the corner, and scanned the room. *Clear.* So clear, in fact, that last night's meal was still half eaten on the table. There was a single door that didn't appear to open to the exterior. A cupboard, a closet—maybe a threat. He trained his rifle on it.

"In, in, in," Darman said. Etain slipped through and he gestured her to the corner opposite, then pointed: *Me, that door, you, back door.* Etain nodded and drew her lightsaber. He walked up to the closet and tried to raise the latch, but it didn't open, so he took two steps back and put his boot to it, hard.

They didn't build well around here. The door splintered and hung on one rusted hinge. Behind it was a storeroom. It made sense now: in a poor country, you locked away your food supply.

"They left in a hurry," Darman said.

"Are you wearing your armored boots?" Etain said.

"I wouldn't be kicking down a door without them." He'd covered them in tightly wound sacking. "No boots, no soldier. As true as it ever was." He stepped through the gap into the store and studied the shelves. "You're just learning the first step in clearing a house."

"What's that?" Etain reached past him for a metal container marked GAVVY-MEAL.

"Who's watching the door? Who's watching our kits?"

"Sorry."

"No problem. I expect it never occurs to you when you have Jedi senses to rely on." There: he hadn't even tried to call her *ma'am* this time. "If we knew why the occupants left in such a hurry, this might have made a decent place to lay up. But we don't. So let's grab some supplies and move on."

He took dried fruit and something that looked like cured leathery meat, making a mental note to test all of it with the toxin strip in his medpac. It was too kind of the locals to leave all this. There was, of course, every chance they had fled in terror from the same violence that he had witnessed looking down from his observation point just after he landed.

Etain was filling a couple of water bottles from a pump outside.

"I've got a filter for that," Darman said.

"Are you sure you weren't trained by Neimoidians?"

"You're in enemy territory."

She smiled sadly. "Not all soldiers wear uniforms."

She'd catch on. She *had* to. The thought that a Jedi might be unable to offer the leadership he had been promised was almost unbearable. His emotions didn't have names. But they were feelings that had memories embedded in them—finishing a fifty-kilometer run thirty-two seconds outside the permitted time, and being made to run it again; seeing a clone trooper fall on a beachhead landing exercise, weighed down by his pack and drowning, while no directing staff paused to help; a commando whose sniping score was only 95 percent, and whose whole batch disappeared from training and were never seen again.

They were all things that made his stomach sink. And each time it did, it never quite regained the same level as before.

"Are you all right?" Etain asked. "Is it your leg?"

"My leg's fine now, thank you," he said.

Darman wanted his trust back, and soon.

They resumed their path along the dirt track that was gradually liquefying into mud, the rain at their backs. By the time they got to the next farm the rain seemed to have set in for the day. Darman thought of his squad making their way through sodden countryside, perfectly dry in their sealed suits, and he smiled. At least this made it harder for anyone to track them.

A woman with a pinched expression like a gdan stared at them from the front step of the farmhouse. It was a grander building than the last one: not by much, but thc walls were stone and there was a lean-to shelter along one side. Etain walked up to her. Darman waited, looking, aware of an outdoor refresher to the right that might contain a threat, keeping half an eye on a group of youngsters tinkering with a large machine on rollers.

They all looked so different. *Everyone was so different.*

After some conversation, Etain beckoned him and indicated the lean-to. So far, so good. Darman still didn't plan on relinquishing his ordnance. He reached into the barq for his helmet and detached the comlink, just in case Niner tried to contact him.

"Are you coming?" Etain asked.

"Just a moment." Darman took out a string of AP micromines and trailed them around the front of the house as far as the cable would stretch. He set them to run off a remote signal and tucked the transmitter section of the detonator in his belt. Etain watched him with an unspoken question, perfectly clear from her expression. "In case anyone gets any ideas," Darman said.

"You've played this game before," Etain said.

He certainly had. The first thing he checked when he entered the farmhouse, one hand against his rifle, was where the best observation point might be. It was a perforated air-brick that gave him a good view of the road. There was a large window in the far wall with a brown sacking sheet tied across it. Reassured—but only slightly—he sat down at the table that dominated the front room.

The family that took them in consisted of the thin gdan-faced woman, her sister, her even thinner husband, and six youngsters ranging from a small boy clutching a piece of grubby blanket to the nearly full-grown men working outside. They wouldn't give their names. They didn't want a *visit,* they said, as if a visit was much more than it seemed.

Darman was riveted. These people were humans like him; yet they were all different. But still they had features that looked similar—not the same, but similar—to others in the group. They were different sizes and different ages, too.

He had seen diversity in training manuals. He knew what different species looked like. But the images always came to mind with data about weapons carried and where to aim a shot for maximum stopping power. This was the first time in his life that he had been in close contact with diverse humans who were in the majority.

To them, perhaps, he also looked unique.

They sat around the rough wooden table. Darman tried not to speculate on what the stains in the wood might be, because they looked like blood. Etain nudged him. "They cut up the merlie carcasses here," she whispered, and he wondered if she could read his mind.

He tested the bread and soup placed in front of him for toxins. Satisfied that it was safe, he dug in. After a while he was aware that the woman and the small boy were staring at him. When he looked up, the child fled.

"He doesn't like soldiers much," the woman said. "Is the Republic coming to help us?"

"I can't answer that, ma'am," Darman said. He meant that he would never discuss operational matters; it was an automatic response under interrogation. *Never just say yes, never just say no, and give no information except your ID number.* Etain answered for him, which was her prerogative as a commander.

"Do you want the Republic's help?" she asked.

"You any better than the Neimies?"

"I'd like to think so."

The table fell silent again. Darman finished the soup. Politics was nothing to do with him; he was more interested in filling up on something that had flavor and texture. If all went according to plan, in a few weeks he'd be far from here and on another mission, and if it didn't, he'd be dead. The future of Qiilura was genuinely of no relevance to him.

The woman kept refilling his bowl with soup until he slowed up and eventually couldn't manage any more. It was the first hot food he'd had in days, and he felt good; little perks like that boosted morale. Etain didn't seem so enthusiastic about it. She was moving each chunk cautiously around with her spoon, as if the liquid contained mines.

"You need to keep your strength up," he said.

"I know."

"You can have my bread."

"Thanks."

It was so quiet in the room that Darman could hear the individual rhythm of everyone's chewing, and the faint scrape of utensils against bowls. He could hear the distant, muffled sound of merlies nearby, an intermittent gargling noise. But he didn't hear something that Etain suddenly did.

She sat bolt upright and turned her head to one side, eyes unfocused.

"Someone's coming, and it's not Jinart," she hissed.

Darman flung off his cloak and pulled his rifle. The woman and her relatives jumped up from the table so fast that it tipped despite its weight, sending bowls tumbling to the floor. Etain drew her lightsaber, and it shimmered into life. They both watched the entrance; the family scrambled through the back door, the woman pausing to grab a large metal bowl and a bag of meal from a sideboard.

Darman doused the lamps and peered out through a hole in the air-brick. Without his visor, he was completely dependent on his Deece for long-distance vision. He couldn't see anything. He held his breath and listened hard.

Etain moved toward him, gesturing at the far wall, indicating *seven*—a whole hand then two fingers.

"Where?" he whispered.

She was marking something on the dirt floor. He watched her finger draw an outline of the four walls and then stab a number of dots outside them, most around the one she'd been pointing to, and one dot near the front door.

She put her lips so close to his ear it made him jump. "Six there, one here." It was a breath, barely audible.

Darman indicated the far wall and pointed to himself. Etain gestured to the door: *Me?* He nodded. He gestured *one, two, three* quickly with his fingers and gave her a thumbs-up: *I'll count to three.* She nodded.

Whoever was outside hadn't knocked. It didn't bode well.

He clipped the grenade attachment to his rifle and aimed at the far side. Etain stood at the door, lightsaber held above her head for a downward stroke.

Darman hoped her aggression would triumph over her self-doubt.

He gestured with his left hand, rifle balanced in his right. *One, two—*

Three. He fired one grenade. It smashed through the sack-covered window and blew a hole in the wall just as he was firing the second. The blast kicked him backward, and the front door burst open as Etain brought her lightsaber down in a brilliant blue arc.

Darman switched his rifle to blast setting and swung his sight on the figure, but it was an Umbaran and it was dead, sliced through from clavicle to sternum.

"Two," Etain said, indicating the window, or at least where it had been seconds earlier. Darman sprang forward across the room, dodging the table and firing as he came to the hole smashed in the wall. When he stumbled through the gap there were two Trandoshans coming toward him with blasters, faces that seemed all scales and lumps, wet mouths gaping. He opened fire; one return shot seared his left shoulder. Then there was nothing but numb silence for a few moments, followed by the gradual awareness that someone was screaming in agony outside.

But it wasn't him, and it wasn't Etain. That was all that mattered. He picked his way across the room, conscious of the growing pain in his shoulder. It would have to wait.

"It's all clear," Etain said. Her voice was shaking. "Except for that man . . ."

"Forget him," Darman said. He couldn't, of course: the soldier was making too much noise. The screams would attract attention. "Load up. We're going."

Despite Etain's assurance that there were no more waiting outside, Darman edged out the door and kept his back to the wall all the way around the exterior of the farmhouse. The wounded soldier was an Umbaran. Darman didn't even check how badly hurt he might be before he shot him cleanly in the head. There was nothing else he could do, and the mission came first.

He wondered if Jedi could sense droids as well. He'd have to ask Etain later. He'd been told Jedi could do extraordinary things, but it was one thing to know it, and another entirely to *see* it in action. It had probably saved their lives.

"What was that?" she asked when he returned to the lean-to. She already had the extra pack slung on her back, and he realized she'd actually moved the micromines even though they were still live. Darman, swallowing anxiety, disabled the detonator and added it to the list of things he needed to teach her.

"Finishing the job," he said, and pulled on his bodysuit section by section. She looked away.

"You killed him."

"Yes."

"He was lying wounded?"

"I'm not a medic."

"Oh, Darman . . ."

"Ma'am, this is a war. People try to kill you. You try to kill them first. There are no second chances. Everything else you need to know about warfare is an amplification of that." She was horrified, and he really wished he hadn't upset her. Had they given her a lethal lightsaber and not taught her what it really meant to draw one? "I'm sorry. He was in a bad way, anyway."

Death seemed to shock her. "I killed that Umbaran."

"That's the idea, ma'am. Nicely done, too."

She didn't say anything else. She watched him attach the armor plates, and when he finally replaced his helmet he knew he didn't care how conspicuous he looked in it, because he wasn't going to take it off again in a hurry. He needed that edge.

"No more safe houses," Darman said. "There's no such thing."

Etain followed him into the woodland at the back of the house, but she was preoccupied. "I've never killed anyone before," she said.

"You did fine," Darman told her. His shoulder was throbbing, gnawing into his concentration. "A *clean* job."

"It's still not something I would care to repeat."

"Jedi are trained to fight, aren't they?"

"Yes, but we never killed anyone in training."

Darman shrugged and it hurt. "We did."

He hoped she got over it fast. No, it wasn't enjoyable, killing: but it had to be done. And killing with lightsaber or blaster was relatively clean. He wondered how she'd handle having to stick a blade in someone and see what ran out. She was a Jedi, and with any luck she'd never have to.

"Them or us," he said.

"You're in pain."

"Nothing major. I'll use the bacta when we reach the RV."

"I suppose they turned us in."

"The farmers? Yeah, that's civilians for you."

Etain made a noncommittal grunt and followed silently behind him. They moved deeper into the woods, and Darman calculated how many rounds he'd expended. If he kept engaging targets at this rate, he'd be down to his sidearm by nightfall.

"It's amazing how you can sense people," Darman said. "Can you detect droids, too?"

"Not especially," she said. "Usually just living beings. Maybe I can—"

A faint whine made Darman turn in time to see a blue bolt of light streaking toward him from behind. It struck a tree a few meters ahead, splitting it like kindling in a puff of vapor.

"Obviously not," Etain said.

It was going to be another long, hard day.

A warning siren sounded: three long blasts, repeated twice. Then the peaceful fields northwest of Imbraani shook with a massive explosion, and terrified merlies bolted for the cover of the hedgerows.

"Blasting today, then," Fi said. "Lovely day for it."

Niner couldn't see anything but droids—industrial droids—moving around the quarry. He ran his glove across his visor to clear the droplets of rain and tried several binoc magnifications, flicking between settings with eye movements. But if there were organic workers around, he couldn't see any.

The quarry was a massive and startling gouge in the landscape, an amphitheater with stepped sides that allowed droid excavators to dig out rock for processing. The depression sloped gently at one side; it was a towering cliff on the other. A small site office with alloy-plated walls and no windows sat beside a wide track at the top of the slope. Apart from the steady procession of droids laden with raw rock for the screening plant, the area was deserted. But someone—something—was controlling the detonations. They had to be in the building. And structures with solid alloy walls like that tended to have interesting contents.

The all-clear siren sounded. The droids moved in to scoop up the loose rock, sending spray and mud flying as they rumbled up the slopes.

"Okay, let's see what we can liberate from the hut," Niner said. "Atin, with me. Fi, stay here and cover."

They darted out of the trees and across a hundred meters of open land to the edge of the quarry, dodging between giant droids that took no notice of them. One droid, its wheels as high as Niner was tall, swung its bucket scoop unexpectedly and struck his shoulder plate a glancing blow. He stumbled and Atin caught his arm, steadying him. They paused, waiting for the next droid to return up the slope, then jogged alongside it until level with the site building.

They were now exposed, pressed close to the front wall. The building was only ten meters wide. Atin knelt at the door and studied the single lock.

"Pretty insubstantial if this is where they store the explosives," he said.

"Let's take a look."

Atin stood up slowly and placed a scope on the door to listen for movement. He shook his head at Niner. Then he slid a flimsi-thin flat endoscope around the jamb, working it back and forth, slowly and carefully. "Now that's a tight fit," he said. "Can't get it in."

"We could always just walk in there."

"Remember, we're probably heading into a store full of explosives. If I could get a probe through it could at least get a sniff of the air and test for chemicals."

"Okay, let's walk in *carefully,* then."

There was no handle. Niner stood to the hinge side, Deece in one hand, and pressed silently on the single plate that made up the door. It didn't yield.

Atin nodded. He took out the handheld ram, ten kilos that had seemed like dead, useless weight in their packs until now. He squared it up to the lock.

Niner raised one finger. "Three . . . two . . ."

It applied a force of two metric tons.

"Go."

The door fell open, and they both leapt back as a stream of

blasterfire shot out. It stopped suddenly. They squatted on either side of the entrance. Usually this was simple: if someone inside didn't want to leave, a grenade coaxed them out, one way or another. But with a high chance of explosives being inside, that method was a little too emphatic. Niner shook his head.

Atin moved the endoscope carefully, getting a glimpse of the building's interior. Then he edged the probe into the doorway, drawing another stream of blasterfire.

"Two moving around," he said. "Light's out. But the probe got a sniff of explosives."

"Spot-lamp and rush them, then?"

Atin shook his head. He took out a grenade and locked it in the safety position. "How nervous would you be if you were sitting on enough stuff to put this quarry into orbit?"

"Drink-spilling nervous, I'd say."

"Yeah." Atin hefted the grenade a few times. "That's what I thought."

He bowled the disabled grenade into the doorway and jerked back. Three seconds later, two Weequays rushed out. Niner and Atin fired simultaneously; one Weequay dropped instantly, and the other's momentum carried him on a few meters farther, until he fell in the path at the top of the ramp. The quarry droids trundled on, oblivious. If the shot hadn't killed him, the advancing droid did.

"Sarge, you need some help down there?"

Niner motioned Atin inside. "No, Fi, we're set here. Keep an eye out in case we get company."

The building reeked of cooking and unwashed Weequay. A small droid, lights blinking on standby and caked in dried mud, stood by a console. The rest of the space—three rooms—was taken up by explosives, detonators, and various spare parts and stenciled crates.

"There's your demolitions man," Atin said, tapping the droid on its head, and retrieved his grenade. He wiped it with his glove and put it back in his belt pack.

"I'd rather have Darman," Niner said. He studied the inert droid, which seemed to be waiting for the dislodged rock to be cleared. It jerked suddenly into life, made its way toward a crate of explosives, opened the safety lid, and took out several tubes. Then it turned toward the room where the detonators were kept. Niner reached out and opened its control panel to deactivate it. "Take some time off, friend," he said. "Blasting's over for the day."

It didn't appear that the Weequay had been employed here. The droid sorted all the charges and oversaw the blasting. On an upturned crate were the remains of a meal, eaten off makeshift plates fashioned from box lids. It looked like the Weequays had been hiding out here, and Niner was pretty sure he knew who they had been avoiding.

Atin checked the various charges and detonators, selecting what appeared to take his fancy and piling it in a clear space on the muddy floor. He was a connoisseur of technology, especially things with complex circuitry. "Lovely," he said, with genuine satisfaction. "Some dets here that you can set off from fifty klicks. That's what we need. A bit of a pyrotechnics show."

"Can we carry as much as we need?"

"Oh, there's some beauties here. Darman would think they were pretty basic, but they're going to work fine as a diversion. Absolute *beauts.*" Atin held up spheres about the size of a scoopball. "Now this baby—"

Crash.

Something fell to the floor in one of the rooms off the main one. Atin held his rifle on the doorway and Niner drew his sidearm. He was edging toward the door when a sudden voice almost made him squeeze the trigger.

"Ap-xmai keepuna!" The voice was shaking, and judging by the accent it probably belonged to a Weequay. "Don't kill! I help you!"

"Out. *Now.*" Projected from his helmet, Atin's voice was intimidating enough without a rifle to back it up. A Weequay stumbled out from behind a stack of crates and sank to his knees, hands held up. Atin pushed him down flat with his boot, Deece aimed at his head. "Arms behind your back and don't even breathe. Got it?"

The Weequay appeared to have got it very quickly. He froze and let Niner cuff his wrists with a length of wire. Niner did a sweep of the rooms again, worried that if they'd missed one target they might have missed more. But it was clear. He walked back and squatted down by the Weequay's head.

"We don't need a prisoner slowing us down," he said. "Give me a good reason why I shouldn't kill you."

"Please, I know Hokan."

"I'll bet you know him pretty well if you were hiding out here. What's your name?"

"Guta-Nay. I were *right-hand man.*"

"Not anymore, though, eh?"

"I know places."

"Yeah, we know places, too."

"I got key codes."

"We've got ordnance."

"I got codes to Teklet ground station."

"You wouldn't be messing around, would you, Guta-Nay? I don't have time for that."

"Hokan kill me. You take me with you? You Republic guys nice, you *gentlemen.*"

"Steady, Guta-Nay. All those syllables might burn you out."

Niner looked at Atin. He shrugged.

"He'll slow us down, Sarge."

"Then we either leave him here or kill him."

The conversation wasn't designed to scare Guta-Nay, but it had that effect anyway. It was a genuine problem: Niner was reluctant to drag a prisoner around with them, and there was no guarantee the Weequay wouldn't try to buy back favor from Hokan with intelligence on their strength and movements. He was an unwelcome dilemma. Atin clicked his Deece, and it started to power up.

"I get you Neimie boss, too!"

"We definitely don't need him."

"Neimie's really mad at Hokan. He put droids in his nice shiny villa. Floors messed up."

Guta-Nay's breathing rasped in the silence of the room. Niner weighed the extra baggage against the prospect of some edge in gaining access to Uthan.

"Where's Uthan now?"

"Still in villa. Nowhere else to hide."

"You know a lot about Hokan, don't you?"

"Everything." Guta-Nay was all submission. *"Too much."*

"Okay," Niner said. "You got a reprieve."

Atin waited a couple of seconds before powering down his rifle. He seemed doubtful. Niner couldn't see his expression, but he heard the characteristic slight exhalation that was Atin's silent *oh-terrific.*

"He'll leave a trail a worrt could follow."

"Ideas?"

"Yeah." Atin leaned over Guta-Nay, and the Weequay turned his head slightly, eyes wide with terror. He seemed more terrified by the helmet than the gun. "Where do the droids take the raw rock?"

"Big place south of Teklet."

"How far south?"

"Five klick maybe."

Atin straightened up and indicated with a pointed finger that he was going outside. "Technical solution. Wait one."

His predilection for gadgets was becoming a blessing. Niner was tempted to take back the unkind thoughts he'd had about the man's training sergeant. He followed him outside. Atin jogged alongside one of the excavation droids, matching its pace before jumping up scrambling onto its flatbed. The machine rumbled inexorably up the slope as if nothing was going to divert it from its progress to the screening plant. Then it stopped and swung around, narrowly missing the droid bringing up its rear. It paused a couple of meters from Niner; Atin, kneeling on the flatbed, held up two cables.

"You can't get it to do tricks," he said. "But you can start, steer, and stop it now."

"Brain bypass, eh?"

"I've seen a few people with those . . ."

"So we ride it into town?"

"How else are we going to move all this explosive?"

They couldn't pass up the chance. Niner had plans for the charges, places to lay them all around the Imbraani countryside. They also had a temptingly neat window of opportunity to take out the ground station at Teklet, and rendering Hokan's troops deaf to what was happening around them would double their chances of pulling off the mission. It meant they could use their own long-range comlinks at last.

"Tell you what," Niner said. "I'll take this one to Teklet. You hotwire another and take Fi and our friend as far back down the road to Imbraani as you can get with as much as you can carry." He took out his datapad and checked the chart. "Lay up *here* where Jinart suggested, with the droid if you can, without it if you can't."

A bulldozer droid on a steady path to the screening plant would attract no attention. It just had to overshoot by a few kilometers. It would be dusk soon, and darkness was their best asset when it came to moving around.

Niner hauled Guta-Nay out of the building. "Is the ground station defended in any way?"

Guta-Nay had his head lowered, looking up from under his brows as if blows to the head normally accompanied questions. "Just fence to stop merlies and thieving. Only farmers around, and they scared anyway."

"If you're lying to me, I'll see that you get back to Ghez Hokan alive. Okay?"

"Okay. Truth, I swear."

Niner summoned Fi from his cover position, and they loaded two droids. One carried enough explosives to reduce the ground station to powder several times over, and the other took everything they could lay their hands on, except for some detonators and explosives to keep the blasting droid busy for a few more hours. There was no point letting the quarry's silence advertise the fact that they had liberated some ordnance. It would spoil the whole surprise.

They loaded Guta-Nay last, bundling him into the huge bucket scoop with his arms still bound. He protested at being stuck on top of spheres of explosive.

"Don't worry," Atin said dismissively. "I've got all the dets here." He bounced a few detonators up and down in his palm; Guta-Nay flinched. "You'll be fine."

"Jinart's quite an asset," Fi said. He took off his helmet to drink from his bottle, and Guta-Nay made an incoherent noise.

"She could be right behind us now and we'd never know. I hope they stay on our side." Niner removed his helmet, too, and they shared the bottle before handing it to Atin for a last swig. "What's that Weequay whining about now?"

"Dunno," Atin said, and took his helmet off as well. He paused, bottle in hand, and they all stood and stared at Guta-Nay, loaded in the scoop of the droid like cargo.

His mouth was slightly open and his eyes were darting from one commando to the next. He was making a slight *uh-uh-uh* sound, as if he was trying to scream but couldn't.

"It's Atin's face," Fi said. "Don't stand there being so ugly, man. You're scaring him."

Niner gave the Weequay a quick prod with his glove to shut him up.

"What's the matter?" he asked. "Haven't you ever seen commandos before?"

They were *here.*

The break that Ghez Hokan had been waiting for had come: a farmer had rushed to notify the authorities that Republic soldiers—one man, one woman, both very young—were at a house on the Imbraani–Teklet road.

Hokan studied the dripping foliage at the side of the farmhouse. The maze of footsteps in the mud and the crushed stalks were no different from those on any farm, and they were disappearing fast in the rain. Behind the ramshackle collection of sheds and stone walls, the land sloped away to the Braan River.

"It's a mess in there, sir," Hurati said. "One wall nearly blown out. All dead. And that was just two enemy commandos."

"One," Hokan said.

"One?"

"Only male clones in the front line. The other had to be a Jedi." He turned over the body of an Umbaran with his boot and shook his head. "That wound was made by a lightsaber. I know what a lightsaber wound looks like. Two people. I wouldn't even have that information if it hadn't been for informants. Do I have to rely on dung-caked *farmers* for intelligence? Do I? *Do I?*"

He regretted having to shout. But it seemed necessary. "Why can't anyone manage to *call it in* when they make an enemy contact? Think! Use your *di'kutla* heads, or I'll show you how to recognize a lightsaber wound the hard way." Two droids began lifting the Umbaran's body onto a speeder. "Leave that thing where it is. Get after your comrades and find me some enemy."

Hurati put his hand to the side of his head. "Droids have found something else in a house up the road, sir." His expression fell blank as he listened to his comlink. "Oh. *Oh.*" He turned to Hokan. "I think you should see this for yourself, sir."

Hurati didn't strike him as an officer that would waste his time. They mounted the speeder and worked their way back up the road to another small, dilapidated hovel set among the trees. Hokan followed Hurati into the farmhouse, where a couple of droids had illuminated the rooms with spot-lamps.

For some reason he would never fathom, the first aspect of the chaos that caught his eye was the soup tureen lying on its side on the filthy floor. It was only when he turned his head that he saw the bodies.

"Ah," Hokan said.

Soldiers used blasters. In a pinch, they would use knives or blunt objects. But he had never known anyone in uniform, not even his ragtag militia, who used *teeth.* The three adults were ripped and torn as if a large carnivore had attacked them. All had crush injuries to what was left of their throats. One woman had so little intact tissue in her neck that the head was bent over at almost ninety degrees. Hokan found himself staring.

"There are others outside in the shed," Hurati said.

Hokan had never considered himself easily disturbed, but this worried him. It was an act by something he didn't recognize and couldn't comprehend, beyond the scope of a sentient creature's simple revenge. It might have been coincidence, an animal attack on someone who happened to be an informer—but he couldn't think of any species on Qiilura that could or would bring down humans.

Hurati studied the bodies. "I didn't think killing civilians was the Republic's style."

"It's not," Hokan said. "And commandos wouldn't waste time on work that wouldn't aid their effort."

"Well, whoever killed them wasn't motivated by robbery." Hurati picked up a large metal bowl from the floor, dusted it with his glove, and set it on a shelf. "This is probably our informer. I wouldn't count on much assistance from now on. Word will get around fast."

"You're certain there are no blaster wounds?" It might have been simple predation. He knew in his gut that it wasn't. But what had done this?

"None," Hurati said.

Hokan didn't like it at all. He beckoned Hurati to follow him and walked out briskly to summon two droids. "I want a ring around Imbraani. Pull all the droids back. I'd rather lose Teklet than risk Uthan's project."

"We could arrange for Doctor Uthan to be evacuated."

"Moving her and her entourage is going to be slow and conspicuous. We're better off defending a position than moving. I want half the droids blatantly visible at the facility and the other half around the villa—but discreetly, understand?"

There was a rattle of metal in the distance, and Hokan spun around to see droids swarming toward the riverbank.

"Have they found anything?"

Hurati pressed his hand to his head, listening to the comlink. "Two enemy sighted five klicks west of here, sir. The droids have engaged them."

"That's more like it," Hokan said. "I'd like at least one alive, preferably both if the girl's a Jedi."

He swung onto the speeder bike and motioned Hurati to sit up front and drive. The speeder zipped down the track heading west as Hurati confirmed coordinates with the droid patrol.

Hokan hoped the droids could manage an instruction like *take them alive.* He needed real troops for this, actual soldiers who could get into awkward places and see subtle things. He now had just thirty organic officers remaining and slightly under a hundred droids: ideal for a small set-piece battle, but next to useless for countering a commando force spread over terrain with plenty of cover.

They'd definitely have to come to him. Just this once, though, he'd humor them and join the pursuit.

11

Owing to shortages, we regret to inform you that we have been forced to increase the price of the new season's barq. Shortages are due to local difficulties at source. We will of course be giving preference to our most favored regular customers.
—Trade Federation notice to wholesalers

Darman had taken down quite a few tinnies on Geonosis, and one thing he'd learned was that they were built for conventional infantry combat on nice, flat ground.

They weren't so clever on treacherous terrain—or without an organic officer calling the shots.

He could see a group of trees a hundred meters away that appeared to be skylined against nothing, and he hoped that meant there might be an escarpment on the other side. "Down there," he yelled to Etain, pointing. "Come on, and get ready to *jump*."

He'd almost forgotten the pain in his shoulder. He clutched his rifle tight to his chest and sprinted for the tree line. It took him ten seconds. The land sloped away below, all thorn bushes and muddy soil right down to the river, broken only by a natural back-sloping terrace that formed a small gully. When he looked back, Etain was right behind him—and he wasn't expecting her to be.

"Keep going!" she panted. "Don't keep looking back."

The blasterfire of the advancing droids was hitting branches far too close for comfort. When they got to the edge he simply shoved her. She tried to right herself for a second before falling and rolling down the slope. He launched himself and rolled after her.

Darman had the protection of Katarn armor, but she didn't. When they came to a halt at the bottom of the gully, Etain was minus her outer cloak and plus a lot of scrapes. But she still had two sections of the E-Web cannon strapped to her share of the pack. She was clinging to them with grim determination.

"Next time, let me jump, will you?" she hissed. "I'm not completely helpless."

"Sorry." He checked his grenades. "I'm going to run short of ammo soon. I'm going to have to sacrifice some demolition ordnance."

"Tell me what you're planning."

"Bringing down the slope. With them on it." He paid out the line of micromines and scrambled a few meters back to string them horizontally between the trees. "Can you dig out some of the bore-bangs from that pack, please? Four should do it."

"What are they?"

"The long red sticks. Custom ordnance."

He heard her gasping her way up the slope behind him. When he turned his head she was gripping a bush with one hand, and holding out tubes of explosive in the other. Her fingers were covered in blood. He felt suddenly guilty, but he'd have to worry about that later.

"Thanks, ma'am," he said automatically. He balanced precariously, feeling the strain in his calves, and scrambled from bush to bush. He held each bore-bang perpendicular to the slope and twisted the end cap; the cylinder whirred and burrowed deep into the ground. He spaced them at five-meter intervals.

The chinking noise of droids on the move was getting closer, carrying on the still, damp air.

"Run!" Darman hissed.

Adrenaline was a wonderful thing to see in action. Etain grabbed her pack and bolted along the gully. Darman followed. Fifty meters—a hundred—two hundred. He paused to look back and saw one thin metal faceplate peer over the edge.

"Down!" he yelled, and squeezed the detonator in his palm.

A chunk of Qiilura blew apart at approximately eight thousand meters a second. Darman heard it and regretted not seeing it, but his head was shielded by his crossed arms and he was facedown in the dirt. It was pure instinct. He should have told Etain to cover her ears, although it wouldn't have helped her much. He should have made her run a lot sooner. He should have done a lot of things, like ignoring Jinart, and instead stayed on the mission.

He hadn't. He'd deal with it.

The noise of the blast overloaded his helmet for a few moments; there was a crackling silence. Then sound rushed back in again and he could feel clods of soil plopping against his back like heavy rain. When he got to his knees and turned around, there was a brand-new landscape to be seen. Trees jutted out from a sharp cliff of packed mud at bizarre angles. Some had intact branches, and others were snapped off and splintered. A single metallic leg protruded from the debris. Dirt was crumbling away from the face of the cliff like wet permacrete, and one tree was sliding slowly downward.

Darman looked around for Etain. She was a few meters ahead, kneeling back on her heels with her hand to one ear. When he drew closer he could see a thin trickle of blood running down the side of her face.

"Okay?" he asked.

Etain stared at his mouth. "I can't hear you," she said. She nursed her left ear, face contorted with pain.

"You've blown an eardrum. Take it easy." Stupid: she couldn't hear, and she couldn't see his lips with his helmet on. It was reflex reassurance. He was about to look for his bacta spray when she looked past him and pointed frantically. He turned. A droid was peering over the edge of the crater. It didn't appear to have seen them.

Darman didn't know how many there might be. He debated whether to deploy a remote, then wondered what he'd do if it showed him a hundred more tinnies coming. He wasn't sure where else to run. He estimated that he could hold them off for about an hour, and then they'd be out of everything except his vibroblade and Etain's lightsaber.

Then he heard a shout.

"Droids, report!"

Darman flattened himself into the side of the slope beside Etain. He could hear the voices, even if she couldn't. She stared up at the cliff and squeezed her eyes shut. For a moment Darman thought it was plain terror, and he wouldn't have blamed her. He'd blown away half a hillside and still hadn't stopped the droids. He was starting to feel a gnawing emptiness in his gut as well.

He concentrated on the voices, trying to guess numbers. Two humans, two *men*.

". . . they've booby-trapped . . ."

". . . can you see anything?"

". . . there's nothing else down there."

Darman held his breath.

"No, they're gone. Must have speeders."

"Droids, form up and return . . ."

The metal face pulled back and the clinking gait faded on the air, along with the whir of a speeder engine. Then there was silence, broken only by the occasional creak of a splintered tree being pulled slowly apart on its journey down the shattered slope.

Darman glanced at Etain. Her eyes were still shut, and she was breathing hard.

"I didn't think I could do that," she said.

"Do what?" She stared at him. He took off his helmet so she could see his mouth. "Do—what?" Darman mouthed, exaggerating the syllables. Her gaze fixed on his lips.

"Influence them. Both of them."

"Was that some sort of Jedi thought trick?"

She looked baffled. She obviously wasn't used to lip-reading. "It's sort of a Jedi thought trick," she said.

Darman stifled an urge to laugh. It wasn't funny at all. She'd achieved something he found almost magical. At that point in the crisis, it was the best military option, better than letting loose with all the ordnance at his disposal, and something even Kal Skirata couldn't do.

They were alive. They could move on.

"Nice job, commander," he said. "Very nicely done." He touched his glove to his forehead and grinned. "Let's get ourselves sorted, eh?"

Darman took out his medpac and removed two sharps of painkiller and the bacta spray. He fixed his own shoulder first, jabbing the needle hard into the blue vein in the crook of his left elbow so that the drug dispersed faster. But it still made his eyes water when he sprayed the blaster burn.

Etain watched with grim resignation and swallowed visibly.

"Come on, Etain," Darman said. "Hold still."

He aimed the spray like a pistol into her left ear.

Darman had no idea that Jedi could curse fluently in Huttese, but he was learning more about them every minute. A *lot* more.

The excavation droid rattled down the road, managing to find every pothole and rut between Imbraani and the screening plant. Niner bounced each time, too. Buried in the scoop under a layer of loose rubble, with enough explosives to level everything within half a kilometer, he was . . . *anxious*.

The detonators were disabled. He kept checking that.

Now that night had fallen and the rain stopped, he could ease himself into a position where he could see ahead. Blue navigation lights picked out the droid's front fender, and an amber hazard light whirled on its canopy, illuminating the trees on either side of the track. It was a lumbering thing that wouldn't get out of anyone's way. Behind it, a convoy of identical droids followed. They were an intimidating procession.

Even the column of tinnies marching toward Niner moved to one side of the road.

He picked them out in his night-vision visor, although the sound alone identified them. *Clink-rasp-clink-rasp.* It was the knee joints. Nothing but battle droids marched that regularly, not even clone troopers. There were no voices, not even the occasional command to form single file, or *shut it back there.* It was all grim mechanical purpose.

Niner closed his fingers around the grips of the DC-17. He really didn't want to engage them. It was going to be hard enough to direct the excavator to the target and get away in one piece without pausing for skirmishes along the route. *Walk on, will you? Just walk on.* He didn't want to test the manufacturer's assurance that a few blaster bolts wouldn't set off the charges. He was sprawled on top of them. Proximity made you skeptical.

There were fifty battle droids in the column heading for Imbraani. If he managed to knock out the ground station, that would be the first message he'd send on his long-range comlink.

The *chunk-chunk-chunk* of their feet drew level with him and he froze.

Chunk-chunk-chunk-chunk-chunk.

It began to fade behind him. He breathed again. Once the excavator droid was coaxed past its logical destination of the screening plant, it would be that much more conspicuous. At least the tinnies looked busy. The worst part was having a pretty good idea about what orders they'd been given.

Just ten klicks. He was minutes away from the point where the droid would attempt to deliver its load. At that moment, he'd divert it toward Teklet itself, through the center of the town and into the ground station compound. At least the aerial recce appeared to have been right about that. Teklet was a sprawl of storage silos and shipping facilities for getting produce off the planet, and not much else.

The worst that the Trade Federation had ever anticipated dealing with was a band of angry farmers. It was going to make his job a good deal easier.

Just ahead, the droid's flashing light bounced off a sign pointing left: ALL CONTRACTOR TRAFFIC—NO ENTRY VIA MAIN GATE. The excavator knew its way and began slowing for the turn. Niner took Atin's jury-rigged cables and unplugged one strand. *Go on. Go on. Go . . .*

The droid was almost at the turn. It was moving at around twenty-five klicks now, threatening to veer off. But it carried on, past the sign, past the slip road, and on toward Teklet. "That's my boy," Niner said. The sweat prickled between his shoulder blades, despite his suit's environment controls. "Couldn't speed up a bit, could you?" Maybe that was asking for trouble. When he eased his head clear of the layer of rubble and peered around the side of the scoop, he could see a procession of droids strung out behind him along the curve of the road, neatly line astern like battle cruisers, each flashing an orange hazard light with its outline picked out in blue.

It was actually pretty, all things considered. Then the nearest droid slowed and peeled off down the slip road, the light show behind Niner fading, then disappearing altogether. He was on his own. He settled back under the rubble with his head tilted so that he could see ahead through a channel in the debris.

Teklet had little in the way of street lighting, and there were few people about. As architecture went, this wasn't tasteful, elegant Tipoca. It was a service depot and it looked like one. A couple of Trandoshans were sitting under an awning outside a hut, blasters across their laps; they stared at the droid with vague curiosity but didn't appear to move. Niner was almost past the ribbon of huts when the thought struck him that a five-hundred-meter blast zone would take out a lot of Teklet, and people with it. Not all of them were Separatists.

Once you make that your concern, they'll always have a weapon to use against you. Skirata said they had to get used to it. Achieving your objective sometimes had a high price.

A bonded cargo transporter with red security straps sealing its containers crossed in front of him. The droid missed it by two seconds. If the driver was cutting it that close, then they hadn't taken much notice of the machine. So far, so good . . . and getting better. As the droid pressed on, Niner was checking his escape route. It was a good two-hundred-meter sprint to the nearest cover from any part of the road. It was going to be tight.

He had to get the droid to halt right alongside the ground station. If it kept going, the blast would be centered elsewhere. He could set the dets now, slide out of the scoop, and run for it, but that meant observing the droid up to the last second, and that meant he'd probably be too close when it blew.

But he was committed now. The ground station had to go. It would put a serious dent in the Separatists' defenses for a few critical days, maybe even weeks, and that was an edge they needed.

Working some rubble aside with his finger, Niner could see the lights of the compound. He flicked to night vision, and the green image showed him flimsy mesh fencing and a waist-high retaining wall. The excavator would roll right over it on its path to the building itself.

They'd know he was there, all right.

He'd left the dets until last. The charges were linked by cord in series, just waiting for the final connection to the three detonators that—in theory—Niner could trigger remotely. He clamped the cords together and shoved them into the aperture of the det housings, snapping them shut.

The explosives were now live. He wasn't just sitting *on* a bomb; he was sitting *in* one. The charges, dispersed among the rubble, were up to his neck. He began to ease his legs clear, ready to jump.

If he didn't walk away from this, then that was the way it had to be. For a moment Niner felt a cold spasm in his gut that he recognized from a dozen all-too-real exercises. He was probably going to get killed. He was *possibly* going to get killed. If anyone thought intensive training wiped out the fear of dying, they were wrong. He was as afraid as he was when live rounds had flown past him for the first time. It never went away. He just learned to live with it, and tried to learn well enough that he could use it to work for him, and get him out of trouble faster.

Niner fumbled with the cabling. He steered the droid in a gentle arc so that it was square-on to the fence. It wasn't the best course he'd ever steered, but with a five-hundred-meter blast zone, it was going to be good enough. He ducked. The wire mesh loomed in his face at the edge of the scoop, then strained and vibrated, tearing up posts with it as the droid pushed through, oblivious.

It was nearly at the wall. The building was five meters high; flat roof, no windows. They didn't seem to like windows here. He heard a single shout, something like *chuba,* and he had to agree. This was going to fierfek someone's watch with a lot of reports.

Niner yanked the cables apart and cut the droid's power. Its momentum carried it on a few more meters, and metal twanged and squealed as the chain-link fence was stretched to the breaking point.

The wires finally snapped back like a bowstring under the excavator's wheels.

One, two, three . . .

The droid was at a dead stop hard against the wall. The blocks were beginning to crack, and gaps were opening between them. He had a sudden vision of finding himself buried in collapsing masonry and unable to move, and a combination of animal panic and a lifetime of training propelled him out of the rubble and over the edge of the scoop. He fell flat from two meters and struggled to right himself. Then there was shouting and, fifty-kilo pack or not, he executed the fastest bugout of his career, Deece in one hand and the remote det control in the other.

There was one way out and that was through the gap he'd smashed in the fence.

It wasn't covert. A human in an overall was standing open-mouthed in his path, and Niner knocked him flat on his back as he ran full-tilt for the hole in the mesh.

He had about a minute to put distance between himself and the ground station before he blew the charges. At twenty klicks an hour, that meant he'd be about —

Fierfek, just do it.

Niner was past the first line of trees and into long grass when he dropped and pressed the remote det in both hands.

Teklet was a sudden ball of light. Then the roar of air and the shock wave shook him. He crouched as debris rained down on him, hoping—really *hoping*—that Katarn armor was all that it was cracked up to be.

Ghez Hokan was the first to admit that it was taking a lot less to get him irritated lately. He'd waited long enough. He tapped the comlink console impatiently.

"I asked to be out through to CO CISCom ten minutes ago, *di'kut.*"

"I realize that, Major. He'll be with you as soon as he's free."

"Enemy forces have infiltrated and I need to speak to your commanding officer. Do you understand what we have on Qiilura? Could you possibly shift your *di'kutla shebs* long enough to find out why this is so vital to the war?"

"Sir, we have Republic troops infiltrating more places than I care to name right now, so—"

The screen flickered and broke up in noise. Hokan switched to another channel and got the same crackling, shimmering display. It was the same for every channel he tried. His first thought was that someone had disabled his receiver. They were closer than he'd thought, and a lot more daring. He put on his helmet and edged cautiously down the passage to the exterior door, his Verpine shatter gun in one hand and a hunting vibroblade in the other.

The droid sentry stepped aside to let him pass. On the roof, the comm relay was intact. Hokan took out his personal comlink and called Hurati.

All Hokan could hear was the chatter of static. It struck him that the Republic troops might well have done what he would have, faced with the same target.

"Droid, can you make contact with your fellows?"

"Affirmative sir."

The droids had their own comlink system. They could communicate instantly on any battlefield. What they didn't need was the main relay at Teklet in order to do it.

"Can you contact Lieutenant Hurati?"

The droid paused for a few moments. "I have him, sir."

"Ask him if he has any news of Teklet."

Pause. A much longer pause.

"Large explosion seen in the direction of Teklet, sir."

It's what I'd do if I was preparing an assault, Hokan thought. *I'd render my enemies blind and deaf.*

There was nothing he could do on the ground to deal with an invasion, if one was coming. There was a Republic assault ship in Qiilura space, and that didn't bode well.

He had two options for his immediate task. He could defend Uthan's project—the technical knowledge invested in her and her staff, and the nanovirus itself—or, if he was overrun, he could prevent it falling into enemy hands to be studied and neutralized.

It was a big planet. If he had to run, they'd have to find him. In the meantime, he'd sit tight and wait for them to come.

"Tell Hurati I want every functioning droid back here now," Hokan said. "We're digging in."

12

Coruscant Command to Republic Assault Ship *Majestic,*
Qiilura Sector

Cruiser *Vengeance* will RV with you at 0400. You have clearance to intercept any vessel leaving Qiilura space, prevent landing by non-Republic vessels, and engage any vessel failing to comply. Have biohazard containment standing by.

Niner struggled to his feet and stared back at the ground station.

It wasn't there anymore. Neither were the few small huts scattered along the approach road. There was billowing smoke and fires burning, including one that looked as if it were a blowtorch. Another explosion made him shield his head, and more debris peppered his armor.

Apart from that, the area was silent. He set off through the trees again, feeling as if he'd been picked up and shaken hard by someone really angry. A small pack of gdans began chasing him, snapping on his leg armor, but they caught on fast that he was going to be impossible to eat and fell back. He opened his long-range comlink for the first time in days.

"Niner here, anyone receiving?"

He could hear his own breath rasping as he ran. He was down to a stumbling jog now and feeling the reality of his exhaustion. He'd take a stim or two later. He had to.

"Sarge? Fi here. Target acquired, then."

"Wow. P for plenty."

"You sound busy."

"On my way to the RV."

"You're running."

"You bet. Sitrep?"

"Had to dump the droid and cache a lot of stuff. But the Weequay can carry a surprising amount if you ask him nicely. ETA an hour or so."

"Call Darman, in case Jinart hasn't caught up with him yet."

"Copy that. ETA?"

"Depends. Looking for transport right now."

"You sure about that?"

"You can do fast or you can do covert. Right now fast looks good to me. Out."

Niner kept close enough to the road to hear vehicles. He needed a speeder. The mangled chassis of a personal transport of some kind was upended at the side of the road, testimony to the force of the blast.

Eventually, someone would show up to take a look at the damage. Then he'd have his chance.

After a few minutes Niner was starting to see intact buildings through the trees. He was nearing the farthest edge of the blast zone. Farther ahead he could see lights coming toward him, and his visor told him they were approaching fast. He dropped down into the cover of the grass. As they got nearer, he could pick out one landspeeder and a speeder bike.

Niner couldn't face walking back into the blast zone to take one. He'd have to stop them here. And he'd have to stop them with minimum damage, or else he'd still be hiking back to the RV point.

He aimed his rifle on sniper setting and waited until the landspeeder was within three hundred meters. It didn't surprise him that it wasn't an emergency vehicle. He could see the driver clearly: a Trandoshan. They didn't have a record in humanitarian public service. He was probably rushing to see if his slave traffic had been affected by the blast. The speeder was carrying a Trandoshan as well.

Niner squeezed gently, and the bolt shattered the landspeeder's screen. The vehicle veered right off the road, spraying mud and gravel in the air, and the speeder bike swung left and pulled up dead. For a moment the rider hesitated, instinctively looking around in the dark as if unsure what had happened, but then he appeared to work it out just as Niner's second bolt caught him full in the chest. The speeder bike hung motionless a meter above the ground.

There was a lot to be said for night-vision visors.

Niner ran from cover and swung onto the speeder, catching his pack on the back of the seat. He savored the moment. Taking the weight off his feet ranked near the top of the list of primeval human needs, along with a long drink of ice-cold water. The relief was wonderful.

A good night's sleep and a decent hot meal would have rounded it off perfectly. The sooner he got back to his squad and finished the job in hand, the sooner he'd be able to indulge. He steered the speeder into the woods and headed south with newly uplifted spirits.

Pinpricks of light formed a small constellation ahead of Etain. They might have been a kilometer away, or they might have been within arm's reach: she couldn't tell by sight alone.

But she could certainly smell their breath. It was a cloying, sickly scent of raw meat. She swiped her lightsaber across the entrance to the shelter, and the gdans scattered. She had tried using the Force to persuade them to bother someone else, but it only succeeded in making them more curious, although they had stopped trying to take bites out of her.

How do you do it, Jinart? How do you keep them at bay? She sat huddled under the covering Darman had constructed and listened to the water working its way down through the leaves. The rain had stopped, but the runoff was still trickling through and plopping on the sheet of plastoid above her head. She could hear again, at least in one ear.

She could also see very clearly. What she saw was the face of the Umbaran she'd almost decapitated with her lightsaber. Panic and fear had pushed the event from her mind, but now that she was quiet and tired, it flooded back and wouldn't go away.

Etain tried to meditate for the first time in days, shutting out the irritating drip of water on her head. Darman prowled around outside, silent and unnerving. She could feel him ebbing and flowing; anxious, even a little scared, but focused and devoid of violence or inner conflict.

She wanted to ask him how he achieved that balance. They had both been raised in complete isolation from the everyday world, with their own set of values and disciplines, not because they had been chosen to be different but because they had been *born* that way. Their calling was random, genetic—unfair. He'd obviously succeeded brilliantly; she had failed in equal measure. She let the sensation of his clarity wash over her.

It was almost soothing. Then it was suddenly gone and a wave of pure exhilaration hit her like a body blow. Darman thrust his head through the entrance to the shelter.

"They're coming," he said. "My squad's on its way." He paused as if he was listening to something, his glove held against the side of his helmet. It was odd to watch someone so obviously delighted without having the slightest idea of his facial expression. "An hour or so. Niner's taken out the comm station at Teklet. Fi and Atin have acquired a bit more kits that'll come in handy. Plus a prisoner." He paused again. His head was moving as if he was talking. He appeared to be able to switch back and forth between being audible and inaudible to her, as if his helmet was a separate environment into which he could retreat at will. "A *Weequay,* of all things. Oh well, they've got their reasons."

He was utterly still for a few moments before nodding vigorously. He eased off his helmet and his face was one broad grin, aimed at nothing in particular.

"They're all right, I take it," Etain said.

"They're fine."

"I'm glad. You're brothers, right?"

"No, not really."

"All right, you're clones."

"They're not my original squad," Darman said. His expression was still all delight and good humor. "My brothers were all killed at the battle of Geonosis, and so were theirs. We didn't even know each other before this mission. But three of us had the same training sergeant, so I suppose we feel like family. Except Atin, of course."

It was an extraordinary statement. Darman showed not the slightest sign of being wounded by his recent loss. Etain knew little of biological families, but she knew that losing Master Fulier would still hurt badly in three months' time, and even in three years. Perhaps they'd bred grief out of clones, too.

"You don't miss your brothers, then."

Darman's grin slowly relaxed. "Of course I do," he said quietly. "Every day."

"You seem to be taking it . . . calmly."

"We know we're likely to get killed. If we dwell on that, we won't be any use to anyone. You just get on with it, that's what our old training sergeant used to say. We're all going to die sometime, so you might as well die pushing the odds for something that matters."

Etain wanted to ask him what mattered to him about the Republic's cause. She was almost afraid to, but she needed to know.

"What do you think you're fighting for, Darman?"

He looked blank for a moment. "Peace, ma'am."

"Okay, what do you think you're fighting *against*?"

"Anarchy and injustice." It was a rote response, but he paused as if considering it for the first time. "Even if people aren't grateful."

"That sounds like your training sergeant, too."

"He wasn't wrong, though, was he?"

Etain thought of the locals who had betrayed them to Hokan's men. Yes, she'd learned a lot about the reality of conflict in the last few weeks. But it still wasn't enough.

"It's getting light," Darman said. He sat down cross-legged in the hide, armor plates clacking against something. "You look cold. Need any more painkillers?"

Etain had achieved a consistent level of dampness and pain that she could live with. She was too tired to think of doing anything else. She'd even stopped noticing the persistent odor of wet merlie wool. "I'm okay."

"If we light a fire we'll be a magnet for half the Separatist army." He rummaged in his belt and held out a ration cube to her, still that incongruous amalgam of fresh naïveté and utterly clinical killer. She shook her head. He pulled out a bag. "Dried kuvara?"

She realized from the way he had put the fruit carefully in his belt and not in his pack that he prized it. He lived on rations with all the taste appeal of rancid mott hide. The sacrifice was rather touching; she'd have plenty of time to gorge herself on the galaxy's varied foods, provided she got off Qiilura alive, but Darman wouldn't. She managed a smile and waved it away. "No. Eat up. That's an order."

He didn't need encouraging. He chewed with his eyes closed and she felt desperately sorry for him; yet a little envious of his delight in ordinary things.

"I know a good way to warm up," he said, and opened his eyes.

Etain bristled. Maybe he wasn't as naïve as he seemed. "You do?"

"If you're feeling up to it."

"Up to *what*?"

Darman made a *wait-and-see* gesture with one raised finger and got up to go outside. No, Etain thought, he wouldn't have meant *that* at all. She was suddenly embarrassed that she'd even imagined he might. She stared at the backs of her hands, suddenly appalled at their abrasions and broken nails and general ugliness. A roughly trimmed pole was thrust into the shelter. She jumped. She didn't need any more surprises.

"If that's supposed to be funny, Darman, I'm not laughing."

"Come on, commander." He peered down the length of the pole. "Lightsaber drill. Let's do it now before you have to for real."

"I just want to rest."

"I know." He squatted down and stared at her. "I don't know much about swords, either, but I'm trained in hand-to-hand combat."

He didn't move. His persistence annoyed her. Actually, it suddenly *angered* her; she'd had enough. She was exhausted, and she wanted to sit numbly and do absolutely nothing. She jumped to her feet, snatched the pole, and ran at him.

He sidestepped her, but only just.

"Relatively safe way to perfect your lightsaber skills," Darman said.

"Relatively?" She held the pole two-handed, furious.

"Relatively," Darman said, and brought his own mock lightsaber around sharply on her shin.

"Ow! You—"

"Come on. Do your worst." Darman leapt back out of the range of a savage and uncontrolled lunge. "That's it. Come at me."

That was the point at which she always stumbled—the fine line between giving maximum effort and being blinded by angry violence. *You have to mean it. It's not a game anymore.* She came at him with a two-handed sweep from right to left, cracking hard against his weapon and feeling the impact in her wrists and elbows, forcing Darman onto his back foot. Three more rapid sweeps, right, right, left—and then one immediately downwards, unexpected, hitting him so hard between neck and shoulder that if the pole had been a real lightsaber she would have sliced him in half.

She heard the sickening *thwack.* It was the first time she'd seen him in pain. It was a split second of a grimace, no more, but she was instantly appalled at herself.

"Sorry—" she said, but he came straight back at her and sent the stake flying from her hand.

"You have to press home your advantage," Darman said, rubbing his neck. "I've never used an energy blade and I don't have the Force to call on. But I do know when to go all-out."

"I know," Etain said, inspecting her shin and catching her breath. "Did I do any damage?"

"Nothing serious. Good move."

"I don't want to let you down when you need me most."

"You've done fine so far, Commander."

"How can you do all this, Darman?"

"Do what? Fight?"

"Kill and remain detached."

"Training, I suppose. And whatever was in Jango Fett that made him . . . detached."

"Were you ever afraid in training?"

"Almost always."

"Did you ever get hurt?"

"All the time. Others died. It's how you learn. Getting hurt teaches you to shoot instinctively. That's why our instructors began training us with simunition that would hurt us without causing permanent damage. Then we moved on to live rounds."

"How old were you then?"

"Four. Perhaps five."

She hadn't known that. It made her shudder. She couldn't recall any Jedi dying in training. It was another world. She picked up her pole and made a few slow passes with it, her gaze fixed on its tip. "I find this accelerated growth difficult to comprehend."

"It's a Kaminoan industrial secret."

"I mean that it's hard for me to reconcile what you appear to be and what you can do, with—well, with someone who's had less experience of the profane world than even a Padawan."

"Sergeant Skirata told us we *perplexed* him."

"You talk about him a lot."

"He trained my squad and also Niner's and Fi's. That might be why they put us together for this mission when our brothers were killed."

Etain felt ashamed. There was no self-pity in him whatsoever. "What will they do with you in thirty years, when you're too old to fight?"

"I'll be dead long before then."

"That's rather fatalistic."

"I mean that we'll always age faster than you. We've been told decline for clones is mercifully swift. Slow soldiers get killed. I can't think of a better time to die than when I'm no longer the best."

Etain really didn't want to hear anything more about death right then. Death was happening all too easily and frequently, as if it didn't matter and had no consequences. She could feel the Force being distorted around her; not the regular rhythm of life as it was meant to be, but the chaos of destruction. She felt she could neither accept it nor influence it.

"We're supposed to be peacekeepers," she said wearily. "This is ugly."

"But war always is. Calling it peacekeeping doesn't change anything."

"It's different," Etain said.

Darman pursed his lips, looking slightly past her as if rehearsing something difficult in his mind. "Sergeant Skirata said that civvies didn't have a clue, and that it was all right for them to have lofty ideas about peace and freedom as long as they weren't the ones being shot at. He said nothing focuses your mind better than someone trying to kill you."

That stung. Etain wondered if the comment were just an unguarded recollection, or a subtle rebuke of her principles. Darman appeared equally capable of either. She still hadn't come to terms with his duality, killer and innocent, soldier and child, educated intelligence and grim humor. Undistracted by a normal life, he seemed to have spent more time in contemplation than even she had. She wondered how much the intense experience of the outside world would change him.

She'd killed just one fellow living being. It had certainly changed her.

"Come on," he said. "Sun's coming up. Might dry out your clothes."

It was definitely autumn. A mist had blanketed the countryside like a sea. A puddle had formed in the sheeting stretched over the top of the shelter, and Darman went to scoop it out but stopped.

"What *are* these things?" he asked. "I saw them on the river, too."

Ruby- and sapphire-colored insects were dancing above the surface of the puddle. "Daywings," Etain said.

"I've never seen colors like it."

"They hatch and take flight for a day, and they die by the evening," she said. "A brief and glorious . . ."

Her voice trailed off. She was appalled at her own insensitivity. She began assembling an apology, but Darman didn't appear to need one.

"They're amazing," he said, completely absorbed by the spectacle.

"They certainly are," she said, and watched him.

Lik Ankkit's villa had been splendid. It was still splendid in its unnecessary way, but the polished kuvara floors, with their intricately inlaid flower motif borders, were now scuffed and gouged by the metal feet of droids.

Ankkit hovered in the doorway while these four droids screwed alloy sheets across the window frames, shutting out the sunrise. Ghez Hokan watched the progress of the conversion from mansion to fortress.

"You'll split the *wood,*" Ankkit hissed. "Careful! Do you know how long it took to have those panels carved?"

Hokan shrugged. "I'm not a carpenter."

"They were not made by *carpenters.* They were made by artists—"

"I don't care if Supreme Chancellor Palpatine carved them himself with a dinner fork. I need to secure this building."

"You have a perfectly adequate purpose-built facility not three kilometers from here. You could defend *that.*"

"And I have."

"Why? Why ruin my home when Uthan is no longer here?"

"For a devious and treacherous little bean counter, Ankkit, you show a surprising lack of tactical creativity." Hokan walked over to the Neimoidian and stood close to him. He would *not* be intimidated by this grocer's height. He didn't care if he had to crane his neck to look him in the eye; *he* was the bigger man. "I know she's no longer here. The enemy might believe she is. If I observed *my* enemy making lavish preparations to defend an installation, I might assume it was a bluff and investigate an alternative target. If I found that alternative target discreetly prepared against intruders, I would make an educated guess that it was the real objective, and attack it."

Ankkit appeared unconvinced. He glared at Hokan with half-lidded red eyes, which was a rare show of courage for him. "And how will they spot this discreet reinforcement?"

"I've made sure that supplies have been seen arriving here with an accompanying degree of security procedure. Movement by night, that sort of thing. Given the nobility of the local population, I'm sure someone will trade that information for some bauble or other. It always worked for me."

"This reinforcement will not save my home from destruction."

"You're right, Ankkit. Wooden structures don't bear up well to cannons. That's why I've moved Doctor Uthan back to the facility. If I have to, I can actually defend metal and stone more successfully."

"So why did you move her here in the first place?"

"I'm surprised that you even have to ask. To keep everyone guessing, of course."

It had seemed like a sensible idea at the time: he hadn't known what he was dealing with. Now he was fairly sure that he was facing no more than ten men. Had an army landed, he'd have known by now. Moving Uthan—not a task he could achieve in complete secrecy anyway—had helped thicken the fog of confusion.

Hokan was leaving nothing to chance. He was laying a trail of clues that would lead the enemy commandos to one conclusion: that Uthan and the nanovirus were barricaded in Lik Ankkit's villa.

A droid dragged a heavy alloy joist through the salon, plowing a furrow in the golden floorboards. Ankkit let out a muffled squeal of frustration. The droid's comrades lifted the joist and aligned it with a horizontal beam, knocking over a fine Naboo vase and smashing it. Droids weren't programmed to say *Oops* and sweep up the fragments. They simply crunched through them, oblivious.

Ankkit was shaking again. He screamed for a servant. A sullen-looking local boy appeared with a brush and swept the debris into a pan.

"Oh dear," Hokan said. He didn't think it was the right time to mention that the labyrinth of wine cellars and secure vaults beneath the villa was now packed with explosives. He didn't know how to revive a Neimoidian who had fainted, and he had no intention of learning.

Lieutenant Hurati was waiting outside the front door. Even when not under scrutiny, Hurati stood with military composure. Hokan had never caught him sneaking a drink from a flask or scratching himself. Hurati didn't straighten up when he saw Hokan, because he was already at attention.

"Sir, Doctor Uthan is getting irritated about the disruption," the lieutenant said.

"I'll talk to her. How is our droid signal chain working out?"

"It's adequate, sir, but I would feel more secure if we had comm monitoring online."

"My boy, there was a time when we had no listening stations, and we had to fight wars by observation and our own wits. It can be done. What have the droids spotted?"

"The incursions appear to be limited to Teklet and the area to the south, sir, and quite specific in nature. At least we know why they attacked the quarry office. I have to say I haven't encountered an excavator bomb before." Hurati licked his lips nervously. "Sir, are you sure you don't want any patrols to search the Teklet road? I'd be happy to do it myself, sir. It's no trouble."

Hokan took it for the genuine concern it was rather than a criticism. "No, we could be chasing gdan trails all over the region. Our enemy is obviously good at diversionary tactics, and I'm not going to take any bait. I'll wait for them to take mine." He patted Hurati's back. "If you're anxious to be busy, keep an eye on Ankkit. I don't want him interfering. Restrain him by any means you consider necessary."

Hurati saluted. "Will do, sir. Also—Lieutenant Cuvin . . . I don't think he will make captain, as you said."

Hokan liked Hurati more every day. "Has his removal from the promotion list been noted by your fellow officers?"

"It has, sir."

"Good. Well done."

Hurati was proving to be a loyal aide. He was eager to obey. Hokan decided he would have to watch him. He promoted him anyway. There was nothing to be gained by willfully ignoring excellence in another.

13

CO *Majestic* to Republic Command, Coruscant

On station and awaiting contact from Omega Squad. All communications from Teklet ground station have ceased. Separatist vessel has approached and is standing off our port bow at 50 kilometers—has not responded to signals but is believed to be a Techno Union armed transport. Will engage if vessel appears to be taking hostile action. Standing by.

"Turned out nice again," Fi said, somewhere ahead of the column.

"You been on the stims?" Niner asked.

"I'm just naturally cheerful."

"Well, I'm not, so where did you get it from?"

Niner didn't like being tail on a patrol. He walked backward, scanning the trees, wondering why he was this close to Imbraani without a sign of enemy contact since Teklet.

Tinnies couldn't climb trees. It was the wets he was worried about.

"Want to swap?" Fi said.

"I'm fine."

"Just say the word."

Fi was about a hundred meters ahead on point. Atin walked behind Guta-Nay. The Weequay was carrying a fair share of the ordnance and equipment they'd had to load on their backs since abandoning the excavator droid and the speeder bike.

"Very quiet, all things considered," Atin said. "Mind if I send up a remote?"

"Might as well," Niner said. "Patch visual through to all of us, will you?"

"We there yet?" Guta-Nay asked.

"Soon." Niner hadn't found the Weequay much use so far except as a pack animal. All he seemed to know about Hokan's tactics was that they *hurt bad.* "Now, are you going to be cooperative, or am I going to return you to your boss?"

"You not do that! It *cruel* it is!"

"He'll probably just give you a big kiss and tell you how much he's missed you."

"He gonna cut my—"

"I'm sure he will. Want to tell us more about the droids?"

"A hundred."

"Any SBDs?"

"What?"

"Super—battle—droids." Niner indicated the bulky shape with his arms held away from his sides, letting his rifle hang on its webbing. "Big ones."

"No. I seen none, anyway."

"I told you we should have slotted him," Fi said. "Still, he carried a bit of kit. I suppose we ought to cut him some slack for that."

The metallic sphere of the remote rose just above the level of the trees and shot off. Niner's field of vision was interrupted in one quadrant by an aerial view of the countryside. As the remote tracked along paths and swooped among branches, it was clear that nobody was about, a worrying thing in itself. Then it dived in to show a familiar figure, stripped to the waist, bending over a makeshift basin of soapy water fashioned from a section of plastoid sheet.

The remote hovered above Darman as he reached for his rifle, not even raising his eyes.

"Sarge, is that you?"

Niner was staring into the business end of Darman's Deece. It was a sobering close-up. "We're about ten minutes from the RV. Going anywhere nice?"

The rifle disappeared from the frame and Darman, half shaved, stared back. "Knock first, will you?"

"I'm glad to see you, too. Where'd you get that wound?"

"This one? Or *this* one?"

"The burn."

"A Trandoshan. Ex-Trandoshan, actually. We've had a little more attention than we'd have liked."

"The commander's still in one piece?"

"Well, *this* bruise is hers. I'm teaching her to fight dirty. She's catching on."

"Get the kettle boiling, then. We're bringing a guest."

Darman's faintly impatient expression dwindled below the remote and was replaced by an open view over Imbraani. It wasn't so much a town as a scattering of farms, with a few knots of industrial-looking buildings dotted among them. Atin sent it higher and a few more remote buildings were visible.

"Take it in over the villa," Niner said.

"Open country, Sarge. Bit risky."

"I think we've lost the element of surprise."

"Okay. Long lens, though."

"What you doing?" Guta-Nay asked. To him, they were traveling in silence. He couldn't hear the conversations going on between helmet comlinks. Niner switched channels with a couple of deliberate blinks.

"Taking a look at that villa."

"I know about villa."

"We all know about the villa."

Niner would have welcomed a visit from Jinart. They hadn't seen the shapeshifter since yesterday. She could have been anywhere, of course, but she hadn't made herself visible. He hoped she hadn't run into problems.

Five minutes now. No time at all. They'd be a squad again, and they'd have a commander. They'd be at the RV, and then they could rest up, eat, have a wash, and generally clear their heads. It began to feel like good news.

There was just the matter of taking Uthan and the nanovirus, then getting out in one piece.

Etain had almost grown used to thinking of Darman's armored anonymity as a friendly face. Then three more exactly like him emerged from the trees and disturbed that fragile equilibrium.

And then they took their helmets off.

It was rude, she knew, but all she could do was stare, and she found herself slowly putting her hand to her mouth in an attempt to disguise her shock.

"Yes, sorry about the Weequay, Commander," one of them said. He had Darman's voice and Darman's face. "He's a bit ripe, I know. We'll have him clean himself up."

They were utterly identical, except for one with a terrible scar across his face. The other two seemed like different moods of the same man, one serious, one pleasantly calm and unconcerned. They were all staring at her.

"I can't tell you apart," she said.

"I'm CC—"

"No, you have proper names. I *know* you have names."

"It's—it's not policy, Commander."

Darman lowered his eyes. "It's a private thing."

"Everyone calls me Fi," said the calm one, clearly not bothered by policy. "And this is Atin."

"Niner," the serious one said, and saluted. Etain couldn't sense a great deal from either of them, but the scarred Atin exuded a sense of loss that was almost solid. She could feel its weight. She tried to concentrate on the Weequay. She didn't need to tap into the Force to tell that he was terrified. He was bent over as if about to drop to his knees, staring up at her.

Weequay didn't all look the same. She *knew* this one. He had chased her across a barq field. He was a rapist and a murderer, not that the descriptions set him apart from any other of Hokan's thugs. She reached for her lightsaber.

"Whoa," Darman said.

"Girlie?" Guta-Nay said.

"I'll give you *girlie,*" she said, but Darman caught her arm and she was instantly ashamed of her reaction. Again, it was anger. It was what stood between her and making sense of her calling. She had to get the better of it. If Darman could exercise force without venom, then so could she.

"What's he here for?" she asked, thumbing off the blade.

"We thought he might have useful information," Niner said.

Etain was desperate to be useful. She felt as if she were only capable of performing conjuring tricks: enough skills to distract, but not enough to be a functioning soldier. She also wanted Darman to stop treating her as if she were merely in need of a little more instruction. She wanted him to tell her how much he despised all that potential power wasted on a girl with no discipline or focus. He wasn't stupid. He *had* to be thinking that.

"What do we need to know, Niner?"

"How Hokan thinks, Commander."

"Give me some time with him."

Guta-Nay straightened up and took one step back, shaking his head. He was expecting Hokan-style treatment.

Fi chuckled. "Guta-Nay thinks you're going to cut off his . . . er, braids, ma'am."

Braids. She'd forgotten. She pulled a section of hair free of her collar, plaited it as fast as she could, and fumbled in her pocket for a piece of cord to fasten it. *This is what you are. Live up to it, if only to justify Darman's faith in you.*

"We're going to have a little chat," she said. She let her braid fall back inside her collar. "Sit down . . . Guta-Nay."

It wasn't easy for him to settle down on the ground with his hands still tied, but Etain wasn't taking any chances. He knelt and then fell sideways in an undignified sprawl. She hauled him into a sitting position and they sat outside the shelter in silence. She wanted him to calm down before she attempted to influence him.

A sudden clack of armor made her glance over her shoulder, and she was astonished to see Atin giving Darman an awkward hug, slapping him on the back. She caught Darman's eye: he looked bewildered.

Whatever had given Atin his huge emotional burden had been slightly relieved by finding Darman well. Then the two men parted as if nothing in particular had happened. Etain turned back to Guta-Nay, suddenly very aware that for all their calm manner and unnatural appearance, these soldiers were every bit as painfully human as she was.

Bred to fight.

A new doubt was growing in her. She shook it off and turned to Guta-Nay, who wouldn't meet her eyes.

"You're not afraid," she said quietly, and visualized the gentle trickle of water from the fountain of her clan home on Coruscant. "You're relaxed and you want to talk about Ghez Hokan."

He certainly did.

"Haven't seen Jinart?" Darman said.

"Not since yesterday." Niner cleaned his armor. It didn't matter how visible they were now, and he hated scruffy rig. Darman had stripped down his Deece and was wiping the ignition chamber more than it needed it. Fi wandered around the temporary camp, cradling his rifle, keeping watch.

"Well, whether she's here or not, I think we go in sooner rather than later."

"The villa or the facility?"

"Latest intel we have from Jinart indicates the villa."

"But . . ."

"Yeah, but. I'd find it hard to walk away from a place I could defend, too. That villa's nothing but firewood." He put down the shoulder plate he was cleaning. "Show me that plan again."

Darman clipped the DC-17 back together and reached into his belt for the holochart sphere. "She did okay to get this."

"Our commander? Jinart seemed dismissive of her."

"C'mon, Niner. She's a Jedi. She's an *officer.*"

"Well? What do you think?"

Darman rubbed the bridge of his nose. "She's got a lot of fight in her."

"And?"

"She's . . . well, she's not exactly Skirata. But she's learning fast. And you should see the Jedi stuff she can do. There's more to it than just the fighting skills."

Niner occasionally had his doubts about nonclone officers. They all did. They never admitted it publicly, but Skirata had warned them, quietly, privately, that outside officers sometimes needed help, and while you always obeyed *orders,* you needed to be able to make *helpful interpretations* if the officer was less than specific. Officers could unintentionally get you killed.

"*Nobody's* Skirata," Niner said. He was watching the commander discreetly. Whatever she had done to Guta-Nay had transformed him into a true conversationalist. She was actually looking bored, as if she'd been cornered by someone who really, really wanted to explain every engineering detail of a repeating blaster.

"You have to admit that's quite a skill," Darman said.

Niner tried not to think about it. It made him uneasy, not knowing how many of his actions were his own choice. He didn't like the other conflicts she created in him, either. He had never been this close to a human female before, and he was relieved that she was emaciated, unkempt, and generally less than appealing. The proximity still made him feel edgy, though, and from the way Darman was looking at him, it seemed they shared the realization.

They both watched Guta-Nay unburdening himself to the commander until she seemed to tire of it and got up from her cross-legged position. She walked over and looked at both of them uncertainly.

"I'm sorry, Darman," she said to Niner. Then she gave an embarrassed shrug. "Sorry. Of course—you're Niner. I got a little detail out of him, but he isn't the analytical type, I'm afraid. I can tell you that Hokan carries a Verpine shatter gun and a custom KYD-twenty-one blaster. He's got a lot of Trandoshan equipment, and as far as any of the militia knew, there were no more than a hundred battle droids at the garrison. Hokan is also apparently something of a game player—he likes to bluff and double-bluff."

Niner considered the information. "That's useful, Commander. Thank you."

"I was going to see if I could summon Jinart. She could probably see what's happening down there at the villa."

"Can you do that?" Darman asked.

"I can sense her, when she wants me to. I'll see if she can sense me." She stared down at her boots. "And please don't call me *Commander.* I haven't earned the rank. Until I do—if I ever do—I'm Etain. Darman knows that, don't you, Darman?"

He nodded. Niner didn't feel comfortable with that. He liked to know who stood where in the hierarchy of things. "Whatever you say. Can I ask you a question?"

"Certainly."

"Why did you say *of course you're Niner*?"

She paused. "You feel different. All of you. You might look the same, but you're not. I don't normally identify individuals by their effect on the Force, but I can if I concentrate."

"We seem different to you?"

"You know you are, surely. You know you're Niner and he knows he's Darman. You're as self-aware as I am, as any other human."

"Yes, but . . ."

"All beings are individuals, and their essence in the Force reflects that. The act of living makes us different, and in that way you're like twins, only more so. Atin's *very* different. What happened to him to make him so burdened?"

The answer stunned Niner. He was used to being a product. His squad and his sergeant had treated him like a man, but the Kaminoans certainly hadn't. This was the first time that a Jedi, a commander, had confirmed the clone commandos' intensely private suspicion that they were no less than normal men. It was no longer a secret dissent that had to be hidden.

"Atin was the only survivor of his first squad, then he was reassigned and lost all three brothers in action again," Niner said. "He feels guilty."

"Poor man," she said. "Does he talk about it?"

"Not much."

"Perhaps I could help him see he has nothing to feel guilty about. Just a little encouragement. Nothing like the influence I used on the Weequay, I promise."

"That's kind of you."

"We have to look out for each other."

Right then Niner didn't care if she had less idea of guerrilla warfare than a mott. She possessed one fundamental element of leadership that you couldn't teach in a lifetime: she cared about those she led.

She had earned her rank on the strength of that alone.

"Contact, five hundred meters," Fi said.

The squad abandoned their impromptu meal of stewed dried meat and put their helmets back on. Etain was again surprised at how fast they moved. They were lying prone in the undergrowth, rifles trained, in the time it took her to turn and check where the Weequay was.

You're not going to make a sound, Guta-Nay. You want to be totally silent.

He was. But she felt what was approaching. She scrambled into the bushes on her hands and knees and leaned close to Darman. "It's Jinart," she said. "Relax."

Darman, Fi, and Atin sat back on their heels. Niner stayed prone, still lined up on his sights, and held his hand away from the trigger in a conspicuous gesture.

"Niner likes to be sure," Darman said. "No offense."

The grass shook visibly, and then a living oil slick flowed past the kneeling commandos. It seemed to be carrying something horrific in its black swirls. The slick resolved itself into Jinart's natural form, and she had a huge lump of raw meat in her jaws. She laid it on the ground.

"I gave you plenty of warning," Jinart said, staring at Niner. She sniffed the air and appeared to follow an invisible beacon with her long snout. Her gaze settled on Guta-Nay, dozing against a tree, bound hands in his lap. "What possessed you to collect *that* souvenir?"

"We thought he might come in handy," Fi repeated.

"You can't even eat Weequays," Jinart said, and metamorphosed into her human form. "Better not let the creature see me for what I am, just in case. Have you eaten? Would you like some merlie?"

Fi took his helmet off and grinned. "We've got time for that, have we?"

"You might as well fight on a full stomach," Jinart said. "You have a tough job on your hands."

Fi picked up the leg of merlie and rinsed it with water from his bottle. "Dar, you got any of that dried fruit left?" He ejected the vibroblade from his knuckle plate and began cutting the leg into chunks. Etain wondered how he had developed his relentless good humor; she couldn't imagine him shooting anyone. One thing she had discovered in the last few days was that professional soldiers were neither habitually angry nor violent.

They didn't even talk tough. They were a mass of contradictions. They washed their clothing and they shaved and cooked and generally conducted themselves like well-behaved, well-educated Padawans. Then they went out and blew up installations and killed total strangers and cracked bad jokes. Etain was getting used to it, but slowly.

While Atin kept an eye on Guta-Nay, the rest of them sat listening to Jinart in the shelter.

"I have been observing," she said. "Hokan has made much of reinforcing the Neimoidian villa under strict security, and he does indeed have most of his hundred droids there. The whole building is packed with explosives, most of them in the wine cellars. But he has also moved Uthan back to the installation."

"Our fragrant Weequay friend was right about the double bluff, then," Etain said.

Niner shrugged. "It's what I'd do. Defend the strongest position."

"So we go for the installation, then," she said.

"We'll have to deal with both targets. They're only two or three kilometers apart. Once we start on the main facility, the droids from the villa will pop over for a visit in a matter of minutes."

Etain rubbed her forehead. "If they followed the plans when they built the facility, then the only way in will probably be through the front door."

Darman shrugged. "We can make our own doors. That's what frame charges and water cuts are for."

"Sorry?"

"We blow holes in the walls. But I'd rather avoid that if we're dealing with hazardous materials. Don't want to break any bottles, I reckon."

"There isn't even a fire exit. One door, no windows, no large ventilation shafts."

"Doesn't look like anyone enforces building regulations around here." Darman shrugged. "Front door, walls, or drains. Walls would be best, but how we can get into position unnoticed is another matter."

Niner looked at Darman as if waiting for a suggestion. "A split attack could divert them if it's noisy enough."

"Well, if Hokan's been kind enough to load up the villa with things that go bang, it would be a shame for them to go to waste."

Darman studied the holochart plan of the villa. "They won't fall for a droid bomb again, but we do have a lot of explosives we could introduce to the mix."

"You make it sound as if it's going to be relatively easy," Etain said.

"No, it's going to be hard. But that's what we're trained for."

"I'd rather have you effecting rapid entry to the main facility," Niner said.

"But we should place our own explosives inside the villa, in the cellars if we can," Darman said. "A high-energy explosion will set off the rest of their charges. If we can place one, it'll direct the blast upward, and if the droids are on top of the pile, it'll solve that problem, too."

"Okay, in real terms, there's a layer of solid droid on top of the cellars. Can't free-fall in. So it's through the front door, the wall, or the drains. And the drains look like thirty-centimeter diameter."

"Bore-bangs?" Fi said.

"They won't drill far enough into the ground to penetrate the cellars, and they're not powerful enough anyway." Darman's gaze was fixed on the holographic plan. "Although they might be if Atin modified them and packed in a bit of the thermal tape. I was saving it for the blast doors in the facility, but I could spare a meter. That'd be ample."

"How about a remote?" Atin said. "If we can direct it into the building, that is. If you took out the recording components, you could pack in the thermal tape—about a couple of meters, easily."

"They'll be able to spot anything that's flying."

Jinart, in aged crone mode, looked from face to identical face. "What size is this device?"

Darman formed a fist. "About this big. I'll show you one."

"I could carry that to the villa, right to the walls, if you can direct it from there."

Niner pointed into the shimmering image of the building. "Down the roof vent, which would put it in the main hall running front to back."

"Or maybe along the main drain from this culvert about two hundred meters behind the house. I like that better."

Etain joined in the communal ritual of staring at the holographic display as if an answer would eventually emerge on its own. "The only point in blowing up the villa is if you could hit as many droids with it as possible."

"Then we have to convince them we're going all out for the

villa," Niner said. "That means a feint of some sort, which would be fine if we had more men. But we don't."

Then Etain did have an idea, and it was one that she wasn't proud of.

"How about sending Hokan a direct message?" she said. "What if Guta-Nay were to escape and tell him we were planning to attack the villa?"

"But he knows there are only four of us," Darman said. "Sorry, five."

"Six," Jinart said sourly.

"We could convince the Weequay that we have another squad or two in the area," Etain said. "At this point, he'll believe anything I tell him. But I'll be sending him to his death."

Fi nodded. "Yeah, if Hokan skewers him without waiting to hear what he's got to say, we're stuffed."

He was cheerfully, benignly callous. Etain was briefly appalled before letting the reality wash over her. Given the chance, Guta-Nay would have abused and killed her without a second thought. Aside from that, the squad's target was effectively a weapons factory, a weapon that would kill millions of men just like Niner, Fi, and Atin. *And Darman.* If they didn't kill, they would be killed.

It didn't take her long to move from her reverence for all living things to thinking *waste the Weequay.* She wondered if that was the true nature of corruption.

"I'll do my best to give him a good opening line," Etain said.

"He's scum," Jinart said suddenly. "If his death can help remove the Trade Federation and all their minions from my world, then it is a cheap price to pay."

My world? Etain obviously had the same thought as the commandos, because they all reacted, looking at the shapeshifter expectantly.

"We didn't realize this was your homeworld," Niner said.

"It is," Jinart said. "I'm among the last of my kind. Various invaders have driven us from our habitat without even seeing us—and now I doubt they would have done any differently had they known we were here. Yes, we'll help you rid this world of Neimoidians and every other hostile alien species that's here. That's our bargain with the Republic. You help us; we help you. That's why we risk our lives. It is *not* for the greater glory of your cause."

"Nobody told us," Etain said. "I'm sorry. I can't speak for the Republic, but we'll do our best to see that they keep their word."

"Mark that you do," Jinart said. She indicated the commandos with a swing of her fine black head. "Like your young friends here, we are few, but we have no problem inflicting a great deal of damage."

Etain could only nod. At least Jinart was brutally honest. Perhaps telepaths, deprived of secret thought, had no other style of interaction. The creature was staring at her, all unblinking orange eyes, and she could see for the first time that the four fangs protruding over the Gurlanin's lower lip each ended in a double point.

"I'll place scent marks around this camp," Jinart said stiffly. "The gdans won't bother you tonight." She slipped away and merged with the land, leaving a trail of rustling noises as she moved through the bushes.

"Okay, let's see what Guta-Nay can manage," Niner said. "If we don't see signs of movement toward the villa by midday tomorrow, we'll go in anyway, and that'll mean splitting the squad and taking both groups of droids. We really don't want to do that if we can help it."

"This has the makings of a diverting evening," Fi said. "Anyone for supper?"

It was an elaborate charade, and the bizarre thing was that it needed no rehearsal. Guta-Nay was entirely unquestioning: Etain had begun to see him as a monstrous and sadistic child, unable to comprehend the feelings of others, or control his own. They sat around and ate the merlie stewed with dried kuvara, talking about leaving enough for the "other squad" when it showed up. They discussed in hushed tones about how "the villa" was their target. If this was the misinformation game, it was an easy one.

Even so, Etain definitely didn't feel proud of her subterfuge when she cut the ties around the Weequay's wrists, ostensibly an act of kindness so that he could eat. It was designed to send him to his death. At least she felt some relief that as soon as it was dark, and they made a show of turning their backs on him and being preoccupied, Guta-Nay would try to escape, and vindicate Jinart's judgment that he was *scum*.

The decision still sat heavy on her.

Fi and Darman were asleep, judging by the position of their heads. It was impossible to tell with their helmets on, but they were sitting against a tree, chins resting on their breastplates and arms folded over the rifles clutched to their chests. She had no doubt that if she walked over to them, they'd wake and be on their feet in a second.

She glanced up. Niner was on watch, perched in the fork of a tree with one leg dangling, occasionally peering down his rifle scope at something.

"What can he see?" she asked.

Atin, cross-legged with an array of wires and detonators spread around him, looked up. He'd taken off the armor section that protected his backside and was using it as a convenient plate for components while he worked.

"Line of sight? Up to thirty kilometers in good viz. Connected to a remote ship system? Well, you name it, Com—sorry, *Etain.*" He pointed to his rifle, and then went on packing tight-coiled black and white ribbons of explosive into the remote. "Have a look through the Deece. Safety's on, but don't press anything."

Etain shouldered the rifle. It was a lot lighter than it looked, and the view through the scope was startlingly vivid despite the failing light. She found it difficult to shut out the display that was superimposed on her field of vision. It narrowed the view to a tight focus on the target. "Is this what you see through that visor?"

"Sort of."

"Can I try the helmet? I want to know what it's like to be inside it."

Atin gave her a dubious look and shrugged. "You won't get all the readouts without the rest of the armor system, but you'll see enough. It's top shelf. They upgraded it just for this mission."

She lifted the helmet and held it above her head, a bizarre coronation. As she lowered it into place, the feeling of confinement and stifling heat almost made her nauseous, but she steeled herself to tolerate it.

"Hot," she said.

"It's fine when it's sealed to the rest of the suit," Atin said. He got to his feet and loomed in her field of vision. "See the red light in the top corner?"

"Mm."

"Look at it and blink twice, fast."

She did. It unleashed chaos. All she could see now was a riot of lines and numbers and flashing symbols. She was aware of a normal view beyond it, but the rest of the data dancing before her eyes was overwhelming.

"That's the HUD," Atin said. "Heads-up display. Real lifesaver. The proverbial eyes in your backside."

"It's distracting. How do you cope with it?"

"You get used to it fast. We've used these systems all our lives. You can filter the information out, like listening to a conversation in a crowd."

Etain lifted the helmet off and inhaled cool evening air. "And you can communicate without any audible sound outside the helmet?"

"Yes, and even without Command and Control hearing us on certain frequencies. I don't think ordinary troopers can do that, but we're different."

"Separate specialized training?"

"They're trained from day one to be more obedient than us. And we're more obedient than ARC troopers. They're pretty well raw Jango."

He was talking about himself as if he were a commodity. Etain found it uncomfortable: yes, these young men were odd because they were externally identical, but they were still individual men, and not exotic houseplants or strains of grain. She understood that the Republic faced desperate times. She just wondered how many desperate measures that could justify. Somehow it seemed an affront to the Force to do this to fellow humans, even if they seemed remarkably sanguine about it.

She handed him back his helmet. "We use you, don't we, Atin? All of you."

"No soldier has it easy." He fumbled with a length of wire, clearly embarrassed, brow furrowed in mock concentration. The fresh scar from cheek to chin was all the more shocking etched into fresh young skin, and not a battle-hardened, wrinkled face that indicated a full life. "But I like this job. What else would I do?"

It was a painfully good question. What would any of them do if they were discharged from the Grand Army? She reached out and squeezed his arm instinctively, but all she grasped was plastoid-alloy plate.

"I know what happened to you," she said. She concentrated, a precision job: just enough to influence him to see what was true and reasonable, but not to make mockery of his natural grief. "What happened to your brothers wasn't your fault. You're a good soldier. Sometimes the odds are too far against you."

He stared down at his boots. Eventually, he looked up and shrugged. "I'll do my best to make sure this bunch stays alive, then." There was little indication on his face that the gentle push toward acceptance had worked, but Etain felt less of a jagged tear in the Force around him. He might heal, in time.

And time was something none of the clone commandos would have. It made her ashamed.

"Can I help with anything?" Etain said.

"You could help me put some remote dets into these. I told Dar I'd finish them for him." Atin indicated small packs of mining explosive, and handed her something that looked like a packet of steel toothpicks. "Slide these between the ribbon and the main charge. Makes any party go off with a bigger bang."

"What are they?"

"IEDs," he said. "Great for planting down drainage systems and air-conditioning ducts."

"Not more acronyms."

"Improvised explosive devices. Be sure you make them look neat. Dar's fussy about his devices."

It was a relatively simple but fiddly task: Etain was a quick learner. They sat in silent concentration, making bombs as casually as if they were shelling qana beans. *This is how it happens,* she thought. *This is how you slide from peacekeeper to soldier to assassin.*

"Can I ask you a favor?" Atin said, not looking up from the bomb in progress.

"Of course."

"May I look at your lightsaber?"

Etain smiled. "Well, you've shown me yours, so it's only fair I should show you mine." She took out the hilt and held it up to him. He wiped his palms on his bodysuit and took the saber carefully. "*That's* the dangerous end, and *this* is the control."

He showed no inclination to activate it. He seemed absorbed by the hilt and its markings.

"Go on," Etain said.

The lightsaber flared into blue light with a *vzzmmm.* Atin didn't even flinch. He simply stared down the length of the blade and seemed to be checking it for true.

"It doesn't feel like a weapon," he said. "It's a beautiful thing."

"I made it."

That changed his expression. She had struck a chord with him, one builder of gadgets to another. "Now that *is* impressive."

Etain enjoyed the respect. Being treated with deference as an officer made her squirm, but this felt good. *So I think I'm pretty good at something. And someone else thinks I'm good at it, too.* It was a boost that she sorely needed.

Atin thumbed off the blade and handed the hilt back to her with suitable reverence. "I'd still rather have plenty of distance between me and the enemy," he said. "This is a close-in weapon."

"Maybe I need to practice my more remote skills," Etain said. "You never know when telekinesis might come in handy."

They went on bundling explosives with ribbon charges and stacking the packages in a heap. She heard and felt Darman relieve

Niner on watch: their respective presences ebbed and flowed, merging at one point as they crossed paths.

Through the night Etain alternated between dozing and checking on Guta-Nay. She was careful not to give him the idea that she was watching him, and instead concentrated on sensing whether he was still there, sitting in the lee of a tree with his knees drawn up to his chest. Sometimes he slept; she could feel the absence of mental activity, almost like sensing a plant. Other times he woke and felt more vivid and chaotic, like a predator.

It was getting light again. It had been a long and restless night.

And still Guta-Nay sat there. He'd made no attempt to escape.

Of course he won't. Etain felt her stomach knotting. *He's terrified of Hokan. He wants to stay with us. We're the good guys, the civilized guys.*

Once again she was horrified by her ruthless and almost involuntary calculation of benefit against evil. She wandered past the shelter made of leaves, tarpaulin, and a camouflage net that seemed to be handmade. Niner, now clearly asleep, still wearing full armor, was curled up on his side, one arm folded under his head. Atin was reading his datapad; Fi was finishing the cold remains of the merlie stew. He glanced up at her and held out the mess tin.

"I'll pass, thanks." Fat had congealed in unappetizing yellow globules on the surface. It seemed soldiers could sleep anywhere and eat anything.

This couldn't be a moral dilemma. It was obvious. These men had become her responsibility, both as an individual and as a Jedi: she owed it to them to see that they survived. She liked them. She cared what happened to them, and she wanted to see Atin live long enough to overcome his demons.

And she could do something that even they couldn't.

"Guta-Nay," she said, putting her hand on the Weequay's shoulder. He opened his eyes. "Guta-Nay, you're not afraid. You want to go to Ghez Hokan and tell him what you know. You want to offer him information about the Republic forces in exchange for your life. You want to tell him that they plan to attack the villa because they think the forces at the facility are a decoy."

Guta-Nay stared past her for a moment, and then stood up. He picked his way through the bushes and headed east toward Imbraani.

Etain knew she had now taken a second life.

She pinched the bridge of her nose, eyes screwed shut, and wondered what had happened to her, what Master Fulier would have thought had he been alive. Then she was aware of someone watching her.

She looked up. Darman, perched in the same fork of branches as Niner had been, stared down.

"It's hard to send someone to their death," she said, answering his silent question.

His expression was hidden behind the visor of his helmet. She didn't need to call on any of her abilities as a Jedi to know what he was thinking: one day she would do the same to men like him. The realization caught her unawares.

"You'll get used to it," he said.

She doubted it.

14

There is nothing wrong with fear. You need never be ashamed of it, as long as it doesn't stop you functioning. Fear is your natural warning system; it keeps you alive so that you can fight. Show me a man who isn't afraid, and I'll show you a fool who is a danger to his entire ship. And I do not tolerate fools in my navy.

—Admiral Adar Tallon, addressing the new intake at a Republic academy

Hokan stood on the veranda of Ankkit's villa and stared out at a bright autumnal morning. There were still too many leaves on the trees for his liking.

They were out there somewhere. Republic forces. A handful.

But they were not an army.

He walked to Uthan's laboratory complex, a comfortable fifteen-minute stroll. It occurred to him that he was a good target for a sniper, if a sniper had been able to penetrate Mandalorian armor. Even so, he decided to divert via a coppice. His path took him along a dry-stone wall to the rear of the installation, and he made a complete circle of the farm building before walking up to the single entrance at the front.

As a lure, this was a good one. The line of droids across the entrance was spectacular. Hokan made a point of inspecting them at a leisurely pace and then engaged them in conversation about their cannons. If anyone was observing—soldier, spy, or talkative farmer—they would get the message.

Inside, though, Dr. Uthan was losing her glamorous cool.

"Is this the last time you're going to move me?" she said, tapping her nails against the polished metal of her desk. Her files and equipment were still in packing crates. "My staff members are finding this extremely stressful, as am I."

Hokan took out his datapad and projected a holochart of the installation above the surface of the desk. The place was a cube within a cube: below ground level, the accommodations, storage, and offices lay in a ring around a central core. The core contained a square of eight small laboratories with one more—the secure room—nestled in the center. The rest of the complex had bulkheads that could be brought down and sealed to isolate a biohazard escape. It could be defended.

But it wouldn't come to that. He'd laid a careful trail to Ankkit's villa and a greeting from fifty droids, along with cannons and powerful explosives.

He wanted to get it over with.

"Yes, Doctor, this is the last time I'll move you," he said. "Try to understand why I've done this, Doctor. I believe I'm facing a small commando force. Rather than chase them, which could be diversionary, I've decided to bring them to me. This means they'll be facing a conventional infantry and artillery battle that I don't think they're equipped to fight. Those are battles of numbers."

"I'm not sure if I do see your point, actually."

"We can defend this installation. I have the numbers and the firepower. Sooner or later, they'll take casualties."

"You're certain about this?"

"Not certain, but everything I see suggests they have landed a minimal amount of troops—for example, no evidence of large-scale transport. They hijacked explosives from a quarry to destroy the Teklet ground station. If they had the matériel, they wouldn't have bothered."

"And then again, maybe that's a diversionary tactic, too."

Hokan looked up from the holochart. "Nobody has perfect knowledge in battle. No plan survives contact with the enemy. Yes, I'm making an educated guess, as every commander in history has had to do."

Uthan considered him with cold black eyes. "You should have evacuated my project from the planet."

Hokan folded his arms. "When you move, you're vulnerable. You're vulnerable crossing the countryside between here and the spaceport. You're even more vulnerable attempting to leave Qiilura with a Republic assault ship on station. And now we have no communications beyond runners, and a bunch of droids relaying messages. No, we sit tight."

Uthan indicated the warren of rooms behind her with one hand. "If this comes to a pitched battle, what about my project? What about my staff? Those five scientists represent the best microbiologists and geneticists in the CIS. In many ways, they're more important than the biomaterial we hold. We can start again, even if the work so far is lost."

"It's as dangerous for them to leave as it is for you."

"I see."

"You specified a very secure layout when you had this facility built. You must know it's defensible."

Uthan seemed suddenly fixed on the holochart in front of her. It showed hydraulic emergency bulkheads and chambers within chambers. It showed ventilation systems with triple filters. It could be sealed as tightly as a bottle.

"It's not secure enough to stop anything getting *in,*" she said carefully. "It's to stop anything getting *out.*"

"You said the nanovirus was only lethal for clone troops."

There was a pause, the sort of pause Hokan didn't like. He waited. He stared at her, and he was disappointed to see for the first time that she was nervous. He waited for her to continue. He would wait all day if necessary.

"It will be," she said at last.

"You said that it might make other organisms merely—what was the word—unwell?"

"Yes."

"How unwell, then, if you go to all this trouble to contain it?"

"Very unwell."

"*Dead* unwell?"

"Possibly. Depending on whether the exposed subject has certain sets of genes . . ."

Hokan experienced a rare moment of uncertainty. It wasn't because he was closer to a dangerous virus than he supposed. It was because someone had lied to him, and his instinctive way to deal with that was a violent one. The fact that he was dealing with a woman was the only thing that made him hesitate.

But it was only hesitation. He leaned forward, seized her by her elegant designer collar, and heaved her sharply out of her seat across the desk.

"Never lie to me," he said.

They were eye-to-eye. She was shaking, but she didn't blink. "Get your hands off me."

"What else haven't you told me?"

"Nothing. You didn't need to know the details of the project."

"This is your final chance to tell me if there's anything else I should know."

She shook her head. "No, there isn't. We're having some problems isolating the parts of the virus that will attack only clones. They're human. All human races share the majority of genes. Even you."

He held her for a few more seconds and then let go, and she fell back into her chair. He really should have shot her. He knew it. It would have made her staff more compliant. But she was a significant part of the asset. He hadn't gone soft because she was a woman, he was certain of that.

"Understand this," he said, feeling suddenly very uncomfortable. "This means we're sitting on a weapon that might destroy us as easily as it will destroy the enemy. It places constraints on how we fight." He went back to the holochart and indicated various features of the installation with his forefinger. "You're sure it can't escape into the environment?"

Uthan was staring at his face, not at the chart. It was as if she didn't recognize him. He snapped his fingers and pointed at the chart.

"Come on, Doctor. Pay attention."

"That's—that's the biohazard containment area. Impregnable, for obvious reasons. I was thinking we might retreat in there for the time being."

"I would prefer to keep you and the biomaterial separate. In fact, I would prefer also to keep you separate from your staff. I dislike having all my eggs in one box—if the enemy ever breaches this facility, then they won't be able to destroy the project in one action. If they eliminate one part, we can still salvage the other components, be they personnel or materials."

"These rooms aren't as secure in biohazard terms."

"But they *are* relatively secure in terms of stopping someone from getting at them. The hazardous materials can stay in the central biohazard chamber."

"Yes," she said. "I concede that."

"Then get your people moving."

"You think it'll come to that? To a battle?"

"No, not here. But if it does, this gives me the best chance of succeeding."

"You're prepared to fight while sitting on a bomb, effectively."

"Yes. Your bomb. And if we're both sitting on it, it'll motivate us to prevent its detonation, won't it?"

"I think you're a dangerous and foolhardy man."

"And I think you're a woman who's lucky that she has relative immunity through her value to the Separatist cause." Hokan straightened up. Maybe she wanted an apology. He saw no reason to give one. A scientist, expecting half the relevant facts to be acceptable in the solution of a problem? It was sloppy, unforgivably sloppy. "I'll have a droid help you if you like."

"We'll do it ourselves. I know how careful they are with fragile objects."

Hokan closed the holochart and walked out into the corridor.

Outside, a droid approached him. "Captain Hurati is bringing a prisoner and a visitor," he said. "He says he disobeyed your orders on both."

Maybe promoting the man hadn't been such a good idea. But Hurati was smart. He'd taken them alive when he should have taken them dead, and that was significant. The young officer wasn't squeamish.

Hokan decided to give him the benefit of the doubt. When the droids at the entrance parted to let him pass, Hurati was waiting, and he had two others with him.

One was a Trandoshan mercenary. He carried his distinctive tool of the trade, an APC repeating blaster.

The other was no stranger at all. It was Guta-Nay, his former Weequay lieutenant.

"I got information," the Weequay said, cowering.

"You better have," Hokan said.

With one pair of shoulders missing, Niner had some hard choices to make about what equipment they could take with them. He stared down at the various weapons and piles of ordnance laid out on the ground, astonished by what they had managed to carry as well as in consideration of what they couldn't take into battle.

"We could always cache some stuff near the target," Fi said.

"Two trips—double the risk."

Atin picked up one of the LJ-50 concussion rifles. He had been most insistent on saving those. "Well, I'm taking this conk rifle and the APC array blaster if I'm going into that facility."

"Don't trust Republic procurement, then?" Fi said.

"No point being a snob about kit," Atin said.

"Don't get stuck in any confined spaces."

It was a fair point: with a backpack, Deece, rifle attachments, and sections of cannon, there wasn't a lot of room left to load much else.

Niner didn't want to say it aloud, but they were trying to do two squads' work. Something had to give.

"Come on, you know I can carry equipment," Etain said. She didn't look like she could even carry a tune: battered, disheveled, and ashen, she seemed about to drop. "Ask Darman."

"That right, Dar?" Niner said on the helmet link.

Darman glanced down from his observation point in the tree. "Like a bantha, Sarge. Load her up."

They could split the E-Web across five of them. That meant an extra piece and a decent supply of extra power cells and ordnance.

"Okay, plan A," Niner said. He projected a holochart from his datapad. "The nearest suitable laying-up point is just under one kilometer from the facility in this coppice *here.* We tab down there now and deploy two surveillance remotes to give us a good view of both the facility and the villa. Depending on the situation, we can try to come back for the spare kit during the day. It's two klicks each way. Not a lot, but it's daylight, and if Guta-Nay did the business, we'll have a lot of attention."

"I'm up for it," Atin said. "We're going to need it."

"Go on with plan A," Etain said.

"As we agreed—get a remote loaded with ribbon charge into the villa and do what damage we can, while Fi lays down fire at the rear of the facility, Darman blows the main doors, and I go in with Atin. If we can't get the remote into the villa, then we have to tie the droids down with a split attack—plan B."

Etain chewed her lower lip. "That sounds almost impossible."

"I never said we had good odds."

"And I'm not that much use against droids."

"You would be if you had one of these," Atin said, and offered her the Trandoshan array blaster. "Lightsabers are all very well, but we don't want to get too intimate with the enemy, do we? It's got a good close-range spread so you don't even have to be an expert marksman to use it." He made a gesture with his hands. "Bang. *Serious* bang."

She took the weapon and examined it carefully, then shouldered it like a pro. "Never used one of these. I'll get the hang of it fast."

"That's the spirit, ma'am."

"You should also know that I can move things, too. Not just carry them."

"Move?"

"With the Force."

"Handy," Fi said.

Niner slapped a clip of plasma bolt rounds in Fi's hand to shut him up. "We might need you to keep Doctor Uthan cooperative, too. Worse comes to worst, we've got sedation for her, but I'd really rather have her walking than as a deadweight."

"Is there a plan C?"

"The nice thing about the alphabet, ma'am, is that it gives you plenty of plans to choose from," Fi said.

"Shut up, Fi," Niner said.

"He has a point," Etain said. She spun around to face the undergrowth. "Jinart?"

The Gurlanin slipped out of the bushes and wandered among the selection of weapons, a glossy black predator again, picking her way between the equipment with careful paws. She sniffed at it.

"Show me what I need to carry," she said.

"Can you manage three remotes?" Atin asked.

"All bombs?"

"No, two holo-cams, one bomb."

"Very well. You can explain to me what you want done with them when we reach your . . ."

"Laying-up point," Niner prompted. "LUP."

"You enjoy not being understood, don't you?"

"Part of our mystique and charm," Fi said, and strapped more webbing onto his armor.

They followed the line of the woods, a route that took them a couple of kilometers out of their way, but offered the shortest distance over open terrain. Etain—Niner still struggled with first-name familiarity, even in his mind—kept close to Darman. She seemed to like him. She was polite and sympathetic to the rest of them, but she certainly *liked* Darman. Niner could see it on her face. She exuded concern. He heard snatches of conversation.

"How did you ever carry all the E-Web sections alone?"

"No idea. Just did, I suppose."

She was a Jedi. Skirata said they were fine people, but they didn't—and couldn't—care about anyone. But you got close very quickly under fire. He wasn't going to ask Darman what he was playing at. Not yet.

They reached the edge of the woodland and came into a hundred-meter stretch of waist-high grass. Fi went forward as point man. Sprinting and dropping was now beyond them, but there appeared to be nothing around to spot their gray armor anyway, so they walked at a crouch. Niner's back was screaming for a rest. It didn't matter how fit you were when you pushed yourself this hard: it hurt.

When they reached the coppice, it was painkiller time. Niner stripped off his arm plate and peeled back a section of suit. He didn't bother finding a vein. He stabbed the needle into muscle.

"Know the feeling," Darman said. He dropped his pack and sat down, legs outstretched. "Anyone taken any stims so far?"

"Not yet," Niner said. "I reckon we should all dose up one hour before moving, just to make sure we're a hundred percent." He glanced at Etain, wondering how she might appear after a week of normal meals, unbroken sleep, and clean clothing. She looked worryingly frail now, even though she was doing a valiant job of keeping up. "You, too. *Especially* you. Can Jedi take stimulants?"

"What exactly do they do?"

"The equivalent of ten hours' good, solid sleep and four square meals. Until they wear off."

"I ought to draw on the Force to sustain my stamina," she said. "But the Force could do with a bit of help right now. Count me in."

She sat down and rested her head on her folded arms. Maybe she was meditating. Niner switched to helmet comms.

"Dar, she's not going to collapse on us, is she? We can't carry anything else."

"If she drops, it'll be because she's dead," he said. "Trust me, she's tougher than she looks. Physically, anyway."

"She'd better be. Let's get those remotes deployed."

Jinart had identified a couple of high points to place the cam remotes. One was on the gutter of a farm building overlooking the entrance to the facility; the other was a tree whose canopy gave a good 270-degree view of the villa. The third remote—the one loaded with ribbon charge—needed more careful placement. She sat up on her hind legs and a pouch formed on her stomach like a cook's apron.

"Normally I would carry my young around in this," she said. She placed the three spheres in the pouch, giving the impression that she'd swallowed some particularly lumpy prey. "But if I don't help you, my chances of raising another litter are remote. So I consider it an appropriate act."

Niner was as fascinated as ever by the Gurlanin. The more he saw of the creatures, the less he knew about them. He hoped he might have the chance to find out more one day.

In an hour it would be midday. Atin took out his ration pack and mess tin, a flat sheet that snapped into shape. He placed his remaining ration cubes in it and held it out. "How much have we got among us?"

"I'm down to half a day's worth," Fi said.

"Me, too," Niner said.

Darman reached into his pack and pulled out a carefully wrapped brick-sized bag. "A day's worth of cubes and this dried kuvara and jerky. Let's pool this and have two meals before we go in. If we pull this off, we'll be running too fast to have lunch. If we don't, it'd be a shame to die hungry."

"Gets my vote," Atin said.

Niner was going to ask Etain, but she was sitting cross-legged with her eyes shut and her hands in her lap. Darman put a finger to his lips and shook his head.

"Meditating," he mouthed silently.

Niner hoped she emerged from it transformed. He was still one squad short of an adequate force for this job.

"You have ten seconds to live," Ghez Hokan said. He took out Fulier's lightsaber, and the blue shaft of energy buzzed into life. He wondered what made the blade a consistent, finite length each time. "Speak."

Guta-Nay, looking more bemused than he recalled, ignored the lightsaber. "I been captured by soldiers. I get away."

"Republic troops? Human?"

"Yes. They catch me, they make me carry stuff."

Hokan sheathed the blade. "They obviously spotted your talents. How did you get away?"

"They were sleeping. They not care. I go."

"How many soldiers?"

"Four. And girlie."

"Girlie?"

Guta-Nay pointed at the lightsaber. "She got one like that."

So the woman with them *was* a Jedi. "Just four?"

"They got another lot." He pursed his lips, grappling with a new word. *"Squad."*

"Very well, so we have two squads. Eight men. That would fit." Hokan turned to Hurati. "And our Trandoshan friend?"

"He says he's highly irritated about his business being interrupted, sir, and he offers himself and three colleagues to help you deal with the inconvenience."

"Thank him and accept his offer." Hokan turned back to Guta-Nay. "I want you to think very hard. Did they say what they were going to do? Where they were going?"

"The villa."

How predictable people were. The locals would tell you anything for money, sell you their daughters, inform on their neighbors.

Hokan had half expected the ruse to be almost too obvious. "You're doing well. Tell me what equipment they have."

"Blasters. Explosives." The Weequay made an indication of great width with his hands. "*Big* gun. They got armor with knives in gloves."

"Describe."

"Like yours."

"What do you mean, like mine?"

Guta-Nay indicated his head and made a T-shape with his fingers. "Your helmet."

It was difficult to take in. Guta-Nay was an inarticulate brute, but there was no ambiguity in his description. "Are you saying they were wearing *Mandalorian armor*?"

"Yeah. That it."

"You're sure about that."

"Sure."

"Anything else?" Hokan wondered how he expected this creature to be able to assess intelligence. "Anything else unusual?"

Guta-Nay concentrated on the question as if his life depended on it, which it did not; Hokan would kill him anyway. "They all look the same."

"They were wearing uniforms?"

"No, the men. Same faces."

Children could be unerringly accurate in their observation of detail, and so could stupid adults. Guta-Nay was describing something that Dr. Uthan had told him about: soldiers, identical soldiers, mindlessly obedient soldiers—*clone* soldiers.

Hokan couldn't believe that clone troopers could operate like this. And the one weapon that would work against them was denied him, because in its present state it would kill everyone, Uthan and her team included.

But there were probably only eight of them. He had nearly a hundred droids. He had weapons.

"Hurati? Hurati!"

The young captain came running and saluted. "Sir?"

"I think we face a two-pronged attack. There are two squads, and I find it unlikely to imagine that they would *not* have one squad attack the villa, while the other made an attempt on the most obvious target. Divide the droid platoons between the locations."

"That's what you would do with two squads, sir? Not concentrate your forces?"

"Yes, if I weren't sure my objectives were consolidated in one place. They can't know who and what is in which building. And they'll attack at night, because while they're bold, they're not stupid." He shook his head, suddenly interrupted by his own preoccupation. "Who would have thought clones could carry out this sort of operation? Uthan said they were no more than cannon fodder."

"Commanded by Jedi, sir. Perhaps our tactician is the woman."

It was an interesting idea. Hokan considered it for a moment, then realized that Guta-Nay was waiting expectantly, oddly upright and apparently unafraid.

"Well?" Hokan said.

"I tell you stuff. You let me live?"

Hokan activated the lightsaber again and held it out to his side, just above the level of his right shoulder.

"Of course not," he said, and swung the blade. "It would be bad for morale."

15

So how do we justify what we are doing now? Breeding men without choice, and without freedom, to fight and die for us? When do the means cease to justify the end? Where is our society heading? Where are our ideals, and what are we without them? If we give in to expedience in this way, where do we draw the line between ourselves and those we find unacceptably evil? I have no answer, Masters. Do you?

—Jedi Padawan Bardan Jusik, addressing the Jedi Council

Etain jerked involuntarily, as if falling in a dream. She opened her eyes and stared straight ahead.

"He's dead," she said.

"Who is?" Darman had been watching her meditate, worrying what might happen to her in the coming battle, afraid both for her and because of her. She could be either a liability or an unimaginable asset. "What's wrong, Etain?"

Niner caught his eye with a look that suggested he thought Darman was being too familiar with an officer, whatever she had ordered. Then he went back to checking his datapad.

"Guta-Nay." She rubbed her forehead and looked defeated. "I felt it in the Force."

Fi looked about to say something, and Atin silenced him with a frown. Darman gave both of them a *shut-up* look. There was a way of saying unpalatable things to people, and Darman thought it would be better coming from him than from his comrades.

"Hokan would have found him sooner or later," he said. "If the

Weequay's managed to mislead him about our true target, he's at least redeemed himself a little."

"Dar," she said. It was shockingly familiar, the squad nickname for him. "I killed him as surely as if I'd cut him down."

"You told us yourself that he was a rapist," Fi said, sounding irritated. "The world won't miss him."

"Shut up, Fi." Darman tried again. "It'll save lives in the end."

"Yeah, ours," Fi said.

Darman twisted around, angry. "I said shut up, didn't I?"

Niner stepped in. "You can *both* shut it," he said. "We're all tired and we're all testy. Save it for the enemy."

Darman swallowed a sudden and unexpected desire to tell Fi to lay off Etain, and in no uncertain terms. Fi knew nothing about her, *nothing.* Darman was ambushed by a split second of protectiveness and was immediately embarrassed by it.

He turned back to her. "He's right. It's one life for many."

"Means justify the end, right?" Etain stood up from her cross-legged position in one movement. "And what about you? What happens if I send you or Fi or any of you into a situation where you're going to die?"

She was genuinely upset. He could see it in her face, and in the way she held one thin, scratched, bony hand clenched tightly into a fist. He stood up as well, walking after her as she headed for the edge of the coppice.

"We were all made for this," Darman said. It was true, wasn't it? He wouldn't exist at all if it hadn't been that someone needed soldiers, utterly reliable soldiers. But it didn't feel that way right then. Her reaction told him he was wrong, and suddenly he saw Kal Skirata, in tears, a drink in his hand. *You poor boys. What sort of life is this?* "Etain, we all do what we have to. One day you really *will* have to give an order that's going to get some of us killed."

"Us?"

"Soldiers, troopers. Whatever."

"Perhaps, but the day I can accept that without being diminished by it is the day I'm not fit to be a Jedi."

"Okay," he said. "I understand that."

"How do *you* feel when you kill?"

"I never had time to think about it. On Geonosis, they killed my brothers and they were trying to kill me. They weren't like us."

"So what if it was someone you knew?"

"But you didn't know Guta-Nay, and he isn't like you. Or me, come to that." Darman hadn't a clue what she was going on about.

She was new to killing. It was inevitable that she'd have a few problems dealing with it. "Etain, this squad needs you to be sorted and alert. Think about that."

He turned and walked back to where Niner and the others were sitting. It seemed too obvious to replace their helmets and discuss privately whether the commander was going flaky on them. She wasn't giving orders anyway. But a simple glance could convey a great deal. Darman hoped Fi understood that his fixed stare meant *Lay off.*

Apparently, he did. Fi made a quick palms-out movement with his hands as if in submission. The subject was dropped.

Niner was right. They were all frayed by the last few days, hovering on short fuses. They busied themselves checking and rechecking weapons.

We've never fought as a squad before.

They were probably all thinking the same thing. Darman took the hydraulic ram apart and reassembled it, then checked the hand pump for pressure. It came with an assortment of claws, and at least having the original plans and specs of both buildings meant he knew which ones to leave behind. It could exert eight metric tons, so if the charges didn't get them through the door, the ram would. The hand-operated ram was lighter to carry, but packed less than half the punch.

He'd have liked cutting equipment, too, but he'd opened steel blast doors on Geonosis with thermal tape charges, and the ribbon version was even more powerful. Explosive moved at eight thousand meters a second, enough to slice through steel: rapid entry didn't get much more rapid than that.

This wasn't a silent job. It was an application of force against an enemy who knew they were coming.

"Whoa, receiving," Niner said. He shoved his helmet back on his head in a hurry. Darman could hear the *blip* of the alarm from where he was sitting. "Jinart's got the remote cams in place." He was looking at something only he could see, and judging by his quick head movements, it was interesting. Darman and the others followed suit.

"What are they doing?" A platoon of tinnies was marching down the track from the villa and into the facility. There appeared to be some urgency in their pace. "It looks like they're going back to the laboratory."

The remote was looking down on the scatter of small structures around the former farmhouse. It didn't have a complete view of all the approaches to the building, but it did look out on both the front path and the land to the rear. It had no view of the rear slope of the roof or the land immediately at the back.

There was a man in armor very similar to their own, standing with a familiar helmet tucked under one arm. He was middle-aged and his hard face and confident attitude said clearly that he was a Mandalorian. It had to be Ghez Hokan.

Darman heard the collective holding of breath in his helmet comlink. Hokan was talking to a Trandoshan mercenary, making short stabbing gestures with a finger pointed at nothing in particular. He was agitated but in control. He was marshaling troops.

"Yeah, Dar, I think that's *exactly* what they're doing. Looks like he's making some last-minute changes."

"Why would they be doing that?" Darman said, but he had an unpleasant feeling that he knew.

"Because we've been too clever by half," Niner said. "*Fierfek.* Guta-Nay did his job, all right. Too well. What would you do if you thought you were really facing two squads?"

"Assume two separate attacks were really possible."

Atin made a noise that sounded like a controlled exhalation. "Oh well. We were going to meet the whole tinnie family sooner or later. Plan C, anyone?"

They waited, standing in an awkward group. Within half an hour they would know if Jinart had managed to get a remote cam close to the Neimoidian villa as well.

Darman felt a hard rap on his back plate and jerked around to see Etain standing with her hands on her hips, looking anxious. "What's got everyone upset?" she asked. "Come on, I felt it. What's gone wrong?"

Darman took off his helmet. "Guta-Nay did a pretty good job of convincing Hokan we were targeting the villa. But we overplayed our hand by hinting that we had another squad."

"Why?"

"It looks as if Hokan thinks one squad will be going after each target. So our chances of getting most of the droids in one location have taken a bit of a tumble."

Etain raked her fingers through her hair and shut her eyes. "Time for a rethink, then."

Darman replaced his helmet to watch the feed from the remote. Then the second cam came online. There was a shaky but clear view of the Neimoidian villa and its outbuildings, seen from the branches of a swaying tree. A wide path stretched away out of shot from the front of the house.

At least they could now see the size of the problem facing them. If Hokan tried to move Uthan, they had a high chance of spotting her.

But whichever remote view Darman switched to, there were an awful lot of droids.

"Okay," Niner said. "Fi, you take the first watch on the remotes. I'm going to see if we can get some backup. *Majestic* should be on station by now."

"We were ordered to keep comm silence until we needed extraction," Darman said, looking at Etain.

"Commander?" Niner said. "We've taken out the comm station. They can't intercept our signal."

Etain didn't even pause. "Sergeant, you go right ahead and call up *Majestic,*" she said. "Ask for whatever help you think we need."

Fi held up one hand. "Hey, we might have a break here. Check out the remote at the villa."

Darman switched channels with a double blink. The display in his HUD showed him a shot of a young boy in a scruffy smock walking around to a side door at the villa, a fruit-laden basket clutched in both arms. He knocked, and the door was opened by a droid. The youngster went in. There was something familiar about him, even though Darman had never seen him before.

He had a very characteristic walk.

"Tinnies wouldn't have sent out for fruit, would they?" Fi said.

The kid's gait reminded Darman of an old woman he'd recently slammed up against a barn wall.

"You've got to hand it to Jinart," he said. "She's certainly got guts."

"Let's hope she manages to get that fruit into the cellars."

"Let's hope she comes back out," Etain said.

Dr. Uthan appeared to have forgotten that Hokan had hauled her across a desk by her collar, at least for the time being. She sat in one of the beige brocade chairs that really didn't match her utilitarian office, listening to him with apparent patience.

"This is an unprecedented opportunity," she said at last.

Hokan agreed completely. "I realize that you haven't managed to create a delivery system for the nanovirus yet, but I think we might be able to help with that. Inhalation will work, yes? Could we introduce it into a sealed room?" He had ideas for ambush and entrapment. "Can that be done?"

"It's one of several vectors," she said. "And skin contact, too. But that isn't quite what I had in mind."

"Which was?"

"A live subject. I would like you to take one of the clones alive."

"That wasn't quite what *I* had in mind. I tend to have problems with the *alive* bit. Not my forte."

"You can't simply spray this agent around, Major. I told you we haven't ironed out the genome specificity."

"I have droid troops. While rust might be a health issue for them, I suspect that viruses aren't."

"Having a live test subject would almost certainly enable us to achieve weaponization faster."

"If you allow me access to the nanovirus, I'll do what I can to save one for you."

Uthan shook her head. Her vivid red-and-black-streaked hair was scraped up in a tight bun on the top of her head, giving her an even more severe appearance. Not a wisp of hair escaped the top-knot. "I can't do that. While you might be an expert in combat, you're not a microbiologist, nor used to handling hazardous substances. This is far too dangerous a pathogen for you to use at this stage of its development. I'm also not prepared to expend what limited samples we have on a risky counterassault."

Hokan knew he could have taken it by force. But it would have been pointless. She was right; if the virus wasn't in a state that could be weaponized, it was a long shot compared to the proven weapons he had at his disposal.

"Pity," he said. "I'll endeavor to learn more about this technology after we've dealt with the current difficulty."

"So what happens now?"

"Sit tight. Stay in this suite of rooms with your staff until further notice."

"What do we do if shooting starts?"

"The same."

"What if they get through your defenses?"

"They won't, but if it makes you feel safer, I'll provide you with hand weapons for your personal protection."

Uthan gave him a regal nod of the head and reached for a pile of notes. Then she went on reading, pausing occasionally to write something in the margins of the papers. Despite the brief showdown earlier, she didn't seem afraid of him in the least: perhaps working with deadly organisms on a daily basis gave her a different perspective on threats.

"Something highly effective, please," she said as he turned to leave.

* * *

"Commanding Officer *Majestic,*" the voice said. "That was fast. Position?"

Niner couldn't get a video image on his HUD, but the sound was crystal clear. "That's a negative on the extraction for the time being, *Majestic.* Requesting gunnery support."

"Say again?"

"We'll be needing gunnery support. It might get a bit hectic down here. A hundred droids."

There was a second or two of silence. "Omega Squad, be aware that it might get busy up here, too. We have a Techno Union vessel standing off our port bow."

"Is that a negative, *Majestic*?"

"No. If we cease firing, though, it may be because we're repelling an attack ourselves."

"Understood. Coordinates uploading now. On receipt of code Greenwood, direct cannon at *this* location. On receipt of code Boffin, *this* location. Enemy now has no comm apart from droid networks, repeat comm disabled. Knock yourselves out."

"Received. My, you've been busy boys. Standing by, Omega."

Niner shut his eyes and felt the relief flood through his stomach. He wasn't exactly sure how they were going to deploy *Majestic*'s massive firepower, but at least they had it to fall back on.

"Are you making this up as you go along, Sarge?" Fi asked.

"You got a better idea?"

"I meant the code names."

"Yes."

"Classy."

"And I meant it about the better idea."

Fi drummed his fingers on the thigh plate of his armor. "I wish Skirata was around. What was it he always said? *Turn the problem upside down.* See it from the enemy perspective."

Etain glanced up, now a sure sign that Jinart was approaching. They seemed to share a kind of radar. The Gurlanin slunk into the laying-up point and swung her head around. Darman and Fi gave her a mute round of applause and a show of thumbs up.

"Nice job, ma'am," Darman said. "Amazing deception."

"Thank you, gentlemen," she said. "Uthan is definitely not in the villa. And your device is now sitting in Ankkit's wine cellars, between a case of vintage Naboo tarul wine and a crate of thermal detonators. When you're ready, you can give Qiilura its own asteroid belt."

"That'll make their eyes water," Fi said.

"And ours if we're too close," Niner said.

"So what now?"

"Let's do what Skirata taught us. Turn it upside down."

The holochart plans of the facility once again hung in midair as the squad, Etain, and Jinart sat around it, seeking inspiration.

"Is this how you plan operations?" Etain asked.

"It's not meant to be like this, no. You gather intel and then you plan and execute. This is what Skirata called a *self-adjusting screwup.* When the problem actually provides the solution to another problem. It's there. All we have to do is work it out." Niner didn't mind admitting it was more guesswork than anyone should have indulged in. But then he'd been on two real missions now, and they'd both been the same. They hadn't known what they were going into until it was too late. *Intel.* It was all about having reliable intelligence. "There's three things you should never believe—weather forecasts, the canteen menu, and intel."

Skirata said soldiers always complained. Niner was not given to complaining, but he was definitely not satisfied with the situation. This wasn't what special forces were best designed to do. They should have been there to gather intel themselves, identify the target, call in air strikes, and maybe recover hostages or data. They might even carry out assassinations. They weren't meant to be artillery and infantry as well.

If the Republic hadn't wanted Uthan alive, they needn't have been here at all. *Majestic* could have targeted the facility from orbit, and everyone would have been home in time for supper. Nobody would have needed to get their backside shot at, or spend days hauling forty-five-kilo packs across farmland.

"I'm glad you're not just accepting this," Etain said.

Fi shrugged. "If you can't take a joke, you shouldn't have joined."

"I *didn't* join," Atin said.

At least they all managed to laugh. It was the first time that anyone had found any humor in the situation, apart from Fi, of course.

"What do we normally do?" Darman said suddenly. "How do we normally take a target? Break it down."

Niner concentrated. "We isolate a target, go in, and neutralize it."

"Okay, say we *don't* fight our way in."

"Not with you."

"We're expected to pull off a rapid entry and fight our way *in.*

What if we fought our way *out*?" Darman prodded his finger into the hologram. "Can we get in under the facility to this central room?"

"This plan only shows drains. The bore's too narrow to get a man down there, and this really isn't a job for Jinart."

The Gurlanin twitched visibly. "I wasn't offering, but if there was anything I might do—"

"You've done more than enough already." Darman tilted his head this way and that, studying the plans. "The main drain chamber is nearly a hundred centimeters wide here, though. It only tapers to thirty centimeters at the wall. Is there any other way of getting into that main?"

"Short of walking up to the wall and digging under it like a gdan, in full view of the droids, no."

Jinart sat upright. "Gdan warrens."

"They tunnel, don't they?"

"Everywhere. They even cause subsidence."

"Are there tunnels around there? Could we locate them? Would they be wide enough?"

"Yes, there are warrens, because it was once a farm site and gdans like eating merlies. The tunnels can be quite wide. And I can certainly locate them for you. In fact, I will lead you through the warrens. You might have to excavate some of the way, though."

"Basic sapper procedure," Darman said. "Except we don't have proper equipment, so we'll be digging with these." He took a folding sharp-edged trowel from his belt. "Entrenching tool. Also used for 'freshers. Apt."

"What is it between you and the gdans?" Etain asked. "Why do they avoid you and your scent?"

"Oh, we eat them," Jinart said casually. "But only if they try to approach our young."

"That's it, then," Darman said. "Get me into that central chamber from below, and I'll work my way out through the facility."

"Take Atin with you," Niner said. He didn't want to say *in case you get killed,* but he wanted another technically minded man in there to lay charges and blow doors. "Fi and I can lay down fire out front and deal with any droids we see. When you bring Uthan out, Etain can help us get her clear and then you blow the place. Then we do a runner for the extraction point."

"Gets my vote," Atin said. "You okay with that, ma'am?"

Etain nodded reluctantly. "If that's plan C, it sounds as impossible as plans A and B." She patted Darman's arm, not quite focusing, as if she was lost in thought about something. "But I don't have a better suggestion."

"Okay," Niner said. "Everyone take a stim now. Be ready to move out at nightfall. We've got four hours to prep for this. I'll notify *Majestic*."

"What if this fails?" Etain asked.

"They'll send in another squad."

"And lose more men?" She shook her head. "If it's down to me, I'll happily give the order for *Majestic* to pound this facility to dust, with Uthan inside or not."

"Do you think we're going to fail?"

Etain smiled. There was something mildly unnerving about the way she was smiling. "No. I don't. You're going to pull this off, believe me."

Niner kept a tight grip on his breathing. If he gave the slightest hint of a sigh of doubt, they'd pick it up. It was crazy. But, as Skirata said, they went where others wouldn't, and did what nobody else could.

And fighting your way out from the heart of an alloy-plated, heavily guarded facility designed to be impregnable to any life-form certainly lived up to that boast. For some reason he felt fine about it all.

You're going to pull this off, believe me.

He wondered if his thoughts were actually his own. If Etain was influencing his mind to improve his confidence, that was okay by him. Officers were supposed to inspire you. Right then he didn't much care how she did it.

16

What do I think about it? I don't know, really. Nobody's ever asked me for my opinion before.
—Clone Trooper RC-5093, retired, at CF VetCenter, Coruscant. Chronological age: twenty-three. Biological age: sixty.

An autumnal mist had settled over the countryside. It wasn't dense enough to provide cover, but it did give Darman a sense of protection. He tabbed behind Atin as Jinart led the way.

He was a walking bomb factory. Why was he even worried about being spotted? The ram and its attachments clunked against his armor and he adjusted them, fearing discovery. Atin walked ahead, Deece held in both hands with his finger inside the trigger guard, a small but significant expression of his anxiety level.

"Matte-black armor," Darman said. "First thing we ought to slap in for when we get back. I feel like a homing beacon."

"Does it matter?"

"Does to me."

"Dar, it's one thing for the enemy to spot us coming. It's another thing entirely for them to do anything about it." Atin was still checking all around him, though. "I was knocked flat by a round and it didn't penetrate the plates."

Atin had a point. The armor might have been conspicuous, but it worked. Darman had taken a direct hit, too. Maybe in the future the sight of that armor alone would deter enemies, a touch of what Skirata called *assertive public relations.* Myth, he said, won almost as many engagements as reality.

Darman was all for a little help from the myth department.

They were four hundred meters southeast of the facility. Jinart stopped in front of a gentle slope and thrust her head through a break in the foliage. Her sniffing was audible.

"We enter here," she said.

There didn't even appear to be a hole. "How do you know what's in there?"

"I can detect solid surfaces, movement, everything. I don't need to see." She sniffed again, or at least Darman assumed she was sniffing; it occurred to him that she might have been echolocating. "Do you want to stand here and present a target all night?"

"No ma'am," Darman said, and got down on all fours.

Jinart might not have needed to see, but he did. He could have relied on the night-vision visor, but he felt the need for real, honest light. He switched on his tactical spot-lamp. He switched it off again, fast.

"Uh . . ."

"What's wrong?" Atin asked.

"Nothing," Darman said. It was natural not to like confined spaces, he told himself. With the light projected forward, he could see just how suffocatingly small a space he was in. With his night vision in place, he was simply looking down a narrow field of view, safe inside his armor, cocooned from the world in a way he was not only used to, but actually *needed.*

Get a grip.

He could hear the sound of scurrying farther ahead, but it was moving away from him. His pack caught the roof of the tunnel, occasionally scraping loose soil and stones. The warren had been excavated by thousands of small paws, circular in section because gdans obviously didn't need as much floor space as a tall human male. Darman almost felt that his hands and knees were against the sides of the tunnel because of the curvature of the floor, like negotiating a chimney when rock climbing. At times he felt he was losing his orientation and had to shut his eyes and shake his head hard to regain accurate proprioception.

"You okay, Dar?" Atin asked. Darman could hear labored breathing in his helmet and he thought it was his own, but it was Atin's.

"Bit disoriented."

"Let your head drop and look at the floor. The pressure on the back of your neck is going to make you feel giddy anyway."

"You, too, eh?"

"Yeah, this is weird. Whatever we inherited from Jango, it wasn't a love of caving."

Darman let his head hang forward and concentrated on putting one hand in front of the other. He switched to voice projection. "Jinart, why do such small animals dig such big tunnels?"

"Have you tried dragging a whole merlie or vhek home for dinner? Gdans work as a team. That's what enables them to take prey that's many times their size. A point, I think, that would not be lost on men such as yourselves."

"On the other hand," Atin said cautiously, "you could say that sheer numbers overwhelm strength."

"Thank you for that positive view, Private Atin. I suggest you select the interpretation that inspires you most."

They didn't talk much after that. As Darman progressed, sweating with the effort, he was aware of a particular scent. It was getting stronger. It was sickly at first, like rotting meat, and then more bitter and sulfurous. It reminded him of Geonosis. Battlefields smelled awful. The filtration mask was active against chemical and biological weapons, but it did nothing to stop smells. Shattered bodies and bowels had a distinctive and terrifying stench.

He could smell it now. He fought down nausea.

"Fierfek," Atin said. "That's turned me off my dinner for a start."

"We're near the facility," Jinart said.

"How near?" Darman said.

"That odor is seepage from the drainage system. The pipe work is local unglazed clay."

"Is that all we can smell?" said Darman.

"Oh, I imagine it's also the gdans. Or rather their recent kills—they have chambers where they amass their surplus. Yes, it's an unpleasant stench if you're not accustomed to it." She stopped unexpectedly, and Darman bumped into her backside. She felt surprisingly heavy for her size. "That's good news, because it means we're near a much larger chamber."

Darman almost felt relief that it was simply rotting meat, although that was bad enough. It wasn't *his* meat. He crawled farther, encouraged by the promise of a bigger space ahead, and then his glove sank into something soft.

He didn't need to ask what it was. He looked down despite himself. In the way of men exposed to memory triggers, he was immediately back in training, crawling through a ditch filled with nerf entrails, Skirata running alongside and yelling at him to keep going because this was *nothing, nothing compared to what you'll have to do for real, son.*

They called it the Sickener. They weren't wrong.

Fatigue made nausea inevitable. He almost vomited, and that wasn't something he wanted to do in a sealed suit. He fought it, panting, eyes shut. He bit the inside of his lip as hard as he could, and tasted blood.

"I'm okay," he said. "I'm okay."

Atin's breathing was ragged. He had to be feeling it, too. They were physiologically identical.

"You can straighten up now," Jinart said.

Darman flicked on his spot-lamp to find himself in a chamber that wasn't just larger; it was big enough to stand up in. The walls were lined with what looked like tiny terraces spiraling up around the chamber from the floor. There were scores of twenty-centimeter tunnels leading off them.

"This is where the gdans retreat if rain floods the warren," Jinart said. "They're not foolish."

"I'll thank them one day," Atin said. "How close are we to the drain? Can you locate it?"

Jinart put a paw against the wall where there were no tiny escape tunnels. "The gdans know there's a solid structure behind this." She paused. "Yes, there's water trickling back there. The soil feels a meter thick, perhaps a little more."

Darman would have removed his helmet, but thought better of it, and settled for letting his pack drop off his shoulders. He took out his entrenching tool and made an exploratory stab at the chamber wall. It was about the consistency of chalk.

"Okay, I do five minutes, then you do five," he said to Atin.

"And me," Jinart said, but Darman held up his hand to stop her.

"No ma'am. You'd better go back to Niner. We're on our own now, and if this all goes wrong he'll need your assistance even more."

Jinart hesitated for a moment, then raced back up the tunnel without a backward glance. Darman wondered if he should have said good-bye, but good-bye was too final. He planned on coming out that front door with Atin and Uthan.

He scraped out a guide circle with the tip of the tool and hacked into the hard-packed soil. It felt like slow going and he was surprised when Atin tapped him on the shoulder and took over. A man-sized hole began to emerge.

"Should we shore this up?" Darman said, wondering what he might have to sacrifice as a pit prop.

"We should only be going through it once. If it collapses after that, it's too bad."

"If we have to blast our way in, it might collapse. Alternative exit?"

"You want to be pursued through those tunnels? They'd fry us. One flamethrower volley and we'd be charcoal."

Atin was slowing. Darman took the other side of the opening and they worked together, removing progressively damper and darker soil, flattening out the sides of the excavation so that they had access to drill through without having to lean through a short tunnel. It was weakening the integrity of the soil wall: Darman willed it to hold together until they were through.

Maybe he should have brought Etain. She could have held the wall with that Jedi power of hers. Suddenly he realized that he missed her. It was amazing how fast you could form a bond with someone when you were under fire.

Atin's tool hit something that made a distinctive *chink* noise.

"Drain," he said. "Drill time."

A few quick rounds from the Deece would have blown a good-sized hole in the thickest clay pipe. It would also have brought down the chamber roof, Darman suspected, and summoned a lot of droids. It was time for the slow, quiet route. A hand drill was part of their basic rapid entry kit, and they each took half the rough circle, drilling at five-centimeter intervals around the circumference, starting from the top. It wasn't until they got down to the bottom that the ooze started appearing from the holes.

It had taken them an hour to excavate and drill. Darman couldn't stand the sweat trickling down his face any longer and took off his helmet. The stench really was worse than ever. He shut his mind to it.

Atin took a swig from his water bottle and held it out to Darman. "Hydration," he said. "Five percent fluid loss stops you thinking straight."

"Yeah, I know. And above fifteen percent kills you." Darman drank half the bottle, wiped the sweat away, and scratched his scalp vigorously. "Another thing to tell Rothana's geeks when we get back—up the temperature conditioning in these suits."

He lifted the ram and took a side-on stance to the disc of clay pipe visible through the soil. He gripped hard, fingers tight around each handle. He had to swing carefully this time or he might collapse the pipe. "Ready?"

"Ready."

One, two—

"Three," Darman grunted. The ram hit with a couple of metric tons of force and the perforated section fell inward as a waterfall of stinking dark slime shot out and splashed across Darman's legs and boots.

"Oh, that's just great," he sighed. "Definitely matte black next time, okay?"

Atin took his helmet off and Darman realized he was struggling not to laugh. Now that the drain was open to the air, it was a perfect conduit for sound to the building above. Atin put his hand to his mouth, bent over slightly, and appeared to be biting down hard on the knuckle plate. He was actually shaking. When he straightened up, tears were streaming down his face. He wiped them away and gulped, then bent over again.

Darman had never even seen the man smile. Now he was in hysterics because Darman was spattered with the accumulated waste of total strangers. It wasn't funny.

Yes, it was, actually. It was *hilarious.* Darman felt his stomach begin to shake in a completely involuntary reflex. Then he wasn't certain that it *was* funny, but he still couldn't stop. He shook in painfully silent laughter until his abdominal muscles ached. Eventually, it subsided. He straightened up, inexplicably exhausted.

"Shall I let Niner know we're through?" he said, and they both managed to stay completely calm for a count of three before the hysteria overtook them again.

Once you knew what laughter really was, and what primitive reflex triggered it, it wasn't funny at all. It was the relief of danger passed. It was a primeval *all-clear* signal.

And that wasn't the reality of their situation at all. The real danger was just starting.

Darman, suddenly his usual self again, replaced his helmet and opened the comlink.

"Sarge, Darman here," he said quietly. "We're into the drain. Ready when you are."

Niner and Fi set up the E-Web repeating blaster half a kilometer from the front of the facility. That was pretty close. If anyone had spotted them, they weren't reacting.

"Copy that, Dar." Niner checked the chrono on the forearm of his left gauntlet. "Can you see the drainage cover yet?"

The comlink crackled. Niner was yet again faintly pleased with himself that he'd decided to take that trip to Teklet. They'd never have stood a chance of pulling this off in comm silence. There were too many unknowns to do it by op order and chronosynch.

"I just followed the trail of crud and there it was," Darman said. "Want a look?"

Niner's HUD flashed up a grainy green image of huge dripping tubes that could have been a klick wide or just a centimeter. Come to that, it could have been an endoscopic view of someone's guts. It didn't look like fun, either way.

"What's above you?"

"Dirty square plate and it's not a drain. The water's feeding down here from other pipes." The image jerked as Darman's head lowered to look at his datapad. It threw up eerie ghost images of the building. "If they stuck to the blueprints, then this is a hazmat filter and the maximum containment chambers are above it." There was a scraping noise. "Yeah, the serial numbers match the schematic. If they had to hose down after a mishap in there, this is where the screened water or solvent would come out."

"Are you going to need to blow it?"

"Well, it doesn't look as if I can unscrew it with a hairpin. It's permacreted in place. It's not the sort of thing you want coming loose, I suppose."

"Good timing for a spot of pyro at the villa, then. Let's sync that up."

"Okay. Give me a couple of minutes to set the charges."

Two minutes was a long time. Niner counted it down in seconds. He was aware of Etain pacing up and down behind him—but you didn't tell a commander to pack it in and stop fidgeting. He focused on Fi, who was kneeling behind the E-Web tripod, checking the sights, utterly relaxed. Niner envied him that ability. His own stomach was churning. It always did on exercise: it was much worse now. His pulse was pounding in his ears and distracting him.

Darman responded eleven seconds late. "All done. I'll count you down. We're moving back out of the drain now. If we bring the outer chamber down, then we might take a little time to work our way back in."

"What's *a little time* in your book?"

"Maybe forever. It might kill us."

"Let's avoid, that, shall we?"

"Let's."

Etain was hovering at Niner's shoulder. He glanced at her, hoping she'd take the hint.

"You've never worked as a complete team before, have you?" she said unhelpfully.

"No," Niner hissed, and withheld the *ma'am*.

"You're going to do fine," she said. "You're the best-trained, most competent troops in the galaxy and you're confident of success."

Niner was close to responding with a few words of pithy Huttese, but he suddenly saw her point. His stomach settled into a peaceful equilibrium again. He could hear Darman clearly. His drumming pulse had faded. He was perfectly content not to think how she had achieved that reassurance.

"In ten," Darman said. He still had his forward helmet cam patched through to Niner's HUD. He was scrambling through a tunnel. Niner had a sensation of rushing down a flume and half expected to splash into a deep pool at the other end.

"Five . . ." It went dark. Darman had his head tucked into his chest. "Three . . ." Niner felt for the remote detonator. "Two . . . *go go go*."

Niner squeezed the remote.

For a fraction of a second the landscape was picked out in brilliant, gold, silent light. Niner's antiblast visor kicked in. Then the ground shook, and even at two klicks the roar was deafening. It seemed to go on for several seconds. Then he realized he was hearing two blasts—one at the villa and one below the facility.

As the fire blazed and clouds of amber-lit smoke roiled into the air, the droids on watch outside the facility started reacting.

"Hold, Fi." Niner swallowed to clear his ears. "Dar, Atin, respond."

"Was that us or you?"

"Both. You okay, Dar?"

"Teeth are a bit loose, but we're fine."

"Nice job with the custom ordnance, you two. I think the villa's got a new indoor swimming pool."

"The chamber's holding down here, just about. Going in."

Silence had fallen on the countryside. It was as if everyone was waiting for the next move. Fi moved the five-pack of energy cell clips a little closer to him. Niner aimed his Deece to get a better view of the front of the villa, and saw droids milling around and an Umbaran officer with binocs scanning left to right across the fields.

"Ready, Sarge."

"Wait one."

A few more droids came out of the farmhouse door. If Niner hadn't seen the plans, he would never have believed what was concealed inside and beneath the convincingly shabby wooden siding. Etain stood to one side of him.

"Ma'am, you might want to duck and cover."

"I'm all right," she said. She looked longingly at the Trandoshan concussion rifle. "Let me know when I'm needed."

Darman's voice cut in on the comlink. "We're about to enter the drain cover," he said. "Time for distraction, Sarge."

"Got it." He knelt beside Fi and touched him on the shoulder. "Put a couple down a little short of that barn. Just to say hello. Then fire at will."

Fi hardly moved. The characteristic *whoomp* of the energy cell was followed by a ball of fire and a fountain of splintered wood. The barn rained back down, burning as it fell.

"Oops," Fi said.

It got the droids' attention, all right. Six formed a line and began marching down the field.

Fi opened up. Niner could feel the roar of noise in his chest as droid shrapnel rained down on them and incoming fire whisked over their heads. A large chunk of metal flew in an arc: Niner heard it fizzing in the air as it cooled while it fell. He didn't see where it landed, but it was close. His night vision saw the sprays of shrapnel as brilliant white irregular raindrops. A few tinnies were getting through. Niner picked off two with the grenades.

The next rank of droids advanced. Fi was firing in short bursts; Niner picked off whatever was still standing. Hot metal shrapnel continued to rain down on them. At the E-Web's rate of fire he was going to run out if he simply hosed them, and they were only minutes into the engagement. They'd dropped around twenty droids. That meant twenty more inside the facility, at least. Then the tinnies stopped coming.

The field fell silent, and it rang in Niner's ears as loudly as the cacophony of battle.

"I hate it when they work out what's happening," Fi said. He was panting from the effort.

"They'll sit tight."

"If it's just twenty or so in there, I say we go in now."

"Let's make sure we haven't got guests arriving." Niner opened the long-range comlink. "*Majestic,* Omega here, over. *Majestic*—"

"Receiving you, Omega. That was some fireworks display. Got trade for us?"

"*Majestic,* extra target for you. Have you got a visual between targets Greenwood and Boffin?"

"If you've got a remote you can patch us into."

Niner slipped off his pack and took out a remote, releasing it into the air. "Droids, estimated strength no more than fifty. If they're heading toward us, do me a favor and spoil their day, will you?"

"Copy that, Omega. Sitrep?"

"We've breached the facility and we've got twenty or thirty droids and an unknown number of wets holed up in there."

"Say again?"

"Two of our squad are inside. Ingress via the drainage system."

"You guys are off your repulsors."

"The thought did cross our minds."

"Okay, some fireworks coming your way, Omega. Be advised we still have a Techno Union vessel standing off, and we're expecting a response when we train the lasers."

"Watch how you go," Niner said. "Omega out."

Apart from the ticking of cooling metal, it was silent. Even the chatter and whistling of Qiilura's nocturnal species had stopped. Smoke was billowing across the field from the wrecked barn.

"You okay, ma'am?" Fi said.

Niner glanced around and expected to see Etain in some state of distress, but she wasn't. She was kneeling in the grass, alert, as if listening to something. Then another huge explosion shook the ground to their north.

She closed her eyes.

"Ma'am?"

She gave a little shake of her head as if loosening stiff neck muscles.

"It's fine," she said. "It just took more out of me than I imagined."

"What did?"

"Diverting all this debris. Droids make a terrible mess when they explode."

Niner hadn't a clue what she was talking about. It was only when he turned around that he saw the meter-long jagged sheet of metal right behind him. It had almost given him an unwanted haircut. Etain managed a grin.

"Can you open doors as well, ma'am?" Niner asked.

Darman and Atin looked around the plastoid-lined chamber and decided not to remove their helmets.

"This is one way to find out if a nanovirus can breach our filtration masks," Atin said.

Darman checked the cupboards, looking for booby traps and other surprises. "I don't feel dead yet. Anyway, they don't leave this stuff lying around. It'll probably be sealed in something."

He checked the room. It was exactly like a medic's station on Kamino, except it was completely constructed from plastoid ceramic. Some of the cupboards had transparent fronts; he could see racks of vials in them. In the middle of the room there was a separate sealed booth, running floor-to-ceiling, with a glove box in it. It was empty. There was also a refrigerated cabinet full of flasks and small boxes. He had no idea what might be live virus and what might be the lab technician's lunch, and he wasn't going to open everything to find out. This was another case of using P for plenty.

"Seeing as they're not helpful enough to label this stuff with a skull and crossbones, I'm going to set an implosion device in every room, to be on the safe side." He ran his hands over the walls, testing for signs of metal substructures that might block his signal. The HUD showed zero from his glove sensors. He checked his comlink to be sure that he could get a signal outside. "Darman here. Anyone receiving, over?"

"Fi here."

"The inner chamber's clear. I'm setting charges and then we're going to move out into the rest of the building."

"We're approaching the front. It's gone quiet out here and we think you've still got up to thirty tinnies for company."

"Is that you shaking the ground?"

"Majestic."

"Good to know the navy's here."

"Leaving the helmet comlink channel, by the way. Make sure you leave us your visual feed."

"We'll let you know if it spoils our concentration. Darman out."

He gave Atin a dubious thumbs-up and took the implosion charges out of his pack. He could improvise most devices, but these were special, guaranteed to create such a high-temperature fireball and shock wave that they would destroy not only everything standing in a half-klick radius, but also every microorganism and virus as well. They were disappointingly small for such massively destructive power, a little smaller than the average remote.

Darman still had two. It was overkill, and overkill made him feel safer. He picked up the lidded boxes in the refrigeration unit and tested each for weight—very carefully—before finding a lighter one that suggested it was half empty. He set it on the table, held his breath, and eased the lid off.

It held a few metal tubes with sealed caps, and enough space for one of the devices. He placed the thermal carefully inside and replaced the container.

"Go careful," Atin said, indicating the boxes.

"I will." He found another lightweight box and peered inside. "There. And if they get to searching, they might even stop after they find one device." He closed the refrigerator door.

"That won't reduce the blast any, will it?" Atin asked.

"Not so you'd notice, believe me."

"Time for the tour of the building, then."

There were status panels to the right of the door, set to warn some monitoring system if the chamber was opened, and a hand-sized button marked EMERGENCY CLOSE, a smart precaution if you were handling deadly viruses. Opening the door would advertise the fact that they had gained entry to the building. Atin moved in and carefully unclipped the control plate. He took out a disruptive device about the size of a stylus and held it just clear of the exposed circuits. It was much the same technology as a mini EMP, only with a less powerful electromagnetic pulse. Nobody wanted a full-strength EMP going off a few centimeters from their HUD, hardened or not.

"Next big bang," Atin said. "Then they might think they've just taken a hit."

The ground shook again, and Atin touched the mini EMP against the control panel. Status lights winked out; the door gave a sigh as it lost its safety vacuum seal. A thin vertical gap opened in the smooth ceramic. Sound now filtered in from outside: explosions, shouts from officers, the occasional monotone responses of tinnies. He stood back and gestured to Darman.

The gap was big enough to admit a flat endoscope, as well as the claws of the ram. He slid the probe cautiously through and checked the image it was receiving. The corridor lights were flickering. There was no movement.

"I'll force the doors and you stand by. I'll be ready to lob in an EMP grenade and a flash-bang."

"Both?" Atin said.

"Yeah, I don't want to waste any, either, but we've got wets *and* tinnies out there somewhere."

Darman wedged the ram's claws into the gap and locked the bars in place. It was more awkward to configure it as a spreader than as a simple ram, but he didn't want to blow it open. He pumped the ratchet handle furiously. An eight-metric-ton force slowly pushed the doors apart.

Atin checked outside with the endoscope again, then stepped through the opening with his Deece raised. "Clear."

Darman dismantled the ram and hurriedly hooked it back into his webbing. "Room by room, then. Killing House time."

That was something they'd done many, many times before. Each time they entered the Killing House on Kamino for an exercise, the walls and doors had been reconfigured. Sometimes they knew what they were going to find, and sometimes it was like a real house clearance, a sequence of nasty surprises that they had to take as they came.

But there was a lot more at stake now than their individual lives.

Atin gestured left. The inner corridor was a ring with doors leading off it and a single passage to the front entrance. At least there were no stairs or turbolifts to cover. They moved almost back-to-back, pausing at the corner to slide the endoscopic probe out far enough to check.

"Oh boy," Atin said, just as the first droid swung around and blasted. Darman heard the clatter of metal feet from exactly the opposite direction, and for a frozen moment he found himself staring down his scope at a very surprised Umbaran officer.

Darman fired. So did Atin. They both kept firing down their respective ends of the corridor.

"Okay, plan D," Atin said. "Niner, we're pinned down here, over."

"We're concentrating fire on the front." Niner's voice cut back in with a background of explosions both near and farther away. That was why Darman didn't like a having a four-way open comlink during an engagement. The noise and chatter were overwhelming. "They've pulled back inside. But nobody's coming out."

"We haven't located Uthan yet."

"Can you hold the position?"

"Can you see where we are? West side corridor, left of the entrance."

Atin emptied a clip into two droids that came around the corner. Then there was no noise except for their respective panting.

"Dar?"

"Still here, Niner." Back-to-back with Atin, he waited and stared down the polished hallway twenty meters ahead. There were two doors on the right, unconventional hinged doors. He glanced up at the ceiling to locate the emergency bulkheads: one was on the other side of Atin, and the next was between them and the inner chamber. If those were activated, they'd be cut off on both sides, boxed in and waiting to be picked off. And then anyone could easily enter the biohaz chamber and defuse the implosion device.

It seemed that someone had the same idea at the same time, because there was an *uh-whump* noise and then the quiet whine of a small motor.

The bulkheads were descending from their housing.

"Atin, chamber, *now*!" Darman yelled, even though he didn't need to, and they both sprinted back toward the chamber. The bulkhead was down to waist level when they reached it and skidded under on their knees.

It sealed with a *clunk* behind them. It was suddenly so silent that Darman knew another bulkhead had closed somewhere along the ring, sealing them in. There was the sound of a door unlocking manually, a real *clunk-click* noise, and then nothing.

"Start again," Darman sighed. "Let's see what's around there."

Atin moved forward and edged out the scope. He paused. He sat back on his heels and shook his head.

"Show me," Darman said, and switched his HUD to the scope view, expecting disaster.

"I think it's called irony."

Darman crawled up to him and patched the endoscope into his own helmet.

Yes, *irony* was a good word for it. He almost laughed. Between the corner and the next bulkhead, he could see two doors, one closed and one partly open. Someone—someone humanoid—was peering around the edge of it.

"Women don't half look different, don't they?" Atin said. "That's the most amazing hair I've ever seen."

Darman agreed. They hadn't seen a lot of females in their lives, but this one would have been memorable even if they had seen millions. Her blue-black hair was streaked with brilliant red stripes. They were trapped with Dr. Ovolot Qail Uthan.

And she was clutching a Verpine shatter gun.

17

CO *Majestic* to Coruscant Command

Techno Union vessel is now drifting. Damage assessment is incomplete but it is no longer returning fire. *Vengeance* is standing by to dispatch a boarding party. Will continue to provide turbolaser gunnery support to Omega Squad.

"Who activated the emergency systems? Which *di'kut* hit the button? Tell me!" Ghez Hokan found himself shouting. He had abandoned dignity. "Open this *di'kutla* bulkhead!"

Captain Hurati's voice was strained. They were both on the wrong side of the first safety bulkhead, in a single unforgiving corridor that led to the entrance, and the main doors were jammed shut. It was a very secure building: and, as Uthan had said, it was designed to stop anything from getting out if things went wrong. It was doing that well.

"We've been infiltrated, sir."

"I worked that out for myself, *di'kut.*" He was interrupted by a grenade exploding against the front wall. "How in the name of—"

"I don't know yet, sir, but the bulkheads activated because the containment chamber doors weren't registering on the system as closed, and it triggered the emergency systems."

"Stuck open, in other words."

"Yes."

Hokan swung around on the nearest droid. "Anyone up on the surface see signs of entry?"

A pause. "Negative."

Oh, how he longed for decent communications again. He could guess from the strength and direction of some of the explosions that the area was coming under laser cannon fire, which meant the Republic assault ship had finally showed its hand. It could even be landing more troops.

But that wasn't his immediate concern. The bad news was that somebody had already managed to get in, and not through the front door. They couldn't have come in through the drains. They *shouldn't* have been there. But there was firing, and droids were reporting casualties.

There were Republic commandos inside the facility.

Hokan had never thought himself infallible, but he had at least imagined he was exceptionally competent. He'd locked down the facility and they'd still found a way in. His first thought was that Uthan had wanted a live subject so badly that she was prepared to lure them in and trap one, but that was ludicrous: she hadn't the means or the opportunity to bypass security.

The nanovirus was out of Hokan's reach behind bulkheads that wouldn't yield. Droids patiently fired blasters into the face of the alloy. But, as in his earlier test, they were making no impression beyond heating the sealed corridor to tropical temperatures.

"Do we know if all the bulkheads are down?" he asked the droid. Its comlink with its peers made it suddenly a lot more useful than Hurati. "All of them?" Hokan was trying to work out if he had any way of getting to Uthan or the nanovirus. The control board in the office off the main corridor was showing red throughout, but he didn't know whether to believe it or not.

"All of them. Droids trapped in sections four, five, seven, and twelve."

It felt like being in the middle of a brawl and then finding yourself dragged off your opponent. The enemy couldn't get at him, but now he couldn't get at them, either. And if the biohazard chamber doors were open, then both the nanovirus and Uthan were on the commandos' side of the barrier. If they had managed to get in, they could probably get out the same way.

The front wall shuddered.

Even if any droids had survived the assault on the villa, how would reinforcements help him now?

Hokan turned to Hurati. "Can you get into the system and override the safety controls?"

"I'll do my best, sir." Hurati's face said that he doubted it, but he'd die trying. He retreated to the office with Hokan, and they rummaged through the cabinets and drawers looking for operating instructions, tools, anything that might be used to release the bulkheads. In one cabinet Hokan found a crowbar. But its edges were too thick to get any purchase in the flimsiplast-thin gap between the two sections of the front door or the lower edge of the bulkhead. He flung it to the floor in frustration, and it clattered across the tiles.

The doors needed a blast of some magnitude. And he didn't have the ordnance.

Hurati removed the cover from the alarm panel and began poking the tip of his knife experimentally into the maze of circuits and switches. Hokan took out the lightsaber and took a swipe at the bulkhead, more out of frustration than any expectation of success.

Vzzzmmm.

The air took on an oddly ozonic smell, almost irritating in its intensity. He stared at the bulkhead's previously smooth surface. There was a definite depression.

He made another pass with the blade, more slowly and controlled this time. He pressed his face close to the cooling metal at one edge and squinted across the flat surface, one eye closed. Yes, it was definitely warping the alloy.

But at this rate it would take him hours to cut through. He suspected time was a luxury he couldn't afford.

Something thudded into the wall of the corridor.

Darman didn't even hear the shatter gun fire. The Verpine projectile was never in danger of hitting anyone, but he suspected they'd have known all about it if it had.

"Wow, that's some dent," Atin said. "I don't think the good doctor is going to come quietly, though."

"Niner, are you picking this up?" Darman said. "Found her. Just like that."

There was a faint sound of movement in his earpiece. He'd switched off the video feed. Niner sounded almost relaxed. "That's the first bit of luck we've had."

"Yeah, but she's got a Verpine on her."

"They're fragile weapons and they don't bounce. Give her a fright."

"I've got a few frighteners ready."

"If you need a hand, we're going to have trouble getting in. I reckon *all* the emergency doors have shut tight."

"All quiet out there?"

"Apart from *Majestic* getting too on-target for comfort, yes. We don't want to take the whole building out with you still inside."

"Can you go back for the other ram and try to force the front doors?"

"Do you need us to?"

"We'll try getting Uthan out via the drains. If we can't, it's plan D."

"Cheer up, still got E through Z plans," Fi's voice said.

"One day, Fi, I'm going to give you a good slap." Darman said.

Atin held up his hand for silence. Darman heard the faint sibilance of whispered conversation, and then the door slammed and the lock clunked. So it wasn't an automatic safety door. Uthan had company.

"She really doesn't know me, does she?" Darman said, and peeled off a few centimeters of thermal tape. He checked around the corner with the probe, loath to test his armor against a Verpine. "It's going to take more than a lock to keep me out, sweetheart."

He hugged the wall. He was nearly at the door when it opened and he found himself face-to-face with two Trandoshans who seemed pretty surprised to see him. Maybe it was the armor. It seemed to have that effect.

There was nowhere to run.

There were times when you could pull your rifle and times when you couldn't, and Deeces weren't much good at point-blank range unless you used them as a club. Darman aimed an instinctive punch before he thought about what he would do with the explosives in his hand. Even with an armored gauntlet, it was like hitting a stone block in the face. The Trandoshan fell back two paces. Then his comrade came at Darman with a blade. There was a frozen second or two of bewilderment as the Trannie looked at his knife, and then at Darman's armor.

"Atin, want to give me a hand here?" Darman said quietly, taking one step back with vibroblade extended.

"What do—oh."

"Yeah. *Oh.*"

The nice thing about a fixed vibroblade was that nobody could knock it out of your hand, not unless they took your arm off with it. The Trannie seemed to be considering that as an option before taking a huge lunge, the blade of his weapon skidding off Darman's arm plate.

Darman ran at the Trannie headfirst and cannoned into him, throwing him against the wall and pinning him there while he tried to drive the vibroblade into soft tissue. He tried for the throat—big blood vessels, quick effect—but the Trannie had his wrist clamped tight. It was taking Darman all his strength to keep the enemy's blade from his own throat. It seemed like deadlock.

The bodysuit was stabproof. Wasn't it? He couldn't see Atin. He had to concentrate on his own predicament, and he wasn't getting anywhere fast with the Trannie. It was time for one of those bar-brawl tactics that Skirata made sure they all learned. Darman scraped his boot along the Trannie's shin and brought it down hard on his instep. It gave him the split second of loosened grip he needed, and he plunged the vibroblade in up to its hilt, over and over, not sure what he was hitting, but noting that the Trannie was shrieking and that the shrieks were gradually getting fainter.

Skirata was right. Stabbing someone was a slow way to kill them. He pressed his forearm against the Trannie's neck and held him pinned while he slid down the wall. Darman followed him all the way down and finally knelt on his chest to make sure he didn't move while he jammed the blade up under his jaw and across his trachea.

He waited for him to stop moving, then scrambled to his feet to see Atin standing over the other Trandoshan, still cursing. There was a lot of blood, and it didn't look like Atin's.

"I could have done without that interruption," Darman said.

"Ruins your concentration," Atin said. "Where were we?"

"About to use my universal key." Darman retrieved the ribbon charge from the floor, wiped it on his sleeve, and set it with its detonator against the lock. They moved quickly to the hinge side, and Atin drew the Trandoshan array blaster he'd been so unwilling to abandon.

"Atin, it's *capture alive,* remember?"

"She's got company."

"You make sure you need to use it, then. If they'd wanted her disintegrated they'd have said." Darman took out the stun grenade and the mini EMP: she might have droids in there, too. He juggled both spheres in one hand. "Okay, I blow the lock, and in these go. They're down for five seconds. I take Uthan and you shoot anything else still moving."

"Got it."

"Cover."

Whump. The door exploded, showering kuvara splinters, and Darman leaned forward and threw in the surprises. A blinding three-hundred-thousand-candlepower white light and 160 decibels of raw noise flooded the room for two seconds, and Darman was inside before he realized it, pinning Uthan flat to the floor as Atin pumped the array blaster across the room.

The dust and smoke settled. Darman had cuffed Uthan. He didn't actually recall doing it, but that was adrenaline working. For some reason he had expected a fight, but she was simply making an odd incoherent groan. He'd become used to Etain's resilience. Uthan was a regular human, untrained, unfit, and—apart from her intellect—nothing special.

Darman picked up the Verpine and aimed it at a wall. It made the faintest of whirring noises, then jammed. Niner was right. Verpines didn't bounce, or maybe the mini EMP had temporarily fried its electronics.

"Darman here. We have Uthan, repeat, we have Uthan."

Fi's whoop hurt his ears. Niner cut in. "Are we done here?"

"Let's check we haven't missed anything. Atin?" He glanced over his shoulder. Atin was cradling the array blaster, staring down at four bodies on the floor. It was all a bit of a mess, as Fi would say.

Three of the dead were Trandoshans, and the fourth was a young red-haired woman who wasn't pretty any longer, or even recognizable. Darman wondered if the girl was Uthan's daughter. Then he had another thought.

"How many staff do you have here, ma'am?" He took his helmet off and rolled her over so they were face-to-face. "How many?"

Uthan seemed to be regaining her composure. "You murdered my assistant."

"She had a blaster," Atin said, almost to himself.

Darman shook her. "Ma'am, I'm going to detonate an awful lot of ordnance under this building very soon, and your staff, if you have any, will be dead anyway."

She was staring up into his face, seeming totally distracted by him. "Are you really a clone?"

"I'd like to say the one and only, but you know I'm not."

"Amazing," she said.

"Staff?"

"Four more. They're just scientists. They're civilians."

Darman opened his mouth, and Kal Skirata's voice emerged unbidden again. "Not all soldiers wear uniforms, ma'am. High time those scientists took responsibility for their role in the war effort."

Yes, it was personal. War didn't get much more personal than a virus aimed specifically at you and your brothers. "Darman here. Sarge, Uthan's staff members are somewhere in the building, too. What do you want to do? Retrieve them as well?"

"I'll check with *Majestic.* Wait one." Niner's link went dead for a few moments and then crackled into life again. "No, not required. Get her clear and let us know when you're going to detonate."

"They were just following orders," Uthan said.

"So am I," Darman said, and trussed, gagged, and hooded her with salvaged parasail cord and a section of sheeting. He replaced his helmet and heaved her over his shoulder. It was going to be a tough job getting her down those tunnels. Atin followed.

They slipped back down the drain. Darman hoped that they could find their way back to the surface without Jinart as their guide.

Hokan could feel the sweat stinging his eyes. He withdrew the lightsaber and examined the substantial dent in the bulkhead.

It wasn't deep enough or fast enough, and he knew it. This was displacement activity. He was little help to Hurati, so he vented his frustration on the alloy and all he seemed to succeed in was making the stale atmosphere even hotter and more suffocating.

Then he heard a hiss of air, and he wondered if it was the seal breaching: but it wasn't.

It was Hurati.

Hokan ran the few steps along the corridor to the office. He feared that the young captain had electrocuted himself, and whether he wanted to admit it or not, he actually cared what happened to him. But Hurati was intact. He was leaning over the desk, both hands braced on the surface, head down, shoulders shaking. Then he looked up, and his face was a big, sweaty grin. A bead of perspiration ran down his nose and hung there for a moment before he batted it away with his finger.

"Check the status board, sir."

Hokan swung around and looked for the board. The unchanging pattern of red lights had now become a pattern of red and green.

"Bulkheads two, six, and nine, sir," he said. "Now I can clear the rest. I had to try every sequence. That's a lot of permutations." He shook his head and went back to carefully prodding a piece of circuit board with the tip of his knife. "They'll be jammed open, though."

"Better than jammed shut."

As Hokan watched, the lights changed from red to green, one by one, and a cool draft hit his face.

The front doors had opened.

Hokan expected a missile or blaster volley to punch through them, but all that entered was the silent, refreshing, fire-scented night air.

"Hurati," Hokan said, "Right now, I couldn't love you more if you were my own son. Remind me I said that one day." He drew his blaster and raced down the corridor, past droids, stumbling over shattered metal plates and the body of an Umbaran, and into the room where he had left Uthan with her Trandoshan guards.

He had half expected to see her lying dead on the floor with them. In a way he had hoped for it, because it would mean the Republic hadn't stolen her expertise. But she was gone. He picked up the Verpine and tested it for charge: it made a faint whir and then ticked. Either Uthan hadn't managed to get a shot off or they'd used an EMP grenade.

Hokan worked his way down the passage to the biohazard chamber, pausing on the way to check inside prep rooms and storage cupboards, wary of booby traps. As he opened one door, he heard whimpering in the darkness. He switched on the light.

The remaining four members of Uthan's research team—three young men and an older woman—were huddled in the corner. One of the men held a blaster, but its muzzle was pointed at the floor. They blinked at Hokan, frozen.

"Stay here," he said. "You might be all that's left of the virus program. Don't move." There seemed little chance that they would.

When Hokan reached the central chamber, the only sign that anything untoward had taken place was that the concealed drain in the center of the floor was now a charred, gaping space.

He looked around the walls, shelves, and cupboards. *A mistake.* He'd made a mistake, a terrible oversight. He hadn't taken the time to check what the virus containers looked like, or how many there had been. He could see gaps on shelves through the transparent doors; he pulled on the handles, but they were still locked.

He ran back up the corridor and grabbed one of the young men from Uthan's team. "Do you know what the nanovirus looks like?"

The boy blinked. "It has a structure based on—"

"Idiot." Hokan jabbed fiercely toward his own eye, indicating *look.* "What does the *container* look like? How many? Come on. Think."

He hauled the scientist to his feet and dragged him down the corridor to the biohazard chamber.

"Show me."

The boy pointed to a plain-fronted cabinet. "Fourteen alloy vials in there, inside their own vacuum-sealed case."

"Open it and check."

"I can't. Uthan has all the security codes and keys."

"Is it conceivable that the enemy could have opened it and simply shut it again?"

"Normally I'd say that was impossible, but I also remember thinking that it was impossible for anyone to breach this building."

The hole where the drain had been was now a jagged fringe of scorched, broken tiling and twisted metal frame. Hokan looked down into the void and saw debris.

For a moment he wondered if he was actually dealing with human beings and not some bizarre, unknown life-form. He knew where they'd gone. Now he had to hunt them down and stop them from taking Uthan off the planet with whatever was left of the nanovirus project.

If this was what a handful of clone soldiers could achieve, he was almost afraid to think what millions might do.

18

You never have perfect knowledge in combat, gentlemen. It's what we call the fog of war. You can either sit around worrying what's real and what's not, or you can realize the enemy hasn't got a clue either and fire off a few rounds of psychology. A truly great army is one that only has to rattle its saber to win a war.
—Sergeant Kal Skirata

"Omega to *Majestic. Check check check.* Cease firing."

Niner waited several minutes before moving. There had been trees to the northwest of the facility that weren't there anymore. You couldn't stake your life on the accuracy of gunnery support. He edged forward on his stomach and propped himself on his elbows to check the area, first with his binoc visor and then through the scope of the DC-17.

Nothing was moving, although nothing with any sense would present itself in a bright-lit doorway anyway.

The facility was now stripped completely of its wooden farmhouse shell, and its alloy doors were wide open. For a few seconds, Niner almost expected to see Darman and Atin walk out into the yard, and for Kal Skirata to shout *Endex, endex, endex*—end of exercise. But there were no more exercises, and this night wasn't over, not by a long shot.

Behind him, Fi switched to his Deece and trained the sniper attachment on the entrance, waiting to pick off anything insane enough to walk out. Niner wasn't sure if Fi would pause for thought if anyone did come out, even with raised hands.

"Dar, Atin, can you confirm your position?"

Niner waited.

"Somewhere pitch black and smelly, and dragging a semiconscious woman behind me," Atin said.

"Sounds like happy hour at the Outlander," Niner said, although he had no idea what a nightclub was really like, and probably never would. The comment sprang from his subconscious. "Is Uthan injured?"

"Dar got fed up with her struggling and sedated her."

"How long before you can detonate?"

Muffled noises filled Niner's helmet. It sounded as if Atin was conferring with Darman without the comlink. Maybe he'd removed his helmet to sip some water. A woman was making incoherent noises, and Niner heard Darman's voice clearly: "Shut up, will you?" He didn't need a medic to check Dar's stress levels.

Atin was back on the link. "At this rate, half an hour."

"Fi, how fast could you cover one klick right now?"

"Unladen and suitably motivated? 'Bout three minutes."

Now it was the timing that was giving them grief. They needed to keep whoever was in the facility right where they were until Darman was in position to detonate the implosion device. Niner wondered how long *Majestic* could wait, and how long it would be before they had more company. He decided to ask.

"Omega here, Majestic. What's that Techno warship doing?"

"Listing to port and smoking a bit, Omega."

"You've been busy."

"If we get busier, we'll let you know. We're dispatching the gunship now. It'll be waiting when you reach the extraction point."

Niner crawled back to Fi's position and nudged him. "You might as well make a move for the EP now with Etain. I can hold this position."

"No."

"Can I give you an order?"

"I might call you Sarge, but right now I'm ignoring you."

Etain appeared on the other side of Fi, with Jinart. "What's happening?"

"The gunship's on its way. I suggest you and Fi head out and meet it."

"Where's Darman?"

"About fifty meters down the tunnel. It's heavy going."

"It's still the quickest path through the warren," Jinart said. "Short of digging them out."

"Digging through five meters of soil without power tools or explosives is going to take a long time." Niner turned to Etain. "Is there anything you can do, ma'am?"

Etain pushed her tangled hair back from her face. "If Jinart can find the shallowest point of the tunnel, I can try to part the soil. If you explain to me what needs to happen, I can picture it. The more accurately I can picture it, the better my chances of bringing the Force to bear. I have to *see* what's happening in my mind."

"I can find their position," Jinart said.

"By all means bring your lightsaber, ma'am," Fi said. "But only use it if you miss with this." He handed her his blaster.

Etain shoved it in her belt. "You persuaded me."

Jinart was fast. Etain had trouble keeping up with her when she was running on all fours, her snout to the ground. The Gurlanin's rhythmic sniffs were in counterpoint to Etain's gasping breath.

They were moving in a square search pattern across the field to the east of the facility, trying to locate the exact section of tunnel that Darman and Fi had taken. Etain could sense Darman now. They were close.

"Are you following scent?" Etain panted.

"No, I'm listening for echoes."

"With your nose?"

"Where I keep my ears is my own business." Jinart stopped dead and pressed her snout into the soil with a few short, strong snorts. "Here. Dig here."

"I hope they know we're right above them."

"We aren't. They're about ten meters back up the tunnel. If you excavated where they are you could bury them completely."

Etain wasn't sure if Jinart was making a general point about rescue procedure, or commenting on her competence. She didn't care. Darman was down there and he needed her help. Atin was down there, too, but the thought of Darman focused her because . . . because he was a *friend.*

She could almost imagine him advising her that sentimentality was a luxury that a commander could never afford.

"Here we go," she said, more to herself than to Jinart.

Etain knelt to one side of the line of the tunnel and placed her hands flat on the ground. When she closed her eyes, she visualized the warren, seeing its uneven walls with tree roots emerging from them like knotted rope. She saw small stones and seams of amber clay.

Then her focus became more intense. She saw smaller roots, and then the individual grains of mineral and veins of organic material. She felt her breathing slowing, changing, as if her lungs weren't moving within her but rather the air outside her body was pressing and relaxing, pressing and relaxing, slowly and rhythmically.

And she finally saw the space around each microscopic grain. It wasn't empty. It was invisible, but it was not a void. Etain felt it. She had control of it at a fundamental, subatomic level. She could feel the pressure throughout her body.

Now all she had to do was shape it.

At the sides of the tunnel, she pictured the space thinning and reducing, compacting the walls, strengthening them against collapse. Overhead—and she now felt like she was lying flat on her back looking up at the vault above her—she saw the space expand.

The grains moved farther apart. The space flowed in to displace them. The space flowed upward to lift them. And then the space was suddenly all there was.

Etain was aware of something cold and slightly damp across the backs of her hands and opened her eyes. She was kneeling in fine, friable soil. It looked as if a patient gardener had sieved it to prepare for planting seeds.

She was looking down into an open trench. There was a domed line of soil along both sides, as neat and regular as if an excavator had done the job.

"That," said Jinart's voice beside her, "was quite extraordinary." The Gurlanin's tone was almost reverent. "*Quite* extraordinary."

Etain knelt back on her heels. Instead of the exhaustion she normally felt after using the Force to shift objects, she felt refreshed. Jinart slipped down into the trench and disappeared. A few moments later, a familiar blue-lit, T-shaped visor popped up from the darkness below, and it didn't alarm her at all.

"There's always a career for you in the construction industry, Commander," Darman said.

He scrambled out of the trench, and Etain threw her arms around him without thinking. Her blaster clunked against his armor plates. It was odd to hug something that felt like a droid, but she was overwhelmed by relief that he'd made it. She let go and stepped back, suddenly embarrassed.

"Yeah, I've been in a sewer," he said, all guilt. "Sorry."

Atin's voice carried from the trench. "Dar, are you going to stand there all night posing for the commander, or are you going to help me lift this?"

"As if I could forget," Darman said.

After some grunting and cursing, thc two commandos managed to lift a thoroughly trussed body onto the edge of the trench. Etain pulled off the hood and stared into the half-closed eyes of Dr. Uthan. She was drifting in and out of consciousness.

"How much did you give her?" Etain asked.

"Enough to shut her up," Darman said.

Etain hoped the woman didn't vomit and choke to death. It was always a risk with heavy sedatives. They hadn't come this far to lose her. Atin leaned forward, and Darman heaved Uthan onto his back.

"Ten-minute shifts," Atin said. "And I'll be counting."

"I hope she's worth the effort," Etain said.

"So do I," Jinart said. "You must make your own way now. I've done all I can. Remember us, Jedi. Remember what we have done for you, and that we expect your help in reclaiming our world. Honor that promise."

Jinart looked the Padawan up and down as if measuring her, and then the Gurlanin lost her outline and became black fluid again, vanishing into the undergrowth.

"To think I nearly shot her," Darman said, shaking his head. They moved off toward the extraction point across country remarkably empty of gdans.

Ghez Hokan lined up the young scientists on the other side of the door. He gestured to Hurati.

"On my mark," he said. "Kill the lights."

"Sir, if the speeders have been destroyed, what are we going to do?"

Hokan thought it an unusually stupid question for such a fine officer, but perhaps he was thinking about just how far untrained civilians might get on foot before falling to the enemy.

"Run," he said. "Just run."

He turned to the four biologists, hoping terror would speed them up, as it often did. "What's your name?" he asked the woman.

"Cheva," she said.

"Well, Cheva, when the lights go out, hang on to me and run like crazy, understand?"

"Yes."

"And if the captain or I shout *drop,* you drop down flat. Got that?"

"I can assure you I have."

"Hurati, you take the rear. Don't lose any of them."

Hokan was expecting more laser bombardment. It was quiet outside, but he felt that it would begin again as soon as they emerged. He couldn't defend a facility with its doors jammed open. There was at least one squad of enemy commandos still out there. His last chance was to make a run for it with the remnants of Uthan's team and hide them somewhere. Then he would look for Uthan.

One way or another, he would salvage what he could of the nanovirus program. Beyond that, he hadn't made plans.

"Ready, Hurati?"

"Ready, sir."

Hokan slid on his Mandalorian helmet, as much for comfort as protection.

"Lights!"

19

CO *Majestic* to Coruscant Command

Standing by to retrieve LAAT/i from Qiilura. Be aware we have detected two Trade Federation warships approaching from the Tingel Arm to reinforce Qiilura. *Vengeance* is moving to protect our flank.

"We're almost at the one-klick line," Darman's voice said. "Ready when you are."

Niner clapped his glove to the left side of his helmet. He feared it was becoming a nervous tic. "Good. See you at the EP."

"Give me a few minutes."

Fi made a casual thumbs-up gesture and adjusted his shoulder plate. Five minutes felt like forever right then.

"Whoa, what's happening here?" Niner said. "Dar, hold off. Wait one."

The light from the front doors had died, and his night-vision visor kicked in.

He thought he saw Darman or Atin, another odd flashback now that the stims were wearing off, but then he realized the T-slit visor coming out the door was Hokan's. He opened fire. The hesitation had cost him half a second, an eternity, and he didn't see anyone fall.

Fi laid down a burst of plasma bolt rounds, and they waited. Nothing. Then there was another flurry of movement and someone yelled "Drop!" but the three shapes didn't, at least not until the plasma rounds hit them.

It was silent again. Niner paused. As he and Fi began edging forward to check, someone got up from the blast-cratered ground and sprinted around the far side of the building.

Niner and Fi sprayed more rounds and paused again. But there was no more movement.

"If there's more inside that lobby, Sarge, can I put a bit of anti-armor in there? I don't fancy running with droids behind us."

Standard grenades wouldn't trigger the thermal detonator. "Lob in six," he said. "And then set the E-Web to self-destruct."

Fi lined up the blaster, easing it a little on its tripod. Niner heard a high-pitched noise like a repulsorlift drive starting up, but then it was drowned out by the *whump-whump-whump* of the first three grenades launching and exploding.

The doorway of the facility belched black, rolling flames and smoke.

"Now that's *endex,*" Niner said, and they ran. They ran over rutted fields and crashed through two hedges and were into the trees before Niner managed to open his comlink and gasp out the *take-take-take* command to Darman.

The white flash illuminated the track before them a second or two before the shock wave smacked Niner hard in the back. It threw him forward. His mouth smashed against the interior of the visor and he tasted blood. When he turned his head and tried to get up, Fi was also flat on his chest, arms out in front, head turned toward him.

"No, Sarge," Fi said, still seeming totally pleased with life. "*That* was endex."

Ghez Hokan found himself on the ground with his speeder bike upended, its drive still running. The blast was ringing in his ears. He froze, head covered, waiting for incoming cannon fire. But only silence followed.

He struggled to his feet and managed to heave the speeder upright again. A steering vane was slightly bent, but it was serviceable. He dusted himself down and then swung back into the rider's seat.

He could see his hands gripping the bars. The tan glove on his left hand looked black; it was still wet. Cheva had hung on to him. She'd run, as he'd told her. Her blood had sprayed over him when she was hit. It was the closest he had come to feeling pity in many years.

Enough of this. You're going soft, man. Concentrate.

"Sir." It was hard to identify the voice from a single shout. Hokan turned to check, but there was really only one man who would have struggled to stay with him. "Sir!"

Hurati rode up from behind and stopped his speeder level with his. He had no second rider. Hokan didn't need to ask.

"I'm sorry, sir," Hurati said. "They froze when the shooting started. They didn't even drop."

"Civilians tend to do that," Hokan said wearily.

"That blast was the facility. Judging by the color, that was a high-temperature implosion. Not laser cannon."

"Does it matter?"

"Nothing could have survived that, even in a blastproof container. If there were any samples of the nanovirus, they're gone now."

So there was now no nanovirus in Separatist hands, and no scientists with any degree of expertise in the program, either. That made it imperative to retrieve Uthan.

Given the blast area of an implosion device, they were using sensitive remote detonators. Hokan was relieved that he had some EMP grenades in his cargo pannier.

"Find them," Hokan said.

He couldn't even trace their route from the drainage system now. Where would he start? The enemy would need to leave Qiilura. They would have a vessel somewhere. If intelligence from Geonosis was any guide, they would have gunships to extract them and evacuate wounded.

It was a quiet, backward, rural planet. You could hear motors and drives for kilometers, especially at night.

Hokan powered down the speeder and waited, listening.

Etain could feel it long before she saw or heard it.

She hadn't been able to detect droids, or so she thought, but she could feel something *big* disturbing the Force, and it was getting nearer. She wasn't sure if it was mechanical or organic. And it didn't communicate any sense of threat beyond a mild anxiety.

Then she heard the rushing air and steady drone of a vessel's propulsion drive. She stopped and craned her neck. Atin and Darman stopped, too.

"Oh, I love that sound," Darman said.

"What is it?"

"The sound of us getting out of this cesspit in one piece. A *larty*. A gunship."

The sound was practically right overhead. As Etain scanned the night sky she picked out a silhouette against the stars. The vessel wasn't showing any navigation lights. It dipped slightly, its drive changing pitch, and Darman reacted as if someone were talking to him. He gestured and nodded. Then he waved. The gunship picked up speed and lifted higher before shooting away.

"They tracked us by our comlink transponder," Darman said. "Good old Niner. Bless him for knocking out Teklet."

Atin jerked his shoulders to heave Uthan a little higher on his back. "Your carriage, princess," he said to her, far more cheerful than Etain had imagined him capable of being. His presence felt almost healed, but not entirely. "Want to sit up front?"

Uthan had recovered from the sedation enough to squirm. Etain realized that the scientist was the only person she had ever seen who could convey such rage just by writhing. She didn't envy the soldier who had to untie her.

"Your turn, Dar," Atin said.

"Okay." He seemed elated as well as edgy. Etain could feel it. It was nearly over: they'd pulled it off. She wanted to ask him what he was going to do when he got back to base, but she could guess that it involved a lot of sleep, a hot shower, and food. His dreams were modest. She thought that was a fine example to set, even for a Padawan.

She just hoped that she could become a competent officer. She wanted Darman's respect.

"Come on, Dar," Atin said irritably. "Uthan's starting to weigh a ton. Your turn."

"Try this," Etain said, and *lifted* with the Force. Atin half turned to check what was relieving the weight on his back. Darman had almost caught up with him.

Crack. Atin pitched forward.

Etain thought he had merely tripped, but Darman was now down on the ground, and she followed suit. He was sprawled across Atin with his rifle raised. Atin wasn't screaming, but he was making a rhythmic *ah-ah-ah* noise as if he was trying to gulp air. Uthan was lying in a heap on the grass.

"Man down," Darman said, unnaturally calm. Etain heard him clearly: he still had the voice unit open. "Sarge, Atin's hit."

Whatever Niner's response was, Etain didn't hear it. Darman fired rapidly and she saw the brilliant rounds fly over her head.

Why hadn't she felt anyone behind her? Because she'd been distracted. *This was her fault.* If Atin died, she would have him on her conscience for the rest of her life.

The firing stopped. It was over inside thirty seconds. The world had somehow gone back to the way it was before, except for Atin.

Darman could obviously see something through his rifle sight that Etain could not. She watched him get up, run forward, and aim at an object on the ground. He switched on his helmet lamp.

"One of Hokan's officers," Darman said. "A captain."

"Is he dead?"

A single shot. "He is now," Darman said.

This time Etain wasn't quite as appalled as she had been when Darman had dispatched the wounded Umbaran. She was wrapped up in concern for Atin. Her perspective had shifted radically.

Atin was now worryingly quiet. When Darman turned him carefully onto his side, there was a shattered hole in his armor plate about twenty centimeters below his right armpit that was leaking blood. Darman took a small, gray oblong container with rounded edges from his belt and emptied the contents on the ground. He shoved what looked like a field dressing in the gaping hole and taped it to the armor.

"Get on," Atin said. His voice was shaking. "Go on. Leave me."

"Don't go all heroic on me or I'll smack you one."

"I mean it. Get Uthan out of here."

"Atin, shut up, will you? I'm not leaving anyone anywhere." Darman was working with all the precision of someone who'd been drilled repeatedly in combat first aid. He nodded at Etain. She grasped Atin's hand and squeezed it hard. "That's what a Verpine projectile can do to Katarn armor . . . easy, brother. I've got you." He removed one of Atin's thigh plates, peeled back the section of bodysuit, and exposed the skin. He held two short single-use syringes in his hand. "It's going to hurt a bit, okay? Steady."

Darman stabbed both needles into Atin's thigh in quick succession. Then he scrawled something on Atin's helmet with a marker and replaced the thigh plate.

Etain stared at the letters P and Z now written on the forehead of the helmet.

"P for painkiller," Darman said. He laid Atin flat on his back. "And Z for blood-loss control agent, because B looks too much like P when you're in a hurry. It's for the medics, just in case they don't scan him, so they know what I've dosed him with. Now, this is going to look really odd, but trust me . . ."

Atin was flat on his back, breathing heavily. Darman slid on top of him, back-to-chest, then slipped his arms through Atin's webbing and rolled both of them over so he was lying underneath. Raising himself on his arms, he drew his legs to a kneeling position and then stood up with Atin secure across his back. He tottered slightly. But he didn't fall.

"Easiest way to lift and carry a heavy man," Darman said, his voice sounding a little strained.

"I could have done that for you," Etain said.

"Yeah, but he's my brother. Besides, you're going to carry Doctor Uthan."

Etain felt momentary guilt for not checking on her. But the scientist was still lying there trussed, quite silent, and no doubt bewildered. Etain leaned over her.

"Come on, Doctor," she said. She went to lift her, but her hands touched something cold and wet. There was a jagged sliver of pale gray plastoid alloy protruding from just under her ribs. It was shrapnel from Atin's armor. The doctor was bleeding heavily.

"Oh no. Not this. Look. Darman, *look.*"

"*Fierfek.* After all this rotten—"

"No, she's alive."

"Just get her to the extraction point. They better have a medic on board."

The disappointment was sudden and crushing. Etain felt it. It almost made her stop in her tracks, too overwhelmed by the unfairness of it all to move, but it didn't stop Darman, and so she was determined to go on. His absolute discipline was tangible. In a few days she had learned more from him than she had ever been able to learn from Fulier. Being seconds from death so many times drove the lessons home that much harder.

Etain also knew it had forged a bond that would cause her enormous pain in years to come. It was worse than falling in love. It was a totally different level of attachment: it was shared trauma. Master Fulier said you could fall out of love, but Etain knew you could never fall out of *this,* because history could never change.

She lifted Uthan across her back by her own arm and jerked her forward until she was comfortably across her shoulders.

"Let's move it, Darman," she said, and hardly recognized her own voice. For a moment, she didn't sound like a Jedi at all.

Hokan was still on the loose. Niner knew it. He'd seen him—or at least someone in his armor—come out of the facility. The officer whom Darman had shot had just been a young captain. And Hokan was probably doing what the dead captain seemed to have done, and tracked them by the gunship. Their salvation might also prove to be their undoing.

"About one more klick," Fi said. "Any word on Atin?"

"Haven't you got your long-range switched through?"

"No. It's one more distraction I can't face right now."

Niner was beginning to understand how Fi coped: the man just switched off, sometimes literally. He wondered who or what had taught him to do that, because it wasn't Skirata. Kal Skirata *felt,* all too visibly sometimes.

"I hope we get an urban deployment after this," Niner said. *Stay positive. Look ahead.* "A nice, noisy, confusing city with places to hide and lots of running water. Surveillance. Data extraction. Easy Street."

"Nah, jungle."

"You're sick."

"Jungle's like a city. Lots going on."

"You're worried about Atin."

"Shut up, Sarge. I'm just worried about me, okay?"

"Of course you are."

"Why didn't we just pound this whole region from space?"

"No intel. Virus could have been at several locations. We might not have hit them all and we'd never have known until it was too late."

"Just when we were making a good team."

"He's still alive, Fi." Niner began walking backward, playing the tail role. "He's still alive. Jedi can heal. Darman's done all the right first aid—"

Niner never did like being tail on patrol, especially at night. He liked it even less when the point man shouted, "Down!"

He dropped flat in the grass and looked where Fi was aiming his Deece.

"Speeder," Fi said. "Guess who. Crossing right-to-left ahead. It's got to be Hokan."

"Can you take him?"

"Clear shot when he passes the trees."

"Don't hang about, then."

Niner counted the seconds, following the speeder bike with his rifle scope. The speeder's movement behind the avenue of kuvara created a strobe effect. A flare of energy lit up his night vision and the rider was thrown off the vehicle in a cloud of vapor.

"That's the way to do it," Niner said.

They waited the mandatory few seconds to check that Hokan was truly down. There was no movement at all. Niner could see the glint of gdans' eyes in the grass, a sign that at least someone thought the fighting was over and that it was safe to come out again.

Niner was on his feet and Fi was up on one knee when Hokan

rose from the grass like a specter. He staggered a few steps and raised his weapon.

Niner didn't hear him fire. But he heard a projectile whistle pass him and hit something with a loud *crack.* Verpine shatter guns were silent, and they were accurate. If Hokan hadn't been winded by Fi's round, then Niner would have had the same hole blown in him as Atin."Sarge, when I kill him, can I have his armor?" Fi asked.

"You get to take it off him personally."

"I needed that motivation. Thanks."

"Still see him?"

"No . . ."

A blaster round hit the grass a meter in front of Fi and sent sparks swirling. Their enemy wasn't a mindless tinnie or a stupid Weequay. He was a Mandalorian, a natural-born fighter, dangerous even when wounded.

He was very much like them.

"You think that gunship's going to wait?" Fi asked.

"Not once they have Uthan."

"Fierfek." Fi snapped on the grenade attachment and aimed. "Maybe we shouldn't have ditched the E-Web." The night lit up with the explosion. Fi raised his head a little and blasterfire flowed back, a meter farther off target than before. "You go right of him while I keep him busy."

Niner edged forward on his elbows and knees, Deece crooked in his arms. He'd moved about ten meters when the air above him made a frying noise and a blaster bolt took the seed heads off the grass above him.

If it hadn't been for that Verpine, things would have been a lot simpler.

Majestic wouldn't wait much longer. The stims had worn off fully now, and Niner was feeling the impact of days of hard tabbing, little sleep, and too much noise. He made himself a promise there and then. If he and Fi weren't getting off Qiilura, then neither was Ghez Hokan.

But Mandalorian or not, Hokan was just one man, and he was facing two men who were at least his match. Niner didn't underestimate him, but the end result was almost certain: sooner or later he would deplete the power cells. Still, time wasn't on their side right then.

"Not good at all," Niner said. "Darman, Niner here. What's your position?"

He sounded out of breath. "Slow going, Sarge. About ten minutes from the EP."

"Ask them if they'll keep the meter running, will you? Just saying good-bye to Ghez Hokan."

"I'll drop Atin off and—"

"Negative, Dar. We can handle this once we crack his armor. Stand by."

Fi was edging forward looking for a clear shot. Niner, running out of patience, looked about for some cover he could use to get a position to the side of Hokan. The flash of a weapon discharge caught his eye but he didn't hear anything except Fi beginning to say something over the comlink and then a very brief searing peak of high-pitched noise.

Then everything went silent and black.

For a moment Niner thought he'd been hit. He couldn't hear Fi and he couldn't see the data from his HUD. There was no green image of the field and the trees behind it in his night-vision visor. But he could feel his elbows squarely braced in the soil and he could feel his Deece still in his hands. No pain—but if you were hurt badly enough you sometimes didn't feel a thing.

It took him several slow seconds to realize his helmet's systems were totally dead. His face felt hot. He wasn't getting air.

He pulled off the helmet and squinted through the scope of his DC-17. The night-vision scope picked up his image; Fi had taken his helmet off, too, and had his hand inside it, pressing controls frantically.

EMP grenade, Niner thought. *Hokan's droided us.*

You used electromagnetic pulse charges against droids. But they were equally effective against delicate electronics attached to wets. The enhanced Katarn helmets, three times the price of an ordinary trooper's version, were packed with sophisticated prototype systems, *vulnerable* systems.

Niner crawled slowly and carefully toward Fi. A couple of blaster bolts went wide. He lay flat, head-to-head with him.

"He's fried our helmets," Fi whispered. "Don't they test these things properly?"

"I bet some civvy thought nobody would use EMPs against wets."

"Yeah, I might look him up when we get back."

"They should reset."

"How long?"

"No idea. Deece still works, though."

"As long as he puts his head up."

"I could do with one of Dar's flash-bangs."

"Doesn't fit the Deece anyway."

"Can you see him at all?"

"No . . . no, wait. There he is."

Niner had to track back and forth a couple of times before he spotted Hokan through the scope. "Got any of the IEDs in easy reach?"

"Six."

"How far can you throw?"

"Far enough."

"Wide as you can. Scatter them across him."

Niner laid down suppressing fire while Fi bounced up and down, lobbing the little makeshift bombs and dropping flat again. Niner took the detonator control.

"When I hit this, you go wide that way and try to get side-on to him."

Fi rolled slightly to one side, bracing on his right arm for a quick start. Niner hit the det. Fi bobbed up.

Nothing happened. A blaster round seared the grass between them, and Fi threw himself down again.

"We really must talk to procurement about hardening our electronics," Fi said mildly.

"I fear we might be back to old-fashioned soldiering."

"I'm fresh out of bayonets."

"Sergeant Kal would have an idea."

"You got his number on you?"

"I'm going to scream."

"What?"

"Don't laugh. This man's a nut. If he thinks I'm down and badly injured, he won't be able to resist coming over and slitting my throat."

"And then I give him a surprise party?"

"Anything that resolves this *fast.*"

"Okay, kid. Off you go."

Niner suddenly realized he didn't actually know how to scream. But he'd heard enough terribly wounded men to make a fair stab at it.

He threw back his head and let go.

20

I don't know who the good guys are anymore. But I do know what the enemy is. It's the compromise of principles. You lose the war when you lose your principles. And the first principle is to look out for your comrades.
—Kal Skirata

The gunship was the most beautiful craft Darman had ever seen.

It came into view as he staggered through the line of bushes and into the newly plowed field. Its cockpit bubbles gleamed like a holo of Cloud City, and its cannon turrets had the symmetry of the finest Naboo architecture. He even loved its rust and the dents in its wings.

"Look at that, Atin," he said. "Sheer art . . . Atin?"

". . . yeah."

"Nearly there."

". . . uh."

White trooper armor came running toward him with a Gran in a medic's uniform just behind them. Atin's weight lifted from his back, and he struggled to pull his arms free of the webbing. He followed the stretcher, trying to talk to the medic.

"Verpine projectile, right side of his chest," he said. "Painkiller, five ccs of—"

"I can see," the Gran said. "Neat job, Private. Now get in that ship."

When he looked around, troopers had taken Uthan from Etain and she was walking toward the gunship, stopping to look over her shoulder every few steps. General Arligan Zey stepped down from the troop cabin and bowed his head very slightly in her direction. She slowed down and stopped to return it.

It struck Darman as a remarkably formal greeting under the circumstances. Behind this tableau of Jedi etiquette was a scene from a nightmare, with medics working on both Atin and Uthan, removing armor, cutting garments, hooking up transfusion lines, calling for more dressings. It was like watching two parallel worlds, each wholly oblivious to the other.

Zey didn't look at Darman at all, but the ARC trooper who jumped down beside the general took off his helmet and simply stared at him in silence. Something black moved in the shadows of the ship and then emerged slowly to sniff the air with a long glossy snout.

It was Valaqil. He had come home. Darman could hardly say that he recognized the Gurlanin, because this one looked indistinguishable from Jinart. But he could guess.

"Private Atin is still collecting scars, I see," Valaqil said. "And my consort is impatient and waiting for me. I have to go."

"Jinart?" Darman shrugged, embarrassed. "She's been an extraordinary help to us, sir. A fifth—a sixth member of the squad, in fact."

"I'm sure she will tell me all the details of what has made her so very excited for the past few days."

And then he was gone, loping across the field and into the bushes. Darman hoped the Republic wouldn't disappoint the Gurlanins. They'd served as well as any soldier.

"You've done remarkably well, Padawan," Zey said. "Especially without the guidance of a Master. Quite exceptional, in fact. I think that this may hasten your progress toward your trials as far as the Council is concerned. With the supervision of a Master, of course."

Darman expected delight or embarrassment or something equally positive to soften Etain's expression. He knew she believed she was unfit to be a Jedi Knight, or even a Padawan at times. He knew it was the one thing she lived for.

But the elevation didn't appear to move her at all. She didn't even appear to hear what Zey had said.

"Master, where are Niner and Fi?" Etain asked.

Zey looked bemused. "Who?"

"Sorry, Master. The two other men from Omega Squad."

Darman felt the scrutiny of the ARC even more keenly now. He'd only seen ARCs a couple of times before, and they came as close to scaring him as anyone supposedly on his side ever could. Zey shook his head. "You're the first to make it here."

"They'll be here, sir," Darman said. He flicked open his helmet-to-helmet comlink. If the ARC was listening in, it was too bad. "Sarge? Fi? Time to get a move on."

There was no sound at all in his ear, not even static. He switched to the alternative frequency, and still there was nothing. "Niner, Fi, are you receiving?" He checked the diagnostics mode of his HUD: his helmet was fully functional. He could see the crevasse on Geonosis again, standing behind the cooling, ticking E-Web, trying to raise Taler, Vin, and Jay. He couldn't see the biometric data from their suits on his HUD.

No, not again. Not again, please . . .

"Ma'am, I'm not getting any response."

"What does that mean?"

He could hardly bear to say it. "Their helmets are offline. I don't think they made it."

"They're dead?" Zey asked.

"They're *not dead,*" Etain said firmly.

"Ma'am, I can't raise them at all."

"No, I don't care, they're alive. I know they are."

"You have to go," Zey said. "If you don't go now, you could be flying straight into a battle with Trade Federation vessels. We've attracted a lot of attention." The general turned back to the two medics working on Uthan. "Is she going to survive?"

"She's in a very bad way, sir. We need to move her."

"Keep her alive any way you can. Prepare to lift off. Etain—"

"Master, there are two men still out there."

"They're dead."

"No, I can feel them. I know them, sir, I know where they are. They're not even hurt. We *must* wait for them."

"We must also save Uthan and get you two out of here."

"They've destroyed the virus. Isn't that what matters? You can't abandon them now."

Darman could see she was at that point where she would either collapse or do something extreme. Her face was drawn tight, and her pupils were dilated. It was an expression that scared him. He'd seen it a few times in the last few days.

The gunship's drives were throbbing now. Etain still had one boot on the platform and the other firmly on Qiiluran soil.

Etain swallowed hard. *Oh,* Darman thought. *Just bite your tongue, ma'am. Don't react.* But he felt what she was feeling. All that sweat and terror and pain for nothing. All that, when they could have bombed the facility and gone home. All that—and Atin fighting for his life, and Niner and Fi either dead or marooned here.

"I will *not* leave without them," Etain said. "I regret disobeying you, Master, but I must."

Zey registered visible annoyance. "You will do as I order," he said quietly. "You're compromising the mission."

"We need these men. They are *not* expendable."

"We are *all* expendable."

"Then, sir, I'm expendable, too." She lowered her head slightly, looking up at Zey, more challenging than coy. "An officer's duty is the welfare of her men."

"I see that Master Fulier taught you little about obedience but a great deal about sentimentality—"

Darman dared to interrupt. He couldn't stand seeing Jedi Masters arguing. It was painfully embarrassing. "Look, I'll stay, ma'am," he said. "Go with Atin. See he's okay."

Despite Skirata's frequent assurances that their lives had meaning, Darman had accepted the hierarchy of expendability: it was not only natural in the Grand Army, but also necessary and inevitable. His life was a more valuable defense asset than a clone trooper's; the ARC's life was more valuable than his. But the mirror that Etain's loyalty and care held up in front of him had made him see himself as a man. Yes, Niner and Fi deserved better. They all did.

Zey ignored Darman. "You must go. More Separatist vessels are heading this way, and I know how this pains you, but—"

Etain bounced off her back heel into the troop cabin in one move. For a moment Darman thought she had changed her mind, but that wasn't Etain at all. She took out her lightsaber and held the glowing shaft a handspan away from the power conduit running along the spine of the airframe. She could ground them with one move. Zey's jaw was set. Nobody else moved except for the Gran medic working on Atin, who seemed oblivious to the drama, a quality Darman suspected was honed by working under fire.

"Master," Etain said, "either *all* of Omega Squad leaves Qiilura or *nobody* does."

"This is a foolish act, Etain." His tone was very calm. "You must see the necessity of this."

"No, Master. I don't."

He's going to do some of that Jedi stuff on her, Darman thought. *No, no, please . . .* He couldn't see the ARC's expression but he could guess it was one of astonishment.

"Etain, this is precisely why you must resist attachment."

Oh, he doesn't know her at all, Darman thought. *If only he'd—*

Her lightsaber was still ready to slice through the conduit. "As

Jedi we say we revere all life. Are we prepared to *live* that belief? Are these soldiers' lives worth any less than ours because we had them created? Because we can *buy more of them* if these are destroyed?"

"They are *soldiers,* Etain. Soldiers die."

"No, Master, they're men. And they've fought well, and they're *my* responsibility, and I would rather die than live with the knowledge that I abandoned them."

It was so silent that time seemed to have frozen. Zey and Etain were locked in a wordless argument. Then Zey shut his eyes.

"I feel your certainty has its roots in the Force," he said. There was a sigh in his voice. "What's your name—*Darman*? So you have names, do you? Darman, go where she directs you. She values your lives more than she values becoming a Jedi Knight."

Etain made as if to follow him. "You stay, ma'am. Please."

"No," she said. "I won't leave you, *any* of you." She was holding her lightsaber as if she were part of it now, not like something she feared would bite her. "I realize this is gross disobedience, Master Zey, but I really don't think I'm ready to become a Jedi Knight yet."

"You're completely right," Zey said calmly. "And we do need these men."

Darman followed her, looking back for a second at the general.

He looked as if he was smiling. Darman could have sworn he seemed almost proud.

Ghez Hokan had expended almost every round he had. He was down to his vibroblade, the lightsaber, and the last two projectiles in his Verpine now. He pressed his glove hard into his thigh and checked again to see if the wound was weeping fluid.

He couldn't feel any pain. His glove came away wet: the blaster burn had gone deep through skin, nerves, and fat, cauterizing blood vessels but exposing raw tissue that wept plasma.

He wondered what kind of injury was making the commando scream like that, a high-pitched, incoherent, sobbing scream that trailed off and then started up again.

Hokan couldn't see the man's comrade. He knew he had one because he had been hit from two separate positions. Maybe the other was dead. He listened a little longer. He'd heard many men die. Whatever their species, whatever their age, they almost always screamed for their mothers.

Clone soldiers didn't have mothers as far as he knew. So this one was screaming for his sergeant. The sergeant was called Kal or something like it. It was hard to tell.

For some reason that made it unbearable. For once, Hokan could not despise weakness. Whatever he thought of the Republic and the loathsome, sanctimonious Jedi, this was a Mandalorian warrior out there, used and discarded.

He would finish him. It was the decent thing to do. A wounded man could also return fire, so he wasn't going soft, not at all. He was simply ending the battle.

Hokan knelt and looked around. It was clear. Even so, he struggled to crawl with his head down toward the direction of the screams.

They were quieter now, a series of gulping sobs.

"Sarge . . . don't leave me . . . Sargeant Kal! *Sarge!* Uhhh it hurts it hurts it hurts . . ."

How dare the Republic use Jango Fett to create this abomination. How had Fett let this happen? Hokan edged closer. He could see a body in the grass now. He could see light-colored, dirt-caked metallic armor very similar in design to his own, but bulkier and more complex.

And now he was close enough to see the face with the mouth wide open. The man had his arms folded tight across his chest. He was sobbing.

It was Jango Fett, many years before.

Hokan drew himself up on his knees and knelt a couple of meters from the wounded commando, absolutely astonished.

"I'm sorry, my brother," he said. The lightsaber would have been fast, but it was a disgrace to use a Jedi weapon to kill a Mandalorian man. It was too much like reenacting Jango's fate at Geonosis. Hokan drew his vibroblade instead. "It's not your fault. They made you like this."

The commando opened his eyes and focused at a point just past him, as Hokan had seen many dying men do. They all seemed to see ghosts at the final moment.

It was only then that Hokan heard the sound of a lightsaber. And it was too late.

"You cut that fine," Niner said.

It was the only time Darman had ever seen him look shocked. He wiped his face with the palm of his glove.

"And where were you, Fi? Thanks a bunch. I could have been filleted. You were suppose to slot him."

Fi searched through the decapitated Hokan's jacket. "Ah, I could see Dar and Commander Etain behind him. I knew you were probably okay." He paused, and the rifling grew more vigorous. "Here you go, ma'am. I think you ought to have this." Fi handed a short cylinder back to Etain. It was Master Kast Fulier's lightsaber. It was a matter of honor to return it. "They do work well against Mandalorian armor, don't they?"

Etain didn't seem remotely triumphant. She took the hilt and turned it over in her hand before placing it in her pocket. Darman wondered how long it would be before she sheathed her own lightsaber. She was still clutching it in one hand, its blue blade humming and shimmering as she trembled. She wasn't focusing. Darman willed Fi not to make the obvious comment that killing someone with a lightsaber was nice and clean, no guts, no mess. For once he kept his gallows humor to himself, and simply walked a few paces away to recover the genuine Mandalorian helmet he had decided to appropriate.

"You want to put that away now, ma'am?" Darman said gently. "We're done here."

Niner got to his feet and saluted her in best formal parade fashion. "Thank you, Commander. You don't mind me calling you that now, do you?"

She seemed to come back to the here and now. The shaft of blue light vanished.

"It's an honor," she said.

Darman called back on the comlink: General Zcy had kept his word. The gunship was still waiting. They set off in column, picking up speed until they broke into a trot.

The gunship was surrounded by a skirt of billowing dust. Its drive had been idling so long that the heat of the downdraft had dried the top layer of soil.

Etain didn't care if the ship had taken off. She hadn't abandoned her squad. Nothing else mattered after that. And although she knew it had been a deliberate decoy, the sound of Niner screaming would haunt her forever. He must have heard that for real at least once in his life to have mimicked it so horribly well. She felt sick, and it was not because she had killed Ghez Hokan, and that filled her with shame.

She understood fully now why attachment was forbidden to Jedi.

The ARC trooper was pacing a slow, regular square, hands clasped behind his back, head down, and Etain would no longer make the assumption that he was lost in thought. He was probably listening to comm traffic in the private world of his helmet.

General Zey was sitting patiently on the ship's platform. "Are you ready now?"

She held out Master Fulier's lightsaber to him. "Omega Squad recovered it. I felt I should return it to you."

"I know what you're going through, Padawan."

"But that's no comfort, Master."

"A concern for those under your command is essential. But it carries its own pain if you identify too much with your troops." Yes, it did sound as if Zey had known that dilemma. "There are always casualties in war."

"I know. But I also know them now as individuals, and I can't change that. No clone trooper, no commando, not even an ARC trooper will ever be an anonymous unit to me now. I'll always wonder who's behind that visor. How can I be a true Jedi and *not* respect them as beings, with all that entails?"

Zey was studying his hands a little too carefully. "Every good commander in history has had to face that. And so will you."

"If I'm a commander, then may I accompany them on their next mission?"

"I suspect that would not be for the best."

"And what do *I* do now? How can I go back to everyday duties after this?"

"There *are* no everyday duties now we're at war. I will not be leaving. I have come to do what work I can here."

"Work?"

"What will happen to our allies—the Gurlanins—if we abandon them now, with enemy forces in the area? I'm here to operate with them, and try and make Qiilura as inhospitable to Separatists as we can."

"I'm glad we're honoring our commitment, Master."

"You know this land better than anyone now. You would be a valuable asset here."

"And when will more troops join you?"

"I'm afraid we'll have to continue the covert work for the time being. We would need to *disappear.*"

We. Etain could think of nothing worse than staying on Qiilura, with its terrible memories and uncertain future. The nearest she had to friends was a squad of commandos who would be deployed on another mission within days. She would be working with a Master she didn't know. She was alone again and scared.

"Etain, you have duties," Zey said quietly. "We all have. We talk about duty when it's easy, but living it is hard." And he didn't need to add what she knew he was thinking—that she needed to be separated from the object of her recent and desperate wartime attachment. She needed to let her squad go.

It was no different from what was asked of soldiers every day.

"I—I would like to play a useful role in the future of Qiilura, Master." She hoped Darman wouldn't think she was turning her back on him and that he was after all just a glorified droid to her, an asset to be used in battle and expended if necessary. "But I would still find it a comfort one day to know how Omega Squad is faring."

"I understand," Zey said. "The choice is yours, though. You can go with Omega Squad. Or you can stay. You might even request that one of the squad remain here."

One of the squad. Maybe he thought she was just a girl who'd become too attached to a young man when neither of them would ever be able to take the relationship farther. He was testing her, challenging her to make the choice a proper Jedi Knight should make. Yes, she had become close to Darman: he'd been the making of her. But she cared at an inexplicably fundamental level about all of them.

"I don't think caring about your troops is a weakness," she said. "The day we stop caring is the day we turn our back on the Force."

She dug her nails into her palms. Zey was right, though. And it was going to hurt. She sat on the platform beside Zey in silence, eyes closed, composing herself.

The ARC trooper suddenly jerked his head up. "General, sir, we absolutely *must* go now."

"General Zey," Niner said, and touched his glove to his temple. "Sorry we kept you. Are we ready to lift?"

"We don't have time for a mission debriefing, but perhaps you'd like a moment with your commander," Zey said, and beckoned the ARC trooper to follow him. It was a gracious gesture. Etain watched him walk to the rear of the ship to offer her some privacy, apparently supervising the offloading of equipment. She wondered if they had managed to land Zey's starfighter somewhere.

She'd worry about that later. She beckoned the commandos to her.

"What's going to happen to you now?" she said.

"Next mission. Have they assigned us to you?"

She wondered whether a lie might be in order. She looked at Darman. "Not exactly," she said. "I'm staying here with General Zey."

Darman and Niner both averted their eyes, looking at the ground, nodding as if in agreement. Fi raised his eyebrows. "I'm really going to miss you, Commander. Just when we were shaping up. Typical of the army, eh?" He rapped his knuckles on Niner's back plate, pushing him a fraction toward the gunship. "Make a move, then, Sarge."

"Hope to serve with you again, Commander," Niner said, and saluted her. "And don't ever think you didn't earn that rank, will you?"

Etain wished they hadn't left her alone with Darman. She wanted a quick exit with no time to think and make a stupid, emotional comment.

"I chose to stay," she said. "I really would have liked to have stayed part of the team, but I'm not the officer you need."

Darman said nothing. Of course: how could he ever have learned how to take his leave of a friend? All his brief life had been spent among his own kind, immersed in warfare real or virtual. This was where he became a ten-year-old child again. His embarrassment and confusion were palpable.

"You could remain here with me and General Zey," she said. *And I'd know you were safe.* "You have that choice."

He really was a child now. His eyes were fixed on the ground. He was flicking one of the switches on his rifle, back and forth, over and over.

"Just me, ma'am?"

She felt she was testing him now. "Yes."

The gunship's drive rose in frequency, a high whine: the pilot was more than impatient to leave.

"I'm sorry, Commander," Darman said at last. For a moment, he really did seem to be considering it seriously. "I have a job to do."

"I can't pretend I won't miss you," she said.

Darman's gaze didn't flicker. "I've got about ten years left. But I'll be with my brothers, doing what I do best. It's all I've ever known—like going home, really." He bent his head and snapped on his helmet, becoming one of the faceless again. "You take care, Commander."

"And you," she said, and watched him run to the platform and grasp Fi's outstretched arm to be hauled inboard.

The drive roared into higher gear, and the gunship shook slightly.

Etain turned and walked away in a crouch to steady herself against the downdraft. She speeded up into a hunched run until she found a tree and sat down in the lee of it with her back to its trunk.

And she let the tears run down her face.

All that she was, and all that she would be in the future, was because a clone soldier had put such undeserved faith in her that she had become that Jedi he imagined she was. She could now harness the Force in a way she had never been able to at Fulier's side.

She thought of that look of complete faith. She thought of his stoic acceptance of his duty and of the fact that his life would be brief and bright, whatever happened. He had never known a moment of self-pity. She had learned the most important lesson of all from him.

She wiped her eyes with the heel of her hand and hoped Zey wasn't watching.

Etain didn't know if she would ever see Darman or Omega Squad again. She did know, though, that in days to come, every clone trooper or commando or ARC that she might have to order into battle would be neither anonymous, nor meaningless, nor expendable. Under that grim helmet was a man, someone just like her, a human being, but one without the freedom or the life span afforded to her.

Etain Tur-Mukan stood up and walked back into the clearing at the edge of the field to watch the gunship lift into the early-morning sky.

STAR WARS®

REPUBLIC COMMANDO

TRIPLE ZERO

For the ship's company of HMS *Dunedin,* including my uncle Albert Edward Traviss, who died in the sinking of the cruiser on November 24, 1941—a seventeen-year-old boy unable to join the Royal Navy because of poor eyesight, but who insisted on serving as a warship's NAAFI assistant instead, and so gave his life for his country before it had hardly begun.

ACKNOWLEDGMENTS

I've been blessed with the best help any writer could wish for. My grateful thanks go to the editors who know no fear—Keith Clayton (Del Rey), Shelly Shapiro (Del Rey), and Sue Rostoni (Lucasfilm); my agent Russ Galen; the Lucas-Arts *Republic Commando* game team; Bryan Boult, Simon Boult, Debbie Button, Karen Miller, and Chris "TK" Evans—insightful first readers; and Ray Ramirez (Co A 2BN 108th Infantry snipers, ARNG) for technical advice and generous friendship.

And without the following, there would be no book: Jesse Harlin—inspirational composer and lyricist of the *Vode An* theme, which focused me as surely as it did the clone army; Ryan "ER" Kaufman—my professor in GFFA Studies, mentor and friend; the many *Star Wars* fans who've made this the most enjoyable job I've ever had; and the 501st Legion, Vader's Fist—my boys!

It's been a privilege. Thank you.

DRAMATIS PERSONAE

Sergeant KAL SKIRATA, mercenary (male Mandalorian)
Sergeant WALON VAU, mercenary (male Mandalorian)
Null ARC Trooper Captain N-11 ORDO
Null ARC Trooper Lieutenant N-7 MEREEL
Republic Commandos:
  Omega Squad:
    RC-1309 NINER
    RC-1136 DARMAN
    RC-8015 FI
    RC-3222 ATIN
  Delta Squad:
    RC-1138 BOSS
    RC-1162 SCORCH
    RC-1140 FIXER
    RC-1107 SEV
Clone Trooper CT-5108/8843 CORR
General BARDAN JUSIK, Jedi Knight (male human)
Captain JALLER OBRIM, Senate Guard, seconded to Coruscant Security Force Anti-Terrorism Unit (male human)
General ETAIN TUR-MUKAN, Jedi Knight (female human)
General ARLIGAN ZEY, Jedi Master (male human)
ENACCA, associate of Skirata (female Wookiee)
QIBBU, entrepreneur (male Hutt)
LASEEMA, employee of Qibbu (female Twi'lek)
BESANY WENNEN, a GAR logistics employee (female human)

PROLOGUE

Republic Commando covert insertion on Fest, Atrivis sector,
Outer Rim, ten months after Geonosis

Private journal of RC-8015, "Fi"

You have to see the funny side of things in the army. I think they have a real sense of humor in Defense Procurement, too.

"So," I ask. "How long ago did you put in a request for *black* stealth armor?"

"Seven standard months," says Darman, staring out the gunship's crew bay onto an unbroken plain of snow. *White* snow. The freezing wind is whipping flurries of it into the open bay. "When we got back from Qiilura."

"And *now* they issue it to us? To do a raid on *Fest*? The whole planet's covered in snow from pole to pole."

I can hear the gunship pilot laughing over the comlink circuit. He can't resist it. "Want to borrow *my* armor? It's nice and white."

Yes, they've deployed us in black Katarn armor. It'll take a direct hit from laser cannon to put a dent in us, but it would be nice to have the comfort of camouflage when we hit the ground.

Even Atin's laughing. But Niner, who tries to take the place of Sergeant Kal and reassure us it's all going to be okay, is *not.* He's worried that we've run out of luck for this mission.

And so am I. Republic Commando losses in the first year of the war are running at 50 percent. Today we have to infiltrate a Separatist factory developing some new supermetal called phrik—whatever that is—and carry out a little asset denial, known in the trade as blowing stuff up. It's not a complicated mission: avoid droids, get in, lay charges in the processing plant and the foundry, avoid droids, get out. And then press the detonator.

One of Captain Ordo's Null ARC trooper brothers found this place: Clone Intelligence Units, they call them. I must write to thank the *di'kut* sometime.

So I try to keep the squad laughing, because it takes our minds off calculating the odds.

"Okay," I say. "What do we all want most right now?"

"Roba steak," says the pilot.

"White-clad camo," says Niner.

"A really thick slice of uj cake," says Atin.

Darman pauses for a moment. "To see an old friend again."

Me? I'd like to go back to Arca Company Barracks on Coruscant. I want to see Coruscant before I die, and so far I've seen next to nothing of the place. Someone promised to buy me a beer there once.

The pilot is skimming a couple of meters above the snow, taking us through a narrow pass to avoid detection. It's all mountains and ravines now. And snow.

"I've got visual on the factory," the pilot says. "And you're not going to like it."

"Why?" Niner asks.

"Because there're an awful lot of battle droids out there."

"Are they made of phrik?"

"I don't think so."

"No problem, then," says Niner. "Let's spoil their entire day."

The gunship slows enough for us to jump clear, and we scramble through knee-deep snow to take up a position in the lee of an outcrop. There's nothing like a quick hello from a Plex rocket launcher to show droids who's boss. No, they're *definitely* not made from phrik.

I reload the Plex and keep turning the droids into shrapnel while Darman and Atin make their way to higher ground to reach the factory.

Yeah, a nice beer on Coruscant, on Triple Zero. Dreams like that keep you going.

1

Find Skirata. He's the only one who can talk these men down. And no, I'm not going to obliterate a whole barracks block just to neutralize six ARCs. So get me Skirata: he can't have traveled very far.

—General Iri Camas, Director of Special Forces, to Coruscant Security Force, from Siege Incident Control, Special Operations Brigade HQ Barracks, Coruscant, five days after the Battle of Geonosis

Tipoca City, Kamino, eight years before Geonosis

Kal Skirata had committed the biggest mistake of his life, and he'd made some pretty big ones in his time.

Kamino was damp. And damp didn't help his shattered ankle onc little bit. No, it was *more* than damp: it was nothing but storm-whipped sea from pole to pole, and he wished that he'd worked that out before he responded to Jango Fett's offer of a lucrative long-term deployment in a location that his old comrade hadn't exactly specified.

But that was the least of his worries now.

The air smelled more like a hospital than a military base. The place didn't look like barracks, either. Skirata leaned on the polished rail that was all that separated him from a forty-meter fall into a chamber large enough to swallow a battle cruiser and lose it.

Above him, the vaulted illuminated ceiling stretched as far as the abyss did below. The prospect of the fall didn't worry him half as much as not understanding what he was now seeing.

The cavern—surgically clean, polished durasteel and permaglass—was filled with structures that seemed almost like fractals. At first glance they looked like giant toroids stacked on pillars; then, as he stared, the toroids resolved into smaller rings of permaglass containers, with containers within them, and inside those—

No, this *wasn't happening.*

Inside the transparent tubes there was fluid, and within it there was *movement.*

It took him several minutes of staring and refocusing on one of the tubes to realize there was a body in there, and it was alive. In fact, there was a body in *every* tube: row upon row of tiny bodies, *children's* bodies. *Babies.*

"Fierfek," he said aloud.

He thought he'd come to this Force-forsaken hole to train commandos. Now he knew he'd stepped into a nightmare. He heard boots behind him on the walkway of the gantry and turned sharply to see Jango coming slowly toward him, chin lowered as if in reproach.

"If you're thinking of leaving, Kal, you knew the deal," said Jango, and leaned on the rail beside him.

"You said—"

"I said you'd be training special forces troops, and you will be. They just happen to be growing them."

"What?"

"Clones."

"How the fierfek did you ever get involved with *that*?"

"A straight five million and a few extras for donating my genes. And don't look shocked. You'd have done the same."

The pieces fell into place for Skirata and he let himself be shocked anyway. War was one thing. Weird science was another issue entirely.

"Well, I'm keeping my end of the deal." Skirata adjusted the fifteen-centimeter, three-sided blade that he always kept sheathed in his jacket sleeve. Two Kaminoan technicians walked serenely across the floor of the facility beneath him. Nobody had searched him and he felt better for having a few weapons located for easy use, including the small hold-out blaster tucked in the cuff of his boot.

And all those little kids in tanks . . .

The Kaminoans disappeared from sight. "What do those things want with an army anyway?"

"*They* don't. And *you* don't need to know all this right now." Jango beckoned him to follow. "Besides, you're already dead, remember?"

"Feels like it," said Skirata. He was the *Cuy'val Dar*—literally, "those who no longer exist," a hundred expert soldiers with a dozen specialties who'd answered Jango's secret summons in exchange for a *lot* of credits . . . as long as they were prepared to disappear from the galaxy *completely.*

He trailed Jango down corridors of unbroken white duraplast, passing the occasional Kaminoan with its long gray neck and snakelike head. He'd been here for four standard days now, staring out the window of his quarters onto the endless ocean and catching an occasional glimpse of the aiwhas soaring up out of the waves and flapping into the air. The thunder was totally silenced by the soundproofing, but the lightning had become an annoyingly irregular pulse in the corner of his eye.

Skirata knew from day one that he wouldn't like Kaminoans.

Their cold yellow eyes troubled him, and he didn't care for their arrogance, either. They stared at his limping gait and asked if he minded being *defective.*

The window-lined corridor seemed to run the length of the city. Outside, it was hard to see where the horizon ended and the rain clouds began.

Jango looked back to see if he was keeping up. "Don't worry, Kal. I'm told it's clear weather in the summer—for a few days."

Right. The dreariest planet in the galaxy, and he was stuck on it. And his ankle was playing up. He really should have invested in getting it fixed surgically. When—if—he got out of here, he'd have the assets to get the best surgeon that credits could buy.

Jango slowed down tactfully. "So, Ilippi threw you out?"

"Yeah." His wife wasn't Mandalorian. He'd hoped she would embrace the culture, but she didn't: she always hated seeing her old man go off to someone else's war. The fights began when he wanted to take their two sons into battle with him. They were eight years old, old enough to start learning their trade; but she refused, and soon Ilippi and the boys and his daughter were no longer waiting when he returned from the latest war. Ilippi divorced him the *Mando* way, same as they'd married, on a brief, solemn, private vow. A contract was a contract, written or not. "Just as well I've got another assignment to occupy me."

"You should have married a *Mando* girl. *Aruetiise* don't understand a mercenary's life." Jango paused as if waiting for argument, but Kal wasn't giving him one. "Don't your *sons* talk to you any longer?"

"Not often." *So I failed as a father. Don't rub it in.* "Obviously they don't share the *Mando* outlook on life any more than their mother does."

"Well, they won't be speaking to you at all now. Not here. Ever."

Nobody seemed to care if he had disappeared anyway. Yes, he *was* as good as dead. Jango said nothing more, and they walked in silence until they reached a large circular lobby with rooms leading off it like the spokes of a wheel.

"Ko Sai said something wasn't quite right with the first test batch of clones," said Jango, ushering Skirata ahead of him into another room. "They've tested them and they don't think these are going to make the grade. I told Orun Wa that we'd give him the benefit of our military experience and take a look."

Skirata was used to evaluating fighting men—and women, come to that. He knew what it took to make a soldier. He was good at it; soldiering was his life, as it was for all *Mando'ade,* all sons and daughters of Mandalore. At least there'd be some familiarity to cling to in this ocean wilderness.

It was just a matter of staying as far from the Kaminoans as he could.

"Gentlemen," said Orun Wa in his soothing monotone. He welcomed them into his office with a graceful tilt of the head, and Skirata noted that he had a prominent bony fin running across the top of his skull from front to back. Maybe that meant Orun Wa was older, or dominant, or something: he didn't look like the other examples of aiwha-bait that Skirata had seen so far. "I always believe in being honest about setbacks in a program. We value the Jedi Council as a customer."

"I have *nothing* to do with the Jedi," said Jango. "I'm only a consultant on military matters."

Oh, Skirata thought. *Jedi. Great.*

"I would still be happier if you confirmed that the first batch of units is below the acceptable standard."

"Bring them in, then."

Skirata shoved his hands in his jacket pockets and wondered what he was going to see: poor marksmanship, poor endurance, lack of aggression? Not if these were Jango's clones. He was curious to see how the Kaminoans could have fouled up producing fighting men based on *that* template.

The storm raged against the transparisteel window, rain pounding in surges and then easing again. Orun Wa stood back with a graceful sweep of his arms like a dancer. And the doors opened.

Six identical little boys—four, maybe five years old—walked into the room.

Skirata was not a man who easily fell prey to sentimentality. But this did the job just fine.

They were *children:* not soldiers, not droids, and not units. *Just little kids.* They had curly black hair and were all dressed in identical dark blue tunics and pants. He was expecting grown men. And that would have been bad enough.

He heard Jango inhale sharply.

The boys huddled together, and it ripped at Skirata's heart in a way he wasn't expecting. Two of the kids clutched each other, looking up at him with huge, dark, unblinking eyes: another moved slowly to the front of the tight pack as if barring Orun Wa's path and shielding the others.

Oh, he *was.* He was defending his brothers. Skirata was devastated.

"These units are defective, and I admit that we perhaps made an error in attempting to *enhance* the genetic template," Orun Wa said, utterly unmoved by their vulnerability.

Skirata had worked out fast that Kaminoans despised everything that didn't fit their intolerant, arrogant society's ideal of perfection. So . . . they thought Jango's genome wasn't the perfect model for a soldier without a little adjustment, then. Maybe it was his solitary nature; he'd make a rotten infantry soldier. Jango wasn't a team player.

And maybe they didn't know that it was often imperfection that gave humans an edge.

The kids' gaze darted between Skirata and Jango, and the doorway, and all around the room, as if they were checking for an escape or appealing for help.

"Chief Scientist Ko Sai apologizes, as do I," said Orun Wa. "Six units did not survive incubation, but these developed normally and appeared to meet specifications, so they have undergone some flash-instruction and trials. Unfortunately, psychological testing indicates that they are simply too unreliable and fail to meet the personality profile required."

"Which is?" said Jango.

"That they can carry out orders." Orun Wa blinked rapidly: he seemed embarrassed by error. "I can assure you that we *will* address these problems in the current Alpha production run. These units will be reconditioned, of course. Is there anything you wish to ask?"

"Yeah," said Skirata. "What do you mean by *reconditioned*?"

"In this case, *terminated.*"

There was a long silence in the bland, peaceful, white-walled room. Evil was supposed to be black, jet black; and it wasn't supposed to be soft-spoken. Then Skirata registered *terminated* and his instinct reacted before his brain.

His clenched fist was pressed against Orun Wa's chest in a second and the vile unfeeling thing jerked his head backward.

"You touch one of those kids, you gray freak, and I'll skin you alive and feed you to the aiwhas—"

"Steady," Jango said. He grabbed Skirata's arm.

Orun Wa stood blinking at Skirata with those awful reptilian yellow eyes. "This is uncalled for. We care only about our customers' satisfaction."

Skirata could hear his pulse pounding in his head and all *he* could care about was ripping Orun Wa apart. Killing someone in combat was one thing, but there was no honor in destroying unarmed kids. He yanked his arm out of Jango's grip and stepped back in front of the children. They were utterly silent. He dared not look at them. He fixed on Orun Wa.

Jango gripped his shoulder and squeezed hard enough to hurt. *Don't. Leave this to me.* It was his warning gesture. But Skirata was too angry and disgusted to fear Jango's wrath.

"We could do with a few wild cards," Jango said carefully, moving between Skirata and the Kaminoan. "It's good to have some surprises up your sleeve for the enemy. What are these kids really like? And how old are they?"

"Nearly two standard years' growth. Highly intelligent, deviant, disturbed—and uncommandable."

"Could be ideal for intel work." It was pure bluff: Skirata could see the little twitch of muscle in Jango's jaw. He was shocked, too. The bounty hunter couldn't hide *that* from his old associate. "I say we keep 'em."

Two? The boys looked older. Skirata half turned to check on them, and their gazes were locked on him: it was almost an accusation. He glanced away, but took a step backward and put his hand discreetly behind him to place his palm on the head of the boy defending his brothers, just as a helpless gesture of comfort.

But a small hand closed tightly around his fingers instead.

Skirata swallowed hard. *Two years old.*

"I can train them," he said. "What are their names?"

"These units are *numbered.* And I must emphasize that they're unresponsive to command." Orun Wa persisted as if talking to a particularly stupid Weequay. "Our quality control designated them Null class and wishes to start—"

"*Null*? As in no *di'kutla* use?"

Jango took a discreet but audible breath. "Leave this to me, Kal."

"No, they're not *units.*" The little hand was grasping his for dear life. He reached back with his other hand and another boy pressed up against his leg, clinging to him. It was pitiful. "And *I can train them.*"

"Unwise," said Orun Wa.

The Kaminoan took a gliding step forward. They were such graceful creatures, but they were loathsome at a level that Skirata could simply not comprehend.

And then the little lad grasping his leg suddenly snatched the hold-out blaster from Skirata's boot. Before he could react the kid had tossed it to the one who'd been clinging to his hand in apparent terror.

The boy caught it cleanly and aimed it two-handed at Orun Wa's chest.

"Fierfek." Jango sighed. "Put it down, kid."

But the lad wasn't about to stand down. He stood right in front of Skirata, utterly calm, blaster raised at the perfect angle, fingers placed just so with the left hand steadying the right, totally focused. And *deadly* serious.

Skirata felt his jaw drop a good centimeter. Jango froze, then chuckled.

"I reckon that proves my point," he said, but he still had his eyes fixed on the tiny assassin.

The kid clicked the safety catch. He seemed to be checking it was *off.*

"It's okay, son," Skirata said, as gently as he could. He didn't much care if the boy fried the Kaminoan, but he cared about the consequences for the kid. And he was instantly and totally *proud* of him—of all of them. "You don't need to shoot. I'm not going to let him touch *any* of you. Just give me back the blaster."

The child didn't budge; the blaster didn't waver. He should have been more concerned about cuddly toys than a clean shot at this stage in his young life. Skirata squatted down slowly behind him, trying not to spook him into firing.

But if the boy had his back to him . . . then he *trusted* him, didn't he?

"Come on . . . just put it down, there's a good lad. Now give me the blaster." He kept his voice as soft and level as he could, when he was actually torn between cheering and doing the job himself. "You're safe, I *promise* you."

The boy paused, eyes and aim still both fixed on Orun Wa. "Yes sir." Then he lowered the weapon to his side. Skirata put his hand on the boy's shoulder and pulled him back carefully.

"Good lad." Skirata took the blaster from his little fingers and scooped him up in his arms. He dropped his voice to a whisper. "Nicely done, too."

The Kaminoan showed no anger whatsoever, simply blinking, yellow, detached disappointment. "If that does not demonstrate their instability, then—"

"They're coming with me."

"This is not your decision."

"No, it's mine," Jango interrupted. "And they've got the right stuff. Kal, get them out of here and I'll settle this with Orun Wa."

Skirata limped toward the door, still making sure he was between the Kaminoan and the kids. He was halfway down the corridor with his bizarre escort of tiny deviants before the boy he was carrying wriggled uncomfortably in his arms.

"I can walk, sir," he said.

He was perfectly articulate, fluent—a little soldier way beyond his years.

"Okay, son."

Skirata lowered him to the floor and the kids fell in behind him, oddly quiet and disciplined. They didn't strike him as dangerous or deviant, unless you counted stealing a weapon, pulling a feint, and almost shooting a Kaminoan as deviant. Skirata didn't.

The kids were just trying to survive, like any soldier had a duty to do.

And they looked four or five years old, but Orun Wa had definitely said they were two. Skirata suddenly wanted to ask them how long they'd spent in those awful suffocating transparisteel vats, cold hard tanks that were nothing like the dark comfort of a womb. It must have been like drowning. Could they see each other as they floated? Had they understood what was happening to them?

Skirata reached the doors of his stark quarters and ushered them in, trying not to dwell on those thoughts.

The boys lined up against the wall automatically, hands clasped behind their backs, and waited without being told to.

I brought up two sons. How hard can it be to mind six kids for a few days?

Skirata waited for them to react but they simply stared back at him as if expecting orders. He had none. Rain lashed the window that ran the whole width of the wall. Lightning flared. They all flinched.

But they still stood in silence.

"Tell you what," Skirata said, bewildered. He pointed to the couch. "You sit down over there and I'll get you something to eat. Okay?"

They paused and then scrambled onto the couch, huddling together again. He found them so utterly disarming that he had to make a rapid exit to the kitchen area to gather his thoughts while he slapped uj cake onto a plate and sliced it roughly into six pieces. If this was how it was going to be for—for *years* . . .

You're stuck, chum.

You took the credits.

And this is your whole world for the foreseeable future . . . and maybe forever.

It never stopped raining. And he was holed up with a species he loathed on sight, and who thought it was okay to dispose of units who happened to be living, talking, walking children. He raked his fingers through his hair and despaired, eyes closed, until he was suddenly aware of someone staring up at him.

"Sir?" the boy said. It was the courageous little marksman. He might have been identical to his brothers, but his mannerisms were distinctive. He had a habit of balling one fist at his side while the other hand was relaxed. "May we use the 'freshers?"

Skirata squatted down, face level with the kid's. " 'Course you can." It was quite pathetic: they were nothing like his own lively, boisterous sons had once been. "And I'm not *sir.* I'm not an officer. I'm a sergeant. You can call me *Sergeant* if you like, or you can call me *Kal.* Everyone else does."

"Yes . . . Kal."

"It's over there. Can you manage on your own?"

"Yes, Kal."

"I know you don't have a name, but I really think you *should* have one."

"I'm Null Eleven. En-one-one."

"How'd you like to be called Ordo? He was a Mandalorian warrior."

"Are we Mandalorian warriors?"

"You bet." The kid was a natural fighter. "In every sense of the word."

"I like that name." Little Ordo considered the white-tiled floor for a moment, as if assessing it for risk. "What's Mandalorian?"

For some reason that hurt most of all. If these kids didn't know their culture and what made someone a *Mando,* then they had no purpose, no pride, and nothing to hold them and their clan together when home wasn't a piece of land. If you were a nomad, your nation traveled in your heart. And without the *Mando* heart, you had nothing—not even your soul—in whatever new conquest followed death. Skirata knew at that moment what he had to do. He had to stop these boys from being *dar'manda,* eternal Dead Men, men without a *Mando* soul.

"I can see I need to teach you *a lot.*" Yes, this was his duty. "I'm Mandalorian, too. We're soldiers, nomads. You know what those words mean?"

"Yes."

"Clever lad. Okay, you go and sort yourselves out in the 'freshers, and I want you all sitting back on the couch in ten minutes. Then we'll sort out names for everyone. Got it?"

"Yes, Kal."

So Kal Skirata—mercenary, assassin, and failed father—spent a stormy evening on Kamino sharing uj cake with six dangerously clever small boys who could already handle firearms and talk like adults, teaching them that they came from a warrior tradition, and that they had a language and a culture, and much to be proud of.

And he explained that there was no Mandalorian word for "hero." It was only *not* being one that had its own word: *Hut'uun.*

There were an awful lot of *hut'uune* in the galaxy, and Skirata certainly counted the Kaminoans among them.

The kids—now trying to get used to being Ordo, A'den, Kom'rk, Prudii, Mereel, and Jaing—sat devouring both their newfound heritage and the sticky sweet cake, eyes fixed on Skirata as he recited lists of Mandalorian words and they repeated them back to him.

He worked through the most common words, struggling. He had no idea how to teach a language to kids who could already speak fluent Basic. So he simply listed everything he could recall that seemed useful, and the little Null ARCs listened, grim-faced, flinching in unison at every blaze of lightning. After an hour Skirata felt that he was simply confusing some very frightened, very lonely children. They just *stared* at him.

"Okay, time to recap," he said, exhausted by a bad day and the realization that there was an unknowable number of days like this stretching ahead. He pinched the bridge of his nose in an effort to focus. "Can you count from one to ten for me?"

Prudii—N-5—parted his lips to take a quick breath and suddenly all six spoke at once.

"Solus, t'ad, ehn, cuir, rayshe'a, resol, e'tad, sh'ehn, she'cu, ta'raysh."

Skirata's gut flipped briefly and he sat stunned. These kids absorbed information like a sponge. *I only counted out the numbers for them once. Just once!* Their recall was perfect and absolute. He decided to be careful what he said to them in the future.

"Now that's *clever,*" he said. "You're very special lads, aren't you?"

"Orun Wa said we couldn't be measured," Mereel said, totally without pride, and perched on the edge of the couch, swinging his legs almost like a normal four-year-old. They might have all looked identical, but their individual characters seemed distinct and . . . obvious. Skirata wasn't sure how he managed it, but he could now look at them and see that they were *different,* distinguished by small variations in facial expressions, gestures, frowns, and even tone of voice. Appearance wasn't everything.

"You mean you scored too high for him to count?"

Mereel nodded gravely. Thunder slapped the platform city: Skirata felt it without hearing it. Mereel drew up his legs again and huddled tight up against his brothers in an instant.

No, Skirata didn't need a *hut'uunla* Kaminoan to tell him that these were extraordinary children. They could already handle a blaster, learn everything he threw at them, and understand the Kaminoans' intentions all too well: no wonder the aiwha-bait was scared of them.

And they would be truly phenomenal soldiers—if only they could follow a few orders. He'd work on that.

"Want some more uj?" he said.

They all nodded enthusiastically in unison. It was a relief. At least that gave him a few minutes' respite from their unrelenting, silent attention. They ate, still miniature adults. There was no chattering or high spirits.

And they flinched at every bolt of lightning.

"Are you scared?" asked Skirata.

"Yes, Kal," said Ordo. "Is that wrong?"

"No, son. Not at all." It was as good a time to teach them as any. No lesson would *ever* be wasted on them. "Being afraid is okay. It's your body's way of getting you ready to defend yourself, and all you have to do is use it and not let it use you. Do you understand that?"

"No," Ordo said.

"Okay, think about being scared. What's it like?"

Ordo defocused slightly as if he were looking at something on a HUD he didn't have. "Cold."

"Cold?"

A'den and Kom'rk chimed in. "And spiky."

"Okay . . . okay." Skirata tried to imagine what they meant. *Ah.* They were describing the feeling of adrenaline flooding their bodies. "That's fine. You just have to remember that it's your alarm system, and you need to take notice of it." They were the same age as city kids on Coruscant who struggled to scrawl crude letters on flimsi. And here he was, teaching them battle psychology. His mouth felt oddly dry. "So you tell yourself, okay, I can handle this. My body's now ready to run faster and fight harder, and I'll be seeing and hearing only the most important things I need to know to *stay alive.*"

Ordo went from his wide-eyed dark stare to slight defocus again for a moment and nodded. Skirata glanced at the others. They had that same disturbing concentration. They had also stacked their plates neatly on the low side table. He hadn't even noticed them doing it.

"Try thinking about your fear next time there's lightning," Kal said. "Use it."

He went back to the kitchen area and rummaged through the cupboards for some other snack to keep them going, because they seemed ravenous. As he stepped back into the main room with a white tray of sliced food-board that looked even less appetizing than the tray itself, someone buzzed at the door.

The Nulls immediately went into a defensive pattern. Ordo and Jaing flanked the door, backs hard against the wall, and the other four took cover behind the sparse furniture. Skirata wondered for a second what flash-learning program had taught them that—or at least he *hoped* it was flash-taught. He waved them away from the door. They hesitated for a moment until he took out his Verpine shatter gun; then they appeared satisfied that he had the situation under some sort of control.

"You scare me," Skirata said softly. "Now stand back. If anyone's after you, they've got to come through *me* first, and I'm not about to let that happen."

Even so, their reaction prompted him to stand to one side as he hit thc panel to open the doors. Jango Fett was standing in the corridor outside, a small sleepy child in his arms. The boy's curly head rested on his shoulder. He looked younger than the Nulls, but it was the same face, the same hair, the same little hand clutching the fabric of Jango's tunic.

"Another one?" Skirata said.

Jango glanced at the Verp. "You're getting edgy, aren't you?"

"Kaminoans don't improve my mood. Want me to take him?"

He shoved the shatter gun in his belt and held out his arms to take the boy. Jango frowned slightly.

"This is my *son,* Boba," he said. He pulled his head back to gaze fondly at the dozing child's face. This wasn't the Jango that Skirata knew of old; he was pure paternal indulgence now. "Just trying to settle him down. Are you sorted now? I've told Orun Wa to stay away from you."

"We're fine," Skirata said. He wondered how he was going to ask the question, and decided blurting it out was probably as good a way as any. "Boba looks just like them."

"He would. He's been cloned from me, too."

"Oh. *Oh.*"

"He was my price. Worth more to me than the credits." Boba stirred, and Jango carefully adjusted his hold on the kid. "I'll be back in a month. Orun Wa says he'll have some commando candidates ready for us to take a look at as well as the rest of the Alpha batch. But he says he's made them a bit more . . . reliable."

Skirata had more questions than seemed prudent under the circumstances. It was natural for a *Mando'ad* to want an heir above all else, and adoption was common, so cloning was . . . not *that* much different. But he had to ask one thing.

"Why do these kids look older?"

Jango compressed his lips into a thin line of disapproval. "They accelerate the aging process."

"Oh, fierfek . . ."

"You'll have a company of a hundred and four commandos eventually, and they should be less trouble than the Nulls."

"Fine." Did he get help? Were there Kaminoan minders to tackle the routine jobs, like feeding them? And how would the non-Mandalorian training sergeants deal with them? His stomach churned. He put on a brave face. "I can handle that."

"Yeah, and I'll be doing my bit, too. I have to train a hundred." Jango glanced at the Nulls, now watching warily from the couch, and began walking away. "I just hope they aren't like *I* was at that age."

Skirata pushed the controls, and the door sighed shut. "Okay, lads, bedtime," he said. He dragged the cushions off the couch and laid them out on the floor, covering them with an assortment of blankets. The boys gave him a hand, with a grim sense of adult purpose that he knew would haunt him for the rest of his days. "We'll get you sorted out with decent quarters tomorrow, okay? Real beds."

He had the feeling they would have slept outside on the rain-lashed landing pad if he'd asked them to. They didn't seem at all unmanageable. He sat down in the chair and put his feet up on a stool. The Kaminoans had done their best to provide human-suitable furniture, something that struck him as a rare concession given their general xenophobic arrogance. He left the lights on, dimmed, to soothe the Nulls' fears.

They settled down, pulling the blankets over their heads completely. Skirata watched until they appeared to be asleep, laid his Verpine on the shelf beside the chair, and then closed his eyes to let the dreams overwhelm him. He woke with an explosive jerk of muscles a couple of times, a sure sign that he was past the point of tiredness and into exhaustion, and then he fell into an unending black well.

He slept, or so he thought.

A warm weight pressed against him. His eyes jerked open and he remembered he was stranded on a perpetually overcast planet that didn't even seem to be on the star charts, where the local species thought killing human kids was merely quality control.

Ordo's stricken little face looked up into his.

"Kal . . ."

"You scared, son?"

"Yes."

"Come on, then." Skirata shifted position and Ordo scrambled up onto his lap, burying his face in his tunic as if he had never been held or comforted before. He hadn't, of course.

The storm was getting worse. "The lightning can't hurt you here."

"I know, Kal." Ordo's voice was muffled. He wouldn't look up. "But it's just like the bombs going off."

Skirata was going to ask him what he meant, but he knew in an instant that it would make him angry enough to do something stupid if he heard the answer. He hugged Ordo to him and felt the boy's heart pounding in terror.

Ordo was doing pretty well for a four-year-old soldier.

They could learn to be heroes tomorrow. Tonight they needed to be children, reassured that the storm was not a battlefield, and so was nothing to fear.

The lightning illuminated the room in brief, fierce white light: Ordo flinched again. Skirata laid his hand on the boy's head and ruffled his hair.

"It's okay, *Ord'ika,*" he said softly. "I'm here, son. I'm here."

Eight years later: Special Forces SO Brigade HQ Barracks, Coruscant, five days after the Battle of Geonosis

Skirata had been detained by Coruscant Security Force officers and for once in his life he hadn't put up a fight.

Technically, he'd been *arrested.* And now he was the most relieved man in the galaxy, as well as the happiest. He jumped out of the police patrol speeder and winced at the sharp pain in his ankle as he hit the ground. He'd get that sorted out sooner or later, but now wasn't the time.

"Wow, take a look at *that,*" the pilot said. "They're holding off special ops squads there. You sure there's only six of 'em?"

"Yeah, six *is* overkill," Skirata said, discreetly patting his pockets and sleeves to make sure the assorted tools of his trade were in place and ready for use. It was just habit. "But they're probably scared."

"*They're* scared?" The pilot snorted. "Hey, you know Fett's dead? Windu topped him."

"I know," Skirata said, fighting the urge to ask if he also knew what had happened to little Boba. If the kid was still alive, he needed a dad. "Let's hope the Jedi don't have a problem with *all* of us *Mando'ade.*"

The pilot closed the hatch, and Skirata limped across the barracks landing pad. Jedi general Iri Camas, hands on hips with his brown robes flapping in the breeze, watched in a way that Skirata could only describe as *suspicious.* Two clone troopers waited with him. Skirata thought the Jedi should get his long white hair cut: it wasn't practical or becoming for a soldier to wear his hair to his shoulders.

"Thank you for responding, Sergeant," Camas said. "And I apologize for the manner of your return. I realize your contract is completed now, so you owe us nothing."

"Anytime," Skirata said.

He noted the blasterproof assault shields erected across the main entrance: four squads of Republic Commandos stood behind them, DC-17 rifles ready. He glanced up at the roof, and there were two commando sniper teams spread out along the parapet as well. Yes, if a bunch of Null-class Advance Recon Commandos didn't want to cooperate, then it would take a lot of equally hard men to persuade them otherwise. And he knew that none of the commandos would be happy about being ordered in to do the persuading. They were brothers, even if the ARCs were rather different men at heart.

Skirata shoved his hands in his jacket pockets and focused on the doors. "So what started all this, then?"

Camas shook his head. "They're scheduled to be chilled down now that they're back from Geonosis, because nobody can command them."

"I can."

"I know. Please, get them to stand down."

"They're even more of a handful than the regular Alpha-batch ARCs, aren't they?"

"I know that, Sergeant."

"So you wanted the hardest troops you could buy to take on the enemy, and then you got cold feet when they turned out to be *too* hard."

"Sergeant—"

"I'm a civilian at the moment, actually."

Camas took a silent breath. "Can you get them to surrender? They've shut down the whole barracks."

"I *can*." Skirata wondered if the clone troopers were looking sideways at him, or in the direction they appeared to be facing. You could never tell with their helmets on. "But I won't."

"I really don't want any casualties. Are you holding out for an increased fee?"

Skirata was a mercenary, but the suggestion insulted him. Camas couldn't be expected to know how he felt about his men, though. He made an effort not to be annoyed. "Enlist me in the Grand Army of the Republic and give me back my lads. Then we'll see."

"What?"

"They're terrified of chill-down, that's all. You have to understand what happened to them as kids." Camas gave him an odd look. "And don't even *think* about mind influence, General."

Skirata didn't give a mott's backside about pay. Eight years spent on Kamino training special forces for the Republic's clone army had made him wealthy, and if they wanted to press more credits on him, that was fine; he'd have a good use for them. But what he wanted most right then, and what had made him happy to return with the CSF officers instead of showing them just how handy he was with a fighting knife, was *not* being safe in a soft civilian life when his men were fighting a desperate, bloody war.

And he *needed* to be back with them. He hadn't even had the chance to say good-bye when they suddenly shipped out to Geonosis. He'd lasted five miserable days without them, days without purpose, days without *family.*

"Very well," Camas said. "Special adviser status. I can authorize that, I suppose."

Skirata couldn't see the commandos' faces behind their visors, but he knew they'd be watching him carefully. He recognized some of the paint schemes on their Katarn armor: Jez from Aiwha-3 Squad, and Stoker from Gamma, and Ram from Bravo up on the roof. Incomplete squads: high casualties on Geonosis, then. His heart sank.

He began walking forward. He got to the blaster shields, and Jez touched his glove to his helmet. "Nice to see you back so soon, Sarge."

"Couldn't stay away," Skirata said. "You okay?"

"It's a laugh a minute, this job."

Camas called out, "Sergeant? Sergeant! What if they open fire—"

"Then they open fire." Skirata reached the doors and turned his back on them for a few moments, unafraid. "Do we have a deal? Or do you want me holed up in there with them? Because I won't be coming out unless you guarantee them no disciplinary action."

It struck Skirata that Camas might be the one to fire on him right then. He wondered if his commandos would obey that order if it were given. He wouldn't have minded if they had. He'd taught them to do their job, regardless of their own feelings.

"You have my word," Camas said. "Consider yourself in the Grand Army. We'll discuss how we're going to deploy you and your men later. But first let's get everyone back to normal, shall we, please?"

"I'll hold you to every last word, General."

He waited at the doors for a few moments. The two sheets of reinforced durasteel parted slowly. He walked in, relieved, and home again at last.

No, Camas really needed to understand what had happened to these men as young boys. He had to, if he was going to cope with the war that had now been unleashed.

It wouldn't just be fought on someone else's planet. It would be fought in every corner of the galaxy, in every city, in every home. It was a war not just of territories, but of ideologies.

And it was wholly outside Skirata's Mandalorian philosophy: but it was his war regardless, because his men were its instrument whether they liked it or not.

One day, he would give them back something the Kaminoans and the Republic had stolen from them. He swore it.

"Ord'ika!" he called. "Ordo? You've been a naughty boy again, haven't you? Come here . . ."

2

Yes, I know I should be directing the battle from the ship. Yes, I know we could reduce the surface of Dinlo to molten slag from orbit. But we can extract more than a thousand men, and that's worth doing. I asked for volunteers and I got the whole ship's crew and every man in Improcco Company, and not from blind obedience. Let me try.

—General Tur-Mukan, in a signal to General Iri Camas, Battle Group Command, Coruscant, copied to General Vaas Ga, Commanding Officer, Sarlacc Battalions, Forty-first Elite Infantry, Dinlo

Republic assault ship *Fearless,* approaching Dinlo, Expansion–Bothan Border, 367 days after Geonosis

General Etain Tur-Mukan watched the HNE news feed with mixed feelings. On one hand the events at home saddened her: on the other, they reminded her what the war was about.

"Fifteen soldiers and twelve civilian support staff are reported dead after today's second bomb blast, this time at a GAR logistics base. No group has yet claimed responsibility for the attack, but a security forces spokesman said today that the proximity to tomorrow's first anniversary of the Battle of Geonosis was significant. It brings the total number of deaths in apparent Separatist terror attacks this year to three thousand and forty. The Senate has pledged to smash their networks . . ."

Clone Commander Gett stood at her side, hands clasped behind his back as they waited on the repulsor platform that shunted ammo boxes from the magazine to the hangar deck.

"No way to die," he said.

Etain turned to look at the troops around them. "Neither is this."

They were set to go. *Fearless* was half an hour out from Dinlo and the gunship pilots were making their way down the passage from the flight briefing to carry out their presortie checks, yellow-trimmed helmets tucked under one arm. They all held the helmets exactly the same way, no doubt the result of thorough drill. General Etain Tur-Mukan noted that.

She stood back from the hatch to let them through and got a salute from each as he passed. One glanced at the somewhat unconventional weapon slung across her shoulder and grinned. He indicated the huge LJ-50 concussion rifle that almost dwarfed her.

"Does that thing light up blue, General?"

"Only if you're on the receiving end, trooper," she said, and gave him her most reassuring smile.

She knew they were afraid, because a commando called Darman had taught her that only idiots didn't fear combat. Fear was an asset, an incentive, a tool. She knew how to use it now, even if she didn't embrace it.

Today she needed to tell Improcco Company that. They knew it already, but this was her first mission with them, and she had learned that a little openness with the troops went a long way. And she wanted them to know that she saw them for the human beings they were. Meeting Republic commandos on Qiilura for the first time had been a painful revelation for her.

"Are you okay with that, General?" Gett seemed to be able to guess what she was thinking almost all the time, and she wondered briefly if telepathy was in their genetic mix. Then she reminded herself that men who all looked the same learned to be very, very sensitive to tiny behavioral cues. "We've got a DC-15 if you prefer. Nice piece of kit."

The LJ-50 was exhaustingly heavy. She'd developed her arm muscles in the last year, but it still took some handling.

"Some very competent gentlemen taught me to use a conc rifle," she said. "They persuaded me to keep my lightsaber for close-combat. Besides, the LJ's got a four-meter spread at a thirty-meter range. I'm a great believer in efficiency over style."

Gett smiled. He knew the stories about the Qiilura mission. They all did, it seemed. Gossip traveled at light speed in a closed community, and it'd had months to make the rounds. "I understand Omega are okay and on TIOPS in the Outer Rim right now."

"It's kind of you to check for me, Commander." She had to ask. "What's TIOPS?"

"Captain Ordo makes a point of giving your signals priority." He lowered his voice. "Traffic interdiction operations. Boarding the bad guys' vessels."

"Thank you. I've never met Ordo, but he does seem to take care of me very well."

"One of Kal Skirata's Null ARCs."

"Oh, *Kal* again . . ."

"You've never met him, have you?"

"No, but I hope I do. I feel as if he's been walking behind me for a long time." She looked around the hangar and noted there was one platoon still missing. She'd wait. She needed them all to hear this. "I envy his ability to inspire people."

Gett said nothing. Tact, perhaps, or merely nothing to add; Etain feared that she still projected her own doubts onto others. She was a Jedi Knight now. She had passed her trials on Qiilura with Master Arligan Zey, working under deep cover with him to mobilize the colonists against the remnants of the Neimoidian and Trandoshan occupation. It was silent, grim, secret work, and even though a Republic garrison had now been established on the planet, she still felt that the dwindling population of native Gurlanins and the human farmers were set on a collision course. The Republic had promised the Gurlanins that they would remove the human colony from their world.

So far, they hadn't.

It would have been a simple case of broken promises—like many others in the galaxy's history—had the Gurlanins not been a race of shapeshifting predators, working as spies for the Republic. This was their bargain: they would provide their unique espionage skills if the farmers stopped driving away the prey on which Gurlanins depended. As far as the Gurlanins were concerned, that meant the removal of the human settlements on Qiilura.

Etain knew Gurlanins made bad enemies. They were more than capable of killing farmers, as they'd proved when they exacted revenge on informers on Qiilura. But the war came first, and diplomacy had to take a backseat.

"All present and correct now, General," Gett said. He flicked the controls of the repulsor platform and it lifted them about a meter above the deck, so that the assembled company of 144 clone troopers could see and hear her clearly. There was no noise apart from the occasional clack of armor plates as one soldier brushed too close to another, or the quiet clearing of throats. They didn't chat.

Gett still defaulted to drill. "Company—a . . . ten . . . *shun*!"

The *chunkkk* of armor and rifles being slapped hard against chest plates was one synchronous noise. Etain waited a few moments and concentrated on projecting her voice across the cavern of the hangar. She hadn't been trained as an officer. It didn't come naturally.

They needed her to *be* one, though, just as Darman had when he had expected all Jedi to be competent commanders. She inhaled slowly and felt her voice lift from her stomach through her chest.

"Stand easy," she said. "And buckets off."

The clack and hiss of helmets being removed was a little more ragged than the snap to attention. They weren't expecting that. She stared down into identical faces, reaching out into the Force to get some sense of who they might be and their state of mind, much as she had with Omega. It was a complex tapestry, and yes, there *was* fear; there was an intense sense of belonging and focus, too. And there was not a trace of the hopeful child that had once so confused her when she *felt* Darman long before she saw him for the first time.

Clones grew fast and learned even faster. A year at war—real war, not just fatally realistic training—had made them a lot more worldly-wise and less idealistic.

"We have two battalions pinned down on Dinlo," she said. "You've seen the op order. We open up that exit route for them by cutting through droid lines so they can reach the extraction point. You'll have air support, but we'll be relying predominantly on your infantry skills." She paused. They listened politely. Whatever focus they had appeared to come not from her but from something inside them. "I'm not going to shoot you any line about glory, because this is about *survival*. That's my first rule as a Jedi, you know that? *Survive*. And so should it be yours. I don't want any wild sacrifices. I want to come out of this with as many of you and the Forty-first alive as possible—not because you're assets we need to use again, but because *I don't want you to die*."

She felt the silence change, not in quality but in the realization that shivered almost imperceptibly through the Force. This wasn't how they were used to seeing themselves.

"We weren't exactly queuing up for it ourselves, ma'am," said a pilot, one boot on the step to his cockpit. There was a ripple of laughter, and Etain laughed, too.

"I'll try to keep my arc of fire under control, then," said Etain, and patted the Stouker. She glanced at Gett's forearm; he tilted it so that she could see his chrono readout. "Ramps down in twenty-four minutes. Dismissed."

The men broke up, replacing their helmets and falling into platoons and squads to make an orderly path to their assigned craft. The squadron of LAAT/c gunships had been stripped out to create troop space on their cargo decks. Gett inspected the interior of his helmet, holding it in both gloved hands.

"Aren't you supposed to wish that the Force be with them, General?"

Etain liked Gett. He didn't treat her as an omniscient military genius but as just another being stuck in a hard place without a lot of choices. She could hear a faint sound coming from his helmet's audio feed; when she concentrated, she could hear singing, and so held out her hand for the helmet. She'd tried on Atin's once and been stunned by the welter of data it flung at the wearer. Helmet held close to her head, she could make out strong male voices, a choir of them, singing an anthem she had heard snatches of but rarely had the chance to listen to: "Vode An."

They were singing, in the privacy of their own helmet comlinks, retreating into their world, like Omega Squad did from time to time. She could hear nothing outside the helmets, of course, and she felt oddly excluded. But they were not her *brothers all,* however much she wished to be part of something greater than herself, even more than the Jedi Order. They were gearing up for battle.

Bal kote, darasuum kote,
Jorso'ran kando a tome . . .

It sounded less martial and more of a lament to her ears right then.

She'd have to ask General Jusik for a translation. He was very much the *Mando'a* speaker these days.

She handed Gett his helmet back and gave him a nod of thanks. "It's not just the Force we need with us today, Commander," she said. "It's reliable kit and accurate intel."

"Always is, General," he said. "Always is."

He slipped his helmet back on and sealed the collar.

She knew without asking that he had started singing, completely silent to her, but one voice with his brothers.

* * *

Special Operations Brigade HQ, Coruscant, twenty minutes after the explosion at Depot Bravo Five, 367 days after Geonosis

Captain Ordo needed General Bardan Jusik, and he needed him *fast.*

He wasn't answering his comlink. That irked Ordo because an officer was supposed to be contactable at all times. And this was precisely the kind of emergency that proved the point.

Ordo settled the two-seater Aratech speeder bike outside the main doors—far enough to one side not to obstruct them, as safety precautions dictated—and strode down the main passage that led to the briefing and ops rooms.

"Location for General Jusik, please," he said to the admin droid that was operating the comlink relays in the lobby area.

"Meeting with General Arligan Zey and ARC Trooper Captain Maze in the CO's office, sir, discussing the incontinent ordnance situation—"

"Thank you," said Ordo. *Just say* bomb, *will you?* "That's why I'm here, too."

"You can't—"

But he could; and he did. "Noted."

The red light above the office doors told Ordo that the general didn't want to be interrupted. He expected the Jedi's Force sensitivity to detect him coming and open those doors, but they remained closed, so Ordo simply made use of the list of five thousand security codes that he had memorized for an eventuality like this. He would never trust them to a datapad alone. Skirata had taught him that sometimes you could only take your own brain and body into battle.

Ordo took off his helmet first, a courtesy Skirata had also taught him, and tapped in the code on the side panel.

The doors parted and he walked up to the meeting table, a pool of dark blue polished stone where Zey, Jusik, and Zey's frankly surprised ARC captain sat staring at him.

"Morning, sir," said Ordo. "My apologies for interrupting, but I need General Jusik now."

Jusik's thin pale face with its straggly blond beard was the picture of horrified embarrassment. Ordo thought all Jedi could sense him coming, but that never seemed to buffer their surprise when he arrived on urgent business.

Jusik didn't move fast enough. Ordo made a gesture toward the door.

"Captain, it's not customary to interrupt emergency meetings," Zey said carefully. "General Jusik is our ordnance specialist and—"

"That's why I need him now, sir. Sergeant Skirata sends his compliments, but he would like the general to join him at the incident scene, seeing as he's the explosives expert and his skills would be best spent on practical matters rather than discussion."

"I think your *sergeant* should be leaving all that to Coruscant Security," said Captain Maze, who clearly didn't understand the situation well enough.

Typical ordinary ARC. Typical stubborn *ARC.*

"No," Ordo said. "Not possible. If I could hurry you a little, General Jusik, I have a speeder right outside. And please remember to leave your comlink active in the future. You *must* be contactable at all times."

Maze looked at Zey, and Zey shook his head discreetly. Ordo caught Jusik by his elbow and hurried him down the passage.

"Sorry about reprimanding you in front of Zey, sir," Ordo said, scattering droids and the occasional clone trooper as they hurried back up the passageway. "But Sergeant Skirata is *livid.*"

"I know, I should have left it on—"

"Like to pilot, sir? I know you enjoy it."

"Yes please—"

It was the rapid thud of boots behind him that made Ordo stop and turn just as Captain Maze put his hand out to tap him on the shoulder. He deflected the ARC's arm and brushed it aside.

Maze squared up. "Look, *Null,* I don't know who your sergeant thinks he is, but you *obey* a general when he—"

"I don't have time for this." Ordo brought his fist up hard and without warning right under Maze's chin, knocking him against the wall. The man swore and didn't go down, so Ordo hit him again, this time in the nose—always demoralizing enough to stop someone dead, but nothing seriously damaging, nothing to cause *lasting* pain. He would never harm a brother if he could help it. "And I only take orders from Kal Skirata."

Jusik and Ordo sprinted the rest of the way to the speeder to make up lost time.

"Ordo . . ."

"Yes?"

"Ordo, you just *flattened* an ARC trooper."

"He was delaying us."

"But you *hit* him. *Twice.*"

"No permanent harm done," Ordo said, lifting his *kama* to slide over the pillion seat behind Jusik. He sealed his helmet. "You can't convince Alpha ARCs of anything by rational argument. They're every bit as obtuse and impulsive as Fett, believe me."

Jusik looked perplexed as he started up the drive. He took the speeder bike into a straight vertical lift and spun it around at the top of the climb. His hair, tied back in a bunch, whipped across Ordo's visor on the slipstream, and the ARC brushed it aside in irritated silence. It was high time the boy braided it or got it cut short.

"Where to, Ordo?"

"Manarai."

"Brief me," Jusik said.

"CSF is struggling with this. If you get in right now and use the Force while the incident scene is fresh, we might get a break."

Jusik banked right to avoid a slim spire and chewed his lower lip. He seemed to be able to fly without thinking. "I've been over the data six or seven times and I can't see *any* consistent pattern in any of the devices. Not the materials, not the method of construction, nothing. Just that they're all very complex devices, and hard to set."

Ordo blinked to switch his helmet audio to filter out the wind noise. Next time, he'd commandeer an airspeeder with a canopy. "Always explosives."

"Say again?"

Ordo adjusted his volume. "I said *always explosives.*"

"Chemical and biological ordnance has limited use on a planet with more than a thousand different species. Things that go bang, though, are guaranteed to hurt *every* race."

"I'd buy that if these devices were being used randomly. They're not. It's all Grand Army targets. Humans."

"Are you sure it's me you need for this?" Jusik asked. "I'm not as adept with the living Force as others."

"You want to go back and have a nice meeting?"

"No." Jusik looked back over his shoulder with a big grin. Ordo had learned not to tell him to keep his eyes straight ahead, but it was still unnerving to watch a Jedi navigate a craft by his Force-senses alone. "I've never seen *anyone* walk over Zey like that."

"I simply had to get the job done, sir. No offense."

"Do you mind my asking you something, Ordo?"

"Go ahead."

"Why do you tolerate me? You don't take the slightest notice of Zey. Or Camas. Or anyone else, for that matter."

"Skirata respects you. I trust his judgment."

"Oh." Jusik didn't seem to be expecting that answer. "I—I have a very great regard for our sergeant, too."

Ordo noted the word *our*. And *that* was what made Jusik different, as far as *Kal'buir,* Papa Kal, was concerned: he had thrown in his lot with his men. But, as *Kal'buir* said privately, you could stick a Weequay officer in front of the clone army and they would still fight well. An army of three million men with very few Jedi officers had to be self-directing.

Ordo was well used to directing himself.

Jusik never asked if Ordo thought of him as his commanding officer, though. He probably knew, and didn't need to be reminded that Ordo answered only to the one man who had stepped physically between him and death once, twice, more times than was decent to count: Kal Skirata. And while Ordo knew intellectually that a detached, unsentimental officer was the kind who won wars and saved the most lives, his heart said that a sergeant who was ready to die to protect his men got the very last drop of sweat and blood from them, and given gladly.

"I think you might *really* be in trouble with Zey this time, Ordo."

"And what do you think he's going to do about it?"

"Aren't you afraid?"

"Not since Kamino."

If Jusik understood that, it didn't show. "Is it true that your brother Mereel hijacked a transport to Kamino?"

"It's known as hardening targets, General. Challenging security to improve it. We do that."

It was a lie, but not entirely: the Nulls tried not to remove GAR assets from the battlefield unless it was absolutely necessary, but in this case *Kal'buir* had said it was. The Jedi command turned a blind eye to the irregularities if they detected them because the Null squad produced unparalleled results. No, Zey wouldn't touch him. If he was foolish enough to try, he would learn a hard lesson.

"General, do you remember being taken from your parents?"

Jusik glanced to his left and a few moments later a CSF patrol appeared on their flank, dipped a wing in acknowledgment, and dropped away below them again.

"They're just pinging us to be sure we are who they think we are," the Jedi said, evading the question. "Can't trust anything to be what it seems these days."

"Indeed."

"I hope CSF aren't offended by our intervention."

Ordo tightened his grip. "It's not their fault they can't handle this."

"They're very competent."

"They're competent at *defense.* They're not used to attacking. We can think like an enemy better than they can."

"*You* can. I fear I never will."

"I was trained to kill and destroy by any means possible. I suspect you were trained to obey some rules."

"I do actually."

"What? Obey rules?"

"No, I remember being taken from my family. Just being *taken.* Not my family, though."

"And what makes you so attached to *us*?" Ordo chose his words precisely, knowing what attachment meant to a Jedi. He knew the answer anyway. "And doesn't that worry you?"

Jusik paused for a moment and then turned with an anxious smile. Jedi weren't supposed to feel powerful emotions like vengeance or love or hate. Ordo could now see that conflict on the boy's face daily.

And Jusik *was* a boy: Ordo was the same physical age as the general—twenty-two—but he felt a generation older, despite being *born* only eleven years ago. And the Jedi drew strength from the things that tore up his heart, just as Kal Skirata did.

He and Jusik were opposites in so many ways and yet so very similar in others.

"You have such a passionate sense of *belonging,*" Jusik said at last. "And you never complain about the way you're used."

"Save your sympathy for the troopers," Ordo said. "Nobody uses *us.* And a clear sense of purpose is a strength."

The southern side of the logistics depot was a wasteland of shattered metal and rubble. From the air, it looked like an abandoned construction site with a brightly colored perimeter fence. As Jusik dropped lower, the perimeter resolved into crowds held back by a CSF cordon. The GAR supplies base was right on the boundary of a civilian area, separated only by a strip of landing platforms, with levels of warehousing operated by droids below it.

It had obviously been a big device. Had the same bomb exploded in the civilian heart of Coruscant, the casualties would have run to thousands.

"Whatever do they find to look at?" Jusik asked. He had trouble finding a space to set down and had to land outside the security cordon. He was clearly offended by the sightseers and didn't wait for

Ordo to clear a path through the crowd for him. For a quietly spoken man, Jusik could certainly make himself heard. "Citizens, unless you have contributions to make here, can I suggest you clear the area in case there's a second device still set to detonate?"

Ordo was impressed at the speed with which most of the crowd melted away. The resistantly curious hung around in small groups.

"You don't want to see this," Jusik said.

They paused, and then walked away. A CSF incident support vessel skimmed across the strip and hovered for a moment beside Jusik. The pilot leaned a little way out of the hatch. "Never seen mind influence in action before, sir. Thank you."

"I wasn't using the Force," Jusik said.

Ordo found a new reason to like this Jedi every day. He took the war as personally as *Kal'buir* did.

A thickset man in gray tunic waved to them from the inner cordon, where a large group of civilians and hovercams waited. Captain Jaller Obrim wasn't wearing his Senate Guard finery any longer. Ordo knew him well: since they'd worked together with Omega Squad on the spaceport siege, Obrim's time had been increasingly taken up with counterterrorism duties. He was seconded to CSF now, but they still didn't seem able to persuade him to wear the blue uniform.

"Can you influence the media to go away, General?" Ordo said. "Or shall I do it *manually*?"

The CSF forensics investigation team was still picking a slow and careful path through the debris of the entrance to Bravo Eight when Ordo and Jusik reached the cordon. Set back ten meters from the inner cordon was a screen of white plastoid sheet with the CSF badge repeated across its surface: the worst debris had been screened from the cams and prying eyes.

It was grim work for civilian police. Ordo knew that they had neither the expertise nor the numbers to handle what was happening lately. And how did they cope with the things they saw if they hadn't been trained to deal with them from childhood, as he had? For a moment he felt pity.

But there was work to do. Ordo flicked on the voice projection of his helmet with a quick eye movement. "Mind your backs, please."

An HNE crew and a dozen other media representatives—some *wets,* as Skirata called organic life-forms, some *tinnies,* or droids—formed a cautious audience for the grisly aftermath of the explosion. They parted instantly, even before they looked around and saw Ordo striding toward them. Then they gave him an even wider berth. An

ARC trooper cut an imposing figure, and a captain—marked in the brilliant scarlet that subconsciously said *danger* to many humanoid species—cleared a *big* path.

Obrim deactivated a section of the cordon to let Jusik and Ordo pass.

"This is General Bardan Jusik," Ordo said. "He's one of us. Can he wander around and assess the site?"

Obrim looked Jusik up and down with the air of a man who believed more in hard data than the Force. "Of course he can. Mind the evidence markers, sir."

"I'll be cautious," Jusik said, meshing his fingers in front of him to do that little Jedi bow that Ordo found fascinating. Sometimes Jusik was one of the boys, and sometimes he was ancient, wisely sober, another creature entirely. "I won't contaminate evidence."

Obrim waited for him to walk away and turned to Ordo. "Not that it'd matter. The forensic is getting us nowhere. Maybe we need the Mystic Mob to give us a break. How are you, anyway?"

"Focused. Very focused."

"Yes, your boss is pretty *focused,* too. He can curse the slime off a Hutt, that man."

"He takes all casualties personally, I'm afraid."

"I know what you mean. I'm sorry about your boys, by the way. They catch it coming and going, don't they?"

Skirata was bent deep in conversation with a CSF officer, their heads almost touching, talking in low and agitated voices. He swung around as Ordo approached. His face was gray with suppressed anger.

"Fifteen dead." Skirata clearly didn't care about civilian casualties, traffic disruption, or structural damage. He gestured toward a large fragment of white leg armor in the rubble of what had been a security post. "I'm going to rip some *chakaar*'s guts out for this."

"When we find them, I'll make sure you're first in line," Obrim said.

There wasn't a lot any of them could do at that moment except to allow the largely Sullustan scenes-of-crime team to do their work. Skirata, chewing vigorously on that bittersweet *ruik* root that he'd recently taken a liking to, stood with his fists in his jacket pockets, watching Jusik stepping delicately between chunks of debris. The Jedi occasionally stopped to close his eyes and stand completely motionless.

Skirata's expression was one of cold appraisal. "He's a good kid."

Ordo nodded. "Do you want me to look after him?"

"Yes, but not at the expense of your own safety."

After a few minutes Jusik made his way back to the cordon, arms folded.

"You didn't pick up anything?" Skirata said, as if he expected Jusik to bay like a hunting strill latching on to a scent.

"A great deal." Jusik shut his eyes for a second. "I can still feel the disturbance in the Force. I can sense the destruction and pain and fear. Like a battlefield, in fact."

"So?"

"It's what I *can't* sense that bothers me."

"Which is?"

"*Malevolence.* The enemy is absent. The enemy was never here, in fact."

Republic Fleet Protection Group traffic inderdiction vessel (TIV) Z590/1, standing off Corellian–Perlemian hyperspace intersection,367 days after Geonosis

Fi really didn't like zero-g ops.

He took off his helmet with slow care and put one hand on the webbing restraints that stopped him from drifting away from the bulkhead of the anonymous utility vessel that had been customized for armed boarding parties. If he moved a little too quickly, he drifted.

Drifting made him . . . queasy.

Darman, Niner, and Atin didn't seem bothered by it at all; neither did the pilot, who, for reasons Fi hadn't yet worked out, was called Sicko.

Sicko had shut down the drives. The unmilitary, unmarked, apparently unimpressive little TIV—a "plain wrapper," as the pilots tagged it—hung with drives idling near an exit point of the hyperspace route, cockpit panels flickering with a dozen weapons displays.

Externally, it looked like a battered utility shuttle. Under the rust, though, it was a compact assault platform that could muscle its way onto any vessel. Fi thought that *traffic interdiction operations* was a lovely euphemism for "heavy-duty military hijack."

"I do like a noncompliant boarding to start the day," Sicko said. "You okay, Fi?"

"I'm sorted," Fi lied.

"You're not going to throw up, are you? I just cleaned this crate."

"If I can keep field rations down, I can handle anything."

"Tell you what, chum, put your bucket back on and keep it to yourself."

"I can aim straight."

Fi had learned the skills of maneuvering in zero-g late in life—just before he turned eight and sixteen, not all *that* long before Geonosis—and it didn't come as naturally to him as those troopers trained specifically for deep-space duties. He wondered why the others had come through the same training with more tolerance of it.

Niner, apparently impervious to every hardship except seeing his squad improperly dressed, stared at the palm of his glove as if willing the wrist-mounted hololink from HQ to activate.

The squad now wore the matte-black stealth version of the Katarn armor that made them even more visibly different from the rest of the Republic Commando squads. Niner said it was "sensible" even if it made them pretty conspicuous targets on snow-covered Fest. Fi suspected he liked it better because it also made them look seriously menacing. Droids didn't care, but it certainly put the wind up wets—organic targets—when they saw it.

If they saw it, of course. They usually didn't get the chance.

An occasional click of his teeth indicated Niner was annoyed. It was Skirata's habit, too.

"Ordo's always on time," Fi said, trying to take his mind off his churning stomach. "Don't fret, Sarge."

"Your *buddy . . . ,*" Darman teased.

"Rather have him for a friend than an enemy."

"Ooh, he *likes* you. Hobnobbing with ARC officers from the Bonkers Squad, eh?"

"We have an understanding," Fi said. "I don't laugh at his skirt, and he doesn't rip my head off."

Yes, Ordo *had* taken a shine to him. Fi hadn't fully understood it until Skirata had taken him to one side and explained just what had happened to Ordo and his batch on Kamino as kids. So when Fi had thrown himself on a grenade during an anti-terrorist op to smother the detonation, Ordo had marked him out as someone who'd take an awfully big risk to save comrades. Null ARCs were psychotic—*bonkers,* as Skirata put it—but they were unshakably loyal when the mood struck them.

And when the mood failed to strike them, they were instant death on legs.

Fi suspected that Ordo was bored out of his brain, stuck in HQ on Coruscant for most of the last year with nothing to kill except time.

So Fi stared at Niner's glove, too, willing his stomach to stay put. At precisely 0900 hours Triple Zero time, right on cue, Niner's palm burst into blue light.

"RC-one-three-zero-nine receiving, sir," Niner said.

The encrypted link was crystal clear. Ordo shimmered in a blue holoimage, apparently sitting in the cockpit of a police vessel, helmet beside him on the adjoining seat. But he didn't look bored. He was clenching and unclenching one fist.

"*Su'cuy,* Omega. How's it going?"

"Ready to roll, sir."

"Sergeant, latest intel we have is that the suspect vessel left Cularin bound for Denon and is headed for your position. The bad news is that it appears to be traveling with a couple of legit vessels as a smokescreen. Commercial freight is getting very edgy about piracy so they're forming up into convoys now."

"We can weed out the target," said Niner.

"It would be very *awkward* if you decompressed a civilian freighter at the moment. It'll be the Gizer L-six."

"Understood."

"And we need the *di'kute* alive. No slotting, no disintegration, no accidents."

"Not even a good slap?" asked Fi.

"Use the PEP laser and keep it nonlethal if you can. Somebody's very keen to have a frank chat with them." Ordo paused, head tilted down for a second. "Vau's back."

Fi couldn't stop himself from glancing at Atin and noted that Darman had done the same. Atin had his chin tucked into the padded rim of his chest plate and was idly scratching the scar that ran from just under his right eye and across his mouth to the left side of his jaw. It was a thin white linc now, a faint memory of the raw red welt it had been when Fi first saw him: and Fi suddenly realized something he hadn't worked out before.

I think I know how he got that.

Atin was from Sergeant Walon Vau's training company, not Skirata's. And over the months, as casualties mounted and more partial squads were regrouped with men from other companies, they all swapped stories. The Vau stories didn't get a laugh at all.

"You okay, *ner vod*?"

"Fine," Atin said. He looked up, jaw set. "So how many bandits are we going to *not* slot, disintegrate, or speak harshly to, then, Captain?"

"Five, best intel says," said Ordo.

"We'll assume ten then," said Niner.

Ordo paused for a moment as if he thought Niner might be resorting to sarcasm. Fi could see it in the way his shoulders braced. He was a knife-edge kind of man, Ordo. But Niner was simply in literal mode, as he tended to be when things were getting intense. He always wanted to err on the side of caution.

Ordo obviously knew that: he didn't bite. "By the way, General Tur-Mukan is operating around the Bothan sector, and appears to be coping, according to Commander Gett," he said. "And she's still packing the conc rifle, so your lesson wasn't wasted."

"Beats swinging the shiny stick," Fi said, winking at Darman. "It'd be fun to see her again, eh, Dar?"

Darman smiled enigmatically. Atin was staring in slight defocus at the bulkhead, jaw clenched. Fi thought it was high time the bad guys dropped out of hyperspace and took their minds off the individual things that were troubling them, which included his stomach.

"Ordo out," the blue holo said, and Niner's glove held nothing but air again.

Darman prepped his helmet, resetting the HUD with a prod of his finger. "Poor *Ord'ika.*" He called him by the affectionate nickname Skirata used in private, a kid's name, *Little Ordo.* In public, it was strictly Captain and Sergeant. And you could call your brother *vod'ika* in the Mandalorian way, but nobody else could, and *never* in front of strangers. "Who'd want to be doing the filing when the rest of your batch are off saving the galaxy?"

"Well, I hear Kom'rk is out at Utapau, and Jaing's cannoned up and gone hiking with extreme prejudice in the Bakura sector," said Fi.

"Fierfek."

"Knowing him, he's doing it for the fun of it. And as for Mereel—well, why has Kal sent him out to Kamino?"

Niner clicked irritably again. "Anyone else you want to discuss classified intel with, Fi?"

"Sorry, Sarge."

The cabin was silent once more. Fi slid his helmet back on, sealed the collar, and concentrated on the artificial horizon of his HUD to convince his stomach which way was up. The Mark III Katarn armor now had more enhancements and was rated blaster-resistant up to light cannon rounds. Every op was full of new surprises from GAR Procurement—like a birthday, according to Skirata, although Fi, like all his brothers, had never celebrated one.

Now they even had a nonlethal pulsed energy projectile, or PEP, for the DC-17 that didn't exactly kill the targets, but certainly made their eyes water. It was police riot control kit, a deuterium fluoride laser: it would probably just annoy a Wookiee, but it sorted out humanoids in short order.

Fi focused on the icons in the frame of his HUD and blinked one into action, sending chilled air across his face. That soothed his nausea. Then he isolated his audio channel and accessed a particularly thumping piece of glimmik music.

Niner cut in on the comm channel override. "*Now* what are you listening to?"

"Mon Cal opera," Fi said. "I'm improving my mind."

"Liar. I can see you nodding to the beat."

Relax, Sarge. Please. "Want to listen in?"

"I'm psyched up enough, thanks," Niner said.

Darman shook his head. Atin looked up. "Later, Fi."

Sicko glanced over his shoulder, excluded from the squad's conversation by their secure helmet-to-helmet comlink. But he could obviously see the body language that indicated they were chatting. Fi flicked to his frequency with a couple of blinks directed at the sensor inside his visor.

"How about you, *ner vod*? Want some music?"

"No thanks." Sicko had much the same neutral accent as most of the infantry trooper clones. They'd learned Basic from flash-instruction and had rarely been exposed to outsiders with interesting accents. "But it's decent of you to offer."

"Anytime."

Commandos owed their lives to the guts of these pilots—Omega had been extracted under heavy fire by their astonishing skill a number of times—and the TIV pilots were the most daring of the lot. Any gulfs among clone trooper, specialist, and the elite commando units had now been swept away by shared hardship and they were *an vode* now—all brothers. Fi was happy to indulge them.

He killed the music feed and switched over to the open squad comlink again. The waiting was eating at him now. If—

"Got trade," said Sicko. "They *should* be jumping out of hyperspace anytime now. Three contacts." He flicked the tracking display from his console into a holoprojection so they could see the pulses of color that represented the ships—no outlines or shapes, just a flickering array of numbers and codes to one side, awaiting a ship to tag. "Intercept in two minutes. They should all be less than a minute apart."

"Bring us in starboard-side-to, please," said Niner.

"There you go . . . the L-six is coming out first." Sicko pressed a pad on the console and Fi heard the grapple arms extend and retract like an athlete flexing muscles before an event. The display picked up the ship, then another. "But the second profile looks like an L-six, too . . ."

"Intel said—"

"Intel has *occasionally* been known to be less than one hundred percent accurate, apparently . . ."

Atin sighed a *ffft* of contempt. "You reckon?" Fi could see that he was checking ships' configuration data via his HUD. "I'm glad I'm shockproofed."

"But we *like* intel," said Fi. *No, not again. Let it be right this time.* "Sergeant Kal never read us bedtime stories, so intel satisfies our innate boyish need for heroic fantasy."

"Is he always like this?" Sicko asked.

"No, he's pretty quiet today." Darman clutched a magnetic frame charge to his chest plate—his *hatch persuader,* as he liked to call it. "So are we going to jump the first crate or what?"

"Play it by ear," said Niner, who always seemed to resort to Skirata's voice under pressure. He hit the release on his restraints. "Let's see how it reacts when we approach. Pressure up helmets, gentlemen, and we're in business."

"Coming about," said Sicko. "And if I can't disable its drive, blow the navigation power conduit. The access ought to be outside the engineering compartment, but it's sometimes inside the port-side bulkhead, three meters from the hatch. So knock the rotten thing out, will you? Or they'll bolt and drag us across ten star systems."

Then the pilot punched the TIV into a ninety-degree roll and the apparently fixed constellations Fi had been watching tilted before his eyes. He understood *instantly* why they called the man Sicko.

Fi grabbed a restraint instictively and his backpack hit the bulkhead.

"Oh *fierfek*—"

"Whoaaa!"

"Uhhh . . ."

Fi could see through the cockpit screen as he steadied himself alongside the hatch. A box-like freighter—yes, a Gizer L-6—loomed out of black nothing.

"Interdict *that,*" Niner said.

Fi reached for his jet-pack controls, hanging right beside Darman in free fall.

Sicko powered the TIV into a slow head-on approach and corkscrewed slowly to line it up and bring the deckhead hatch against the port side of the freighter, landing lights on. The freighter slowed, too. Darman stood ready, fingers flexing over the jet-pack controls on his belt. He'd be first out, blowing the hatch controls when the blastproof coaming sealed against the target's hull, pulling aside to let the others storm in. As the TIV moved sedately along the freighter's flank, the landing lights picked out the bright orange livery of VOSHAN CONTAINERS.

"Oops," said Sicko. "Looks like the legit one."

"Back off, then," Niner said. "If the other ship sees this, we've lost—"

A flash caught Fi's eye at the same time it did everyone else's. The second vessel was heading their way.

"Another L-six," Sicko said. "Please don't let there be three of them."

The first L-6 suddenly altered course with a rapid burn. It had probably picked up the wrong idea about a scruffy little ship in an area of space that was frequently populated by pirates. One of its spars wheeled ninety degrees almost instantly, looming in the TIV's viewscreen on collision course.

"Abort abort abort!" Sicko yelled. *"Brace brace brace—"*

He was cut short by a screech of tearing alloy that shuddered through the TIV, and suddenly it wasn't the tight gut-exhilaration of a boarding but the desperate scramble to survive. The impact spun the TIV off and the last thing Fi saw as he somersaulted involuntarily was Sicko pulling on the yoke and punching a stabilizing burn to stop the spin.

There was nothing Fi or the squad could do. It was all down to the pilot. Fi hated that moment of helpless realization every time. The display in his HUD shuddered like a cheap bootleg holovid as he hit the bulkhead harder than he thought possible in zero-g.

"Incoming! Returning fire."

And then there was light: brilliant blue-white light. The instant hot rain of fragments peppered and pecked on the hull. Sicko had neutralized the incoming missile. The second L-6 powered up and punched back into hyperspace in a flare of light.

"Chew on *that,*" Sicko said, and slapped his fist hard on the console. "Foam deployed . . . hull breach secure."

"What's that?" Fi said, suddenly ice-cold and focused, and not nauseous at all.

"BRB."

"What?"

"Big Red Button. Emergency hull seal."

The remains of the freighter's missile cartwheeled slowly into the distance, trailing vapor. It was the kind of self-defense many freighters felt the need to carry these days: wars created useful opportunity for the criminal community.

Niner sighed. "Oh, fierfek, everyone knows we're here now . . ."

"Anyone get his license number?" Fi said. "Maniac."

"Yeah, and more maniacs along shortly, too." Sicko turned his head toward the scanner readout. "Next one's due in sixty seconds . . . and the next one two minutes later, I reckon. I hope he doesn't call for assistance, or we're going to have to bang out of here *really* fast."

"Tell me they're not going to notice that little fracas."

"They're not going to notice that little fracas."

"*Vor'e,* brother."

"You're welcome." The pilot didn't takc his eyes off the scanner. "Happy to lie to a comrade anytime, if it makes him feel better—there you go . . ."

The next freighter fell out of hyperspace fifteen hundred meters from their port bow, and its pilot definitely *noticed.* Fi knew that because the immediate bright arc of laser cannon shaved the elint mast mounted on the TIV's nose just as Sicko let loose a sustained volley into the freighter's underslung drive. It was still showering debris as Sicko brought the TIV about and swung back under the freighter to loop over its casing from its starboard quarter and bring the TIV, totally inverted, to rest hatch-to-hatch with the target.

And there was nothing the crippled freighter could do about it. Sicko was too close in, too far inside the minimum range of its cannon, and now riding a very angry Ralltiiri tiger.

"This is where you get off." Sicko's voice was just a little shaky. "End of the line."

"Stand to!" Niner said. The skirt of coaming shot out of the TIV's hatch housing and sealed tight against the freighter's hull while the grapple arms held it secure. The pressure equalization light flashed red and the TIV's blastproof inner hatch opened, then the outer one. "*Dar,* take it!"

Dar slapped the frame charges on the freighter's hatch, the inner hatch snapped shut again, and a muffled *whump* vibrated through the TIV.

How Sicko had managed to bring the TIV alongside the port hatch without ramming the vessel—or ripping the deckhead out of the TIV—Fi would never understand, but that was what trooper pilots did, and he was in awe of them. The inner hatch opened again.

Darman bowled in two flash-bangs—blinding, deafening stun grenades—and Niner was first through the hatch.

"Go go go—"

Fi, buoyed up on a wave of adrenaline, plunged through after him, DC-17 set to blaster mode. The TIV and Sicko were swept from his mind from that moment as time disobeyed all the rules and he was caught in an infinite, slow-motion split second while the squad burst through the hatch and the L-6's artificial gravity smacked him down hard on the deck. The impact ran up through the soles of his boots. He was running for seconds before his proprioception caught up with the gravity and his body said *I remember this.*

But there weren't many places to run on an L-6 freighter. It was a cockpit and a couple of cabins bolted to a durasteel box of nothing. Atin moved ahead and simply opened up with the Deece's new PEP laser, knocking two men flat in a massive shock wave of sound and light as they came out of the starboard cabin firing blasters.

Fi's anti-flash visor darkened instantly. Even with armor, he felt the shock of the PEP's unleashed energy. They all did.

Fi ran on over Atin as he dropped to one knee to cuff and search the men, wrists to ankles, as they lay struggling for breath, whimpering. A PEP round was like being flash-banged *and* hit in the chest by several plastoid rounds at once.

It was usually nonlethal. Usually.

Two down, three—maybe—to go.

The cockpit doors didn't open when Niner stood back and hit the controls. Atin caught up with Fi again and they stood catching their breath.

Niner motioned Darman into position at the cockpit doors. "Shame that PEP doesn't work through bulkheads."

"Confirmed, three still inside," Darman said, running the infrared sensor sweep in his gauntlet up and down the seam of the doors. "Nothing in the port cabin."

Intel had it right for once: there *were* five bandits on board.

"Encourage them to step outside, Dar," Niner said, checking his Deece's PEP setting. He peered at the power readout. "This thing actually scares me."

Darman unrolled a ribbon of adhesive thermal charge and pressed it around the doors' weak points. Then he pushed the det into the soft material and cocked his head to one side as if calculating. "All that fuss getting in and now we just walk over them. Anticlimactic, I think the word is . . ."

There was a dull echoing thud and screech of metal that vibrated through the deck. For a second Fi thought the det had gone off prematurely and that it was all a trick of his adrenaline-distorted perception, and that he was dead but didn't know it yet.

But it wasn't the det.

Fi looked at Niner, and Niner looked at Atin, and Fi saw in Darman's viewpoint icon that he was staring at a fragment of flimsi that whipped past him as if snatched by a sudden wind.

It *was* being carried on a stream of air. *Escaping* air. Fi felt it grab him and they all reached instinctively for a secure point to anchor them.

"Hull breach," Fi said, arms tight around a stanchion. "Check suit seals."

They went into an automatic and long-drilled check of their suit systems. Katarn armor was vacuumproofed. Fi's glove sensor confirmed his suit was still airtight and the thumbs-up from the rest of the squad indicated that their suit integrity was holding up too. The temporary gale of escaping air was abating.

"Sicko, you receiving?" said Niner.

Fi had the same thought, and judging by the rapid breathing on the shared comlink, so had Atin and Darman. The decompression was via the hatch. And that meant the seal formed by the TIV had been breached.

On their comlink there was only faint static and the sound of their own breathing and swallowing.

"Fierfek," Atin said. "Whatever it is, he's gone."

Niner motioned Darman to stay by the cockpit hatch and beckoned Fi to follow him. "Let's see if it's fixable. You two stay there."

"Well, we've probably lost two prisoners now," Darman said. "Better make sure we haven't lost the rest."

There was no telling what had dislodged the TIV and whether they were going to meet someone boarding to deal with *them.* They made their way back up the passage to the entry hatch, DC-17s raised, and there was no sign of the two prisoners they'd left cuffed, nor anybody else.

And the hatch—about two meters by two—was wide open, star-speckled void visible beyond.

Fi gripped the rail on one side of it and leaned out a little. It was a good way to get your head blown off but he decided that the urgency of the situation warranted it.

There was no sign of the TIV. There was no sign of *anything.* He pulled himself back inboard. At least the gravity was still functioning.

Niner checked the environment sensors on his forearm plate. “Atmosphere’s fully vented now.”

“They have to have a foam system in these things.”

“Yeah, but if you had us running around *your* vessel, would *you* seal the hull and help us out?”

“Is the cockpit airtight?” Fi asked.

“We won’t know for sure until they go cold and we can’t pick them up in the infrared.” Niner switched on his tactical spot-lamp and began searching the bulkhead for panels. “And by that time we’ll be ice cubes ourselves.”

Katarn armor—even the Mark III version—was only good against vacuum for twenty minutes without a backup air supply. And they hadn’t counted on being exposed that long.

For some reason Fi was distracted by Sicko’s fate. It was a strange thing to discover when you were on borrowed time yourself. But Sicko had said the power conduits were routed via a panel three meters from . . .

. . . here.

Fi ejected the vibroblade from his knuckle plate and pried open the panel. Niner stood behind him and directed his spot-lamp into the recessed mass of cabling, pipes, and wires.

“That one’s labeled ISOLATION BULKHEAD,” Niner said.

“Yeah, but where does that come down?”

They looked up at the deckhead for shutter housings. There were at least three back down the passage that they could see.

“Let’s play safe and withdraw to the one nearest the cockpit,” Niner said.

“We could blow the whole panel here and shut everything down.” *Including the gravity. Lovely.* “Usually triggers emergency containment.”

Niner put his glove to the side of his helmet. It was a nervous habit of his, just like the way he grew increasingly irritable with Fi as his stress levels peaked. “Dar, are you getting this?”

“Halfway there already,” said Darman’s voice.

Fi’s chrono said they had fifteen minutes left to make this work. “Okay, if Dar blows this remotely and it activates the emergency bulkhead, then we’ll be stuck between that and the cockpit hatch.”

“And if there’s atmosphere in there, we can open it and cozy up to the other three *hut’uune.*”

“Or,” Fi said, “we find it’s hard vacuum, too, and then we’ll be completely stuffed.”

"Stuffed if we *don't,*" said Darman, appearing at Fi's shoulder with a ribbon of thermal detonator tape. "Go on. Get back there and wait for me while I set the timer."

"We ought to call in a Red Zero."

"Let's wait until we know if there'll be anything left of us to make it worth rescuing," Niner said, trotting back down the passage. Fi watched him go, shrugged at Darman, and then patted the wide-open cover of the control panel.

"Thanks, Sicko," he said.

3

MRU. Already committed.
—Much Regret Unable, signal relayed from CO, RAS *Fearless,*
on receipt of request to withdraw to Skuumaa and abort extraction
of Sarlacc Battalions

The windchill factor in the open troop bay of a LAAT/c gunship flying at five hundred kph was sobering, but then so was the deafening roar of air and the swoops and dips of the flight path as the pilot jinked to stop ground-based AA fire from getting a lock.

Etain realized why the troopers' sealed armor and bodysuit was a good idea. She had only her Jedi robes and the sensible precaution of upper-body armor plates, which did little to insulate on their own. She summoned the Force to help her withstand the icy blast and made sure her safety line was hooked securely to the bulkhead rail.

"You're going to be in the dwang when you get back to HQ, General," the clone trooper sergeant said with a grin. He slipped on his helmet and sealed it. His nickname was Clanky. She'd made a point of asking.

"I really did not see the signal," she said carefully. "Or at least I looked at it a little too late."

His voice emerged now from the projection unit of the anonymous helmet. "It was very funny, signaling *MRU.*"

"Funny? Oh . . ."

There was a frozen pause. "It's how you decline a social invitation, an *RPC. R*equest the *P*leasure of your *C*ompany? *M*uch *R*egret *U*nable."

Yes, she was in the dwang indeed, as he put it. She wasn't fully up to speed with the mass of acronyms and slang that had erupted in the last year. She could hardly keep up with the clone troopers' inventiveness: their extraordinary capacity to appropriate language and habits and shape them to their needs had spawned subcultures of clone identity everywhere. She almost felt she needed a protocol droid.

But she knew what a larty was. Darman had said the LAAT/i—or in this case, the bigger cargo variant—was the most beautiful vessel imaginable when you needed an urgent lift out of trouble. It certainly felt like it now.

MRU indeed. How could I be so stupid? So the troopers thought she was a smart-mouth like Fi, flourishing a little bravado. Instead, she was simply ignorant of the rapidly evolving and idiosyncratic jargon and used it carelessly. "I'm sure they'll forgive me if you pull this off, Sergeant."

Her voice was drowned by the roar and falling note of V-19 Torrent drives as two of the fighters streaked past them and disappeared into the distance. They were heading off to soften the droid positions that stood between the heavily forested terrain where both Sarlacc Battalions were pinned down and there was a narrow ribbon of delta shoreline where pilots could land. Droids, as Darman had once pointed out, were *rubbish* in dense forests.

Etain hoped so.

The gunship dropped suddenly, now level with the tree canopy, and the streaked image of green foliage showed her just how fast they were flying. Another larty came up on their port side. There were thirty-four gunships somewhere near, strung out in a loose formation, heading for the extraction zone.

"Three minutes, General," the pilot's cockpit intercom said. There was a crack and flare of something exploding off to their starboard side. "Getting some attention from the tinnies' triple-A, so we'll drop a little more. Hold tight."

It hardly made her flinch now. She had reached the saturation level of adrenaline where she was vividly aware of every hazard but running on some primeval automatic level of painless cold reason—too scared to panic, as one of the clone troopers had described it.

Three minutes became three hours became three seconds.

Red blasterfire from droids lit up the tree line as the larty banked to come around in a spiral descent. Etain didn't think, and she didn't feel, and she simply jumped the last ten meters from the open deck over the fast-roping four-man squad of clone troopers and the green-trimmed sergeant. Force skills came in very useful at the most unlikely times. She landed in front of the squad and brought the conc rifle up level—one hand on the stock, the other on the barrel grip—to sweep the forest edge in front of her.

She felt other gunships landing all around them, whipping up soil and leaves, but she saw only what was in front—about two platoons of Sarlacc men exchanging fire with super battle droids on the edge of the clearing—and her squad to either side of her.

A spread of ten EMP grenades from the squad and a volley from her conc brought half the super battle droids to a halt. It was at times like this that she longed for the comlink convenience of a helmet instead of one strapped to her arm in just the wrong place: the Force was short on specifics like *SBD strength one hundred units, closing up at green twenty.* And there was so much chaos and pain in the Force right then that she couldn't harness it to focus.

So she did what she had been drilled to do without thinking since she was four years old. She *fought.*

She ran, the squad matching her pace and firing a blue stream into the droid line in odd silence until Clanky activated his voice projector and she heard him say, "—they're closing up all along the shoreline. Sorry, General! Big holes now in the droid lines."

"No link," she said, superfluous words stripped from her mind. The concussion rifle was getting heavy and running out of charge: the power indicator was edging back down to zero. Two more volleys knocked three SBDs flat and a small tree with them. "How many more?"

"Forward Air Control says two hundred SBDs and tanks bearing twenty degrees with four Torrents on their case—"

More V-19s screamed low overhead and a yellow-fringed ball of white fire backlit the forest, suddenly throwing silhouetted trees and running men into sharp contrast. *Fearless*'s air group commander certainly had a grip on the reality of the situation. No wonder everybody loved pilots.

Clanky dropped flat and began firing prone at the stream of SBDs that had turned toward the gunship landing area. Etain followed him without thinking. He was listening to data in his helmet, judging by his occasional emphatic nod.

"Sarlacc's breaking out all along the shoreline, General, and *Fearless* is directing the rest of the larties north."

"Any word on General Vaas Ga?"

Clanky went silent for a moment, to her at least. "One klick north with Commander Gree, calling in air strikes."

Two gunships moved in close enough to catch Etain's peripheral vision and knots of men broke from the trees, some carrying wounded comrades between them. Etain hoped the single IM-6 medical droid on each larty could handle the triage of dozens of men at once. One gunship set down again at right angles to the tree line, its starboard hatch shut tight and taking droid fire that scattered sparks while it trained composite beam lasers on the SBDs.

The starboard gunner—horribly exposed in the transparisteel bubble set in the wing—was hosing the droids at waist height. Etain saw movement and white-armored shapes race behind the vessel and disappear, presumably into the port side of the troop bay. The torrent of comp beam laser was like a freeze-frame in its unbroken, steady stream.

For a slow-motion moment Etain reasoned: using the forward cannon and deploying the heavier and nastier armaments—radiation burst missiles—would cause heavy trooper casualties in this position. Her mouth was dry, her heart pounding so fast that she could hardly distinguish between beats, and yet she could stop the chrono to think these odd things.

She resumed firing. She held her fingers tight on the trigger until the conc died in her hands.

"Whoa, tinnies breaking *this way*—"

Her focus narrowed. She no longer saw the five men around her except as white blurs and vortices of raw energy in the Force. The lead battle droid overran their position and she simply swung the dead rifle in a Force-driven arc right up into the thing's chest, smashing the alloy and sending the droid's sunken head assembly flying into the air.

She was suddenly aware of blue energy behind the next droid like a continuous backdrop, although it had to be interrupted bursts of DC-15 fire. She let the conc rifle drop and drew her lightsaber because she had nothing else left.

The blade of blue light sprang into life and she didn't recall touching the control at all. She swept her arm around in a clean arc that brought the mountain of metal down without its legs, tipping like a felled tree to one side of her, falling flat on its firing arm and shuddering as its own discharging weapon tore it apart. Hot shrapnel sizzled on her robes and skin but she felt nothing.

And she was on her feet now, lightsaber gripped in both hands, point-blank with the next droid. She saw two of her squad blasting away from a prone position while Clanky scrambled to one knee to fire a grenade into the advancing rank of a dozen SBDs.

Droids kept advancing. So did clone troopers. And so did she.

We're all the same. None of us is thinking. We're just reacting.

She fended off a barrage of red fire, whirling and flicking the lightsaber without conscious decision. Each *snazzz* of colliding energy was the first and last: she went on, and on, and on, blocking each shot as if it would never end. And the next droid was upon her. She slashed. Cables and alloy fragments showered her. A white-gauntleted fist grabbed her shoulder and pulled her bodily out of the way.

"Bang out, General, the larty's ready to lift." Clanky almost had to drag her off the pile of shattered droids and shove her into a run toward the gunship. "We've done all we can here and the bay's full. Go! *Run!*"

She grabbed the conc rifle as she ran back, retracing their line of advance, blind on adrenaline. But at the gunship's platform she still stopped dead, one foot on the edge of the rail, to look back and count men passing her. One—two—three—*four* troopers, and Clanky. All accounted for. She sprang up just as an armored hand gripped hers and yanked her inboard. She had no idea who the trooper was. But he was one of hers now.

The gunship lifted in a straight vertical so fast that her stomach plummeted back to ground level.

The forest and fertile delta plain of Dinlo shrank beneath the ship and grew dark. The bay hatches slid forward and slammed shut. Then she was standing in a warehouse of scorched, filthy armor and the stench of blood and seared flesh. Her primeval survival mechanisms yielded to shaking anticlimax.

Clanky pulled off his helmet and their eyes met, an odd moment that was almost a glance in a mirror: she knew that the unblinking wide-eyed shock on his face was exactly what he was seeing on hers. Instinctively, they both reached out to clasp forearms and their grips locked for a second or two. Clanky was also shaking.

Then they parted and turned away. It was synchronous.

Yes, Etain thought. *We're just the same, all of us.*

It was very, very quiet once she blocked out the thrum of the gunship's drive as it made 660 kph—off the dial—back to *Fearless.*

And no, the IM-6 droid could *not* deal with forty men crammed into a modified bay better suited to thirty, not if a quarter of them were injured.

Then, when Etain listened more carefully and her adrenaline had ebbed, she realized the bay wasn't as quiet as she had thought. There was ragged breathing and stifled yelps of pain and—the worst, this—

incoherent whimpering that peaked to a crescendo of a single stifled scream and trailed off again.

She picked her way across the bay, stepping over men who were crouching or kneeling. Propped against the bulkhead, a clone trooper was being held in a sitting position by a brother. His helmet and chest plate were removed and Etain needed no med droid to provide a prognosis for a chest wound that was producing blood on his lips.

"Medic?" She whipped around. "*Medic!* Get this man some help, now!"

The med droid appeared as if from nowhere, jerking bolt upright from a knot of troopers where it was obviously working. Its twin photoreceptors trained on her.

"General!"

"Why is this man not being attended to?"

"Triage *X,*" the droid said, dropping down into the unbroken carpet of troopers again to resume its first aid.

Etain should have known. The red X symbol glowed on his shoulder. She hoped the man hadn't heard, but he probably knew anyway, because that was the unsentimental way the Kaminoans had presented their training to the clones. *Triage code X: too badly injured. Not expected to survive despite intervention. Concentrate resources on code 3, then code 5.*

She took a breath and reminded herself that she was a Jedi, and there was more to being a Jedi than wielding a lightsaber. She knelt down beside him and grabbed his hand. The grip he returned was surprisingly strong for a dying man.

"It's okay," she said.

She reached out in the Force to get some sense of the injury, to shape it in her mind, hoping to slow the hemorrhage and hold shattered tissue together until the larty docked. But she knew as soon as she formed the scale of the damage in her mind that it wouldn't save him.

She had vowed never again to use mind influence on clones without their consent: she had eased Atin's grief, and given Niner confidence when he most needed it, both unasked for, but since then she had avoided it. Clones weren't weak-minded anyway, whatever people thought. But this man was dying, and he needed help.

"I'm Etain," she said. She concentrated on his eyes, seeing behind them somehow into a swirl of no color at all, and visualized calm. She held out her hand to the trooper supporting his shoulders and mouthed *medpacs* at him. She knew they carried single-use syringes of powerful painkiller: Darman had used them in front of her more than once. "There's nothing to be afraid of. What's your nickname?"

"Fi," he said, and it shocked her briefly, but there were many men called Fi in an army with numbers for names. His brother said *no* silently and held up spent syringes: they'd already pumped him full of what little they had. "Thank you, ma'am."

If she could influence thought, she could influence endorphin systems. She put every scrap of her will into it. "The pain's going. The drug's working. Can you feel it?" If the Force had any validity, it *had* to come to her aid now. She studied his face, and his jaw muscles were relaxing a little. "How's that?"

"Better, thanks, ma'am."

"You hang on. You might feel a bit sleepy."

His grip was still tight. She squeezed back. She wondered if he knew she was lying and just chose to believe the lie for his own comfort. He didn't say anything else, but he didn't scream again, and his face looked peaceful.

She rested his head on her shoulder, one hand between his head and the bulkhead, the other still clutching his, and held that position for ten minutes, concentrating on an image of a cool pale void. Then he started a choking cough. His brother took his other hand, and Fi—a painful reminder of a friend she hadn't seen for months and might never see again—said, "I'm fine." His grip went slack.

"Oh, ma'am," said his brother.

Etain was aware in a detached way of spending the next twenty minutes talking to every single trooper in that bay, asking their names, asking who had been lost, and wondering why they stared first at her chest and then at her face, apparently bewildered.

She put her hand to her cheek. It stung. She brushed it and a fragment of alloy came away on her hand with fresh, bright blood. She hadn't felt the shrapnel until then. She aimed herself towards a familiar patch of green in the forest of grimy white armor.

"Clanky," she said, numb. "Clanky, I never asked. Where do we bury our men? Or do we cremate them, like Jedi?"

"Neither, usually, General," said Clanky. "Don't you worry about that now."

She looked down at her beige robe and noticed that it was way beyond filthy: it was peppered with burns, as if she'd been welding carelessly, and there was a ragged oval patch of deep red blood from her right shoulder down to her belt, already drying into stiff blackness.

"Master Camas is going to fry me," she said.

"He can fry us, too, then," Clanky said.

Etain knew she'd think about the deftly evaded answer to her question sometime, but right then her mind was elsewhere. She thought of Darman, suddenly conscious that something was wrong: but something was always wrong for commandos on missions, and the Force was clear that Darman was still alive.

But the other Fi—the trooper—wasn't. Etain felt ashamed of her personal fears and went in search of men she could still help.

Bravo Eight Depot crime scene, Manarai, Coruscant,
367 days after Geonosis

Skirata took every clone casualty as a personal affront. His frustration wasn't aimed at Obrim: the two men respected each other in the way of time-served professionals, and Ordo knew that. He just hoped Obrim knew that *Kal'buir* didn't always mean the sharp things he said.

"So when are your people going to get off their *shebse* and tell us how the device got in here?" Skirata said.

"Soon," Obrim said. "The security holocam was taken out in the blast. We're waiting on a backup image from the satellite. Won't be as clear, but at least we have it."

"Sorry, Jaller," Skirata said, still chewing, eyes fixed on the rubble. "No offense."

"I know, comrade. None taken."

It was another reason why Ordo adored his sergeant: he was the archetypal *Mando'ad.* A Mandalorian man's ideal was to be the firm but loving father, the respectful son learning from every hard experience, the warrior loyal to constant personal principles rather than ever-changing governments and flags.

He also knew when to apologize.

And he looked exhausted. Ordo wondered when he would understand that nobody expected him to keep up with young soldiers. "You could leave this to me."

"You're a good lad, *Ord'ika,* but I have to do this."

Ordo put one hand square on Skirata's back and one on Obrim's to steer them both a little farther from the scene of destruction, anxious not to make it obvious in front of the *aruetiise*—the non-Mandalorians, the foreigners, sometimes even the traitors—that his sergeant needed comforting. Waiting was the worst thing for *Kal'buir's* mood.

Obrim's comlink chirped. "Here we go," he said. "They're relaying the image. Let's play it out to Ordo's link."

The images emerged as a grainy blue aerial holo rising from the palm of Ordo's gauntlet, and they replayed it a few times. A delivery transport came up to the barrier and was waved in to land on the strip. Then the scene erupted in a ball of light followed by billows of smoke and raining debris.

The explosion blew out the transparisteel-and-granite walls of the Bravo Eight supply depot fifteen times before Ordo had seen enough.

"Looks like the device came in on that delivery transport," Obrim said. Some of the recognizable debris scattered around the blast site confirmed that there had been a transport caught up in the explosion. "Nobody running away. So the pilot was inside, and . . ." He stopped to look down at data loading into his own 'pad. "I'm getting confirmation that it was a routine delivery and the pilot was a regular civilian driver. Nothing to suggest that it was a suicide mission, though. Just a routine run with some extra unwanted supplies."

"Can we go back over the recordings from previous days?" Ordo said. "Just to see if anyone was doing a recce of vessels and movements in the run-up to this?"

"Archived for ten days. Won't be any better in terms of angle and clarity than this."

"I'll still take it."

Ordo looked to Skirata, who was silent and visibly angry, but clearly thinking hard. Ordo knew that calculating defocus all too well.

"Okay, the best lead we have right now is to track back the other way down the line—from confirmed explosives supply chains," Kal said.

"Omega's on a TIOPS run checking that right now," Ordo said. "They might come back with some suspects for Vau to work on."

"I'm turning a blind eye to that, right?" said Obrim, a man who left the impression he would have given a lot to be back in the front line instead of supervising others. "Because suspects are *my* part of ship to deal with. But I do have this annoying eyesight problem lately."

"Long-term condition?" Skirata asked, moving Ordo out of his way with a gentle pat on the forearm.

"As permanent as you want it to be, Kal."

"Make it incurable for the time being, then."

Skirata picked his way past the forensics team, who were still setting marker holotags at various points in the rubble: red holos for body parts, blue for inorganic evidence. Ordo wondered if the civilians who'd been gawking from behind the barrier would see anything about *that* on the HNE bulletin.

Skirata paused and leaned over a Sullustan technician who was sensor-scanning the rubble on hands and knees. "Can I have the armor tallies when you find them?"

"Tallies?" The Sullustan sat back on her heels and looked up at him with round black liquid eyes. "Explain."

"The little sensor tags that identify the soldier. On the chest plates." Skirata held finger and thumb a little apart to indicate the size. "There'll be fifteen around here somewhere."

"We can sort the admin for you, Kal," Obrim said. "Don't worry about all that."

"No, it's not to account for them. I want a piece of their armor. To pay our respects, the *Mando* way."

Ordo noted Obrim's puzzled expression. "Bodies are irrelevant to us. Which is just as well, really."

Obrim nodded gravely and ushered them behind another plastoid screen where the SOCO team was assembling and logging fragments of alloy and other barely identifiable materials on a trestle table. "You can take over all this if you want."

Skirata motioned Ordo across to the trestle. "It's Ordo's area, but I'm happy for your people to process it. I've got faith in Sullustan diligence."

Maybe it was just Skirata indulging in harmless hearts-and-minds work. But it seemed to do the job for the SOCO personnel.

One of them looked up. "It's good to know that military intelligence respects CSF."

"I've never been called military intelligence before," Skirata said, as if he hadn't realized that was what he had been doing every waking moment since five days after Geonosis.

Ordo held out one hand to the nearest scenes-of-crime officer and crooked a finger to gesture for their datapad. "You'll need this," he said, and linked it to his own 'pad. "Here's our latest IED data."

Yes, the CSF's anti-terrorism unit and Skirata's tight-knit team had become very close indeed in the last year. Going through official Republic security clearance channels just wasted time, and there was always the chance its civil servants would behave like petty fools across the galaxy and mark data as top secret for their own dreary little career reasons. Ordo didn't have time for that.

He was checking that the data had transferred cleanly when the hololink on the inner side of his forearm plate activated again and his hand was filled with a small scene of blue chaos.

For a split second he thought it was an image in his HUD, but it was external, and it was Omega Squad.

"Omega—Red Zero, Red Zero, Red Zero, over."

The holoimage showed the four commandos pressed against a bulkhead with an occasional fragment of debris floating into view. They were all alive, anyway.

Skirata whipped around at the sound of Niner's voice and the code they all dreaded: *Red Zero,* request for immediate extraction.

Ordo switched instantly and without conscious thought into emergency procedure, capturing coordinates from the message and holding up his datapad so that Skirata could see the numbers and open a comlink to Fleet. Their language changed: their voices became monotone and quiet, and they slipped into minimal, direct speech. The SOCO team froze to watch.

"Sitrep, Omega."

"Target's boarded. Unplanned decompression, and our pilot and the TIV are missing. No power, but no squad casualties."

"Fleet, Skirata here, we have a Red Zero. Fast extraction please—on these coordinates. Pilot down, too, no firm location."

"Stand by, Omega. We're scrambling Fleet assistance now. Time to critical?"

"Ten minutes if we don't get the hatch on this side of us open, maybe three hours if we do."

Skirata stopped, comlink still held to his mouth. Obrim was staring at the little blue hologrammic figures with the expression of a man realizing something terrible.

We could be watching them as they die.

"Go on," Ordo said.

"Three suspects the other side of that hatch, and they can't open it now even if they wanted to. Dar's got to blow it."

"In a confined space?"

"We've got the armor."

Well, that was true: Fi had withstood a contact blast from a grenade in Mark II armor. "You don't have any choice, do you?"

"We've had worse days," Fi said cheerfully.

Ordo knew he meant it. He could feel the other part of him, the *Ord'ika* who wanted to cry for his brothers, but he was very distant, as if in another life: there was just absolute cold detachment in the physical shell where his mind was situated now.

"Do it," he said.

"The Red Zero's been transmitted to all GAR ships in striking distance," Skirata said. Ordo didn't want him to watch the hololink in case things didn't go as planned, and turned his back to him. But Skirata turned him around by his arm and stepped into the holo pickup's field of view so the squad could see him. "I'm here, lads. You're coming home, okay? Sit tight."

There was a certainty about Skirata regardless of how impossible that assurance sounded in cold reality. But Ordo could feel his utter helplessness, and shared it: Omega was light-years from the Coruscant system, far beyond the sergeant's ability to step into the firing line in person. The two soldiers turned together to shield the holoimage, and then Obrim moved in close, diplomatically blocking the view of his own team.

"Your lad Fi," he said, "—my boys *still* want to buy him that drink."

It was Obrim's men Fi had saved from the grenade. And that was probably as openly sentimental as Jaller Obrim would ever be.

"In *five,*" Darman said. *"Four . . ."*

Like a HoloNet drama whose budget hadn't run to a decent set, the image in Ordo's cupped hand showed the squad curling themselves against the far bulkhead, grasping conduit to anchor themselves in zero-g, heads tucked to their chests and hunkering down.

The image disappeared as Niner—whose gauntlet obviously carried the holofeed—buried his head, too.

"Three, two, go!"

The picture flared into a ball of blue light and the silent explosion looked even more like a poor-quality holovid whose audio track had failed.

The holoimage dimmed for a moment and then the squad's jet packs ignited and they surged forward in free fall, rifles raised, and the video feed broke up into wildly random movement with two more blinding flashes.

"Okay, three bandits down, *not* slotted, *not* fragmented, but *not* very happy either," said Fi's voice, clearly relieved. "And oxygen."

"Nice one, Omega." Skirata had his eyes shut for a moment. He pinched the bridge of his nose hard enough to leave a temporary white mark. "Now take it easy until we get to you, okay?"

Obrim's face was ashen. "I wish the public realized what those boys do," he said. "I hate kriffing secrecy sometimes."

"Shabu'droten," Skirata muttered, and walked away. No, he didn't care much for the public at all.

"What's that mean?" Obrim asked.

"You don't want to know," said Ordo, mulling over Jusik's tenuous analysis of the Force around the blast scene.

The enemy was never here.

So . . . maybe there was nobody watching.

There was *nobody waiting for precisely the most damaging moment* to detonate the device from nearby.

Remote detonation of a moving device required one of two things: either a very good view of the target, or, if the target wasn't visible, a precise timetable so the terrorist would know *exactly* where the device might be at any given time.

And that meant either a very good knowledge of GAR logistics, or—if the terrorist wanted to see the whole area, not just the immediate base—access to security holo networks.

Ordo felt a sudden cool clarity settle in his stomach, a satisfying sense of having learned something new and valuable.

"Gentlemen," he said. "I think we have a mole."

RAS *Fearless:* hangar deck

Clanky kept a tight grip on Etain's upper arm until she felt the drag of deceleration and the thud through the soles of her boots as the gunship docked in *Fearless*'s hangar.

By the time she teetered on the edge of the troop bay, somehow more wary of jumping down one meter than ten, Gett was waiting, expression carefully blank.

"The general's got a taste for making shrapnel," Clanky said approvingly. "You're instant droid death, aren't you, ma'am?"

Helmet off, he lowered his voice as he bent his head close to Gett's, but she still heard him. She heard the words *rough time.*

"We'd better get you cleaned up," Gett said. "I fear it's the proverbial interview without caf when we get back to Fleet."

Commander Gree limped past them with General Vaas Ga, both looking smoke-streaked and exhausted. "Oh, I don't think so," Vaas Ga said. "Well done. Thank you, *Fearless.*"

"Let me walk this off a little, please, Commander." Etain looked around the hangar deck, now crowded with gunships disgorging men. Medical teams moved in. The smell of burned paint and lube oil distracted her. "Anyone want to give me the numbers?"

Gett glanced down at the panel on his left forearm. "Improcco Company—four KIA, fifteen wounded, total returned—one hundred and forty out of one hundred and forty-four. Sarlacc A and B Battalions, one thousand and fifty-eight extracted—ninety-four KIA, two hundred and fifteen injured. No MIA. Twenty Torrents deployed and returned. That's *seven point five percent* losses, and most of those were during the Dinlo engagement itself. So I'd call that a result, General."

It sounded like a lot of deaths to Etain. It was. But most had made it. She had to be content with that.

"Back to Triple Zero, then." She'd called it *Zero Zero Zero* originally—the street slang—but the troopers had told her that was confusing, and that over a comlink it wouldn't be clear if she meant Coruscant or was simply using the standard military triple repeat of important data. She decided she liked *Triple Zero* better anyway. It made her feel part of their culture. "And not before time."

"Very good, General," Gett said. "Let me know when you want to refresh yourself and I'll call a steward."

Etain didn't want to be back in her cabin on her own, not right now. There was a mirror on the bulkhead above the tiny basin, and she didn't like the idea of looking herself in the eye yet. She wandered around the crowded hangar.

The bacta tanks were going to be fully occupied on the journey home.

And the clone troopers of the Forty-first Elite who were trying to find somewhere to get a few hours' sleep seemed a different breed from the four almost-boys who had been her rough-and-ready introduction to unwanted command on Qiilura.

Men changed in a year, and these soldiers around her *were* men. Whatever naïve purity of purpose—this *kote,* this *glory*—fueled them when they left Kamino for the last time, it had been overwritten by bitter experience. They had seen, and they had lived, and they had lost brothers, and they had talked and compared notes. And they were not the same any longer.

They joked, and gossiped, and evolved small subcultures, and mourned. But they would never have a life beyond battle. And that felt *wrong.*

Etain could feel it and taste it as she wandered across the hanger deck, looking for more troopers she might be able to help. The sense of *child* that had so disoriented her when she first met Darman on Qiilura was totally absent. There were two shades of existence that tinted the Force in that vast hangar: resignation, and an overwhelming simultaneous sense of both self and community.

Etain felt irrelevant. The clones didn't need her. They were confident of their own abilities, very centered in whatever identity had evolved despite the Kaminoan belief that they were predictable and standardized units, and they were bonded irrevocably with each other.

She could hear the quiet conversations. There was the occasional word of *Mando'a,* which few ordinary troopers had ever been taught, but had somehow flowed through their ranks from sources like Skirata and Vau. They clung to it. Knowing what she knew about Mandalorians, it made perfect sense.

It was the only rationale that *could* make sense when you were fighting for a cause in which you had absolutely no stake. It was the self-respect of a mercenary; internal, unassailable, and based on skill and comradeship.

But mercenaries got paid, and eventually went home, wherever that might be.

One trooper was waiting patiently for the medic. He had a triage flash stuck on his shoulder plate: the number "5," *walking wounded.* There was blood streaked across his armor from a shrapnel wound to his head, and he was holding his helmet in his lap, trying to clean it with a scrap of rag. Etain squatted down and patted his arm.

"General?" he said.

She had so ceased to notice their appearance that it took her a few seconds to see Darman's face in his. They were identical, of course, except for the thousand and one little details that made them all utterly unique.

"Are you all right?"

"Yes ma'am."

"What's your name, and *not* your number, okay?"

"Nye."

"Well, Nye, here you go." She handed him her water bottle. Apart from two lightsabers—her own and her dead Master's—her concussion rifle, and her comlink, it was the only item she was carrying. "I have *nothing* else I can give you. I can't pay you, I can't promote you, I can't give you a few days' R and R, and I can't even decorate you for valor. I'm truly sorry that I can't. And I'm sorry that you're being used like this and I wish I could put an end to it and change your lives for the better. But I can't. All I can do is ask your forgiveness."

Nye seemed stunned. He looked at the bottle and then took a long swig from it, his expression suddenly one of blissful relief. "It's . . . okay, General. Thank you."

She was suddenly aware that the hangar deck had fallen completely silent—no mean feat given the vast space and the numbers of men packed in it—and everyone was listening.

The unexpected audience actually made her face burn, and then a little ripple of applause went through the ranks. She wasn't sure if that meant they agreed, or that they were just being supportive of an officer who—now that she had some embarrassing clarity of mind—looked like a walking nightmare and was clearly having trouble dealing with the aftermath of battle.

"Caf and a change of clothes, General," Gett said, looming over her from nowhere. "You'll feel a lot better after a few hours' sleep."

Gett was a gracious commander and a perfectly competent naval officer. *He* ran the ship. He was, to all intents and purposes, the commanding officer. She wasn't. And had he been born to a family on Coruscant or Corellia or Alderaan, he would have had a glittering career. But he'd been hatched in a tank on Kamino, and so his artificially shortened life would be very different because of that.

When she got back, she would seek out Kal Skirata and beg him to help her make sense of it all. She would find Omega Squad and tell them face-to-face how much she cared about them before it was too late. She would tell Darman that most of all. She never stopped thinking of him.

"You meant what you said, General," Gett said, steering her back toward her cabin.

"Oh yes. I did."

"I'm glad. However powerless you feel, solidarity means a great deal to us."

She suddenly wanted to see Gett go home to a house full of family and friends, and wondered if she wanted it for him or for herself.

"I was once taught to see while blindfolded," she said. "It was a far more important lesson than I ever imagined. At the time I thought it was just a way of teaching me to strike with my lightsaber using the Force alone. Now I know what purpose the Force had. I look beyond faces."

"But you won't change anything by blaming yourself."

"No. You're right. But I won't change anything by pretending I have no responsibility, either."

At that point she knew as surely as she had ever known anything that the Force had lifted her from one existence, turned her around, and dropped her on another path. She could *change* things. She wouldn't change them immediately, and she couldn't change them for any of the men here, but she would somehow change the future for men like this.

"If it's any comfort, General, I'm not sure what we'd do if we weren't doing this," Gett said. "And you do get to hear an awful lot of good jokes."

He touched his fingers to his brow and left her at her cabin.

They actually found things to laugh about even surrounded by pain and death. Gett had that understated, inventive, and irreverent humor that seemed common to anyone in uniform: if you couldn't take a joke, apparently, you shouldn't have joined. She'd heard Omega quote that Skirata line more than once. You had to be able to laugh or else the tears would ambush you.

Etain stared at the dried blood on her robes and, while the memory appalled her, she couldn't bring herself to obliterate it by rinsing it away. She shoved the garment under the mattress of her bunk, shut her eyes, and then didn't even recall lying down.

She woke with a start.

She woke, and *then* the ship changed course and picked up speed: she *felt* it. That hadn't woken her. Some disturbance in the Force had.

Darman.

She could feel the very slight vibration that told her *Fearless*'s drives were straining flat out.

She sat up and swung her legs over the side of the bunk, rubbing a painful cramp from her calves. A clean set of robes was hanging on a peg behind the hatch door of her cabin. She had no idea where the crew had acquired them, but she washed her face in the basin, and looked up at last at the small mirror to see the scratched, ashen, rapidly aging face of a stranger.

But at least she could meet her own eyes now.

She pulled on the clean robes and was pocketing both her own lightsaber and Master Kast Fulier's—which she always carried out of sheer sentimentality and pragmatic caution—when there was the sound of boots padding down the passage outside. Someone rapped on the hatch. She eased it open using the Force. It was reassuring to know she wasn't too beaten to do that.

"General?" Gett said. He handed her a mug of caf, remarkably relaxed for a man whose ship was clearly driven by new urgency. "Sorry to disturb you so soon."

"That's very kind of you, Commander." She took the caf and saw her hands shaking. "I felt something. What's wrong?"

"I took a liberty, General. I hope you won't be offended, but I overrode your orders."

She couldn't imagine *that* ever bothering her. She'd once *or-*

dered Darman to do that if he ever felt she was screwing up. The clones knew their trade far better than she ever would.

"Gett, you know I trust you implicitly."

He had a disarming grin, not unlike Fi, but with less of a sense of desperately trying to jolly everyone along. "I've diverted the ship to the Tynna sector. We received a Red Zero call and I thought you'd really want to respond. An extra day or so isn't going to make any difference to the survival rate of casualties now."

Red Zero. An emergency command for all vessels to respond to a disaster of some kind, something very serious indeed. Even extracting the Forty-first hadn't been a Red Zero signal.

"I'd always give a Red Zero top priority, too. Good call, Gett."

"Thought you might." He watched her drain the cup and held out his hand to take it. "Especially because this one's from Omega Squad. They're in very deep dwang, General."

Darman, she thought. The Force always made sure she got the most important intel after all. *Dar.*

4

DELTA SQUAD TO FLEET OPS. RESPONDING TO RED ZERO. POSITION: CHAYKIN SECTOR, ETA: 1 STANDARD HOUR 40. CAN ASSIST: MEDICAL AND OXYGEN. PLEASE NOTE: DEPLOYING IN REQUISITIONED NEIMOIDIAN VESSEL. NO DEFENSIVE CAPACITY. REPEAT: NEGATIVE ARMAMENT. STRONGLY ADVISE ANY GAR VESSELS TO PING TRANSPONDER BEFORE OPENING FIRE. BE AWARE THAT SEPARATIST TRAFFIC IN SECTOR HAS INCREASED IN LAST 20 MINUTES IN RESPONSE TO FLEET MOVEMENTS. PREP FOR UNWANTED COMPANY.

—Signal received at Fleet Ops. Passed to MILINT N-11 Captain Ordo and acknowledged. Vessels responding now: *Fearless, Majestic,* and impounded enemy shuttle. Advised to assume extraction may be opposed.

367 days after Geonosis

It was cold and pitch-black in the cockpit, but it certainly beat being dead.

Fi kept his suit temperature at the bare minimum to conserve power. He flicked on his spot-lamp briefly and checked the trussed and shivering suspects who were lying against the deck: a human, and—disturbingly—two Nikto. Fi had only seen Nikto in obscure databases devoted to identifying the best part of their anatomy to aim at to stop them dead. They were *tough.* Intel said they could defeat Jedi. They were even rumored to have a weapon that could deflect and destroy a lightsaber blade. Maybe Jedi needed to tool up with PEP lasers, then.

And all the prisoners had tested positive for explosives residue when Darman had run his sensor over them. With the intel and the heavily encrypted data on their 'pads, the three looked like being *dead to rights,* as Skirata would say. But it was a long way from being satisfied that they'd snatched the right people to actually extracting useful information from them.

Fi took his thermal plastifoil survival blanket from his backpack and folded it carefully over the human, who seemed to be more affected by cold than the Nikto. Losing a suspect to hypothermia after going to all this trouble to grab them wasn't an option. Wrapping a body wasn't an easy maneuver in zero-g, but at least he'd stopped feeling sick.

The ultralight plastifoil kept drifting away every time the man shuddered. Fi sighed and took out his universal solution to any problem, a roll of thick adhesive tape, and hooked his leg around a handrail to stop himself floating while he tore off lengths. He taped the blanket to the suspect. Then he secured the trussed suspects to the deck with more of the tape. It was *amazing* how handy tape could be.

"And don't ask me to tuck you in and read you a story." The human just stared balefully at him. He had a lovely black eye now from resisting Darman a little too vigorously. "They never have happy endings."

The man's ID said Farr Orjul but nobody took that too seriously. He was about thirty: fine blond hair, sharp features, very pale blue eyes. The Nikto claimed to be M'truli and Gysk, or at least their mining licenses did, because none of the suspects was talking.

SOPs—standard operating procedures—said they had to stop prisoners from talking to each other before processing. But SOPs hadn't allowed for the little complication of running out of air before an interrogator could be found.

Niner turned his head slightly to Orjul. "You can talk to us. Or you can wait until Sergeant Vau sits you down with a nice cup of caf and asks you to tell him your life story. He's a good listener. And you'll *really* want to talk to him."

There was no response. Apart from the brief curses and grunts of pain they'd emitted when Omega stormed the cockpit and *subdued* them—Fi loved military understatement—none of the suspects had said a single word, not even name, rank, or serial number. And, of course, the two who were dry-frozen somewhere in the vacuum of space weren't going to provide many answers of their own free will, either.

"Look, shall I try to get some information out of these gentlemen just in case the taxi doesn't get here before our air runs out?" Fi asked.

"We're not trained to interrogate prisoners," said Niner.

Fi maneuvered himself above the human. He didn't know what Nikto felt or feared, and suspected that it wasn't much, but he knew plenty about his own species' vulnerabilities. "I could improvise."

"No, you'll bounce off the bulkheads, expend too much oxygen, and then we'll have to slot them to preserve the supply for us. It can wait. Vau isn't going anywhere, and neither are they."

Niner was reclining in the pilot's chair, restraining belt buckled and staring straight ahead. The blue-lit T of his visor was reflected in the transparisteel viewscreen, making him look wonderfully droid-like. Fi wasn't sure if Niner was simply saying coldly brutal things to intimidate the prisoners or not. Fi wasn't entirely sure whether *he* was really joking some of the time.

War was nothing personal. But somehow Fi felt differently about people who didn't carry a rifle and who didn't kill in honest combat. They were an invisible enemy. Fierfek, even droids stood up where you could see them.

He put it out of his mind with a conscious effort, and not only because Ordo had insisted on undamaged prisoners. He knew how to kill, and he knew how to resist pain, but he wasn't sure how to inflict it deliberately.

But he was pretty sure that Vau did. He'd leave the job to him.

Darman had positioned himself against the bulkhead with his legs stretched out. He looked asleep. Arms folded, head lowered, his point-of-view icon in Fi's HUD showed only an image of his belt and lap. Dar could sleep anywhere, anytime. At one point he flinched, as if someone had said something to him, but there was nothing audible on the comlink.

Atin, belted in to the copilot's seat, worked on the assortment of datapads, datasticks, and sheets of flimsi that he'd taken from the suspects—dead and alive—and prodded probes into dataports, doing what he seemed to enjoy best: slicing, hacking, and generally dismantling things. Niner occasionally reached out to grab any of his prizes that floated free.

Fi propelled himself forward with a gentle push against the deck and offered his roll of tape. Atin managed a smile and trapped the wayward components on the sticky side, securing the other end on Niner's left forearm plate.

"Fi, you know I don't mean it, don't you?" Niner said suddenly. "When I get on your back about stuff. I'm just venting steam."

It took Fi aback. "Sarge, I think the first thing you ever did was to tear me off a strip, and we're still brothers, aren't we? You're just like Sergeant Kal. He never meant any of it, either."

"Did you see the state of him on the hololink?"

"He looked pretty exhausted."

"Poor *Buir*. He never stops worrying."

Fi paused. It was the first time he'd ever heard Niner use the word *buir* openly: father. Fi preferred to see everyone burying their fears in wisecracks. This was all too raw.

We could be dead in two hours. Well, we've been there a few times before . . .

He shrugged, desperately seeking the other part of him that always had the smart answer ready. "I don't know about you, *vode,* but *I'm* planning on getting back to base because Obrim still owes me a drink."

"And your free warra nuts." So Darman wasn't asleep, then. "Fierfek, I keep getting this weird feeling like someone's here next to me."

"It's me, Dar. But don't ask me to hold your hand."

"Di'kut." He unfolded his arms slowly and turned to Atin. "*At'ika,* if you can't decrypt that data, why not just try to send the whole memory back down the hololink as is?"

"That's what I'm doing," Atin said without looking up. The only light in the compartment now was the blue glow from their helmets. Fi noted that Atin had his night-vision filter in place to see the small ports on the datapads. "You're right. I can't crack the encryption here, but I can dump the data down the link now and let Ordo play with it if I can override the anti-tampering. Otherwise it'll just delete everything on here. Ten minutes, maybe? I'm not letting this beat me."

Niner eased himself out of the seat and gave Atin a pat on the shoulder as he floated past him. "I'm going to keep the hololink open. Time to update Fleet on our rate of drift anyway."

They had nothing to say at the moment. And the link was a power drain that they might regret later if things didn't pan out quite as they were hoping.

But Fi understood. Kal Skirata would be going crazy not being able to keep an eye on them at a time like this. It was what he always, *always* said when things got tough: *I'm here, son.* He felt he had to be there for them. And he always had been.

Buir was exactly the right word. Fi had no idea how he had managed to keep faith with more than a hundred commandos.

The link flared into blue light again. Ordo appeared, in full armor and looking away from the cam. He must have been at Fleet HQ, then, to be working with his helmet on like that, and the hololink unit must have been placed on his desk.

"Omega here," Niner said. "Captain, mind if we keep the link open until further notice?"

Ordo looked around, and Skirata's voice cut in from outside the video pickup's field: "I'd kick your *shebs* if you didn't, *ad'ike.* You okay?"

"Bored, Sarge," said Fi.

"Well, you won't be bored much longer. *Majestic* and *Fearless* are on their way, ETA under two hours—"

"Good old ma'am," Niner said.

"—but you'll probably have help sooner, because Delta Squad are in transit."

"Oh, we'll never hear the last of this . . ."

"You haven't *met* them yet, son."

"*Heard* enough."

"Rough, rude boys," Fi said. "And rather full of themselves."

"Yes, but they have oxygen, a functioning drive, and they're just gagging to get to you first. So play nicely with them." Skirata moved into the hololink's visual range and sat down on Ordo's desk, swinging one leg, his injured one. He looked the way he always looked on training exercises: grim, focused, and constantly chewing something. "Oh, and don't open fire. They're driving a Sep ship."

"How did they get hold of that? Not that the cannon on this crate is working now anyway."

"Well, I don't think the Sep pilot was keen to part with it, but maybe they promised that they'd bring it back when they were finished."

Fi cut in again. "Anyone looking for Sicko, Sarge? Our TIV pilot?"

"Yes. We'll keep you posted." Skirata glanced at Ordo as if he'd said something. "Atin, son, you know Vau's back, don't you?"

Atin paused for a second and then carried on tapping a probe on the entrails of a dismantled datapad. He nodded to himself. "Yes, Sarge. I noted that."

"You're coming back to Brigade HQ when we get you out of there, but you steer clear of him, okay? You hear me?"

Fi was riveted. Atin had never said a word about Vau, other than that he was *hard,* but his reactions were telling.

He didn't even look toward the holoimage. "I promise, Sarge. Don't worry."

"I'll be around to make sure, too."

Atin inhaled audibly, a sign that usually meant he was either exasperated or burying his anger. Fi thought better of asking which.

Niner detached the holo emitter and pickup from his forearm plate, unlatched the small disc from inside the wrist section and stuck it on the flat shelf that ran along the freighter's console with a rolled-up piece of tape. The holoimage of Ordo and Skirata was silent, as was Omega. There was nothing more to discuss. Just having that visual link was enough to comfort everyone.

It was a long, silent half hour. Maybe Darman slept and maybe he didn't, but Fi suspected he was just thinking. Atin's ten-minute estimate had stretched somewhat but he plowed on, head down, completely focused. *Atin* was exactly what he was. Not "stubborn," as Basic translated the word, a negative refusal to change; but *atin* in the *Mando'a* sense—courageously persistent, tenacious, the hallmark of a man who would never give up or give in.

Eventually he let out a breath. "Sorted." He leaned forward to connect the dataport to the hololink. "Downloading now. Plus Dar's explosives profiling and some images of the prisoners. Sorry we didn't get pictures of the dead ones, but they wouldn't look too cute now anyway. All yours, Captain."

"That's my boy," Skirata said.

Well, he was now. He wasn't Vau's batch any longer. They all settled back and relaxed as best they could. Fi could hear it in his helmet. They were breathing in unison now, slow and shallow.

Ordo disappeared from the holoimage, no doubt to take the prized data somewhere else to crack it. Skirata simply stayed where he was, occasionally turning to check a screen behind him.

After an hour he spoke again. "Update position and intended movement, Omega. *Fearless* onstation in forty-three minutes, *Majestic* fifty-nine . . . Delta *thirty-five.*"

"They're so competitive and macho," Fi said. "We're going to have to teach them how to relax."

There was a brief snort of amusement from Darman's audio and then everyone was silent again. The three prisoners shifted from time to time: the human Farr Orjul was shuddering uncontrollably in the cold despite being wrapped like a roasting joint of nerf in all four of the squad's emergency plastifoil blankets. Condensation was forming on the bulkhead next to Fi and he ran his gloved fingertip across it, making the moisture bead and run.

It was just as well that the vessel's electrical power was down. It would be shorting out by now.

And just when things were going so well—all things considered—Skirata jumped upright from the desk and rushed out of camshot. When he came back seconds later it was clear something had gone *osik'la,* as he always put it—badly wrong.

"Omega, you've got company. There's a Sep vessel on an intercept course with you, unidentified but armed and going *fast.* Have you *any* power at all you can divert to cannon? Are you certain it's offline?"

Niner swallowed hard. The problem with a shared helmet comlink was that you heard your brother's every reaction, even the ones you really didn't want to. It was one reason why they checked each other's biosign readouts only when they had to.

"We blew all the power relays to trigger the emergency bulkheads, Sarge. It's dead."

Skirata paused for a heartbeat. "Their ETA at that speed is thirty-five minutes. *Ad'ike,* I'm sorry—"

"It's okay, Sarge," Niner said. He sounded flat calm now. "Just tell Delta not to stop for caf, okay?"

Fi's adrenaline flooded his mouth with a familiar tingling sensation, and a great cold wash of ice flowed into his leg muscles.

You couldn't defend yourself against cannon with a DC-17, not in a sealed and crippled section of a slowly drifting ship. Fi hadn't found himself helpless for a long time. He knew he wasn't going to handle it well.

Darman looked up suddenly. He hadn't reacted at all to the grim news until then. He turned to face Fi, just a ghostly blue T-shaped light on the other side of the cockpit.

"I don't want to throw any more cold water on this party," he said. "But has anyone thought through the logical sequence of this extraction? Because I bet Delta has . . ."

RAS *Fearless,* time to target: twenty minutes

Commander Gett leaned over the ops room trooper, the one he called Peewo.

It had taken Etain a while to realize that he called all the men who took watches at that console *Peewo;* it was simply an acronym for "principal weapons officer." The man's name was actually Tenn.

Tenn's face was blank with total concentration, thrown into sharp relief by the yellow light from the screens in front of him.

"There it is," he said.

The Separatist ship—appearing on the tracking screen as a visibly shifting red pulse—was now within their scanning range. Omega's wasn't, although Tenn had programmed in a blue marker that corresponded with their last position and projected drift.

"How many minutes are we still behind them?" Etain asked.

If Tenn didn't like having a commander and a general breathing down his neck, he showed no sign of it. Etain admired his ability to ignore distractions, even without a little Force help from her. He didn't seem to need it. "Five, maybe four if the velocities hold constant."

"Now, what's that?" Gett said.

A smaller target had appeared on the screen, first red, then blue, then flashing red with a cursor saying UNCONFIRMED.

"Sep drive profile, but the scan is probably detecting a GAR encrypted transponder," Tenn said. "I think we can guess who's in the driver's seat there."

"Wasn't Delta carrying out a rummage of *Prosecutor*?" Gett asked.

"I gather they had expected visitors."

"Doesn't Delta file full contact reports?" Etain interrupted.

"No more detail than they have to, I understand," Gett said. "Silent ops. I think they get out of the habit of talking to the regular forces side of things. Perhaps General Jusik might have a word with them."

Delta, like Omega, was part of Jusik's battalion, Zero Five Commando, which was one of ten in the Special Operations Brigade commanded by Etain's former Master, Arligan Zey. A year before, there had been two brigades; casualties had slashed their strength in half.

And like all the commando squads, Delta was utterly self-reliant and operated largely without command, merely receiving intelligence support and a broad objective. It was the kind of command that was ideal for a very smart but inexperienced general. And there was no other way for one Jedi to run five hundred special forces men: clones led clones, as they did in the regular GAR. So Delta did more or less as they pleased within the overall battle plan. Fortunately, it seemed to please them to be blisteringly efficient, a quality Etain noted and respected in every clone soldier she met.

"Get me a link to them, Commander," she said. "I need to talk to them. As do you. I have no idea how they're going to play this."

Gett just raised his eyebrows and turned to the signals officer to request a secure link via Fleet. It took thirty seconds. They were eighteen minutes to target. Time was running out. Tenn moved his seat a little so Gett could place the hololink transmitter on the console where they could see both the link and the tracking screen.

"Delta, this is General Tur-Mukan, *Fearless.*"

The image that shimmered before her showed one man in a familiar suit of Katarn armor, squatting with a DC-17 across his thighs. The blue light distorted natural color, but the dark patches on his armor suggested red or orange identity markings.

"RC-one-one-three-eight, General, receiving."

It was time for names. "You're *Boss.*"

"Yes, General, Boss. Our ETA is fourteen to fifteen minutes."

"You don't have any armament, do you?"

"No, and we're aware that there's another Sep ship right up our *shebs* that *does.*" Boss appeared to check himself. "Apologies for the language, General. But you're the ones carrying the cannon."

"Boss, how do you plan to execute this?"

"Get there first, get them out fast, and bug out even faster. That usually works pretty well."

She bristled, but she knew that wasn't fair to him. "Could you be more specific?"

"Okay, we get alongside, access the cockpit, seal against vacuum, and extract personnel."

"Access means a big bang, yes?"

"No. Scorch would usually love that, but this is a cutting job if you want those prisoners alive because that'll mean an instant decompression. If you *don't* want them alive, then that's easier. Omega has enough air, so their suits are still good for another twenty minutes in vacuum. In that case we just blow the cockpit viewscreen and haul them out."

Boss had his helmet cocked slightly to one side as if he was asking her to make a command decision. He *was.*

It was the mission objective versus Omega's safety.

And that's what command is all about. Etain suspected this was where she finally stopped playing at being a general.

Omega didn't have to survive, but a few terrorists who might hold the key to a wider terror network *did.* Accessing the cockpit carefully with cutting equipment would take more time, time that might mean the Sep ship arrived before Omega was safe and clear.

Her personal choice was immediate. But she wavered over the professional one. She was aware of Gett glancing at her and then looking down at something of overwhelming interest on the deck.

Boss showed unusual diplomacy for a squad that had a name for being unsubtle. He wasn't blind. He could see her as well as she could see him, and he probably saw a child out of her depth.

"General, I've spoken to Niner," he said. "He's clear. They're *all* clear. This is as close as we've come to grabbing some key players for a long, long time, and it probably cost their pilot his life as well. We *have* to make prisoner retrieval the priority. We all know the game by now. It's a risk for us, too. We might *all* get vaped."

"I know you're correct," Etain said. "But none of you is expendable as far as I'm concerned. And I know you'll do everything you can to get them out alive."

"General, is that an order, and if so, *what is it?* Extract Omega and abandon the prisoners? Or what?"

She felt her stomach fall. It was relatively easy to be the commander who held a trooper as he was dying. It was much, much harder to stand there and say *Yes, rescue three terrorists and let my friends die—let Darman die—if that's what it takes.*

Had they asked Skirata? What did *he* say?

Gett touched her arm and indicated the tracking screen. He held up three fingers. *Three minutes behind the Sep vessel now.* They were gaining on them.

"Extract the prisoners," Etain said. It was out of her mouth before she could think further. "And we'll be right behind you."

Unnamed commercial freighter, drifting three thousand klicks Core-side of Perlemian node: Red Zero first responder ETA six minutes

Fi studied his datapad and considered his brief and busy one-year career as an elite commando.

He'd fought at Geonosis. He'd taken out a Sep research base, nearly slotted his beloved Sergeant Kal, and ended the careers of eighty-five assorted Seps and more droids than he bothered to count. And he'd denied the CIS an awful lot of assets, from replenishment depots to a capital ship and a fighter squadron that didn't even have the chance to fly its first sortie.

Some of it had been fun, most of it had been a grim hard slog, and all of it had been frightening. And now the cheerful euphemism was over; he was probably going to die. And he didn't want Skirata to witness that.

He looked up from the expired op orders on his datapad and saw that the holoimage of Skirata was still much as it had been for the best part of two hours. Sergeant Kal waited. He wouldn't leave.

Niner continued to stare out the viewscreen.

Then he sat bolt upright, prevented from shooting forward by the restraining belt. Fi checked his viewpoint icon and saw he had activated his electrobinocular visor.

"Visual contact," Niner said quietly. "Fierfek, it really *is* a Sep crate. Neimoidian."

The whole squad maneuvered so they could see what he was looking at.

"About time," Niner said. Fi listened in. "Delta, Niner here. You been sightseeing?"

"Boss receiving. Sorry, we had to stop and ask for directions." He had a voice very like Atin's but with a stronger accent. "My boys are now going to show you how to do an extraction *properly,* so take notes because you might blink and miss it. There's a Sep ship with missiles up the spout about three minutes behind us."

"Can we bring some friends?"

"The more the merrier. We're going to align with your cockpit, slap an isolation seal on the viewport, and Scorch will cut through. Then you shift it fast, and we RV with *Fearless* for caf, cakes, and hero worship. Got it?"

"Copy that."

"I love emotional reunions," Fi said. "And hero worship."

"Boss, that Sep's getting awfully close." Another voice: Fi couldn't identify any of them yet. "This might have to beat the galactic record."

"*How* close? Close enough to make me mad?"

"They could launch a missile in two minutes and it'd singe your *shebs* overtaking us."

"Okay. *Close.* Omega, you heard the man." Boss sounded unperturbed. "Powder your noses and get ready to party."

Fierfek, Fi thought. He rolled carefully to peel Orjul off the deck and haul him upright for a hasty exit with jet-pack assist.

The human prisoner looked straight at him. And he *spoke.* "You're really not very good at this, are you?"

"*Now* you decide to get chatty."

"We'll all be charcoal in a few minutes, and that gives me some satisfaction."

"Okay, I'm now *really* motivated to introduce you to Sergeant Vau."

"Whoa, cut it out," Darman said. One of the Nikto tried to gore him with its short horns as he lifted it ready for escape. "Ungrateful *di'kut.*" He brought his helmet hard down in its face in a perfect head-butt; only the pilot's seat stopped them from being catapulted by the inertia of the impact. Darman looked around at the other Nikto. "Want some?"

"Udesii, boys, *udesii."* Niner raised his Deece. "Push comes to shove, we only need one of them alive, so next one to look like a safety risk isn't going home. Okay?"

The small Neimoidian assault vessel now filled their field of vision as it came to nestle partly across the freighter's viewscreen. Fi watched, mesmerized. A hatch opened and something distressingly reminiscent of a widemouthed worm emerged and sucked against the transparisteel. A familiar blue light loomed from the darkness of its maw. Through the plate, Fi saw a helmet very like his and an exaggerated thumbs-up gesture.

"Stand back and watch a pro at work," said a disembodied voice on the comlink.

For a second Fi thought Scorch was attaching a frame charge. *Yeah, that's clever, I don't think.* But the large ring of alloy pipe sat snugly on the plate and began to glow white-hot. Scorch's thumbs-up became a jerked *move away* gesture.

"Scorch, sooner rather than later, okay?" Boss's voice said.

"One minute, tops."

"We haven't *got* a minute—"

"What d'you want me to do, chew through it?"

The transparisteel plate was distorting as the hot frame burned through from the outside. Niner gathered up the hololink and snapped it back on his forearm plate. Atin shoved datapads and tools in his belt.

"Tell you what, shall we just float here and panic incoherently while we're waiting?" Fi said.

"Good idea," Scorch said, unmoved.

"*Very* good idea, panicking," Boss said. "Guess what I just eyeballed from the port-side screen . . ."

RAS *Fearless*, ops room, ETA to target: two minutes

The assault ship had to decelerate to drop from hyperspace and open fire. It cost critical time. Etain watched while Tenn made rapid calculations to see if they could find that single critical firing solution that balanced losing speed with firing missiles and would not only make up those seconds, but also take out the Sep ship before it had a chance to target Omega.

The ops room was crowded with white armor and yet utterly silent as *Fearless*'s crew watched the tracking screen repeater on the bulkhead. It mirrored what Tenn, Gett, and Etain could see in smaller format at the PWO's station.

Tenn didn't seem to have blinked in the last three minutes.

"Firing solution, General." His hand rested on the firing key, his gaze welded to the screen. "Target acquired. Best solution we're going to get and our window is ten seconds or we'll take out Omega and Delta, too. Now, General?"

Etain glanced at Gett, her mind partly sensing the ripples in the Force. And the Force agreed with Tenn, to the very second.

"Take it, Tenn."

"Yes, ma'am." The key made a small snipping noise as he depressed it. "Fire *one,* fire *two.* Missiles away—"

Two huge trails of savage energy sped away from the decelerating assault ship and into the void. Etain could feel too much imminent disaster in the Force: she didn't want to watch it as well. She cupped her hands over her nose and shut her eyes for a second, and then made herself look back at the screen.

The tracking screen followed the missiles as steady white lines. They looked as if they had overlapped the pulsing red point of light that was the Separatist fighter. All the traces winked out of existence at the same time.

"Splash one," said a trooper at another station. "Visual confirmation. Target destroyed."

"And who else?" Commander Gett asked.

"Whoaaaa . . !"

Fi wasn't certain if it was his own cry of shock or Scorch's voice in his comlink, but he saw the ball of white-and-gold flame expanding toward them, silhouetting the section of Neimie ship that partly obscured the shield, and he ducked instinctively.

A hailstorm of debris rained on the screen. Something large and metallic skidded along the casing of the freighter with a long dull screech. Fi straightened up as the hammering faded to the occasional rattle, like stones being tossed onto a roof. Then it stopped completely.

"Fierfek," Scorch said. "Now, if they'd only added a spot of maranium to the warhead, it would have burned a really pretty *purple.*"

"*Fearless Fearless Fearless* calling Delta. Are you clear, repeat, are you clear, respond."

A large rectangle of hot softened glass peeled slowly away from the screen, helped by Scorch's fist, and drifted off serenely into a silent, slow-motion collision with the headrest of the pilot's seat.

"Delta here, *Fearless.* Just extracting Omega and cargo now."

Fi fought to stop himself from sounding breathless and shaky. It would let the squad down. "I'm glad the navy's here," he said. "Because if it had been down to you, Greased Lightning, we'd be an asteroid belt by now."

Scorch's visor poked through the aperture at last, followed by his arm, and he made an unmistakable gesture of displeasure.

Fi felt his mouth take over, fueled by shock. "My hero! You finally made it!"

"You want to walk back to base?"

Niner lifted the plastifoil-wrapped Orjul with one hand and lined him up with the opening. "Fi's going to give his mouth a nice rest now and help me cross-deck the garbage."

"Gift-wrapped? Aww, you *shouldn't* have." Scorch hauled himself a little farther down the access tube and hung motionless at 135 degrees, assessing the three bound prisoners. "Feet first, please. Then if the *di'kut* tries to kick out I can break his legs. Don't want this tubing breached."

It proved harder than expected. But by the time the second Nikto had been rammed up into the connecting tube like a torpedo, the warm air from the hijacked Neimoidian vessel had worked its way into the freighter cockpit and made Fi feel a lot more comfortable. He stood back to let Atin then Darman make their way up the tube.

Scorch hauled Darman inboard by his webbing. Fi waited for his boots to disappear and then rolled to peer up the aperture into a circle of dim light.

"Next!"

Fi lined up and then pushed off with one boot. As he passed through the open hatch at the other end, he felt artificial gravity seize him, and he rolled onto the deck with a clatter of armor plates. It took him a few seconds to get to his feet. Niner collided with him from behind. It wasn't a very big ship.

Boss—his armor daubed with chipped and peeling orange paint—slammed the hatch behind Niner and sealed it. Niner stared at him as if he wasn't sure what should happen next and then the two men simply shook hands and slapped each other on the back.

"Like what we've done with the place?" Boss said, taking off his helmet. The flight deck looked as if someone had been dismantling it the hard way: panels had been ripped out, wires hung from the deckhead, and there were empty slots in the console where units had either been removed or not installed in the first place. "Okay, perhaps it's a little basic, but we call it home."

"You *nicked* this?"

"No, they let us take it on a test drive." Boss gestured at the rest of his brightly painted squad. "Fixer, Sev, and you already know Scorch. Say hello to the boys in boring black."

"Thanks, *vode,*" Fi said. He wondered why Atin wasn't joining in; he had turned away and seemed to be taking a technical interest in a run of conduit. "Any word on Sicko?"

"If that's your pilot, *Majestic*'s been diverted now. They picked up his beacon and that's all we know." Boss looked down at the three prisoners, lined up on the deck like corpses. He gave each of them a nudge with his boot. "You'd better be worth everyone's effort."

Fi eased off his helmet and inhaled almost fresh air. Except for Scorch, they had all taken off their helmets. Delta was one of fewer than a dozen squads that had survived intact since decanting, a true *pod* as the Kaminoans had called it, and they seemed to think that made them an elite within an elite. They had been raised and trained together, and they had never fought with anyone but their brothers. It was a luxury few squads now enjoyed.

Fi suspected it meant they didn't play well with others. He remembered only too well how ferociously competitive and inward looking his own pod had been, and how badly his confidence had been dented when he lost his brothers at Geonosis and was then dumped in Niner's care.

"You do okay for a mongrel squad," Sev said, and Fi chose not to react. He knew he was on autopilot now and that he should shut up. Niner's glance helped him decide. "I don't suppose you did a rummage on that ship, did you?"

"Not with a rapid decompression on our hands, no," said Niner. "Word was that it was carrying explosives."

"Okay, we're going to be coated in Seps anytime now, so let's get this crate into *Fearless*'s hangar and then they can blow the freighter. If there's anything useful in it, at least the Seps don't get it."

Darman slid down a bulkhead onto the deck, and Niner sat down beside him. They were nearly back aboard *Fearless,* and that meant they were nearly home, and home meant Arca Company Barracks and—at last—a good night's sleep after two months on patrol. Fi never got enough. None of them ever did. And fatigue could make you dangerously careless.

"So, Atin . . . ," Sev said. He wandered up behind Atin and stood close enough to be annoying. Atin didn't turn around. "Sargent Vau asked to see you again, *vod'ika.*"

"I'm not your *little brother,*" Atin said quietly. He kept his back to Sev. "I just work with you."

Ah, so there *was* some history between those two. Fi bristled: he rallied to his adopted brother. He could see that the prospect of actually meeting Vau again was stoking something inside that wasn't typically Atin.

Sev didn't let up. "I don't forget, you know."

This time Atin *did* wheel around, face-to-face with Sev, so close that Fi thought his placid brother was actually going to lose it for once. He prepared to intervene.

"It's my business," Atin said. "Stay out of it."

Sev stared into his face. "And disagreements stay *inside* the company."

Atin hooked his fingers in the neck of his bodysuit and yanked it down to the left as far as the edge of the armor, exposing his collarbone. He had a lot of raised white scars. Nobody took much notice of them because injuries in training and combat were so common that they rarely drew comment. "You got worse than that, did you? You spent a week in bacta, *did you*?"

Atin looked about to snap, and Fi stepped forward to intervene. Then Niner was across the cabin in three strides and slammed in between the two men. He had to break them up by putting his arms between them and knocking them apart with his arm plates. But Sev's unblinking gaze was still fixed on Atin as if Niner weren't there.

"I think we all need to reach a comradely understanding," Niner said, blocking Sev with his body. "Back at the barracks, if that's okay with you, *ner vod.*"

Sev looked murderous. His eyes were still fixed on Atin's. "Anytime, *vod'ika.*"

"Okay, you two can shut it *now.* And you, Fi. Stand down. We've all had a bad day, so let's throttle back on the testosterone and play nicely."

Sev held his hands away from his sides in a gesture of reluctant submission and went to sit beside Scorch in the cockpit. Boss didn't say a word, but Niner grabbed Fi and Atin by their shoulders and shoved them farther away.

"You're going to tell me what that's all about."

"No, I'm not, Sarge. It's personal."

"There's no *personal* where this squad is concerned. Later, okay? I'm not having you brawling like a pair of civvies. If there's a needle match between you two, we *all* sort it together. Got it?"

"Yes, Sarge."

Niner emphasized his warning with a prod in Atin's chest and moved back to stand with Boss while Scorch brought the vessel alongside *Fearless* and began negotiating with the flight deck controller on how they might make space in the hangar for it. Fi waited with Atin in case he decided to resume his little chat with Sev. He had never seen Atin flare up even under the most extreme pressure, but he seemed ready to swing at anyone now. And even a brain-dead Weequay could have spotted that it had something to do with Vau.

"*At'ika,* you want to tell me about it sometime?"

"Not really." Atin patted Fi on the shoulder. "I have to deal with it myself sooner or later."

Fi glanced at Sev and got a blank stare that wasn't even hostility, just an absence of anything comradely. It wasn't going to be a bundle of laughs if they ever had to work together again.

Fi hadn't thought he would get on with Niner on first meeting, either. But there had never been anything about Niner that had made Fi want to punch him in the face and get it over with, just to save time.

It was going to happen, sooner or later. Fi *knew* it.

He'd never had a disagreement, let alone a fight, with a brother before. It made him uneasy. He distracted himself with dreams of a hot shower, hot food, and the luxury of five hours' unbroken sleep.

5

To: Officer Commanding SO BDE, HQ Coruscant: CO Fleet Protection Group.

From: CO *Majestic,* off Kelarea: 367 days after Geonosis.

I regret to inform you that we have recovered the wreckage of TIV Z590/1 and the body of pilot CT-1127/549. Perlemian Traffic Control reports that Republic civilian freighter *Nova Crystal* logged that it fired on a vessel it described as a "pirate" attacking its convoy to dislodge it from the hull. I also regret that due to security restrictions, I am unable to tell PTC that the freighter killed a special forces pilot on active service, and so PTC regard *Nova Crystal*'s skipper to be something of a hero.

Fleet Ops HQ, Coruscant, 0600, 368 days after Geonosis: the first anniversary of the battle

Skirata walked out of the Fleet Ops lobby and into a cool, moist morning that he wasn't expecting to welcome.

It was over, for the time being. Omega had survived, and they were coming home. They needed a break from continuous deployment in the badlands and he was certain they were needed here. CSF couldn't handle a big terror operation in the capital system, not even with Obrim around.

The question was how to work that past Arligan Zey. The Jedi was reluctant to commit men to what he saw as security work at a time like this.

But it was what Ordo and the Nulls were ideally suited for—if they had a few commandos to deploy as well.

Skirata stood on the steps for a few minutes inhaling fresh air, eyes stinging from fatigue, and raked his fingers through his crew cut. He could sleep now. Omega was safe; Ordo was here with him; and his five brothers were accounted for, safe and well.

Mereel was on Kamino. If Zey was heard to mutter that the Nulls were Skirata's private army, he wasn't entirely wrong.

There were still ninety of the men Skirata had trained from small boys on active service, and he worried about them, too. But Omega had become as much his closest family now as the Null ARCs. He would move the galaxy for them if he had to.

The gold-veined marble fountain in the center of the plaza beckoned to him. He stopped as he walked past it and simply leaned over and plunged his head in the icy water, holding it there for a few painfully refreshing moments before jerking upright and shaking the water off like a mott.

A couple of early-morning pedestrians stared at him and he returned the stare until they looked away. It was rare for anyone to even notice him: he made a habit of being inconspicuous. But today he didn't care. Did they have *any* idea what was going on around the galaxy on hundreds of battlefields? He resisted the urge to grab them, shake them, and make them listen to what was happening in their name.

It was the first anniversary of Geonosis. Nobody seemed to be marking that.

Ordo walked up behind him. "You should get some rest, *Kal'buir.*"

"I'll sleep when *you* sleep."

"I have more good news."

"I could do with that."

"Darman's explosives profile. The reading from the prisoners matches up with the manufacturing characteristics of at least a quarter of the devices detonated so far. We got a break."

"Good work. And good old Dar." He smiled at Ordo, reminded again of how well his boys had turned out. "Tell you what, *Ord'ika,* fancy some breakfast while the system gets on with unpacking that data? They do a disgustingly greasy fry-up in the Kragget. It's not the Skysitter, but it sets you up for the day."

Ordo shrugged and tilted his head in a conspicuously self-conscious glance down at his spotless white armor. "I don't think we're the Skysitter's type of clientele, anyway."

Skirata couldn't see the expression behind the visor, but he knew Ordo was amused. It was good that a man who'd had an unimaginable nightmare of a childhood could find anything funny. "They have napkins. And I'll try not to splash sauce over you. Deal? Just to celebrate the fact that we're both still here a year on."

Ordo started walking. "What were you doing a year ago today?"

"Wondering where all my boys had gone."

"Sorry, *Kal'buir.* It was a *very* rapid deployment. I should have woken you."

"You did fine. I should have shaped up and realized you had a job to do."

"We certainly accounted for a number of enemy positions," Ordo said.

"I never said good-bye to the lads who didn't come back, that's all. I lost nine out of my batch."

"But the last time you saw them, you left them feeling confident, respected, and loved. That's enough for any *buir* to achieve."

"Thanks, son." *How did he ever grow up this normal?* "Let's enjoy ourselves for a change, shall we?"

For a few brief hours Skirata and Ordo did what normal civilians did and took an EasyRide to the city's lower levels to have a dangerously unhealthy but comforting breakfast.

Skirata had never used public transport with Ordo in tow before, and the reactions of other passengers fascinated him. They sneaked sideways glances. Ordo's custom holster with its twin blasters probably focused them somewhat. The ARC trooper armor was spectacular even in a city jaded by the everyday presence of a thousand exotic species.

Skirata regularly forgot how few of the capital's civilians had ever seen a clone soldier face-to-face. Apart from the heavily publicized display of massed GAR battalions boarding assault ships at the military staging area a year ago, the vast majority of Coruscanti had no contact with them whatsoever.

And *never* without their helmets.

"Ord'ika," he whispered. "Do me a favor. Take off your bucket, will you?"

Ordo paused for a moment and then popped the seal on his collar and lifted off his helmet. Skirata kept an eye on the other passengers' reactions. It was a revelation. Some looked blankly surprised. Others went a little farther.

"Oh no, they're *human!*" one man whispered. "And they're so *young!*"

Did anyone know *how* young? He hated using Ordo like this, but it had to be done. Skirata, tired and permanently irritable, bit back his retort and became a diplomat for a few moments.

"No sir, the war isn't droids fighting droids," he said. "May I introduce Captain Ordo?"

Ordo nodded politely at the man in the seat across the aisle and extended his hand; Skirata had taught his little Nulls to act like nice boys when they needed to. The man hesitated and then reached across to shake Ordo's hand, surrendering soft pale civilian fingers to a black gauntlet. The look on his face said clearly that he hadn't expected to find flesh and blood inside the droid-like shell, or to retrieve his hand uncrushed afterward.

"My pleasure, sir," Ordo said.

It was unusually quiet in the EasyRide after that. At least the reality had registered on them. Skirata nudged Ordo to get off when they reached the Kragget level, and the ARC replaced his helmet.

"You like to shock," said Ordo.

"I like to *educate,*" said Skirata. "Sorry, son."

Strolling around Coruscant with a fully armored ARC captain was hardly blending in, but it got him a good table in the Kragget, which meant one that the service droid actually wiped clean before they sat down. A couple of CFS officers acknowledged them. Police and security officers liked eating here because it was right on the edge of their "manor," as some of them called the rough territory where they plied their trade, handy for a quick response to a call but far enough away to be a haven.

Ordo took his helmet off again to tuck into the plate of fried smoked nerf slices. The eggs were from something Skirata couldn't identify and knew he didn't want to. He concentrated on the seductively unctuous sensation of hot fat and salty yolk in his mouth and washed it down with several cups of caf.

"We can't leave this to the boys in blue any longer," Skirata said. They both knew what *this* was without being specific in a public place. "They're hampered by having to do stuff by the book, and we don't know if they're all playing for our team anyway. This is one for *us.* I'm going to make Zey see sense about it. Once everyone's back in town, it'll be a lot harder for him to say no."

"If the cryptography droid extracts some relevant data from Atin's little haul, it might be even harder."

"Which reminds me. I haven't paid my respects to Vau."

"Promise me you won't pull your knife on him again."

"I'll behave."

The server droid seemed to have been replaced by a female Twi'lek waitress, who looked past prime dancing age but who still distracted Skirata for a second or two. She put another plate of nerf strips in front of Ordo, who—like every clone soldier Skirata had ever known—would eat anything and everything put in front of him.

She smiled and lingered. Ordo froze and returned the smile in the nervous way of a small boy, then busied himself with his breakfast and the waitress moved away.

Skirata reflected on the careless power of youth and looks, and how incomplete a teacher he had been of social skills. "Somehow I don't think *she's* mistaken you for a droid."

Ordo looked uncharacteristically flustered for a moment. "Er . . . I've been assessing our requirements." He cleared his plate again, and Skirata slid his unwanted eggs onto the man's plate and watched them disappear. "Kit is an issue. We need to discuss this before you see Zey. This is going to take some serious resources—vehicles, safe houses, special surveillance equipment, and ordnance."

Skirata had been doing the calculations at the samc time Ordo had.

They'd need two squads, at least, and a couple of Nulls. But two squads of Republic Commandos in their distinctively bulky, bad-boy Katarn Mark III kit and Ordo and Mereel in their spectacular red and blue would be *noticeable* as unusual activity.

They might need to wear that armor sooner or later, even if they could be deployed in civilian clothing the rest of the time.

Skirata chewed the last overdone piece of smoked nerf—he saved the delectable crunchy bits for last—and a solution blossomed as his jaw worked.

Hide in plain sight.

He was good at that. He could become so mundane—unkempt hair, scruffy clothing—that he was almost invisible. And so could his lads, by being the opposite.

All they had to do was be one of *a number of* clone personnel wandering around Coruscant in full armor. And if occasionally they took off that armor and went about in fatigues, then who would really recognize them as individuals?

They all looked the same to most people, other than a few Jedi who cared about them as men, and their own brothers.

Skirata considered it a *very* productive working breakfast.

He opened his comlink and keyed a meeting request to General Zey. Then he leaned across the table, seized Ordo two-handed by his shoulder pauldron, and gave him a noisy and exaggerated paternal kiss on the top of his head.

"Sorted!" he said. *"Plain sight!"*

The Twi'lek waitress watched, fascinated. "Hey, can I try that, too?"

"He's just a boy," Skirata said, and left her a very generous tip. Ordo got up to follow him, pocketing a couple of mealbread sticks for later. "My son."

RAS *Fearless* hangar deck

"Good grief, here comes the armored division," said Commander Gett. He strode toward the Neimoidian vessel. Its casing was streaked and pocked with scorch marks. "RCs look like *tanks,* don't they?"

Republic Commandos did look fearsomely bulky alongside the clone troopers. The first four to clamber out of the seized Trade Federation craft were a riot of color, their battered armor daubed with green, yellow, red, and orange markings.

The second squad was armored in matte black, utterly featureless and grim. But Etain knew instantly who they were and which man was which. She needed no battle livery to distinguish them: their forms in the Force were almost like trails of phosphorescence in a tropical ocean, and they were instantly familiar, instantly old friends.

I was only with them for a few days and I haven't seen or talked to them for months. But it's as if we were never apart.

Fi—oh yes, she knew it was Fi even before he spoke—saluted, lifted his helmet, and winked.

"Ma'am, you look like the back end of a bantha," he said sympathetically. "Are they looking after you properly here?"

"Fi!" She knew she was supposed to remain dignified and aloof, and she'd felt comradeship with many clone troopers in the intervening months, but her first reluctant command with Omega had utterly changed her. "Fi, I've really missed you. What happened to the gray armor?"

"You know how much Dar griped about being too visible on Qiilura. Anyway, he's brought you a present." He gestured over his shoulder. Darman was helping a group of troopers haul the prisoners out of the Neimoidian landing craft while Gett examined it. "They're all in one piece, too. We've been really good boys this time."

Delta Squad had simply disappeared. When Etain looked around, she saw they had settled in a tight knot in a corner of the hangar deck, helmets on, obviously talking intently. She knew the body language now. They didn't feel like Omega in the Force at all. They were a concentrated well, a bottomless pool of something unyielding, and totally enmeshed with each other. The general impression they made on the Force was one of triumphant high spirits.

Niner and Atin approached and clasped hands with her. It didn't feel at all inappropriate. They looked tired and anxious, and she wanted very badly to make things right for them. They were her *friends.*

"I bet you'd like something to eat," she said.

"Any chance of a hot shower and a few hours' sleep first, please, General?" Niner looked apologetic and shoved Fi gently in the back. "Me first. I'm pulling rank."

"He's not *really* a sergeant, General," said Fi. "He just helps them out when they're busy."

"Any news on our pilot?" Niner asked.

"Yes. I'm so sorry."

It was never easy. She tapped her datapad to bring up the copy of the signal that *Majestic* had sent to Fleet and handed the 'pad to him. Niner glanced at it, blinked, and passed it to Fi. Fi parted his lips briefly as if to say something, and then his slight frown almost crumpled into grief. He composed himself and just looked down at the deck.

"He's not the first," Fi said, suddenly grim, and Etain had never seen that aspect of him surface visibly before. "And he won't be the last."

Etain watched them disappear through a hatch on the aft bulkhead, trailing after a trooper. *Fearless* shivered slightly under the soles of her boots, making top speed back to Coruscant, and she waited while Darman spent what seemed like an interminable time fussing about with the prisoner handover. She wondered if he was reluctant to talk after choosing not to remain on Qiilura with her. Perhaps he was just concerned that nothing else went wrong.

She gave up waiting and walked carefully between the troopers still trying to catch some sleep on the hangar deck, curled up wherever they could find a relatively comfortable space.

"Well done," she said, hoping that some were awake to hear her.

Darman had changed.

He bent his head to ease off his helmet, popping the seal, and then shook his hair and smoothed it flat with one glove. And although he smiled, he wasn't the Darman she had been through hell with.

He looked older.

Clones aged faster than normal men. He was eleven going on twenty-two going on—fifty. When she had first sensed him as a child in the Force, his square, high-cheekboned face had been both man and boy, at the stage of life when—had she been able to manipulate time—the slightest push backward would have revealed the child he had so recently been. But now he was a man, quite solidly, and with no hint of the boy about him.

It wasn't simply that he had aged two years in one. The look in his eyes said he was much, much older, as old as the battlefield, maybe as old as war itself. She had seen it in the face of every clone trooper and commando and ARC she had commanded. She knew that she had that same look, too.

But Darman smiled anyway, and the smile broadened into a grin that made the rest of the ship—even the galaxy—utterly irrelevant to her.

"You always cut it fine, don't you, ma'am?"

"It's good to see you, Dar. Whatever happened to *Etain*?"

"She turned into a general and we're on the hangar deck."

"You're right. I'm sorry."

"Is it definitely confirmed that we're going back to base?"

"Unless you want to argue with the officer of the watch, I believe so."

"Good. We need a break. Just a day or two, maybe."

He never did ask for much. None of them did: she wondered if they didn't know what the world had to offer them or if they were just honed down to basic needs, too overwhelmed to think beyond recovering enough to do the job over again the next day.

She patted his armored shoulder and held her hand there for a few seconds. He looked as if he suddenly remembered something and was embarrassed by it in a way he quite enjoyed.

"It must be nice to be able to reach out to someone through the Force," he said.

So he'd felt it. She was glad.

"Get yourself off to the 'freshers," she said. "Come and find me afterward if you're not too tired, and I'll show you over the ship."

"Have you met Sergeant Kal yet?"

"No." *Kal* was always there for Darman, somewhere, even at times like this when she wanted to say so much to him. "When we dock, perhaps you could introduce me."

Darman beamed, clearly delighted. "Oh, you'll like him, General. You'll really *like* him."

Etain certainly hoped so. And if she didn't, then she'd try, for Darman's sake.

SO Brigade HQ, Coruscant, 369 days after Geonosis

The smell hit Ordo long before he reached the meeting room. It was a familiar blend of wet wool, mold, and a pungent oily musk.

Skirata reacted visibly. He straightened his right arm by his side out of old, old habit and let the blade slide into his hand, fall a fraction until the handle touched his palm, and then snatched it.

"*Kal'buir,* it would be better if I *shot* it," Ordo said. He put a restraining hand on Skirata's arm. "I won't let it near you."

"I've often wondered if you're telepathic, son."

"I can smell the strill, you have your knife ready, and we're meeting Sergeant Vau. Telepathy isn't required to work that one out."

Ordo would have been quite content to shoot the strill without a second thought because it upset *Kal'buir.* But it wasn't the strill's fault that it stank, or that it had a master who cherished cruelty, or that it had become savage itself. It had been selected by nature and then trained by people to hunt for pleasure rather than for food, and nothing else had ever been allowed to cross its mind.

He felt some pity for it. But he would still kill it without a moment's hesitation.

The doors slid back. Ordo placed his right hand discreetly on the grip of one of his repeating blasters. His attention went instinctively to Vau, then to the strill lying on his lap, and then to the fact that he had a clear shot at both. It took less than a second to process the information and then to subdue the impulse.

Behind Vau's head, the walls of General Zey's meeting room were a beautiful soothing shade of aquamarine, but they weren't working. Skirata wasn't *soothed.*

And Captain Maze was sitting at the table beside Zey, arms folded across his chest and looking none too impressed, either. There was an ugly purple bruise at the point of his chin, more discoloration around one eye, and a cut on the bridge of his nose.

I didn't think I hit him that *hard,* Ordo thought. *Unfortunate.*

Zey motioned Skirata to enter just after the man strode in of his own accord, and indicated chairs at the lapiz-topped table. Bardan Jusik sat beside him, hands clasped on the tabletop in an attempt at serenity.

"Well," Skirata said, and sat down. He ran his hand across the luxurious polished surface. "*This* is nice. I hope I never hear anyone complaining about the GAR's expenditure on armor and weapons."

"Kal," Vau said politely. "It's good to see you again."

Vau was settled in one of the deeply upholstered hide chairs with the strill draped across his lap on its back, all six of its legs flopping in an undignified sprawl while he scratched its belly. Its huge fanged mouth was slack, tongue lolling, and a long skein of drool hung almost to the floor. Its body was a meter long, lengthened by a whip of a tail covered in more loose skin.

The strill was still prettier than Vau, though. The man had a long square-jawed face that was all bone and frown lines, and graying dark hair cut brutally short. Faces rarely lied about the soul within.

"Walon," Skirata said, nodding.

Zey gestured to Ordo to sit but he remained standing and simply removed his helmet. He transferred the bead-sized comlink connector to his ear, noting Zey's expression without looking directly at him.

Skirata looked up. "Take a seat, Captain."

Ordo obeyed only one man's orders, and that man was *Kal'buir.*

Zey was visibly thrown—again. No doubt all other ARCs and commandos jumped when he said so, but he should have known Ordo by now. Maze certainly did. He was staring at his brother ARC as if one snap of Zey's fingers would give him permission to jump up and return that punch.

"Maze, perhaps you'd like to go and have a break," Zey said. "This is just going to be a tedious administrative matter."

Maze paused for one beat, his eyes never leaving Ordo's. "Yes sir." He grabbed his helmet from the table and left.

Zey waited for the doors to close behind him. "Let's hear your plan, Sergeant."

"I want to deploy Delta and Omega on Coruscant to identify and neutralize the Sep network here, because it *is* here," said Skirata. "It has to be in order to strike us so easily. And CSF doesn't have the expertise or personnel to deal with this, and there might even be someone inside the CSF passing intel to the terrorists."

Zey's eyes were locked on him. "Commandos are a military asset. *Not* an intelligence one. Nor police. We have theaters of war across—"

"I wasn't planning to arrest anybody. This is a shoot-to-kill policy."

"I wasn't aware we had one."

"You haven't, so you'd better get one *fast.*"

"I can't ask the Senate to authorize use of special forces against Coruscant residents."

"Don't ask them." Skirata became pure ice at times like this: Ordo watched him carefully, anxious to learn more nuances of the part of soldiering that required no weapons beyond nerve and psychology. "Is the Jedi Council squeamish about that sort of thing, too?"

"Sergeant . . ."

"Then don't ask them, either. In fact, we never had this conversation. All you've done is tell me you can't ask the Senate to give its blessing to a change in the GAR's terms of reference."

"But *I* know what you're suggesting," Zey said.

Skirata was fidgeting with his blade. Ordo could see it: it was a tiny movement, but he could detect the flex of his forearm muscles through his jacket. Skirata had the point of the blade resting on his curled middle finger and was pressing it ever so slightly up and down, a preparation for dropping and catching the grip.

"The Jedi Council is pretty adept at turning blind eyes," Skirata said. "For an organization that knew it was taking on an army with an assassination capability, you do send out conflicting signals to simple soldiers like me."

Vau was watching the exchange like a man being mildly amused by a holovid. The strill yawned with a thin, high-pitched whine.

"The difference the Senate will see," Zey said, "is that this is *Coruscant.*"

"General, the days when wars were fought elsewhere while the home fires were kept burning are long gone."

"I know. But there are armies, and there are . . . bounty hunters and assassins. And the Senate will be wary of crossing that line on home ground."

"Well, that's what tends to happen when you let a bunch of . . . *bounty hunters and assassins* train your army."

"We didn't know we even *had* an army until a year ago."

"Maybe, but the fact that you're sitting here now with a general's rank means you've accepted responsibility for it. You could have objected, collectively or individually. You could have *asked questions.* But no. You picked up the blaster you found on the floor and you just fired it to defend yourself. Expedience ambushes you in the end."

"You know what the alternative was."

"Look, General, I need to clarify a few things, being just a simple assassin and all that. Answer a few questions for me."

Zey should have been furious that a mere sergeant was treating him as if he were an annoyingly pedantic clerk rather than a battle-hardened general. To his credit, he seemed more intent on a solution. Ordo wondered where expedience ended and pragmatism began.

"Very well," said Zey.

"Do you want to stop attacks on vulnerable targets that are starting to compromise the ability of the GAR to deploy and are destroying public confidence in the Senate's ability to defend the capital?"

"Yes."

"Do you think it's a good idea for some of our hard-pressed special forces lads to have an unprecedented break on Coruscant after months in the field?"

Zey paused, just a breath. "Yes."

"Do you need to ask anyone else to authorize that purely administrative matter?"

"No. General Jusik is responsible for personnel welfare."

Ordo kept his face utterly blank. *Leave?* There was never any leave for the GAR, or their Jedi command in the front line. Neither would have known what to do with free time anyway.

Jusik looked pinned down. "I do believe some R and R would be a good idea, actually." Skirata smiled at him with genuine warmth. Jusik was all right, one of the boys, all desperate courage and desire to belong. It was hard to tell if he was now playing the game or just being a decent officer. "I'll look into it."

"And sir," Skirata said, "is it true that you knew all along that I was a complete *chakaar* who could never follow orders, who kept you in the dark, who treated his squads like his own private army, and was generally a *Mando* lowlife just like Jango and the rest of that mongrel scum?"

Zey leaned back in his seat and pinched the end of his nose briefly, staring hard at the blue stone table.

"I do believe I might realize that at some time in the future, Sergeant." The corners of his eyes crinkled for the merest fraction of a second, but Ordo spotted it. "I have my suspicions. Proving them *is* hard, though."

Zey was all right, too, then.

Vau had been watching the exchange with mild interest, and Ordo had been watching him, because he knew the man all too well.

"Sergeant Vau, do you have any view on this . . . ah . . . *leave* situation?" said Ordo.

"Oh no, I'm just a civilian now," Vau said. The strill rumbled. Vau, apparently distracted, fondled its ghastly, stinking head, his slightly narrowed eyes revealing a doting affection that he never seemed to spare for any other living creature. "I'm just hanging around. When those detainees are released, I'll offer them a room for a while, and I'll have a conversation with them. Nothing to do with the GAR or the Senate at all. Merely a private citizen doing what he can to welcome visitors to Coruscant."

Jusik was watching the exchange with an expression that suggested he was both excited and aware that the stakes had just been raised. They were subverting democracy in one sense, but they were also saving their political masters from a decision they could never be seen to take, yet had to.

"That's the worst thing about having *chakaare* like us around," Skirata said. "We just wander off, find someplace that you don't know about, and hole up in it and get into all sorts of mischief that you also know *nothing* about. And then we bill you for it. Dreadful."

"Dreadful," Zey echoed. "Is this the kind of thing that CSF might notice?"

"Were we to get a little out of hand, I imagine *very* senior officers in CSF might need to be reassured, but not by you."

"Dreadful," Zey said. "Hypothetically, anyway."

Language was a wonderful thing, Ordo thought. Skirata had just told Zey that he was about to *go bandit,* as he called it, running an unauthorized shoot-to-kill operation in a civilian location and simply sending Zey the bill. Vau planned to interrogate the prisoners. CSF senior command would be placated by Skirata should anything go wrong, without any need for Zey to be involved. And yet Zey had authorized it all.

And the subject had still *not been discussed.*

"I wonder if anyone will notice our commandos on leave here," Jusik said, apparently catching on.

"Probably," said Skirata. "And wouldn't it be nice if we also extended that home deployment to honest ordinary clone troopers, *lots* of them? That'd be good for morale."

"And reassuring for the public to see soldiers in armor around the capital."

"I wonder how I can persuade the Senate officers that it's a good idea?"

Zey cut in. "Have you met Mar Rugeyan, the Senate's head of public affairs? Just asking."

Skirata nodded. "I do believe I've had some contact with him, yes."

"Excellent," Zey said. "I know you two will get along very well."

And the conversation that had never taken place was over.

Skirata stood to leave, and Vau gave the strill a gentle shove to persuade it to drop to the floor. It complained in a gravelly rumble but settled at his feet, looking up at Skirata with red-rimmed gold eyes. Skirata's hand was still cupped, arm at his side, in that way Ordo knew often preceded a fight.

"Kal, I hear Atin's returning," Vau said.

Skirata walked out of the room, head down, Ordo right behind him. Jusik followed.

"You stay clear," Skirata said quietly. "I'm meeting them all straight off *Fearless.* That includes Delta. And they're not yours to run anymore, remember? You just sit tight at the barracks and wait for me to give you a location."

Ordo wasn't fooled by Vau's restrained politeness. Seven years ago Vau had loomed over him as a figure of authority in his black *Mando* armor for the first time, the strill at his heels. Its name was Lord Mirdalan. Ordo, like all the Nulls, had perfect recall; he sometimes wished he hadn't. But at least it gave him clarity, and he knew the source of all his fears and anxieties. Lord Mirdalan—Mird—had lunged at him at Vau's command, snapping.

Ordo had drawn the little hold-out blaster that Skirata had let him keep and would have killed the animal had *Kal'buir* not yelled, *"Check!"* and brought him to a frozen halt as his blaster aim came to rest between Mird's eyes. Vau, Ordo recalled, had laughed: he said that Ordo was *ge'verd*—almost a warrior. And Skirata had aimed a kick at Mird to drive it off, saying there was no "almost" about it.

Ordo watched the strill carefully. The creature trotted ahead of them, sniffing noisily in crevices and leaving behind a waft of pungent scent and a trail of drool.

"If that thing's going to accompany you on *jobs,*" said Skirata, "you'd better keep it under control, or find a use for a strill pelt."

He drew up his arm and flicked his wrist before even Ordo could react. The three-sided blade shaved past Mird and thudded into the polished pleekwood floor a pace ahead of it. The knife vibrated to a standstill.

Mird squealed, leaping sideways. Ordo stepped between Vau and Skirata ready to defend *Kal'buir* in yet another confrontation with the man he loathed.

But Skirata just turned to fix Vau with a stare that said he wasn't joking. Vau stared back, his long hard face suddenly a killer's again.

"It's not the strill's fault," Skirata said. He walked a few paces forward and pulled the knife from the floor. The strill backed away from him, lip curled back to reveal its fangs. "But you have your warning, both of you. We need to get this job done, and that's the only reason I haven't gutted both of you already. Understood?"

"I've moved on," said Vau. "And it's time you did, before I end up having to kill you."

Ordo really didn't like that. He ejected the custom vibroblade in his gauntlet, a better weapon at close quarters than his blasters.

Skirata gave him the palm-down gesture: *Leave it.* "Stay useful, Walon." He beckoned Jusik and Ordo to follow him. "And I hope that Atin's moved on too, because I won't stand in his way now."

"How far is *too* far, Kal? Can you answer that? How far did *you* go?" Vau called after him. "I made that boy a warrior. Without me, he wouldn't be alive today."

With him, Ordo thought, Atin very nearly *wasn't.*

"Why didn't you mention to Zey that we might also have a leak within the Grand Army?" Ordo asked.

"Because," Skirata said, "I can't assume I know who it *isn't.* The leak might not even know that they're the one, either. Until then, only the strike team will know we're looking."

"What about Obrim? He's an ally."

"I hope so. But in the end, who are the only people we can really trust?"

"Ourselves, *Kal'buir.*"

"So we make sure we know who's watching our back—*kar'tayli ad meg hukaat'kama.*"

It was good advice to live by. Ordo knew who always watched his.

RAS *Fearless*, inbound, to Coruscant Sector Control,
369 days after Geonosis

"I really should make a holo of this," Commander Gett said. He reached into the assortment of pouches clipped to his belt and took out a small recorder. "It doesn't happen that often."

Etain and the commander of the assault ship stood on the gantry that ran around the upper hangar bulkhead and watched the extraordinary spectacle beneath them on the deck. She had heard of this thing, but never seen it. It was the *Dha Werda Verda*—a Mandalorian ritual battle chant.

Men from the Forty-first Elite and some of the ship's company—about fifty in all, helmets off—were learning to perform it with some instruction from Fi and Scorch. Sev—easy to spot by the blood-red streaks daubed on his helmet—sat on an ammunition crate nearby, cleaning his sniper attachment and looking as if he wasn't interested in joining in.

He was, of course. Etain could sense it, and she wasn't even properly attuned to Sev's presence in the Force.

The *Dha Werda* looked fearsome. General Bardan Jusik—a young man who barely came up to a clone commando's shoulder—said he loved to see it, and drew so much courage from it that he learned to perform it with his men. It was Kal Skirata's legacy; Jusik explained that the veteran sergeant wanted his men to know their heritage and taught them the rite along with Mandalorian language and culture.

Taung—sa—rang—bro-ka!
Je—tii—se-ka—'rta!

The commandos were layering rhythm upon rhythm, hammering first on their own armor and then turning to beat the complex tempo on the plates of the man next to them. Timed precisely, it was spectacular: timed wrong, a soldier could break the next man's jaw.

Dha—Wer-da—Ver-da—a'den—tratu!
Cor—u—scan—ta—kan—dosii—adu!
Duum—mo—tir—ca—'tra—nau—tracinya!
Gra—'tua—cuun—hett—su—dralshy'a!

It was irresistible, ancient, and hypnotic.

The chant rose from the hangar deck in one solid communal voice. She recognized words like *Coruscanta* and *jetiise:* Coruscant, Jedi. That *couldn't* have been in the original Mandalorian chant. Even their heritage had been remolded to serve a state in which they had no stake. It was, Etain recalled, something to do with being shadow warriors and forcing traitors to kneel before them.

They were supremely fit warriors displaying their discipline and reflexes: any flesh-and-blood enemy would have been adequately warned of the power of the forces that awaited them.

But droids didn't have the sense to be scared. That was a pity, really.

Etain winced. The blows looked real. They were putting all their weight behind every one.

Astonishingly, none of the initiates had yet timed the movements badly enough to receive an accidental blow in the face. Fi and Scorch demonstrated another sequence. Armor clashed. Sev abandoned his feigned disinterest, took off his helmet and joined in. Then Darman appeared and they formed a line of four in the front.

It was strange to watch Darman actually enjoying himself, oblivious to his surroundings: she had no idea that he had such a powerful voice or that he could—for want of a better word—dance.

"Jusik always talks about this," said Etain.

"I've seen a few squads do it," Gett said. "It came via Skirata, I hear."

"Yes." Etain was wondering how she would ever measure up to that man. Halfway would have been enough. "He taught all the commandos to live up to their Mandalorian heritage. You know—customs, language, ideals." She was mesmerized by the unconscious precision of men who were all exactly the same height. "It's very weird. It's like they have a compulsion to do it."

"Yes, we do," Gett said. "It's very stirring."

"I'm sorry. That was rude of me."

"No problem, General. It certainly wasn't part of our trooper training on Kamino. It gets passed on from man to man now." He looked restless. She knew what he was thinking. "General—"

"Give me the recorder," she said, and smiled. "Go ahead."

Gett touched his glove to his brow and shot off down the ladder to the deck, sliding the last three meters on the handrails. It was delightful to see the mix of armor—yellow-striped commanders and pilots, plain white troopers, and the motley mix of commando colors—drawn together in one ancient Mandalorian ritual, every face the same.

Etain felt adrift, excluded.

She had never truly felt this degree of bond with her Jedi clan. The connection in the Force was there, yes, but . . . no, the real strength here was attachment, passion, identity, *meaning.*

She thought of Master Fulier, the man who insisted she have a second chance as a Padawan and not be consigned to build refugee camps because she lacked control. The man who was also passionate and prone to taking on causes: the Jedi who lost his life because he couldn't stay out of a fight when Ghez Hokan's militia roughed up the locals on Qiilura.

Etain thought that wasn't such a bad sort of Jedi to be. Not textbook, but centered on fair play and justice. The clone soldiers were worth that, too.

She was suddenly aware of Darman looking up at her, grinning, and if it hadn't been for his armor and surroundings he could have been any young man showing off his prowess to a woman. She smiled back.

She still envied him his focus and discipline, especially as he had somehow managed not to lose it after being exposed to a galaxy that didn't quite resemble the ideal he had probably been taught about on Kamino.

But Kal Skirata had largely been responsible for his training. She didn't know Skirata yet, but one thing she was certain of was that he was—just like a Jedi—a pragmatic man who dealt in reality.

The *Dha Werda* went on for verse after repeated verse. Then the klaxon sounded and the pipe came over the address system.

"Port duties men close up. Damage and fire control parties to stations. Prepare to dock."

Commander Gett broke out of the ranks and came bounding back up the ladder, wiping sweat from his face with a neatly folded piece of cloth.

"General, will you come to the bridge to see the ship alongside?"

"I won't be much help, but I'd like that, yes."

It was as if she were leaving a ship after a long association, a retiring captain. She was only a temporary officer, but still Gett treated her as if she actually had some importance to the crew, and she found that touching. She stood at the command console and watched as the docking grapnels and platforms slipped past the viewscreen and the crew maneuvered *Fearless* on instruments. Gett had the con. "Stop reactor."

"Stop reactor, Commander . . . reactor stopped."

Fearless's secondary propulsion shivered into silence. The vessel slipped gradually into dock on the power of tugs bringing her alongside *port-side-to,* as Etain had now learned to call it. She walked slowly across the bridge to watch the dockside team getting a brow in place to disembark those members of the crew being transferred and to allow maintenance and replenishment teams to board.

There was the slightest of jarring sensations as the ship came to rest against huge dock fenders. *Fearless* was back safely in her home port—for the time being.

Etain held out her hand to Gett. "Gloves off, my friend."

He shrugged, smiling, and slipped off the entire gauntlet. They shook hands as equals. Then she pressed a key on the console, opening the public address system that reached every cabin and flat and hangar and mess deck in the huge warship.

"Gentlemen," she said. "It's been an honor."

6

In five millennia, the Mandalorians fought with and against a thousand armies on a thousand worlds. They learned to speak as many languages and absorbed weapons technology and tactics from every war. And yet, despite the overwhelming influence of alien cultures, and the absence of a true homeworld and even species, their own language not only survived but changed little, their way of life and their philosophy remained untouched, and their ideals and sense of family, of identity, of nation, were only strengthened. Armor does not make a Mandalorian. The armor is simply a manifestation of an impenetrable, unassailable heart.
—*Mandalorians: Identity and Language,* published by the Galactic Institute of Anthropology

RAS *Fearless*, upper dock, Fleet Support Depot, Coruscant, 370 days after Geonosis

The ramp went down, and for once the scene that greeted Fi wasn't hostile droid-infested territory and red blasterfire.

But Coruscant—impossibly high towers and deep canyons of skylanes—was every bit as alien as Geonosis. Fi had seen it once before, all too briefly, on the way to break a siege at the spaceport. It had been an exotic, exciting lightscape at night, but in daylight it was breathtaking in a totally different way.

"Can we have a run ashore?"

Niner stood with his hands clasped behind him, with his Deece slung across his back. "Not my call. I'm not the sergeant now."

Boss and the rest of Delta had formed up behind Omega in a neat line, presenting a more orderly rank. They were on the same comlink. Niner said it was ungrateful to block them out, seeing as they'd ridden to the rescue. But Omega would never hear the end of it, Fi was sure of that.

The Forty-first Elite were disembarked first.

Scorch leaned a little closer to Fi. He was right behind him. The nice thing about Katarn helmet comlinks was that you could switch between circuits and have totally private exchanges without any external sign that you were talking—or even having a stand-up fight, come to that. "So you want a *run ashore*?"

"What's that?" Sev said.

Fi enjoyed Skirata's wide-ranging and often bizarre language. No other squads talked quite like Sergeant Kal's. "A night out on the town. Dinner at a fine restaurant, perhaps take in a Mon Cal ballet . . ."

"Yeah. Right."

"Don't, Fi," Niner said. "You're just being cruel to the Weequay team here."

"Okay, ale and warra nuts. No ballet."

"And maybe a little shopping with your spook squad buddy?" Scorch said. "New *kama,* maybe?"

Ah, news did travel, then. "Don't let Ordo hear you say that," Fi said. "He'll rip your leg off and hit you with the soggy end."

"Yeah? ARCs are all mouth and *kamas.*"

"Ooh, hard man, eh?"

"I've seen Twi'lek dancing girls tougher than you," said Scorch. "How many times are we going to have to save your *shebs,* then?"

"Probably as many times as we have to clean up your *osik,*" said Niner. "Can't you two talk about blowing stuff up and play nicely?"

"Where's the general?" Fi said.

Darman interrupted. "Saying good-bye to Gett." He seemed to be taking a keen interest in Etain's whereabouts. "Can you see Sergeant Kal yet? She said he was meeting us."

"So . . . you've been ordered around by a geriatric *and* a child, have you?"

Darman's voice frosted over. "Scorch, do you like medcenter food?"

"Touchy, touchy . . ."

There was a faint click on the helmet comlink.

"Delta! This is the geriatric. Get down and give me fifty, now!"

"Fierfek," Sev sighed.

Omega parted ranks to give Delta the room to perform fifty

press-ups in full armor, with backpacks. Fi watched appreciatively. He didn't care for Sev at all.

But he was also scanning the landing platform for Skirata, desperate to see his *real* sergeant again: when Skirata was around, Niner ceased to play the senior NCO. Generals tended not to get much of a look in, either. Skirata was his own command chain.

"That was forty, not fifty," Skirata said from somewhere *behind* them. "I hate innumeracy almost as much as I hate cracks about my personal state of disrepair."

Skirata just had a knack for sliding around unnoticed. There had been times when Fi had wondered if he was a Force-user, because only Jedi were supposed to be able to pull those kinds of stunts. But *Kal'buir* was adamant that he was simply good at his job, because he'd been doing it since he was seven years old.

That made him a late starter—by clone standards.

He appeared suddenly from between a knot of Forty-first men and ambled over to Omega, not limping quite as badly as usual and looking rather dapper in a smart leather jacket. In rough working clothes, he could disappear, but the jacket changed him utterly. Yet there was always something about the man that inspired relief and confidence. Fi felt instantly ready for anything, just as he had when Skirata had been the highest authority in his limited world on Kamino.

Skirata paused for a moment in front of him. He didn't seem worried whether Delta had cranked out the extra ten press-ups or not. He just clutched Fi's arm, and hugged Darman, and slapped Niner across the shoulders, and grabbed Atin's hand. He never seemed to have the slightest trouble now in showing how much he cared about them. Over the years he'd changed from shielding his emotions behind a veneer of good-natured abuse to abandoning the pretense altogether.

Nobody had ever been fooled by it anyway.

"Don't scare me like that again, *ad'ike.*" He turned to Delta, easing themselves up from the floor. "And you bunch of *di'kute,* too. I'd better keep a tighter rein on you." He watched the last of the Forty-first men disappearing into transfer vessels, presumably for return to barracks, and something appeared to amuse him. "Scorch, if you're not a good boy then I'm going to make you wear a *kama.*"

"Sorry, Sergeant. Is it true that Sergeant Vau's back?"

"He's back, but he's not a sergeant. *I'm* your sergeant now, Scorch."

"And General Jusik?"

"He's not your sergeant, either." Skirata looked past Scorch and seemed suddenly startled. Fi turned and saw what he was staring at: Etain Tur-Mukan walked across the huge landing platform hauling the LJ-50 as if it were putting up a fight. "That has to be General Tur-Mukan, yes?"

"That's her," Darman said. "She's very keen to meet you."

Fi was distracted by a blip of movement in his HUD. A scruffy civilian air taxi had risen over the parapet of the landing platform. *And it shouldn't have been able to do that.*

His unconscious brain said *danger* and reacted a split second before his ingrained training reminded him that *unidentified civvie vessels shouldn't penetrate the Fleet base cordon.* He was on one knee with his Deece charged and aimed before he even noticed from his HUD that Omega and Delta had both formed up into a single front contact formation.

The taxi stopped dead in midair.

"Check!" Skirata stepped in front of them. Fi froze but Delta aimed around the sergeant. "Stand down!" One fist held up clenched to hold off the squads, Skirata signaled vigorously to the taxi with his other hand held flat, slapping down on the air. *Drop.*

The taxi settled slowly on the platform.

Omega stopped dead at the check command; Delta took a second longer. Maybe it hadn't been drilled into them as it had Skirata's batch. But all of them still had their rifles trained. Fi's heart pounded. They were all wound tight and still alert to any threat, alert enough to let hard-trained reactions take over. It was what kept you alive. You could never switch it off. Your muscles learned to do things and then stopped asking your brain's permission.

"I'm sorry, lads." Skirata spun around to face them. "*Udesii, udesii* . . . relax. It's ours."

"I'm glad you pointed that out, Sarge," Niner muttered. He lowered his Deece. Fi followed his lead, and glanced behind him.

Etain was still lying prone with her concussion rifle aimed in the right direction, no easy task with a weapon that size, but her arc of fire left something to be desired. He hoped that her Jedi sense of right place and right time would have stopped her from blowing them all to pieces if she had opened fire.

Fi gestured to her to stand down, and then gave up and just shook his head at her. *No.* She gestured back, palm up, and jumped to her feet. He wondered if anyone had thought to teach her basic hand signals.

Skirata was still apologizing. "I should have warned you I had transport coming. That was sloppy of me." The taxi's hatch opened and a Wookiee—not a big one, just over a couple of meters tall—unfolded itself from the taxi and clambered out, throwing its head back and yawling in complaint.

"Okay, *my fault,*" Skirata said. He held both hands up in admission to the mountain of glossy brown fur. "They're just jumpy, that's all. We'll load now."

"All of us, in *that*?" Niner asked. It wasn't a very big taxi. "With the Wookiee, too?"

"No, the *prisoners.* Just load 'em in."

"Where are they going?"

"That's all you need to know right now."

Niner paused, then shrugged and beckoned Boss, Fixer, and Atin to follow him back on board *Fearless.*

Etain had moved forward by now and walked up to Skirata, rifle slung across her back; she was so small that she looked more like a bolt-on accessory to the weapon. Darman reacted and stepped in to get Skirata's attention. It wasn't that he needed to, of course. Skirata was watching Etain, and he seemed to have one eye on *Fearless*'s ramp, and he was placating the clearly irritated Wookiee, somehow juggling situations as skillfully as he had ever done.

"General," he said. He paused to nod formally to Etain, which—given Skirata's general contempt for anyone not in armor—seemed quite an encouraging start, Fi decided. "We've got a nice new job, and that includes you."

"Sergeant," she said, and bowed her head. "You're not what I expected."

Skirata raised an eyebrow. "Nor are you, General." He shoved the Wookiee back a few meters, apparently untroubled by the fact that the creature could have used him for a cleaning rag. He rounded on it. "*No,* just put them on the back seat and *drive.* Let Vau do the rest."

The mention of Vau gave Fi a hint of what he couldn't grasp from the Shyriiwook words. So the Wookiee was delivering the prisoners to Walon Vau. It seemed to have volunteered to do something that Skirata preferred to leave to Old Psycho, then. The Wookiee obviously wasn't asking if they wanted to stop for lunch.

"What's happening here?" Etain asked. "What's happening to the prisoners?"

"Civilian matter, General," Skirata said, and stood back as Niner and Boss jogged past steering a medbay repulsor with what looked like three large rolls of blanket on it. They bundled each into the back of the taxi with a little grunting and cursing, then slammed one hatch closed. "Don't you worry about it."

"But I *am* worrying about it."

The Wookiee barked once and folded itself back into the taxi. The vessel lifted off and swung back over the parapet, dropping below their view into one of the artificial canyons that seemed to reach down into Coruscant's core. Fi fought the urge to peer after it, then lost and walked a few paces to gaze over the edge.

It was a long, *long* way down. He was thrilled by the sheer scale and variety of it: polished stone, sparkling glass, a blur of vessels in the skylanes, hazy sunlight. Alien, utterly alien.

Skirata blew out a breath and rocked his head slightly as if easing tense neck muscles. "General," he said. "You and I need to talk. Omega, Delta—a transport will be taking you back to barracks." He paused to check his chrono. "You just relax until fifteen-hundred hours and then you report to the briefing room at HQ Main Admin Building."

"Yes, Sarge," said Niner and Boss, absolutely synchronized.

But Etain wasn't giving up. Fi rather liked that about her, but she could be a pain in the *shebs* when she persisted. She stepped a little closer to Skirata.

"I don't like being left in the dark, Sergeant."

"Then this galaxy is going to be a constant source of disappointment to you, General." For a second Skirata had that edge in his voice that made Fi stiffen. But it softened as soon as it had hit its target. "Things change. You can say no to this, and I'm rather hoping you won't, but if you do, then Omega, Delta, and my Null boys will do it without you."

Etain lapsed into silence. Skirata could motivate a brick if he put his mind to it. She wanted to stick with the squad and everyone *knew* it.

She looked at him as if she was listening to other voices. "If Omega can't say no, then neither can I."

"Good," said Skirata. He peeled back the collar of his jacket and muttered into a tiny comlink. It looked as if General Jusik still had a taste for supplying unusual kit. "Standing by."

Fi peered back over the dock platform parapet, gripping the safety rail to lean out a little more and get a better look. It was the kind of view the very wealthy paid a fortune to see from their window, but you could get it for free in the Grand Army, as long as you didn't mind getting your head shot off to qualify for the privilege.

Skirata leaned against the parapet beside him.

"I'd like to fast-rope down there," Fi said. He'd always enjoyed that in training on Kamino. He preferred endless vistas to cramped spaces, as did many of his brothers. They said it was the legacy of being gestated in glass vats; Ordo claimed he could even remember it. "How long have we got here, Sarge? Can we see some of the city? Please?"

"Yeah, I promised you all a night out, didn't I? How long ago?"

"Eight months." Fi remembered, all right: straight after the spaceport siege, the promise of a drink from Captain Obrim for a job well done—and then Ordo hauled them straight off for another mission. "I'd love to see it once before I—" He paused. "I'd just like to explore a bit."

Skirata's brow creased briefly and he put his hand on Fi's back. "Don't talk like that, son. You'll see plenty of this, I promise."

"Now?" Far below, something that might have been a bird leapt suddenly into the yawning crevasse of buildings and plummeted at high speed with wings folded back until Fi lost sight of it. The platform was at least five thousand meters high. "That'd be a nice change."

"So you like the new battlefield, then."

Fi dragged himself away from the apparently limitless view. "So we get a spell in a stone frigate?"

"What?"

"Just something I picked up from the lads on board *Fearless.*" So he'd taught Sergeant Kal some new slang: *that* was something. "A shore-based job. Filing flimsi and answering the comlinks. Lots of caf breaks."

"Try threat resolution. Interdiction."

"Oh."

"Welcome to the world of euphemism, Fi. We're going to be fighting in the hardest terrain of all. Right in the middle of billions of civvies. Slotting bad guys on Coruscant."

"Good," said Fi. "I hate commuting."

Arca Company Barracks, SO Brigade HQ, Coruscant

Etain trailed Skirata down the long passage that ran from the main doors of the Arca barrack wing and felt like she was following a gdan.

Omega Squad's description had made her think of him as a kindly old uncle, a veteran soldier with a façade of tough talk who had sweated blood to give a generation of boys the benefit of his wisdom. But what she experienced in the Force was very different, just as his appearance was unlike her mental image of him.

He was a whirlpool of balanced conflict—truly cold black violence shot through with deep red passionate loves and hatreds. It marked him out as a complex man who had built a warrior elite. If she looked at him another way, though, he was very much the dark side—everything she had been taught to shun.

Yes, he reminded her of a gdan, the nasty little carnivores that hunted in packs on Qiilura and would take on *any* prey; small by comparison with his strapping troops, but ferociously, tenaciously aggressive.

And he wasn't quite the elderly man the squad had first described, either. To twenty-year-old boys, he must have seemed ancient. But he was about sixty standard years—just middle-aged—and obviously fit except for his tendency to drag his left leg.

And he looked *armored.*

He was only wearing a civilian jacket—polished tan bantha leather with a high black collar—and plain brown pants, but he had that same presence that all the commandos had. He was *ready* for something. Given that he was a head shorter than his squad, had a pronounced limp, and yet *still* looked like trouble, Etain decided he must have once been a formidable soldier. She realized he still was.

"In here, ma'am." He could make *ma'am* sound like *girl* somehow; he could do the same with *General.* But as a Jedi she had no right to feel affronted by lack of deference. She realized that she simply wished he would like her. "Just a little chat and then you can find General Jusik and catch up on events."

Yes, Skirata gave the orders.

He ushered her into a side room that turned out to be a cabin with a table, a chair, and narrow bed with a half-packed carryall sitting on it. There was a neat pile of clothing, military-grade fabric equipment cases with unidentifiable lumpy items in them, and a set of sand-gold, battle-scarred Mandalorian armor.

The Force told her this was a tidy room filled with the wretched chaos of broken lives, pain, and misery. She wondered if it was entirely his, but she stopped herself from probing further in case he felt it and reacted. He was a dangerously perceptive man. She had no sense at all of any animosity directed at her.

"That's a fine helmet," she said. It had detailed crimson and gold sigils, and the alloy section that formed the eyepiece T of the visor was jet black. There were telltale scrapes and gouges as if some huge creature had clawed at it. "Does Fi still have Hokan's armor?"

Skirata nodded. "Certainly has. Niner said he could have it, and he keeps it stashed in his locker."

Etain thought of Ghez Hokan, and how she had first mistaken Darman for Qiilura's brutal enforcer simply because of that sinister helmet with its T-shaped slit. Fi had the helmet now. And that was because Etain had taken Hokan's head off with her lightsaber, nearly a year and a lifetime ago when she was still not used to killing.

It was red armor with a distinctive gray trim. She recalled that vividly.

Mandalorian helmets didn't look half so fearsome now. The shape was familiar: it was even *welcome.* But she had somehow forgotten that Skirata, and most of the training sergeants who had been recruited to forge boys like Darman into elite commandos, had been Mandalorian mercenaries handpicked by Jango Fett.

She wondered if she would have seen Skirata the same way nine months earlier, had he been her enemy on Qiilura. "Packing or unpacking?"

"Packing." He lifted the fabric bags carefully and they made a metallic clunk: *weapons.* "We can't operate out of here. Officially we're off duty and on indefinite leave." He laid the armor plates in the bag and layered the clothing between them, then slid in the fabric-cased weapons. It occurred to her that this was probably all he owned, the nomadic mercenary ready to move on to the next war. "Are you squeamish, General? I mean *ethically* squeamish."

"I'm a Jedi, Sergeant."

"Well, that answers a lot of questions I didn't ask."

"Ask me a *specific* question."

"Do you know what *black ops* means?"

"Oh yes . . ."

"I thought you might. I had no idea you would be coming back with Omega right now, but you spent four months with Zey on Qiilura turning the locals into guerrillas to fight the Seps, right? And be fore that you survived when Master Fulier didn't. So I reckon you're pretty handy in a scrap."

"I know my weaknesses."

Skirata paused and looked up from his packing. "Best knowledge of all."

"Just tell me what's at stake," Etain said.

"Now, there's an interesting request from a Jedi." He put his hand carefully in the side of the carryall and withdrew a small cloth-wrapped package. When he unwrapped it and held it out in his palm, she could see it held small scan bars mounted on fragments of white plastoid alloy. "For me, stopping more of these. For the Republic, stopping activity that limits the ability of the Grand Army to deploy. For the Senate, showing the Seps that they can't strike here at will. Take your pick."

She knew what the objects were now: she'd seen them on hundreds of chest plates. They were armor tallies, the identification devices all clone soldiers wore.

"I'll take the first option." She thought of the other Fi, the one who was no longer alive to be boyishly excited like his namesake at the prospect of seeing the Coruscant that lay beyond the barracks. "You believe I'll be of some use?"

"In urban operations, a woman is always useful, Jedi or not. Another aid to invisibility—old *di'kute* like me and females like you."

Skirata smiled and rewrapped the armor tallies. Etain reached into her bag and realized that she had even fewer possessions than this nomad. "And General Jusik is part of this operation? What about Master Zey?"

"General Zey is not officially aware of this."

"If we're not operating out of here, then where?"

"Oh, somewhere interesting. Give me a couple of days and then we can relocate. Besides, the boys need some rest."

So he wasn't going to tell her. Fine. "Delta seem a little . . . different from Omega. I take it you have confidence in them?"

"Oh, they're good lads." He fumbled in his jacket pockets and pulled out credit chips, scraps of flimsi, and a nasty-looking metal device crested with a row of short, savage spikes and that appeared to have holes for four fingers. She stared. He placed it on the table. "The hormone that makes them hard fighters is the same one that makes them a bit of a handful, too." The contents of Skirata's jacket continued to pile up on the table. A coil of thin wire, a fifteen-centimeter knife with a tapering three-sided blade, a stubby custom blaster, and a length of heavy, sharp-edged chain joined the cache. "Not that the poor *ad'ike* are *ever* off duty, of course. But when you say the word, they're on the case like *that.*" He snapped his fingers to make the point of immediacy. Yes, she'd seen that.

Skirata took off his jacket, revealing surprisingly broad shoulders and an underarm holster holding what looked like a modified Verpine shatter gun. He hung the garment over the back of a chair. Etain estimated he was still exceptionally fit in the wiry way of small men and continued to revise her view of him as a man who could only train others to fight.

And she had never seen so many instruments devoted to injury and destruction in one man's possession—not even a Republic commando. She indicated the weapons with a cocked head and waited for a hint of why he was carrying them.

Skirata paused, one hand raking his short gray hair.

"What?" he said, looking bemused.

"The . . . kit." He was a walking armory. "The weapons."

"Oh, don't worry." He clearly didn't understand. "I don't carry many tools when I'm in civilian areas. Don't want to be too conspicuous. Ordo looks after the rest of it. We'll be properly cannoned up when we deploy. Guess what? Got six Verpine sniper rifles. Custom-made and EMP-hardened. *Exquisite.* Not really *rifles,* 'cos they don't have rifled barrels, but . . ." He grinned suddenly, apparently distracted by a thought, and she had a brief and vivid vision of another man entirely. "You haven't met Ordo yet, have you? He's a fine lad. Pride of my heart, really he is. Him and his brothers."

Etain was totally disarmed by his candor, which seemed both incongruous and yet in keeping with a man who had gone to such extraordinary lengths to equip his young charges to survive.

She knew he was a killer. She knew his people had a long history of killing Jedi, even fighting for the Sith. She knew *exactly* what he was, but she couldn't help liking him and knowing that he would be very, very important to her for the rest of her life.

Her certainty was in the Force. And she knew what was coming in the days and months ahead would take her beyond her limits, and would bring her no sense of peace or understanding as a Jedi. But the Force would show her what it intended her destiny to be.

7

I think it's significant that the casualty rate among commando squads trained by Mandalorians is lower than those trained by other races. Somehow, Mandalorians imbue their charges with a sense of purpose, self-confidence, and almost obsessive sense of clan—of family—that gives them a genuine survival advantage. Let us be thankful they're on our side this time.

—General Master Arligan Zey, Director of Special Forces, officer commanding SO BDE, addressing the Jedi Council

SO Brigade HQ Coruscant, briefing room 8,
1500 hours, 370 days after Geonosis

"I thought we'd have a chat," said Skirata. He turned a chair around and swung his legs astride it, folding his arms on the chair back and resting his chin on them. "Just us *Mando* boys. No *aruetiise* present."

Delta Squad had settled in seats on one side of the briefing room and Omega on the other, with the table between them. Skirata could have sliced through the atmosphere between Atin and Sev with a vibroblade: how could they think he hadn't noticed? He knew how to read every nuance of cloned men like a book, even if they weren't the ones he knew intimately. In fact, he could read most species now. So they either thought he was stupid, or they were so at ease in his company that they felt no need to disguise their feelings.

And the Delta boys—like Omega—were painfully loyal to their

sergeants. They sat around in dark red fatigues, looking disturbingly young without their armor and weapons.

"You don't see Tur-Mukan or Jusik as traitors, do you?" Darman said.

"I was using *aruetiise* in the general sense of non-Mandalorian." Oh, Darman *was* fond of Etain, wasn't he? He'd have to keep an eye on that. "What I've got to say is just squad business, not the officers'." Skirata dropped his knife from his sleeve and fidgeted with the blade, running his fingertip carefully along the honed edge. "I hope you're listening to this, Delta."

"Yes, Sarge." Boss was watching him intently.

"And you, Sev."

Sev glanced at Atin for the merest fraction of a second, but enough to confirm Skirata's hunch. "Yes, Sergeant."

"Okay, number one—any bad blood between me and Vau is *our* business, not yours. If any of you want to fight about it, I'll personally make you regret it. Save it for the bad guys."

The silence was almost solid. Atin stared ahead of him, unblinking; Sev compressed his lips as if choking back protest and flicked a glance at Niner. Darman and Fi simply looked baffled.

"No, Sev," Skirata said. "Niner didn't say a word to me, but I've got eyes in my backside and a *very* good memory. You do *not* have a grudge against Atin, do you understand me? If you want to argue the toss about my little altercation with Vau, then you have it out with *me*."

"Understood, Sergeant."

"Good. Prove it."

"Sorry?"

"You two." Skirata motioned to Atin and Sev with the point of his blade. "Get up and shake hands."

Neither Atin nor Sev moved for a moment.

"I said get up and shake hands. *Now*."

Skirata wondered if he'd lost them, but then Atin stood just a heartbeat before Sev did. They leaned across the table that separated them and shook hands as ordered.

"Now do it again and *mean it,*" Skirata said quietly. "You *have* to be one team now, one big squad, and when I tell you what we're up against you'll understand why. Boss, I expect you to keep your boys in line."

Boss leaned forward and shoved Sev in the back. "You heard the sergeant."

Atin held his hand out again. Sev took it and shrugged.

"Good," Skirata said. "Because we're off the charts now. What we're about to do has no official authorization from the Senate or the generals, so if we screw up, we're on our own."

"Ah," said Scorch. "So Jusik and Tur-Mukan don't know about this."

"Oh yes, they do."

"Then who's *we*?"

"You, our young generals, Ordo, Vau, and me."

Scorch raised his eyebrows. "You're *operational* again?"

It was time for a little theater. "Yes." Skirata hurled his knife with the exquisite accuracy born of decades of surviving by it. It embedded itself in the wooden paneling behind Sev, half a meter to his right. "Bet you can't do *that* with a vibroblade, son."

"He can if I pick him up and throw him," said Fi.

They all laughed. Skirata wondered if they'd still be laughing in a few minutes. Ordo was due back soon. With any luck, he and Vau would have beaten some information out of Orjul; the Nikto were probably too tough even for Vau to crack in that time.

In the end it might not matter. He had his team ready to deploy on Coruscant now—*his* team, not the Republic's—and they could do things that CSF either wouldn't or couldn't. Obrim had his hands tied by laws and procedures, and maybe he even had a mole among his own comrades.

But this strike team had no laws at all: it didn't even exist. On Triple Zero, it was . . . *zero.*

Skirata hadn't asked Zey what would happen to them if they got it wrong. They could end up dead, all of them. It was an academic detail.

Scorch got up, pulled the knife from the wall, and handed it back to Skirata with a grin. Fixer applauded.

"Remember all that dirty black ops stuff that me and Vau taught you way back?" Skirata slid the blade back up his sleeve again. *My dad's knife. All I have of him. I took it off his body.* "Or did you file it with the boring stuff on contingency orders and emergency procedures?"

"I think we *recall* it, Sarge."

Skirata remembered it, and didn't want to. It was training that had to be done. It broke his heart, but it was going to be all that stood between those boys and death sooner or later. They had to be able to face the unimaginable, and—yes, there were even worse things than charging a line of droids with your comrades.

There were the things you might have to face alone, in a locked room, with no hope of rescue.

Maybe Vau was right. Perhaps trainees needed to be brutalized beyond the point where they were just brave, pushed into a state of existence where they became animals intent only on survival. That was how Vau had nearly killed Atin. It was why Skirata had then gone after Vau and nearly killed *him.*

"I'm not proud of what I did to you," Skirata said.

"You crawled through the nerf guts first, Sarge. It looked like so much fun that we followed you in." Fi roared with laughter and leaned back in his seat. "And then you threw up."

The Sickener, they called it. One more endurance test to make sure they could face conditions that would break and kill lesser men, crawling through a ditch filled with rotting nerf guts.

But there were more tests to come. A night out in Fest-like temperatures; no sleep for three days, maybe more; scant water, a full sixty-kilo pack, and blistering heat; and a lot of pain. Pain, pitiless verbal abuse, and humiliation. A captured commando could expect brutal interrogation. They had to be able to cope without breaking, and it took some imagination to test that to the limit.

How far is too far, Kal?

Vau was much more detached about handing out all that punishment than Skirata could ever be. It was very hard to hurt your sons, even if it helped them survive the unsurvivable.

"Well," Skirata said, mortified that Fi could take it in such good spirits. "The nerf guts were the *fun* part. It all goes downhill after that."

Sev seemed quite animated. "Do we get to do assassinations?"

"If we do, they never happened. You imagined them."

"Whoops. My trigger finger just *slipped,* Sarge. Honest."

"You catch on fast about the fascinating world of politics in which we now find ourselves, young man."

"Is it okay if I say politicians are gutless *chakaare*?" Scorch asked.

"Call 'em what you like, son. You still haven't got a vote." Skirata felt the thud of boots striding down the passage outside. The vibration carried; their voices didn't. "Wars are *legal* violence. Everything else is just crime. Fortunately we're Mandalorian, so we're a lot less prissy about that fine distinction."

"Just point us at the bad guys and say go."

"That's the awkward bit."

"What is?" Scorch asked.

"You've got to find them first."

"Well, we found quite a few so far . . ."

Delta laughed like one man, even Sev, and Omega joined in. The coded entry system blipped and the doors slid open. Ordo strode through them, probably aware of the kind of entrance he could make.

Delta had never worked with a Null ARC before. Maybe they thought it would be no different from working with Alpha or any of the other Jango-trained ARC troopers. Skirata watched with interest. Ordo would certainly break some more ice.

"Sir!" Delta said sharply, all at once. Niner and the rest of Omega just touched their brows casually.

"Sorry I'm late, Sergeant." Ordo took off his helmet, tucked it under one arm, and handed Skirata a datapad and a rather heavy flimsi-wrapped package about the size of a small blaster case. "Not much information, but Vau is still working on the problem. And General Jusik sends his compliments."

"Thanks, Captain." Skirata glanced at it and then unwrapped the parcel. But it wasn't a weapon; it was a box of candied vweliu nuts. Jusik was a very thoughtful officer indeed. Skirata broke the seal and got up to place it on the table within the reach of both squads. "Fill yer boots, lads."

Fi had his usual silly grin on his face, the faintest hint that he might be planning to do something at Ordo's expense.

"Ooh, nice new skirt!" said Fi. "You went to all that trouble just for us? What happened to the old *kama*? Did it shrink in the wash?"

He got up and stood a pace or two in front of Ordo, still grinning and clearly expecting some backslapping or some other show of delight at reunion after several months.

" 'Scuse me, Sergeant," Ordo said calmly, and smacked Fi down on the floor with a none-too-playful body press. Fi yelped. Being hit by someone in armor when you weren't wearing your own *hurt.*

Boss's expression was a study in shock. The Delta boys jerked upright in their seats and stared as if they were debating whether to step in and break it up. Ordo looked like cold death; even Skirata had times when he wasn't quite sure which way Ordo would jump.

"Your big mouth is going to get you into a lot of trouble one day," the ARC hissed. Fi, eyes locked on Ordo's, neck tensed, looked ready to fight back. "So you better hope *I'm* there when that happens." Then Ordo burst out laughing and got to his feet in one move. He hauled Fi upright by his arm, slapping his back enthusiastically. "The old firm back together again, eh? Good stuff!"

Boss glanced at Skirata, who smiled enigmatically, or so he hoped. Nulls were either your best friend or your worst imaginable enemy. Fi, luckily, had a devoted friend. He still looked shaken by the nature of the reunion, though.

"Okay, you can thin out now and we'll resume tomorrow morning with our little generals for a full intel briefing at oh-eight-hundred," Skirata said. "Now that we all understand each other."

Ordo took a handful of candied nuts and stepped outside with Skirata. The two men stood in the corridor, giving the squads a chance to chat now that Delta had been suitably unnerved. And maybe they thought he couldn't hear them, but Skirata wasn't as hard of hearing as they imagined, years of exposure to deafening fire or not.

And it wasn't what he expected to hear.

"Fierfek, I remember thinking he was just bent over breathless, but he was actually crying and *throwing up.* And it wasn't the nerf guts."

"He never liked knocking us around."

"And he *always* apologized and made sure we were okay afterward."

"Top man." That was Niner talking. *"Jatne'buir."*

The best father. Well, that was a joke. His own kids had formally disowned him and declared him *dar'buir* instead—no longer a father. It was a very rare and shameful thing for a *Mando* father to be formally shunned by his sons.

But he couldn't have left Kamino, or even told them where he was and that he hadn't completely abandoned them. Not even Ordo knew about the declaration of *dar'buir.*

You put your clones first, before your own flesh and blood, didn't you?

"Are you all right?"

And I don't regret doing that, not a second of it.

"I'm fine, *Ord'ika.* Vau must be losing his touch, then. Nothing useful from our friends?"

"There might be nothing to get out of them, of course. But it's not a quick process, interrogating experienced suspects without killing them."

"What about getting one of our *jetiise* to help out? They're good at persuasion."

"Possibly too squeamish. Jusik is always anxious to please, though."

"He's much more use in the field. Brave lad, handy with tech, and a good pilot. But the girl's got an edge to her. Let's see if she'll put pragmatism above principle."

"Do you dislike them, *Kal'buir*?"

"It's not a matter of liking them or not. It's whether they're reliable. Look, Zey will waste you and every last clone—and me—if he thinks it'll win the war and save civilians. But Jusik hero-worships you. And I don't know which of those two extremes is the more dangerous."

"This is your opportunity to help them become the soldiers you made of us, then."

Ouch. "Why do I always get the feeling that you were more of a man at four years old than I would ever be?"

Ordo gave him a playful shove. He was clearly in a good mood today. "Let me ask General Tur-Mukan to interrogate the prisoners. If she finds that morally unacceptable, then her view of you won't be tainted by it."

Skirata had to bite his lip. Ordo often shamed him with unexpected compassion and diplomacy. "Yeah, I reckon she'll find it easier to do the heroic infantry stuff than get dirty along with us. But leave her to me."

"Very well," Ordo said. "Have you decided where we need to base the operation?"

"I've got a few people who owe me favors. Where would you hide soldiers?"

"*Hide* hide or conceal hide?"

"Not-taking-much-notice-of-activity hide."

"Somewhere with a bar. Somewhere you'd get a lot of off-duty traffic."

"You don't drink. Never seen a clone drink much at all." Skirata was suddenly ambushed again by Ordo's agile brain. For a man who knew little of life beyond warfare, his ability to learn and extrapolate from the smallest scrap of information was breathtaking. "And you never get off duty."

"You said, *Kal'buir,* that you might disguise the presence of some *hulking big boys in armor* by having a lot more of them around. You were going to see Mar Rugeyan about a *smokescreen.*"

"Sorry?"

"Remember Mar Rugeyan? The man who can talk out of all three corners of his mouth at the same time? The man you grabbed by the—"

Kal remembered, all right. "Yeah, if I'd known then that I'd need him I'd have been a little more careful."

“I think I can propose an idea he might find attractive.”

“Would that involve leaving bruises?”

“I wasn’t planning to injure him. Just point out that if troopers were actually allowed leave in considerable numbers, it would reassure the public, too. Eventually we become invisible.” Ordo pondered, that telltale little frown creasing his brow. Sometimes his staggering intellect and perfect recall didn’t help him process the real world one bit, at least not where Skirata was concerned. “Let me try, *Kal’buir.* I promise I’ll be more diplomatic.”

“It was a joke, *Ord’ika.* I think you’d probably stand as much chance of charming him as I would right now.”

“Have I ever let you down?”

It wasn’t a rhetorical question. Skirata was mortified. It was all too easy to swagger out of the meeting full of aggressive confidence and forget that Ordo—muscular, lethal, the ultimate soldier—was vulnerable to the approval of one person alone: *him.* It was as if Ordo became that literal, trusting child again, the one who had decided that the only person in the galaxy who would ever look out for him and his brothers was a down-on-his-luck mercenary who didn’t much like Kaminoans.

“I didn’t mean it literally.” Skirata reached up and ruffled his hair just like he’d done when Ordo was a scared little kid, terrified by the lightning on Kamino, except he hadn’t had to reach quite so far in those days. “You’re my pride and joy. You couldn’t be smarter or better or braver, any of you.”

Ordo looked blank for a moment and then managed a smile, but it was the placatory gesture of a child under threat. “I know I have gaps in my knowledge.”

“Oh, son . . . I’m going to change that. For all of you.”

“I know, *Kal’buir.*” His trust was transparent and absolute. “You’re our protector and we’ll always serve you.”

Skirata winced. Faith was devastating if you weren’t up to being a god.

But I don’t regret it. No, not a second of it.

Logistics center, Grand Army of the Republic,
Coruscant Command HQ, 370 days after Geonosis

“You’re not on the authorized personnel list for this center,” said the security droid at the doors.

Ordo reached past it and tapped a memorized code into the door panel. The sentry was a solid block with four arms, a head shorter than he was. "Well done. You're right to challenge me."

"Sir—"

Ordo reached into his belt and took out a stylus probe. The droid was fast, but not fast enough to avoid the probe Ordo slipped silently into the command port in its chest. There was a *chack-chack-chack* of memory drives and motors stalling for a moment, and then the droid seemed placated.

"You appear to be on the authorized personnel list," it said. "You have access to all areas including those restricted to staff officers, without on-site security tracking."

"Excellent," Ordo said, walking through the doors into the polished white marble lobby. "I'm a very private person."

And it was easy to be private when you were in armor. Nobody took much notice of a clone inside the GAR complex, not even one wearing an ARC trooper captain's livery.

It was simply a matter of looking as if you had every right to be going about your business. And the Null squad's proper business was anything Kal Skirata deemed it to be. Right now that meant identifying a method of inserting covert surveillance into Logistics, the most likely place for a mole who could relay very precise information on transport and contractor movements to the Separatists.

Ordo took out his datapad and consulted it frequently as if he were here for a routine visit. Without the possibility of eye contact, none of the civilian staff seemed even to register his presence. The white armor here was usually clone troopers who were physically unfit for front-line service, Engineer Corps, or ARC troopers carrying out occasional inspections for their generals.

After striding into a few offices, startling the droids and getting an occasional glance from civilian technicians, Ordo walked into the operations room at the heart of the logistics wing, and struck gold.

It was a large circular room with walls that were covered in live holocharts of troop and materiel movements. It danced with brilliant light and color, a HUD on a grand scale. At the room's heart was a large multistation desk staffed by two droids, four humans, six Sullustans, three Nimbanese, and . . .

. . . one clone trooper, minus his helmet.

"Excellent," Ordo said aloud.

The clone trooper jumped to his feet and saluted, even though it was technically a poor example of protocol to do so without his helmet in place. Ordo returned the salute anyway.

"Problem with your helmet, trooper?"

The man lowered his voice. "It makes the civilians edgy, sir. They prefer to see my eyes."

Ordo bristled. He would never defer to civilians' whims. "I'm carrying out a routine survey for General Camas." He didn't give the man his designation. Alpha ARCs rarely bothered to identify themselves to the lower ranks. He glanced at the civilians: one of the Nimbanese and a human female looked up at him. The pale reptilian Nimbanel was interesting as a detail, but the human female was enough to make him stop, stare, and note her as suspicious. She *smiled* at him. He still had his helmet on, but she *smiled* at him, and she was shockingly beautiful; both those facts were worrying in an administrative department. She looked down at her data console, lost in her work again, and flicked long pale blond hair over one shoulder.

"Trooper," Ordo said. He beckoned the man to him. "I'd like you to brief me on the operation of this unit."

They walked outside the main doors, and Ordo removed his helmet to look a brother in the eye and give him due respect. His glove's tally scanner told him the man was CT-5108/8843, an EOD operative: a bomb disposal expert, the kind of man who disarmed booby traps and UXBs so that other troopers could advance, the kind of man who could do work that even droids could not.

The explosives connection wasn't lost on Ordo for one moment.

"What's your name?"

The trooper hesitated. "Corr, sir," he said quietly.

"And what brings you here?"

Corr paused and then pulled off his gauntlets.

He had no hands.

They had been replaced by two simple prosthetics, so basic that they didn't have a synthflesh coating, just the bare durasteel mechanism. Ordo didn't even have to ask how he had acquired them. Somehow losing *both* hands was shocking in a way that losing one was not. Hands defined humanity.

"There's a parts shortage, sir, what with there being so many men injured and needing prosthetics," Corr said apologetically. "And these aren't good enough for me to do my job in the front line. As soon as the parts come through, I'll be back, though."

Ordo knew what *Kal'buir* would have said then, and he was moved to do the same, but this wasn't the time or the place. He held back. "Do they treat you properly here?"

Corr shrugged. "Fine. Actually, sir, the civilians tend not to speak to me that much, except for Supervisor Wennen. She's very kind to me indeed."

Ordo could see it coming. "Wennen would be the blond woman, yes?"

Corr nodded, his expression noticeably softened. "Besany Wennen. She doesn't approve of the fighting, sir, but she doesn't let it affect her work and she's looking after me very well."

Poor naïve trooper. "*How* well?"

"We have lunch together and she's taken me to visit the Galactic Museum."

Fascinating. Ordo had learned the wisdom of mistrust at a very early age. Glamorous woman, EOD expert, logistics hub: he could work it out. *Not* starting his observation here would have been stupid, but there was little to be gained from crashing in yet.

"How many shifts?"

"Three per daily roster, sir."

"I might need to ask you to do something for me, Corr."

"Certainly, sir."

"But when I do, it will be classified and you're to discuss it with nobody, not even your supervisor. It will be part of a routine fraud audit, that's all, and that's why I need your silence." Did it matter if he told him his name? Only the special forces inner circle knew who he was anyway. "My name is . . . Ordo. Mention *that* to nobody."

"Yes sir. Understood."

Ordo wanted to tell him that he understood his loneliness among strangers and his need to be back with his brothers at the front, doing *real* work. But he could tell him nothing. He ushered him back into the operations room, noted the lovely and apparently genuine smile that Supervisor Wennen gave him, and paused on his way out to break into the automated comlink relay and place a monitoring device.

Poor Corr. Ordo patted the sentry droid on the head and strode to his parked speeder.

8

Yes, I know how the Kaminoans did it. They used our genes against us, the ones that make us bond with our brothers, make us loyal, make us respect and obey our fathers—that's what they manipulated to make us more likely to obey orders. They had to remove what made Jango a selfish loner, because that makes a bad infantry soldier, and you can tell from the Alpha ARCs that the Kaminoans weren't wrong. But there's one thing I don't know yet—and that's how they controlled the aging process. That's the key. They robbed us of a full life span. But we will not be defeated by time, ner vod.

—ARC Trooper Lieutenant N-7—Mereel—in an encrypted transmission to N-11, Ordo

Republic Administration, Senate Head of Public Affairs Office, floor 391, Support Services Center, 370 days after Geonosis

Mar Rugeyan's office was very near the top floor of the administration building and had a view that some Senators would have killed for. Ordo wondered how Rugeyan did his killing—metaphorically, anyway—because he had the air of a man who would terminate anyone in his way without a second thought.

It was a long way down. Ordo tucked his helmet under his arm and admired the steady stream of speeders in the skylanes below.

"It's been a while," Rugeyan said, perfectly pleasant. "I never imagined I might be in a position to be any help to *you.*"

The subtle threat wasn't lost on Skirata, at least if his blink rate was anything to go by. "I appreciated your assistance during the siege. You remember my captain, don't you? Captain Ordo? Sir, can Mr. Rugeyan offer you anything to drink?"

"A glass of juice would be very welcome, thank you." Skirata was indeed inferior in rank, but it always made Ordo uncomfortable to hear *Kal'buir* call him *sir.* "We were wondering if you might be able to advise us."

Rugeyan betrayed no discomfort whatsoever at talking to a clone. "Happy to help, Captain." He tapped something on his desk. "Refreshments, please, Jayl. Juice and some cakes." He smiled. "But what could I advise you upon? You seem to have your public image pretty well honed. Smart, efficient, and noble. You can't buy an image like that."

"We feel that our troops should have a little more comfort in life and we're aware how much weight your advice carries with key members of the Defense Department," said Ordo.

"Ah." Rugeyan's eyes narrowed ever so slightly. "Quite right, too. What do you want out of this, then?"

"Leave."

"More of it?"

"*Any* of it. They don't get leave. Any downtime is spent in barracks or in training."

"Oh."

"You didn't know that?"

"No, frankly, I didn't. I never asked." Rugeyan actually seemed surprised, or at least he was feigning it very well. "But that's a command decision. They won't bend easily to public servants like me."

Ordo took a glass of brilliant emerald juice handed to him by Rugeyan's young female assistant, who simply stared, eyes scanning him. *Kal'buir* was right: Civilians never saw clone soldiers face-to-face.

It almost threw him off track. "In strategic terms, the temporary withdrawal of a few thousand troops from the front line makes very little difference," he said. "But I'm sure you know that warfare isn't all about big bangs. There's another front, and that's here." Ordo tapped his temple. "Visible troops around Coruscant. Good for public confidence right now, with the constant threat of terror attacks. And good for our men."

Rugeyan toyed with a cake studded with chunks of glistening red and purple fruit. "I admit that the Senate would like some positive results on the terror attacks. It's making the administration look helpless. Much as I respect our colleagues in the CSF, they're not making much progress, are they?"

Skirata cut in. "But if they did, it would be very timely, wouldn't it? And I'm sure that you'd be told about it right away."

This was the interesting thing about Skirata. He could speak around corners. He was an articulate self-educated man, and that always came as a surprise to outsiders. Jusik fell for the rough-diamond act all too often, but Vau wasn't the only *Mando* with a razor-sharp mind and a fine line in rhetoric. Skirata could switch from *Mando* hard man to politician without a visible change of gear.

Ordo found every conversation an education.

"I always appreciate information," Rugeyan said. "Especially when I know it'll serve some real purpose."

"So," Ordo said, and drained his glass. The assistant popped in again as if she'd been staking out the office and refilled it. "We have two battalions of the Forty-first Elite back in barracks and an assault ship's crew waiting on a refit. If someone could come up with the idea of an extended leave with the men allowed and encouraged to go off base, I think everyone would benefit. And maybe some credits to spend, because they don't get paid. A nice feelgood story for the media."

Rugeyan's expression flickered briefly from professional neutrality to surprise and then back again. "Never even thought of that, you know. So is this going to involve *your* men? The RCs?"

Rugeyan pronounced it *Arr-Sees,* like a soldier would. It was internal jargon and not for outsiders. Skirata blinked for a second, and then shifted down a gear into *Mando* mercenary again, albeit it one in a better mood than usual.

"They're not *RCs*. Arr-See sounds like a droid to the public. My boys are *men.* So please refer to them as Republic Commandos, not just commandos, and the other forces as troopers, or by their rank." He slurped his caf enthusiastically. "Words like RCs, cannon fodder, grunts, gropos, squaddies, pongoes, meat cans, white-jobs, or even shiny boys create the wrong impression. Terminology is everything, I find."

Rugeyan was actually making notes on a sheet of flimsi. He took no offense at all, not visibly anyway.

"Very useful," he said. "Leave this to me."

"And I'm sure Captain Obrim has your comlink code at the very top of his list, should there be any good news for you."

Skirata smiled and looked as if he meant it. Ordo nursed his glass, leaving a little juice at the bottom to fend off more instant attention from Rugeyan's assistant.

"An inevitable fact of life is that some of us are doomed to do the dirty thankless work in the shadows while someone else gets the headlines," Rugeyan said.

"Headlines can be overrated," said Skirata. "The captain has another meeting to attend, but thank you for your time."

It was all *very* civilized: another coded conversation where the unspeakable had somehow been spoken.

And it was all a far cry from the sweaty, anxious hours at the Galactic City spaceport a few months before, when Rugeyan had been no more than a severe irritant and Skirata had taken a rather physical dislike to him. Now the man seemed to have a clear and almost uncanny grasp of exactly what he was being asked to do, and although he must have had questions, he never asked them. It almost made him a soldier.

The descent in the turbolift felt like a rapid insert via gunship as they plunged down a hundred levels.

Skirata began laughing quietly and pinched the bridge of his nose, eyes shut. "I wish I'd realized that Rugeyan would respond to a simple request. Then I'd never have—well, you know."

"If you hadn't captured his attention in such an assertive way at the siege, perhaps he wouldn't have been so accommodating today. That man might even make a useful member of an intelligence bureau one day."

"He just needed me to show some understanding of his own position. Sometimes I think people want more from me than they actually do. So where does this leave us, *Ord'ika?*"

Ordo counted off on the fingers of his glove. "Smokescreen in progress. Team on standby, split into watches. Observation points and potential operational houses collated and identified. Armory and logistics in place. Confirmed link between devices and prisoners."

"But?"

"All dressed up and nowhere to go. Still a large gap in the intel."

"What did the droid crack out of the download from Atin?" Skirata asked.

"A lot of data that needs combing by hand when we have other intel to put alongside it. It's just lists of businesses like any transport company would keep. Nothing leaps out. Sometimes I wish we had to deal with Weequays. They'd label things TOP SECRET and give us a clue."

"Why is this proving so hard? Fierfek, son, Kom'rk and Jaing can track a flitnat across the galaxy and we can't find a gang in our own backyard."

"I'm sorry, *Kal'buir.*" *I should be able to crack this. I'm letting him down.* "This is a double line of surveillance, I'm afraid—the terror network itself and whoever is providing their recce intelligence—and that could be inside our own organization, or in the CSF, and the latter is going to be harder to identify."

"I'm not blaming you. It's just an expression."

"And my brothers do know the identities of the flitnats they're looking for, of course."

"Only one option left, then. Explore every line and dot, and hope for a lucky break while we're doing it to speed things up."

"Unless Vau gets lucky."

"Time to break out the emergency Jedi, I think, son."

"Oh-eight-hundred tomorrow," said Ordo.

"Still got time to do some more preparation, then. Let's go and see a Hutt who owes me one. Well, a lot more than one, actually. And let's pick up Sev and Scorch so they can see how it's done."

There were things Skirata could do that not even a commando or an ARC could, and one of those was to work his contacts.

Ordo committed it all to memory. Tonight would be highly educational.

Qibbu's Hut, entertainment district, Coruscant;
Delta recce troop in attendance

Garish green light framed the pulsing orange sign above the entrance. Qibbu opened late: it was already dark, and Skirata thought it was high time the bar welcomed new customers.

"I'm only a simple trained killer," Sev said, "but something tells me never to eat in a restaurant with a bad pun over the door."

"You haven't tried the food yet," Skirata said. "That'll leave no room for doubt."

"Or dessert," Scorch said. "And did I mention I feel naked?"

"About a dozen times since we left HQ. Get used to it. You can't wear armor all the time."

Ordo drew one blaster. Scorch raised his eyebrows.

"I'm being low-key," Ordo said. "Or I'd draw both."

"I really didn't notice you in that shiny white rig at all, sir . . ."

"Listen up, lads." Skirata slid one hand into his pocket to feel for a reassuring meter of durasteel chain and held his right arm straight at his side. He hadn't seen the Hutt in a long time, years before Kamino, and it was bound to be a nasty shock for the old slug.

"Qibbu might be surprised to see me, especially as he still owes me a fee. So no heroics. I can handle him." Skirata gestured for the two commandos to stand back in the open lobby. "Look casual and read the menu. And don't throw up."

The sprawling maze of rooms passed for a restaurant, bar, and hotel, but only if the Coruscant food hygiene inspectors were looking the other way. It was perfect in every way if you wanted *not* to be bothered. There was a certain anonymity in the rough end of the entertainment district.

It was just the kind of place where an awful lot of clone soldiers could pass in and out without drawing comment, at least after the novelty wore off. Skirata leaned on the intercom.

Qibbu the Hutt *was* at home. He just knew it. It was the skinny Duros suddenly standing in the doorway with a blaster that gave the game away.

"We're closed," the Duros said.

"And I'm Kal Skirata."

The Duros' gray fist closed on the blaster. "And I said we're *closed.*"

Ordo swung around the door and leveled his blaster in the Duros' flat face. "No, I do believe you're *open,* and we'd like to see tonight's special, please."

The Duros paused long enough to gape, which was probably what saved his life. If he'd lifted the blaster, Ordo would have killed him. Ordo grabbed his wrist anyway and twisted it almost as a side effect of wresting the blaster from his grip, and there was the unmistakable *snick* of cracking bone. The Duros squealed.

"I think that means come right in," Skirata said, and made sure he had his blaster in his waistband. Qibbu might have shelled out some credits for competent help after all. He wandered into the deserted restaurant and noted that the carpet didn't quite stick to his boots as much as it used to. He wandered behind the bar, as much to check that nobody was lurking there to give him a Very Unhappy Hour as to see if the glasses were clean.

Ordo's blaster whirred faintly as he raised it. When Skirata looked up, Sev and Scorch were covering one door each. *Good lads.* They'd all do fine out in the big bad world.

"Ka-a-al . . ." Qibbu inched out of the kitchens, a waft of exotic spice and burned fat escaping as the Hutt eased himself into the bar area. "So you come for your bounty at last. I thought you would never come. And you have staff and a *nice* jacket now . . . must be doing better business, yes?"

"Colleagues," Skirata said. "I'll take hard currency, but if you haven't got that, we can negotiate."

Qibbu was unattractive even by Hutt standards. His tongue flicked across his slit of a mouth, and he edged to the bar to slither onto his dais and pour a couple of drinks.

"Your boys want ale?" Qibbu indicated a jar of pickled gorg on the bar. "Snacks?"

"No thanks." Sev and Scorch were a chorus, eyes fixed on the jar of very dead amphibians. "Couldn't manage another thing."

"Okay, you and I talk, then, Ka-a-al."

"I take it you haven't got ready currency?"

"Not that much. Give me time, and—"

"Let me make it easy for both of us." Skirata pulled up a stool and sat down to bring himself level with the Hutt's eyes. "I'm a tourist. Can my boys take a look at your rooms? If we like what we see, we'll stay for a while."

Skirata indicated the turbolift. Sev and Scorch drew their blasters and disappeared for a recce. Ordo locked the main doors again and paced slowly around the bar, probably committing the layout and every detail to memory. A right little holorecorder, Ordo: another superb advantage of perfect recall.

"So . . . you have a project in hand, Ka-a-al?"

"I might have."

"Does it involve . . . dead people?"

"Not this time. I just need a place where my colleagues and I can relax and not be bothered for a while."

Qibbu's yellow slit-pupiled eyes followed Ordo around the bar. Skirata could never see yellow eyes now without thinking of Kaminoans.

"Your colleagues are soldiers."

"Yes. They like to make the most of their leave. They don't get much."

"So they do little . . . *jobs* for you," Qibbu said.

"Yes, and none of those jobs need inconvenience you. You won't get any visits from CSF, because my boys behave themselves."

"You just want . . . *peace and quiet* for them to do those little jobs for you."

You have no idea how much, Slug-Breath. "Yes."

"In exchange, you write off that small sum I owe you?"

"I might." It was five hundred thousand credits plus interest. He didn't need it now. There was a time when he would have risked his life and that of anyone who got in the way to pick up a fee like that. He'd been a successful debt enforcer for a brief time, but it wasn't proper soldiering. "I might also bring some trade your way, because there could be a lot of troopers in town who want to visit somewhere relaxing."

"You offer me more than I owe you. There is a *catch.*"

"The catch," Skirata said, feeling the negotiation slipping away from him, "is that you'll guarantee no trouble here. And my definition of trouble is quite exacting."

"No unwanted attention."

"And no nonsense from your usual low-life clientele. No taking advantage of my soldier boys. As much food as they want—fresh and properly cooked, please—and clean rooms. They don't drink much but they do tend to like a lot of caf and sweet beverages."

Qibbu blinked slowly, still apparently distracted by Ordo, who was taking an interest in the kitchen.

"Mind if I do a food hygiene inspection?" Ordo said, and disappeared into the kitchens without waiting for a reply.

Qibbu's gaze slid toward the kitchen and then back to Skirata. "You ask for a *lot* for your shiny boys."

Skirata closed his hand around the end of the chain in his pocket. The slug needed to learn who had the upper hand in this negotiation. "That's because they *deserve* a lot, you *owe* me a lot, and if you mess me about you'll have a lot more *trouble* than you could possibly imagine—"

Skirata's buildup to giving Qibbu a serious smacking was suddenly interrupted by a stifled shriek from the kitchens. A young Twi'lek female came rushing out the doors. He realized Ordo must have startled her. It might have been the twin blasters.

"And only *respectable* females allowed in the bar," Skirata added. But the Twi'lek looked terrified in a way that said she was used to being that way, and he didn't like that at all. He knew Qibbu only too well. "She doesn't look like your usual . . . kitchen staff."

The girl huddled against the far wall, staring at Ordo, who merely walked out and holstered his blaster with an exaggerated gesture. He didn't do *reassuring* very well at the best of times, let alone with women. It was time to teach him more social graces when carrying firearms.

The Hutt gurgled a laugh. "Females . . . you know how they are—"

Enough. Skirata pulled his durasteel chain out in one movement and whipped it around Qibbu's neck, twisting it in his fist as he wrenched the quivering bulk toward him. The metal cut into the creature's soft fat, leaving a white margin where the blood could no longer circulate.

"Listen, *shag,*" Skirata said, feeling his anger tightening his throat muscles. There was no worse insult for a Hutt than *slave.* "I *like* Twi'lek females. Honest ones, the sort that don't thieve, or worse. So no mistreating the staff or I might discover what a trade union activist I can be. Just look after any of my boys who pass this way. *Eniki?* You step out of line and there'll be a new batch of fresh blubber products at the market first thing in the morning." He twisted the chain a little tighter. "*J'hagwa na yoka,* Fatboy. No trouble."

Qibbu's third eyelid flicked across his reptilian eye like a windscreen wiper. "Your pretty shiny boys die anyway, sooner or later."

That was *it.* Skirata jerked the Hutt's head down and brought his knee up in Qibbu's face as hard as he could with a wet *thwack.* He didn't need this *thing* to remind him of that and mock their sacrifice. Qibbu spluttered ammonia-scented saliva, moaning.

"Are we going to get good service at your establishment?" Skirata said, ignoring the pain in his kneecap. "Or would you prefer to pay me half a million creds plus nine years' interest right *now*?"

"Tagwa, lorda."

"That's more like it." He loosened his choke hold a little. "A bit of customer focus is good for business."

Qibbu balked visibly. "I lose profit."

"You'll lose a lot more than that if you mess around with me. I've always wanted to see if Hutts really can regenerate body parts." Skirata tightened the chain again. *"Ke nu'jurkadir sha Mando'ade . . ."*

Don't mess with Mandalorians. It wasn't bad advice.

Qibbu was no linguist but Skirata knew tone could convey a great deal even to an animal, and maybe even to a Hutt. He hoped the lack of circulation in Qibbu's neck was translating for him.

"*Tagwa* . . . Sergeant," Qibbu said, and let out a long wet gasp as Skirata released the chain.

Sev and Scorch emerged from the turbolift again and gave Skirata the thumbs-up.

"Ideal for a relaxing break, Sarge," Scorch said. "Lovely clear views, platform to park a speeder or six, and *lots* of room to stretch our legs. A whole floor of rooms at the top, in fact."

Good defensive visibility, easy access and escape, and the right layout for moving around and storing kit and ordnance. Excellent.

"If it's good enough for my colleagues, it'll be good enough for me," Skirata said. "You want to take a look just to make sure, Ordo?"

Ordo shook his head, still seeming wary of the Twi'lek female. "I'll go with the majority."

"So, long-stay rates?" Skirata asked.

"As . . . discussed," Qibbu said.

Skirata slid off the stool and wiped the chain clean of Qibbu's slime before coiling it and putting it in his pocket again. He was concerned about the Twi'lek, though. Civilians were hardly his prime concern on this operation, but it didn't cost anything to be courteous.

He walked over to her. She was still cowering. He squatted down almost instinctively: he saw six scared little boys waiting to be *reconditioned.* "I'm Kal, ma'am," he said. "What's your name?"

She didn't meet his eyes. She had that way of looking off slightly to one side that he thought he'd seen too many times before. "Laseema."

"Well, Laseema, if your boss isn't treating you well, you let me know. And I'll have a word with him." He smiled as best he could. "And none of my boys will give you any problems, either, okay?"

"Okay," she said shakily. Her lekku were moving slightly, but Skirata couldn't understand the unspoken language they conveyed. She might just have been twitching out of fear. "Okay."

Skirata gave her as reassuring a smile as he could manage and moved to the doors. "We'll be back tomorrow to move some stuff in. Have the top floor ready for us, will you? Nice and clean."

"And fresh flowers," Scorch said.

They ambled back to the speeder and set off for Arca Barracks, settling into an automated skylane and merging into the stream of glittering taillights. Coruscant was lovely at night, just as Fi said. Skirata had never thought about it much before.

He nudged Sev. "Good operational house, then."

"Tailor-made. It'll take us a day to move the kit in discreet amounts, but we can access via the landing platform when it's dark again."

"Does our host get nervous about storing ordnance?" Ordo said.

"He's a Hutt," said Skirata. "He's stored a lot worse. And what he doesn't know won't keep him awake at night."

Scorch seemed impressed. "You really were a bit of a bad boy in your past, weren't you, Sarge?"

"What d'you mean, *past*?" Sev said.

And they laughed. They were perfect special forces troops, very bad boys in their own right, but they had never dealt with the criminal underworld—and crime was an inevitable partner of terrorism. It was one reason why Skirata didn't feel one scrap of misgiving about going bandit himself.

Fierfek, he'd *impressed* them. The Delta boys were emerging from their closed, tight-knit exclusivity and settling into the larger team. That was one problem solved.

There was still the operation itself, of course.

And keeping an eye on Atin, Vau, and Sev.

And introducing Etain to an element of war that wasn't remotely noble.

And making sure that everyone came out of it alive.

Skirata reached over the back of the seat and gave Sev and Scorch a playful swat, then nudged Ordo beside him.

"I promised you all a night out," he said. "When we get this cleaned up, Zey's going to get a *really* big mess bill from the officers' club."

"Maybe we shouldn't wait until then," Scorch said. "You never know what's around the corner."

No. You didn't. You never did.

9

When the enemy is a droid or a wet with a weapon, then killing them is easy. But in this game you're operating among civvies, on your home ground. You could be working right next door to the enemy. They might even be people you know and like. But they're still the enemy and you'll have to slot them just the same. There's no Mandalorian word for "hero," and that's just as well, because however many lives you save in black ops, you will never, ever be a hero. Deal with it.

—Sergeant Kal Skirata, teaching counterterrorist tactics to Republic Commando companies Alpha through Epsilon, Kamino, three years before Geonosis

Arca Company Barracks parade ground,
0730 hours, 371 days after Geonosis

The missile skimmed the top of Etain's head and bounced off the Force-shield she had instinctively thrown up to protect her face.

Jusik skidded to a halt in front of her, sweat dripping off the end of his nose, a flattened alloy rod clutched in one hand. There was a smear of blood across his cheek, and she wasn't sure if it was his.

"Sorry!" He looked elated. "Look, why don't you sit over there? It's safer."

Etain indicated the blood. "And why don't you use your Force powers?" she said. "This is a dangerous sport."

"That's *cheating,*" Jusik said, lobbing the small plastoid sphere back into the knot of commandos. They pounced on the object like a hunting pack and jostled each other ferociously to whack the thing with rods, trying to drive it hard against the barrack wall.

Etain had no idea what the game was called, if it had a name at all. Nor did it seem to have any rules: the ball, such as it was, was being hit, kicked, and thrown as the whim took the players.

And the teams were Niner, Scorch, Fixer, and Darman against Fi, Atin, Sev, and Boss. Skirata *insisted* that they played in mixed teams.

Several other commandos had paused while crossing the parade ground to watch. The battle was conducted in grim silence except for the clash of rods, gasping breath, and occasional approving shouts of *"Nar dralshy'a!"—Put your back into it!*—and *"Kandosii!"*—which, Jusik had explained, had been appropriated colloquially to mean "classy" rather than "noble."

They had all become much more ferociously *Mando* since she had first met them. It was a phenomenon that made sense given the specific nature of their duties, but it still left her feeling that they were becoming strangers again. Working so closely with Skirata appeared to have focused their minds on a people who seemed to have the ultimate freedom.

Even Darman had fallen happily into it. He was utterly engrossed in the game, shoulder-charging Boss out of the way and knocking Jusik flat. There was a shout of *"Kandosii!"* as the ball thudded against the wall, two meters above the ground.

Then Skirata emerged from the doorway. Etain didn't have to take any hints from the Force as to his state of mind.

"Armor!" he yelled. His voice could fill a parade ground. The commandos froze as one. He did *not* look amused. "I said wear some *armor!* No injuries! You hear me?"

He strode across to Jusik with surprising speed for a man with a damaged leg and came to a halt with his face centimeters from the Jedi's. He dropped his voice, but not by much.

"Sir, I regret to have to tell you that you're a *dik'ut.*"

"Sorry, Sergeant." Jusik was a contrite scrap of bloody robes and sweaty hair. "My fault. Won't happen again."

"No injuries. Not *now.* Okay, sir?"

"Understood, Sergeant."

Skirata nodded and then grinned, ruffling Jusik's hair just as he did his troops'. "You're definitely *ori'atin, Bard'ika.* Just don't get yourself killed."

Jusik beamed, clearly delighted. Skirata had not only told him that he was exceptionally tough, but he had used the most affectionate form of his name: now he was "Little Bardan," and thus one of

Skirata's clan. He jogged off after the commandos and disappeared inside the building.

Skirata ambled across to Etain and sat down next to her on the bench. "He's a gutsy little *di'kut,* isn't he?"

So it wasn't only a term of abuse, then. "If there wasn't a war on, I suspect that Master Zey would have had a serious word with him by now. Bardan's become very *attached.*"

"Being a loner might make a warrior, but it won't make a soldier."

"Where were you educated?"

Skirata was looking straight ahead rather than at her, and his eyes creased at the corners for a brief moment. "On the street, on the battlefield, and by a bunch of very smart little boys."

Etain smiled. "I wasn't being rude. Just curious."

"Fair enough. I had to analyze and explain everything I taught my Nulls for eight years. It wasn't enough for me to show them the right way to fight. They wanted me to rationalize it. They shredded me with questions. Then they'd feed it all back to me in a way I'd never seen it before. Amazing."

"Do we get to meet them all? Are they all like Ordo?"

"Maybe," Skirata said. "They're deployed in various locations." It was his noncommittal answer: *Don't ask.* "And they're all of the same caliber, yes."

"So out of a strike team of twelve, you have eleven tough men—*atin,* yes?—and me. I can't help feeling I'm not going to be much use."

Skirata took out a chunk of something brown and woody and popped it into his mouth. He chewed like a gdan, as if he were gnawing off someone's arm. *"Atin'ade,"* he corrected. "Oh, you'll be plenty of use. I suspect you'll have the hardest job of all."

"Whatever it takes."

"I know."

"Sergeant, is this going to become clear at the briefing?"

"It's not a secret. I just want everyone to have the full picture at the same time. Then we ship out and disappear."

"I hear you've done that before."

"*Cuy'val Dar.* Yes, I've been 'those who no longer exist' before. You get used to it. It has its plus points."

He got up and walked toward the barracks, Etain following. His limp was far less obvious today.

"How did you hurt your leg?" she asked.

"I didn't follow orders. I ended up with a Verpine shatter gun round through my ankle. Sometimes you need to learn the hard way."

"Never got it fixed?"

"I'll get around to it one day. Come on, breakfast before briefing. Some things sound better on a full stomach."

When the briefing started at 0800, Jusik looked freshly scrubbed, but he was developing a fine black eye. He also seemed delighted. Etain envied him his capacity for finding joy in the most unlikely places, just like Darman did. Omega and Delta appeared to have broken up as squads completely. They took their seats, lounging around in their black bodysuits, but they no longer sat in their own tight groups. Atin and Sev still exuded a sense of distance, but Skirata's crash course in being buddies appeared to be working.

There was also the small matter of the Wookiee who had walked in. Skirata directed the creature to a bigger chair and locked the doors. It was the one who'd piloted the taxi.

"Ordo, have you swept the room for bugs?"

"Yes, Sergeant."

"Okay, ladies and gentlemen, this is strictly for those in this room. If anyone wants out, now's the time to say."

"Observe the complete lack of movement, Sarge," Scorch said. "Nobody's passing on this one."

"I didn't think so. From now on, there's no *General* or *sir* or *Sergeant* or designation codes, and no Jedi robes. There is no rank. There is no chain of command beyond *me.* If I'm otherwise engaged or *dead* then you answer to Ordo. Got it?" The Wookiee threw him two bundles of clothing and he lobbed one each to Etain and Jusik. She caught hers and stared at it. "Plainclothes, kids. You clone lads are just soldiers on leave, and us mongrels are . . . well, Etain can pass for my daughter and *Bard'ika* is a useful deadbeat I picked up on my travels. A *go-fer.*"

The Wookiee emitted a long and contented trill. "This is Enacca, by the way." Skirata indicated the Wookiee with a polite flourish. "She's our quartermaster and mobility troop—she'll secure supplies and transport for us. You ever worked with Wookiees?"

The commandos shook their heads, wide-eyed.

"Well, everything you've heard is true." He gestured to Ordo, and a holoprojection streamed from the ARC's glove onto the wall. It was a chart with arrows and labels on it. "So here's what we have so far. One, we have a point of origin for the explosives. Two, we think we have someone in GAR logistics or support, or in the CSF, who is either passing information or being careless with it. Now, what we *don't* have is a link in the chain between the following terror cells: materials to bomb manufacture; bomb manufacture to placement cell; and placement cell to recce and surveillance cell—in other words, the ones who tell them where to place the device and when to detonate it."

Ordo had his projection arm resting on his chair. "And Vau is trying to extract at least one link from the cell Omega lifted."

"But they might not even know what that link is," Skirata said. "It's common to use the equivalent of a dead letter drop to deliver stuff. The prisoners tested positive for explosives, so they might be the manufacturers, but I'd assume the devices are made on Coruscant because it's simpler to ship bulk explosives than complete bombs, given that you can't pretend bombs are for mining use, although neither is easy. So our best guess is that they're the procurement cell that buys the raw material."

Jusik had his head cocked on one side. "I take it that if we don't know this after a day, then Vau is not having much success with his interrogation. May I volunteer to help him? Jedi have some persuasive powers as well as ways of uncovering facts."

"I know," Skirata said. "That's why Etain's going to do it. I need you out and about at the moment."

Etain's stomach somersaulted. *Is this a test?* Jusik was watching her cautiously: he could definitely sense her discomfort. Perhaps he had tried to do the decent thing and save her from the duty. Or perhaps he was so caught up in being one of the boys that he really wanted to have a crack at a prisoner. Jusik had his own wary relationship with the dark side, it seemed.

"Okay," Etain said. *You've killed. You've killed hand-to-hand, and you've killed by unleashing missiles. On Qiilura, under deep cover, you stabbed and crushed and cut, and taught the local guerrillas to do the same. And now you worry about manipulating minds?* "I'll do whatever I can."

"Good," Skirata said, and moved on as if she had simply volunteered to cook dinner. "Now, the data Atin sliced is just a list of thirty-five thousand companies using the freight service that Vau's guests were apparently hitching a ride with. That means a lot of physical checking we can't do ourselves. So Obrim's running it through his database—his personal, special one—to see if any of them have form in customs irregularities, shady dealings, or even a speeding ticket. While he does that, we ship out. Jusik, Enacca is going to turn you into the galaxy's scruffiest taxi pilot, and the rest of you can draw your *extra* kit—by which I mean discreet body armor, plainclothes rig, and civilian weapons."

"Aww, Sarge . . ."

"Fi, you'll love it. You might even get to wear Hokan's helmet."

"Just for you, then, Sarge."

"Good boy. Okay, we all RV back here at twenty-one-hundred hours when it's nice and dark." Skirata gestured to Ordo to kill the holoprojection and then beckoned to Etain. "General, Ordo—with me."

He led them into the passage and, instead of taking her into a quiet alcove to discuss matters, simply hurried her down the length of the corridor and out onto the parade ground, where yet another battered speeder with darkened transparisteel windscreens was waiting.

"Are you starting up a used-speeder dealership with Enacca?" Jokes always seemed to work for Fi, but Etain found they offered her no comfort at all. "They don't draw attention, though, I'll admit that."

"Get in. Time to go to work."

Like the clone army, she had become very good at following orders. Ordo took the speeder at a sedate pace into the main skylanes and dropped it into a gap in a route heading south.

"This is where it gets difficult, Etain," Skirata said.

In a way, she knew what was coming. "Yes."

"This is harder than taking on a column of battle droids and playing the hero." Skirata was still chewing the ruik. She could smell it on his breath, sweet and floral. "I won't insult your intelligence. I want you to torture a man. It's the first intelligence break we've had in months and we need to make the most of it. Men died making sure we got those prisoners."

She wasn't sure if it was a test of her loyalty or not. It was certainly something that Skirata knew would be the ultimate line for a Jedi to cross. But Jedi crossed the lines of decency all the time, and it was supposed to be fine as long as you didn't commit violence out of anger, or dare to love.

She was finding it harder to follow her path than ever before, and yet she was now clearer about her own convictions than she had ever been in her life.

She was aware of Ordo, too.

He appeared perfectly calm in the pilot's seat, but the eddies and deep dark pools in the Force around him spoke of a man who was *not* at ease with himself or the world. Great peaks of fear and pain and helpless trust and desolation and . . . and . . . *sheer overwhelming speed* and complexity hit Etain like a spray of cold water. He felt as foreign as a Hutt or a Weequay or a Twi'lek.

He was a man in frequent agony. His mind was racing at full throttle, and it felt as if it never stopped.

She must have been staring at him. "Are you all right, ma'am?" he asked, still veneered in calm.

"I'm fine," she said, swallowing hard. "What . . . what can I possibly do that Walon Vau can't?"

"Are you ready to hear some unpleasant things?" Skirata said.

"I have to be."

He rubbed his forehead slowly. "You can train people to resist interrogation. That's a fancy phrase for torture, and I don't like using it. I know, because I've done it, and hard-line terrorists get trained much like soldiers do. But they don't get trained to resist *Jedi.* And that gives you a psychological advantage as well as a real one."

"Nikto are supposed to be tough."

"Humans can be tough, too."

He seemed distressed. It was severe enough for her to feel the Force around him become that dark vortex again. "Kal, who's finding this more unpleasant, you or me?"

"Me."

"I thought so."

"It comes back to you at times like this."

"So who . . . trained Omega?" She felt the faintest shimmer of distress in Ordo now.

"Me," said Skirata.

"Oh."

"Would you have let anyone else do it if you were me?"

"No." She knew immediately; she didn't even have to think about it. It would have been an act of abandonment, letting someone else do the dirty work to salve your own conscience, with the same outcome. "No, I wouldn't."

"Well . . ." He shut his eyes for a moment. "If I can *train* my boys, then you should have no trouble doing what Vau can't."

"Tell me what's at stake."

"For who? The Republic?" Kal asked. "I think it's marginal, to be honest. In real terms, terrorism doesn't even dent it. Casualties in the thousands, that's all. It's fear of it that does the damage."

"So why are you in so deep?"

"Who's getting hit hardest? Clone troopers."

"But thousands of troops are dying in the front line every day. Numerically—"

"Yeah, I can't do much about the war. I trained quite a few men to stay alive. But all that's left for me is to do what I can, where I can."

"Personal war, isn't it?" Etain said.

"You think so? I don't care if the Republic falls or not. I'm a mercenary. Everyone's my potential employer."

"So where does the anger come from? I know anger, you see. As Jedi we guard against it all the time."

"You won't like the answer."

"I don't like a lot of things lately, but I still have to deal with them."

"Okay. Day by day, I get more bitter when I see Mandalorian men—and that's what they are, whether you like it or not—used and discarded in a war in which they have *no stake.*" Skirata, sitting right behind Ordo, put his hand gently on the captain's armored shoulder. "But not on my watch."

Etain had no answer to that. She hadn't articulated it in racial terms, and she knew that Mandalorians weren't a race as such. But there hadn't been one day since she had parted from Omega Squad on Qiilura nine months ago that she hadn't agonized over the use of soldiers who had no choice, no rights, and no future in the Republic that they gave their lives to defend.

It was *wrong.*

There was a point somewhere at which the means did *not* justify the ends, no matter what the numbers argued. Like this violent, passionate little man beside her, Etain didn't refuse her role in the war out of principle, because that would have been no more than shutting her eyes to it.

Men would still die.

And if the Jedi Council could accept the need to let that happen to save the Republic, then she could sink to a level she had never believed possible to save soldiers she knew as people.

"I'll try not to let you down," she said.

"You mean *me*?" said Skirata.

And you, she thought.

Safe house, Brewery zone, Coruscant Quadrant J-47, 1000 hours, 371 days after Geonosis

Skirata had been expecting the safe house to be in another seedy part of the city where unusual activity was part of the landscape.

But Enacca had surpassed herself this time. The property was a small apartment in a refurbished quarter known as the Brewery; the construction droids were still working on some of the buildings, facing them with tasteful durasteel wroughtwork. Zey was going to have a fit when he saw the bill for this one land on his desk.

"I think that's what our brothers might call *kandosii,*" Ordo said, bringing the speeder up to the landing platform. It had a discreet awning to shield it from view, although Coruscant was so traffic-packed that enemy surveillance from tall buildings—Skirata's dread—was less of a threat than usual here. Lines of sight were frequently obscured. "I'll be back later. Errands to run, *Kal'buir.*"

When the lobby doors closed behind them, the constant throb and hum of Coruscant was completely silenced. *Ah. Top-range soundproofing.* Enacca was a very smart Wookiee. Vau's job could be noisy. There was no point upsetting the neighbors in cheaper parts of town that had less efficient soundproofing.

And it was the last place Orjul's colleagues would come looking for him.

Etain had her arms folded tightly across her chest, her light brown wavy hair scraped back in a braid except for the wiry bits that had escaped and sprung into coils. Even her new civilian clothes already looked as if she had slept in them. She had a veil of freckles and an awkward gait; just a schoolgirl armed with a lightsaber, nothing more.

"You up to this, *ad'ika*?" Little one: Skirata slipped accidentally into being the reassuring father. But he reserved judgment. Like him, she might just have made a point of looking a lot less trouble than she actually was. "If not, walk away *now.*" And if she did, what would he have to do? She already knew dangerous numbers of people and places.

"No. I'm not backing out now."

He thought she might suddenly reveal a powerful charisma or sweetness that would explain why this scrap of skin, bone, and unkempt hair had so riveted Darman. But she was just a kid, a Jedi kid with a lot of responsibility that showed in her young face and old eyes.

Skirata pressed on the entry buzzer into the main apartment, and after a moment the doors whispered apart. The strong smell that hit him on the moist air reminded him of walking into a barn full of frightened animals. It was so distinctive that he almost didn't notice the scent of the strill. But Mird was nowhere to be seen.

Vau, sitting at the table, looked tired. He still seemed like a professor who wasn't very happy with his class, but the physical effort showed in deeper lines from nose to mouth and the way he was drumming his fingers on the table in front of him. It was his trick for staying awake.

The man who had his head resting on the same table in front of him didn't look awake at all. Vau leaned forward and lifted the man's head by his hair, peered into his face, and set him down carefully again.

"You're the relief watch, then, Jedi?" Vau got up and stretched extravagantly, joints clicking, and indicated the empty chair. "All yours."

Etain looked surprised. Skirata had expected her to register horror at the blood spatter on the otherwise pristine cream walls, but she just looked at Vau as if she was expecting to see someone else.

"Where are the other two?" Skirata asked.

"Nikto number one is M'truli, and he's secured in the small bedroom." Vau was perfectly polite: this was just business after all, and even Skirata felt too centered on the task at hand to resume their feud where it had left off. "Nikto number two is Gysk, and he's in the study."

"Your tunic could do with a wash."

"It's the little horns. You can't punch a Nikto. Had to use something else."

Etain sat down in Vau's seat and placed her hands flat on the table, still looking puzzled. Skirata leaned against the wall. Vau wandered into the 'fresher: water tinkled into a basin.

"You want to tell me what you know," Etain said soothingly. "You want to give me the names of the people you operate with."

Orjul twitched. He raised his head from the table with some difficulty and stared into her face for a second.

Then he spat in it.

Etain jerked back, visibly shocked, and wiped away the pink-stained spittle with one hand. Then she composed herself again.

"Keep your stinking mind tricks to yourself, Jedi," Orjul hissed.

Skirata didn't expect her to break at that point. And she didn't: she simply sat there, although he knew it wasn't blank inactivity. She had been trained from childhood just like the clone army, except the first weapon she seized would be her control of the Force and her ability to read it like clamoring comlink signals.

Darman had told him. *She could tell us apart right away by how we felt and thought, Sarge. Wouldn't that be a handy trick to have?*

"Can I see the Nikto?" she asked suddenly.

Vau came out of the 'fresher, wiping his face on a fluffy white towel. "Help yourself." He gave Skirata a *you-know-best* look and unlocked the doors for her. "They're securely trussed. You know we keep them from talking to each other, don't you?"

"I worked that out," Etain said.

She disappeared into one room for a minute and then came out and went into the other. When she emerged again, she walked up to Skirata and Vau and lowered her head.

"I'm pretty sure those Nikto have no information, and *know* they don't have it," she said quietly.

"People have useful information all the time and don't know it," Skirata said. "*We* piece the apparently useless stuff together and come up with connections."

"What I mean is that they have this distinct sense that they're just afraid of dying."

Vau shrugged. "So much for Nikto grit, eh?"

"Every creature avoids death. The difference is that Orjul is afraid of *breaking.* It feels different to me. It's not animal dread. It's not as deep in the Force." Etain had her fingers meshed in that Jedi way that made her look as if she were wringing her hands. "I might as well concentrate on him. He has information he's afraid to reveal."

They watched her walk the few meters back to the main room and settle down at the table opposite Orjul again and stare at him.

Vau shrugged. "Oh well. At least I can have a nap while she's minding the shop. Then I can get back to work with more *tangible* methods."

There was a sharp gasp from Orjul and Vau looked around. Whatever Etain was doing, she wasn't even touching him. Just *staring.*

"Kal, *those* people scare me more than Orjul does," Vau said. "I'm just going to get my head down for a couple of hours. Wake me if she gets anywhere—or kills him, of course."

It was about 1030 in the morning, when people were going about mundane business in the city. It felt like an odd time of day to be conducting an interrogation. Skirata somehow felt they were always carried out in some permanent night.

And Etain showed every sign of being up to the task.

From time to time, she would lower her head as if to try to get a better view of Orjul's expression while he sat facedown at the table, fingers knotted in his pale hair as if he had a blinding headache. Skirata wanted to ask her what she was doing to him but he was worried it would break her concentration.

And she was fixed completely on the task in hand. Her blink rate had slowed so much that she appeared to be frozen, except for the pulse in her throat. Orjul would occasionally pant and squeal, writhing as if he were attempting to crawl into the very surface of the table.

Skirata walked away and went to stare at the Nikto for a while. When he came back into the room, Orjul was making little hiccuping sobs. Etain, face level with his, was talking quietly to him.

"Can you see it, Orjul? Can you see what happens?"

Skirata watched.

"Orjul . . ."

The man whined exactly like a strill, a thin animal noise. "I can't . . ."

"Fear of being wrong is worse than pain, isn't it? It just eats you and you can't shut it off. Are you right? Or are you as bad as the Republic you hate? Are we really the enemy, or are you? Look at the helpless pawns you kill."

So *that* was what she was doing. Skirata had wondered if she was using her Force powers to cause real physical pain. But she had cut to the chase and re-created the stuff that pain did to you anyway: it made you fear for your sanity long before your life.

He had to hand it to her. It was nonlethal and not that far beyond the usual mind influence. Maybe she was struggling to find an ethical limit in her own mind. Maybe it was her own nightmare, the worst thing she could conceive.

She kept it up for an hour. He had no idea whether she was suggesting terrible images and consequences in his mind, or if she was simply flooding him with adrenaline against his wishes, but whatever it was it was exhausting him and her with it. Eventually Orjul broke down sobbing, and Etain shuddered and looked disoriented as if coming out of a trance.

Skirata grabbed Vau's shoulder and shook him awake. "Get in there. She's broken him down enough for you to finish the job."

Vau looked at his chrono. "Not bad. What's up? Don't want to let her face the real consequences?"

"Just do it, will you?"

Vau swung his legs off the bed and stalked into the main room to usher Etain from the chair and steer her and Skirata toward the doors. "Go and have some fizzade, Jedi." He turned to Orjul, who was staring after Etain with wide-set eyes. "She's just stepping out for some refreshment. She'll be back later."

Skirata caught Etain's elbow. He wasn't used to grabbing small people: his lads were solid muscle, bigger and stronger than Etain. He felt as if he were clutching a kid's arm. He sat her down on the little bench at the back of the landing platform and took out his comlink to call for transport.

"No, I'm going back in," said Etain.

"Only if Vau calls us back."

"Kal . . ."

"Only if he really needs you. Okay?"

They were still waiting for Ordo to collect them when Etain flinched and then looked back at the lobby doors.

They opened and Vau wandered out, rubbing his eyes. There was a distinctive tang of ozone clinging to him, like a discharged blaster.

"Retail zone, Quadrant B-Eighty-five," said Vau simply. He held out his datapad with coordinates. "But he hasn't given me a date, if he knows one. He was supposed to drop the explosives off in the warehouse, and someone would be along to collect it. He never knew who."

Skirata sniffed the ozonic scent again and switched to *Mando'a,* although he was sure Etain had flinched because she had sensed what had happened.

"Gar ru kyramu kaysh, di'kut: tion'meh kaysh ru jehaati?" You killed him, you moron: what if he was lying?

Vau made an irritated pfft sound. *"Ni ru kyramu Niktose. Meh Orjul jehaati, kaysh kar'tayli me'ni ven kyramu kaysh."* I killed the Nikto. If Orjul's lying, he knows I'll kill him.

Orjul would be dead sooner or later anyway. No prisoners: not on this run. It was amazing how many people overlooked the inevitable while hoping for a way out.

Etain said nothing. She almost bolted for the speeder when Ordo settled it down on the platform. Skirata settled beside her. She simply seemed subdued.

"Result?" Ordo said calmly, helmet on the seat beside him, eyes straight ahead.

"Potential drop-off location," said Skirata. "Someone might be expecting to collect a stash of explosives. So we'd better have something ready for them to collect."

"Intel doesn't suggest they've noticed the loss of the consignment yet."

"Well, if the cells are as isolated for security reasons as we think, then there's nobody to notice for a while, is there?"

"There's the small matter of getting hold of a cache of explosives, but we could make this work for us."

"I can hear the cogs working, son." Skirata patted Etain's hand. "And you did fine, *ad'ika.*" Ordo glanced over his shoulder and then appeared to realize that Skirata meant Etain, not him, this time. There was no gender in *Mando'a.* "It's never easy."

She accepted his touch without reaction, and then seized to his hand so tightly that he thought she was going to burst into tears or protest. But she maintained the façade of calm, except for that desperate grip on his hand. He had always been a soft touch for a desperate child's grasp.

"Sowing doubt is a very corrosive thing when you're dealing with people who believe in causes," said Etain.

Skirata decided he'd have no trouble treating her as his daughter. He forgot his real, estranged daughter all too often. He'd enjoyed returning to little Ruusaan's excited welcome, but each time he came home from a war, wherever home happened to be, she was unrecognizably older and less excited to see him, as if she didn't know him at all.

But I have sons.

"That's why I stick to causes nobody can take from me," Skirata said.

A Mandalorian's identity and soul depended only on what lived within him. And he relied only on his brother warriors—or his sons.

10

Clone troopers are well disciplined. Even the Alpha-batch ARC troopers—surly though they are—are predictable, in the sense that Fett gave them precise orders that they continue to obey. But the commando batches are almost as unpredictable as the Nulls, and the Nulls are as good as being Skirata's private army. That's the problem with having intelligent clones trained by a ragbag of undisciplined thugs—they've turned out at best idiosyncratic, at worst disobedient. But they'll probably win the war for us. Tolerate them.

—Assessment of Republic Commando cadre by Director of Special Forces general Arligan Zey, explaining discrepancies in stores and armory inventory to General Iri Camas

Qibbu's Hut, entertainment sector—strike team operational house—early evening, 371 days after Geonosis

"This is plain *unnatural,*" Boss said. He stood in front of the mirror. "I can't help noticing what this body armor *doesn't* cover."

"It covers your torso and thighs, and that's where your major blood vessels and organs are." Atin tugged at his tunic. They had all defaulted to GAR-issue fatigues, the standard red tunic and pants. Outside the barracks, the casual rig made Fi feel ludicrously naked. "That's all you need. See? Doesn't show under fabric."

"You can live without an arm," Fi said. "They can always bolt on a new one."

"What about my *head*?"

"Like I said, they can always replace nonessential parts."

Boss didn't even look up from the inspection of his tunic. "I love this guy. He'll make such great target practice."

He had a point: they were fighting without helmets. *That* was going to be tough. Everyone from clone trooper to ARC captain lived by his bucket. The *buy'ce* was a command and control center in itself.

Fi picked up a coil of razor-sharp wire and stretched it out between his hands. Skirata had taught him to use this: a garrote, flicked around the neck—if your target had a neck—and pulled tight to slice or choke. There were all kinds of interesting devices and techniques that Skirata recommended. Other instructors had their own favorites, according to their commando training batches, but Kal's were clearly close-range, personal ones. What was it he used to say? *You need to be able to fight if you're cornered in just your underpants, son. Nature gave you teeth and fists.*

Sergeant Kal sounded as if he knew *exactly* how that felt. He certainly knew his techniques.

The main room at the top of the seedy hotel—hastily soundproofed with a micro-anechoic coating over the walls and windows—was filling with jostling bodies. Jusik bounced in, clearly pleased with himself, and laid out a row of small beads and devices on the scratched black duraplast table. Atin wandered over and peered at the haul.

"Where'd you get all that, Bardan?"

Jusik trapped one of the beads on his fingertip and held it out to Atin. Fi moved in. Whatever it was, he wanted one, too. "ARC trooper aural stand-alone comlink. One each. No need for your *buy'cese* or anything too obvious—just stick it in your ear. Plus . . ." The Jedi took out a small transparent sac of what looked like powdered permaglass. "Tracking marker."

"Never seen it before."

"Brand new from the labs. It's called Dust. Microscopic transmitters. Scattered on a battlefield for pretty much invisible monitoring. You never know when you might need it."

"You liberated all that from stores?" asked Fi.

"And Procurement Development. It all ended up in my pockets somehow."

"Captain Maze is going to go spare."

"That's okay. Ordo can explain the necessity to him later. He *listens* to Ordo."

"Where's Skirata?" Sev asked. "Maybe they're having trouble cracking the prisoners."

"Not Vau." Fixer pocketed a comlink bead.

"Why did he need Etain, then?"

"Maybe to show her how it's done."

Fi watched Darman bristle. He waited for his brother to say something, but Dar swallowed whatever retort was forming and went on fussing with the fit of the armor plates under his tunic. It wasn't exactly a secret that he had a soft spot for Etain, but nobody teased him about it, either. It was one of those aspects of life that Skirata had taught them about, but that none of them entertained much hope of pursuing.

It was easy back on Kamino, where the real world had never intruded—not beyond the risk of getting killed in training, of course. But the last nine months' exposure to people outside the tight fraternity had made ordinary life feel much more dangerous than combat itself.

Because other people's lives were *not* ordinary at all.

Fi went to the window, now obscured by a fine film of anti-surveillance gauze, and watched the promenade of tourists and locals along the walkways facing Qibbu's Hut. He didn't envy them their day-to-day existence: Skirata had told his commando batch just how grim and dreary it could be to earn a living, and how much cleaner it was to have a clear purpose in life.

But he hadn't told them how it might feel to watch couples and families of all species. Skirata stuck to the basics. *I've been kicked out by so many females that I can't tell you anything useful about relationships, so just avoid them if you can.* Again, it struck the class as something he said and didn't mean—like the way he called them Wet Droids and said they were here to fight, not socialize. It just meant it was a painful topic for him to face.

He also called them Dead Men. But they were not Dead Men any longer. They had learned to be Mandalorian, and that, Kal said, meant they had a soul and a place in the *Mando* eternity. Fi thought that was probably worth having.

The doors opened and all eight commandos spun around to train a motley collection of modified civilian blasters on the opening. Security code or not, you could never be too careful. Skirata entered with Ordo and Etain at his heels. The squads lowered their weapons.

"Been shopping," Skirata said cheerfully. And he meant it. Fi expected it to be his usual euphemism for acquiring illicit weapons—or worse—but it seemed he really *had* been buying things. He tipped a bag of assorted fruit, candies, ices, nuts, and other delicacies that Fi couldn't identify onto the table next to Jusik's haul. "Go on. Fill yer boots."

Delta hung back. Omega didn't. Then Delta appeared to remember that *fill yer boots* meant "eat your fill." Fi peeled bright green wrapping from something that smelled of sour fruits and found it to be frozen and covered in something appetizingly crunchy.

But Etain looked tired. Jusik was watching her warily as if something unspoken was going on between them. Jedi could do that kind of thing, just like soldiers on helmet comlinks, silent to the outside world. Then Etain muttered something about having a hot soak in the 'freshers and disappeared into the next room.

"We have a drop location," Skirata said. "And a few thousand or so clone troopers on leave for a few weeks thanks to our totally unexpected friend Mar Rugeyan."

"Mmm, crushed nuts," Fi said, identifying the topping on the ice. "That was very helpful of him."

They all stopped in midcrunch. Fi noted Jusik wasn't eating, just watching the sergeant with a rapt expression. The young general had a very bad dose of the Skiratas. As diseases went, it was one of the best to catch.

"So do we get to drop *them,* or do we have to do the boring thing and let them stroll off?" Boss asked. Niner gave him one of his funny looks, the kind that said he thought a bit of quiet contemplation was called for. Niner and Boss didn't see their newly reduced roles in quite the same way: Niner liked to lead by being certain, and Boss seemed to like being *first.* "This is a tracking job, right?"

"Vau made you into very impatient boys," Skirata said. "Yes, this is where it gets boring. And you know what? You won't be any less dead if you get it wrong." He picked up some shuura fruits and lobbed one each to the Delta team. "And I really hope Vau schooled you well in this, because I'll be pretty hacked off if you get trigger-happy and blow this op."

Boss looked hurt. Fi didn't think Delta ran to such delicate emotions. "We're pros, Sarge. We know how to do this."

"What did I tell you?"

"Sorry. *Kal.* It's just that we haven't even seen the enemy yet."

"Welcome to anti-terror ops, hotshot. They aren't droids. They don't line up and march at you. Didn't you listen to *any* of my lectures?"

"Well—"

"They can kill you and not even be on the planet when it happens. But you can track and kill them the same way. This is about patience and attention to detail."

"Delta's really good at that, so I hear," Fi said. Sev gave him that blank cold stare. It simply provoked Fi all the more. "That's why they do their op planning with finger paints."

Skirata lobbed a rolled-up ball of flimsi at Fi and it hit him in the ear—hard. "Okay, Ordo is going to score some credible explosives over the next few days, because that's going to be handy if we need to infiltrate the cells. And we'll start surveillance of the drop point now because we don't have a time window when the explosives were due to be picked up. Four shifts—Fi and Sev as Red Watch, relieved by Dar and Boss as Blue Watch, relieved by Niner and Scorch as Green Watch."

Fi noted Atin's process of elimination. He looked as if he'd been doused in cold water. Fi suspected he'd wanted to be paired with Sev, and for all the wrong reasons.

"That leaves you and *Fixer* as White Watch, so you stay focused," Skirata said, giving Atin a friendly prod in the chest. He'd spotted it, too. But then, Skirata spotted *everything.* "One watch on observation, one on intel collation, and two stood down."

"What about everyone else?"

"Ordo's going undercover to find our mole, and Bardan and Etain will join the normal shift rotations until we need to break into a new phase. If needed, Vau and Enacca will turn to as well, and give us a hand."

Jusik—looking convincingly unsavory in ordinary clothing and with his hair unbound—checked his snazzy S-5 blaster. Yes, Zey *would* go nuts when he saw the bill for this op. "Can we use the Force, Kal?"

" 'Course you can, *Bard'ika.* As long as nobody notices. Or as long as you don't leave witnesses, anyway. Same goes for lightsabers. No witnesses. Might look a bit obvious."

"When do we start?" Boss asked.

Skirata looked at his chrono. "Three hours. Time to eat, I think."

Sev elbowed Fi, a little too hard to be friendly but not hard enough to start a fight. "So, you and me. The brains and the mouth. Don't get me killed."

"I'm slumming it. I usually work with ARC captains." *Watching normal people leading normal lives? I'd rather charge a droid line. What happened to my certainty? Do the others feel like this?* "But there's a war on, so sacrifices have to be made."

"Can you do the dumb-trooper act?"

"You mean you're not doing it now?"

"I hope you're as good as you talk, *ner vod.*"

"Count on it," Fi said, and noted that Darman had wandered off in the direction of Etain's exit. "Sometimes I'm not very funny at all."

Etain felt she had held out pretty well, all things considered.

It was only when she closed the refresher door that she let herself vomit uncontrollably until tears spilled down her face and into her mouth. She ran water into the basin to cover the sound, and choked on her sobs.

She'd been so convinced she could handle it. And she *couldn't.*

Ripping into Orjul's soul had been even harder than outright physical violence. She had stolen his conviction from him, which was no great evil until set in the context of the fact that he would, she knew, die very soon without even the comfort of his beliefs, broken and abandoned and *alone.*

Why am I doing this? Because men are dying.

When do the ends cease to justify the means?

She vomited until she was convulsed by dry heaves. Then she filled the basin with cold water and plunged her head into it. When she straightened up and her vision cleared, she looked into a face she recognized. But it wasn't hers: it was the hard, long face of Walon Vau.

Everything I've been taught is wrong.

Vau was all brutality and expedience, as clear an example of the dark side for a Jedi as any she could imagine. And yet there was a total absence of conscious malice in him. She should have sensed anger and murderous intent, but Vau was just filled with . . . nothing. No, not *nothing:* he was actually calm and benign. He thought he was *doing good work.* And she saw her supposed Jedi ideal in him—motivated not by anger or fear, but by what she thought was *right.* She now questioned everything she'd been taught.

Dark and light are simply the perpetrator's perception. How can that be right?

How can Vau's passionless expedience be morally superior to Skirata's anger and love?

Etain had struggled for years with her own anger and resentment. The choices were to be a good Jedi or a failed Jedi, with the assumption—sometimes unspoken, sometimes not—that failure meant the dark side awaited.

But there *was* a third path: to leave the Order.

She wiped her face on the towel and faced a hard realization. She remained a Jedi because she knew no other life. She pitied Orjul not because she had tortured him, but because he had been robbed of the one thing that held him together, his convictions, without which he had no direction. The truth was that she pitied *herself*—devoid of direction—and projected it onto her victim by way of denial.

The only selfless thing I have ever done that was not centered on my own need to be a good, passionless, detached Jedi was to care about these cloned men and ask what we're doing to them.

And *that* was her direction.

It was so very clear; but she was still raw and aching within. Revelation didn't heal. She sat on the edge of the tub with her head resting on her knees.

"Ma'am, what's wrong?" It was Darman's voice. It should have been the same as every other clone's, but it wasn't. They all had their distinct nuances in accent, pitch, and tone. And he was *Dar*.

She could sense Darman across star systems now. She'd wanted to reach out to him in the Force many times, but feared it might distract him from his duty and endanger him, or—if he knew it was her and didn't welcome it—annoy him.

After all, he'd had the choice of staying on Qiilura with her. And he had opted to stay with his squad. What she felt for him now, the longing that had developed only after they parted, might not be mutual.

He called out again. "Are you okay?"

She opened the doors, and Darman peered in.

"I don't want to be *ma'am* right now, Dar."

"Sorry, I didn't mean to interrupt—"

"Don't go."

He moved a couple of steps into the room as if it were booby-trapped. She had been here before; she had been utterly dependent on his military skills when her life was at stake. He had been so focused, so reassuring, so competent. Where she had doubts, he had certainties.

"So you still don't find it any easier, then," said Darman.

"What?"

"Giving in to anger. You know. Violence."

"Oh, any Jedi Master would have been proud of me. I did it all without anger. Anger makes it the dark side. Being serene makes it okay."

"I know it must have been hard. I know how Sergeant Kal reacted when he had to—"

"No. I was harming a stranger. No personal dilemma at all."

"It doesn't make you a bad person. It has to be done. Is that what's upsetting you?"

"That, maybe. And having doubts."

She didn't want to be alone with all that in her head. She could have meditated. She had the strength of will and the ancient skills to pass through this turmoil and do what Jedi had done for millennia—detach from the moment. But she didn't want to.

She wanted to risk living with those terrible feelings. The danger suddenly seemed to lie in denying them, just as she tried unsuccessfully to deny what she felt for Darman.

"Dar, do you ever have doubts? You always said you were certain of your role. I always felt you were."

"You really want to know?"

"Yes."

"I have doubts all the time."

"What kind?"

"Before we left Kamino, I was so sure what I had to do. Now . . . well, the more I see of the galaxy . . . the more I see of other people, the more I wonder, why me? How did I end up here, and not like the people I see around me in Coruscant? When we win the war, what will happen to me and my brothers?"

They weren't stupid. They were highly intelligent: bred for it, in fact, and if you bred people to be intelligent and resourceful and resilient and aggressive, then sooner or later they would notice that their world wasn't fair, and begin to resent it.

"I ask that, too," Etain said.

"It makes me feel disloyal."

"It's not disloyal to question things."

"It's dangerous, though," Darman said.

"For the status quo?"

"Sometimes you can't argue with everything. Like orders. You don't have the full picture of the battle, and the order you ignore might just be the one that should have saved your life."

"Well, I'm glad you have doubts. And I'm glad I do, too."

Darman leaned against the wall, all concern. "Do you want something to eat? We're going to risk Qibbu's nerf in glockaw sauce. Scorch reckons it's probably armored rat."

"I'm not sure I can face crowds right now."

"You might be overestimating the popularity of Qibbu's cuisine." He shrugged. "I could probably get the cook to stun the thing with my Deece and send it up by room service."

That was Darman all over: he had a relentlessly positive nature. It was her job to inspire him, but he'd been the one on Qiilura who had made her get up and fight time after time. He'd changed her forever. She wondered if he had any idea how much he was still changing her life now.

"Okay," she said. "But only if you keep me company."

"Yeah, eating armored rat alone is probably asking for trouble." He grinned suddenly, and she felt illuminated by it. "You might need first aid."

Niner's voice interrupted from down the passage. "Dar, you coming with us or what? Fi and Sev are supposed to be on watch."

"No, I'll get something sent up. They can head on down with you. We'll do the duty." Darman cocked his head as if to listen for some rebuke. "That okay?"

This time it was Skirata's voice. "Two *steaks*?"

"Please."

"Not something safe, like eggs?"

"Steaks. We fear *nothing*."

Suddenly Etain felt an urge to laugh. Fi might have been the comedian, but Dar was genuinely uplifting. He wasn't trying to suppress pain.

She also found him distractingly handsome, even though he looked identical to his brothers. She adored them as friends, but they were *not* Darman, and somehow they didn't even look like him. Nobody else ever would be that precious to her, she knew that.

"Well, what shall we do now?" he asked.

"Not lightsaber training, for a start."

"You really whacked me with that branch."

"You told me I had to."

"So you take orders from clones, do you, General?"

"You kept me alive."

"Ah, you'd have done fine without me . . ."

"Actually, no," said Etain. "Actually, I wouldn't have done fine at all."

She looked him in the eye for a few moments, hoping that Darman the man would react to her, but he simply stared back, a bewildered boy again. "I'd never been that close to a human female before. Did you know that?"

"I guessed as much."

"I wasn't even sure if Jedi were . . . real flesh and blood."

"I wonder sometimes, too."

"I wasn't scared of dying." He put his hands to his head for a moment and then raked his fingers through his hair, that gesture she'd seen in Skirata. "I was afraid because I didn't know what I was feeling and—"

The service droid buzzed to be let in.

"Fierfek." Darman's shoulders sagged a little. He got up and took the tray from the droid, looking pink-faced and annoyed. He peeled back the lids and inspected the contents as if they were unstable explosives, and she felt the moment was now lost.

"Is it dead?" Etain asked.

"If it isn't, it's not getting up again anytime soon."

She chewed a test-mouthful thoughtfully. "Could be worse."

"Ration cubes . . ."

"Oh, *that* brings back memories."

"Now you know why we'll eat *anything.*"

"I remember the bread, too. Ugh."

He prodded something in the container with his fork, looking concerned. "You *did* reach out to me in the Force, didn't you? I wasn't imagining that."

"Yes, I did."

"Why?"

"Isn't it obvious?"

"How would I know? I'm not sure if I know that much about you."

"I think you do, Dar."

Darman suddenly took exceptional interest in the remains of the steak, which might have been nerf after all. "I don't think anyone believed females would matter to us, given our life expectancy. And it wasn't relevant to combat."

That was freshly agonizing. Of all the injustices piled on these clones who had never been given choices, that was the worst: the denial of any individual future, of hope itself. If they beat the odds of battle, they were still doomed to lose the war against time. Darman would probably be dead in thirty years, and she wouldn't even be halfway through her life by then.

"I bet Kal thought it was important."

Darman chewed his lip and averted his gaze. She wasn't sure if he was embarrassed or if he simply didn't know what she was really asking.

"He never mentioned what to do about *generals,*" he said quietly.

"My Master never specifically mentioned soldiers, either."

"I hear you ignore orders anyway."

"I was afraid I'd never see you again, Dar. But you're here now, and that's all that matters."

She held her hand out to him. He hesitated for a moment and then reached across the table and took it.

"We could be dead tomorrow, both of us," she said. "Or the next day, or next week. That's war." She thought of the other Fi, whose life had ebbed away in her arms. "And I don't want to die without telling you that I missed you every day since you left, and that I love you, and that I don't believe what I was taught about attachment any more than you should believe that you were bred only to die for the Republic."

This was breaking all the rules.

But the war had broken all the rules of peacekeeping Jedi and a civilized Republic anyway. The Force wouldn't be thrown into turmoil if a mediocre Jedi and a cloned soldier who had no rights broke just one more.

"I never stopped thinking about you, either," said Darman. "Not for a moment."

"So . . . how long does it take two squads to finish their meals in the bar?"

"Long enough, I think," said Darman.

11

I'd rather have little Jedi like Bardan and Etain working with us than the likes of Zey. They're sharp, no preconceptions, no agenda. And they're more concerned with pulling their weight in the team than all this philosophical osik about the dark side. Zey might be a seasoned man, but he seems to want respect from me just because he can open jars of caf with his mind.
—Kal Skirata, having a quiet drink with Captain Jaller Obrim, well away from prying eyes

Retail sector, Quadrant B-85, nine days later, observation vehicle in position overlooking warehouse space, 1145 hours, 380 days after Geonosis

Jusik was enjoying himself.

"So," he said, and let the trendy dark visor slide down his nose so he could look over the top. "Do I look like a low-life taxi pilot?"

"Pretty convincing," Fi said. He wondered if Jusik ever had the sense to be scared. "Do I look like a fare?"

Sev, sitting beside Jusik in the taxi's front seat, had a detached DC-17 scope balanced on the vessel's console and patched into a datapad by a thin yellow wire. He was *pinging,* as Skirata called it. Each time a delivery transport or other craft passed through the dead-end canyon of warehouses that lay beneath the retail levels above, Sev checked the registration transponder against CSF's database. He also checked the cargo with the scope's sensor scan.

Fi was impressed by the ease with which Fixer and Atin had set up the remote link without CSF spotting it. They hadn't even had to call in Ordo to sort it out. Ordo had melted into the city again two days ago, no mean feat for an ARC trooper captain.

Fi tried not to wonder where he might be. It was bad enough thinking about Sicko.

"Okay, that one was routine. Garment delivery." Sev made a low rumble in his throat, almost like an animal. "What do we look like from the outside now?"

"At the moment, one Rodian taxi driver reading a holozine while he's parked and waiting."

Fi could see out, but nobody could see in—or at least they could see something that wasn't actually in the taxi, thanks to the thin film of photoactive micro-emitters coating the interior. "Clever stuff, this gauze."

"Thank you," Jusik said. "It took me a long time to work out how to program moving images into it."

"Are you bored?" Sev said, looking around at Fi. He still seemed wary of directing any of his comments at Jedi, even if all rank had been swept aside. " 'Cos I'm not. And your constant yakking is getting to me somewhat, *ner vod.*"

Jusik cut in. "Sorry, Sev. My fault."

Sev looked embarrassed for a moment. "If you're interested, fifty-one of the seventy crates I've clocked on this watch show up on the CSF database tagged as criminal. Theft is a bigger industry than legit business here."

Jusik raised an eyebrow. "Isn't that the sort of thing Obrim's people might like to know?"

"Isn't it the sort of stuff that would bring the boys in blue crashing in here and blowing our op?"

"Point taken."

"No offense . . . Bardan."

Delta hadn't worked with Jedi much, at least not the junior ones. Fi savored a moment of delight at seeing Sev's stone-cold pretense reduced to embarrassed deference. All Jedi were supposed to be humble, but Jusik actually *was.* He seemed to see himself as nothing special, just a man with some accidental skills that didn't make him any more important than the next person, only *different.*

So they waited.

And that was a *lot* harder than it looked.

"Whoa," Sev said. "Look at this one . . ." Fi and Jusik followed the angle of Sev's scope. "CSF database has this tagged as RESTRICTED."

"Could mean it's of interest to us, or could mean organized crime."

Jusik's visor had slipped to the end of his nose. "Or both."

It was a medium-sized delivery transport with dull green livery caked with dust. The identity transponder was evidently fake, because when the crate aligned itself with the platform at the doors to Warehouse 58, and the hatches sprang open, there were just a few boxes inside. The warehouse doors eased open far enough to let a repulsor cart edge out, and two droids began loading the small containers onto the repulsor's flatbed.

"Small but heavy load by the look of it," Fi said.

"And we've got company." Sev realigned the scope, and the datapad hummed into recording mode. "Second transport backing up to it."

Another delivery vehicle hovered, edging astern until it was level with the other side of the landing platform. The boxes were transferred to it. They didn't go into the warehouse at all.

"That's irregular," Sev said. "And we don't like irregular, do we? ID transponder says a legit rental vessel."

A female human in coveralls—white skin, wavy ginger hair to the shoulders, medium build, short—stepped out of the green transport onto the platform to be met by a male Falleen who'd jumped out of the rental. He was young, as far as Fi could tell, with light green skin, and his mundane pilot's rig was a little too long in the leg for him. All details were worth noting.

The two turned their backs to the skylane and appeared to be talking.

"Well, that's a rare sight, and I bet *he's* not on the CSF database," Sev said, checking the 'pad. Images flicked across the screen at a blinding speed while the system sought a match from the image the scope had grabbed. After a few moments the screen read: NO MATCH. "Falleen don't venture offworld very often, and he certainly isn't here to check out the tourist sights. Let's try the woman."

Fi watched. There was a match indeed, and one that came up rapidly.

"Fierfek," Sev said. "Her name's Vinna Jiss. And she's a government employee."

"I'm not going to like this, am I?"

"Not when you hear she works in GAR logistics, no."

"Chakaar," Fi said. "She could be on legit business, of course, but then I'm such a trusting soul."

"Falleen male and GAR clerk? Hello? Do I have to draw you a

picture?" Sev sighed to himself. "They certainly put those Falleen pheromones to good use. I bet she'd do him any favor he asked. Getting security information out of her would be even easier."

The two transports closed their hatches, leaving the woman and the Falleen on the platform, and lifted back into the skylane. It looked like any other delivery—except that it was a transfer of cargo, which was not usual, and the two waiting on the platform oozed *bad guys* from every pore and scale.

The two targets looked at their datapads just like warehouse staff checking a consignment. Then the Falleen turned and began walking up a pedestrian ramp to the retail level, and Vinna Jiss hung around.

"I'm naturally curious," Sev said. "Fi, you up for a discreet trail of those two?"

Fi's heart was pounding. Training and instinct took over. He was back on Kamino again, stalking an armed target in the simulated urban training terrain in Tipoca City. It was just the town that was simulated: the ammunition was real, *deadly* real. "Ready."

"Bardan, back up behind that pillar, will you?"

"We can't abandon this position until the next watch arrives, Sev. Let me call for backup. What if they've pinged *us* and it's a decoy?"

"Okay, you let us out on foot, and call in Niner and Scorch to relieve you. Then you stand by via the comlink just in case."

"That's not standard operating procedure."

"This isn't standard operating terrain, either." Sev almost said *sir.* Fi heard the beginning of a hissed *s*. Delta's self-appointed hard man poked his finger hard in his right ear as if he was afraid the bead-sized link would fall out. "There goes Jiss. Up the ramp, too. Come on, Fi. Move it."

They slipped out of the taxi's twin hatches and activated Fi's holochart of the sector to check where the ramp led and where the exits were. They stared at the meshed blue and red lines on the holochart, courtesy of the fire department's database. Fi hoped it was up to date.

"That takes them straight up to the retail plaza."

Fi's immediate thoughts were of civilians, obstructed arcs of fire, and his own limited senses being a poor substitute for his Katarn helmet's gadgetry. *But I'm more than my armor. Sergeant Kal said so.*

He edged along the wall, staying out of sight. *Can't deploy tracking remotes, not here, not in public.* "I might do a little shopping myself."

"Just keep that dumb-grunt expression on your face, Mongrel Boy. It suits you."

Sev took out his datapad and switched the screen to reflective mode, turning his back and holding the device a little out to his right. "She's just going over the top of the ramp . . . yeah, she's peeled off on the first level. She's following Lounge Lizard so far. Come on. Let's go around the bridge route and pick them up *here.*"

"You have as bad an attitude toward ethnic diversity as you have toward the regular army," Fi said quietly, relaxing his shoulders with every intention of just being a soldier on leave in his dark red fatigues—with a blaster on his belt, like any sensible Coruscanti.

The next hour was unplanned, unexpected, but not *untrained for.* Fi hoped he'd make it through alive.

Coruscant Security Force Staff and Social Club, 1300 hours, private booth, senior officers' bar

Kal Skirata had his peripheral vision and half an ear trained on the general murmur at the bar. He felt bad about applying caution to these men: they had much the same thankless task as his boys. But there was a possibility that the leak was within their ranks. He couldn't let comradeship cloud his judgment.

He hoped Obrim wasn't offended by the distortion field he'd set up. The little emitter sat discreetly on the table between the glasses like a rolled-up pellet of flimsi, ready to bounce any bugging signals.

"If it's one of mine, I'll personally put a round through him," Obrim said.

Skirata didn't doubt it. "You could put a fake lure in the system and see who goes for it."

"But even if it's one of us, then they'd still need data from the GAR to complete the loop. It's one thing having the holocam images of military targets and movements. It's another knowing where they'll be to start with."

"Okay, then. I have to put someone inside GAR logistics." There was only one choice: Ordo. "If we find a link to your people, though, I have to cut you loose. I'm sorry."

"I'm not exactly being kept in the loop on all this anyway, am I?"

"If I told you where my squads were operating, and they happened to get into a bit of trouble that attracted the attention of your people, you might have to call them off. Then everyone would know we had a strike team deployed."

"I know. I'm just worried that your personnel will attract the attention of some of my overzealous colleagues, and one of us will be sending wreaths to next of kin."

"My boys don't have next of kin. Only me."

"Kal . . ."

"I can't. I just can't. This has to be deniable." He liked Obrim. He was a kindred spirit, a pragmatic man who didn't trust easily. "But if something looks like it's going to get out of hand, and I can warn you off, I will."

Obrim swirled the dregs of his ale in the glass. "Okay. Sure you don't want one of these?"

"I only have one at night to help me sleep. Habit from Kamino. Sleep got pretty hard to come by."

"You'll have to tell me about that one day. I bet they didn't have any crime in Tipoca City."

"Oh, there was crime, all right." The worst kind: if he ever met another Kaminoan, he knew what he'd do. "Nothing you could have arrested anyone for, though."

"When's your boy Fi going to stop by for a drink? We owe him one from the siege. Brave kid."

"Yeah. He throws himself instinctively on a grenade, and he's a hero. If he fires instinctively and slots a civilian, though, he's a monster."

"And don't *we* know it, pal. Happens to us, too."

"Anyway, Fi's on a routine patrol at the moment." Skirata checked his chrono. Green Watch was due to relieve Red in two hours. "I'll bring him down here, don't worry. He's probably bored out of his skull at the moment. Anti-terror ops can be tedious."

"Sitting around, more sitting around, even more sitting around, then scramble, sheer panic, and *bang*."

"Yeah, I think that sums it up." Skirata drained his glass of juice. "I just hope we get to the *bang* part in time."

Level 4 retail plaza, Quadrant B-85, Coruscant, 1310 hours; Red Watch observing targets on foot

They should have called it in and let one of the other teams pick it up. But sometimes you had to run with it.

Fi was now on autopilot, reacting to training he hadn't realized he'd absorbed so thoroughly, and Sev was matching him pace for pace.

The shopping plaza was a mass of color, random people, and

even more bewildering smells and sounds. This was life in the field without a helmet, and Fi didn't like it. Just ahead, Vinna Jiss wandered casually, moving along one diagonal line then another, and then pausing to stare into transparisteel windows full of things Fi had no idea that people bought—or wore.

Sev glanced at him. He didn't even have to say it.

She looks in an awful lot of shop windows. She doesn't follow a straight path. She thinks she knows how to avoid a tail, but she's learned it from the holovids. Amateur. Weak link.

"Bardan . . . ," Sev said quietly.

The Jedi's voice was a whisper in Fi's ear. "I know where you are. Don't worry."

"Not worried." Sev glanced away from the target and Fi turned around casually toward her, looking past her but keeping her in his peripheral vision. "Can't see the Falleen now . . ."

"Moving on," Fi said.

They let Jiss walk on until she was almost lost in the crowd, and then started moving again. A well-planned surveillance operation would have positioned mobile and fixed teams in the area to simply watch and hand off the target to the next team along the route. But they were on their own. And they had never planned to follow a suspect.

"This is what Kal said we should *never* do," said Fi.

"You got a better idea?"

"Reckon she's seen us?"

"If she has, she hasn't reacted."

"Why would she? If she's what we think she is, then we're just targets to *her.*"

The plaza was busy. There was a restaurant on the left-hand side with tables and chairs in the open air. Jiss sat down. Sev and Fi walked on past her, and if Fi looked like an overwhelmed clone who'd spent his life cloistered in military environments, then he wasn't acting. Even Qibbu's Hut felt more familiar than this.

It wasn't the urban environment. It was the sheer mass of *civilians.*

They had no choice. They walked on farther.

"Fierfek," Sev said. "She'll have doubled back or disappeared by the time we can turn around safely."

Fi was looking straight ahead. He could see splashes of dark red between the multicolored shoulders of the dozens of species strolling around the plaza.

"Here comes the Forty-first," he said. "You can always rely on the infantry . . ."

A dozen or so brothers were ambling along, gazing around them and being gazed at by shoppers who had clearly never seen clones before. No matter how many times Fi saw that reaction, he always found himself wondering what they found so strange about it, and then had to see his own world as the rest of the galaxy saw it.

The Forty-first were level with them now.

Fi smiled fraternally and got a bewildered nod or two in return. *They don't recognize me!* That felt strange. *All* his commando brothers knew him. And he could tell infantry from ship's crew by the way they walked. He walked between the men of the Forty-first with Sev like a marching band merging, and spun around at the back of the group to walk back toward the target.

She was still sitting there. But she was looking the other way.

She was staring at another group of clone troopers heading toward her from the other direction.

"I love being a familiar face," Fi said. His anxiety gave way to a sense of heightened awareness, the thrill of the hunt. The woman's spine straightened as if she was going to jump up, but she sat tense for a few seconds until the clones drew level with her and met the group coming from the other direction. They stopped to chat. Fi and Sev melted into the group at the rear.

"I'm heading around the back of the plaza," said Jusik's voice in their ears. "Niner's on station now. I'll give you some aerial recon."

"Gotcha," Fi said quietly.

It's bad personal security to cluster like this. But that didn't matter right then. The woman dithered, trying not to look at the group and failing miserably: Fi, like any clone, was exceptionally attuned to small gestures. Then she got up to walk briskly into the nearest shop.

"Maybe she owed Jango credits." Fi shrugged and noted with a sinking heart that the shop looked to be exclusively for females. The garments on display were truly bizarre. "Or we're just not her type."

"So, smart-mouth, you going to follow her in there?"

"I could."

"What, tell them you're looking for a present for your girlfriend?"

"Don't push your luck. Is there a back way out?"

Sev stepped into a doorway and shielded Fi while he took a quick look at the holochart and snapped off the image quickly.

"No, but there's a landing platform for deliveries."

Sev dropped to a whisper. "Bardan, you with us yet?"

Jusik's voice was almost a chuckle. "Fascinating," he said. "I'm waiting at the delivery platform. A taxi is just what she needs right now." Sev and Fi looked at each other. They could hear Jusik, but the taxi wasn't visible even when they stood back and glanced up discreetly at the roofline. Then they heard his voice, utterly level, utterly calm—utterly worrying. *"Yeah? Yeah, I am, lady . . . where d'you want to go? I've got a booking, but . . ."*

"Sev, tell me he isn't doing what I think he is."

"He's doing it."

"He's nuts."

Sev lowered his voice to a whisper in the comlink. "Bardan, if we lift her now, we'll blow this op. Don't overplay it."

"Okay, lady, but the spaceport isn't my regular run, so that'll be extra."

There was the sound of someone getting into the taxi and a woman's voice. *"Yes, just drop me off at the domestic terminal, please."*

Fi wondered for a moment if ordinary people had shared thoughts like the one he knew Sev was sharing with him. They'd been trained to think the same way, the soldier's way. Where was Jusik going with this? If he dropped her off like a normal taxi, they'd lose her in the terminal anyway. He couldn't follow her in there and check where she went without blowing his cover. And if he *didn't* drop her off . . .

Sev was staring past Fi. "Lizard on your six," he said quietly.

Fi turned very, very slowly and stopped when he caught the Falleen male in his peripheral vision at the point where the plaza funneled into a spiral ramp down to another level. He was searching. So the woman hadn't caught up with him when he expected, and he was looking for her. And that meant she had no comlink, or she'd have used it.

"Now *he's* going to be bad news. He's carrying some serious cannon. Look at the line of his jacket."

Jusik's voice was a quiet descant to Fi's pulse pounding in his head. *"Oh, fierfek. That's great. Being rerouted again . . . this is going to cost, lady . . . another detour . . ."*

"He's way too smart for his own good." Sev looked exasperated. "Bardan, are you doing what I think you're doing? Are you heading back our way?"

"I pay good license money not to have to use automated lanes," said Jusik's voice in their ears. He really didn't sound at all like a nice Jedi Temple boy now. *"And then I still get diverted. What do we pay our taxes for?"*

"I'll take that as a yes."

The Falleen moved off, pausing occasionally to look around, and ambled slowly down the ramp. Fi and Sev leaned on the edge of the parapet like any tourist might to take in the view below.

Fi dropped his voice. "He's calling someone." The Falleen had the back of his hand raised to his mouth. *Oh, for a helmet comlink.* Fi might have been able to pick up the frequency. "Is it her? Or backup?"

"We could call this in and get Niner and Scorch to pick him up."

"And then we drag another team off station. No, let's see this through."

Sev sat down on a bench, looking suitably disoriented. "Bardan, where are you?"

"Let me try this shortcut, lady . . . hey, who you calling? You making a complaint about fares already?"

"I bet she's calling Lounge Lizard. Great."

"Yeah, and now that our driver's got a very dodgy passenger, has he thought what we're going to do with her?"

"Same as we did with Orjul and the Nikto," Sev said, getting up to walk across to the taxi platform at the end of the plaza. They had to get in fast when Jusik appeared and opened that hatch. Fi had visions of the potential grief that would be unleashed if a passenger was screaming her head off when the taxi hatch opened in a very public place.

"Land at ninety degrees, Bardan. Sev will access via the port hatch and I'll go in the other, and we'll pin her down."

"Yeah, I think Fi can manage to subdue a civilian," Sev said.

"Remind me to show you my unfunny side later, *ner vod.*"

"Skirata's going to kill us for this—"

"Better get it right then," Fi said.

"Here he comes . . ."

"Steady, Bardan."

"Too fast."

"He's a Jedi. There's no such thing as too fast."

The battered taxi, its anti-surveillance gauze now showing a human driver that wasn't Jusik, dropped onto the platform scattering dust and grit. The two commandos ran to their respective sides.

Jusik's voice filled their heads now. *"Hatches in three . . . two . . . one!"*

They threw themselves in. The hatches snapped shut so fast that Fi felt his pant leg snag in the seal but he was flat on top of a squealing, struggling woman and then she went quiet because Sev clamped his hand over her mouth.

"You waiting for a tip?" said Fi.

The taxi lifted in a straight vertical and nearly shaved the paintwork off another cab trying to drop off passengers. It was just as well that Enacca had done something creative about the identity transponder.

"Fi, I don't suppose you brought any restraints?"

"No, but this usually works." Fi freed his right arm and put his blaster to Jiss's head. "Ma'am, shut up and stop struggling. I have no problem shooting women."

No, he didn't. Enemies were enemies. Females were soldiers, too.

Jusik took the taxi high into what appeared to be a commuter lane and shot off in a complex loop that first took them away from Qibbu's and relative safety, and then dropped down between lanes where the layers of traffic overhead gave some protection against visual surveillance.

"We've been tagged," Jusik said. He shut his eyes, far too long for Fi's comfort. It was the first time he'd seen the Jedi fly with his eyes closed, and the fact that the good ones could do that didn't reassure the simple animal part of him that said it shouldn't be possible. "Yes, we're being followed."

Fi wanted to ask how he knew but Jiss had no reason to know Jusik was a Jedi, and the less she knew, the easier it would be to *process* her, as Skirata put it.

"You can evade them, right?"

"About as well as anyone can."

"Any idea who they are?"

"None, other than they're very persistent, and if it's CSF, it's an unmarked vessel."

"You can sense all that information?"

He opened his eyes again. "Yes, because they're only two or three speeders behind us and I can see them in the mirror."

Sev looked at Fi with the unspoken count of *one, two, three.* Sev released his grip on Jiss as Fi clamped his arm tight around her neck, blaster pressed so hard into her temple that the muzzle was ringed with a little patch of white bloodless skin. He could feel her heart pounding through her back against his chest even through the thin sheet of body armor under his tunic. He wondered for a moment if it was his own frantic heartbeat.

Sev reached under the rear seat for his DC-17 and took out the grenade attachment. "Okay, it lacks finesse, but we're late for lunch. And if they track us, we're finished."

"Here? In daylight, in traffic?" Jusik said.

"Not yet." Sev tried to aim his Deece and snapped on the grenade launcher. "Open the rear screen a crack. Can you hold steady?"

"You wanted me to outrun them—"

"Can't. We've got to drop them."

Jusik looked in the rearview. "In a *skylane*? You haven't got a clear shot and the debris will—"

"Me sniper, you pilot. Understand the difference?"

Jusik's grip on the steering vane tightened. "Too many vessels and too much debris. Let's head for somewhere less crowded."

"Maybe Qiilura?" Fi said.

"Hold on *tight.*"

Jusik dropped the taxi like a stone and plummeted ten, then fifteen, then twenty levels to the lower skylanes, slipping in between two transports and then jumping between horizontal lanes.

"Still there," said Sev. "Three vehicles behind."

"Have they alerted anyone?"

"I can't sense anything." Jusik kept shaking his head as if trying to clear it. "They might not want to risk using comlinks."

"Who the fierfek are they?"

"I don't know! I'm not a mind-reader and if you'd just *shut up* because I'm trying to concentrate on flying and listening and—" His voice trailed off. "Just *aim.*"

Fi pressed his blaster harder into the woman's head. She flinched and shut her eyes tight. He could feel no emotion whatsoever, just the cold clarity of his life and his comrades' against her existence, and it seemed an easy equation.

"Move and you're dead, ma'am, okay?" *Move?* Even Fi wasn't sure he could make an escape from a speeder moving this fast and this erratically—and not at this height, either. "Start thinking of all the helpful information you're going to give us."

Jusik broke from the automated lane and fell another five levels like a stone, drawing screaming protests of klaxons as he skimmed other vessels. But the speeder dropped with them, delayed only by a few seconds. Then he banked right into a service vessel tunnel, and Fi had no idea where they were. It was enclosed. And that was *bad.* Fi wasn't a pilot but flying fast down a tube struck him as suicide.

"Look, I know where I'm heading," Jusik said, as if he were suddenly telepathic. Fi wondered if he had protested aloud and hadn't realized. "I *know.* And they can't get a signal through down here."

And then he fell silent. And this was where it became very, very frightening to have a Jedi on the squad, because Jusik had shifted from a skill that Fi could see to something beyond his comprehension.

Jusik was now skimming a meter above the surface of a conduit lit at regular intervals by a dim green light. Sev was struggling to get a steady shot through the narrow opening in the rear screen. All Fi could do was watch one madman or the other while he held a gun to a woman's head, and Fi didn't enjoy not being in control of his environment. He thought of Sicko again and the moment when he and Omega were helpless and utterly dependent on that pilot's skill. *Poor Sicko.*

"Sev, he's twenty meters behind us, right?" said Jusik.

"Spot on."

"Are you going to be ready when I say fire?"

"Try me."

"Only on my mark."

"Get on with it, *sir.*"

Fi felt his left arm going numb around the woman's neck, and he struggled to keep the blaster hard against her head. The taxi was veering from side to side. "I just hope they're not CSF."

"They're not *ours* . . . ," Sev said. "And they're in pursuit. So they're a *target.*"

Fi dug the blaster into the woman's skin. "Are they your people, ma'am?"

"I don't know! *I don't know!*"

"If they are, it's too bad," Sev said. "We can't let them track us back."

Jusik speeded up. "Stand by."

Fi noticed that he had his eyes shut again.

"Fierfek."

"Fire!" Jusik said, and the taxi suddenly flipped up ninety degrees and climbed in an agonizing vertical. Fi braced for impact.

They had to be dead.

But the taxi was still climbing.

They were in a vertical shaft and a ball of blue-white flame roared beneath them. Fi was thrown against Sev but he locked his arm tight around the woman's neck, and all three of them hit the partly open rear screen as the sound of ricocheting debris faded behind them in the service duct.

The light dimmed fast beneath them and suddenly disappeared as Jusik slammed the taxi into another right angle and they were flying horizontally along a channel again.

"Target down." Sev shut his eyes.

"That better *not* be CSF," Fi said. "That's going to be very messy."

Suddenly they were bathed in hazy sunlight. Jusik brought them out into passenger traffic and slipped into the automated lanes of private speeders again.

"What do we look like from the outside now?" Sev asked.

Jusik wiped his forehead with his palm and looked as breathless and battered as he ever had after performing the *Dha Werda.* Fi could have sworn he looked just as elated, too.

"Family of Garqian tourists with a Gran driver," the Jedi said. "Now let's try to explain this to you-know-who without getting our heads ripped off." He opened his comlink. "Returning with a prisoner, Kal . . ."

Sev grumbled in his throat. "*Never* use real names."

"Least of our worries now," Fi said.

So Jusik was scared of Skirata, too. It was supposed to be a quiet *obs job,* as he'd put it, observation duty; it had turned into kidnapping and blowing up unidentified vessels. *Scared* wasn't the right word, though.

He'll be disappointed *with us. We let him down.*

Fi, like anyone who came into Skirata's circle, desperately wanted *Kal'buir* to be proud of him. It was more effective motivation than fear any day.

"Remember he even shoves Wookiees around," said Fi. He adjusted his grip on the woman's neck to stop the tingling in his fingers. "And they take it."

The taxi was silent except for the occasional whimpering gulp from Jiss and the rumble of the vessel's hard-pressed drive. Eventually Jusik came to a shuddering halt on the platform at the top level of Qibbu's Hut. Sev called on his comlink for a hand with the woman, and Atin came running out with Fixer.

"What have you been playing at? Skirata's going nuts in there." Atin slid into the taxi and put cuffs on Jiss. "Get out and we'll take her to the safe house. You've got some explaining to do."

Safe house for them, maybe. Safe for her? No. But then she had picked the wrong side. She wasn't a helpless victim.

So much for whining that we never get to see the enemy.

The taxi lifted off, leaving Fi, Sev, and Jusik standing on the platform, exhausted by adrenaline.

"Thank you for flying Jedi Air." Jusik grinned, and shook their hands. "Have a nice afternoon."

"You're all insane," said Sev, and stalked off.

12

Definitely not one of our speeders, Kal. Look, I know why you think I don't need to know what your boys are getting up to. But someone's going to notice you blew up their people. And so is CSF. What do you want me to tell them?
—Captain Jaller Obrim, to Kal Skirata

Operational house, Qibbu's Hut, 1600 hours,
380 days after Geonosis

"You're *sure* nobody followed you?" Skirata said quietly.

The strike team, minus Ordo, was assembled in the main room, sitting where they could. For a moment Skirata was distracted by the way Darman and Etain were positioned. It told him something, but he had more pressing issues right now.

He'd calmed down, too. Red Watch was back safely. Jusik, predictably, was taking his roasting like a man.

"I'm sure, Kal. I *felt* it."

"Don't go mystic on me. Did you go through the procedures? Give me tangibles."

"I didn't return via a direct route. I looped back on myself several times. *Nothing.*"

There was no point yelling at them. Skirata knew he probably would have done the same. It was all very well to talk about painstaking surveillance and meticulous planning before resolving a threat, but when a truly ripe target walked in front of your scope—no, he *would* have done the same.

And he was simply relieved that they'd made it back in one piece.

"Okay, surveillance is off for the day. We change vehicles again, and we'll start defense watches, just in case the Force has deceived *Bard'ika* and we've got a load of bad guys on our case now. Enacca is identifying a second location we can pull back to if this place is compromised."

Jusik looked crushed. "I'm sorry, Kal."

"You weren't in command. I should have made sure you were ready for this." Skirata turned to Fi and Sev. Fi looked crestfallen; Sev was complete blank insolence. "And what have you two got to say for yourselves?"

"It won't happen again, Kal." Fi looked at Jusik. "And it was me and Sev who decided to go for it. If Bardan hadn't done some clever flying, we'd all be dead now and the op would be over."

"And you, Sev?"

Sev turned his head with slow deliberation. "What he said."

"Son, I know you *think* you're a hard case because you survived Walon Vau, and you probably *are.* But anti-terrorist ops are more about *this.*" Skirata walked over to him and rapped his head so hard with his knuckles that the *thunk* of bone was audible. Sev blinked but didn't move a muscle. "If you'd thought about it for two minutes, you could have relayed that identification back here and we could have planned some intelligent surveillance. But now we've got *another* prisoner plus a bunch of dead guys, and we have to explain why a GAR employee isn't going back to the office anytime soon. Because if she wasn't working alone, then some *di'kut* is going to notice she's absent. Have I missed anything?"

Niner, arms folded, looked up. "Yes, who's helping Vau now? He must have his hands full."

"Enacca. Wookiees are good at looking like a crowd."

Boss had been remarkably quiet for the last ten days. He'd worked his watches without complaint and had shown none of the swaggering confidence that the Delta boys were known for. Now he was pacing up and down the length of the window, slow and deliberate, and glancing occasionally at Niner. Skirata wondered if it was the displacement from the sergeant role that was getting to him.

Might as well lance the boil. "You want to say something, Boss?"

"With respect, Kal, we have different approaches, don't we?"

"Spit it out."

"Delta does rapid *neutralization.* Omega does the more *considered* stuff. Why not split our tasking that way?"

For once, rock-solid Niner took the bait. "Yeah, you blow up everything without checking and we think first. I certainly agree with your analysis, *ner vod.*"

"And we have the unbroken track record of successful missions."

"Like we don't."

"You said it."

Skirata wasn't quite fast enough crossing the room and Niner had slammed Boss hard against the wall without a moment's warning. If Skirata hadn't yelled "Check!" Niner would have smashed his drawn-back fist into Boss's face. The two men stood almost nose-to-nose, locked in a frozen standoff.

"This stops right *now,*" Skirata barked. "You hear me? Stand *down!*"

He'd never seen Niner react like that. Soldiers got into scraps all the time; it was an inevitable part of being encouraged to fight. Sometimes they took a swing at each other, but it was rarely serious, no more than a bit of bravado. But not his boys—and certainly not Niner.

There was a switch in all men somewhere, no matter how deeply buried, that could be thrown.

"You have *never* lost brothers." Niner took one grudging step back from Boss. "*Never.* You have no idea."

"Ever wondered why?" said Boss.

"Enough." Skirata put an arm between them. "Next one to open his mouth gets a thump from *me,* okay?"

This was the brief moment where the fight would erupt or vanish, and Skirata was secretly uncertain if he had what it took to separate two bigger, younger, fitter men. But Niner muttered, "Yes, Sarge," and sat down in a chair on the far side of the room, face white with anger. Boss paused, then followed him to hold out a placatory hand.

"Apologies, *ner vod.*"

Niner just looked up at him, unblinking. Then he took Boss's hand and shook it, but his mind was clearly elsewhere, and Skirata knew *exactly* where. Some things didn't go away with time. Niner had lost another Sev, plus DD and O-Four, at Geonosis; and during training he'd lost Two-Eight. Republic Commandos never forgot the brothers they grew up with in that tight pod from the time they were decanted.

But Delta still had their pod intact. The world was different for them. They thought they were invincible; death only happened to others.

"I think we need to take a step back," Skirata said, bleeding for Niner. He'd thought the squad was as close as a true pod, but they still nursed their loss. "Delta, you break off and get a meal downstairs and report back at nineteen-hundred. Omega, you break when they get back. Maybe we'll all feel better on a full stomach."

There was no point turning this into a contest between the squads. But mixing them hadn't helped that much. Skirata watched Delta troop out toward the turbolift. It was going to take more than food to distract them, although it usually did the trick.

"Are we all okay?"

Atin looked up from a datapad he was cannibalizing. Dismantling things seemed to keep him happy. "We're okay, Sarge. Sorry. I just don't feel happy calling you *Kal.* Except in public, of course."

"That's okay, son."

Skirata made a point of sitting down where he could see Darman and make a discreet assessment. There was something about the way he was turned slightly toward Etain in his seat, and she made a lot more eye contact with him than she had earlier. Skirata wondered why he hadn't spotted it earlier, and also when it had happened.

If he was right . . .

It was bad for discipline to let an officer and an enlisted man have a relationship. But Etain wasn't an officer, and Darman had never chosen to enlist. The risk lay more in how Darman would handle it, and how left behind his brothers might feel now that they were out in a world where everyone who wasn't wearing armor was free to love.

Skirata stood up and limped across to Etain."Come and explain some Jedi stuff to me," he said quietly. "I'd ask *Bard'ika,* but he's still in disgrace at the moment." He winked at Jusik to indicate he was joking: the kid took his ribbing far too seriously sometimes. "Outside."

It wasn't subtle, but Darman obviously didn't think anyone else had noticed what was going on between them. He probably thought Skirata wanted to discuss the unsavory side of interrogation with her.

Skirata sat down next to Etain on the rickety bench against the landing platform wall. It was late afternoon and the air smelled of hot speeder drives and the powdery sweet scent of a solitary mayla vine that had taken root in a crack in the permacrete. Etain folded her hands in the lap of her pale blue tunic. Without the dull brown robes she didn't look like a Jedi at all.

"You and Darman," Skirata said carefully.

She closed her eyes for a second. “He told you, then. I suppose he tells you everything.”

“Not a word. But I’m not stupid.” It was amazing how easily people told you things when you didn’t even ask a question. Perhaps she actually wanted people to know. But it seemed Darman didn’t, and he had a right to keep what little privacy he had. “I heard the squad’s comments after Qiilura.”

“Are you telling me to stop?”

“No, I’m asking where this is heading.”

“Are you going to tell *him* to stop?”

“Not if you make him happy.” Skirata trod carefully, but he knew where he drew the line and whose interests he would put first, war or not. “See, I know that much about Jedi. You can’t *love.*”

“We’re not *supposed* to. But we sometimes do. *I* do.”

“You’re serious about him, then.”

“I never stopped thinking about him after Qiilura.”

“Have you *really* worked this out?”

“That I’ll outlive him? Women outlive their men all the time. That I might be thrown out of the Jedi Order? As prices go, that’s worth paying.”

“Etain, he’s more vulnerable than you think. He’s a grown man and he’s a killing machine, but he’s a kid, too. Crying over girlfriends can be dangerously distracting for him and the whole squad.”

“I know that.”

“I’d hate to see him used. If you’re going to carry on with this, you’d better mean it.” He paused to make sure she understood what he was saying. “You know I’ll protect him come what may, don’t you?”

Etain’s lips parted slightly and her cheeks looked suddenly pink. Her gaze flickered slightly. “I want him to be happy, Kal. I’d never use him.”

“I’m glad we agree,” he said.

Threatening a Jedi general was probably a court-martial offense. Skirata didn’t care. Darman and his last remaining sons came before everything, before the needs of a likable young Jedi, before even his own life—and certainly before the interests of the Republic’s politics.

It was a matter of honor, and love.

But Etain would give Darman a little comfort and tenderness in his life that would tide him through the dark and inevitable days ahead, days that for him and his brothers were already destined to be limited.

Skirata would just have to keep an eye on the situation. “Make him happy, then, *ad’ika,*” he said. “Just make him *happy.*”

Qibbu's Hut, 2100

The sign above the 'freshers read PATRONS PLEASE OBSERVE THE NO WEAPONS RULE. But although it was written in five languages as well as Basic, most of the patrons appeared not to understand it.

Ordo slipped among the motley assortment of drinkers and gamblers, now diluted considerably by a sea of dark red GAR fatigues, and hoped none of the species here were scent-followers. That was the trouble with some explosives. They had a distinctive smell. He'd scrubbed himself as thoroughly as he could and changed into the ubiquitous red fatigues as well.

Laseema, the Twi'lek female who had fled from the kitchens when he found her cowering behind a table, smiled nervously at him across the bar. By the time he reached it, she had his favorite muja juice waiting for him without the prompt of his distinctive armor.

"How do you know I'm me?" he said, puzzled. "I could be any clone."

"The way you hold yourself." She had a very soft voice, and he had to strain to hear her in the noisy bar. "You stand as if you're still wearing that skirt."

"Kama," he said patiently. "Belt-spat. It's based on a traditional Mandalorian hunting *kama.* It was designed to protect your legs." Yes, the pauldron and *kama* did tend to make him stand more upright out of habit, his back a little arched. He'd have to watch that if he wanted to pass for an ordinary clone trooper. "But it's just for show now."

"Ah," she said. "It's certainly very showy."

Ordo was getting used to the attention of Twi'lek females, and he rather liked it. "Is Qibbu treating you properly?"

"Yes. Thank you." Laseema sounded as if she really was grateful. She leaned forward a little. He was still taken aback by the vivid blue of her skin, but he was willing to get used to it. She had a little scar on the point of her chin that was turquoise and more decorative than disfiguring. "Is your friend a captain?"

She glanced sideways and Ordo followed her gaze to Omega Squad and Skirata, who were eating something unidentifiable and occasionally lifting a lump of it on a fork to inspect it communally with worried frowns. "The one with the scar. He's nice."

"That's Atin," Ordo said, crushed. *Oh.* "He's . . . not a captain. He's a private." The vast majority of the army was made up of privates: it wasn't restricted information. Atin glanced up with that unerring soldier's sense of knowing when someone was targeting you. He managed a shy smile. "Yes, he's very reliable."

"He's got a lot of scars. Has he been in many battles?"

Oh, she really *had* been studying Atin carefully: apart from the thin diagonal scar across his face, the rest were harder to spot, just a couple on his hands and one telltale line that was visible above the neckline of his red tunic.

"Yes," Ordo said. "They've all been in quite a few battles."

"Poor Atin," she said, looking smitten. "I'll bring your meal over in a moment."

He forced a smile as *Kal'buir* had taught him, picked up his glass, and went to join Omega's table.

"What d'you reckon *this* is, Ordo?" Darman said. He held his fork so that Ordo could inspect the object skewered on it.

"A *tube* of some sort."

"That's what we were afraid of."

"It's all protein." Ordo stared at Atin. "Laseema has taken a fancy to you, *ner vod.*"

There was no jeering or barracking as Ordo had seen ordinary males do at the mention of females. The squad simply sat in silence for a moment and then resumed their debate on the anatomical content of Qibbu's dish of the day. Skirata got up and moved along the bench to sit next to him.

"Successful *shopping* trip?"

"I have everything on the list now. Sorry for the delay. And I have a few extras."

"How extra?"

"*Surprising* extras. Very noisy, too."

Laseema glided up to the table and placed a dish in front of Ordo. She smiled at Atin before making her way back to the bar. Ordo picked up his fork to eat, and the squad studied his plate intently.

"But that's all *vegetables,*" Niner said accusingly.

"Of course it is," Ordo said. "My intelligence score is at least thirty-five percent higher than yours."

It happened to be true. Skirata laughed. Ordo cleared his plate as fast as he could and then indicated the turbolift. Skirata followed him up to their rooms, where Delta Squad sat cleaning their DC-17s.

"Just *dusting,*" Fixer said, subtle as a bantha.

"Dust away," Skirata said. "They'll see action soon enough. So, Ordo, what did you get?"

"A hundred kilos of thermal plastoid plus five thousand detonators."

Even Scorch looked up from his dismantled rifle at the mention of *that.* "That's a lot of ordnance to make disappear without anyone noticing, let alone store it."

"I liberated it in stages from different sources."

Skirata tapped him on the arm. "Now explain the extra surprise."

"The delay was because I enriched it all—minus a pack or two."

"How?"

"A little chemical refinement that'll make it unstable if anyone attempts to use it in devices."

"How unstable, exactly?" Skirata asked.

"If they don't work a stabilizer compound into the plastoid, it'll blow their workshop into orbit as soon as they attach a det to it."

Scorch sniggered appreciatively.

"Just a precaution," Ordo said. "If we end up using it for a sting operation and by some chance it goes wrong, then we'll at least remove a few *hut'uune* in the process."

"And half of Galactic City." Sev grunted to himself and peered through his scope to calibrate it against the view from the window. "You spook boys overdo it sometimes."

Skirata patted Ordo's arm. "Nice job, son. Now tell me where you've stored it."

"Half at the safe house and half under Fixer's bed."

Scorch guffawed. Boss smacked his ear but it didn't stop him from laughing. "I'm sharing Fixer's room, *di'kut.*"

"Well, you won't even wake up if *that* blows."

Ordo accepted it was a risk, but risks were relative. And Skirata hadn't expressed interest at his advanced ordnance skills, so he could still keep Mereel's return as a surprise.

He was going to be pleased with Mereel's news on Ko Sai, too.

"So all we have to do now is work out how we get them to take the bait," said Skirata. "Maybe Vau is getting somewhere with our GAR colleague."

Boss looked up. "You more interested in using the stuff to kill them, track them, or make them think everything's going fine on the terror front?"

"I'll take all three."

"Does it usually take this long to get anywhere?"

Skirata laughed. "*Long?* Son, it normally takes *years* to shut down a network. This is lightning speed. It might still take years, and it's just a fraction of the trouble out there."

"Makes you wonder why we bother."

"Because we can't *not* bother," Skirata said. "And because it's for *us.*" He sat back in the chair in the corner and put his boots up on the low table, shutting his eyes and folding his arms on his chest. "Vau's calling in shortly. If I don't hear the comlink, somebody wake me up."

Ordo had rarely known Skirata to sleep before his men did. And he had seldom seen him use a bed. He always slept in a chair if he had the choice, and while it might have been a mercenary's need to be ready to wake and fight immediately, Ordo suspected it had a lot to do with that first night on Kamino. His normal life had ceased, and would remain suspended until that elusive normality had been achieved for his troops. He always seemed to be waiting for the Kaminoans to come through the door.

His breathing changed to the shallow, slow rhythm of a man asleep.

Scorch started whistling, distracted by his task. Ordo walked up behind him and clamped his hand hard over his mouth. *Quiet. Quiet for* Kal'buir.

Scorch took the hint.

Ordo waited, memorizing Mereel's download from his datapad with a single glance at each screen.

Then Skirata's wrist comlink chirped. He opened his eyes and lifted his hand nearer his mouth.

"Walon . . ."

"Try Jaller," a weary voice said.

Skirata sat bolt upright. Delta Squad froze.

"Where are you?" said Skirata.

"Sweeping up a pile of dead guys with colleagues from the Organized Crime Unit."

"Sorry?"

"I think your boys just kicked off a gang war. Can I borrow a Jedi, please?"

13

Ten members of a criminal gang have been killed in what's thought to be a gang feud in the lower levels. Sources close to Coruscant Security Force suggest the crimelords' battle broke out in a row over gun-running territories.
—HNE late bulletin

Forensics Unit morgue, CSF Divisional HQ, Quadrant A-89, 2345 hours, 380 days after Geonosis

"There's your lizard," Obrim said, pulling back the sheet. "Paxaz Izhiq."

Fi and Skirata looked at the elegant green-scaled face, or at least the half that was still intact. Blasterfire was cleaner than ballistic damage but it still did nothing for your looks.

"Not very attractive to the ladies now, is he?" said Fi.

The morgue was cool and quiet. Fi had never seen one before and he was both fascinated and disturbed, not because it was full of dead things but because he now wondered what would happen to his own body.

Left on a battlefield. Does it matter? Mandalorians don't care about remains. We have our soul. My brothers can retrieve some of my armor, and that'll be enough.

The pale green room with its polished durasteel doors also had an antiseptic smell that reminded him of Kamino. He wasn't comfortable here.

"You okay?" Obrim said.

"Just interested." Fi stared. "Yes, that's him. You can match him with the images Sev grabbed, too. Is he important?"

"Not on our files, but Falleen don't visit Coruscant to get nice jobs in the clerical service. Best guess is Black Sun or an offshoot."

"So," Skirata said. "Purely *hypothetically,* if we picked up a woman friend of his who had access to GAR weapons shipments . . ."

"Purely hypothetically, because *you don't exist* . . . imagine she's diverting a few weapons for his business, but you snatch her and so he refuses to complete the deal because he thinks you're the customer trying to intimidate him." Fi listened, riveted. Obrim's mental gymnastics were hard to follow. "But the real customer thinks the Falleen just made an excuse to run out on their agreement. So they come after you, thinking you're his foot soldiers. And you waste them. So their buddies come back to settle a few scores with young Scale-Face's colleagues." Obrim took one final look at the Falleen's face and covered it up again. "And if they were all waiting on a shipment of explosives anyway—the one you intercepted—then you have a *very* jumpy assortment of bad guys around town."

"You're going to have to spell out why this is good news," Skirata said.

"Well, we're minus some criminal scum, and we've found more we didn't even know about. Plus we now have some good forensics. The SOCO team has been all over his apartment like a rash."

"And?"

"Solid gold for the Organized Crime Unit."

"Whoopee for them, but was he or was he not *handling explosives*?" Skirata was getting agitated, chewing that ruik root again. "I'm not interested in gangsters stealing Republic weapons for their own purposes. Is his gang supplying explosives to anyone?"

"Yes, we found traces everywhere. Your Jedi colleagues seem to be finding the disturbance in the Force useful—whatever *that* means."

"Does this mean that your Organized Crime Unit is going to be getting in our way now?"

"Share operational details with me and they won't."

"You know the rules of this game."

"Kal, your boys are coming awfully close to being targeted by CSF themselves. It could easily have been you and them in a shooting match. I don't want any friendly-fire incidents if we can avoid them."

Fi watched Kal's jaw muscles working as he chewed. This wasn't warfare. It had crossed over into armed politics. Skirata and Obrim seemed to be conducting a private war by their own rules, and Fi didn't envy them.

"You know that we're not taking prisoners," Skirata said. "And I can't see your people turning a blind eye to that once they know what we're up to."

"But I've got something you need," Obrim said.

Skirata switched instantly from lovable rogue to a creature of pure ice. "Don't ever, *ever* try to bargain with me about *this.*"

"Are we on the same side or not?"

Skirata was ashen. "We'll go it alone then." Fi had rarely seen him truly angry, but when he had been pushed too far he went white and quiet and *dangerous.* "Come on, son. We've got work to do."

He took Fi's elbow and steered him to the doors. It didn't bode well. Fi looked back over his shoulder at Obrim—a man equally white, equally tense—and the captain shook his head.

"Okay, Kal, I'll give it to you anyway, but may the Force save your sorry backside if this goes wrong."

Skirata turned. He seemed genuinely surprised: he hadn't been bluffing. He really *had* been storming off and cutting Obrim out of the loop. "What happens if it does go wrong, Jaller? You get into trouble with your bosses. But my boys *die.*"

"Yeah, and so might mine if they get in the way by accident."

"Then don't get in the way."

"Okay, what time did your people grab the woman?" Obrim asked.

"Midafternoon."

"Well, there was someone trying to get hold of our irresistible friend here via a government comlink shortly before CSF went to his home an hour ago."

"You mean there's someone else in the GAR working with him?"

"Yes, and if we could pin down the transmission source, I'd have given it to you."

Skirata's shoulders sagged. "Thank you, my friend."

"Don't mention it. Just try to give me a warning before you start another war here, okay?"

"That was a nice smokescreen line to the media, by the way. Gang war indeed."

"It's very nearly true. But thank your oily friend Mar Rugeyan for that. You'll owe him one, I'm sure."

Skirata rolled his eyes. Fi continued to be surprised by the machinations of political life in Coruscant. He was grateful—and not for the first time—that all he had to do was shoot or be shot. There was no time to worry or plan: either you did a better, faster job than the enemy at that particular moment or you died.

"Rugeyan wants good news," Skirata said. "Let's see if we can find some for him."

Obrim smiled ruefully at Fi and made a gesture of tipping back a glass of ale. "Don't forget that drink, will you?"

They left Obrim in the morgue and took the service turbolift to disappear into the late-night crowds around the CSF complex and emerge at a taxi platform to wait for Jusik to collect them. Skirata simply glanced at three innocent Coruscanti citizens waiting there, too, and they decided they had urgent business elsewhere. *Kal'buir* could look anything but paternal when he felt like it.

Fi pulled his collar up, still feeling horribly exposed without his armor. Skirata rummaged in his pocket, took out a bar of candied fruit, and broke it in two. He handed Fi the bigger piece.

"What now?" Fi said.

"It's the only solid lead we've got," Skirata said. "And it's a mess, but I'm reluctant to let it go and start over."

"I bet the Seps are looking for another source of supply for their explosives now. If this were Qiilura or any other mining planet, they could do it easily. On an urban world like this . . . well, scoring a few blasters is easy, but shopping for explosives is going to attract attention. Maybe this is where we use Ordo's little cache of stuff that goes bang."

Skirata stopped chewing. "I'm never sure if we have the same ideas because they're common sense, or because I trained you and now you're as crazy as I am, son."

"Well, they know their original consignment didn't arrive, so now you might as well use the stuff as bait."

"And there's Qibbu."

"Now, *that's* dangerous."

"No, that's when Hutts come in *useful.* They're like one big scum want-ad service. Seeing as he thinks we're doing a bit of private business without the GAR's consent anyway, why disappoint him? He can put the word out that Kal has something to sell."

"But then we've pinpointed our operational base for them."

"You think Qibbu will want to advertise that we're in his precious hotel, with the possibility of unpleasantness and lots of damage following him home, too? He won't discuss locations. He likes being alive."

"But you're going to tell Obrim, right?"

"Only the location when we have a delivery set up with our new customers," Skirata said. "And then only to warn off CSF."

He lapsed into silence. Around them—keeping a sensible distance, because Skirata looked remarkably gangsterish himself right then—ordinary citizens and tourists from dozens of species were making their way in and out of brightly lit clubs, restaurants, and shops. They were dressed in exotic, colorful clothes, chattering and enjoying themselves: they were arm in arm with friends, or holding hands with lovers, or accompanied by gaping children who had never seen a city-planet like this at night.

Fi knew how those kids felt. It was still as much a spectacle of miraculous delight to him as it had been when he first saw it from the crew bay of a police cruiser. But it was also now something alien to him, something he had no stake in and could never fully understand.

The civilians around him could have no idea of what was happening right in the middle of their safe daily lives. A few meters from them, a mercenary and a soldier who had no official orders were planning to unload enough explosives on the black market to destroy whole quadrants.

But it was a fair trade. Because Fi had no idea of what their lives were about, either.

We live in parallel worlds. We can see each other, but we never meet.

At least Darman seemed to have found a bridge to a normal life, if you could call a Jedi normal. Fi wondered if his brother realized that everyone knew what was going on with him and the general.

If he were Darman, he wouldn't care.

Operational house, Qibbu's Hut, 0056 hours, 381 days after Geonosis

Ordo placed the tight-wrapped packs of five-hundred-grade thermal plastoid explosive on the table and stacked them in piles of ten. Darman picked one up and fondled it with the fascinated expression of a connoisseur of explosives.

It was interesting, Etain thought, to note what made Darman feel relaxed and confident, because sitting on fifty kilos of ultrahigh explosives didn't reassure her at all.

"Dar, cut it out," Niner said. "We'd like the hotel to still be here when Vau arrives. Reckon you can avoid blowing the place up for the next hour?"

"This stuff is perfectly safe unless you stick something metallic in it and trigger an electrolytic reaction," Darman said. He smiled at Etain before lobbing a hand-sized pack at Niner. *"Udesii, ner vod."*

Niner caught it and swore. Then he threw it back.

Etain could hear the shower running in the 'fresher. She could also see Atin wandering around, eyes fixed in defocus on the grubby carpet as if he was rehearsing a speech in his head, and he was trailing a disturbance in the Force that felt like the aftermath of a battle. She'd felt Atin's raw grief on Qiilura, the pain at losing his original brothers at Geonosis, and she could taste the dark depths in him all too easily.

Fi, even without the ability to use the Force, seemed to be able to do the same. From time to time he got up and gripped his brother by his upper arm, talking very quietly and earnestly to him.

Much of the conversation was in Mandalorian, which she didn't understand well enough, but she certainly picked up one word that needed no translation: *Vau.*

Boss, Jusik, and Scorch had gone back down to the bar. Sev and Fixer were out on the landing platform—now looking like a normal hotel roof covered with assorted transport from speeder bikes and airspeeders to a couple of taxis—providing a discreet perimeter defense in case someone had tracked the strike team back to Qibbu's. The whole place simmered with tension and—yes, it was there, very subtly, but it *was* there—fear.

"If Vau's bringing the rest of the thermal, who's minding the prisoners?" Darman said.

"I don't imagine they'll take much minding now," Ordo said. "But Enacca's around."

"So who's going to help him haul fifty kilos of deadweight?"

Ordo looked faintly irritated. He still felt to Etain like a disjointed turmoil of emotions held in place by a ferociously intelligent logic. She had classified him as dangerous without really knowing why.

"Vau," he said carefully, "is still a fit man. A soldier since childhood, just like you and like *Kal'buir.* He can carry fifty kilos on his own almost as well as you can." Ordo adjusted the pile of sealed packs so they lined up perfectly, as if that mattered very much to him. "And if Enacca doesn't need to guard prisoners, she'll help him carry the ordnance. Either way, stop worrying."

"Yeah, that's *my* job," Niner said.

Etain had a very good idea what *doesn't need to guard prisoners* meant. If they had ceased to be useful, then they were a liability here, just as they were on Qiilura. And they would be shot.

Darman killed Separatists when he couldn't take them prisoner. She'd watched him do it: clean, quick, passionless. And—was this the dark side finally pulling her over the edge?—even if she would hesitate to do it herself, she was no longer appalled that he or his comrades did.

He looked up from the packets and gave her a broad smile. There was never even a hint of darkness in him.

"It's perfectly safe," he said. She realized she was frowning at him and that he had taken it to be a comment on the pile of instant destruction on the table. "Don't you trust me?"

She smiled back instinctively. "Of course I trust you." *Yes, I do: you're my friend, my lover.*

Skirata emerged from the 'fresher toweling his hair and wearing a change of clothes with his Verpine in its light gray holster. He leaned over Niner to look at the holozine he was reading.

"Don't you ever watch the holonews?" he asked, pointing at the darkened screen on the wall.

"Too much to take in." Niner resumed reading. "Other people's complicated lives."

Atin had settled in the corner with his DC-17 on his lap. They all kept the rifle close to them when they weren't in public. It was too obviously a commando weapon in the street, and had to be replaced by a discreet blaster. But back here, they lavished affection on the Deece again. It was the weapon they had been raised with and now lived by.

Fi had his slung over his shoulder, and he was looking out the window onto the catwalk opposite, the one that linked another level of seedy bars with the concourse below. He was invisible to the Coruscant beyond the transparisteel, but clearly it was painfully visible to *him.* Etain could feel his longing.

Fi had changed since Qiilura. Etain had first sensed him in the Force as good-natured and calm. A year later his façade was as unfailingly cheerful, but the undertow was darker, more desperate. He'd seen too much of the war. And he had glimpsed something even more painful and guaranteed to trouble him: ordinary people on Coruscant, leading normal lives of the kind he would never have.

She didn't need the Force to help her taste that. She could see the constant question on his face when he glanced at couples and families, of all species. *Why not me? Why is this life not for me?*

It was what Darman had asked.

Family and clan—family and fatherhood—seemed of overwhelming importance to Mandalorian men. They certainly drove Skirata.

Then Etain knew exactly what the Force had in mind for her, and it was not the path of a Jedi any longer. It was to ensure that at least one cloned man was given back the future that had been taken away from him at birth, or whatever cold distant process served for birth in those Kaminoan laboratories.

Etain would make him a father one day. She would give Darman a *son.*

But neither of them had the luxury of a normal life in this war. Her dream would be a secret—even from him for the time being.

Then Etain put the thought from her mind and closed her eyes to meditate, unself-conscious because she was among true friends.

She drifted in formless calm, hearing only the slowed pace of her own heartbeat, until the door buzzed.

She snapped alert again. So did Omega and Skirata.

Etain saw the squad individually as clearly as she did any other beings, and not just because the Force tinted them with their unique shades of character. She had ceased to see their identical faces or their armor, and experienced instead only their distinct personalities and habits.

And yet when they moved—when they switched to their soldier state of being—they were like a single perfect predator.

The buzz made them all look up together, not like ordinary men responding by staggered milliseconds one after the other, but in *one movement,* absolutely synchronized, and their expressions and the angle of their heads and their frozen alertness were *one.* Then, with another perfect single movement, they split like a fist opening into fingers and snapped to positions around the room, rifles trained on the door.

Not a word: not one hand signal from Niner. They hadn't even had time to put on their helmets and activate the shared comlink. Whatever told them to move *there,* do *this,* watch *that,* was so thoroughly ingrained in them from drilling that they seemed almost to be operating on instinct.

Their dark, high-cheekboned, exotic faces were expressionless. Except for the rapid blinking, they were completely and utterly still. Etain suddenly saw them as that single exquisite predator again, and it scared her.

Their DC-17 rifles all blipped once in unison as each weapon charged up to fire.

"Vau's not due yet. And Delta's on perimeter." Skirata had his Verpine shatter gun trained this time, not his small blaster—an indication of how much higher he felt the stakes were. "Etain, you feel anything?"

"Nothing." She was certain she would have perceived a threat by now. She was suddenly aware that she had drawn her lightsaber. She hadn't even felt herself move. "Nothing at all."

"Okay . . . on *three* . . . one . . . two . . . th—"

And the door opened. Etain flinched involuntarily, grasping her lightsaber two-handed. A scent hit her, a foul damp musk.

"Fierfek," Skirata said. "You *di'kut.* We could have blown your head off."

Niner, Ordo, Darman, and Fi made annoyed clicks and sighs and lowered their Deeces. Atin didn't.

Vau walked in with two straining carryalls and a six-legged, loose-skinned shambles of pale gold short fur ambling behind him. So that was the strill. And the absence of malice and tension had been . . . ice-cold, calm, utterly detached Walon Vau.

"*At'ika,* lower your Deece," Skirata said softly.

"If you say so, Sarge." And although Atin obeyed, his steady stare at Vau was an eloquent loaded weapon.

"Come on in," said Fi. "Ain't nobody here but us clones."

"You could have called ahead," Skirata said.

Vau lowered the carryalls to the floor, and Ordo pounced on them. "Just challenging your security, like I ought to."

"Well, either Delta and Jusik got instantly stupid or they let pass someone they knew, so don't get too cocky. Anything you want to tell us?"

"I've shut down the safe house and Enacca has cleaned up."

Etain listened intently to the language, spoken in the code of euphemism out of long habit. *Cleaning up* certainly meant removing bloodstains, because she'd seen them, but she had the feeling it was more than that.

"No further business with our two friends?" Skirata said.

"That's the trouble with Coruscant," Vau said. "High balconies are safety risks. At least that confirms our two guests weren't Jedi, eh?" Vau found a seat, and the strill scrambled onto his lap: it took Etain a moment to work out what he meant, and the realization shocked her. "The other fortunate thing is that I was able to talk to Vinna Jiss's supervisor at GAR logistics as her . . . *landlord* and complain that she had skipped owing me rent. The supervisor was sympathetic and said she was an unreliable employee."

"So?" said Skirata. Omega had disappeared back to the rooms that led off the main one. Except Atin: Atin waited, a block of black hatred, and Ordo stacked the explosives.

"So at least we don't have to worry about her being missed too badly." Vau glanced at Atin, almost as if he was seeking a greeting, but got no reaction. "And she confirmed that there was one other person in logistics that she had to leave information for in an agreed place, a dead letter drop inside the GAR complex, whenever she could manage it. In a locker in the female 'freshers."

"What? You're kidding me."

"I know. We spend millions on the latest ships but we're stuffed by a simple security leak that wouldn't baffle a Kitonak grocer."

Etain felt Skirata generate a little dark vortex of rage. His face drained of color. "Why are they so *shabla* clueless?"

"Because they're a bureaucracy, and they're not the ones in the front line. Anyway, none of the traffic information is impossible to dig out by other routes. It's just quick and easy—all wrapped up in one chip. Worth having because it saves them a lot of time, which means they don't have many personnel. Small and opportunistic network, I reckon."

Skirata was rubbing his face slowly with both hands, exasperated and weary. "So she didn't know who collected the data, other than that they could use the female 'freshers without attracting attention? Or what their schedule was?"

"If she had known, I can guarantee she would have told me."

"I'll bet."

"So we need someone in there to flush that person out."

"That's me," Ordo said, and went on making the thermal plastoid into neat piles. Etain had counted two hundred small rectangular packets so far. "All I have to do is withdraw the trooper who's seconded to the transport division and step in."

"And what happens to him?" Vau said.

"He stays here until I'm finished," Ordo said. "You can make a commando of him in the meantime, *Kal'buir.*"

"Well, this is going to be very cozy." Vau rubbed the strill's back, and it shuddered with visible delight. "Because you have to find room for me, too."

"Then the strill sleeps on the landing platform," Skirata said.

"Then I do, too," said Vau.

Fi emerged from the room he shared with Atin and stared at the animal. "We could always leave it downstairs in the bar as an air freshener."

"One day, RC-eight-oh-one-five," Vau said, smiling with unusual sincerity, "you might be very glad of Mird's natural talents."

Etain suspected they were not dissimilar to its master's.

Qibbu's private rooms, Qibbu's Hut, 1150 hours,
381 days after Geonosis

"So *this* is why you write off my debt," Qibbu said. He swallowed a pickled gorg whole and sighed. "You use my fine establishment as a base so that trouble does not follow you home."

Too right, Skirata thought.

"My little girl needs to start up her own *business,*" he said, beaming convincingly at Etain. "So she can look after her old dad in his dotage."

Etain looked suitably sullen. She continued to surprise him with her capacity to do whatever was needed. She could act brave, and she could act calm, and now she could act the wayward and spoiled daughter of an overprotective mercenary.

"She is too skinny to make a living as a bounty hunter," Qibbu said, and shook with laughter. *"Mando* females are supposed to be big and *tough."*

"Her mother, the *chakaar,* was a Corellian and she left me to bring the girl up," said Skirata. "What Etain lacks in muscle she makes up for in business acumen."

"Ah, I *thought* your fondness for the Republic's army would prove to have a financial motive. You care nothing for your . . . *boys.*"

Kal bit the inside of his cheek. "No. You ever met a *Mando'ad* who cared about the Republic?"

"No. So what is for sale?"

"Something armies have a great deal of."

"Ah . . . you follow the news closely."

Skirata made a silent vow to be very, *very* kind to Mar Rugeyan in future. That turf war cover story had worked all too well and the man probably didn't even know it. "There does seem to be a sudden gap in the arms market, yes."

"You *made* that gap, yes?"

His stomach somersaulted. He managed a grin. "I'm not that big a player."

Qibbu swallowed the hint whole like a gorg. "So what can you obtain?"

"Blasters, assault rifles, thermal plastoid, ammunition. Anything larger than that I'll treat as a special order and it might take longer. Don't ask for any warships, though."

Qibbu laughed. "I put out the word and we see if it attracts customers."

"I'm sure I can rely on your discretion. You like this place, don't you?"

"I want no trouble finding its way back here. But I will expect . . . commission. Twenty percent."

"That's my dowry," Etain said sourly. "Papa, are you going to let this *chakaar* steal from me?"

Fierfek, she was getting *good,* this kid. " 'Course not, *ad'ika.*" Skirata leaned toward Qibbu and jangled his length of chain in his pocket as a little reminder. "Five percent, and I'll see that your lovely establishment here remains in one piece and unvisited by the riffraff of this world."

Qibbu gurgled. "If this partnership is successful, we renegotiate terms later."

"You get the business and we'll see."

Skirata stood up as calmly as he could and led Etain out onto the walkway to get some fresh air. The smell of frying, stale ale, and strill was getting to him.

"I thought *chakaar* was a nice touch," he said.

"I pick up the odd word."

"You okay?"

"Actually, that was hard. I envy your nerve."

"You reckon?" Skirata held out his hand, fingers spread, palm down. It was shaking. She needed to know that in case she thought he was invincible, and her misplaced faith got her killed. "I'm just a soldier. A commando, you'd call it. I'm groping my way through all this."

"But Qibbu's scared of you."

"I don't have any problems with killing people. That's all." The reality of his situation had become starkly clear now: edging farther and farther out on that limb, either to safety or to plummet into the torrent rushing beneath, with a breath between one extreme and the other. *And no way of stepping back onto the riverbank.* "If anything happens to me, I need to know someone will look out for my boys."

"You're asking me?"

"There's only you and *Bard'ika* to ask."

"Nothing is going to happen to you."

"The Force is telling you that, is it?"

"Yes."

"What else does the Force tell you?"

"What I have to do."

"If and when we meet these scum face-to-face, are you up for it? Can't have my boys visible. Too obvious."

"Not Bardan?"

"I don't have to ask *Bard'ika.* He'll want to be there anyway. I'm asking *you.*"

"I'll do whatever you command. You have seniority here."

Skirata was hoping for an expression of confidence rather than obedience.

But it would have to do.

14

Word from our undercover team and their informants is that someone is offering explosives and arms on the black market. It's amazing how fast this scum flows in to fill the gaps. Time for us to move in. And only one warning before you open fire, okay? Let's see how much we can clean up once and for all.

—Organized Crime Unit squad briefing, CSF HQ, 383 days after Geonosis

Logistics center, Grand Army of the Republic,
Coruscant Command HQ, 1000 hours, 383 days after Geonosis

Ordo walked through the center's doors unchallenged this time.

"Good morning, sir," the sentry droid said.

Ordo shoved his stylus probe in the droid's dataport again and downloaded its latest recognized-personnel file. "Carry on," he said.

Before he reached the operations room of the logistics wing, he stepped into the male 'fresher and ran the downloaded images of all the center's organic staff through his helmet's HUD to memorize every face. About 5 percent had changed since his last visit. Civilian staff moved on. Supervisor Wennen, he noted, was still there.

Then he copied all the data stored in his helmet to his datapad and wiped the HUD's memory. His armor was completely clean now, with no trace of who or what he was other than a classified ARC trooper tally ID. His sole connection to the special forces world would be the tiny bead comlink in his ear. His final task was to slide a wide-angle strip cam into the ventilation grille that passed between the male 'freshers and the female ones.

Then he replaced his helmet and walked into the operations room. There was no sign of Besany Wennen; the third-shift supervisor, a Nimbanel, was on duty.

" 'Morning, sir," Corr said.

"Just observing today, trooper," Ordo said. He stood back as if watching the array of live traffic holocharts that covered the circular wall of the ops room, making it feel like the inside of an illuminated drum. In fact, his gaze was on Corr as he worked and occasionally moved around the room. Ordo was taking a crash course in how the trooper moved so that he could mimic him. He already had the measure of his voice with its faint flash-learned accent.

And the civilians always seemed to think he was looking in the direction that his helmet was facing. The basic trooper helmet's specification was available to anyone working in logistics, but they seemed to be unaware of its visual range. Who cared what a trooper could and could not see?

They ignore so much data, these civilians.

"Corr, I need you to show me something," Ordo said. The civilians also seemed to ignore conversations between clones. "Come with me."

Corr picked up his helmet, put the security code lock on his workstation with his gauntlet tally—*good man, follows the regulations*—and followed Ordo out of the room. They walked back down the corridor and Ordo gestured him into the 'freshers, marching him into the far end where the lockers were.

"This is where you have to follow my orders to the letter," Ordo said.

Corr looked suddenly wary. "Yes sir."

"Armor off. We're swapping suits."

"Sir?"

"Remove your armor. I need it."

Corr began unfastening the gription panels without argument and stacked the plates on the floor. Ordo did the same. They both stood there in black bodysuits, suddenly without visible rank, and Ordo was reminded of the price Corr had paid. He looked at the trooper's artificial hands.

"Was it very painful?" asked Ordo, who had never been that badly injured.

"I don't remember a thing, sir, but it hurt when I woke up in the bacta tank." He pushed back his sleeves: he had lost both arms from just above the elbow. "I manage okay."

Ordo had no idea what to say. "You should be invalided out. You shouldn't be going back to the front."

"What about my brothers? What am I without them?"

He had no answer to that, either. He snapped Corr's plates onto his own suit. It was a tight fit: he had always known that the experimental genotype that had so disappointed Kaminoan quality control had made the Nulls slightly heavier in build than the clone trooper and clone commando batches. His armor would be a little loose on Corr.

"At least you get to play captain, then. Enjoy it."

Corr attached the plates and had some trouble snapping the *kama* into place. Ordo adjusted it and put the pauldron on his shoulders, then handed him the helmet.

"Wow, this feels different," Corr said, looking down at himself. The ARC trooper armor was built to a higher spec. "It's heavier than I thought."

"Get those shoulders back a bit farther and let the *kama* and the holsters hang like *that*." Ordo placed the helmet on Corr's head and was suddenly surprised to be staring back at himself: so *that* was how he looked to the world. "Take this datapad and walk out of the front doors. You'll be met by a taxi piloted by a Wookiee. Do *not* stop and do *not* talk to anyone. Just walk out as if you were me, and you'll be taken to a place where you'll be among brothers."

"Very good, sir. How long?"

Ordo tried on Corr's helmet. It felt foreign. It smelled of a stranger: different food, different soap. "I don't know. Just savor the break and I'll see you later. What do you call the civilians?"

"I address them by their last name, except for the supervisors, whom I call *ma'am* or *sir*."

"Even Wennen?"

Corr paused. "We use first names when not in the center itself."

Ordo tucked Corr's helmet under his arm. "Good. Off you go."

They left the 'freshers a few seconds apart, and Ordo watched Corr disappear up the corridor. The weight of the *kama* and blasters gave him an authentic swagger. Ordo found it quite touching and turned back to the operations room to get used to being a simple *meat can,* a clone trooper that nobody—except the enemy, of course—dreaded or feared or avoided.

He had at least one shift to settle in before the biggest risk to his cover turned up. Besany Wennen seemed to be the one taking the most interest in Corr. He would have to be careful to get past her scrutiny. But he had a few hours to practice.

He unlocked the workstation and became compliant, conscientious CT-5108/8843, invisible to the world. The job of checking that supplies had reached the correct battalion in the field and that contractors' schedules hadn't slipped was a simple one, and he occupied himself thinking of ways to make the system more efficient. He resisted the urge to upgrade the system there and then.

And he watched those around him.

"Sorry I'm late," said a woman's voice behind him, a level, mellow voice with an undertone of warmth that sounded as if she were permanently smiling, the higher frequencies betraying a shortened vocal tract. "I'll work an extra hour for you tomorrow. Thanks for holding the fort."

Ordo had no time to perfect his simple-trooper act. He glanced over his shoulder as he imagined Corr might, and gave Besany Wennen a slight nod that felt like it came a little too easily to him.

She smiled back. Ordo suspected she too was a consummate actor. But something in him greatly enjoyed that smile.

Operational house, Qibbu's Hut, 2015 hours,
383 days after Geonosis

"Name your time for a discussion about the goods," the stranger's voice said over the comlink. "And we'll name the place."

Skirata didn't like the sound of that. Nor did Vau, evidently. He was listening to the comlink, too, scanner in one hand, and shaking his head slowly, tapping out a random pattern in the air with a forefinger. *Can't trace the transmission point. Multiple relay. Just like us.*

Ordo grabbed his gauntlet from the table and activated a holochart, holding it where Skirata could see it. The whole strike team was waiting on the conversation, including the clone trooper called Corr whose life had suddenly taken a turn for the bizarre that day.

"I'm going to need a little more reassurance than that," Skirata said.

"I'm an intermediary," the voice said. *Coruscanti accent. No clue at all.* "What reassurance would you like?"

"A very public place. If we both like what we see, and we trust each other, we meet somewhere more private to iron things out."

"And you bring a sample."

"Assault rifles? In *public*?" This was the test question, the one that would sort the gangsters from the Separatists. Weapons were instantly useful to criminals: raw explosives weren't, not unless you wanted to resell them. "Don't *takis* me, *di'kut*. My father didn't raise a stupid son."

"My clients suggested you could obtain military-grade explosives."

"I can. So you want a sample of *that*?"

Silence. Vau listened, head cocked.

"We do. What are you offering?"

"Top military-spec five-hundred-grade thermal plastoid."

Pause. "I think that fits the bill."

There was a forest of enthusiastically raised thumbs in the hushed room. For some reason Skirata found himself focused on the anxious face of clone trooper Corr, perched on the edge of a chair with one of Dar's custom dets dismantled in his prosthetic hands.

"Noon tomorrow," Skirata said. He winked at Jusik. "And I'll have my *nephew* with me, just in case."

"On the south side of the Bank of the Core Plaza."

"You'll spot me easily enough. I have a strill."

Vau's face was a study in shock, but—like the professional soldier he was—he said nothing.

"What's a strill?" the disembodied voice said.

"A disgustingly ugly, smelly Mandalorian hunting animal. You can't mistake it for any other species, not even in *this* menagerie of a city."

"Noon, then."

The link went dead.

"Nobody but Seps would want five-hundred-grade thermal," Vau said. "Too exotic for the average criminal. They certainly bit on the bait fast. Should that worry us?"

"They've lost their usual supplier, and this is far better stuff." Skirata watched Delta descend on the holochart and begin planning sniper positions around the banking plaza. "This is purely surveillance unless they start shooting, okay, lads? Killing them there won't help us trace their nests. Least of all in broad daylight."

"Understood, Sarge."

Sev managed a smile. "As long as we get to use lethal rounds later. We like *dead.* Dead is very us."

"I added some Dust to the unenriched thermal," Jusik said. "You want some made into Verpine projectiles, so you can tag anyone you spot and track them, too?" Jusik was a ferociously clever lad and

Skirata prized intelligence very much, as much as loyalty and courage. "I thought I'd make sure we didn't have to follow a suspect the hard way again. Am I forgiven for my lapse of judgment the other day?"

"*Bard'ika,* if you ever want a father, then you have one in me," Skirata said.

It was the highest compliment he could pay him: he was fit to be his son. Jusik might not have fully understood Mandalorian culture yet, but he certainly grasped the sentiment if his embarrassed glance down at the floor and the broad grin were any guide.

Boss gave Skirata a cautious glance. "Does that mean we get to use your Verp rifles?"

"You're such a pushover for fancy kit," Skirata said.

"They're the business, Sarge . . . *kandosii*!"

"But you bend them, and I'll bend *you.* They cost me a fortune, and they *do not bounce.*"

"How you going to get the caliber of those marker pellets right, though, Bardan?" Sev said.

"Multicaliber magazine and bore," Skirata said. "You could load these Verps with stones if you needed to. That's what cost the money. That and the full-spectrum range of filters, variable velocity, and anti-reflective device."

"Kandosii," Sev said, almost sighing. "Shame you didn't pay a bit extra to make them more robust."

"Cheeky *di'kut* . . . okay, I reckon you're good enough to use them. Take a look."

Skirata went to the cupboard and slid out one of the precious rifles, disassembled into three discrete parts: thirty-centimeter barrels, matte drab green, silent, horribly accurate, and Jaing's weapon of choice for *going hiking with extreme prejudice,* as he described it. Sheer ballistic beauty. An assassin's tool: a *craftsman's* tool.

He hadn't seen Jaing in months. He missed him. He missed all the Nulls badly when they were on long, distant missions.

Boss and Sev fondled the rifles and beamed. Even Fixer looked happy. The Delta boys didn't respond to food treats and pats on the head, then, but they loved new toys and praise. Skirata noted that.

"I need accurate ranges from your recce," Jusik said. "I've got to pack the Dust into a medium that'll stay together until it's right at the target, or the stuff will disperse too soon. This has to splatter them close to the face so they inhale it, or it'll just sit on their clothing. If they dump their jackets, we'll lose them."

"Fun," Sev said, and obviously meant it.

Vau got up and wandered out toward the landing platform, no doubt to fuss over Lord Mirdalan before the slobbering thing did a real job for once in its life. When he was out of earshot, Boss turned to Skirata.

"Sargeant Vau loves that animal. Don't let anything happen to it. *Please.*"

"I won't. It knows I carry a knife."

Corr, who had been the subject of much fussing and attention since Jusik had brought him back to Qibbu's, watched cautiously. Skirata ruffled his hair. He flinched. "Sorry about all this, son. Learning a lot?"

"Yes, Sargeant."

"Want to be useful? I mean even more useful than you are now?"

"Yes. *Please.*"

Poor little *di'kut.* Skirata fought the urge to collect another damaged young boy, another stray in need of belonging, and lost immediately. He had been that orphan, and a soldier had rescued him.

"Dar, give him a crash course in using a DC-17, will you?"

Boss and Sev slid the discreet body armor plates under their tunics and checked their hand blasters. "Just off for a recce of the location, then," Boss said. "Back in two hours, and then I suggest we insert as soon as possible so we're there before the bad guys."

"What makes you think they won't be doing the same right now?" Etain said.

"Because it looks like a very hard location to lay up in for any length of time, and we're pros, and they're not," said Boss. "So they'll probably go in closer to the rendezvous time."

Skirata made a point of looking around the group so that he could see the reaction of the two Jedi. Both of them were very capable warriors but assassination—killing someone who was not about to kill you—was psychologically *very* different from using a lightsaber or blaster in combat.

The silent excitement that had gripped the room was palpable.

"Gentlemen—ma'am—this is a shoot-to-*kill* operation," he said. "Not *arrest.* We want as many *hut'uune* identified, located, and dead by any means possible at the end of this deployment. Nothing else. We're cutting out a big chunk of this network in one slice. Are we all clear that's what we're doing?"

"Yes Sarge!"

It was one voice. And Jusik and Etain were part of it.

That was good. Anyone who hesitated would get the rest of the strike team killed, or worse.

“Okay, recce team, move out,” Skirata said. “And don’t you *dare* drop my Verps.”

15

Mandalorians are surprisingly unconcerned with biological lineage. Their definition of offspring or parent is more by relationship than birth: adoption is extremely common, and it's not unusual for soldiers to take war orphans as their sons or daughters if they impress them with their aggression and tenacity. They also seem tolerant of marital infidelity during long separations, as long as any child resulting from it is raised by them. Mandalorians define themselves by culture and behavior alone. It is an affinity with key expressions of this culture—loyalty, strong self-identity, emphasis on physical endurance and discipline—that causes some ethnic groups such as those of Concord Dawn in particular to gravitate toward Mandalorian communities, thereby reinforcing a common set of genes derived from a wide range of populations. The instinct to be a protective parent is especially dominant. They have accidentally bred a family-oriented warrior population, and continue to reinforce it by absorbing like-minded individuals and groups.

—Mandalorians: Identity and Its Influence on Genome, published by the Galactic Institute of Anthropology

Logistics center, Grand Army of the Republic, Coruscant Command HQ, 0815 hours, 384 days after Geonosis

This was no place for a fighting man to be when his brothers were out in the field, but Ordo reasoned that the faster he identified and neutralized the informant, the sooner he could leave this office job.

"Clone," the Nimbanel voice said. The creature was riding him today. It was a bad idea—normally. "*Clone!* Have you input the overnight batch of data yet?"

I know at least ten ways to kill you without a weapon, lizard. I'd like to try them all.

"Yes, Guris," Ordo said, being nice, compliant Corr. "I have."

"Then you should have told me immediately."

Ordo heard Skirata's constant admonishment in his head and kept his temper: *Udesii, udesii, ad'ika—easy, easy, son.* This clerk wasn't fit to clean Corr's boots. He certainly wasn't fit to clean *his.*

"My apologies," Ordo said, acting the calm man that he definitely wasn't right then. "It won't happen again."

Besany Wennen raised her head from her screen very slowly. She was distressingly pretty. The symmetry of her features made him uncomfortable because he wanted to stare, and his male instinct said *pursue,* but his brain said *suspect.*

"Guris, if you have a concern about data management, may I suggest you raise it with me first?" The warmth in her voice had disappeared completely. The frequency dropped as her lips compressed. Ordo could see her in his peripheral vision: she had a way of switching off that vivid smile and just freezing for a few moments. This was someone used to obedience in those around her. "Trooper Corr is doing what I asked of him."

Ordo had no idea if that was true or if she was saving him embarrassment. He managed a placatory smile anyway. Watching Corr last night had honed his act a little more.

As he worked, inputting vessel pennant codes and supply routes into the program that fed the wall display, he pondered on the one solid piece of information he had. The advance schedule for movements of men and matériel was stripped out to provide confirmation messages. One internal stream went to GAR logistics battalions and Fleet Ops, and one external stream was relayed to the thousands of civilian contractors who provided supplies and transport. The two sets of data were different.

So this had to be the data that was left on a chip at the drop point within the complex—the one that Vinna Jiss had helpfully described to Vau whether she wanted to or not. The bomb attacks had been spread throughout the contractor and military supply networks; whoever executed the attacks had both sets of data.

And copying data showed no audit trail. Relaying data from the system did. And *that* was what routine security watched. Old tech beat state-of-the-art with depressing frequency.

All Ordo had to do now was watch the surveillance images of the drop point at the female 'freshers. So far it had picked up nothing. He had no idea how frequently the Separatist contact—and he had to assume it was one—checked the locker, but nobody had shown up. Maybe they hadn't missed Jiss yet.

It was nearly noon when Supervisor Wennen got up and left the operations room. On a whim, Ordo laid his helmet on its side on the desk next to him at an angle where he could discreetly view the feed from the 'freshers playing out on his HUD.

Wennen was *not* the kind of woman who belonged here. Some uneasiness told him so. *Kal'buir* had told him that a strong hunch was usually based on subconscious observation of hard facts, and was to be treated with respect.

The grainy blue image showed Wennen entering the 'freshers. She didn't glance around. She paused at the lockers, scanned along them with her head moving visibly, tucked a strand of pale hair behind one ear, and bent to open several unlocked doors until she appeared to tire of it and left again. She reappeared in the ops room a minute later and gave him a regretful smile that appeared utterly sincere.

Something had irked her.

Ah, Ordo thought, disappointed.

Then he wondered why he felt that disappointment, and realized it was due to impulses unconnected to the business in hand. And business, of course, had just taken a turn for the better.

His shift finished when hers did, at 1600.

He would spend the next few hours working out exactly how to remove her without alerting any other Separatist contacts that might be in her cell. He wanted them *all.*

1100 hours, 384 days after Geonosis, commercial zone, Quadrant N-09: agreed meeting point to open negotiations with interested parties

"Lazy *chakaare,*" Fi said, glancing at his chrono. "What time do they call this?"

"Well, if they got here before us and we can't see 'em . . . we're probably dead meat."

Darman was somewhere on the opposite side of the Bank of the Core Plaza, three floors above the pedestrian area in a storeroom he had infiltrated. Fi couldn't see him, but his voice was clearly audible in his head: the bead comlink was so sensitive that it picked up subvocalization via the eustachian tube.

They'd been here since 2330 last night. They had observed and noted every cleaning droid, automated walkway sweeper, late worker, early-morning commuter, shopper, drunk, CSF foot patrol, delivery repulsor, unlicensed caf vendor, and truant schoolkid that had passed in and out of the plaza from any direction. They had also swept the cliff walls of office buildings and—to Fi's great interest—noted that some employees did *not* catch up with the filing after hours if they had colleagues of the opposite sex with them.

And every couple of hours, Etain Tur-Mukan had walked briskly across the plaza as if she had business somewhere, sweeping the area with whatever extra sense Jedi had that enabled them to detect concealed people. Etain was said to be good at that. She could place the squad to within a meter. Each time she passed, Fi heard Darman move or swallow, and he wasn't sure if it was because he could see her or because she was reaching out to him in the Force.

Fi suddenly wanted the uncomplicated focus of a totally military life on Kamino.

You're getting distracted. Think of the job in hand. Maybe they'd let him keep the bead comlink after this op. They'd never miss a few back at HQ. *Surely.*

"I want my HUD back," Darman said. "I want my enhanced view."

"But you get to wear face camo instead. Makes you feel wild and dangerous."

"I'm wild," Sev's voice said. Sev was behind a roof balustrade under a pile of discarded plastoid sheeting. "And then I get dangerous. *Shut up.*"

"Copy that," Fi said cheerfully, and clicked his back teeth twice to exit Sev's open comlink channel. It was far too noisy an environment for their quiet conversation to be heard anyway. "Miserable *di'kut.*"

"Don't mind him." Scorch was at walkway level about fifty meters west of the meeting point, lying prone in a disused horizontal access shaft. "He'll be fine once he's killed something."

Darman had a Verpine rifle with live rounds, as did Sev. Fi and Scorch had the nonlethal tracking projectiles, twelve rounds each. The Verp was truly lovely. Fi had always wondered just how many credits Sergeant Kal had made over the years. His growing collection of expensive, exotic weapons and the modest extravagance of his bantha jacket were the only visible signs that it might have been a *lot.*

"Dar—"

"Possible contact, first walkway level, my left of the bank entrance . . ."

Fi adjusted his scope and tracked right. It was a boy he'd seen before: human, very short scrubby light hair, gangly. He was still hanging around the plaza. If he was a Sep, he was a disgracefully amateurish one. They watched for a few minutes, and then a young girl in a bright yellow tunic raced up to the boy and flung her arms around him. They kissed enthusiastically, drawing glances from passersby.

"I think he knows her," Fi said. He felt his face burn. It bothered him and he looked away.

"Well, that's just you and Niner left on the shelf now that your brothers are spoken for," Scorch said.

There was a pause. Darman cut in. "You got a point to make, *ner vod*?"

"I think it's kind of encouraging." Scorch chuckled. "Atin gets a cute Twi'lek, Dar gets his very own general—"

"—and Scorch gets a thick ear if he doesn't *shut it right now.*"

The comlink was suddenly silent except for the occasional sound of swallowing. Darman wasn't in a joking mood when it came to Etain. He never had been, not even on Qiilura, when there hadn't been anything going on between them.

Why is this hurting so much? Why do I feel I've been cheated?

Kal'buir, *why didn't you prepare me for this?*

It was too distracting. Fi shut his eyes for a few moments and went into the sequence he had learned to center himself when the battlefield pressed in on him: controlled breathing, concentrating on nothing except the next inhalation, ignoring everything that wasn't of the next moment. It took a while. He shut out the world.

Then he found that he had his eyes open without even realizing and he was simply following movement on the plaza below through the breathtakingly accurate scope of the Verpine rifle.

"Now, do we get the best kit or what?" he said, becoming the confident man he wanted to be again. "Name me another army where you get handcrafted Verps to play with."

"The Verpine army," Scorch said.

"Do they have an army?"

"Do they need one?"

Silence descended again. At 1150 Sev cut into the comlink circuit. "Stand by. Kal's moving into position."

Skirata wandered into the plaza from the direction of the Senate with Jusik one on side and an excited Lord Mirdalan straining on a leash on the other. He was doing a credible job of looking as if the strill were his constant companion. The animal seemed remarkably content with him, given the number of times Skirata had driven it off or thrown his knife at it over the years. Maybe the riot of strange new scents had thrilled the strill enough that it didn't much care that the man who usually shouted at it was holding the leash. Fi watched as they took up a position near the door, sitting down on an ornate durasteel seat shaped like a bow.

Skirata's voice came over the comlink circuit.

"How's my boys?"

"Cramp, Sarge," Darman said. "And Fi's dribbling over your Verpine."

"He can clean it, then. Ready?"

"Ready."

At 1159 a human male in his forties—green casual tunic, brown pants, collar-length brown hair, beard, tall, lean build—walked toward Skirata and Jusik in a purposeful line. Fi tracked him.

"Got him, Fi," Darman said. If anything went wrong, the man would be dead in a fraction of a second from a silent high-kinetic round in his back.

"Escort," Sev said. "Looks like three . . . no, four. Three male, one female, all human . . . one male twenty meters south of Darman. Spread out but all moving toward Skirata."

"Got him."

"Got the female," Scorch said.

"You sure they're with the Beard?"

"Yeah, check their eyeline, Fi. They're watching him, nothing else. They're pretty cool about it but they're obviously not professionals. They shouldn't even be looking his way."

Etain's voice cut in. "There's another female approaching slowly on the Senate side of the bench. I'm moving in behind her so you can spot her."

Sev cut in. "Any more?"

"I can only sense four others plus the man approaching Kal."

"Aww, look. They've taken up positions to block the main pedestrian routes off the plaza. Thank you! I love a target that identifies itself."

"I hope this doesn't turn into a shooting match," Scorch said. "Too many civvies."

"I can get a clear shot," Sev said. "And I can take at least three out from here. Relax. You just worry about tagging 'em."

Tagging. Would they feel it?

Fi dropped in an EM filter with a touch on the optics housing. He focused the scope on the woman now standing almost under Darman's position by the walkway heading toward Quadrant N-10: shoulder-length red hair, blue business suit, tan leather document bag. The filter detected electromagnetic emissions, which made it not only handy for locating someone operating a comlink but also just *perfect* for seeing if Dust had hit its target. It cast a pinkish brown tinge across the image.

He checked for indications of wind speed. The woman's hair was moving slightly in the breeze: a flimsi cup discarded near the caf vendor rolled a little way along the paving. Fi adjusted his scope and checked the air temperature, which had crept up a fraction in the last twenty minutes. He adjusted the Verp's settings again and settled the weapon on his forearm.

Relax. Power coil set to medium. Don't want her to feel the projectile hit her. Don't want to spray the Dust over the whole plaza, either . . .

The crosshairs settled.

"So that's a strill." The man's voice was a little fuzzy but Fi could hear the accent, even if he didn't recognize it. *"Charming. Call me Perrive."*

"And you can call me Kal."

Fi closed his eyes for a second and slowed his breathing. When he opened them, the aim was still dead center of the woman's chest.

"So let's see the goods."

Fi exhaled slowly and held his breath.

"Here. Take it and have it tested."

Fi's finger tightened on the end of the trigger. The Verp was so finely constructed that all he felt was a sudden lack of resistance under his finger and the rifle fired—silent and without recoil.

"How much stuff in all?"

"Hundred kilos. More if you need it."

A smoke-like white puff billowed in Fi's filter. The projectile had burst on contact, showering the woman with microscopic tracking powder, each tiny fragment capable of relaying its location back to the base receiver at Qibbu's—or even to a HUD. She glanced down as if an insect had landed on her and then simply brushed the end of her nose as if she'd inhaled pollen.

"Five hundred grade?"

"All of it," said Kal.

"Dets?"

"How many?"

"Three or four thousand."

"Five-hundred-grade—I have it. Dets—just a matter of acquiring them discreetly. A day maybe."

"Confirm—female target in blue, *marked.*" Fi tracked the rifle ninety degrees to his left. "Targeting the male farthest from Kal. Black jacket."

Breathe easy. Relax. He aimed and adjusted the scope again, held his breath at the comfortable point of exhalation, and fired for a second time. Again, the man reacted and looked for something on his chest, then carried on watching Skirata as if nothing had happened.

"Male, black jacket—*target marked.* So they *can* feel it strike, then."

"Don't hog them all," Scorch said. "I want a go."

"All yours, *ner vod.*"

"Targeting the male right of Skirata, gray robe . . ."

Fi lined up his EM scope on Scorch's target to observe. Scorch's breathing paused, and then Fi saw a puff of white smoke bloom on the gray robe. He didn't react at all.

"Now the other male, red vest, left of Skirata by the caf vendor . . . no, keep still, you *di'kut* . . . that's better." Scorch was silent again. Fi watched through the EM filter. The projectile burst neatly on the man's shoulder and he brushed his nose without noticing, just like the first woman. Maybe it was a combination of seeing absolutely nothing as the pellet's binding agent vaporized, and being hyped up on adrenaline during a mission. They weren't tuned in to much beyond seeing and not being seen.

"Okay, who's taking Beard Guy? Perrive."

"Me," Fi said. "If I make it three for three, do I get to keep him? Y'know, stuffed and mounted?"

"He'd make a nice stand for your Hokan armor."

Perrive—Beard Guy—stood at a slight angle, moving a little as he spoke to Skirata. He held the small pack of thermal plastoid in his hand, about a hundred grams of it, and was squeezing it between his fingers while glancing at the wrapping. It looked for all the world like a spice deal, and Fi wondered for a moment if they were all blind to how obvious that might appear.

Worry about that later. Tag him.

"Turn around, *chakaar.* I don't want to hit your back."

Fi had settled into a rhythm now. He watched through the scope as Perrive slipped the plastoid into his pocket and stood with one hand on his belt, turning idly back and forth, presenting a good expanse of back and then a narrow angle of shoulder.

Fi relaxed, aimed and went for the shoulder, anticipating the turn.

Whuff.

The tracker projectile struck home and got no reaction.

"Okay, we'll take a look at this and get back to you tomorrow at noon," Perrive said. *"If we like it, we meet somewhere private. If we don't, you never hear from me again."*

"Suits me," said Skirata.

"What about the second woman?" Fi said. "Etain, where are you?"

"About three meters to her left."

"Can you edge her clear of the civvies?"

"Okay . . ."

Fi listened. Skirata could hear all this on his comlink bead, too. It took some skill to carry on talking with someone having a five-way conversation in your ear.

"Excuse me," Etain said. "I'm hopelessly lost. Can you show me how I get to Quadrant N-Ten?"

Fi watched as the woman simply paused, looked at Etain with surprise, and then began pointing out the connecting walkway. Etain moved. The woman stepped out farther, pointing again.

"Thank you," Etain said, and walked on.

Whuff. The projectile plumed light on the woman's shoulder. And she brushed her nose.

"All six tagged," Fi said. He changed channels with an exaggerated click of his molars. "Niner, you receiving?"

"Got 'em all," said Niner's voice, several quadrants away in Qibbu's. "Nice vivid traces on the holochart."

"Okay." Fi let his head drop to ease his neck muscles. "You can wind up now, Sarge."

"The old *di'kut*'s good at it, isn't he?" Scorch betrayed a grudging fondness. Skirata could hear the conversation and Scorch knew it. "I'd love to know where he learned to do all that."

Skirata's face didn't even twitch. Nor did Jusik's. Jusik was just looking around as a gangster's errand boy was supposed to, appearing alert but not too bright.

"My intermediary says you have lots of army friends," Perrive said.

"Contacts," Skirata said. *"Not friends."*

"Don't like our army, then?"

"Just useful. Just clones."

"Not worried what happens to them?"

"You're not some di'kutla *liberal, trying to recruit me, are you, son? No, I don't give a mott's backside about clones. I'm in this for me and my family."*

"Just curious. We'll be in touch, if we like the goods."

Skirata simply sat with his hands thrust into his pockets, apparently watching the strill, which had stretched out in an ungainly pile of loose skin with its head under the bench, trailing drool. Jusik chewed vacantly, also staring ahead. Fi and the sniper team watched Perrive and the five targets disperse into walkways and downramps.

They waited.

"Anyone else spot a Jabiimi accent there?" Jusik asked.

Skirata leaned over and appeared to be about to pat Mird. "I reckon so." Fi waited for it to sink its teeth in him, but he stopped short of touching it and the animal simply rolled over to watch his hand with malevolently curious eyes.

Fi remembered the strill from Kamino. It seemed smaller now that he was a grown man. Once, it was bigger than he was.

Eventually there was a long sigh of relief. "I sense they're all gone," Jusik said. "Niner, are they clear of the plaza area?"

Niner grunted. "Confirmed. You can move now."

"Stand down, lads," Skirata said at last. "Well done."

"Nice job, Etain," said Darman's voice.

"Yeah, okay, well done the Mystic Mob, too." Skirata tugged on Mird's leash; the pile of fur scrambled onto all six legs and shook itself. "Let's thin out carefully, and don't forget to wipe off the face camo before you move. We'll RV back at Qibbu's by thirteen-fifteen. Then get some rest."

"Sounds good," Fi said. It was only when the tension had passed that he realized how stiff his joints felt and how much parts of him hurt from twelve hours and more lying prone on the makeshift padding of his jacket. "Hot bath, hot meal, and sleep."

Skirata cut in. "You know I didn't mean that, don't you?"

"What?"

"About clones. Qibbu obviously mentioned you to his scum associates."

"Of course we know, Sarge," Scorch said. "You said you were in this for your *family,* didn't you?"

* * *

Logistics center, Grand Army of the Republic, Coruscant Command HQ, 1615 hours, 384 days after Geonosis

Ordo listened to his concealed comlink with a practiced expression of blank disinterest while he keyed in traffic movements. The holochart that covered every centimeter of wall space shifted and pulsed as consignments turned from red to green—now laden, cross-checked, and en route—and requests for replenishment stacked up in a panel of blue horizontal bars.

The holochart gave no numbers of troops, but a little common sense would have told anyone who wanted to spend the time thinking through the obvious that they were thinly stretched. There were, Ordo knew, at least a million troops now in the field spread over hundreds of worlds: small forces on some, multiple battalions on others. It meant long supply chains, and those were inherently vulnerable. So . . . why didn't the Separatist terror networks target them off-world? *No ability.* No suitable vessels or skills. Or . . . maybe the point was to intimidate the seat of galactic government after all.

Motive mattered. Motive gave you the capacity to think like the enemy, want what they wanted, and then snatch it from them.

And killing clone troopers—mainly troopers, if you didn't count the unfortunate civilians who were also in the way—made the point that the Seps could come and go as they pleased.

Ordo took it personally. He drew on the memory of sharp, cold fear and focused hatred that he had learned on Kamino before a total stranger had stepped in front of him and saved his life.

We can trust nobody but our brothers and Kal'buir.

Over the comlink, he could still hear Niner's exclamations of satisfaction. The six men and women tagged by Fi and Sev were dispersing all over Galactic City, leaving routes and stopping points that Niner and Boss were logging on a holochart that showed every skylane, quadrant, and building on Coruscant. Judging by their occasional descent into the rich Mandalorian invective that *Kal'buir* considered an important part of their continuing education, they were learning more than anyone had bargained for.

Ordo would evaluate it all when he returned, but the number of locations that the tagging had registered had now reached twenty; it was growing into something larger than a fourteen-man team might be able to handle.

Ordo wanted to tell them to concentrate on the clusters, the areas of most traffic, but it would have to wait. The strip cam had yielded nothing, except the fact that females of all species employed in the center seemed to spend a lot of time in the 'freshers rearranging their appearance. Whoever had been used to collecting the data probably knew Vinna Jiss was gone now and was no doubt trying another route. He kept a careful eye on Supervisor Wennen because she seemed to be getting increasingly agitated as the day wore on. He could hear it in her voice. She didn't like Guris. She was checking something: when he went to the 'freshers, she was still on the same screen when he returned, scrolling up and down an inventory.

She was checking rifle shipments going back two or three months. *If it's you, Wennen, what is your motive?*

He didn't have to stop to read the screen over her shoulder. He could simply glance at it, focus, and walk back to his workstation to close his eyes discreetly and recall what he had seen.

Whatever errors the Kaminoans had made in their attempt to improve Jango Fett's genome, the efforts had not been wasted.

Wennen looked up toward the doors. Her fine-boned face, while still aesthetically pleasing, suddenly froze into genuine anger and lost its prettiness.

"Jiss," she said sourly. "You'd better have a *good* excuse this time."

Ordo fought every instinct to jerk around and stare. He simply turned his head casually to focus on a sheet of flimsi to his right, and there she was: Vinna Jiss.

You're dead.

"I've been unwell, Supervisor."

But you're dead. So who are you?

"Heard of comlinks? I even had your landlord calling me, complaining you'd skipped without paying rent."

I know you're dead because you fell a few thousand meters from a balcony after a chat with Walon Vau.

"Sorry, Supervisor."

Wennen was all acid, lips compressed. "See me first thing in the morning. I'm off shift now."

She shut down her workstation, grabbed her jacket, and made a move toward the doors. Then she paused and turned to Ordo.

"Corr, it's sixteen-thirty," she said. "Come on. Time to go. Nobody will thank you for sitting there all night. Want me to drop you off at the barracks?"

Jiss, either you're dead or you're an imposter. So who did Vau kill?

"Thank you, Supervisor." Ordo logged off and replaced his helmet, suddenly glad of the chance to hide behind an anonymous white plastoid visor and stare horrified at the face of a dead woman who seemed to be doing pretty well for a corpse. "I'm . . . I'm going to meet some comrades from the Forty-first. Could you drop me off at the first taxi platform in the entertainment sector, please?"

"I'm glad you're taking the opportunity to relax, Corr." She seemed genuinely pleased. "You deserve it."

Ordo took one last look at the woman who appeared to be Jiss, memorizing every pore and line, and followed Wennen outside to the speeder bays. He slid into the passenger's seat with a hundred questions that had, for once in his life, yielded no fast answers.

Wennen powered up her speeder and sat still for a moment, staring at the console.

"Honestly," she snorted, all exasperation. "That's the most unreliable employee I have *ever* known. Sometimes I could just *kill* that woman."

Operational house, Qibbu's Hut, 1630 hours, 384 days after Geonosis

"There they go . . . ," Niner said.

Beads of red light were now dotted throughout the blue holochart of grids and lincs that had expanded to fill a space a meter high and two meters long. The tracking Dust was transmitting the movements of the six Separatists they had tagged a few hours earlier.

Etain walked around the 3-D chart, studying tracks that were strung like necklaces with occasional solitary beads placed at intervals. The virtual representation of a section of Galactic City spanned the table. Some of the threads crossed and merged. Niner and Boss were still taking data from it and listing each location while Vau watched with Jusik.

"They do get around," Vau said. "Jusik, my boy, has anyone ever told you you're a genius?"

Jusik shrugged. "And my friends are excellent shots. Good team, aren't we?"

Friends was an unusual way for a Jedi to describe clone troops who were technically his to command and use as he thought fit. But Jusik simply didn't see the world that way. Etain found it deeply touching.

"Yes, *excellent* team," Vau said. Boss glanced up, evidently pleased. "It's wonderful to watch a job done well."

That wasn't quite the Walon Vau that Etain had sensed and found to be sheer passionless brutality. He was no less complex and contradictory than Skirata. Atin, reading from his datapad, ignored him completely; Vau sometimes glanced at his former trainee but got no reaction.

Atin loathes him. He wants revenge of some kind. Etain found it hard to reconcile that with the methodical, considerate, and courageous man she knew, the one who had felt he had no right to survive Geonosis when his brothers had died.

While the locations were collated, another frustrating hiatus had forced the squads into rest and recovery. They seemed to need to be busy fighting, especially Delta. Etain could taste their collective impatience. Maybe it was youth; but maybe it was that they didn't enjoy having time to think.

Fi, Sev, Fixer, and Scorch had gone down to the restaurant to eat with Corr, but Darman was asleep in his room. Etain went to check on him and watched him for a while. He lay on his stomach, head turned to one side, cheek resting on folded arms, and twitched occasionally as if dreaming.

They grabbed every small moment together that they could find. And it wasn't enough. Etain kissed his temple and left him to sleep. Skirata, wandering around with his hands deep in his pockets, gave her a conspiratorial wink.

"Looks like we've got three clusters in residential areas," Boss said. "And now about twenty-five other places they've at least stopped for a while, including shops."

Skirata stood looking at the mesh of colored light. "We can't cover them all," he said. "The clusters are the priority."

"Probably their safe houses or bomb factories." Boss indicated a static point of red light that hadn't moved in an hour. "I think that's our marked pack of thermal plastoid."

"Could well be. Got a list now?"

"It gets longer by the hour. How long did you say that Dust can transmit?"

Jusik cocked his head, calculating. "Four, perhaps five weeks."

"Well, I say we recce the cluster points for a day or so, confirm the activity, and then decide which are the priority targets and leave the rest to CSF." Niner jabbed his finger into the holochart again to indicate another thread growing as the tagged suspect moved to a new location. "This target is trailing the other. No idea why. Maybe providing tail cover."

"Okay, you draw up a surveillance roster for the next twenty-four hours and be prepared to pull people off it if I get the call from Perrive, or whatever his real name is."

"Okay, Sarge."

Skirata finally allowed himself a little satisfied grin, which put Etain more in mind of a gdan than ever. He gave both Boss and Niner ferocious pats on the back; Boss flinched while Niner turned and smiled, pleased with life. "Nice job. You two go and get something to eat."

Etain fought an urge to walk across to Skirata and hug him. She had finally worked out what was happening. Omega—and Ordo—were clearly used to genuine affection from him: they touched all the time, from roughhousing and crushing hugs to hair ruffling. Delta didn't. They were uncomfortable with it. Whatever relationship they had with Vau was much more distant, more competitive, more a desperate quest for his approval. Skirata played the good father even now, dispensing treats, unashamedly pleased and proud of everything his boys achieved. Vau looked as if he played the master, and being judged good enough was rare.

It made her wonder more than ever about Atin. She would have seized the moment and taken him aside to ask, because it troubled her, but she was interrupted by the return of Fi and Sev. Fi strode up to Atin and grabbed the datapad from his hand.

"A strange blue woman with no taste in men wants to see you," he said. "Go on. Laseema's complaining you haven't said hello to her today."

Fi had a knack for teetering on the edge of offense. He also did a very good job of pretending that Atin's good fortune with Laseema didn't bother him one bit. The aching little void at the core of him, so plainly detectable in the Force, said otherwise.

Jusik caught Etain's eye: he spotted it, too. Then he looked past her toward the doors, and she felt something as well—anxiety and distress, very clearly emanating from a presence that could only be Ordo.

He strode into the room and began unfastening his armor, jaw clenched. Skirata just waited.

"So, did you have a good day at the office, dear?" said Fi.

"She's not dead," Ordo said. "Vinna Jiss is not dead."

"Start again, son," Skirata said.

"A woman my supervisor identified as Vinna Jiss walked back into the logistics center at sixteen-fifteen today." He stacked the plates and sat down on the edge of a chair, completely calm except for the telltale gesture of one fist clenched on his knee. He looked up at Vau. "And it *was* her, or at least she looked the image of the woman Jusik picked up. In one piece. Are you *sure* you killed her?"

Vau raised an eyebrow. "Oddly enough, yes. Humans don't bounce. I would have spotted that, I think."

"Then who was that at work today?"

"You couldn't be mistaken?"

Ordo didn't even blink. "I remember *everything* I see in complete detail. I have eidetic memory. What I saw was the identical image of the woman we detained and who you took for interrogation. Of that much I am *absolutely certain.*"

"Fierfek," Skirata said. "Options?"

"One, she's a twin or a clone." Ordo counted off on his fingers. "Two, she's some kind of droid designed to mimic her. Three? A Clawdite. Shapeshifting is a useful skill for a terror group to recruit. But why would they want to mimic a dead colleague?"

"How about that supervisor?"

"I've logged her going into the 'freshers and searching lockers, but now I have no idea if she's working alone or with this Jiss woman. She was genuinely angry when she saw her, though."

"Because the other Jiss fouled up, maybe."

"We need to do some surveillance on this resurrected Jiss. She's supposed to be on the evening shift, so I'm going back to the center just before midnight and I'll follow her when she leaves."

Jusik's lips parted but Etain was faster off the mark. "I'll come with you," she said. "I'll be able to tell you whether she's a droid, at least."

"I can do that with sensors," said Ordo.

"I'll come with you anyway."

Ordo turned to Skirata. "I don't like mysteries." He was clearly embarrassed. "I'm sorry, *Kal'buir.* I'm not resolving this as fast as I should."

"Son, this is *never* a fast game. We're making good progress. Take it easy."

But Ordo wasn't the type to take it easy. He joined the contemplation of the holochart and picked up Niner's datapad.

"I'll take a clip of those Dust rounds, please, *Bard'ika,*" he said. "Just in case."

Skirata drew his stubby Verpine handgun from his holster. "Better use this, then. More compact than the rifle."

"Thank you."

Etain stood with Vau, watching the erratic progress of the markers around the chart. A hard decision lay within it: at what stage would Skirata feel it was safe to bring CSF in on the surveillance? When would he share information with them? Etain understood his anxiety, but the simple mathematics of the situation was that CSF would be needed sooner or later.

Ordo began logging more locations into the datapad. His jaw muscles were working visibly. It must have been hard for a man used to being smarter than anyone else except his five brothers to handle the ordinary mortals' world of being dumbfounded a lot of the time.

"Oh," Vau said suddenly.

"What?"

"Tell me what this building is."

Jusik interrogated the database in the holochart emitter. "CSF Divisional Headquarters."

"Well, well," said Vau. "How illuminating. Why is one of our tagged bad guys going in *there*?"

16

Mhi solus tome
Mhi solus dar'tome
Mhi me'dinui an
Mhi ba'juri verde

We are one when together.
We are one when parted.
We will share all.
We will raise warriors.

—Traditional Mandalorian marriage contract
and ceremony, in its entirety

Logistics center, Grand Army of the Republic, Coruscant
Command HQ, 2340 hours, 384 days after Geonosis

There was a lot to be said for having a matte-black army-issue bodysuit.

It provided a reasonable amount of protection against blaster and projectile weapons, and it was low visibility at night, unlike ARC trooper armor. Ordo felt in the pockets of the knee-length dark gray jacket that Vau had lent him and felt compelled to inhale the unfamiliar scent of its wearer: antiseptic soap, weapon-lubricating oil, and a maleness that was not his. But it disguised the skintight suit. That was all it had to do.

It also disguised the Verpine shatter gun in his holster.

"What makes you think she's going to stick to her shift hours?"

Etain said, looking slightly past him, head almost touching his. They sat in the closed cockpit of a speeder parked a hundred meters from the logistics center, where they could watch the doors. To anyone watching, they were just a young couple in a parked speeder late at night, like a thousand others at that moment.

"The fact she bothered to return to work at all. That means she wants her pattern to appear normal again."

Etain just nodded. She seemed to be finding it hard to keep up a conversation. Ordo could smell Darman on her, which fascinated him: Darman seemed able to step beyond the community of brothers and not feel adrift, just as his Null brothers could. But Ordo found it distressing, and Fi seemed to as well.

Ordo wasn't sure if he would ever trust a female, not after Chief Scientist Ko Sai first towered above him, gray and cold and unfeeling. He wondered if having a human mother would have made it easier.

Etain shut her eyes again. She shuddered.

"It's not cold," Ordo said.

"Are there Jedi working here?"

"Of course. Jedi make great clerks."

"I'll take that as a no."

"It's a *definite* no. Why do you ask?"

"I felt someone in the Force, very faintly."

Fierfek. Zey? Jusik being helpful? "Close?"

"Gone now."

She went back to silent contemplation of something beyond him.

"Is your PEP laser fully charged?"

"Yes, Ordo."

"Very noisy and visible. *Last resort.*"

"As is a Verpine round."

"I have the chamber loaded two and one," Ordo said.

"What?"

"Two marker projectiles between each live round, and one live round already *up the spout,* as *Kal'buir* so aptly puts it."

"And you can—"

"Count? I do believe so."

"I seem to offend you without meaning to. I realize you have an astonishing intellect."

It wasn't that his mind was so remarkable that seemed worth comment, but that hers and others' were *not.* He felt the need to explain.

"In an emergency, it's better that I'm able to fire a killing shot without needing to discharge two nonlethal rounds first." He stared into her eyes: they were light green, flecked with amber. Except for

Skirata's, the only eyes so unlike his own that he had ever studied at that range were alien, and shortly before he killed their owner. "Anyway, I can execute a triple tap with a Verpine. So it's academic."

"*Triple* tap? I've heard Dar talk about double—"

"*Three* rounds in quick succession. Some species need a little more stopping power."

"Oh."

"The PEP laser will stun most humanoids."

"And if it doesn't?"

Ordo simply tapped the Verpine under his jacket.

They waited. Maybe they really did look like a couple having a private moment. Randomly created people did strange things.

Staff in groups, ones, and twos began entering the building for the night shift.

Soon . . .

Movement behind the transparisteel doors made him focus and check his chrono: 1155. *Staff sloping off early.* "Stand by," he said quietly.

Etain turned very slowly away from him in her seat, ready to open the speeder's hatch and slide out.

Ten or eleven workers emerged. Ordo and Etain slipped from the speeder and feigned ambling around in conversation. There was still frequent pedestrian traffic around the center.

By 0005 the trickle of staff in and out had slowed, and there was still no sign of Vinna Jiss.

"She has to come out that entrance."

"You're sure—oh, okay, Ordo."

They waited. He wondered how long the two of them would look inconspicuous.

And then he spotted the ginger wavy hair and the beige tunic he'd seen earlier. *Jiss.* He watched her turn along the path and walk down the ramp toward the walkways that connected the complex to the business district around it; then he made his move.

Etain walked briskly at his side and grabbed his hand. "For goodness' sake, Ordo, try to look like a *couple.*"

Ordo didn't much like that, but the mission came first.

They kept twenty meters behind Jiss, hampered by the lack of crowds of office workers to hide among at this time of night. Maybe they should have waited until daylight. But nobody knew how much time they might have to act. It was a case of *now.*

Etain did that side-to-side head movement as if she was straining to hear something. "Okay . . . people behind us, but they seem to have their minds on matters other than us . . ."

"How do you know that?"

"No feeling of focus on me, or you."

"Handy," Ordo said, but he hitched back his jacket and hooked his thumb in his belt to be ready to grab the Verp.

They had followed Jiss for about half a klick along the shrub-lined office walkways when the few pedestrians became none and they had no cover between her and them. Jiss turned right into a side alley and Ordo picked up speed, drawing his weapon and holding it as discreetly as he could against his chest.

"Where's she gone?"

"The alley," Ordo hissed. "Are you blind?"

"No, I mean she's gone. *Gone.* I can't feel anybody there."

Ordo cocked the Verp and checked the status indicator. He might need that live round after all. He slowed at the corner and froze for a second before stepping into the opening with the gun raised, two-handed.

He was looking at a *man's* back about fifty meters ahead. *No sign of Jiss. Maybe that really is a Clawdite.*

"Oh my . . . ," Etain said.

Ordo was about to discharge the lethal round into the containers of shrubbery and try for a tag pellet but the man appeared to crouch into a low run. There was a reflection, a split-second gleam that said *metal, alloy—weapon.*

He fired instinctively.

The silent shot hit something with a wet *ssssputt* and whoever or whatever he had hit rolled, stumbled, and raced off to the left down another passage. Ordo broke into a sprint, Etain pounding after him. He reached the point of impact and saw fluid—dark, oily—before discharging both tag pellets into the shrubs and lining up the next lethal round. This had gone wrong. *He* had got it wrong. But he couldn't turn back now: this had to be resolved. He swung left and there was someone lying on the paving, writhing, and he aimed the Verpine.

"Check!" Etain yelled. *"Check!"*

And in the fraction of a second that he froze on the safety command she had heard Skirata use, a shock wave of air and heat flared past him and hit the figure on the ground in a blinding, deafening flash. Without his visor he was stunned for a second, too. But he dropped on the body, holding the Verp clear, and grabbed an arm.

Its limb melted away in his grip.

That second became endless, a layered image.

I'm going to throttle that Jedi.

What the fierfek have I grabbed?

It's a Clawdite.

He looked up at Etain but she raised her blaster again and spun around. There was a second deafening, blinding crack of a PEP laser discharging.

Ordo had a tight grip of something very heavy and black and sleekly furred that had stopped moving. And that was an odd thing for a wounded Clawdite—a humanoid when not shapeshifting—to become.

A few meters from Etain, a human female lay crumpled on the paving, gasping for breath. It was Supervisor Wennen, *not* Jiss. Ordo defaulted to training and opened his comlink.

"Bard'ika? We need extraction urgently. Two prisoners, both injured. *Now!"*

His instinct told him to find some cover *fast.* The PEP laser would bring someone running before long. He dragged whatever creature he had shot into an alcove and motioned furiously at Etain to do the same with Wennen. It was amazing how heavy a weight a little Jedi could haul.

But he wanted to hit her, and hard.

"You *di'kut,"* he hissed. "I could have been killed. *Never* use that command. Do you hear me? *Never!* If you try that again, I'll shoot you."

Etain's wide-eyed stare was either fury or shock. He didn't care.

"I thought you were going to finish it off!" She knelt over the black creature at his side and put her hands on it. "It's *alive.* I have to keep it alive. You shouldn't have fired."

"That's my call to make."

"You shot a Gurlanin—"

There aren't any Gurlanins currently on Coruscant, so Zey says. "Spare me your hindsight lecture." *Gurlanin. Shapeshifter. Qiiluran. Spy. Never seen one before.* "Jusik, can you hear me? Can Vau handle shapeshifter first aid?"

Jusik's voice was breathless. "With you in ten minutes, Ordo, hang on. Where's your speeder?"

"Not here. Just *move* it, please."

Etain had her fingers spread on the creature's black coat, her eyes shut tight. "I can use the Force to control the bleeding."

"Okay, you do that, Jedi." He squatted over Wennen and

checked her breathing with the Verp held to her head. "So, Supervisor, why were you following us?"

Wennen looked in bad shape. Her eyes were streaming and she curled up into a ball, clutching her chest. Etain had fired the PEP laser at close range. "Republic . . . Audit . . . you shoot me, chum . . . and you're in big trouble . . ."

"What?"

"Treasury officer."

"Show me, or you're the one in trouble, ma'am."

She let out an anguished gasp and fumbled for her pocket. Ordo decided to play safe and extract the contents for her. Yes, it was an identichip: Republic Treasury Audit Division.

"You've nearly fouled up a GAR operation," he said.

"I was following Jiss."

"Why?"

"Supplies going missing. So did she. Who are you?" She pulled back her head a little to focus on his bare hand gripping the Verp. "Well, that tells me you're not Trooper Corr."

"Obviously."

"Are you the captain who came in the other day? Because you certainly recognize me . . ."

So much for deniability: this would be all over the Treasury in hours if he let her get up and walk away—not that she seemed able to. "We need to have a little chat."

"And what's *that*?" Wennen tilted her head to look at the Gurlanin, lying inert while Etain struggled to stabilize its wound.

Etain opened her eyes a little.

"This," she said, "used to be one of our allies."

Operational house, Qibbu's Hut, 0045 hours,
385 days after Geonosis

Skirata assembled a makeshift deployment tote board from three large sheets of flimsi and stuck them to the wall.

It was old technology, real words on real flimsi, not shifting lights and code. He needed its solid reassurance right now. Things were turning *osik'la.*

Corr—assigned to the team on Skirata's whim—stood beside him, dutifully listing target locations by numbers of visits and tagged suspects on one sheet while Skirata kept a tally of which commando was deployed, and where they all were for the next twelve standard hours. Without his armor and bodysuit, Corr was just a very young man with durasteel mechanisms where he should have had real hands, and it broke Skirata's heart.

Droid. They're making you into what they always thought you were, son.

Skirata shook himself out of it and concentrated on the flimsi. He *hated* holocharts. He liked solid things that he could grab hold of, even if they had their limitations. It also kept his hands occupied when he was reaching the limits of his confidence. He had to stand firm. His men needed to see him in control, reassuring, believing in them.

Believing in *them* was easy. He had doubts about himself. He glanced over his shoulder. "Is that thing dead yet?"

"*Kal'buir,* I'm sorry I got this wrong," Ordo said. Somewhere, no matter how much reassurance Skirata gave him, he still seemed to fear that not being good enough meant a death sentence. Skirata hated Kaminoans with renewed passion. "I should have known what the creature was. I knew they existed."

"Son, *none* of us knew any of them were on Coruscant."

But they were. And that changed everything.

Etain and Jusik were kneeling on either side of the Gurlanin, hands flat on its flanks in some kind of Jedi healing process. Vau watched with interest. He was the anatomy expert, although he was more skilled at taking bodies apart than repairing them. Darman and Niner seemed unwilling to go back to sleep and joined the audience.

They'd become close to a Gurlanin on Qiilura. It must have been very hard to think of them now as possible agents for the Separatists.

It was a black-furred carnivore about a meter high at the shoulder, with long legs, four double-tipped fangs, and hard, unforgiving orange eyes. It now looked exactly what it was: a shapeshifting predator.

"It's recovering," Jusik said.

"Good," Vau said. "Because we want a chat with it."

Etain looked up with that pinched expression she tended to adopt when she was angry in her rather righteous kind of way. "I lived alongside them. We promised we'd give them back their planet and so far all we've done is move in a garrison and train the human colonists to look after themselves."

Vau stared slightly past her, straight-faced. "I believe that was you personally, General. You and Zey. And you were only following orders. That's it, isn't it? *Following orders.*"

"Knock it off," Skirata said. He didn't want Darman pitching in to defend Etain. Everyone's nerves were raw: tired, stressed people were dangerous, and they needed to be dangerous to the enemy, not each other. "Ordo, what are we going to do with Supervisor Wennen?"

Besany Wennen was propped in a chair, arms folded gingerly across what must have been a very painful bruise to her whole chest. She was lucky that Etain's close-range PEP round hadn't killed her, but now the woman was just an extra complication they didn't need. Ordo was looking her over as if she was a new species.

And she *was.* There was a comfortable zone of attractiveness in females, and then there was a point beyond which it became too much. The very beautiful were intimidating and unwelcome. Wennen had passed that threshold, and Skirata was ambushed by his own unexpected hostility toward her.

"You've probably guessed what we're doing, ma'am," Ordo said.

"Anti-terrorist operations?"

"Correct."

"I'm sorry. I had no idea." But there was no screaming outrage or threats that *her* boss would rip the guts out of *their* boss, the usual response of bureaucrats. She just indicated the unconscious Gurlanin with a shaky hand. "Where does the Gurlanin fit into all this?"

"Other than mimicking Jiss, we have no idea."

Wennen seemed to be taking refuge in investigation, continuing to do her job even though she knew she was in a serious situation. Skirata respected that. "So if you two are Jedi, why didn't you spot the creature?"

"Gurlanins can hide in the Force and shut us out," Etain said. "When I first encountered them I even thought they *were* Jedi. They're telepathic, we can't detect them, we don't know how many there are, and they appear to be able to mimic any species up to tall humanoid size."

"Perfect spies," Jusik said. "And perfect predators."

"And we didn't honor our pledge to help them, so I suspect they've run out of patience."

"Look, no disrespect to our Treasury colleague, boys and girls, but can we refrain from discussing classified intelligence in front of Agent Wennen?" Skirata said."I need to talk to CSF. Corr, you call up the recce teams and see how far they've got on the main locations."

Skirata wandered out onto the landing platform and breathed in cool night air. The strill was curled up under the bench where, true to his word, Vau had slept each night. He probably thought it proved the point that he was a hard case, but there was no doubt that he worshiped that stinking animal and it loved him.

Atin's going to take a knife to him when this is over. I know it. Well, worry about that when it happens . . .

He raised his wrist comlink to his lips. "Jaller?"

There was a pause and the sound of a woman grumbling and sheets rustling. Of course: Obrim had a wife and kids. Skirata often forgot that other people had lives beyond their jobs. "You know what time it is, Kal?"

"To the second. Look, which of your people was on surveillance in the Bank of the Core Plaza?"

There was a long, sleepy, irritable pause. "What, today? None of my people, I guarantee it."

"Organized Crime Unit?"

"I could ask, but they play these things close to their chests . . . getting to be an epidemic, this secrecy, isn't it?"

"Tell you what," Skirata said, dropping his voice. "Pay your OCU buddies a visit and tell them that anyone we see in our scopes who isn't *us* gets slotted as a matter of course, okay? You think they'll understand that?"

"I can but try."

"Try *hard,* then. I don't want them crashing in like the *di'kutla* Treasury did tonight."

"Really?"

"Yeah. An audit officer was sent in to monitor GAR staff siphoning off supplies. But that isn't my biggest problem right now." *Don't mention the shapeshifter yet.* "Okay, here's my offer. I now have forty-three individual locations that we believe the Separatists are using or visiting in Galactic City. We have to concentrate on the high-value targets, and you really don't want to know what we'll be doing *there,* so what if we give you a list of the others to pick off as you see fit?"

"When?"

"When we've recce'd the high-value ones and have an op order planned out—you know, precise timings. That way we don't fall over each other."

Obrim had gone rather quiet. "I can authorize that. But I've got no control over the OCU."

"Then find someone who does. I mean it, Jaller. We're not playing by rules of evidence."

"You've *really* gone bandit, haven't you?"

"Do you really want to hear the answer to that?"

"Fierfek . . . my eyesight problem has now affected my hearing, too."

"I thought it might. I'm waiting on a meeting right now and after that, I'll have a list for you, a reliable one. Just remember that if there's any talk of explosives sales being of interest to CSF, tell them to steer clear until further notice."

"I'll just say military intelligence and leave it at that."

"Good."

"You go careful, friend. And those rather hasty boys of yours. Especially Fi."

Skirata closed the link and went back into the main room. The Gurlanin was breathing more steadily, although its eyes were still closed and the two Jedi were still leaning over it. It was just as well they could stop the bleeding. There wasn't a medic on Coruscant who knew a thing about the physiology of a shapeshifter like *this* one.

And Wennen was watching the whole scene suspiciously. Okay, so she had a Treasury identichip. Skirata didn't trust anybody, because this leak of information was still very much an inside job. Until he knew otherwise, everyone except his assortment of clone soldiers—and the two Jedi, he conceded—was a potential risk.

"Ma'am," he said. "I hear you don't approve of the war." Civilians did odd things in the name of peace. "How much don't you approve of it? And why?"

Wennen chewed over the question visibly, and both Jusik and Etain flinched at something Skirata couldn't see. Wennen's expression changed to anguish. She stood up with some difficulty, and Skirata noted that Ordo's hand went unconsciously to his blaster.

"This," she said quietly, "is why I don't like the war." She went up to Corr, who was still conscientiously collating data and writing it on the flimsi with an expression of intense frowning concentration. "Corr, show me your hands. Please?"

The trooper put his stylus aside and held them out, metallic palms up. Corr placed her hands underneath so that his rested on hers for a moment and looked him straight in the eye. Single prosthetic hands—efficient, unnoticeable—were common; but to lose both hands seemed to pass beyond a threshold of what was flesh and blood.

"It's not *right,*" she said. "It's not right that Corr and men like him should end up like this. I'm wondering what kind of government I'm working for. *One with a slave army,* that's what. You know how that makes me feel? Disgusted. Betrayed. *Angry.*"

Skirata knew that feeling only too well. He just hadn't expected to hear it from someone who did an office job and could switch off HNE with its heroic and sanitized images of the war anytime she liked. Jusik caught his eye and nodded discreetly: *She really means it, she's upset.*

Skirata acknowledged Jusik with a slow blink. "You said it, ma'am." *Got her. We have an ally. She'll come in useful one day.* "Believe me when I say that what we're doing here is aimed at stopping things like that happening to more lads like Corr."

Wennen seemed satisfied, if someone that upset could reach that state of mind. She made her way back to the chair and handed Skirata her datapad. "Go on."

"What?"

"I don't know what data might be of use to you, and you're not going to discuss detail with me. So take the datapad and copy what you like."

"You're very trusting. You're sure we're who we say we are?"

Wennen laughed and stopped abruptly. That *had* to hurt her ribs. "Look, I know what I'm seeing. Now, if I'm out of contact for more than forty-eight hours, the Treasury will notice. So think about what you're going to do with me."

Skirata hefted the little 'pad in his hands. *Treasury data, codes, encryption algorithms. Oh, my Null boys will* love *slicing this.* "And who else is going to notice you're gone?"

"Nobody. Absolutely nobody."

Skirata pondered on that revelation for a while as he watched the unconscious Gurlanin. Jusik and Etain knelt back on their heels and looked as if they'd run a very tiring race.

"It'll be regaining consciousness soon," Etain said. "And I still have no idea how you restrain a shapeshifter."

Ordo picked up one of the Verpine rifles, checked the charge level, and stood over the inert black body.

"This does the job," he said.

Recce team observation point, residential area,
business zone 6, 0110 hours, 385 days after Geonosis

"I wish I hadn't eaten that hot sauce," Sev said.

"Told you so." Fi held out his hand for the infrared scope. "My turn."

They had found a spot to hide between two top-floor apartments facing the building they were watching, a six-floor tower of a house with closed blinds at every window. A climate-conditioning access space nearly at the top of their vantage point gave them an uninterrupted view below of a very quiet, very private group of homes away from the skylanes in a dead end.

The upper floors arched into a fashionable overhang only seven meters from the facing building. No passing traffic could enter from the front to bother them here, not even a taxi, and the rear access was nonexistent, which left only the roof for access by a small green speeder. It was private and a good place to defend—or get trapped. Fi rather liked the idea of the latter.

The access space felt like being in a drawer. They could just about crawl through it on all fours. Fi knew he wouldn't have enjoyed serving in a tank company at all.

"Roll on your back for a while," Fi said helpfully.

Sev hesitated then surrendered to the suggestion with a groan. "How many?"

Fi tracked from right to left with the scope. "Well, I think we've got ten bodies in there, judging by the GPR image, and they've been in there for an hour now, and they're not moving around much. I call that an operational base. Agreed?"

"Okay. Let's set up the remote holocam and get out of here."

"Given the layout of that place, it's going to be a bit busy slotting them all when we go in."

"I like busy," Sev said.

"Have Scorch and Fixer reported in yet?"

Sev held his datapad level with his eyes. "Now, *that* sounds like fun."

"What does?"

"Scorch says they've confirmed the third cluster is a small commercial docking area. CoruFresh fruit and vegetable distributors. Loads of spacegoing vessels of all sizes."

"Yes, that's my idea of fun, too."

"If we could get them all to meet up for a nice ride . . ."

"Dream on. But we could certainly stop them from leaving in a hurry."

Fi backed out of the space, pushing himself on his elbows with his DC-17 crooked in both arms, collecting more dust and dead insects on his bodysuit. He turned sideways on to a narrow shaft that opened into the building's plant maintenance room and dropped his left leg into the gap, searching for a foothold with his boot before finding the ledge and scrambling down to the floor. Sev simply rolled off and landed with a thud beside him.

"Okay, where next?"

Fi cocked his head. "Want to wander over and take a closer look at the roof? Evaluate it for rapid entry?"

"You know how to engage my enthusiasm."

Fi projected the fire safety holoplans of the building, which had proved to be Ordo's best illicit data slice of the mission. There was no point asking the fire department to provide them; it just invited awkward questions about why lads in white armor wanted detailed floor plans of most of the planet's buildings. "I hope they update these. Okay, go left along the passage; the roof access is the set of doors at the end."

"I love the fire department."

"They're so helpful. Nice uniforms, too."

They crawled across the flat roof along the side of the climate-conditioning machinery room, over lengths of durasteel ladder laid flat on the waterproofing. Some buildings still had them to provide access to maintenance spaces. There were also the remains of a barbecue. They flattened themselves behind the parapet to peer through the breaks in the punched durasteel at the roof opposite.

"Ooh, a Flash speeder," Fi whispered.

"Don't even think about it."

"I meant that we could bolt on a few surprises, not wander off with it."

"Look, what does the word *recce* mean, *ner vod*?"

"It almost sounds like *wreck* . . ."

"You scare me," Sev said. "And that's saying something."

"It's an opportunity we might not get again."

"So you fly, do you? Going to do a Jango?"

"You've got no style." Fi genuinely wanted to place a thermal detonator on the speeder. It could be set off remotely, giving them a relatively easy extra option for striking at the Seps that they might need soon. But he was also itching to smack Sev down a little. The man thought he was the galaxy's gift to adventure. So if he wanted adventure, Fi would show it to him, Omega-style.

It also just happened to be the safest way to cross the six-meter gap to the other roof—safer than asking the Seps across the way if they minded two commandos taking a look at their roof, anyway.

Fi edged backward and began placing the sections of ladder end-to-end. They slotted together neatly. Then he crawled back to the parapet and gave the chasm an appraising glance.

He peered across, then down six floors. "That'll reach."

"I reckon." Sev leaned over next to him. "So you're going to crawl across."

Fi took the end of the ladder and began to move it carefully to avoid loud scraping sounds. Sev took the other end and they balanced it lengthways on the parapet.

"No, I'm going to run."

"Fi, they say someone spiked my vat. But I reckon someone *really* spiked yours."

"Lost your nerve?"

"Di'kut."

"If I plummet heroically to my doom, then you can crawl across. Deal?"

"I hate it when you try to provoke me into showing you how it's done."

"Like this?"

Fi had seconds. They needed to be across the gap and gone before anyone spotted them. He leaned down hard on one end of the ladder, lifting it enough to swing it out horizontally and drop the other end on the facing parapet.

Thirty meters below, death waited. And if it wasn't death, it was paralysis.

He stepped up on the parapet, tested the first rung with his boot, and then focused straight ahead on the other side.

Then he sprinted.

He still had no idea how his body calculated the gaps but he hit every rung and landed on the far side, dropping flat. When he knelt upright, Sev was staring at him.

Fi beckoned. *Come on.*

Sev ran for it. Fi broke his landing as he jumped off the parapet. He noted Sev's clenched jaw with satisfaction.

"Easy," Fi mouthed.

Sev gave him a hand signal, one of his especially eloquent gestures of disapproval.

The roof had a few steps down to doors that the holoplans showed as access to the top floor of the living area and the turbolift shaft. They didn't look that substantial in the flesh, but the plans appeared to be accurate: they didn't always get updated after renovations. A quick application of thermal tape on the doors and it would be easy to lob a few grenades down the hole to soften up the residents before going in. Fi gave Sev a thumbs-up and took a magnetic det out of his belt. It slid into place in the speeder's air intake with a faint *thack.*

Back, Fi gestured.

He teetered on the parapet and then ran across the dura-steel rungs again, feeling them flex and spring back under his boots. When he looked back, Sev was lining up for the sprint, too. Fi beckoned encouragingly. Sev went for it.

He was two-thirds of the way across when he slipped. He grabbed for a rung and hung motionless from his right hand. Fi's gut somersaulted.

If anyone looks up here now—

Most people screamed when they fell. Sev, to his credit, was utterly silent. But his eyes were wide and scared. He tried to reach up with his left arm but for some reason didn't seem able to do it. Fi scrambled across the ladder on his belly and reached down to grab Sev's arm and haul him up. It was a potentially lethal maneuver on a narrow ladder, but Fi managed to get a grip on Sev's belt and pull him across the ladder crosswise.

Sev was using his right arm. It was only when Fi gripped his left shoulder to pull him in line with the ladder that he heard his sharp gasp and understood why he wasn't using that arm, and why he hadn't been able to lunge up to get a grip with his other hand. He'd hurt himself badly.

"Udesii . . . ," Fi whispered. "Take it easy."

There was pain, and there was whatever had happened to Sev. Fi dragged him back across the ladder a few centimeters at a time and rolled him onto the safety of the roof before hauling the ladder back in. When he dropped flat again, Sev was kneeling in a ball, clutching his left shoulder.

Fierfek, this is my fault for goading him. "Can you walk?" Fi whispered.

" 'Course I can walk, you *di'kut.* It's my arm."

"I'll let you drop next time, you ungrateful *chakaar.*" Fi hauled him upright and decided to risk taking the service turbolift down to the ground level. By the time they reached the end of the walkway it was clear that Sev had dislocated his shoulder and had to hold the arm against his chest to tolerate the pain at all. He said nothing but it had made his eyes water. Fi had long used that phrase to indicate extreme pain but it was the first time he'd seen it up close, and it wasn't funny.

"If I miss this mission, I'm going to show you a really interesting trick with a vibroblade."

"Sev, take it easy." Fi always kept his medpac on his belt. He fumbled for the single-use sharp of painkiller and stabbed it into Sev's triceps. "We'll slap some bacta on it back at base."

"Yeah, and maybe that'll work when I rip your head off, too."

"It was an accident."

"It was a stupid stunt. I never had accidents with Delta."

"Well, you're just Vau's perfect little soldier boys, then, aren't you? We screw up. And then we get up and go on."

"I *have* to complete this mission."

"Not if you're a liability you don't. Look, injuries happen. Stay at base and monitor the comlinks."

"You don't understand."

"Really?" Fi racked his brains for first-aid training. "Funny, I thought we did the same job. Look, get in here and let me have a look."

They slipped into the sheltered lobby of an office block and hid behind a pillar. Fi detached Sev's bodysuit sleeve from the shoulder seam and took a look in the dim security lights.

The line of the shoulder looked unnaturally square where the ball of the humerus had shifted out of the socket and was pushing the deltoid muscle up and out of shape. This was going to *hurt.*

"Okay, on the count of four," Fi said. He took Sev's wrist in his right hand, stretching out the arm, and braced his left hand against the man's chest. Then he paused and looked him in the eye in his most reassuring *I-know-what-I'm-doing* way. "See, when you get a dislocation like this, you have to do what they call *reducing* it by—*four!*"

Sev yelped. The joint made a wet *shhhlick* sound as it slipped back into the socket.

"Sorry, *ner vod.*" Fi folded Sev's arm back against his chest and held it there while he struggled to get the sleeve section reattached. He could almost feel the torn ligaments and muscle fibers screaming. Sev's face was white, his lips compressed. "Nothing worse than bracing for it, though."

"For a moron, you're not a bad medic."

"Kal said that if we could take a body apart, we ought to learn a bit more about putting it back together again if we needed to."

"Fi, I *have* to be fit to fight."

"Okay, okay. Bacta and ice packs. Right as rain in no time."

"Vau'll kill me."

"Look, what is this thing with Vau?" Fi pulled Sev out into the walkway again, and they jogged back to the speeder they'd left a block away. "I know he had a reputation for beating the stuffing out of trainees, but why are you ready to gut Atin?"

"Atin's sworn he'll kill Vau."

Fi almost stopped dead. "Atin? Old don't-interrupt-me-I'm-working-on-a-really-interesting-circuit? Our *At'ika*?"

"Seriously?" Sev asked.

"Yeah, sometimes I get serious. It happens."

"Okay. Atin's pod was the only one that ever lost men."

"Geonosis. Ruined Vau's clean record?"

"It's not that simple. Atin was doing that survivor guilt thing when he got back, and Vau just *focused* him a bit."

Odd: Skirata hadn't been around when Fi returned from Geonosis. But he'd worry about that later. "That explains the scar on his face."

"You got it."

"Doesn't explain the rest of the scars he was showing you."

"You ask *him* about that."

Sev was as near to scared as Fi had seen him. He couldn't imagine being afraid of Skirata. The man might have sworn himself to a standstill when he was angry, but nobody in Skirata's company ever felt they had to *fear* him. He was *Kal'buir:* he lavished ferocious care on his commandos to the exclusion of all else.

But Sev didn't want Vau to know that he'd injured himself doing something reckless. Whatever the reason, Fi owed his brother some support.

"Okay, we don't mention the shoulder." Fi started up the speeder. "We'll get it sorted ourselves. *Bard'ika* can do that Force healing if the bacta doesn't do the trick. But Vau needn't know."

For the first time since he'd met the man, Sev softened visibly.

"Thanks, *ner vod,*" he said. "I owe you."

17

So you want a knife, a nice sharp knife. You hone that blade to its limits. It even cuts through stone when you want it to. It saves your life. And then you're outraged when it cuts you accidentally. You see, knives don't switch off. And neither do people, not when you hone them to a fine edge.
—Sergeant Kal Skirata to General Arligan Zey, on the nature of training

Operational house, Qibbu's Hut,
0115 hours, 385 days after Geonosis

The Gurlanin opened its eyes, panting.

Etain couldn't tell one Gurlanin from another unless they allowed her to. They could shut out her Force-senses just as easily as they could reach out to her. She could detect nothing from the creature: no sense of identity, no emotion, and no purpose.

And then the air around her came to life with a shuddering sense of past, of long memory, and of *betrayal.*

"Girl," it said in a familiar liquid voice. "Can you do *nothing* right?"

"I . . . I know you," Etain said.

"Several of you know me." The creature lifted its head and tried to rise, but sank back down again. "Darman, is Atin well?"

"Fierfek." Darman edged forward and knelt down by the head of someone who had carried out vital intelligence work for the squad on Qiilura. Etain could see the pain on his face. Niner caught her eye and simply looked resigned, as if he expected everyone to betray them in the end. "Jinart?"

"Yes. I expect we all look the same to clones."

Darman almost grinned but appeared to stop himself. "Atin's fine."

Ordo cut in. "Just explain why you think killing my brothers is going to help Qiilura."

Jinart focused wild orange eyes on Etain and struggled into a sitting position, flanks heaving. Etain could sense her fully now, bitter and determined, calling out to the void with her mind: she was probably reaching telepathically to her consort Valaqil, once General Zey's agent both on Coruscant and Qiilura. Skirata had his right arm across his body, almost but not completely casual, clearly ready to reach for his Verpine and take a shot if Jinart moved.

"You think I am giving the Separatists information."

Ordo stepped in and Darman got out of his way. "I'm inclined to think that anyone who bothers to shapeshift into Vinna Jiss might do that, yes."

"She disappeared, like she often did. I simply adopted her form to move around unnoticed."

"*I* noticed. We'd already executed her."

"Then I made an error in taking her form."

"Too right you did. Now, what's your problem with the Grand Army? Why not target politicians? You could walk in anywhere—even the Senate chamber itself."

"You assume too much. Are you one of the renegade clones that Zey so dreads?"

"That's me," Ordo said.

"I am *not* the one leaking information to the Separatists. And I am *not* targeting anyone."

"Are you still working for General Zey?" Etain asked.

"No. My people no longer serve the Republic—if we ever served you at all. We had an agreement. You broke it."

"But—"

"We had an *agreement,* Jedi. You said you would give us back our world and stop the farmers from destroying us."

"In the middle of a war?"

"We *served* you in the middle of a war! When my people were dying of starvation, when our prey was being driven away by the colonists, we kept our bargain. And all you did—*you,* Jedi, you and Zey—was make them better able to fight and hold their land."

Etain didn't look at Darman. She didn't want to provoke him

into defending her or—more probably—catch a hint that he might agree with Jinart.

She thought that all she had done was to ensure the farmers were a guerrrilla force able to resist the Separatists, but the native Gurlanins didn't see it that way.

"We'll root out the informants sooner or later," Ordo said. "You can cooperate or not, but I might as well execute you now if you're not going to be useful. We can't handle any more prisoners."

It was always hard to tell if Ordo was playing the interrogation game or simply stating his intentions. Judging by Skirata's quick glance at him, it was the latter. He motioned Etain to stand clear and charged up the Verpine.

"I can identify the informants for you," Jinart said calmly.

Ordo simply held the muzzle to Jinart's head. Etain looked to Jusik, and then to Darman and Niner and Vau, but they were all simply watching impassively. Corr was engrossed in the holochart, still logging movements. Wennen sat in the chair, her hand to her brow as if shielding her eyes, but nobody was making any attempt to intervene. Etain's gut said it was *wrong.*

But she did nothing.

"You're bargaining," Ordo said. "I'll kill you anyway."

"You're the one who needs to bargain. This isn't about my life."

"Game's over." Ordo held the Verpine steady. Etain waited, torn by indecision. She could stop Ordo for a fraction of a second—

"Remove your forces and the colonists from my world and I will identify the Separatists for you."

Ordo—unblinking, passionless—lined the muzzle up about level where a normal animal's ear might be. "You haven't told me *why* you were mimicking Jiss. That actually interests me more."

"Ordo, I'll deal," Skirata said. "Stand down."

Ordo simply raised the Verp and held it back against his shoulder without hesitation. Etain imagined he would need to be coaxed into withdrawing: she'd seen the potential violence swirling within him constantly. But he obeyed Skirata without murmur.

The sergeant prodded Jinart with his boot. "You tell *me,* then, shapeshifer."

"I observe," Jinart said. "I watch to see when you move troops to and from Qiilura and how much you send to the farmers by way of aid to keep them loyal. All the things you never tell us, but that show your true intentions. I spy on you."

"Let me explain something," Skirata said. "I'm not the Republic. The work I do for them is actually for my own people—these lads here. So if you're not helping me keep my people alive, I'll make certain that Qiilura gets reduced to molten slag. And that's a promise. I'm not a Jedi and I'm not a politician, so I can do pretty well what I like. Your whole species is expendable. Understand?"

Jinart managed to get to her feet, or at least raise herself on her front legs.

"I will identify the people you want. But the Republic *must* agree to withdraw from Qiilura and remove the colonists within a year."

"Okay, let's get hold of Zey now," Skirata said. "If he doesn't agree, we move on and I'm not letting you melt back into the city."

"Do you know how many of us there are, or *where* we are?"

"I don't care. Zey might."

"My people are *here,* on Coruscant itself. You'll never track us down and we can be far more damaging than bombs."

"Look, the logistics leaks are a sideshow right now. Save it for Zey." Skirata opened his comlink. If the general was sleeping, then someone could go and wake him. War didn't keep office hours. "Supervisor Wennen, why don't you make us all some caf?"

He expected some complaint, but none came. She stood up, still clutching her ribs, and made her way unsteadily to the kitchen area.

"It's Besany, Sergeant," she said.

Yes, she's on our side. Result. "Okay, I'm Kal."

"Who likes it sweetened?"

"All of us," Skirata said. "Two big spoonfuls. It's going to be a long night."

Operational house, Qibbu's Hut,
0200 hours, 385 days after Geonosis

Darman sat cross-legged on the floor next to Jinart, hands clasped in his lap, as if he was watching her. Jinart watched him in return, orange eyes closing occasionally, her legs tucked under her.

Etain sometimes had to look closely to see if Darman was just thinking or actually asleep, because the impression he was making in the Force was so ambiguous. When she knelt beside him to check, though, his eyes were closed. For a brief moment she wondered if Jinart could make telepathic contact with him.

His eyes opened. He glanced behind Etain and then brushed his lips against her cheek.

"No word from Zey yet?"

Etain shook her head. There was nothing to hide any longer and she rested her forehead against his, not caring what anyone else thought: it was impossible to hide their relationship in a tight-knit group of soldiers living in one another's pockets. "He's got to consult people. Even Zey can't make those decisions on his own."

"You should have been a healer, you know. You're good at it."

"Well, let's see if I'm any good at healing rifts. I need to clear something up with Kal."

"Problem?"

"Nothing to worry about."

Etain knelt back on her heels and stood up in one movement. Skirata was talking to Niner and Ordo by the flimsi sheets on the wall, cleaning his beloved Verpine gun with slow care while they discussed the concentration of Separatists in various locations on the brightly colored 3-D grid of the holochart.

She caught Skirata's eye and beckoned him to follow her. He inclined his head in mute agreement and laid the dismantled Verpine parts on the table beside him, where they sat wrapped in distorted lines of colored light from the holochart projection.

They walked onto the landing platform. The strill was asleep on its stomach, all six legs spread out like an ill-shaped furry insect.

"I did something very foolish," Etain said.

"Again?"

"Ordo."

Skirata looked stunned then balanced on the brink of anger. *"Ordo?"*

"No, nothing like *that* . . . I used a command that I heard you use. It upset him. I called *check* to stop him from killing Jinart outright. He told me why I should never use it."

Skirata blew out a long breath. "And you understand *now*?"

"Yes. I'm sorry. He . . . he said he'd shoot me if I ever did it again."

"He would. Don't ever doubt it."

"I believe you."

"I never taught the Nulls that Jedi were their betters, you see, and I never taught them to obey the Republic, and no Kaminoan engineered them to be more cooperative than Jango. But they obey me for some reason, and even then I encourage them to question everything."

"Is he *programmed*?"

Skirata looked at her with sudden disgust. Then he simply swung his fist at her without warning, a savage punch, a street brawler's punch. She leapt back and drew her lightsaber in one movement, but his fist went past her head. *Deliberately.* She could see the calculation on his face. She held her breath, waiting for him to lash out again.

"So are *you* programmed?" he said.

The blue blade of energy thrummed as she brought the lightsaber down from a raised position and then thumbed it off, feeling stupid and ashamed.

She was also shocked at Skirata's reflexes: he could have landed that punch, and he clearly wasn't afraid of her lightsaber skills. She would *never* take him for granted again.

"No. I'm sorry."

"*You* should know better than anyone. You've been drilled in weapons handling from the same age that those boys were. Do you *think*? Or are you so well trained that your body just reacts"—he snapped his fingers—"like *that*?"

She had reacted all right. Her muscles remembered years of light-saber practice. Her Masters taught her to rely on instinct, on the Force, and *not* to think.

"I said I'm sorry."

"And so you should be. I taught *all* my boys that command from the very start. I drilled them over and over and over until they'd stop whatever they were doing *instantly.* And I did it for them, for times when it was needed to save *them* from something."

"I swear I'll never do it again."

"Ordo will never trust you now."

"But it only stopped him for a—"

"—a fraction of a second that could *get him killed.* You just used him. Like all the *aruetiise* do."

Skirata was furious: even in the dim light on the platform she could see that the skin of his neck was flushed, that telltale sign of strong reaction. In the last few weeks Etain sometimes felt that he saw her as the personification of the Republic, using his men for their own agenda, and that she was a handy target on which to vent his spleen. He didn't seem to view Jusik the same way, though.

Exploitation was a raw nerve in Skirata. Etain desperately wanted him to like her and make her feel like family, the way he did everyone else.

"I'll apologize to Ordo."

"Yeah, it really is him you need to make your peace with."

She wondered why she hadn't realized that to start with. *Do I really see them as men? Do I regret angering Ordo, or do I just want to be Skirata's little girl?* She turned on her heel and decided to confront it.

Ordo was having a tense conversation via his bead comlink, forefinger pressed to his ear. Jusik fiddled with some piece of circuitry, glancing up at him from time to time. The side of the conversation that Etain could hear suggested that someone on Zey's staff wasn't moving as fast as Ordo wished.

Jusik mouthed *Captain Maze* at her.

She waited. Ordo grunted. "I'll stand by." He shook his head and turned to her. "What's wrong?"

"Ordo, I owe you an apology. I was wrong to use the check command and you're right to be angry with me."

He just nodded. It still surprised her that a man who was physically identical to Darman could somehow look so different.

"I realize you had a bad deal, Ordo."

"On Kamino?"

"Even now, I think."

Ordo blinked a couple of times as if she wasn't making sense. She had no idea where his mind ranged in those split seconds other than that he felt like a flurry of activity in the Force.

"I didn't have a mother or a father, but a stranger willingly chose me to be his son. You had a mother and father, and they let strangers take you. No, General, don't pity me. *You're* the one who's had the worse deal."

It was shocking and it was *true.* The extraordinary clarity of his assessment hit her so hard that she almost gasped. It told her things she didn't want to know about herself. None of them changed her intentions. But she knew her motives better now, uncomfortable as they were.

She wondered if her real parents ever thought of her.

She would never know.

18

Withdraw from Qiilura? If that's what it takes to keep the Gurlanins from turning on us, it's a price we were going to pay anyway. We're too thinly stretched to maintain the garrison, and the Senate has no interest on continuing to support a mere two hundred thousand farmers on a backworld. Let me talk to Jinart and reassure her. The damage her people can do is enormous—far beyond the scope of one anti-terror operation. And we need them on our side.

—General Arligan Zey, to General Iri Camas and the chair of the Senate Committee on Refugees

The Kragget all-day restaurant, lower levels, Coruscant, 0755 hours, 385 days after Geonosis

Jinart the Gurlanin had kept her word and provided the information she had promised—and no more. Zey appeared to have kept his. The sleek black predator had slipped out into the Coruscant night and vanished.

But Skirata would always feel that she was standing right next to him in some guise or another. Like the Jedi, her hypernatural abilities—especially telepathy—made him wary and suspicious.

But she could only sense the thoughts of her own kind, they said. *Like that's some kind of comfort.*

Skirata finished his eggs, rubbed his hand across his chin, and realized he needed to shave again. But things that had seemed crushingly impossible in the early hours of the morning looked a lot more encouraging on a full stomach in broad daylight.

"Gurlanins on the loose?" Jaller Obrim's voice was almost a groan. "That's all we need."

"Yeah, that'll be one of the best-kept secrets of the war, I reckon."

"You believe them?"

"That they might be everywhere? You have to, Jaller. And I can't lose any sleep over a few Qiiluran farmers."

They sat side by side, looking out toward the walkway through the Kragget's grimy transparisteel front. Neither of them were men who wanted to sit with their backs to any door. Obrim leaned in a little toward him.

"So do you want us to pick up the suspects the Gurlanin identified?"

"No thanks."

"Is this where my eyesight and hearing fail again?"

"Right now, you can't even see me, let alone hear me," said Skirata.

"Okay. Organized Crime Unit isn't happy, but they understand the words *armed special forces* really well."

"It *was* OCU in the plaza, then?"

"I gather so."

"How did they end up there?"

"Your friend Qibbu uses well-worn channels of communications in the scum strata of society. OCU isn't stupid and it isn't deaf."

"Ah." *There is no monopoly of information.* Skirata's happily full stomach chilled a little. Obrim showed no signs of being smug. But he was almost certainly aware that Skirata was planning a sting operation involving explosives. "So they knew who the Seps were and didn't bother to—"

"No. That wasn't the route."

"What, then?"

"They were carrying out surveillance on a known criminal and that criminal happened to meet up with one of the group that you were watching. Message boy, one chance encounter." Obrim picked a chunk of smoked nerf from Skirata's plate and crunched on it thoughtfully. "You just be careful. I hate finding friends on the slab in the morgue."

Apart from Jusik, Obrim was one of the few nonclones Skirata felt he might be able to trust completely one day. He was still undecided on Etain. While he didn't doubt her sincerity, she had an emotional, impulsive streak of the kind that got people killed.

Like you. You're a fine one to talk.

"Your boys okay?"

"Tired, edgy, but giving it all they've got. One of 'em has sworn to gut Vau, another is having a love affair with a woman he shouldn't even look at, I'm collecting waifs and strays like an animal shelter, and we nearly killed a Treasury agent. But if I told you the *really* bad stuff, you'd think I had problems."

Obrim laughed raucously. "And people think they're good little droids . . ."

"Discipline apart, they're still lads."

The Twi'lek waitress topped up their caf and smiled alluringly. "Where's your son today?"

"At the office, sweetheart," Skirata said. "Won't I do instead?"

Her lekku coiled ever so slightly but he didn't have a clue what it meant. She glided away, glancing back to smile again. Obrim sniggered. "I see Ordo made an impression."

"They all have this naïve streak about them. It's fatally charming, apparently. Youth, muscle, heavy weapons, and a trusting expression. Maybe I should try it."

"Forty years too late."

"Yeah."

And then Skirata's communicator chirped. He lifted his wrist as close to his mouth as he could. Even in a restaurant full of police officers, he took few chances.

"We like what we see," said a voice with a Jabiimi accent.

It was interesting how accents were more noticeable over a comlink. Skirata, still looking toward the walkway, scanned his field of view without moving his head. He was sure he hadn't been followed—but this was a bad place to be spotted if he had. "It's not noon yet."

"I know, Kal. We're keen."

"What next?"

"Can you get to the bank plaza again in half an hour? I can't locate your comlink signal. But then I can understand why you're a *very* cautious man."

Too right, you chakaar. Bard'ika *went to a lot of trouble to make me invisible.* Skirata was ten minutes by speeder bike from the plaza. "I can just about make it if I hurry."

"This is just for a conversation. Be there, and don't bring anyone else."

The comlink went dead. Obrim chewed, silent, but his look said it all.

Skirata reached in his pocket and put some credits on the table to cover the bill. "You're deaf *and* blind, remember?"

Obrim pushed the credits back at him. "You pick up the tab *next* time."

It was his good-luck ritual. Obrim seemed to hope that by saying it, he'd ensure there *was* a next time.

Skirata had every intention of making sure there would be.

Lower level, skylane 348, 0820 hours, 385 days after Geonosis

Skirata kept the speeder at a steady pace and looped back on himself a couple of times. There was no reason to expect anyone to be following him, but he assumed it anyway. The maneuver also padded out the ten-minute journey to a credible half hour.

No point being too early.

His ankle was agony today.

"*Bard'ika,* how are you doing?"

Jusik's voice came over the comlink. "We've tracked a target moving to the plaza from the house that Fi and Sev recce'd. I think that confirms it's Perrive."

"But he won't come alone."

"So that means he'll probably have minders nearby that we haven't tagged. New ones."

"Fine."

"Vau's on his way," Jusik said. "They won't recognize him."

"And you?"

"I'm already there."

"Fierfek. He *knows* you. Wait for orders—"

"Trust me, he won't see me at all."

"Stand down. Get out of there."

"Okay."

"I mean it. And I'm going off the comlink now, unless I hit real problems."

He shut the link, exasperated. But it was his own fault. You couldn't delegate that much to a kid and then expect him to read your mind and work out when he was supposed to wait for specific orders again.

And he was a Jedi, after all. He could take care of himself.

Skirata pushed a bead comlink into his ear and brought the

speeder down in the public parking area. Enacca said she was fed up collecting abandoned speeders from around the city, and wanted to know why they couldn't bring their vessels and vehicles back with them every time. The logistics of operations like this depended on a lot of grim drudgery. He'd have to sweeten her up somehow when all this was over.

Out in the plaza, by the bench where he had awaited the Separatists the day before, stood Perrive.

He was busy looking like an executive waiting for a colleague: suit, document case, polished shoes. Skirata walked up to the man as briskly as he could with a complaining ankle.

"Okay, what's the deal?" Skirata said. He tried to focus on Perrive and not look over his shoulder for possible threats or—to be precise—Walon Vau. "I can get you the dets in twenty-four hours."

"Let's discuss this somewhere less crowded."

Those were often the worst words to hear at times like this. "Where?"

"Follow me."

Fierfek. He hoped Vau was watching him or Jusik was monitoring the conversation carefully. If Perrive moved too far out of the comlink's limited mike range, he'd have to make stupidly obvious comments to clue them in. Perrive didn't strike him as quite that naïve, even if his surveillance team was some way short of professional.

If Vau was here, Skirata couldn't see him.

But that was the point, and Vau was a very skilled operator.

Skirata followed Perrive across the plaza and back to the speeder parking area, a few moments that made him glad that he had a limp. It gave Vau, he hoped, a little more time to work out what was happening. Perrive stood looking around, and a shiny new green speeder with a closed cabin rose from below the level of the parking platform and maneuvered sideways to set down.

Ah well, Skirata thought. *I'd have done the same. But Perrive's lungs are coated with marker Dust, and Jusik can track this crate all the way.*

"Off you go," Perrive said.

"You're not coming, too?" *Oh no, no, no. Why didn't I dose myself with some of that* di'kutla *Dust?* "Forgive me if I get nervous about the quality of your associates' driving."

"Don't worry. All they'll do is blindfold you. Keep whatever weapons I'm sure you're carrying. I'll see you at our destination."

Skirata had no choice but to get in. Two human males—both

about thirty, one shaven-headed, one with thin blond hair scraped back in a tail, neither of them the hired help they had tagged yesterday—sat in the front seat, and the bald one leaned over to place a black fabric bag over his head in total silence. Skirata folded his arms to feel the comfort of his assorted hardware in his sleeve, holster, and belt.

"Well, this is fun," he said, hoping for a display of verbal stupidity that might help Jusik locate him.

But neither man responded. He didn't expect them to.

Concentrate on the movement. Work out the direction.

Skirata tried to count the number of times they seemed to swing right or left to get some idea of the route. They were in an automated skylane, so he could count the seconds and try to calculate the distance between turns, but it was a massive task. Ordo, with his faultless memory, would have had the skylane network memorized and calculated the times and distances at the same time. But Skirata was not a Null ARC trooper, just a smart and experienced soldier whose natural intelligence had been sharpened by having to cope with six hyperintelligent small boys.

He had no idea where he was. The speeder continued toward either a nerve-racking deal that would take them a step closer to striking at the heart of this Separatist network, or a lonely death.

Service tunnel beneath skylane 348, 0855 hours, 385 days after Geonosis

"*Bard'ika,* you'll never need to shave again when Kal catches you," Fi said.

"You seriously think I'm not going to follow him?" Jusik raced Ordo's Aratech speeder bike along the service tunnel that ran parallel to the skylane serving the southern edge of the plaza. Fi decided that Ordo had no sense of danger if he was happy to ride pillion with the Jedi at speeds approaching five hundred kph. But then the man was nuts anyway. Fi held on to the handgrip behind him for grim death. "Vau, can you still hear me?"

The comlink was breaking up, but audible. "I'm a few vehicles behind Perrive. He's transmitting like a Fleet beacon."

"Where's he heading?"

"Looks like Quadrant N-Oh-Nine."

"What's there besides offices and residential?"

"That's about it. Stand by."

Jusik made an irritated grunt that he seemed to have picked up from Sev and accelerated. At times like this Fi had passed beyond the first flush of adrenaline and into a cold and rational world where everything made sense to his body if not to his brain. He found an instinctive sense of effortless balance as Jusik wove through the ducts, clearing some of the transverse durasteel joists by a breath. Speed no longer felt like conscious fun, as it had in training, but he was beyond fear for himself at that moment.

All he could think of was Sergeant Kal.

"He can take care of himself," Jusik said. "He's packing more weapons than the Galactic Marines."

"Are you telepathic?" The thought disturbed Fi, because his mind was the only private retreat he had. "I was just—"

"If you're not as worried for him as I am, then I've read you all wrong, my friend."

"Bard'ika . . ."

"Yes? Too fast? Look—"

"Even if you didn't have your Force powers, you'd still be a terrific soldier. And a good man."

Fi couldn't see the Jedi's expression. For once, Jusik didn't scare the living daylights out of Fi and look back over his shoulder with a silly grin when they were hurtling toward a wall, only to bank sharply at the last moment. Jusik dropped his head for a second and then raised it again. His slipstreamed hair slapped Fi in the face.

"I'll try to live up to that."

"Yeah, but you still need to get your *shabla* hair cut."

Jusik didn't laugh. Fi wasn't sure if he was moved or offended. And it seemed impossible to offend Jusik.

"Hang on."

Whatever element of the Force was guiding the Jedi, it was completely instinctive. He could find Skirata.

The speeder swung hard left and Fi feared for the Verpine rifle under his jacket, its folded stock wedged in his armpit. He was used to wearing the scruffy assortment of dull civilian clothing that Enacca had sent over with Vau. He wondered how he'd cope with his all-encompassing Katarn armor after being out of it for two weeks.

Jusik's head jerked around as if someone had summoned him. "He's heading for business zone six."

"Been there. Recce'd that place last night. Stuck a remote holocam opposite the house, in fact."

"Maybe the Force is giving us a break."

"That's *got* to be their hub."

"Let's try that." Jusik banked right to shoot up a vertical channel. Fi decided zero-g had its appeal. "At least we'll be able to see Kal if that's where they're heading. I bet that's reassuring."

"It would be."

"But?"

"But if they're using the speeder that was parked in their roof space last night, I clamped a remote thermal detonator in its air intake."

"Just remote? Not timed?"

"Yeah."

"That's okay then."

If—when—they got Skirata back in one piece, Fi would tell him. He had a sense of humor.

"There's somebody following him," Jusik said.

"Yeah. You, me, Vau . . ."

"No, not us."

"Escort for the speeder?"

"No, nothing like that at all. Someone else. I don't get any sense of malice. But it's not the strike team."

"What's that feel like?"

"Like someone standing behind me." He took one hand off the steering and tapped the back of his head behind his ear. The speeder swerved. "Right *there.*"

"Both hands, *Bard'ika* . . ."

"Sorry. Whoever it is, they're focused on Kal."

"Should we be worried?"

"No."

Jusik twisted the handlebars and the speeder accelerated as if it had been fired from a Verpine. Fi bit his lip and couldn't stop his knees from pressing harder into the speeder bike's fuselage.

If he dropped the precious sniper rifle, Skirata would be heartbroken.

"That's all right, then," Fi said. "I won't worry at all."

Residential area, business zone 6, 0930 hours,
385 days after Geonosis

The airspeeder settled, hot alloy clicking as its drive cooled, and someone pulled the black hood off Skirata's head.

"This way," said the shaven-headed man. "Mind the steps."

Skirata walked down from a rooftop parking area through doors to a tastefully decorated room with a large, grainless pale wood table and thick deep gray carpet. They weren't short of credits, then. Some terrorism was the war of the dispossessed, and some was the handiwork of the rich who felt secondhand outrage. Either way, it was an expensive sport.

He was a mercenary. He knew the price of everything.

He sat down in the chair offered, elbows braced on the table, and tried to take in as much useful detail of his surroundings as he could. *Two visible escape routes: back out those doors, or down the turbolift.* After ten minutes, a middle-aged human male entered with a woman of similar age: there was nothing remarkable about either of them. They simply nodded to Skirata and sat down facing him. Four more men followed, one of them about Jusik's age, and Skirata found himself surrounded at the table by six people.

Then Perrive walked in.

"You'll excuse us for not introducing ourselves, Kal," he said. "I know you and you know me, and that's probably all you need to know."

"Apart from the bank details, yes."

Perrive stood by the chair opposite Skirata and glanced pointedly at the man sitting in it, who then moved to another chair. *You're definitely the boss, then.* And the others around the table—who were obviously assessing him as a supplier—didn't look like junior minions. This was either the terror cabinet or a rare gathering of cell leaders. It had to be. Perrive handed the man next to him the small sample pack that Skirata had supplied the day before, and he examined it carefully before passing it around the table.

Yes, they'll be the ones distributing this. I should blow this place now. But that's not sensible. Just satisfying.

"We'd like all hundred kilos of your goods and four thousand detonators."

Skirata did a quick calculation. About twenty-five grams of five-hundred-grade thermal per device, then: a Bravo Eight Depot incident took the equivalent of two of those. Enough bomb-making kit for that level of carnage every day for five years, or a lower body count and mutilation for more than ten. A very economical war.

"How much?"

"Two million credits."

Skirata didn't even pause to think. "Five."

"Two."

"Five."

"Three."

"Five, or I need to go and talk to my other customers."

"You don't have any others who want *this* kind of explosive."

"If you think that, then you're new in this galaxy, son."

"Three million credits. Take it or leave it."

Skirata got up and really did intend to walk. He had to look as if he meant it. He skirted the table as far as Perrive and then the man turned and put his hand on Skirata's right arm. Skirata jerked it back, and he wasn't acting the jumpy mercenary. It was his knife arm. Perrive noticed, eyebrows raised for a fraction of a second.

"Four million," Perrive said.

Skirata paused and chewed the inside of his cheek. "Four, credits to be deposited and confirmed as being in my account before I release the goods, and I want the deal done in the next forty-eight hours."

"That requires trust."

"If I don't have any other customers, then why would I want a hundred kilos of explosives hanging around my premises until Mustafar freezes over?"

Perrive paused and then almost smiled. "Agreed."

Skirata reached in his pocket and handed him a datachip, stripped of all information except a numbered account that would exist only from noon for forty-eight hours. He had a constant stream of accounts like that. All the Nulls could slice like top pros, but Jaing was an artist among data deceivers. *My clever lad.* "Time and place, then."

"All in one delivery."

"Okay. But it stays wrapped in quarter-kilo packs bagged in tens, because I'm not going to unwrap every *di'kutla* bar and get covered in forensic evidence." He paused, trying to look as if he was thinking of another reason. "And that's two and a half kilos a bag, which is going to be easier for you to move."

"What makes you think we're going to move it?"

Smart, eh? "If you're keeping that all in one place, you're insane. I'm used to handling the stuff and even *I* don't like it around me. You do know what five-hundred-grade does, don't you?"

"Of course I do," Perrive said. "It's my business. Let's say midnight tomorrow. Here."

"If I knew where *here* was, I might agree."

"We'll let you walk out and then you'll see."

"I can land speeders on your roof, can I?"

"Up to Metrocab size."

"I'll probably bring two small speeders. I'll call you half an hour before."

"I haven't given you my number."

"Better do that, then, or you won't get your goods. I don't want any further contact until then—and I don't want anyone following me when I leave here. Okay?"

Perrive nodded. "Agreed."

And it was that simple. It never ceased to amaze Skirata how much simpler it was to buy and sell death than it was to pay taxes. "Show me to the front door, then."

Shaven-Head took him down in the polished durasteel turbolift—it always reminded him of Kamino, that brutally clinical finish—and walked him through a ground floor that was just one square room with no rear exit and one door at the front.

Easier to defend—if you were confident you could escape via the roof.

The doors parted. Kal Skirata stepped out onto a secluded walkway and found himself in affluent Coruscanti suburbia. He checked the position of the sun and began walking in the direction of the main skylanes. If he kept walking east, he'd come to the office sector sooner or later. Besides, the holocam that Fi and Sev placed a few hours earlier was watching him right now from the building opposite.

There were a lot of pedestrians about.

Skirata clicked his back teeth and opened the comlink channel. He didn't like the bead comlink any better than he liked wearing a hearing enhancer.

"Listen up, *ad'ike,*" he said as quietly as he could. "Game on. *Game on!*"

Logistics center, Grand Army of the Republic, Coruscant Command HQ, 0940 hours, 385 days after Geonosis

"Do I look as if I've been flattened by a . . . *PIP* laser?" Besany Wennen asked.

"*PEP* laser." Ordo, posing as Corr again, helmet tucked under his left arm, let her pass through the logistics center's doors ahead of him as *Kal'buir* had told him. It was the polite thing to do. "And no. You just look tired."

"I can't say it's been a typical day's duty for me."

"I respect your willingness to accept this without wanting to complain to your superiors."

"If I did, I'd compromise your mission, wouldn't I?"

"Possibly."

"Then it's just a bad bruise and an interesting evening. No more."

She was as tall as he was and looked him straight in the eye: her dark eyes made her light blond hair seem exotic in contrast. *She's different. She's special.* He made a conscious effort to concentrate.

"I'll make sure you have acceptable records for your bosses to show that the investigation was completed," Ordo said.

"And that the suspects . . . let's say that I learned they were of interest to military intelligence, so I withdrew from further involvement."

"Well, I can guarantee they won't be troubling you any longer."

Ordo was still waiting for her to ask exactly what Vau had done to the real Vinna Jiss, and what Ordo was going to do to the employees leaking information—Jinart had identified two—and a thousand other questions. He would have wanted to know *everything,* but Wennen just stuck to what she needed to know to close down her part of the surveillance. He didn't understand that reaction at all.

"What happens to you now?" he asked.

"I go back to my own department in the morning and pick up the next file. Probably corporate tax evasion." She slowed him down with a careful hand on his arm. He let that touch thrill him now. He was still uneasy, but he was less disturbed by the attraction. "What about you?"

"Reducing payroll numbers. Fi suggested we call it *staff turnover,* in the spirit of military euphemism."

It seemed to take her a couple of moments to work out what he meant. She frowned slightly. "Won't whoever they're reporting to notice they're missing?"

"Jinart says they only call in every four or five days. That gives us a time window to work within."

"Aren't you ever afraid?"

"When the shooting starts, frequently." It struck him that she probably found the idea of assassination uncomfortable, but she didn't say so. "But not as afraid as I would be if I were operating without weapons. Your superiors really should arm you."

They reached the doors to the operations room. She stopped dead.

"I know this has nothing to do with me any longer, but will you do something for me?"

"If I can."

"I want to know when you make it through this." She seemed to lose some composure. "And your brothers, and your ferocious little sergeant, of course. I rather like him. Will you call me? I don't need details. Just a word to let me know that it went okay, whatever *it* is."

"I think we can manage that," Ordo said.

This was where he turned left to go to Accounts, to find Hela Madiry, a woman clerk nearing retirement age—just an ordinary woman who happened to have distant cousins on Jabiim. Then he would pay a visit to Transport Maintenance, and look up a young man who had no family allegiance or ideology in this war but who liked the credits that the Separatists paid him. Their motives made no difference: they would both die very soon.

"Be careful . . . Trooper Corr," Besany said.

Ordo touched gloved fingers to his forehead in an informal salute.

"You too, ma'am. You too."

Business zone 6, walkway 10 at the junction of skylane 348,
0950 hours, 385 days after Geonosis

Fi braced for a verbal barrage as Jusik brought the speeder to a stop at the end of the walkway and settled it on the edge of the taxi platform. Skirata walked up to them straight-faced through the scattering of pedestrians and stood with his hands thrust in the pockets of his leather jacket.

"You're leading Fi astray, *Bard'ika.*"

"I'm sorry, but you told me that you should never enter an enemy stronghold without backup if you could help it."

"I hate it when people take notice of me. Fi, what's wrong?"

Fi was still looking around, trying to cover three dimensions that might conceal a threat. Jusik had said that whoever was following Skirata had no malicious intention, but Fi reasoned that not everyone who was going to kill you had a sense of malice. He'd killed plenty of people without any ill feeling whatsoever. While the Force was fascinating, Fi liked to see things through the scope of his Deece, preferably with the red target acquisition icon pulsing.

He put his hand under his jacket to slide the rifle from under his arm. This was when the unusually short barrel and folding stock came into their own. You could still use the weapon at short range. "*Bard'ika* thinks there's someone following you."

"I normally notice."

"But you're deaf."

"Partially, you cheeky *di'kut."* Skirata resorted to his reflex of straightening his right arm to have his knife ready. "Well, maybe we'd better move on before they catch up."

"Nobody with ill intent," Jusik said. He slid his hand to the opening of his jacket, suddenly edgy. Fi took his cue and swung off the speeder to stand in front of Skirata. "And they're very, very close."

"Steady, son. Public place, people around. No lightsaber, okay?"

"*Very* close." Jusik looked past Skirata.

A young man with short white-blond hair was striding toward them through the sparse crowd, arms held a little away from his sides, a large bag over one shoulder. His knee-length dark blue coat was wide open. But that didn't mean he wasn't carrying an armory under there somewhere. Fi unfolded the Verp's stock one-handed under his jacket and prepared to draw it and fire.

The man then held both hands up at shoulder level and grinned.

"Fierfek," Skirata breathed. "*Udesii,* lads. It's okay."

The blond man—Fi's height, very athletic—walked straight up to Skirata and crushed him in an enthusiastic hug. *"Su'cuy, Buir!"*

Father. Fi knew the voice.

"Suc'uy, ad'ika. Tion vaii gar ru'cuyi?"

"N'oya'kari gihaal, Buir." The man looked almost tearful: his pale blue eyes were brimming. He wiped them with the heel of his hand. "If I'm not careful I'll wash out this iris dye."

"That hair doesn't suit you, either."

"I can change that, too. I've got lots of different colors. Did you like what I added to the five-hundred-grade thermal?"

"Ah. I did wonder."

"I'm still a better chemist than *Ord'ika, Kal'buir.*"

Fi finally saw the face in front of him as a negative image, and suddenly imagined dark hair and eyes, and realized why the man was familiar. He wasn't one of Skirata's own sons. He was a clone, just like Fi: or, to be precise, just like Ordo. It was astonishing how much difference pigmentation alone made to someone's appearance: a simple but effective disguise, for casual use anyway.

Skirata beamed at him with evident pride. "Lads, this is ARC Trooper Lieutenant N-7," he said. "My boy Mereel."

So this was Mereel. And even though Fi's *Mando'a* wasn't perfect, he understood that Skirata had asked him where he'd been, and that the ARC trooper had said that he'd been hunting fish-meal.

Fi was fascinated. But he kept his fascination to himself.

19

I had no mother and no father. I was four years old when they first put a weapon in my hands. I was taught to suppress my feelings, and to respect and obey my Masters. I was encouraged to be obsessive about perfection. It wasn't the life I would have chosen, but the one ordained because of my genes—just like the men I'm expected to command. But now I have something wonderful, something I have chosen. And I will never let anyone take the child I'm carrying.

—General Etain Tur-Mukan, private journal

GAR logistics center, 1230 hours, 385 days after Geonosis

It was lunchtime.

The biggest decision most people made at that time of day in the logistics center was whether to eat in the cafeteria or find a spot in the public courtyard nearby to enjoy an open-air snack.

Ordo's decision was whether to use the Verpine, or walk up to the traitor Hela Madiry, maneuver her into a shadowy alcove, and then garrote her or cut her throat.

Verpine. Best choice. Fast and silent, as long as the projectile didn't pass through her and hit something that made a noise.

Madiry sat in the shadow of a planter filled with vivid yellow shrubs, eating a mealbread stick and reading a holozine, oblivious to her life expectancy. Ordo sat in the shade of a manicured tree with his datapad on his lap, calculating her remaining life in minutes.

There was nobody within ten meters of her, but there *was* a security holocam.

A man sat down on the bench beside him. "Well, our young friend in Transport Maintenance just had an unfortunate accident with a repulsorlift platform. Thanks for the use of your security codes."

"And he didn't turn into a Gurlanin, I hope."

Mereel looked utterly alien with light hair and eyes. Even his skin was tinted two shades paler. It didn't suit him. "No, *vod'ika,* he turned into a dead human. Skulls and repulsorlifts don't mix. Trust me."

"Just checking."

"You haven't told *Kal'buir* about Ko Sai yet, have you?" Mereel asked.

"I thought he might be less distracted if we wait until this mission is completed."

"He's a true *verd,* a warrior. He's never distracted when the shooting starts."

"There's no rush," Ordo said.

Mereel shrugged. Out of armor and *kama,* he slouched in a convincingly civilian manner. "So, shall I wander off?"

Ordo was watching the security holocam that covered the area between the woman and the public refreshers twenty meters beyond. "Can you disrupt that holocam circuit for me on my mark?"

Mereel felt in his coat for something and pulled out a slim stylus. It was an EMP disruptor. "I can do it without leaving my seat, *ner vod.*"

"Okay, I'll give you a reminder to kill the cam when I'm five meters from her."

Mereel tapped his ear. "Comlink on."

Ordo took a few slows breaths. He had removed the folding stock from the Verpine rifle; it was now short enough to conceal under a document holder. He looked like any other anonymous, helmeted, convalescing clone trooper playing office boy and carting archived flimsi around.

"Go," Ordo said, and stood up.

He walked toward the refreshers, which took him on a path past the Madiry woman.

"Mereel, kill the cam."

He had a few moments now before a security console spotted the outtage and tried to fix it. He took five fast strides and bent over Madiry as if to ask her a question.

She looked up as if an old friend had startled her. "Hello, trooper."

"Hello, *aruetii,*" Ordo said. He drew the Verp and put two rounds point-blank through her forehead and a third down at an angle through her upper chest. One round thudded through into the planter of soil behind her. Ordo had no idea where the other two went, but the informant was now dead and she simply slumped, head down as if still reading, a pool of her bright blood on the holozine's screen.

Ordo slipped the Verp back under the document folder and walked away. It had taken less than ten seconds from cuing Mereel to walking away.

Nobody even looked at him as he strode calmly toward the GAR complex, passed it, and met Mereel on the other side of the speeder parking bays. They disappeared into the sea of vehicles and mounted the Aratech speeder bike to head back to base.

Kal'buir had always told the Nulls they were instant death on legs. Ordo liked to live up to that assessment. His thoughts were on Besany Wennen as he rode off, and how it was good that he hadn't had to kill her, too.

Operational house, Qibbu's Hut, 1330 hours,
385 days after Geonosis

The more the tagged targets moved around Coruscant, the clearer the strike team's task became.

"That," Fi said admiringly, "gets better every time I look at it, *Bard'ika.*"

Jusik stared at the Coruscant holochart with a big grin and basked in the approval. The telltale red traces of the marked terrorists as they moved around the city were forming a pattern that firsthand surveillance would have struggled to build up.

"It was obvious, really," he said. "You'd have come up with it yourselves sooner or later."

Vau put down a bowl of milk in front of the strill. It lapped noisily, showering droplets across the carpet. "I vote that Dust-tagging becomes standard surveillance procedure. It's a matter for your sergeant, of course."

The police interloper's trace had been removed. Jaller Obrim had given her a painless and unnoticeable EMP sweep to kill transmissions from the marker powder she had inhaled. Now just five marked targets moved around the grids of blue light, building an accurate picture of where they went and where they stayed. The division between the two was now very much easier to see. Four locations—the house in banking sector 9, the landing strip used by the fresh farm produce importers, and two apartments in the retail sector—were clearly the most visited.

"But we probably only tagged Perrive's hired help," Fi said. "We want the bigger guys."

"The bigger guys," Vau said, "need the hired help by their side. All this activity is connected to the fact that they're about to receive explosives they badly need. Now, we know they used dead letter drops, for want of a better phrase, to avoid direct contact between the various terror cells in the network. It's how they ensure there's no way of tracing them back. So what does this tell you?"

Fi studied the hypnotic blue and red light in front of him. "They're moving back and forth between locations over and over."

"And therefore?"

"Therefore . . . they're either one cell . . . or they're several cells who have abandoned security precautions and are making direct contact with each other."

"Well done, Fi."

Fi didn't care for Vau but he enjoyed praise. He savored the moment. "So what do you think we've got here?"

"Given that this centered on the explosives, I think we're looking at the manufacturing cell—the people who make the bombs. Possibly also the ones who place them. Setting a complex device in a location or on a vessel can be a fiddly business, and I reckon this lot would do it themselves. They need to be mobile to get to different target locations, too, hence the need for a busy landing strip—nobody notices more traffic movement there. Now, Fi, *that's* a group of people worth taking out. Those are hard skills to replace in a hurry."

Jusik gave Fi a playful punch on the shoulder, elated. "Result!" He seemed to see it as a big puzzle to be taken apart. If Fi hadn't seen Jusik use a lightsaber, he would have taken him for a boy who just liked playing with complicated kit. "Time to make their eyes water, eh, Fi?"

"You got it."

"Delta has recce'd the landing strip. You've recce'd the house in the banking sector. That just leaves the two apartments, and Ordo and Mereel have stopped off to recce those now."

The strill had finished its milk, most of which had ended up on the carpet. Vau—a sergeant who believed in thrashing courage into his men, a sergeant who had scarred Atin badly—grabbed a cloth from the kitchen area and mopped up the damp patches. Then he took a clean rag, soaked it, and wiped the strill's mouth and jowls as if it were a baby. The animal accepted the indignity and rumbled with happiness.

Fi wasn't sure he would ever know what went on in the heads of nonclones.

Delta and Omega assembled in the main room, finding seats where they could, and spent the next hour planning three house assaults and a raid on an airstrip. They were basic maneuvers they had drilled for time and again on Kamino; they'd done it for real more than once, too. They had fairly recent plans of the buildings—not to be relied upon absolutely, of course—and covert holocam surveillance. Apart from the fact that the squads were used to operating alone, it was as near a done deal as an operation could be.

Planning. It was all about *planning*.

But there was always a surprise, always one more factor you hadn't allowed for or didn't see.

Fi planned for that, too. They all did, deep down.

Operational house, Qibbu's Hut, 1530 hours, 385 days after Geonosis

Etain knew.

She had known it would happen in time, but it had happened *now,* in two brief, wonderful weeks. The Force landscape that surrounded her had changed subtly and she felt strangeness and purpose within her, purpose that was *someone else's*.

It was said that Force-sensitive females could often detect the moment that they conceived. And it was true.

Etain stood on the landing platform for a while, searching for the fear she always imagined might come with taking that irrevocable step and not knowing its full consequences. But there was no fear. There was simply a pleasant sensation of certainty, almost like hands pressing on her shoulders.

And a clear vision, in the part of her brain that saw the universe without images, showed a new path through trails of webbed, colored light. In her prosaic way, it reminded her of a holochart, but it was less solid, its threads and lines shifting.

The new path that was marked through the tangle of colored threads was pale, silver, and thick, and from it sprouted silver tendrils that snaked into the tangles of the rest of the image. This new life she carried would be significant, and it would touch many others.

The Force was clear if you listened carefully to it: and this time it said *This is not wrong.*

On Qiilura, I envied Jinart her certainty. I envied Master Fulier that quality, too. And now I have it at last.

It was almost blissful. She savored the warm sun on her face, eyes closed for a few moments, and then walked back into the main room. It seemed oddly empty: Delta and Omega were catching up on sleep, doors shut. Ordo had disappeared with Mereel, and Corr had left a datapad running to log movements of suspects on the holochart while he went for a meal.

Vau stretched out in one chair with the strill on his lap while Skirata sat opposite him, boots up on the low table, eyes closed, hands clasped on his chest. Etain watched him, knowing that she might need to tell him even before she told Darman: she would need Skirata's help, his list of contacts and places to disappear.

Darman would be overwhelmed by it all when he needed to keep his mind on fighting. But Skirata was a man of the world, never fazed by anything; he would understand what she was giving Darman, and want to help.

Not yet, though.

While she watched Skirata, Niner wandered out of his room in his red fatigues, scratching his head with both hands. He poured a glass of water and walked across the room in slow silence to stand contemplating the sleeping Skirata with a slight frown. Then he went back to his room. He emerged a few moments later with a blanket and eased it over his sergeant, tucking it around him carefully. For once the man didn't stir.

Niner stood over him for a while, simply looking down at his face, lost in thought.

"He's okay," Etain whispered.

"Just checking," Niner said quietly, and returned to his room.

Etain defocused for a few moments and sought Darman in the Force: as ever, he was a well of calm and certainty, even while sleeping. When she focused on the room again, she realized Skirata had opened his eyes.

"You okay, *ad'ika*?" he said. "Was that Niner just now?"

"I'm fine." He *was* in a better mood now. Perhaps he regarded the matter between her and Ordo as closed. "Yes. He was checking on you."

"He's a good lad. But he ought to be getting some sleep." He raked his hair with his fingers, yawning. "Fatigue affects your judgment."

"But not yours," Vau said quietly.

Skirata was alert in a heartbeat and swung his legs off the table onto the floor. Vau could wind him up as surely as a mechanical toy. "If I don't move fast enough when the shooting starts, that's my problem. I'm used to it."

"Yes, we all know." Vau turned to Etain. "This is normally where he starts lecturing me on his ghastly childhood as a starving war orphan living feral on some bomb site, and how I just ran away to become a mercenary because I was bored with my idle, rich family."

"Well, that saved me some time," Skirata said irritably. "What he said."

"You have a family, Vau?" Etain was suddenly mesmerized by people who had lives and parents. "Are you in contact with them?"

"No. They cut me off when I declined to choose the career they wanted for me."

"Wife? Children?"

"Dear girl, we're *Cuy'val Dar*. People who have to disappear for eight years or more aren't the family kind. Except Kal, of course. But your family didn't wait for you, did they? That's all right, though. You've got a *lot* more sons now."

If Etain had known nothing of Skirata, or even Vau, it was the kind of jibe guaranteed to start a fight. Skirata was absolutely and instantly white with anger. One thing she knew about Mandalorians was that clan was a matter of honor. Skirata walked up to Vau very slowly and the strill woke, whining.

Etain checked that Skirata's jacket with its lethal array of blades was still hanging over the back of the chair.

Skirata shook his head, slow and deliberate. Vau was much taller and a few kilos heavier but Skirata never seemed to worry about that kind of detail.

"But that's the good thing about being *Mando*. If you don't get the family you want, you can go and choose one yourself." He looked suddenly older and very sad, small, crushed by time. "You going to tell her? Okay, Etain, my sons *disowned* me. In Mandalorian law, children can legally disown a parent who's shamed them, but it's rare. My sons left with their mother when we split up, and when I disappeared to Kamino and they couldn't locate me, they declared me *dar'buir*. No longer a father."

"Oh my. Oh, I'm sorry." Etain knew how serious that would be for a *Mando'ad*. "You found that out when you left Kamino?"

"No. Jango brought the news back that they were looking for me about . . . oh, four years in? Three maybe? I forget. Two sons and a daughter. Tor, Ijaat, and Ruusaan."

"Why were they looking for you?"

"My ex-wife died. They wanted me to know."

"Oh . . ."

"Yeah."

"But you could have told them where you were at the time. Jango could have talked to them."

"And?"

"You could have made your peace with them."

"And?"

"Kal, you could have *explained* to them somehow and stopped it."

"And reveal we had an army in training? And compromise my lads' safety? *Never.* And not a word to any of the boys, you hear? It's the only thing I ever kept from them."

He'd sacrificed his good name and the last possibility of his family's love and forgiveness for the men he was training. It hit Etain hard in the chest like a blow.

She turned to Vau. "Do you see your men as your sons?"

"Of course I do. I have no others. It's why I made them into survivors. Don't think I don't love them just because I don't spoil them like kids."

"Here we go," Skirata said, all contempt. "He's going to tell you that his father beat the *osik* out of him and it made a man of him. Never did *him* any harm, no sir."

"I've lost just three men out of my batch, Kal. That tells me a *lot* about my methods."

"So I lost fourteen. You making a point?"

"You made yours *soft.* They don't have that killer edge."

"No, I didn't brutalize mine like you did yours, you *hut'uun.*"

Etain stepped between them, arms held out, pieces of old conversations falling into place with awful clarity. The strill began rumbling in its throat and dropped to the floor to pace protectively in front of Vau.

It was just as well the bedroom doors were shut.

"Please, stop this. We don't want the men to hear you fighting right now, do we? Like Niner says—save it for the enemy."

Skirata turned his head with that sudden total focus that left Etain tasting a ripple in the Force. But it wasn't the angry reaction of a man who had been stung by painful observation. It was genuine anguish. He glanced down at Mird as if considering giving it a good kick, then limped off to the landing platform.

"Don't do this to him," she said to Vau. "Please. Don't."

Vau simply shrugged and picked up the huge strill in his arms as if it were a pup. It licked his face adoringly. "You can fight ice-cold or you can fight red-hot. Kal fights hot. It's his weakness."

"You sound just like an old Master of mine," Etain said, and went out to the platform after Skirata.

Coruscant's skylanes stretched above and below them, giving an illusion of infinity. Etain leaned on the safety rail with her head level with Skirata's as they gazed down. She searched his face.

"Kal, if you'd like me to do something about Vau—"

He shook his head quickly, eyes still downcast. "Thanks, *ad'ika,* but I can handle that heap of *osik.*"

"Never let a bully manipulate you."

Skirata's jaw worked silently. "I'm to blame."

"For what?"

"Sending boys to their deaths."

"Kal, don't do this to yourself."

"I took the credits, didn't I? Jango whistled and I came running. I trained them from boys. *Little boys.* Eight, nine years of nothing but training and fighting. No past, no childhood, no future."

"Kal . . ."

"They don't go out. They don't get drunk. They don't chase women. We drill them and medicate them and shunt them from battle to battle without a day off, no rest, no fun, and then we scrape them off the battlefield and send what's left standing back to the front."

"And you alongside them. You gave them a heritage, and a family."

"I'm as bad as Vau."

"If you hadn't been there, your place would have been taken by another like *him.* You gave your men respect and affection."

Skirata let out a long breath and folded his hands, elbows still braced on the rail of the balcony. A speeder horn blared far below them. "You know something? *Live-fire exercises.* They started five years into their development. That means I sent ten-year-old boys to die. And eleven, and twelve, and right on up to the time they were men. I lost four of my batch in training accidents, and—some of those were even down to me, *my* rifle, *my* realism. Think about *that.*"

"I hear that happens in any army."

"So ask me the question, then. Why didn't I ever say, *Whoa, enough*? I've had some unkind thoughts about you, *ad'ika,* why your kind never refused to lead an army of slaves. And then I thought, Kal, you *hut'uun,* you're just the same as her. You never stood up against it."

"Your soldiers worship you."

Skirata closed his eyes then screwed them tight shut for a moment. "You think that makes me feel better? That stinking strill loves Vau. Monsters get loved irrationally all the time."

Etain wondered whether to soothe him by judiciously influencing his mind that *he would not feel guilty.* But Skirata was his own man, tough-minded enough to spot her mind influence and shrug her manipulation aside. If she asked him for his cooperation . . . no, Skirata would never take the easy path. She had no comfort to offer him that wouldn't make matters worse.

That was part of his unique and appealing courage. Her first impression was that he would be a man whose bluff exterior was simply embarrassed machismo. But Skirata wasn't embarrassed about his emotions at all. He had the guts to wear his heart on his sleeve. It was probably what made him even more effective at killing: he could love as hard as he could punch.

Force, stop reminding me. Duality. I know. I know you can't have light without dark.

Her spiritual struggles were irrelevant now. She was carrying Darman's child. She longed to tell him and knew she had to wait.

"You love them, Kal, and love is never wrong."

"Yes, I do." His hard, lined face was an icon of passionate sincerity. "All of them. I started with one hundred and four trainees, plus my Null lads, and now I've got ninety commandos left. They say parents should never have to outlive their kid. But I'm outliving them all, and I suppose that punishment serves me right. I was a rotten father."

"But—"

"No." He held up his hand to stop her, and she paused. Skirata was benign but absolute authority. "It's not what you think. I'm not using these lads to salve my conscience. They deserve better than that. I'm just using what I've *learned*—for them."

"Does it matter, as long as they're loved?"

"Yes, it *does.* I have to know that *I* care about them for who *they* are, or I've consigned them to being *things* again. We're *Mandalorian.* A Mandalorian isn't just a warrior, you see. He's a father, and he's a son, and your family matters. Those boys deserve a father. They deserve sons and daughters, too, but that isn't going to happen. But they can *be* sons, and the two things you have a duty to teach your sons are self-reliance, and that you'd give your life for them." Skirata leaned on folded arms and gazed down into the hazy abyss again. "And I would, Etain. I *would.* And I should have had that degree of conviction when I started this sorry mess back on Kamino."

"And walked out? And left them to it? Because it wouldn't have shifted the clone program one bit, even if it made you feel like you'd taken a brave stand."

"Is that how you feel?"

"That stalking out and refusing to lead them is more for my comfort than theirs?"

He lowered his head on his folded arms for a moment.

"Well, that answers my question."

As a Jedi, Etain had never known a real father any more than a clone had, but in that moment she knew exactly who she wanted him to be. She moved closer to Skirata to let her arm drape on his shoulder and rested her head against his. A tear welled up in the wrinkled corner of his eye then spilled down his cheek, and she wiped it away with her sleeve. He managed a smile even though he kept his gaze fixed on the traffic far below.

"You're a good man and a good father," she said. "You should never doubt that for a moment. Your men don't, and neither do I."

"Well, I wasn't a good father until they made one out of me."

But now he would also be a grandfather, too; and she knew it would delight him. She had given Darman back his future. She closed her eyes and savored the new life within her, strong and strange and wonderful.

Qibbu's Hut, main bar, 1800 hours, 385 days after Geonosis

Ordo shouldered a space for himself at the bar table between Niner and Boss and helped himself to the container of juice.

Corr was showing Scorch a dangerous trick with a vibroblade that required lightning reflexes to withdraw his hand before the blade thudded into the surface of the table. Scorch seemed wary.

"But your hand's metal, you cheating *di'kut,*" he said. "I *bleed.*"

"Yaaah, jealous!" Corr jeered. His blade shaved Scorch's finger and went *thunnkk* in the table to cheers from Jusik and Darman. "You shiny boys always did envy us meat cans."

The two squads seemed in good spirits, good enough to be telling long and elaborate jokes without the usual competitive edge of bravado between Sev and Fi. They had a task to complete in thirty hours and it seemed to have focused them completely, erasing all squad boundaries. It was what Ordo had expected. They were professionals; professionals put the job first. Anything less got you killed.

But now they were having fun. Ordo suspected it was the first time they'd ever let their hair down in an environment like this, because it was certainly a first for him. Skirata looked as happy as he had ever seen him. And Jusik sat among them, wearing of all things a chest plate of Mandalorian armor under his jacket.

"We presented it to *Bard'ika* as a souvenir," Skirata said, rapping his knuckles on the plate. "In case we don't manage to have that fancy dinner."

In case some of us are dead by the end of tomorrow.

That was what he meant, and everyone knew it. They lived with it. It just seemed the more poignant now for knowing that a rare bond had been formed between unlikely comrades: two Jedi who openly admitted they struggled with the disciplines of attachment—and Ordo was sure now that he understood that—and a very mixed bag of clone soldiers from captain to trooper who had abandoned rank to answer to a sergeant who didn't answer to *anyone.*

Fi, with his uncanny talent for spotting a mood, raised his glass. "Here's to Sicko."

The mention of the pilot's name brought instant reverence to the noisy table.

"To Sicko," they chorused.

There was no point grieving: settling a score with Separatists was a far more productive use of their energy. Jusik winked at Ordo, clearly happy in a way that reached beyond noisy laughter in a crowded bar. Whatever moat of serenity and separateness surrounded men like Zey, Jusik's had vanished—if he had ever had it. He was daring to feel part of a tight-knit group of men. Whatever brotherhood was like within the Jedi Order, it didn't appear to be like this.

Mereel, his hair rinsed clean to its natural black, was now holding court and reciting an astonishing list of obscenities in forty different languages. So far he hadn't repeated himself once. Fi was bent double over the table, roaring with laughter.

Even Niner was enjoying it, contributing the odd word of Huttese. "It's nice to know that your advanced linguistic skills were devoted to something useful."

"Urpghurit," Mereel said, deadpan.

"Disgusting," said Fi.

"Baay shfat."

"What does that mean?"

Mereel whispered a translation in Fi's ear and his face fell slightly. Mereel frowned. "Don't tell me you've never heard that one."

"We were raised to be polite boys," Fi said, clearly aghast. "Can Hutts really do that?"

"You better believe it."

"I'm not sure I like civilian society," Fi said. "I think I felt safer under fire."

Coming from Fi, it would usually have been a joke. But like all his jokes, bitter reality lay not far beneath. Fi hadn't adjusted gracefully to the outside world. There was a moment of silence as reality intruded on all of them.

"I'll shoot you and cheer you up, then," Sev said suddenly.

Everyone laughed again. Darman drained his glass and got up to go. Scorch flicked a warra nut at him with impressive accuracy, and it bounced off his head. "Where you going, Dar?"

"I'm off to calibrate my Deece."

There was more raucous laughter. Darman didn't look amused. He shrugged and walked off in the direction of the turbolift through a crowd of men from the Forty-first Elite who were shipping out in a few days. At least they'd had something few troopers ever would: two weeks without fighting. They didn't appear to be enjoying it, though. *Kal'buir* said that was what happened when you let someone out of prison after a long sentence. They didn't fit in and they didn't know how to live outside a cell or without a familiar routine.

I know, though. And Fi wants *to know.*

"Don't wind him up about Etain, son," said Skirata.

Scorch looked wary. "He's not breaking any regulation, is he?"

"I don't think so, but she is."

The best thing was *not* to think.

"What happens to us when the war's over?" Corr asked.

Mereel smiled. "You'll have the thanks of a grateful Republic. Now, who can guess what *this* Ubese word means?"

Ordo glanced at Skirata, who raised his glass. Atin came to take Darman's place at the table with the Twi'lek Laseema on his arm: the man obviously wasn't as shy as he seemed. Except for Vau and Etain, the entire strike team had gathered here, and there was some sense of an important bond having been accomplished. It also felt very *final.*

"You and Mereel are up to something," Skirata said. "I can tell."

"He has news, *Kal'buir,*" Ordo said.

"Oh."

Should he tell him now? He'd thought it might distract him too much. But he didn't need to provide detail. It would give *Kal'buir* heart for what was to come.

"He's traced where our mutual friend fled immediately after the battle."

There was no need to say that the *friend* was Kaminoan scientist Ko Sai, the head of the cloning program, or that she had gone missing after the Battle of Kamino. The hunt—and it was a private matter, not Republic business, although the Grand Army footed the bill—was often reduced to just two words: *Any news?*

And if any of his other brothers—Prudii, A'den, Kom'rk, Jaing—found anything as well, Skirata would be told. They might have been carrying out intelligence missions for the Republic, but their true focus was finding elements of Kaminoan cloning technology that only Ko Sai had access to.

Skirata's face became luminous. It seemed to erase every crease and scar for a few moments.

"This is what I want to hear," he said softly. "You *will* have a future, all of you. I swear it."

Jusik was watching him with interest. There was no point trying to conceal anything of an emotional nature from Jedi as sensitive to the living Force as Jusik and Etain, but it was unlikely that Skirata had shared that secret with him. He hadn't even told his commando squads. It was too fragile a mission; it was safer for them all not to know for the time being.

Jusik raised his glass. It was just juice. Nobody would drink before a mission if they had any sense. Alcohol had proved not to be a major preoccupation with commandos anyway: and, whatever had been rumored, *Kal'buir's* only concession to alcohol was one glass of fiery colorless *tihaar* at night to try to get to sleep. He found sleep increasingly elusive as the years of training progressed on Kamino and his conscience tore him apart piece by piece.

He'd sleep well without it tonight, even if it was in a chair.

"This is very, very good news," Skirata said, a changed man for the moment. "I'd dare to say it bodes well."

They drank and joked and argued about Hutt curses. And then Skirata's comlink chirped, and he answered it discreetly, head lowered. Ordo simply heard him say, "Now? Are you *serious*?"

"What is it?" Ordo said. Mereel paused in midcurse, too, and the table fell silent.

"It's our *customer,*" Skirata said, jaw tense again. "They've hit a small snag. They need to move tonight. There's no preparation, *ad'ike*—we have to roll in three hours."

20

You know that thing that sergeants are always supposed to yell at new recruits? "I am your mother! I am your father!" Well, what do you do when that's actually true? Kal Skirata was all they had. And the troopers didn't have anyone. How can you expect those boys to grow up normal?

—Captain Jaller Obrim, to his wife over dinner

Operational house, Qibbu's Hut, 1935 hours, 385 days after Geonosis: whole strike team ready to deploy

"So what's your *shabla* problem, then, Perrive?" Skirata conducted the conversation with his wrist comlink propped on the table while he strapped on his *Mando* armor. Ordo stood out of range of the comlink's mike, holding Obrim on the line via his own link. "Cold feet? Can't get the finance in place? What, exactly?"

Skirata didn't need to act angry. He *was*. Everyone in the team was used to working on the fly, but all the planning—the careful positioning to take out the maximum number of bodies—now teetered on the brink of disaster. Around him, Delta and Omega were armoring up in full fighting order: Katarn rig with DC-17s, grenades, rappelling lines, rapid entry ordnance, and a Plex rocket launcher per squad.

For a moment he was unsettled to see Omega and Vau both in black armor. *But they're mine. They're my squad.* He renewed his concentration on Perrive's voice.

"One of our colleagues has been picked up by the police." Perrive's Jabiimi accent was very noticeable now. It was an indication of stress. And that was encouraging at an animal level for a mercenary. Skirata gestured frantically to Ordo but his head was already lowered, chin tucked into his chest as he relayed the information to Obrim. "We need to move our operation."

"And you want me to drop by with the groceries when you've got CSF crawling all over you? I'm still wanted for seven contract killings in town."

Ordo gave a *standing by* signal: hand at shoulder level, fingers spread.

Perrive swallowed audibly. "They're not *crawling all over us,* as you put it. One man was arrested. He might be a weak link."

Cross-check this with Obrim. "Where? This better not be in my backyard."

"Industrial sector, pulled over for an illegal cannon upgrade to his speeder."

Ordo nodded once and then gave a thumbs-up. *Confirmed.* Skirata felt his shoulders relax immediately. "Call me suspicious, but last time somebody did this to me they didn't plan on paying. You're not sticking to our timetable."

"I'm afraid it's just a good old-fashioned screwup."

"I'll be at your location at twenty-two-hundred hours, then. But you won't mind if I bring a couple of my colleagues just to be on the safe side."

"Not there. We have transport issues."

"What does that mean?"

"I mean we need to move our vessels somewhere safe. Bring the consignment to us at our landing strip and load it straight on."

Scorch stepped in front of Skirata with as near to an expression of boyish delight as the man was ever going to manage. He mouthed *CoruFresh* at him. Any good mercenary could lip-read, because if he wasn't already deafened by long exposure to gunfire, he couldn't hear a word in battle anyway.

"I need a location."

"We have a few vessels laid up in the commercial sector in Quadrant F-Seventy-six."

Skirata watched Scorch clench both fists and pull his elbows hard into his sides in a gesture of silent, total triumph. They were heading for at least one site at which they'd done a thorough recce.

"I need coordinates and I need to know *exactly* what I can expect to see when I show up—so I know I'm not walking into a CSF welcoming committee."

"You really do have a record, don't you?" said Perrive.

"Isn't that why you're doing business with me?"

"Very well. Six speeder trucks with CoruFresh livery and four passenger airspeeders—two Koros, two custom J-twelves."

"For a hundred kilos of thermal? I can carry that with my nephew in two shopping bags, *chakaar.*"

"You're not our only supplier of equipment, *Mando*. And I have personnel to move. I know you'll spit on this, but we're soldiers, and we have a code of honor. We want the goods for the price we agreed. No trap."

Skirata paused for effect. "So I'll meet you there."

"No, it'll be my deputy. The woman you saw at our meeting earlier. I'm moving via another route."

"Transmit the coordinates now and we'll start packing our bags."

"Your credits will be in the account you specified at twenty-one-fifty."

"Pleasure doing business. But the minute I see CSF-issue blasters or even a hint of blue uniform, we're banging out."

Skirata closed the link and for a moment there was absolute silence in a room full of fifteen hot, anxious, adrenaline-laden bodies. Then there was a loud collective whoop of satisfaction. Even Etain joined in, and Skirata hadn't reckoned her for wild displays of enthusiasm.

"So all was not lost after all, *vode,*" Vau said. Lord Mirdalan was frantic, bouncing on its front legs while the other four scrabbled for purchase on the tattered carpet. Adrenaline excited strills and made them eager to hunt. "Plan B. Disable the vessels and slot the occupants."

"Disable . . . ," Scorch said.

"Minimum force required to do the job. We're in a city, remember."

"Holochart," Ordo said. "I've still got Obrim on this link. Quick sitrep, people."

They clustered around Corr, who was collating the moving red lines and points of light with quiet enthusiasm. *Methodical, calm lad.* He'd need to be that in bomb disposal. "They've been going all shades of crazy *here* and *here.*" He zoomed into the holoimage and indicated two tangled masses of red lines like loose balls of thread, both in the retail sector of Quadrant B-85, where Fi had carried out the surveillance of Vinna Jiss. It suggested that tagged suspects had done an awful lot of repeated movement. "I'd say they're shifting kit by hand. Plenty of it, in two locations. But the two apartments

Captain Ordo recce'd have been totally dead for hours. They've left."

Skirata knew what he'd do in their position. He'd assemble what kit he had, move it discreetly to a central point, and then ship out. He wouldn't send a big, conspicuous repulsor truck to pick up from a dozen locations.

"It's all going out via the crates on that landing strip," he said.

"Agreed." Ordo and Mereel nodded.

Scorch just grinned.

A red point of light suddenly moved from the location of the house in the banking sector where Skirata had met Perrive. They watched it moving fast: someone had left the house in a speeder. "Holocam," Skirata said.

Ordo played out the remote image from his glove emitter. A speeder had taken off from the roof.

"I'd bet that was Perrive leaving," said Vau.

Skirata knew they'd lose some of the key players, but this was about making as big a dent in the Sep terror ranks as possible. "Pity. Maybe we can catch up with him later."

Fi held out his palm with a remote detonator on it. "If he's flying that green speeder . . ."

"The one they took me in?"

"Yes."

"Fi . . ."

"You can blow it anytime you like, Sarge." The commandos had slipped back into calling him Sarge. It seemed to happen when they put their armor on again. "I stuck a nice big surprise in his air intake last night."

"I was in that speeder."

"I know. Clever, wasn't it?"

Skirata took the det and checked that it was disabled before slipping it in his pocket.

"*Ord'ika,* let me talk to Jaller." He held his hand out for the comlink to Obrim. "Can your people cover the locations we gave you?"

Obrim's voice was tight with tension. "We're pulling people back off shifts now. We're synchronizing this for twenty-two-hundred, are we?"

"Correct. I'll patch you into my comlink for the duration, but don't talk to me unless it's critical. Other than that, stay away from the area coordinates we're going to transmit to you, and pretend we never existed."

"Sorry about the arrest—not my team. A routine firearms control stop, I'm afraid."

"At least it made them bolt. They're *vulnerable* when they bolt."

"I'll talk to you in twelve hours if all goes smoothly, then. Next breakfast's on you, remember?"

"You take care, too, friend."

The tangle of possibilities and risks in Skirata's mind had become crystal clear. Two key parts of the operation were now as pinned down as they could be: the synchronized raid on the lower-priority terrorist targets by CSF, and the interception of an unspecified number of key players at the landing strip, along with their vessels.

"Remember, *vode.* No prisoners." Skirata took out his medpac and prepared a one-use painkiller syringe. Then he rolled down the soft leather of his left boot and stabbed the needle deep into his ankle. The pain made his muscles shake but he clenched his teeth and let it pass. This was *not* the night to be slowed down by a limp. "Shoot to kill."

Fourteen men and one woman to kill maybe twenty terrorists. Very expensive use of manpower compared to droid kill rates. But worth it.

There were a few more targets still wandering around out there, ones they hadn't even tagged. But when it came to destroying a small organization like a group of terror cells, taking out a cell like this one would have enormous impact. It slowed them down. It set them back while they recruited and reorganized and retrained.

Even a few *months* made all the difference in this war.

"Walon," he said. "Take one of my Verpine rifles tonight. Might come in handy."

"I'm grateful, Kal."

"Okay, *vode.* This is now Captain Ordo's command as ranking officer—even if we have no ranks right now."

Skirata swung his arms through the full range of movement to check the fit of his armor, the sand-gold suit that his adoptive father Munin had given him. He put his knife—the knife he had retrieved from his real father's dead body—up his right sleeve, handle uppermost. He could barely remember his parents or even his original name, but Munin Skirata was as vivid as life and still with him every day, one of the precious departed whose names he recited each night.

He hit his gauntlets against his chest plate to snap himself out of memories. Both squads jumped.

Lord Mirdalan, jowls flapping, threw its head back and let out a long, low, moaning howl. The preparations had worked the strill into a hunting frenzy. It could see its master in full Mandalorian armor, and it smelled and heard men who were tense and ready to fight. All its instincts and training said *hunt, hunt, hunt.*

And Vau held his gloved hand out to Atin. Astonishingly, Atin took it. There was nothing but the battle in mind now. They were all saving it for the enemy.

Skirata felt the visceral thrill tighten his throat and stomach. It had been many years since he'd put on *this* armor to fight.

"Buy'cese!" he said. Helmets on!

It was, he knew, a sight few would believe—Walon Vau and a Jedi Knight *both* in full Mandalorian armor, and Republic Commandos, ARC troopers, and a clone trooper in fighting order so closely modeled on that armor he wore himself that they looked like one united army. He pulled on his own helmet before anyone noticed the tears in his eyes.

"I ought to get a holo of this," Corr said.

Etain stood among them, incongruously fragile.

"I could have lent you my Hokan armor, General," Fi said. "Only one careless owner."

Etain lifted her tunic to reveal plates of body armor. "I'm not stupid." Then she pulled out two lightsabers. Skirata winced. "Mine, and Master Fulier's. He'd have relished a fight like this."

She was not herself tonight, if her usual self was that worried, awkward, but tenacious soul who found it so hard to be a Jedi. She was utterly *alive.* Darman seemed to be able to strike sparks off her. Skirata hoped she did the same for him.

Vau flung out his arm to signal the strill to race ahead. *"Oya! Oya!"* Let's go hunting! "*Oya,* Mird!"

The strill bayed at the top of its voice and shot out the doors to the landing platform.

Ordo turned to the strike team. *"Oya! Oya, vode!"*

It was electric. It had never happened before, and it would probably never happen again.

And they went hunting.

21

Buy'ce gal, buy'ce tal
Vebor'ad ures aliit
Mhi draar baat'i meg'parjii'se
Kote lo'shebs'ul narit

A pint of ale, a pint of blood
Buys men without a name
We never care who wins the war
So you can keep your fame

—Popular drinking chant of Mandalorian mercenaries—
approximate translation, edited for strong language

Landing area, CoruFresh Farm Produce distribution division, Quadrant F-76, 2035 hours, 385 days after Geonosis

The produce distribution depot was as familiar as Arca Barracks now. Everything was as the holochart and holocam images had modeled it, although some of the vessels had been moved in the last hour. Ordo took a small risk and flew the airspeeder over the CoruFresh landing strip at a cautious height just for reassurance. The depot was a lake of harsh white light dotted with loader droids, trucks, and an assortment of speeders. There were more vessels parked there than Perrive had said. They were probably legitimate transports shipping nothing more deadly than fruit.

"I think CoruFresh might be annoyed about the damage to their fleet in the morning," Ordo said.

"That's their problem for not being too choosy about the company they keep." Sev secured one of the Verpine rifles to his webbing. He seemed to take Skirata's warning about bending anyone who bent his kit quite literally. "They must be bankrolled by crime gangs themselves."

"We'll be doing CSF a favor, then."

It was always a challenge to insert teams into a busy location. Air traffic data said the strip clocked an average of 120 trucks and cargo lifters passing through the strip every twenty-four hours; 2000 to 2300 hours seemed to be the period when it almost shut down completely. That was probably why the Separatists had picked the 2200 time slot for Skirata to deliver the explosives. They'd be loaded and gone by the time the overnight deliveries started again at 2300.

If the teams had gone in early, they would have needed to avoid an awful lot of people and droids.

"You ever carried out an assault on an urban objective before?" Sev said.

"Yes. N'dian. Heard of it?"

Sev paused to check his HUD database. Ordo could see the icon flash up on his own HUD over the shared link. He heard Sev swallow.

"I meant one where you had to leave the place pretty well intact, sir."

"In that case, Sev, no. It'll be a first."

"Me, too."

"Glad we could share this moment, then."

Ordo parked the airspeeder next to the small substation that routed utilities to the industrial area where the CoruFresh depot was located. A meter-wide conduit carrying pipes and cables stretched out twenty meters from the substation to span a gap that was five hundred meters deep. That was their route in.

"All tooled up?" Ordo shouldered two Plex missile launchers against his pauldron, one on each side.

"Yes sir."

"Shoulder okay?"

"Fi has a big mouth."

"Fi knows that I need to know if any of my team is compromised by injury."

"I'm fine, sir."

Ordo nudged him. *"Oya, ner vod."*

Ordo led the way across the conduit, checking Sev's progress in his HUD. A man who'd nearly fallen to his death could get a little nervous at heights like this. But Sev advanced as if he were on solid ground, and they slipped into the cover of crates and containers at the rear wall of the warehouse.

"Omega, are you in position?"

Niner's voice crackled slightly in Ordo's comlink. "We're one hundred fifty meters from the perimeter, sir. Southeast of the strip at the waste processing depot."

"Any activity in the vessels parked on the eastern edge of the strip?"

"All quiet except for maintenance droids. Dar sent up a surveillance remote and all the wets are clustered at the warehouse entrance moving boxes. They've backed up two of the trucks against the loading bay."

"We're going to position ourselves on the roof, then."

The warehouse was a single-story building with an unforgiving flat roof that meant anyone in the two repulsor trucks on the far side of the landing area would notice troops moving around. It was the only high vantage point overlooking the floodlit landing area to direct fire as well as pick off a few targets for themselves. Ordo had decided it was asking for trouble to take up a position in the residential towers nearly a thousand meters away. If they wound up on the receiving end of returned fire, there would be a lot of dead civilians to explain.

"Up you go," said Ordo.

Sev fired his rappelling line over the roof and tugged on it to ensure it was secure. The small winch in his belt took most of his weight but he pushed off with his boots, looking almost as if he were walking up the vertical surface. Ordo waited as Sev rolled flat over the edge of the roof, Verpine rifle in his right hand.

"Roof clear, sir."

Ordo fired his own line and let the winch lift him until he could reach the roof with his hand. He handed Sev the Plex launchers and hauled himself over the top to crawl flat on elbows and knees until he was near the front edge of the roof.

They both flipped down the scopes in their visors at the same time. Ordo saw the same image repeated in Sev's viewpoint icon on the margin of his HUD.

"In an ideal world, we could have left a timed charge on that utility conduit and paralyzed this whole sector before we went in," Sev said.

"And that just advertises the fact that the Grand Army was here. We don't exist, remember? We've gone bandit."

"Just fantasizing."

The textbook approach was to knock out the two illumigrids and then move in. But timing was critical. Skirata and Jusik needed to make the delivery of explosives and then get clear before the party started.

"Omega, we're in position."

"Copy that." This time it was Mereel's voice.

"On my mark, we'll knock out both lights and then provide covering fire while you advance from the south side. Delta, what's your location?"

"Boss here, sir. We'll be in position behind the warehouse in two minutes. Atin and Fixer will enter from the front. Scorch and I will cover the north side of the strip."

Atin seemed to have slipped easily into the temporary gap left by Sev. There wasn't the slightest hint in their voices that their former brother wasn't welcome. Ordo supposed that once you were one of Vau's trainees, you could merge back into the batch without comment when there was a job to be done.

"Okay, *vode.* Now we watch and wait."

Mereel, Fi, Niner, Darman, and Corr crouched in the cover of a conveyor belt of bins outside the waste depot, where droids collected the contents for compaction and disposal.

Fi sniffed dubiously. There was the distinct sulfurous tang of rotting vegetables: harmless, or his helmet's filter would never have let the aroma through, but nauseating nonetheless. On Niner's signal, they sprinted from the bins and dropped down by a pillar at the end of the walkway that led across to the CoruFresh depot.

"You're very shiny, you two," Niner said, jerking his thumb at Corr and Mereel, who were almost glowing in the light from the red flashing sign of a seedy caf bar. "Why don't you just write SHOOT ME HERE on that *di'kutla* white armor?"

"You rely on that black stuff way too much," Mereel said. "It's all about a stealthy approach, you see." He heaved a massive Merr-Sonn Reciprocating Quad Blaster onto his hip and powered up the microrepulsorlift to take some of its weight. Four huge double-barreled blaster muzzles loomed from the weapon's body. It was close on eighty centimeters long and looked more like a cruiser's close-in defense cannon. "Stealth, and a nice big Cip-Quad, of course."

Fi patted Corr's conspicuously white shoulder. "His men will follow him anywhere, *ner vod.* But only out of curiosity."

"Okay, get curious, then." Mereel indicated the direction of the landing strip. "They've moved some of the vessels, so we're going to have to cover a little extra open ground. At least most of the cockpits are facing the same way so we might have a blind spot to take advantage of."

Darman, Verpine rifle slung across his back, was still examining the other impressive item of Merr-Sonn firepower excess that was balanced across his thighs, the Z-6 Rotary Blaster. It was almost as big as the Cip-Quad. He looked wary of it and passed it to Corr. "We really *did* say no prisoners, didn't we, sir?"

"Not exactly a sniper weapon, I know."

"Etain would like that," Fi said. "Bit classier than her Trannie LJ-50."

Mereel snorted. "The general can get her *own* rotary. That's *my* baby."

"Beats a bunch of flowers, Dar . . ."

"Has she called in yet, by the way?"

Ordo's voice cut in. There was no privacy on *this* frequency. "She and Vau followed Perrive's trace to an apartment in zone three, Quadrant A-Four. They're watching him now."

"Isn't that a diplomatic quarter?" asked Mereel, whose capacity for memorizing data seemed as unlimited as his brother's.

" 'Fraid so," said Ordo. "That could get interesting. If we go in there, we're into a whole new level of deniability."

Fi watched Darman's head drop for a moment, but there wasn't so much as a breath or a click of teeth. He snapped back to his alert position. Fi wasn't sure if he was afraid for Etain's safety or of what she might do, and he didn't plan to ask. "Vau doesn't need that strill when he's got a Jedi with him."

"He takes Mird everywhere," Mereel said. "Like *Mando* fathers take their sons into battle."

"If I didn't know Old Psycho was a head case, I'd say that was cute. What is it going to do?"

"You've never seen a strill hunt, have you?"

Mereel didn't say another word. He signaled *advance* to Niner with a sweep of his hand and the squad sprinted for the perimeter of the landing strip.

Diplomatic sector, Quadrant A-4, 2145 hours,
385 days after Geonosis

Etain stood on the ledge of a soaring office tower facing the elegant apartment block and realized exactly what *black ops* truly meant.

Vau stood beside her. The ledge was about 150 centimeters wide, and the breeze at this height was noticeable even on climate-controlled Coruscant.

"What's the matter?" Vau said, his parade-ground voice slightly softened by his *Mando* helmet. "Didn't know how dirty politics could be? That diplomats aren't all nice honest people? That they keep unpleasant company?"

"I think I worked that out already." She felt the strill brush past her legs, padding impatiently up and down the narrow ledge. It had no fear of heights, it seemed. "But the consequences of pursuing Perrive into that building reach far beyond assassinating a terrorist."

"We'll have to get him to come out, then."

"He could lie low there for weeks."

"If he's *hiding,* yes."

"I find you hard to follow sometimes, Vau."

"He might be *collecting* something or somebody. He was in a mad rush to leave."

"I sense he's alone. He isn't picking up a colleague."

Vau leveled the scope of the Verpine, angled down about thirty degrees. The strill teetered on the edge of the ledge.

"I can see Perrive. Yes, he's alone. He's in front of the doors to the balcony—now that's *arrogant,* my friend. Think nobody can see you, eh? Etain, want to take a look?"

Vau handed her the Verpine. She took it nervously, hearing Skirata's constant admonition to take care of the weapon, and was surprised how light and harmless it felt. She peered down the scope and felt Vau reach out and flick something on the optic. A different image appeared in the eyepiece, slightly pink-tinted, of a man rummaging through a desk and sticking datachips into his 'pad, activating them, and then extracting and discarding them. A pale blob of light shimmered from his chest and then from his back as he turned.

"What can you see?"

"He's loading data," Etain said.

"He's shredding someone's files. Told you so."

"What's the white light? The EM emissions from the Dust?"

"Correct."

Etain handed back the rifle. "That datapad is going to contain some interesting material. How do we get hold of it?"

"The old-fashioned way." Vau sounded as if he'd smiled. It was hard to tell under the helmet. "Let's get him to come to the balcony."

"I'm not sure I can influence his mind at this range . . . or at all."

"No need, my dear." Vau folded a cloth one-handed and placed it under the stock of the Verpine at the point where it touched his armored shoulder. "I hate a standing shot without something to lean against, but I'm not as sure-footed as Mird so I'm not going to attempt to kneel." He leaned back slightly against the wall at his back. "But this Verpine is *beautiful.*" He rested his firing hand on his raised forearm. "It's almost a handgun."

"Just tell me what you're going to do."

"Make a noise on his balcony so he steps outside."

"What if he doesn't?"

"Then we'll have to go in and get him the hard way."

"But if you—"

"Let's get him outside if we can." Vau paused to let an airspeeder pass. The narrow skylane was almost deserted. "Most armies I ended up serving had no notion of advance planning. I got to be *very* good at unorthodox solutions."

Etain couldn't help but feel the patterns in the Force right then. Being pregnant seemed to have enhanced her sensitivity to the living Force by an order of magnitude. Vau felt like a pool of utter cold calm, almost a Jedi Master's footprint in the Force. The strill felt . . . alien. It had an unfathomable glittering intelligence and a wild, joyful heart swirling within it. Had it not been for Vau's rifle and the strill's savage teeth, the pair might have felt like a peaceful man and his happy child.

She felt something else, as she did constantly now: the vivid, complex pattern of her unborn child.

It's a boy.

I'm standing on a ledge with thousands of meters of nothing below me. And I am not afraid.

She stopped herself from reaching out to Darman in the Force. It might distract him at a critical moment. She simply felt that he was safe and confident, and that was enough.

"Could you choke him using the Force?" Vau said quietly.

"What?"

"Just asking. Very handy."

"I was never trained to do *that.*"

"Pity. All those fine combat skills wasted."

Vau exhaled audibly and paused. There was the slightest of movements in her peripheral vision as he squeezed the trigger, and a small *snakkk* echoed as a puff of vaporized stone billowed briefly off the corner of the apartment wall.

"Ahh . . . ," Vau said. The rifle's scope was still pressed to the eye slit in his black helmet. He looked like the very image of death.

Much as Etain had grown to find that armor reassuring, it made it no less intimidating. "Now, this is not a man used to avoiding professional assassins. Watch carefully and tell me what you feel."

Perrive paused at the transparisteel doors leading onto the balcony and shoved the datapad inside his tunic. Then he took out his blaster. He opened the doors by a meter, no more, and stood looking around, blaster raised, one foot still inside the apartment, one on the balcony itself.

Etain heard Vau exhale and then Perrive's head jerked backward with a brief plume of dark blood as if he had been punched by an invisible fist. He fell, arms thrown wide.

Dead. Gone. Whatever had been Perrive was now gone from the Force: no pain, no surprise, and suddenly *not there.*

Mird the strill was staring up at its master, unblinking, tail thrashing the ledge in enthusiasm. It began making little whimpering noises deep in its throat.

"I *must* treat myself to one of these," Vau said, still all complete calm and satisfaction, gazing at the Verpine rifle. "Outstanding craftspeople, those little insectoids."

"He's dead."

"I should think so. The hydrostatic shock generated by a Verpine projectile is *substantial.* A clean head shot is instantaneous *kyr'am.*"

"But the datapad is still in his tunic."

"Good!" He turned to the strill and put his finger to his lips. "*Udesii,* Mird . . . silence! *K'uur!*"

The strill stared up into his face, gold eyes fixed on his, head drawn back a little into its cowl-like folds of loose skin. Its whimpering stopped abruptly. Vau crouched down and held out his arm as if pointing, and closed his fingers into a fist. "*Oya* . . . ," he whispered. "Find the *aruetii*! Find the traitor!"

Mird spun around and stabbed its claws into the stonework. Etain watched, stunned, as it climbed the wall and made its way to the next ledge above. The strill appeared to understand what was said to it, even hand signals. But she had no idea what it was doing.

"*Oya,* Mird!"

The strill balanced on its four rear legs and then sprang into the abyss.

"Oh my—"

And then Etain suddenly realized why the strill looked so bizarre. It spread all six legs, and the loose, ugly skin that made it appear such a shambling mess was stretched taut by the air pressure beneath it. It glided effortlessly down in a perfect stoop onto the balcony opposite.

Vau took off his helmet and wiped his brow. His face was a study in complete admiration and . . . yes, *love.*

"Clever Mird," he murmured. "Clever baby!"

"It's a *glider*!"

"Extraordinary animals, strills."

"It's going to fetch the datapad?"

Vau paused. Etain could see a smile forming on his lips. "Yes."

"Is it male or female?"

"Both," Vau said. "Mird has been with me since I joined the Mandalorians. Strills live far longer than humans. Who'll care for it when I'm dead?"

"I'm sure someone will value it greatly."

"I want it to be *cared for,* not valued."

Vau replaced his helmet. They waited. Etain strained to see when the animal emerged from the apartment with, she imagined, the datapad clamped in its teeth. Or maybe it had more surprises in store, like a pouch, as Jinart the Gurlanin had.

She stared, aghast.

Mird had dragged Perrive's body out onto the balcony and was worrying at it. She believed the animal was trying to tear out the datapad right up to the moment that it got a good grip with its massive jaws on the corpse's shoulder and hauled it up onto the safety rail.

"What's it doing?"

Vau laughed. Mird balanced the body on the rail like a sack of stones, wobbled a little, and then launched itself into the air. Etain was stunned by its ability to move a man weighing at least eighty kilos, but not half as stunned as when she saw its free fall turn into a vertical climb as it struck out and its parachute of skin became *wing membranes.*

Mird soared like a raptor, carrying its prey.

Mird *flew.*

"Fierfek . . . ," Etain said. There was no other word for it.

"Language!" Vau said, clearly amused. Mird thudded onto the ledge and hauled Perrive up behind it. Vau crouched as best he could on the narrow strip of stone and felt inside the tunic for the datapad. "Got it. Let's go. Good Mird! Clever Mird! *Mirdala Mird'ika!*" He opened his comlink. "Kal, Perrive's no longer a problem, and we have a useful datapad. See you shortly."

Mird was ecstatic, whimpering and slobbering in delight as Vau rubbed its head. As retrievers went, it could have no equal.

"What about the body?" Etain said, still stunned. "Are we just leaving it here? On an office window ledge?"

"It'll give CSF's forensics team a *fascinating* project to keep them occupied," Vau said. "And we didn't even have to enter a diplomatic compound, did we?"

Etain, now used to death and assassination, couldn't help herself. She reached over and rubbed the strill's head, too, although it stank and could probably kill her in a single vast bite. It was still miraculous.

"Clever Mird!" she said. *"Clever!"*

Somewhere near CoruFresh Farm Produce distribution division, Quadrant F-76, 2150 hours, 385 days after Geonosis

"That armor suits you, *Bard'ika.*"

Skirata sat astride the speeder's pillion seat, datapad and chrono at the ready. The operation was under way. Perrive was dead. Now it was time for Skirata to check that the credit transfer had been made.

He watched the screen that showed the status of the temporary bank account that would vanish without trace or audit trail in just over a day.

"I suspect the Jedi Council wouldn't agree." Jusik adjusted the bags on the bike's cargo straps. "Not even if General Kenobi himself wears armor."

"You don't worry much about that," said Skirata.

"I haven't thought that far ahead."

"A *Mando* mercenary has to plan for the future these days, son, even if there turns out to be no future at all. And so should you."

Jusik laughed. "I thought you *Mando'ade* lived only for the day. You even have trouble using anything but the present tense."

Skirata's eyes never left the datapad's screen. Then it reloaded, and suddenly an anonymous numbered account in a bank on Aargau was four million credits in the black. Skirata hit VERIFY and the credits were *there.*

Yes, this was real. *He had the credits.*

He felt one tension evaporate from his chest and another—familiar, comfortable, an old friend—take its place. He was ready to fight. He opened the comlink to the whole strike team.

"Stand by, *vode,* stand by. The credits have cleared. We're moving in to make the drop now."

"Ordo here, copy that."

"Delta here, copy that."

"Mereel here, copy that."

"Do we get ten percent?" Fi muttered.

Jusik powered up the speeder bike. "You'd be amazed what you might get out of this, Fi." The speeder shot up into the air and spun ninety degrees before Jusik aimed it at the CoruFresh depot. "Preferably not a broken neck, though."

"Sorry, Kal," said Jusik.

Skirata checked his chrono: 2155.

A good rousing chant of *Dha Werda* might have psyched him up better, but this was a different battlefield.

"*Bard'ika,* those explosive packs *are* well wrapped, aren't they?"

"Thoroughly. They're really affecting the handling of this speeder, too."

"We've got a few minutes. Take it easy."

"Udesii . . ." Jusik grinned. "If things get a little hairy out there, I *can* use my Force powers, can't I?"

"No witnesses. Go ahead."

Jusik took the speeder high over the landing strip, and Skirata noted Ordo and Sev flat on the roof of the warehouse as they spiraled down to land. The two soldiers didn't move. Omega and Delta were nowhere to be seen. That reassured him enormously. It had been a joy to train commandos who became better soldiers than he could ever be.

Tonight would test them, though. There were enough explosives in the area now to take out a quadrant and well beyond. Fine on a battlefield—but not in a city.

Careful. Go careful.

The speeder settled and hung at rest just above the ground. A group of five men and the middle-aged woman he'd seen at the meeting earlier were the welcoming committee, and they all had blasters visible on belts or held loosely at their sides. They directed Jusik to a spot between two trucks, sheltered from anyone who might pass by.

Skirata and Jusik got off the speeder bike and stood with their arms at their sides, calm and business-like. Skirata removed his helmet. Jusik kept his *buy'ce* on.

"The credits cleared fine," Skirata said.

The woman inspected the speeder, which was laden like a Tatooine bantha with anonymous bags of rough sacking. "This is *all* the five-hundred-grade?"

"Four hundred quarter-kilo packs, bagged in tens. I suggest you split the load for safety."

The woman shrugged. "We know how to handle explosives." She reached out to unfasten one bag and squatted down to slide the ten bundled packets onto the ground. She squinted at the thick packaging and took out a knife from her pocket.

Skirata didn't need to see Jusik's face to know that the blood had drained from it.

Don't stick anything metallic into it. The electrolytic reaction will set it off.

Mereel's little chemical enhancement to thwart the bomb makers in the event of their getting away with any of the explosives was about to kill them all.

"Whoa!" Skirata sighed irritably and hoped to the Force that he didn't sound the terrified man he was right then. "Don't shove a knife in that, woman! Unwrap it properly. Here, let me do it. Are you *sure* you know what you're doing?"

There was a collective involuntary gasp in his comlink earpiece, a very restrained one. He heard Ordo mutter, *"Osik . . ."*

"You insolent little Mandalorian *thug,*" she sneered, but she stood back to let him take over. And she held her blaster to his head.

Skirata ripped the bundle open with nervous hands and broke out one packet, tearing the flexiwrap with his teeth to expose the soft light brown contents. It tasted . . . oddly sweet.

"Here. Believe me?"

The woman scowled at him and squeezed the explosive between her fingers. "I'm checking that this isn't just dyed detonite."

"Tell you what," Skirata said, wondering if Jusik might try a spot of mind influence right then, "pick as many packs as you like at random and I'll unwrap them, and then you can prove to yourself that they're not booby-trapped, either."

He heard Ordo's voice in his ear. "*Kal'buir,* you're scaring us . . ."

"Okay." The woman pointed to another bag on the speeder bike. "That one. Empty it in front of me."

Skirata obeyed. He unwrapped the bundle and waited for her to choose a pack at random. He tore it open and let her inspect it. She repeated the process three times.

Skirata stood up, hands on hips, and sighed theatrically. "I've got all night, sweetheart. Have you?"

The woman looked into his face as if she liked the idea of killing him anyway. "Bag it up and get out of here."

He glanced at his chrono: 2220. Obrim would be getting jumpy now, with squads of CSF officers waiting throughout Galactic City to raid the long list of suspect addresses he'd given them.

"You heard the lady." He shoved Jusik in the back. "Get on with it."

The last few seconds before a hasty exit were always the most terrifying. A hairbreadth lay between victory and defeat, life and death. Jusik secured the last of the bags and dumped the rest from the speeder in a pile between the trucks.

"Now get lost," she said.

"I take it I can't count you as a repeat customer, then?"

She raised the blaster eloquently. Skirata replaced his helmet and swung onto the speeder bike behind Jusik. They lifted into the air and climbed above the warehouse.

"Fierfek," said Darman's voice in his ear. "I hate it when you improvise, Sarge."

"Like you don't."

"Standing by."

Ordo cut in. "The woman's loading all the explosives except a single bag into one truck. The one with the green livery nearest the loading bay. I repeat, *negative* the green truck. Do *not* target the green truck or it's good-bye to half of Coruscant."

"Females never listen to a thing I say, thankfully," Skirata said. He *knew* she'd react like that. "So that means there's only *one* vessel we can't blow up."

"Priority is to isolate the green truck and ground it before engaging other targets."

"Copy that, sir," a chorus said.

Jusik set the speeder down three hundred meters behind the warehouse in a cluster of shuttered wholesalers' units. Skirata sat breathing deeply for a moment to steady himself before opening his comlink again with a double click of his back teeth.

"Obrim, this is Skirata."

"Got you, Kal."

"You can roll now, my friend. Talk to you later."

"Copy that." Obrim's channel snapped into silence.

"Omega, Delta, all units, this is Kal. We're clear. All yours, Captain."

"Copy that, Sargeant." Ordo began counting down. "Five, four, three, two . . . *go go go! Oya!*"

A bitter little war with far-reaching consequences was unleashed in downtown Galactic City.

22

We will watch you, I promise. You will not see us or hear us or even know we stand beside you. How does that feel, Jedi? How does it feel to be at the mercy of a species with powers even you don't have? Now you know how others regard you. Keep your promises, General, or you will see how hard a small, invisible army can strike.
—Jinart the Gurlanin, to General Arligan Zey, on the pledge to relocate all human colonists from Qiilura within eighteen months

CoruFresh depot, 2225—H Hour

At 2225 hours Triple Zero time, Fi and Mereel broke from behind the low wall at the southern edge of the landing strip and positioned themselves between the parked repulsor trucks at the far side facing the warehouse.

Fi focused the infrared scope of his DC-17 on the green truck and saw a bright patch of heat on the fuselage. He tilted up and saw the dim patchwork indicating the varying temperatures of a human's upper body, a pilot waiting to depart.

"I've got a target in the pilot's seat of the green truck, and his drive's showing up warm on the infrared scope. Is the explosive loaded? Can anyone confirm?"

"I can see the rear of the truck. They've closed the hatch with two targets inside as well as the pilot." Ordo paused. "The green truck is now confirmed as laden. We have to keep that vessel grounded, *vode.* We can't detonate it, not here."

"Dar, you got a clear shot at the pilot?"

There was the sound of fast breathing and a grunt as someone dropped next to him. Fi looked left and saw Darman kneeling on one leg with his Verpine rifle raised, elbow braced on his knee. A Verp slug was guaranteed to punch a hole in the truck's viewscreen and kill the pilot without triggering the five-hundred-grade. "Got him lined up. Standing by."

Fi swung his Deece to locate Ordo on the roof. He couldn't see Sev, but Ordo's helmet range finder was just visible as he turned his head.

"Delta," Ordo said, "stand by to take the rear of the green truck when we kill the illumigrids. Omega, target all walking targets on the landing strip."

Kal's voice cut in. "*Ord'ika*—we're at the rear of the warehouse blocking the back doors. Force is estimating twenty-four live targets in all, I'm told."

Fi refocused his scope on the interior of the warehouse. He could see at least nine men and women scurrying around inside, and two more visible via infrared, ripping open crates and bundling small boxes and blasters into bags. "I've got a minimum of eleven contacts around and inside the warehouse and it looks like they've got a small arsenal in there. Good news is that it's just one big empty space with partitioned offices down one wall."

"Once the lights go out, they'll batten down . . ."

Sev cut in. "I've got two loading what looks like DC-15 rifle cases into the small red airspeeder on the northern perimeter fence."

"Six of the trucks look warm and ticking over in my infrared," Mereel said. "Can't see any activity in the rest of the speeders. There ought to be four ready to fly."

"Hit them *all,* then, just to be certain," Ordo said. "Hit everything except the green truck.

"I'm on night vision now," Darman said. "Ready when you are, Captain Ordo."

Corr sprinted into position to Fi's right, sliding behind a truck, with the rotary blaster braced against his belt and his left hand tight on the top grip. From his stance he looked like a man who felt pretty good about his chances. He wasn't even meant to be a commando; he'd just risen to the challenge.

Fi hoped Skirata would find a way of permanently absorbing him into Arca Company. He switched to his night scope and aligned the target icon on a man and a woman carrying a flat crate between them toward one of the trucks.

Fi's finger rested on the trigger.

* * *

"Lights!" Ordo hissed.

He and Sev fired their Plex rocket launchers, and both illumigrids were swallowed simultaneously by two balls of yellow flame.

The roar killed any chances of him hearing the shattering transparisteel viewscreen of the green truck. But he heard Darman an instant later.

"Truck pilot, *clear*!"

"We've lost one!" Jusik said.

"Say again?"

"One target's made a run for it, over in the northeast corner. I felt him go."

There was a split second of frozen time before blue blasterfire sprayed from Fi's position, cutting down the two people moving a crate. Two of the trucks exploded in balls of fire, accounting for six more targets. The landing strip was now a dark void lit by the dying flames of two smashed trucks and sporadic bolts of Deece fire. From the far end of the depot the distinctive blue staccato attack of the rotary blaster hosed every vehicle on that side of the strip. Corr was definitely *getting stuck in,* as *Kal'buir* put it. He sprinted to Ordo's left, firing as he ran, taking out the last gray-and-silver airspeeder in a ball of white light.

"Jusik?" Ordo debated whether to worry about the one escapee. "Jusik, get Vau and Etain onto the one who's bolted."

Beneath Ordo, Boss, Fixer, and Scorch raced to the rear of the green truck, Atin coming in from the other side. Boss fired a stream of bolts from his Deece at a shallow angle, slicing off half the truck's repulsor drive housing. It dropped flat on the ground with a massive crash of crumpling alloy. It definitely wasn't going anywhere now.

Scorch concentrated his fire into the warehouse. Ordo swung over the edge of the roof to rappel down into the mêlée, firing one of his twin blasters as he dropped. The shots sparked and smoked off closing doors. There were probably nine or ten terrorists now shut inside with a good supply of weapons. And right now they weren't Ordo's worst problem.

Sev thudded to the ground beside him and rewound his rappelling line. "Two Verp kills. That's all."

"Two still alive inside the truck," Boss said. "If you had a hundred kilos of thermal explosive, a lot of dets, and no escape, what would you do?"

"Take as many of the enemy out with me as I could," Ordo said. "Storm that *dik'utla* truck *now* before they put us into orbit."

* * *

Two minutes into the engagement felt like seconds. Fi sprinted down to the green truck on Mereel's heels with Corr, Darman, and Niner close behind.

"I make it ten bodies on the landing strip," Niner said.

"One dead pilot and two live targets in this truck." Ordo motioned Niner and Scorch to the front of the truck. "You stand by to distract them when Fixer and Boss go in the rear hatch."

Ordo stood back with both blasters drawn as Fixer and Boss stacked either side of the hatch. He fired at the frame mountings and it buckled and burst open. There was a loud *pee-eww pee-eww* of ricocheting fragments from the front of the vessel and Fixer and Boss burst in with their gauntlet vibroblades drawn.

White lights flared and hissed: hand blasters. Ordo had a split second of thinking *This is it, it's going to blow, we're dead, it's over*—and then silence fell again. Battles seemed to him a mass of deafening noise interspersed with brief, dead silence.

"Fierfek, they didn't even get the dets lined up," Scorch said. "Amateurs." He scrambled out of the shattered truck, his armor blackened by blasterfire. Boss jumped out behind him and shook blood off his vibroblade before sheathing it again.

Ordo took a breath. *"Kal'buir?"*

"We're still at the rear doors. It's gone a little quiet in there. *Bard'ika* says eleven inside."

"Confirmed eleven on the infrared scope, too," said Niner, who always needed to be certain.

"They've locked themselves in. We're just clearing the explosives out of the truck." Ordo motioned to Corr, Niner, and Boss to go. "Mereel and I are going in the front doors. Dar and Fi, open up a hole in the south-side wall."

"Want us to go in from the back, son?" Skirata said. "I'm pumping adrenaline and I'd like to get in on some action. For old times' sake."

"Remember you don't have Katarn armor," Ordo said, instantly more worried for *Kal'buir* than anyone alive.

Skirata snorted. "Remember you're not wearing Mandalorian iron."

Ordo gestured to Mereel. His brother brushed a dusting of debris off his blue lieutenant's pauldron and reached over his shoulders with both hands to draw the massive Cip-Quad blaster strapped across his back.

"In *three . . . ,*" Ordo said.

"What happened to *in five*?"

"I just ran out of patience."

Skirata held up his Verpine in his left hand, knife in his right, listening as Jusik drew his lightsaber, a Jedi Knight in a *Mando* helmet.

Bard'ika, I'll take that image to my grave.

He checked the infrared targeting beam, more out of nervous habit than anything, and hoped the *hut'uune* didn't have night vision.

The deafening double trip-hammer of Mereel's quad blaster shattered the brief calm and the rear doors were blown open. There was an explosion and a pounding rain of debris from the side of the warehouse. For a moment Skirata thought the doors had been blown out by the blast but Jusik punched the air as if it was a rather clever touch.

Fierfek. So that's the Force, is it?

There was no light spilling out of the doorway. Then someone inside the warehouse ran for the doors and a grainy figure shot through his night vision display.

Skirata reacted instantly, without thinking, charging at him and smashing into his face with an armored elbow, then bringing his knife up hard under his ribs before he could even fall backward. It was only when he aimed the Verp in his next breath and concentrated on the face in his HUD for a second, that he realized it was the woman who had called him a Mandalorian thug. He fired the gun before he had even thought of a suitable retort. War was like that. You rarely thought of something satisfying to say until days later, if you had anything to say at all.

"Ten on the infrared," Niner said.

Infrared told you who was still *warm.* Infrared couldn't tell you who was *alive.* Skirata preferred to track movement alone.

"Grenade! Cover!" Atin yelled.

The shock wave lifted Skirata and left his ears ringing. He was sure he was outside the doors but he was now *inside,* and Jusik hauled him cleanly to his feet with one arm. He couldn't hear the comlink clearly now.

The rapid hammering of a rotary blaster started up and then stopped abruptly. For a man trained in the delicate art of bomb disposal, Corr had seized on the crude technique of spraying six barrels with some enthusiasm.

"Grenade—"

Another explosion shook the warehouse. "Man down!"

Someone was cursing—Sev? Scorch?—and Ordo yelled, "Pull back! Clear the building!"

Skirata sprinted after Jusik, following the green glow of his lightsaber. As they cleared the doors, a massive *whooomp* punched Skirata simultaneously under the soles of his feet and in his back. He almost lost his balance.

Silence descended. Skirata strained to listen.

"Lots of scattered *patches* of infrared." That sounded like Niner. "And no idea what's alive and what's just . . . warm."

"Scorch, you okay?"

"Yeah. Yeah. Really. Just shook me up."

"That's it," Jusik said. "I'm coming back in, Ordo." He spun around and ran back into the warehouse. Skirata followed him. "I can find the live ones. Leave it to me."

The warehouse was now almost in darkness and silent except for the ticking, creaking, and crumbling sounds of settling debris and cooling alloy. The air stank of ozone from discharged blasters and from the animal scent of shattered bodies. Nothing moved.

This was taking hours, Skirata was sure. No, this was *minutes.* His brain had slipped into the unreal time frame of combat.

Jusik's green lightsaber left an eerie trail. He didn't seem afraid of drawing fire: he'd just bat it away like an annoying insect, Skirata was sure. "I can feel three lives."

Well, they'll know the Jedi are on the case now.

Skirata imagined lying on that floor in the dark silent chaos, probably deafened, certainly injured, catching glimpses of movement as soldiers stalked the room. The commandos had killed their visor lights, and Fi, Atin, and Darman were nearly invisible in their black armor even to him.

It must have been terrifying. He'd hidden from soldiers, six years old and scared enough to wet his pants.

Now you know what it's like, hut'uune.

Someone made a sound, a little half word, and it sounded like *please.* Skirata swung his Verpine in the direction of the noise. He saw a man kneeling with hands raised: fierfek, he didn't want to take prisoners. That was the last thing they needed. He heard Jusik swallow hard.

"Get over by the wall," Jusik hissed. He was gesturing at the person who seemed to be surrendering. Could the *hut'uun* even see the Jedi? "Get over by the wall!"

Then Darman's voice cut in. "Sarge! *Down!* Flame—"

Skirata swung around and dropped to his knees just as Jusik ducked a sheet of white-hot, roaring liquid flame that lit up the shattered warehouse and overwhelmed his night vision for a split second.

It pumped out in shallow arcs and Darman took it full on. Commandos and troopers leaped back instinctively and Skirata felt the heat even through a layer of ancient Mandalorian iron. Darman was illuminated like a jet black statue, rifle still raised, enveloped in blazing liquid. He didn't even scream.

"Dar!" Skirata found his body responding without intervention from his brain as he pumped Verpine rounds in the direction of the flamethrower. Someone fell. The stream of fire stopped. The *thunk* of a power cell being slapped onto a blaster diverted him from the terrible spectacle of Darman burning like a torch as someone—Fi? Niner?—rushed to roll their brother on the ground in a bid to smother the flames. Skirata caught the faint light of a charge indicator in his peripheral vision and swung the Verpine in its direction, but Jusik waded in instantly, swinging his lightsaber in a blur of light. Skirata could now see that the kneeling man—the apparently *surrendering* man—had drawn a blaster. It was still clutched in his limp hand. For some reason that feint angered Skirata more than anything.

"All clear!" Jusik yelled. *"Dar!"* He looked up at the ceiling. "Hang on, Dar."

Katarn armor could withstand high temperatures but the burning chemical had coated Darman's plates. It was resisting attempts by Niner and Sev to smother it with bundles of sacking they had grabbed. Skirata went to throw his jacket over him. Suddenly a fine sticky rain filled the air.

The fire control system had kicked in.

"I'm glad that worked," Jusik muttered.

A white cloud of hissing gas enveloped Darman and the warehouse plunged back into darkness. The blaze was out; fire retardant rained from the ceiling.

Skirata squatted over Darman, edging Niner and Ordo out of the way. His armor was still radiating heat.

"Son! Are you okay?"

"Sarge—"

"Are you hurt?"

"Not really . . . made me blink a bit, though. That liquid's *nasty* stuff." Darman's plates were hissing audibly as they cooled. His voice was shaky. "Thanks."

"Is this your handiwork, *Bard'ika*?" Skirata helped Darman to his feet. His plates were hot to the touch. "Did you activate the fire system?"

"I'm not just good for blowing stuff up." Jusik picked his way through the rubble and shattered durasteel, boots crunching, then stopped dead. "That's it," he said quietly. "Definitely nobody left alive."

The kid seemed remarkably calm about it, or at least his voice was under control. Darman dusted himself down and Ordo handed him his Deece. Eight helmet spotlamps flared into life and swept the interior, highlighting a scene of smoking wallboard and things Skirata had seen far too much of on too many battlefields. One beam jerked up toward the roof.

"We blew the *shabla* roof half off," Boss said.

"Last time I rely on infrared . . ."

"*Kandosii, Bard'ika!* He's better than a scope any day."

"Is this it?" That was Fixer's voice. "All that, and *still* we don't get to see them? At least you can see droids. They come at you. These scum—"

"You want to look, *ner vod*?"

"They're just so . . . ordinary."

"And now they're so *dead,*" said Sev.

Ordo cut in. "We're done here, *vode.* Time to go." He put his gloved hand on Skirata's shoulder. "Nine minutes, *Kal'buir.* Could have been faster, but it's done. Let's go."

Skirata caught Darman's arm and followed Jusik. *I can still fight: I'm still pretty good.* But he wasn't as good as young men at the peak of their abilities, and he needed to do something about that if he wasn't going to be a liability to them one day.

He'd worry about that later, like his ankle. Now they had to wait on Vau and Etain, who were still out hunting.

Quadrant F-76, somewhere north of the CoruFresh depot, 2305 hours, 385 days after Geonosis

The strill was a little bright light of pure joy as it raced along the walkway ahead of Etain and Vau. There were still a few pedestrians around, leaving factories and workshops for the night, and Vau had taken off his helmet. A dull black armored chest plate didn't attract attention, it seemed, but this wasn't a neighborhood where a distinctive Mandalorian visor would pass unnoticed.

The strill had the man's scent. He had a head start on them but Mird was not to be shaken off, and Etain could follow the trail of panic and fear almost as well as the animal could. She could locate the area: Mird could track by scent once she had narrowed down a search zone for it.

This is a strange thing for a pregnant woman to be doing. Can my son sense what's happening around him yet? I hope not.

Vau kept close behind her, jogging at a steady pace.

"I'm very impressed," he panted. "You and the strill work very well together. I do wish Kal could see this."

Etain imagined this was how Vau hunted with Mird, silent and persistent, covering the ground hour after hour until they had cornered their prey or run it down. The man who had managed to flee the attack on the landing strip had led them into a maze of run-down apartment towers on the edge of the industrial zone.

After a while Etain caught up with Mird and found it crouched impatiently by a set of doors leading into a shabby residential building. A couple of unpleasant-looking youths lounging on the corner of the walkway began ambling toward her, leering, but then Mird opened its huge maw and let out a warning rumble. Vau appeared around the corner, the Verpine rifle raised in one hand.

The youths fled.

"And they say young people today have no intelligence," Vau said. He took a hand disrupter out of his belt and thrust it into the door panel. The doors parted. "In you go."

Mird raced ahead and skidded to a halt at the turbolift, turning its head to gaze pleadingly at its master. Vau put a finger to his lips and pointed up. They got in the turbolift and the strill pressed its nose to the small gap between the doors as the car ascended. As they passed the 134th and 135th floors, it grew frantic and its tail thrashed the floor, but it didn't make a sound. Vau stopped the lift at the 136th floor and they got out. There was an emergency staircase between floors. Etain broke the seal with a Force-assisted push and started down the stairs.

"*Oya,* Mird! Hunt!"

Mird shot past her. She could feel the disturbance in the Force, and their respective instincts took them both to the 134th floor. Mird snuffled along the passage and came to a halt outside an apartment door, settled on its haunches, and stared intently at the door panel.

Vau put a restraining hand on her arm. "I know a Mandalorian regards a female warrior as his equal, my dear, but I feel I should offer to do this job myself."

"I'll do it," she said. She had to.

Vau disrupted the lock. The strill ran into the hallway, almost flat to the floor, and Etain followed it, drawing both lightsabers.

It occurred to her that she might have stumbled upon a family here, and then been presented with a dilemma: a Jedi with two drawn lightsabers, a room full of witnesses, and a cowering terrorist. *What would I do? What* will *I do?* But she sensed that would not be the case. It was just another fear of how far she might be prepared to go.

She burst open each door with the Force, moving at a slight crouch, looking inside.

A stream of blasterfire spat out of one door and caught the strill on its quarters. Etain heard Vau gasp. Mird shrieked and spun around, one leg dragging, and then made to go in after its assailant, but she held out one arm and it stopped dead.

"Leave, Mird!" she whispered.

Etain took a breath then stepped into the room to meet another hail of blasterfire. She crossed the blue blades of energy and batted the bolts aside with a parting motion of her arms. *I didn't know I could do that.* It was pure instinct, drawn from deep within her and many years in the past.

She lunged forward for the kill. As always, she saw little and felt nothing tangible, no shock up her arms, no resistance as she swept the blades, but she felt the Force change. A brief light blazed and died.

She thumbed off Master Fulier's lightsaber and slid it into her tunic one-handed while keeping her own drawn just in case. She sensed nobody else. Mird limped into the room after her and she knew it was looking up into her face even though there was only the scattered light through the window from a city that was never completely dark.

"Oya," she whispered, not knowing quite what the command might mean in this case.

But Mird rumbled quietly and sprang onto the body of the man she had killed. She shut down her lightsaber and walked out of the apartment, and Mird limped out a few moments later, crunching happily. She didn't look too closely at what it had in its jaws. It swallowed noisily.

"Poor Mird." Vau sighed. "Here, baby, come here." He scooped the strill up in both arms and carried it to the turbolift. One of its legs had been seared raw by the blaster.

Etain opened her comlink. "Kal, everyone is accounted for."

"Good work," Kal's voice said. He sounded tired. "See you at the RV point."

Mird let Etain place her hands on its leg to heal it as the lift made its way down to the ground floor. Vau carried it all the way back to the speeder. It was a big, heavy animal, but he refused to let it walk. Etain took it on her lap and eased its pain as Vau started the speeder and they headed for the RV point.

There seemed to be nothing Vau wouldn't do for Mird. He loved that animal.

RV point, two kilometers from Corufresh depot, 2320 hours, 385 days after Geonosis

The strike team rendezvoused at a droid-operated construction site to the north of the depot. The droids needed no light to work by and the presence of a few strangely dressed humanoids in the near darkness would draw no attention.

Skirata counted the six speeders back in, gut churning until the last of the speeders arrived with Mereel and Corr astride. Corr was clutching the rotary blaster like a long-lost friend.

Good lad. I'll shift Coruscant and all its rotten moons to hang on to him, Zey. We can always train more troopers as commandos. Just watch me.

"All thermal plastoid accounted for?"

"Yes, Sarge." Boss leaned against the bodywork of a speeder. "Want to check?"

"I trust you to count. Ordo can slip that back into stores tomorrow after it's been neutralized."

"What's the final score?" Fi said.

Niner eased off his helmet. Even with the environment control inside his sealed suit, he looked as if he'd sweated out an ocean. He rubbed his face slowly with the palm of his glove. "Er . . . I think we took out twenty-six bad guys."

"Twenty-four at the site," Mereel said. "We swept the site and did a tally. It was a bit hard to tell in some places but we logged the blasters that had been fired by their EM traces. So I say twenty-four."

"Plus Perrive and our friend in the apartment block," Etain said.

"Definitely twenty-six." Jusik was subdued. "I felt them."

"Okay, Shiny Boys twenty-six, *Hut'uune* nil," Corr said. He was picking up *Mando'a* fast. "I call that a home win."

Jusik stood staring into the inside of his helmet as he held it in his hands. "No witnesses left standing. Just a nasty argument between crime gangs."

"You'll never get any public praise for this," Skirata said. "But let me tell you now that every last one of you made me a proud man." He looked down at the strill, limping on one of its six legs as it circled Vau, grumbling deep in its throat. "Even you, Mird, you stinking heap of drool."

The strill looked up at Etain and made a musical warbling sound. She'd wrapped one arm around Darman's waist, head resting on his chest plate with her eyes closed, but she opened them and watched Mird.

"Mird likes you," Vau said. "You took care of it and let it have its kill."

Fi gave Darman a weary slap on the back. "She has a way with dumb animals, *ner vod.*"

An exhausted silence settled on the team. The droids labored around them, carrying girders, stacking duraplast sheets, oblivious. If anyone thought wild celebrations followed operations like this, they were wrong. The instant elation of seeing a vessel go up in flames or an enemy drop from a well-placed shot was very short-lived. The hyperalertness of adrenaline lingered for a while, and then was swallowed up quickly by fatigue and a sense of . . . of *void,* of odd purposelessness, of looking for the next task.

The adrenaline had to drain away. They'd be back to normal after some rest. Skirata was determined they'd get some.

"Let's get back to base," he said. "We can clear out of Qibbu's in the morning."

He got no response.

"Anyone hungry? Maybe an ale or two?"

" 'Freshers," Niner said. "Shower."

"Who's on watch roster tonight?"

"Me," Vau said before Skirata could open his mouth. "Go on, Bardan. You head back with Etain and Mird. I'll take Kal."

Skirata hauled himself onto Vau's speeder. The painkiller was wearing off and the ache had started gnawing his ankle again. He opened his comlink and called Jaller Obrim.

"Kal here. How's it going?"

Obrim sounded as if he was in the middle of a riot. There was a lot of shouting in the background and then a loud muffled *whump.* Commandos weren't the only ones who laid charges for a spot of rapid entry, then.

"Busy," said the CSF captain. "We've pulled in around sixty suspects so far. Pretty low on the food chain, but they lead to all kinds of other people CSF has an interest in, and they're off the streets for a while." He paused as another loud *whump* interrupted. "I don't know where we're going to put them all, though. The lockup is filling fast."

"Never had that problem. Our targets don't get out on parole, either."

"I'll bet. You all okay?"

"No serious injury. Everyone's walking. Quite a mess for you to clear up, though."

"My pleasure. CSF Staff and Social Club, *all* of you. End of the week. I will *not* take no for an answer and neither will CSF. Be there."

"Count on it."

Skirata closed the link and let his head drop so that his chin rested on his chest plate.

Vau squeezed into the seat in front of him and powered up the speeder. He reached behind him and passed Skirata a datapad. "Perrive's pad. Enjoy its contents at your leisure, *ner vod.* So, a drink or a fight? What's it to be?"

"Walon, you're very lucky I'm too tired." Skirata pocketed the datapad, another little treasure trove for his Null boys to play with. "I'd just slap you."

"I need to make my peace with Atin."

"He'll still kill you after he's had a good night's sleep."

"The brief unity of triumph, and then back to the fray. Crushing, isn't it? The victories seem so insignificant compared with the size of the war."

"Doesn't mean we shouldn't try," Skirata said. "It's only what individuals do that adds up to history."

"We've written ours, then."

It was one of the few times that Skirata found himself staring at Vau's back without feeling the urge to reach for his knife. "Tell you what," he said. He took out the disabled remote det from his pocket. "Why don't we swing by the diplomatic quarter and pick up that nice green speeder? Perrive's not going to need it now. Can you still hotwire a speeder?"

"You bet," said Vau.

23

When you can no longer know what your nation or your government stands for, or even where it is, you need a set of beliefs you can carry with you and cling to. You need a core in your heart that will never change. I think that's why I feel more at home in the barracks than I do in the Jedi Temple.
—General Bardan Jusik, Jedi Knight

Operational house, Qibbu's Hutt, 0015 hours,
386 days after Geonosis

The suite of rooms on the top floor of Qibbu's hotel looked like inventory day in the GAR equipment stores.

Fi stepped over stacked piles of armor and packs of five-hundred-grade plastoid explosive and flopped into the first chair he found.

"You going to sleep in that bucket?" Mereel said.

Fi took the hint and popped his helmet seal, inhaling warm air scented with sweat, stale carpet, caf, and strill. There were times when the *buy'ce* was a comfort and a quiet haven, insulating him from the world, and he felt in need of that now for reasons he didn't understand or want to think about.

Mereel sat at the scratched, battered table unwrapping packs of thermal plastoid and working a colorless liquid into them. Fi wanted to get up and look but he was simply too tired. He could see Mereel pressing a hollow into the cakes of brown plastoid with his thumb, pouring in a few drops of the liquid from a small bottle, and then kneading it in with a steady folding motion.

"Ah," Fi said, remembering.

"Got to add the stabilizer compound before we put it back into stores or else this is going to kill a lot more *vode* than the bad guys ever could."

"Want a hand?"

"No. Get some sleep."

"Where's Sergeant Kal?" Fi had quite enjoyed calling him *Kal'buir*. But he donned old habits along with his armor. "I hope he hasn't knifed Vau."

"They're liberating a speeder on behalf of the Skirata Retirement Fund."

"Come on, he'll never retire."

"He still wants the speeder. Merc habits die hard."

Fi found it hard to think of his sergeant as having any interest in a life beyond the army. He spent a while wondering what the man might really want, and apart from a wife to look after him, Fi had problems imagining what that might be. It was the same problem he had with his own dreams. They were intrusive and insistent—but they were limited. He only knew there was something missing, and when he looked at Darman and Etain, he knew what it was; he also wondered how it could work out even if he got it. He wasn't stupid. He could count and calculate odds of survival.

"Good night, *ner vod.*" He left Mereel to his task and wandered around, unclipping his armor plates as he went and stacking them in a pile by the bedroom door. Black bodysuits and briefs hung drying on every peg and rail. However exhausted they were, the squads still washed their kit conscientiously.

Fi glanced into some of the rooms to check who might be awake and willing to chat, but the Delta boys were all out cold, not even snoring. Niner and Corr slumped in chairs in one of the alcoves with a plate of half-eaten cookies sitting on the small table between them. Darman was stretched out on his bed in the room he shared with Fi, apparently none the worse for his ordeal, and Ordo was curled up in the next room with a blanket pulled over his head. Odd: he always seemed to do that, as if he wanted total darkness.

There was no sign of Jusik or Etain. Farther along the passage, Fi struck lucky. Atin was sitting in the chair in his room, cleaning his armor.

"I'm on watch until Skirata gets back," he said, without waiting for Fi's question.

"What's wrong?"

"Nothing."

"I'm sure Laseema will wait for you."

"It's not about Laseema."

"So it's *something.*"

"You never give up, do you?" Atin had always been the private type, even though he'd settled into a very different squad culture from the one he'd been raised in. There was always something new to learn about a brother who'd been trained in another batch. "Okay, now that the job's done, I've got matters to address with Sergeant Vau."

"He's not a sergeant any longer."

"I'm still going to kill him."

It was just talk. Men said things like that. Fi closed the doors and sat down on the bed opposite.

"I'm supposed to be on watch," Atin said.

"I made Sev tell me how you got the wound to your face."

"So now you know. Vau gave me a good hiding for being whiny about surviving Geonosis when my brothers didn't."

"It's even more than that. You know it. You wouldn't be the first commando to get in a fistfight with his sergeant."

"You know, I like you better when you're being mindless and funny."

"We need to know."

"Usen'ye." It was the crudest way to tell someone to go away in *Mando'a.* "It's none of your business."

"It is if you pick a fight with Vau, and he kills *you* and we have to get a replacement."

Atin laid the back plate he was cleaning on the floor and rubbed his eyes. "You want to know? Really? Look."

He hooked his fingers inside the neck of his bodysuit and jerked down the front panel. The gription seams yielded. It was nothing Fi hadn't seen before in the refreshers: Atin's shoulders and arms were laced with long white streaks of scar tissue. It was common in the GAR. Men got injured in training and in the field, armor or not. But Atin seemed to have acquired more spectacular ones than average.

Scars happened, especially if you didn't get bacta on a wound fast enough.

"Vau gave you those, too, didn't he?"

"Vau nearly killed me, so when I finally got out of the bacta tank, I said I'd kill *him* one day. Fair enough, yes?"

No wonder Corr said he found commandos a little "relaxed." They must have seemed dangerously chaotic to a clone trooper raised and trained by sober Kaminoan flash-instruction and simulation.

"*Kill* is a bit strong," Fi said. "Break his nose, maybe."

"Skirata did that already. Look, if Vau felt you lacked the killer edge, he'd crank it up a little. He'd make you fight your brother. We had a choice. We could fight each other until one was too badly hurt to stand up, or we could fight *him*."

Fi thought of Kal Skirata, as hard and ruthless as anyone he had ever known, making sure his squads were fed and well rested, finding illicit treats for them, teaching them, encouraging them, telling them how proud they made him. It seemed to work pretty well.

"And?" said Fi.

"I opted to take on Vau. He had a real *Mando* iron saber, and I was unarmed. I just went at him. I never wanted to kill so badly in my life and he just cut me up. And Skirata beat the *osik* out of Vau when he found out. They never did get on, those two."

"So . . . the thing with Sev. You told Skirata."

"No, Skirata just found out. I didn't even know he knew me until we met at the spaceport siege." Atin picked up his plate and started cleaning it again. "So now you know."

Fi thought that a quick swing at Vau might purge Atin's hatred. Then it occurred to him that his brother was absolutely literal.

"*At'ika,* ever thought what's going to happen to you if you *do* kill him?"

"I've killed people outside my legitimate rules of engagement tonight. One more won't make a difference. And I'll die soon enough anyway."

"Yeah, but there's Laseema."

Atin paused, cloth gripped in one hand. "Yes, there is."

"And how *are* you going to kill Vau anyway?"

"With a blade." He picked up his right gauntlet and ejected the blade with a loud *shunk.* "The *Mando* way."

This isn't bravado. Fi struggled for a moment, wondering what the right thing to do might be. *He's really going to do it.*

Fi decided he'd wait near the doors to the landing platform, ready for the moment that Vau walked through them.

Etain found sleep impossible. She sat out on the landing platform with Jusik, meditating. For all the violence of the day she had put behind her, she found a serene core within her that had never been there before, the inner calm she had sought so many years through study and struggle.

All I had to do was have a life beside my own to care for. That is the true detachment we ought to seek, putting another person above ourselves—not denying our emotions. The attachment to self *is the path to the dark side.*

The intricate silver threads of her child in the Force were more complex now, more interconnected. She sensed purpose and clarity and passion. He would be an extraordinary person. She could hardly wait to get to know him.

And when it was the right time, she would explain what she sensed to Darman. She imagined the joy on his face.

She brought herself out of the trance and Jusik was standing a few meters away, looking out over the ravine of towers in the direction of the Senate.

"Bardan, I have a question I can only ask of you."

He turned and smiled. "I'll answer if I can."

"How do I tell Darman in Mandalorian that I love him?"

She waited for Jusik to express some shock or disapproval. He blinked a few times, focusing on a nonexistent spot a few meters ahead. "I don't think he's completely fluent in *Mando'a*. The Nulls are, though."

"I don't want to declare my love for Ordo, thanks."

"Okay. Try . . . *ni kar'tayli gar darasuum.*"

She repeated it under her breath a few times. "Got it."

"It's the same word as 'to know,' 'to hold in the heart,' *kar'taylir*. But you add *darasuum,* forever, and it becomes something rather different."

"That tells me a great deal about the Mandalorian view of relationships."

"They believe that complete knowledge of someone is the key to loving them. They don't like surprises and hidden facets. Warriors tend not to."

"Pragmatic people."

"A pity we Jedi weren't better friends with them, then. We could enjoy being pragmatic together."

"You haven't lectured me on attachment. Thank you."

Jusik turned to her with a broad smile that could only have come from being at complete peace with himself. He indicated his body with a flourish of his hands: dull green Mandalorian armor in the form of body plates and greaves. The matching helmet with its sinister T-shaped slit in the visor stood on the floor beside him.

"You think," he said, "that I'll be walking back into the Jedi Temple wearing this? You think this isn't attachment?"

He really did find it funny. He laughed. The two of them were everything the Jedi Order wouldn't approve of. "Zey would throw a fit."

"Kenobi wears trooper armor."

"General Kenobi does *not* speak Mandalorian." She found Jusik's laughter infectious, and tinged with the exhaustion and frightened relief that was often so evident in Fi. "And his soldiers don't address him as *Little Obi-Wan.*"

Jusik became sober again. "Our code was written when we were peacekeepers. We've never fought a war, not like this, not using others. And that changes everything. So I shall remain *attached,* because my heart tells me it's *right.* If remaining a Jedi means that is incompatible, then I know the choice I'll make."

"You've made it," Etain said.

"And so have you." He made a vague gesture in the direction of her belly. "I can sense as much. I know you too well now."

"Don't."

"This is going to be very difficult for both of you, Etain."

"Darman doesn't know yet. You're not to mention it to *anyone.* Promise me."

"Of course I won't. I owe Darman a great deal. All of the men, in fact."

"You're going to kill yourself trying to live up to them."

"Then that's fine by me," said Jusik.

Jusik didn't want to be a peacemaker. If the Force hadn't manifested itself in him, he could have been a scientist, an engineer, a builder of astonishing things. But he wanted to be a soldier.

And Etain had to be one, too, whether she wanted to or not, because her troops needed her to be one. But as soon as the war was over, she would leave the Jedi Order and follow a harder but sweeter destiny.

Skirata set the green speeder down on the landing platform with a certain amount of satisfaction. He'd get Enacca to change the color and make it disappear from the licensing system, but that was routine work for her. She was furious at having to pick up so many of the team's speeders, sometimes abandoned when they had no choice, but a few extra credits would soothe her.

Vau eased out of the hatch on the passenger's side and Mird loped up to him, rumbling and whining happily.

"I'm going to treat myself to a glass of *tihaar,*" Skirata said. "If the strill wants to sleep inside tonight, it's welcome."

"I might join you in that drink." Vau scooped Mird up in his arms again. "Not a textbook operation by any means, but the men put a decent dent in the opposition in a very short time."

It almost felt like a civilized relationship. It felt that way right up to the moment the doors opened and they almost stumbled over Fi. He held out both arms as a barrier.

"Sarge, Atin's in a foul mood." He turned to Vau, who set Mird down on the carpet and removed his helmet. "I don't think you should go near him, Sergeant Vau."

Vau just lowered his chin slightly and looked resigned. "Let's get it over with."

"No—"

"Fi, this is between me and him."

Skirata's immediate instinct was to intervene, but this time he suspected Vau would come off worse, and that had a certain sense of justice to it. While he respected the man's skill and integrity, he loathed him at a gut level for his brutality. And for him, that erased all the virtues in Vau.

He said he did it for their own good: it was to reinforce their *Mando* identity, to save their lives, to save their souls. His lads even believed it. Skirata never would.

"I've been waiting, Sarge," said Atin's voice.

Skirata pulled Fi back. Ordo and Mereel, still working on neutralizing the booby-trapped thermal plastoid, looked up, wary, waiting for his signal to get involved. He gave them a discreet shake of the head. *Not yet.* Leave it.

Atin wore his right gauntlet and his bodysuit. He extended the vibroblade from the knuckle plate and held his fist up at his shoulder, then sheathed the blade.

"If that strill starts on me, I'll take it out, too."

It was a side of Atin that Skirata had never seen before, but one that Vau had built. It was the little bit of Jango, the gene that said *Stand and fight, don't run,* another genetic tendency that could be nurtured and developed and trained into something much bigger than itself.

Vau held his arms at his sides and looked genuinely frustrated. Atin never understood why he'd done it. *And neither did I,* Skirata thought. *You save a man from being* dar'manda *by teaching him his heritage, not by making him into a wild animal.*

Vau's voice had softened. "You had to be *Mando,* Atin. If I didn't make you *Mando,* you might as well have been dead, because you wouldn't exist as a *Mando'ad,* not without your spirit and your guts." He was *almost* apologetic. "You had to be able to cross that threshold and be ready to do absolutely *anything* to win. Fierfek, if stupid Jedi hadn't used you as infantry on Geonosis, every single one of my commando batch would be alive today. I made you hard men because I *cared*."

Skirata was glad Vau didn't use the word *love.* He'd have put his own knife in the man's guts if he had. He stood clear, hauling Fi away by his arm, and Atin surged forward to seize Vau by his shoulder plates and head-butt him. Vau staggered back a few steps, blood pouring from his nose, but didn't go down. Mird squealed frantically and went to defend its master but Vau sent it back with a hand command.

"*Udesii,* Mird. I can handle this."

"Okay, handle *this,*" Atin said, and swung a punch.

It was hard to fight a man in Mandalorian armor but Atin, true to his name, was going to do it. His blow caught Vau just below the eye and he followed up with a ferocious lunge to slam him against the wall and press his arm across his throat. Vau reverted to animal instinct and brought his knee up in Atin's gut, driving him far enough back to smash his elbow into his face.

Do I stop this? Can I? Skirata stood ready.

The blow stopped Atin for a few seconds. Then he just came straight back at Vau and charged into him, knocking him flat and pinning him to the floor, pounding away at him with his fists, hitting armor as often as flesh. By this time the noise of bodies and the strill's squeals of protest had woken people and Jusik came running just as Atin ejected his vibroblade with a sickening *shunk* and had it raised, elbow held high, to punch it into Vau's exposed neck.

The two men flew apart as if in a silent explosion. Atin cannoned into the table and Vau was rolled back against the wall. There was a stunned moment of silence.

"This stops now!" Jusik yelled at the top of his voice. "That is an *order*! I am your general and I will *not* tolerate brawling, do you hear? Not for any reason. Get up, the two of you!"

Vau obeyed as meekly as any new recruit. The two men struggled to their feet and Atin stood to attention out of long habit. Little Jusik—hair sleep-tousled, wearing just a crumpled tunic and rough pants—stood glaring at the two much bigger men.

Skirata had never seen the Force used to break up a fight before. It was as impressive as ripping open that door.

"I want this feud to stop now," Jusik continued, voice barely a whisper. "We have to have *discipline.* And I can't let you harm each other. We *have* to be united. Do you understand?"

"Yes sir," Atin said impassively, blood streaked across his face. "Am I on a charge now, General?"

"No. I'm just asking you to put an end to this for all our sakes."

Atin was calm reason once again. He didn't even seem out of breath. "Very good, sir."

Vau looked shaken, or at least as shaken as a man like him could be. "I'm a civilian, General, so I can do as I please, but I apologize to my former trainee for any pain I caused him."

Skirata winced. It was enough to start the fight again. But it was as good a concession as anyone would ever get out of a man who believed he had done Atin a favor.

"My fault, sir," Skirata said, doing what a good sergeant should. "I ought to maintain better discipline."

Jusik gave him a look that said he didn't believe that, but it was fond rather than censorious. Skirata hoped he never had to show the lad that he wouldn't obey him, but he suspected Jusik would never want to test that.

The Jedi glanced over his shoulder at the silent audience that had gathered. "We can all get back to bed now." The commandos shrugged and disappeared back to their rooms. Corr's expression of total shock was fascinating. There was no sign of Darman. "And you, Fi. It's been a heavy day."

Jusik grabbed a bacta spray with an expression of weary exasperation and sat Atin down in a chair to clean up his face. He made no attempt to tend to Vau, who walked off to the refreshers, Mird whining at his heels. Ordo and Mereel vanished to the landing platform with bundles of wrapped explosives.

Skirata waited for Jusik to finish and for Atin to return to his room.

"So, no lightsaber and no armor." Jusik was even shorter than he was. He prodded the kid in the chest. "I told you that it's what's *under* the armor that makes a man. A few thousand Jedi like you and the Republic wouldn't be in the *osik* it is now. You're a soldier, sir, and a good officer. And I don't think I've ever said that to anyone in my life."

Skirata meant it at that moment. It didn't make him love Jedi as a kind any the better, but he was very fond of *Bard'ika,* and would look after him. Jusik lowered his eyes, a strange blend of embarrassment and delight, and clasped Skirata's arm.

"I want what's best for my men, that's all."

Skirata waited for him to shut his bedroom doors and went in search of the bottle of *tihaar* and that rarest of things in Qibbu's Hut, a clean glass. He wrenched the stopper out of the bottle and slopped a little into a chipped goblet.

He couldn't identify which fruit it had been distilled from this time, and it didn't taste that good. It never had, but more often than not it got him to sleep. He let it burn the inside of his mouth before swallowing and sat in the chair, nursing the glass in his cupped hands, eyes closed.

I hope Atin's found some kind of peace from this.

He thought he detected a faint hint of jewel-fruit in the *tihaar.*

Four million credits.

That was satisfying, far more than any bounty or fee he had invested over the years on Aargau. Nobody had mentioned it. Ordo and Mereel certainly had to be thinking about it: they knew his plans. Vau was a mercenary but would not interfere, because he had been paid. Etain might ask questions, too. But the commando squads had little interest in the realities of economics. Clones didn't get paid. They never coveted possessions because they had been raised with nothing to call their own. Even Fi's desire for Ghez Hokan's fine *Mando* armor and his lads' general lust for Verpine rifles was a blend of pragmatism and the Mandalorian cultural values that he had taught them himself, not basic civilian greed.

And a copy of a restricted Treasury datapad to play with.

And Perrive's 'pad to pick over. I'll have Mereel copy it before I give it to Zey . . . or give most of it to him, anyway.

He opened his eyes, aware of someone standing over him. Ordo and Mereel stood impatient and excited, looking much more like normal young men having a lark than efficient, disciplined, deadly soldiers.

Mereel grinned, unable to contain his glee. "Want to hear about Ko Sai, *Kal'buir*? She's turned up again."

Skirata drained the glass. *This* was what he wanted most. "I'm all ears, *adi'ke.*"

24

A major terrorist network lies in tatters this morning following the end of a massive overnight operation by Coruscant Security Forces. A total of ninety-seven suspects were detained or killed, and what's described as "a significant amount" of explosives seized. Senator Ihu Niopua described it as a magnificent piece of police work and praised officers.

—HNE evening news, 387 days after Geonosis

Coruscant Security Force Staff and Social Club, 2000 hours, 388 days after Geonosis: ATU and OCU reception for men and guests of Arca Company, Special Operations Brigade

CSF didn't know how brave they'd been until they heard it on the HNE bulletin.

Fi decided to treat the coverage as funny rather than as another case of his brothers' efforts going unrecognized. Skirata had warned him that all special forces personnel had to deal with that, clone or not, so it was nothing personal.

Anyway, it didn't matter. He was leaning on a bar—a clean bar, one that didn't leave your elbows soaking wet—surrounded by people who weren't criminals; unless you counted Sergeant Kal, of course, and he was a special case, because extreme bounty hunting wasn't *really* a crime. And police officers were buying him drinks and shaking his hand, telling him that their buddies would all have been ground nerf if he hadn't thrown himself on that grenade during the spaceport siege. It was amazing how they still remembered that.

Fi didn't have the heart to tell them that he simply did what years of training had made his body do involuntarily, and that he didn't know how to do anything else. He simply grinned and enjoyed the adulation. He liked the comradeship.

Some of them were female officers, too. They were fascinated by his armor. He enjoyed explaining the parts and functions to them, and wondered why they giggled when he told them how easy it was to take off.

Ordo wandered in with Obrim and joined Fi at the bar. Obrim handed them both a glass of a light-colored ale, instantly another brother in uniform with a tacit understanding of how things were.

"I see they've upgraded your armor again," he said, tapping Fi's breastplate with the knuckle of his forefinger. "Different finish. Classy."

"Well, they have to try the new kit out on someone, and we're just so *stylish.*"

"I suppose they can afford to, now that there's fewer of you left to kit out," Obrim said, falling into the grim cynicism of men used to being at the mercy of accountants. "Because body bags are a lot cheaper."

"What body bags?" Fi said.

"Really?"

"Not the *Mando* way. Or the Republic's."

"Kriffing tightwads." Obrim sighed irritably. Then he indicated Mereel, who was surrounded by a small knot of officers plus Delta Squad, laughing noisily. "I see your brother is teaching our boys some bad *Mando'a* words. Is it true you don't have a word for 'hero'?"

"Yes, but we've got a dozen for 'stab.' "

Obrim almost laughed. "And how many for frying someone with a blaster?"

"Loads," said Fi. "We don't know much about art, but we know what we like."

Ordo was scanning the crowded bar with a faint frown. Fi followed his gaze. He wondered if he was checking where Etain and Jusik were, because Jedi didn't fit easily into the raucous atmosphere of a police social club, but there was Jusik, all smiles, engaged in an intense conversation with two Sullustan forensics officers. Darman was deep in discussion with Corr and a couple of men Fi recognized as CSF bomb disposal experts from the spaceport siege. Niner and Boss seemed to have been drawn into a strange game with some other officers that involved throwing a knife at the fine wooden carvings above the bar, much to the annoyance of the service droid.

And Atin had Laseema on his arm, gazing at him adoringly, even if he did still have a striking black eye from his fight with Vau.

But no Etain, and no Vau. Vau had gone off on another job—unspecified, of course. Darman was still here, though, and that meant Etain was, too, for the time being.

Ordo seemed to be concentrating on the doorway.

"What's your problem, *ner vod*?"

"Agent Wennen said she would come," Ordo said. He looked uncharacteristically awkward, seeming for once as if he didn't know what to do next. "I'll have a look around. It's a big bar."

Obrim watched him go. "Fi," he said, "do you mind me asking you something personal?"

"I always try to help police with their inquiries, Captain."

"Seriously, son. Kal talks to me about you all. I never knew how you were . . . bred for all this. Sorry. I can't find another word for it. You don't seem to resent it at all. I'd be furious. Aren't you angry? Not just a little?"

Fi wished Obrim didn't make him think. In a way it was much, much simpler on Kamino. It was also easier being alone with only your squad for company on some *osik'la* planet blowing up droids. There was a clean focus in that. Coruscant had indeed been the hardest battlefield of all, as Sergeant Kal had warned him. But that wasn't because it was rife with the dangers of not knowing if the enemy was standing right next to you. It was because it showed him what he could never have.

"I've done a lot of thinking in the past year," Fi said. "Yes, there's plenty wrong. I *know* I deserve more than this. I want a nice girl and a life and I *don't want to die.* And I know I'm being used, thanks. But I'm a soldier, and I'm also Mandalorian, and my strength is always going to be what I carry around inside me, my sense of who and what I am. Even if the rest of the galaxy sinks in its own filth, I'll die without compromising my honor." He drained his glass and started on the next one that was lined up on the bar. He wasn't that fond of the taste, but he believed in being polite. "That's what keeps me going. That, and my brothers. And that ale you promised me."

"I had to ask." Obrim frowned quickly and looked away for a moment. "Did that drink really keep you going?"

He thought of the insertion into Fest months before. "Yeah, Captain. Sometimes it did."

Fi dreaded where the conversation might take him but he was interrupted by a loud cheer from farther down the bar. Skirata had arrived and was demonstrating his skill in the knife-throwing game. He let fly with his vicious three-sided knife, knocking the other knives out of the woodwork time after time. The bar droid protested.

"He's way too good at that," Obrim said, and turned to Fi again to resume the conversation. "Now, about this—"

Fi didn't want to discuss it anymore. He straightened up and called across the bar to Skirata. "Sarge? Sarge! Want to show 'em the *Dha Werda*?"

There was a whoop of *"Kandosii!"* from the squads. "Yeah, come on, Sarge! Let's show them how it's done!"

"I'm too old," Skirata said, retrieving his knife.

"Nah," Fi said, and seized the chance to drag Skirata away from the game. "You taught us this, remember?"

Skirata took the invitation and limped over to join the two squads, who quickly cleared a space in the bar. Ordo, Mereel, and Jusik joined them; Corr stood back, uncertain. Troopers rarely got the chance to see the ritual chant, let alone learn it.

"I haven't had enough to drink yet," Skirata said, "but I'll give it a go."

Without his armor, he looked even smaller among his commandos than usual. The chant started up.

Taung—sa—rang—bro-ka!
Je—tii—se-ka—'rta!
Dha—Wer-da—Ver-da—a'den—tratu!

He fell into the rhythm instantly, keeping perfect time, taking rhythmic blows on his leather jacket that normally fell on hard armor. He was a battle-hardened warrior like his lads, just older.

Fi winked at him, careful to allow for their difference in height.

Cor—u—scan—ta—kan—dosii—adu!
Duum—mo—tir—ca—'tra—nau—tracinya!

Skirata kept up the relentless pace for verse after verse. Fi caught sight of white armor in his peripheral vision and ARC Trooper Captain Maze appeared from the crowd of CSF officers who were watching openmouthed with glasses of ale in their hands.

"Mind if I join in?" Maze said.

Fi had no intention of trying to stop an ARC trooper. Maze slipped into the line next to Ordo and smiled at his brother captain in a way Fi didn't quite like.

As Skirata always told outsiders, the *Dha Werda* took stamina, timing, and total trust in your comrades. Complex rhythms sharpened your brain and taught you to think as one. Turn too fast or too late, and you'd get a nasty smack in the face. It was performed without *buy'cese.*

Ordo wasn't quite as focused as he should have been. Maybe his mind was still on where lovely Besany Wennen might be. Whatever the reason, as Fi turned right, fists clenched, arms at shoulder height, ready to beat the rhythm on Niner's back plate, he saw and heard Maze's fist connect with Ordo's chin.

Ordo carried on, blood weeping from his lip, refusing to break the rhythm. You didn't stop if you got hit. You carried on.

Gra—'tua—cuun—hett—su—dralshya!
Kom—'rk—tsad—drot-en—t-roch—nyn—ures—adenn!

The line of commandos turned ninety degrees left, hammering the rhythm, and then right again, and Maze hit Ordo neatly and—Fi had to admit it—elegantly in the mouth again without losing the beat. Blood splashed on Ordo's pristine white chest plate. Fi waited for the encounter to erupt in a fight, but the chant finished without incident and Ordo simply wiped his mouth on the palm of his glove.

"Sorry, *ner vod,*" Maze said, smiling with genuine amusement. "You know how clumsy we *ordinary* ARC troopers are. We make lousy dancers."

Fi held his breath. He was ready to back Ordo up against Maze; Ordo was his friend. And Fi also knew that he was utterly unpredictable and totally unafraid of violence.

Ordo merely shrugged, held out his arm, and the two ARC captains shook hands and went to the bar. Skirata watched them carefully and smiled.

All ARCs were crazy. Sometimes Fi was grateful that he'd had the most volatile bits of Jango removed from his genes.

Skirata sat down on a bar stool and wiped sweat from his lined forehead with the palm of his hand.

"I'm not getting any younger," he said, catching his breath, and laughed. "I'll be black and blue in the morning. Shouldn't try that without body armor."

"You could have dipped out after a few minutes," Fi said. He handed him a cloth. "We wouldn't have minded."

"But *I* would have. I can't ask a man to do what I can't or won't do myself."

"You never have." Fi noted that a small silence had formed

around the doorway—and its cause was Besany Wennen. She walked in, looking around, then spotted Ordo and went over to him.

"I'm going out on the balcony to get some air," Skirata said.

The last thing Fi saw before Obrim led him away to meet some officers who were very keen to buy him more drinks was Besany Wennen dabbing at Ordo's split lip with a handkerchief and berating a visibly surprised Captain Maze.

"Hello," Skirata said. "I didn't realize you were out here, *ad'ika.*"

Etain looked up. She had been peering over the balcony at the lane upon lane of airspeeder traffic below. Nightscapes on Coruscant were as entertaining as a holovid. "It's too noisy for me in there. You look like you've been having fun."

Skirata joined her and rested folded arms on the safety rail. "Been showing CSF the *Dha Werda.*"

"I bet that was painful." He seemed a fundamentally good man. She adored him, even if he scared her sometimes. "It's good to see everyone relaxing. It's been tough, hasn't it?"

"We did it, though. All of us. You too, *ad'ika.* Well done."

She was blissfully certain of life now. She felt good. She was also certain that Skirata was a man who understood love and the risks people would take to make those they loved happy. He defied generals and anyone who stood in his way to make sure his soldiers—his *sons,* for that was what they were—got what was rightfully theirs.

There was no reason not to tell him her wonderful news. She should have told Darman first, but she wasn't quite sure how. And—anyway—Skirata was *Kal'buir.* He was everyone's father.

"Thank you for being so understanding about me and Dar," she said.

Skirata rubbed his forehead. "I'm sorry for lecturing you. I'm very protective of them all. But you're both happy, and I'm glad to see that."

"I hope you'll be glad that I'm having a baby, then."

There was a moment's silence.

"What?" said Skirata.

"I'm pregnant."

She watched his face harden. *"Pregnant?"*

She hadn't expected that. An unpleasant coldness spread up from her stomach into her chest.

"Whose is it?" Skirata asked. His voice was level, controlled, distant. It was a mercenary's voice.

That *hurt.* "Darman's, of course."

"He doesn't know, then. He'd have told me if he did."

"No, I haven't told him."

"Why?"

"How could he cope with that? It's hard enough for a normal—"

"He's not *abnormal.* He's what you people made him."

"I meant . . ." Etain struggled. "I meant that he has no experience to enable him to cope with being a father at a time like this."

"Nobody ever has."

"I wanted him to have some kind of future."

Skirata's face didn't change. "You *planned* this? How can he have a future if he *doesn't know he has a son*? Genes don't count for everything."

"If anyone finds out that I'm expecting a child, I'll be thrown out of the Jedi Order and I won't be able to serve. I have to carry on. I *can't* let the men down."

Skirata was furious. She felt it. She could see it, too. And if she thought that was bad, it would be nothing compared with how the Jedi Council would react. She'd be kicked out of the Order. She'd no longer be a general, no longer able to play her part in the war.

But you knew that.

You should have thought that through.

The reality felt very different. And yet she didn't regret it one bit, and that was why she hadn't thought about the Jedi Council's reaction. It was *right.* The Force had guided her to this point.

"And how are you planning to disguise this fact?" Skirata asked, still cold calm. "It's going to be pretty visible."

"I can go into a healing trance and accelerate the pregnancy. I can bear this child in five months." She put her hand on her belly. "It's a boy."

That was probably the worst thing she could have told Skirata. Etain should have known Mandalorians better by now. The father–son bond was paramount. Every scrap of warmth that he had ever shown her had evaporated: and it devastated her. She had grown to love him as a father, too.

And a good *Mando* father put his son first.

"In this great plan of yours, then, this plan to give my lad a future, what did you think his son might become? A *Jedi*?"

"No. Just a man. A man with a normal life."

"No, *ad'ika.*" Skirata's hands were thrust in his pockets now. She could see the rise and fall of his chest as his breathing labored with suppressed rage. A little black vortex in the Force opened up around him. "No, Darman's son *will* be Mandalorian, or he has no son at all. Don't you understand? Unless the kid has his culture and what makes him Mandalorian, he . . . he has no soul. That's why I had to teach them all, *all* my boys, what it was to be *Mando*. Without it they're dead men."

"I know how important it is."

"No, I don't think you do. We're nomadic. We have no country. All we have to hold us together is what we are, what we do, and without that we're . . . *dar'manda*. I don't know how to explain it . . . we have no soul, no afterlife, no identity. We're eternally dead."

Etain repeated *dar'manda* to herself. "That's how he got his name, isn't it?"

"Yes."

It began to dawn on her why Skirata and Vau were both so obsessed with teaching their trainees about their heritage. They weren't just giving them a cultural identity: they were literally saving their lives, their very souls. "He'll be a Force-user. That will make him—"

"Are you *insane*? Do you know what that makes him worth to creatures like the Kaminoans? Do you know how *very* interested people will be in his genetic material? He's in *danger,* you *di'kut*!"

The value of her son's unique genetic heritage had never crossed Etain's mind. She was appalled. She struggled to cope with the hazards that sprang up around her as if from nowhere."But how can Dar raise him?"

"You didn't ask that question when you started all this? Do you really love him?"

"*Yes!* Yes, you *know* I do. Kal, if I don't have his child and he dies—"

"*When* he dies. He's designed to *die young*. I'll outlive him. And you're built to live a *long* time."

"You said it yourself—just one broad generation of men. Then there's *nothing* of the clones left eventually, nothing to show they ever lived and served and *died*. They *all* deserve better than that."

"But again, Darman *isn't given any choice,*" Kal said. "No choice about fighting. No choice about being a father."

He lapsed into silence, walking to the far side of the balcony and leaning on it, just as he had when she'd seen him agonize over whether he had been a monster, a man who turned small boys into soldiers and sent them to fight the *aruetiise's* war.

Etain waited. There was no point arguing with him. He was right: she took choice out of Darman's hands just as every Jedi general did.

"Kal," she said.

He didn't turn.

She put a cautious hand on his back. She felt him tense. "Kal, what do you want me to do to make this right? Don't you want at least one of your men to leave something behind him, someone who'll remember him?"

"You can only remember what you know."

"I'll keep the child safe—"

"You've got a name for him, haven't you? I *know* it. You know you're expecting a boy so you'll have thought of a name. Mothers do that."

"Yes. I—"

"Then I don't want to hear it. If you want my help, I have conditions."

She knew that. She should have known. Skirata took his paternal role obsessively, and he was a hard man, a mercenary, a man whose whole instinct had been honed to fight and survive since he was a small boy.

"I need your help, *Kal'buir.*"

"Don't call me that."

"I'm sorry."

"You want my help? Then here are my terms. Darman is told he has a son when it's safe for *him* to know, not when it suits you. And if that isn't when the kid's born, then I name the boy as a *Mando'ad.* Fathers name their sons, so if Dar can do that, then I'll make sure that he does."

"So I don't have any choice."

"You could skip town to any one of a thousand planets if you wanted to."

"And you'd find me."

"Oh yes. I *find* people. It's my job."

"And you'd tell the Jedi Order. You hate me."

"No, I actually like you, *ad'ika.* I just despise Jedi. You Force-users never question your right to shape the galaxy. And ordinary people never realize they have the chance to."

"I think . . . I think it would be very fitting for Darman's son to know his heritage."

"He'll do more than that. If Darman can't raise him as a *Mando,* then I will. I've had plenty of practice. *Plenty.*"

Etain was helpless. Her only choice was to run—and she knew that wasn't fair to anyone, least of all to the baby. It would have confirmed to her that all she wanted was a child, something to cling to and love and be loved by in return, regardless of how she got it.

This had to be for Darman. His son could *not* grow up an ordinary man. And Etain had no idea how to raise a *Mando* son. Skirata did. If she refused, she knew exactly how far he would go to get his way.

"How will you cope with a Force-using child?" she asked.

"The same way I raised six lads who were so disturbed and damaged by being placed in live-fire battle simulations as toddlers that they never stood a chance of being normal. With a lot of love and patience."

"You actually *want* to do this, don't you?"

"Yes, I do. More than anything. It's my absolute duty as a *Mando'ad.*"

So that was his price. "I can disguise the pregnancy—"

"No, you're going to have a nice quiet few months under deep cover on Qiilura, with one of Jinart's people to keep an eye on you. And just watch me make that happen. Then you return with the child, and I raise it here. A grandson. Given my family history, nobody will turn a hair."

"What will you call him?"

"If Darman is in a position to know when the child's born, it'll be *his* choice. Until then, I'll keep my ideas to myself."

"So you agree Darman shouldn't know yet."

"If I tell him, or you do, then how is he going to go off to war again and keep his mind on his own safety? He ships out again in a few days. So will you. This isn't like telling a regular lad that he's made a girl pregnant, and that can be bad enough. He's a clone with no rights and no real idea of the real world, and he's made his Jedi general pregnant. Do I have to draw you a picture?"

Etain had never truly enraged anyonc. The Jedi who had raised her and trained her all her life had been far beyond that emotion. They allowed themselves a little impatience or irritation, but never anger. And on Qiilura, when she had the responsibility for four commandos thrust upon her for the first time in a desperate, dangerous mission, Jinart's anger at her inexperience had been well short of rage.

But Skirata was now drowning in it. She could feel his blind anger and how he was holding it in check. She could see the ashen tone of his face, drained of blood. She could hear the strain in his voice.

"Kal, you of all people should know how much it matters. Your own sons disowned you for putting your clone soldiers before them.

You *must* know what it feels like to risk hatred and contempt to do the right thing for those you love. And why you'd do the same again."

"If you had been Laseema telling me she was carrying Atin's child, things would have been very different," he hissed.

There was a movement behind them.

"Kal'buir?"

Etain turned. Ordo stood in the doorway. She hadn't felt him approaching; compared with the disturbance Kal was generating in the Force, he was invisible.

"It's okay, son." Skirata looked embarrassed and beckoned him across. He managed to feign a smile. "So Captain Maze got his own back, then?"

Ordo, attuned to Skirata's reactions, looked at Etain suspiciously. He felt like the strill in the Force right then, except there was no joyful sense of a wild infant at play, just ferocity. "Honor has been satisfied, as they say. I wondered if you wanted to join us for a drink. Besany is anxious to see you again."

"Ah, *us* sounds as if you two are getting on very well." Skirata smiled, and it was real: Besany Wennen was not, of course, a *jetii,* a Jedi. She was acceptable. "I'd love to, *Ord'ika.* Etain and I were just finishing our chat anyway."

Skirata left as if nothing had happened. Etain leaned on the rail, forehead on her crossed arms, and felt almost completely crushed. But Skirata was right in everything he had said: and he would honor his promise to help her. The price was inevitable. She would pay it.

She focused on the joy that surrounded her son in the Force. However hard things became, that was one thing nobody could take from her—not even *Kal'buir*.

25

Of course I've planned a way out. I've been a mercenary since I was seven years old. You always plan for what happens when the current war is over. It's called an exit strategy, and mine's been in the planning a long, long time.
—Kal Skirata to Jaller Obrim, discussing the future in an uncertain galaxy

Coruscant Security Force Staff and Social Club, 0015 hours, 389 days after Geonosis

"Well, that was fun," Jaller Obrim said, heaving himself onto a bar stool. The club was almost deserted now. "They don't drink much, your boys, do they?"

"They make up for it with eating." Skirata was working out how he would deal with the current crisis. Jinart the Gurlanin had disappeared in that way that only shapeshifting Gurlanins could. She didn't have a comlink, and he wouldn't run into her eating a fried breakfast at the Kragget. He had to find another way of summoning her. "Enormous appetites. It's the accelerated aging that boosts their metabolisms."

Obrim scratched his cheek, looking embarrassed. "I know, friend. I've not been through what you've been through with them, but anyone in our game will understand just how you feel."

"Yeah." *But Darman has a son now. I'm angry that Etain let that happen without even asking him, but he has a son. Even if I never get hold of that Kaminoan aiwha-bait Ko Sai, he* does *have some kind of future now.* "I'm sorry if I take it out on you sometimes."

"Don't you ever worry about that."

"Thanks."

"What would you do if you could run the galaxy now, Kal? I mean anything."

Skirata didn't even pause to think. "I'd stop the war right now," he said. "Then I'd go back to Kamino and grab those gray freaks by their rotten skinny necks and make them engineer a normal life span for every single last one of our boys. Then I'd take the whole army home to Mandalore and spend the rest of my life making sure they had wives and families, and a purpose that was *theirs,* not some *aruetii's* private feud."

"I thought you might say that," Obrim said. "I ought to be getting home now. Last few days have been a bit rough on my wife. Y'know, never at home. Why don't you come around for dinner sometime?"

"I'd like that."

"Can I drop you off?"

"I'm waiting for Ordo. He's talking to Besany."

"I noticed." Obrim just smiled. "He's a smart boy."

Skirata was left contemplating a future that had seemed no more tangled than it ever had just a few hours ago, but was now totally upended. He stood up and threw his knife into the carvings around the bar a few times and thought about his bank account on Aargau, and the fact that Mereel was very close to finding Ko Sai. Skirata felt he was now in striking distance of making a better life for a handful of cloned soldiers—a tiny number out of so many, but that was all he could do. That had to be enough.

And he had an even sharper focus now. Darman had a son, and he would see that Darman was around to watch the boy grow up.

"Sorry I kept you, *Kal'buir.*" Ordo strode into the bar and attempted a smile, but winced at his split lip. "We can go now."

"Everything working out with Besany?"

"Yes."

"Just yes?"

"Ummm . . . I think it is."

"Good." He resisted the urge to interfere. "I have a question for you. I need to get hold of Jinart. How would I do that?"

"Easy. She's a spy. She monitors the GAR troop movements to and from Qiilura. I can put a message in the logistics system that will get her attention. Something subtle. Give me a time and place, and leave the rest to me."

Skirata had to smile. Almost everything was easy for Ordo. "Back to the barracks then."

"I have a question for you, too, *Kal'buir.*"

"Okay."

"Is it true what Etain said? Did your sons disown you because you stayed on Kamino with us?"

Ordo wasn't stupid and he wasn't deaf. Skirata's family shame was the one thing he never wanted any of them to know about, and not only because it might make them feel guilty. He didn't want them to fear he might abandon *them* with equal ease.

"It's true, *Ord'ika.*"

"Why would you even think of paying such a terrible price for *us*?"

"Because you *needed* me. And I never regretted it for a second. My relationship with my . . . former family was as good as dead before you were even thought of. Don't you ever give it a second thought, because I'd do it again in a heartbeat. No question."

"But I wish we had known."

Do I have the right to keep another secret, then? "I'm sorry."

"So apart from Darman's unborn son, is there anything else you keep from us?"

He'd heard him arguing with Etain, then. Skirata felt the most agonizing shame he had ever experienced in his life. His whole existence now rested on the absolute trust between him and his clone family. He couldn't bear to lose that.

"So you know what I'm going to ask of Jinart, then. I heard the news when you did, *Ord'ika.* And no, there is nothing else. I swore I would never lie to you, and I never have." Skirata pointed to Ordo's matched blasters. "If I ever do, I'd rather you used those on me. Because being there for you was the only decent thing I ever did in my life. Understand?"

Ordo just stared at him. Skirata put both hands up on his shoulders and stood there in silence.

"Okay, son, tell me what I should do about Darman, and I'll do it."

Ordo still had that look of blank appraisal, the expression he adopted when dismantling a new and fascinating puzzle. "I don't think the time is right. We have to do what's best for our brothers."

It was the pragmatic thing to do. Skirata fastened his jacket and checked that his knife was in place, his ritual for leaving any building and walking out into the unknown night.

"Agreed, *Ord'ika.* Now all I need to do is have a little chat with General Zey."

Arca Company Barracks, Special Forces HQ, Coruscant,
395 days after Geonosis

It was an op order—an operational order—like many others they had been given. Niner glanced at the datapad and shrugged.

"Well, that'll be interesting," he said. "Never worked with the Galactic Marines before."

Skirata sat on the table in the briefing room, swinging his legs. Delta Squad had left that morning to prepare the battlefield—a nice military understatement for going ahead of the main assault and sabotaging strategic targets—on Skuumaa. Omega had drawn the slightly longer straw and had a similar task to carry out for the Marines.

"Everyone okay?" The question was directed at Darman as much as anybody. "Any questions?"

"No, Sarge." Fi sounded a little subdued. Atin actually seemed more cheerful than Fi did, which was an interesting reversal of attitudes. "It'll be nice to see Commander Gett again."

"Gett wants you embarked in *Fearless* by oh-seven-hundred tomorrow. So if there's anything you want to do, do it today." Skirata reached in his jacket pocket, took out four high denomination credit chips, and passed them around. "Go on. You know your way around the interesting bits of Coruscant now. It'll be a few months before you're back here."

"Thanks, Sarge." Atin stood up to leave. "You'll still be here when we get back today?"

"I always see you off, don't I?"

"Yeah, Sarge. You do."

Fi took his chip and pressed it back into Skirata's hand. "Thanks. I've got to do some calibration on my HUD. I'll stick around the barracks today."

"He's gone all sober," Niner said. "Don't know what's come over him."

"I'm an unsung hero," said Fi. "I've got my public image to protect."

The Omega boys, like all squads, were well attuned to one another's sensitivities. They knew Skirata was hanging around to talk to Darman on his own. Niner shoved Atin and Fi toward the doors. "See you later, Sarge."

There was no question of Darman joining them for a last day out in town. They knew where he'd want to spend his time. Skirata waited for the briefing room doors to close and slid off the table to stand in front of Darman's seat.

"Now, son, anything troubling you?"

"No, Sarge."

"Etain's off to Qiilura for a few months, to start the rundown of the garrison."

Darman actually smiled. "That's a safe deployment compared with the jobs she's pulled recently. I'm glad."

"She's hanging around the barracks waiting for you."

Darman seemed relieved. He took a deep breath and grinned, but it was that smile Skirata had seen on many mercenaries' faces before they left for a new battlefield.

Fierfek, should I tell this boy now? Should I tell him he has a kid on the way? What if something happens to him before he gets a chance to find out?

Skirata took a sudden and impulsive risk. He could square it with Zey later, like the bill for the anti-terror operation. *Always better to beg forgiveness than ask permission.* "You can go to Qiilura with her if you want."

Darman shut his eyes. The pain showed on his face.

"I've had that choice before, Sarge."

"You love her, though?"

"Yes."

"I can make this happen." *Maybe it wouldn't be right for you, son. But it's your choice.* "All you have to do is say the word, and Corr will take your place in the squad. He's still around. Zey's letting me train him."

Darman let out a long breath and pinched the bridge of his nose, eyes still shut. When he opened them, they were brimming with tears.

"Qiilura's *safe.* My squad deploys in the front line. How can I *not* be there with them? You could have walked away from Kamino with a fortune and never given us another thought, but you couldn't do it, either."

"That was different. I was washed up, a *di'kutla*—"

"No. You were *loyal.*"

"You sure about this?" *Of course you're sure. Your loyalty is overwhelming, too. That's how the stinking Republic uses you.* "I won't think any less of you if you go."

"But *I'll* think less of me."

"Okay, no need to tell her, then. It was my idea, not hers. And Ordo will make sure you two can stay in touch whenever you want."

Darman brushed the tip of his nose and sniffed hard. "You always put us first."

"I always will."

"We know."

Yes. He always would. "There's two ways you can think of females in wartime, son. One is to get obsessed and let them take your mind off your work, and that gets you killed. The other is to focus on them as what you're really fighting for, and draw strength from knowing they're going to be there for you when you get home." He tapped Darman's cheek a few times with the flat of his hand, firm but paternal. "You know which you're going to choose, don't you, Dar?"

"Yes, Sarge."

"Good lad."

Skirata knew that Darman might never arrive home, throw his kit bag on the hall floor, and sob on his wife's shoulder, relieved and grateful and swearing it would be his last tour of duty. But he'd make sure he brought him as close to that sweet normality as a cloned soldier could ever come.

At least Etain understood what a soldier went through. All Skirata had to do was make sure the kid was safe when he was born, and educate him properly. Jinart had held up her end of the bargain and would see that Etain was taken care of on Qiilura. The shapeshifter understood Skirata's obsession with looking after his tribe. She was doing the same thing herself. They were both beleaguered fighters with no love for the Republic, just an uneasy tolerance.

"Go on, then, son." Skirata nodded toward the doors. "Go and find Etain. Have a day out. Be a regular couple for a few hours and forget you're soldiers. Just be discreet, that's all."

Darman smiled and seemed to brighten. He was a resilient lad. "Sarge," he said. "How can I forget I'm a soldier? I don't know how to be anything else."

Skirata watched him go and wondered when the desire to tell him would overwhelm him and it would slip out. Maybe Etain would find the strain too great, too. It was a pity that something that was a source of joy to ordinary people was so dangerous for Darman and Etain.

It was a rotten war. *You should have grown used to all that by now, you fool.* But he doubted he ever would.

Skirata had plenty to occupy him while Omega was away—two datapads' worth and then some. He took a deep breath and opened his comlink.

"Ordo? Mereel? Let's go hunt some Kaminoan aiwha-bait. We have plans to make. *Oya!*"

He was a skilled bounty hunter: they were the best intelligence troops in the galaxy.

There was *nowhere* in the galaxy that Ko Sai could hide from them.

OMEGA SQUAD: TARGETS

KAREN TRAVISS

Headquarters, Special Operations, Coruscant: Arca Company Barracks

"Go on," said Fi. "Shoot me. Do your worst."

He held his arms away from his sides, presenting a clear shot to his comrade. Atin raised the Verpine shatter gun and aimed two-handed, left hand steadying the grip.

"You're all mouth, Fi," he said.

Atin squeezed the trigger. Fi's armored breastplate puffed a cloud of coating with a loud crack, and he fell back against the wall of their quarters. Verps were silent except for the impact and the screaming that sometimes followed the blasts. Fi wasn't screaming. But behind his visor, he had his mouth open in a silent *oh* of pain.

Atin stood over Fi and checked both the breastplate and the Verp's chamber before hauling him back to his feet. They took off their helmets and looked around for the spent projectile. Fi picked up a flattened disc of metal whose edges were split and curled back like a flower, and tossed it in the air for Atin to catch.

"Okay, the upgrade worked," said Atin. "But you can't blame me for checking. I spent a month in the bacta tank thanks to one of these."

Fi didn't trust Procurement any more than Atin did, not when there were more than ten thousand sets of costly equipment to upgrade. They'd griped about the expense, but now everything—from their armor systems to their DC-17 rifles—was hardened against EMP and Verps, the two weaknesses that had almost got them killed on Qiilura.

Fi slipped his helmet back on and rapped his knuckle plate on it.

"Well, nothing short of sustained laser cannon is going to give us a headache now."

The door whispered open. Niner, all grim responsibility, stood in the doorway in his black bodysuit. Darman was behind him, armored up, helmet tucked under one arm.

"What was that noise?" Niner said.

"Testing the new armor, Sarge."

"Testing my patience more like." He made an irritated click with his teeth, just like Kal Skirata used to; Fi could see more of their old training sergeant's habits in Niner with every passing day. He glanced around the room. "You fired a weapon in here?"

"It's okay, Sarge, we were wearing helmets." Atin stood his ground. Sensible precautions often placated Niner. "You can't trust Procurement."

"Well, game over. We've got trade. Armed siege at the GC spaceport."

"Don't they have civil police for that sort of stuff?" Fi asked. "We'll be directing traffic next."

"Not when there are hostages and one is a Senator." Niner held out his hand to Atin for the Verpine, studied it, and then handed it back. "They've never dealt with anything like this before and they heard we were the boys for the job."

Fi lifted his backpack from its locker. "I didn't have anything special planned for this evening anyway." Atin was right: He *was* all mouth. He became two men again, as he always did when it was time to roll—the commando who was eager to put his hard-won skills to the test and the scared kid who wasn't sure he'd be alive tomorrow. He found himself worrying whether he'd signed out the Verpine from the armory. How much trouble could an armed siege be, anyway? He had his Katarn armor and he—and his mates—could take on a small army.

They all knew what the final score would be, more or less.

Atin gave him a shove and tucked the Verpine in his belt. "After you."

Maybe Atin was thinking exactly the same thing.

Halonews Update, 1530: Senator Meena Tills is believed to be among six hostages seized by an armed gang at Galactic City spaceport. Police have sealed off the area and all city traffic and interplanetary flights are being diverted. Expect long delays. More later.

Galactic City, Coruscant, was amazing.

Fi leaned out of the police assault ship's bay with his DC-17 clunking against his breastplate at every swerve and lurch of the vessel. Wind whipped into the hold, flattening his hair and peppering grit against his armor and his face. He'd never seen so many brilliantly colored lights: the walkways and skylanes stretched as far above him as they did below. No wonder they called this place the Abyss.

"Get your head back in," yelled the pilot. "What are you, a tourist or something?"

Fi leaned a little further out, trusting the safety harness. "But don't you think it's amazing?"

"Yeah, every rotten stinking shift," said the pilot wearily. "Get him back inboard, will you?"

Niner jerked on the line. "Fi, don't frighten the civvies," he said. "It's not nice. And put your helmet on."

Cloud cars filled the airspace. The Coruscant Security Force pilot was trying to edge the custom VAAT/e between crammed civilian traffic packed solid in three directions, cursing under his breath. The pulsing wail of the emergency klaxon and flashing lights were enough to make the dead clear a path. But nothing moved in the gridlock. Speeders almost scraping the bodywork tried to escape into gaps that weren't there; 25 meters of assault ship didn't fit well into the tight skylanes.

All that Fi had ever seen of Coruscant was barracks and a compound bounded by security walls. None of the commandos had ever been on a *run ashore,* a social adventure that Skirata had said they should experience at least once in their lives. From the crew bay he could see crowds of every species pressed up against barriers, brightly-lit shops and bars and apartments, exotic and unimaginable places that beckoned. Yes, he'd have that *run ashore* someday.

Omega Squad chatted on the privacy of their helmet comlink, audible only to each other. Fi dragged his gaze from the outside world and settled into the bittersweet cocoon of his helmet, at once both reassuring and confining.

"Receive schematics, people," said Niner. "And real-time view."

A display of lines and fly-through images filled Fi's HUD. The image that Niner had transmitted from his datapad was the plan of the spaceport building; long walkways led off vaulted halls and service areas, cubes of offices lined corridors, and power conduits wove through the image in green light. Superimposed on top of the overview, a real-time image of the main spaceport arrivals area showed knots of blue-armored Senate Guards and CSF squads in yellow vests crouched behind security barricades, some engaged in animated conversation.

A blue hologram figure of a thickset man in uniform shimmered into life in the hold, a little paunchy but still looking like he could give as good as he got. "Commander Obrim here, Senate Guard. Can you see this, Omega?"

Niner spoke for them. "Got it."

"They're holed up in a customs clearance corridor and they've threatened to detonate explosives. Two sets of doors, and we've left them control of one to stop them panicking and doing something stupid."

"How many confirmed?"

"Six passengers, and we're trying to get pictures of them." Obrim might not have played this game before but he had some common sense. "Witnesses report four perpetrators armed with blasters and carrying something in backpacks, which we have to assume are explosives. No ID on them yet, but they were all on the same flight."

"Any contact with the targets?"

A pause. "If you mean the gang, they've issued demands and we have a secure comlink established with them."

"And you have primacy?" *Are you running the show?* Fi could hear the doubt in Niner's voice. "I thought the city came under CSF jurisdiction."

"Not as long as I have a Senator and his aide in danger," said Obrim. The hologram began to waver again. "Obrim out."

The CSF pilot brought the assault ship to a sudden halt. The understated black-and-white marble facade of the spaceport terminal shimmered with ruby under flashing police lights. The front of the building was a crush of speeders and other emergency craft, none of them making a good job of keeping an access corridor open.

"Can't get in any closer, " said the pilot. "You'll have to rope it down the rest of the way."

"Don't wait for a tip," said Fi and wondered where he'd picked up the phrase.

We are citizens of Haruun Kal. The Republic has fueled the civil war on our world and now brings a fresh war to us. Remove your presence from our planet now or your Senator and the passengers die. Now you know we can reach into the heart of the Republic. (Message sent to RHN newsroom by Nuriin-Ar, leader of the group claiming responsibility for the hostage incident.)

Fi braced his legs, placing both boots on the outside rail of the ship's troop hold. He gave the rappel line one last tug to check it was secure before dropping fifteen meters to the walkway, DC-17 ready in one hand, a sea of openmouthed faces staring up at him from behind the police cordon.

A sudden movement in his peripheral vision made him raise the rifle. A hovercam with an RHN logo was sitting motionless 5 meters to his right, too far inside the cordon, outlined against the clean, white facade of the port. There was no point being covert ops if you were on the news and your target might be watching. The rest of the squad could see Fi's field of vision via an icon in their helmet links.

"I don't think that cam's seen a Deece before," said Darman's voice.

Fi's boots hit the walkway and he aimed. The hovercam darted left then right in his scope, fast but not fast enough. "It has now."

A shout of "Hey!" followed the *thwack* of exploding hovercam. The rest of Omega Squad hit the ground and jogged toward the terminal entrance. "You shot my cam!" yelled a woman from the watching crowd. She was wearing a bright yellow tabard emblazoned with the word MEDIA in large letters. "You *shot* it!"

Fi touched his glove to his helmet in apology, just as he'd been taught, but he still thought it was a pretty good shot. "Oops. Beg your pardon, ma'am."

He jogged after the others, conscious of the staring crowd. Fi saw his armor as safe and welcoming. But the expressions on a couple of faces made him realize that ordinary people were scared by it.

And it wasn't just the civilians who found Omega Squad a riveting spectacle. The CSF and Senate Guard officers at the forward control point stared, too. Obrim stopped a head-to-head discussion with a CSF lieutenant and stepped back from the defensive barricade of baggage repulsors and portable blast shields erected 10 meters around the customs hall.

"I see you're tooled up," Obrim said, eyeing the DC-17s with a distinct air of alarm. He almost slid his modest police-issued blaster behind his back. "They're not driving Trade Federation tanks, you know."

Fi decided that the police had a lot to learn about sieges. You could do anything with a Deece: A turn of the wrist, and it was a sniper rifle, grenade launcher or a regular blaster. You could even club someone with it if you had to, although Fi hadn't tried that yet. He checked the vibroblade in his gauntlet out of habit, and the *shunk-shunk* sound as it extended and retracted made Obrim flinch.

Niner made that annoyed click. Fi took the hint.

"Let's get a cam in there first so we can see what's going on," said Niner. He beckoned Darman and Atin forward. "Pictures, Commander? We need to know who to shoot."

"You're a bit keen."

"If you're not a hostage, you're a hostage taker, and that means you're dead a few seconds after we go in. We hate to make mistakes."

"What do you mean by *go in,* exactly?" The CSF lieutenant stepped between them. A name tab on his vest said DOVEL. "I'm incident commander. I say how and when anyone goes in. We've got a Jedi coming down to negotiate with the leader."

Darman took his pack off his back and began pulling out coils of high-yield charges and detonators. He was staring at the security doors as if calculating. "We'll still get the charges in place, just in case."

"No, that's not how *we* do it," said Dovel. "We don't want the hostages char-grilled. No storming, no heroics. Not yet."

Obrim interrupted. "Senate Security Committee wants this ended fast to show Haruun Kal we're in control. They can't just walk in here, grab a Senator, and hold the Republic's finest at bay."

"Maybe the Republic's finest, or you to be exact, should have concentrated on ensuring secure transportation for the Senators," said Dovel. "What about those other hostages? You want to tell their families that they got fried because you called in the heavy mob to save a politician?"

Niner waited, all mild, deceptive patience. Fi had decided on first meeting him that he was a misery-guts, but now he found him solid and reassuring, just the way a sergeant ought to be. "Let's be clear what we're trained to do, gentlemen. We go in and extract hostages by any means necessary. We don't ask for ID. We don't take targets alive. We don't avoid damaging the furniture. When you send us in, there is *no* happy ending." He paused as if waiting to see if the reality of the request had sunk in. "So we'll just wander around and rig the interrupts to the power and light, and you call us when you're ready to roll."

Atin took a couple of strip-cams from his backpack, each no bulkier than a sheet of flimsi. Fi switched to the internal helmet comlink. "You think they're real terrorists or Haruun Kal government agents upping the ante?"

Atin shrugged. "I don't care as long as they fall over when we shoot them."

A commando's life was all clarity. Fi was glad he wasn't Obrim—or Dovel.

Holonews Update, 1700: The family of an elderly couple held hostage with Senator Tills have made an emotional plea for their safe release. Joz and Cira Larutur from Garqi were on their way to see their first grandchild when they were seized. Other hostages have been named as customs officer Berin B'naian and Senatorial aide Vun Merett Jai, but the identity of the sixth hostage remains unknown.

Obrim was talking on the comlink to Nuriin-Ar in carefully restrained tones while Omega listened in. Fi was concentrating on the sounds in the background with the intensity learned from growing up where everyone looked and sounded the same, distinguished only by minute variations in tone and expression.

He could hear the old woman's voice saying, "Oh Joz . . . oh Joz . . . ," over and over very quietly. From time to time, he heard an equally quiet reply from the old man: "Don't you worry."

It made him uncomfortable. He wasn't sure why.

Obrim let out a breath. "The Jedi's here."

Fi's stomach churned when he saw the distinctive red-trimmed visor of an ARC trooper captain through the grimy, white helmets of the CSF line. The line melted away for the ARC: Behind him trailed a human male in a very well-cut business suit, a young Twi'lek Jedi, and . . .

. . . a scruffy, wiry little man who looked old enough to be everyone's father, a man with a face as wrinkled as his clothes, buzz-cut gray hair, and a limp that didn't stop him covering the ground like a racing odupiendo.

"Sarge!" said Fi.

Niner's head jerked up. "It *is*!"

Kal Skirata reached them a stride ahead of the ARC captain. He grinned up at Fi as if he recognized him, but that was impossible. He'd had a hundred identical young commandos in his batch. He couldn't possibly remember. He couldn't possibly see past the visor, either.

"Who let that vagrant in?" demanded Obrim.

"That," said Fi, "is the man who taught us all we know."

Obrim sighed. "We're screwed, then."

Fi touched his fingers to his helmet anyway, even if Skirata was out of uniform. "Sarge, what are you doing here?"

"Where there's trouble, Fi, there's always a job for me. Special security adviser now." Oh, he *knew.* How? *How?* "Nice new armor. Going on a date? And who's he?"

Fi followed Skirata's gaze. "That's Atin. Hang on, how do you—"

"Lads, this is Master Kaim and the Senate Head of Public Affairs, Mar Rugeyan." Fi heard Obrim sigh again. "And ARC N-11. We all want the same outcome—hostages out, scumbags dead, traffic flowing again. Let's get to it."

Kaim looked like a youngster aged early by responsibility. He stared at the door behind the barricades and closed his eyes for a moment, lekku moving ever so slightly, hands clasped in front of him.

"I'm going to ask them to let me in to talk," Kaim said. "When I have their attention, I will help them decide to release the hostages and to talk to me, which will not be easy with Korunnai." He took his lightsaber from his cloak and handed it to the ARC. "I have to show goodwill and enter unarmed."

"You're nuts, sir," said Obrim. "You're giving them another hostage."

"One with a choice," said Kaim. "Captain, if I get inside, you have command here."

The captain just nodded once. Atin took the strip-cams and held one out to Kaim. "If you get a chance, sir, try to leave this inside. Anywhere. Even if we can't get an image, we can pick up audio."

Kaim examined the strip and tucked it in his sleeve, then took out his comlink. "Nuriin-Ar, can you hear me? Will you let me in so we can speak?"

The simultaneous *chunk* and *uuiirrrr* of 20 service-issue blasters powering up made Fi turn and aim in time to see the doors of the customs hall begin to part. For a moment, the commandos were a single wall of rifles with the two police forces. Slowly, the blade-thin gap opened wide enough for Fi to see a few huddled shapes inside.

Kaim went in.

GC spaceport terminal building, 1745.

Fi could see what Atin could see and hear what he heard. The squad had switched to the cam output within their helmets, and they were all focused on an unsteady image of folds of fabric and the muffled but audible conversation.

"Let these people leave," said Kaim. "You don't want to harm them."

"And no doubt you don't want to harm ordinary Korunnai, yet your interference does just that." The view from the cam shifted and Fi could see figures distorted by the wide-angle lens: three men, one in gray, one in dark green, one in light tan, and one in a loose dark brown coat. All had their faces obscured by black scarves. There were figures behind them, two groups of three, also with their heads covered in the same scarves. But they were the hostages, judging by their huddled positions and their clothing: out-of-date fashions from Garqi, a business suit, a customs uniform, a Mon Calamari Senator's formal robe and a cheaper imitation of it.

Fine, thought Fi. His helmet was recording. *I don't need to see your faces. I know what you wear, how you move, how you sound, and that's how I'll know who you are when I blow your brains out.*

Kaim's voice was soothing and reasonable. "These people need food and water."

"That's the least of their worries." The one in gray: Fi noted his voice. The one in light tan turned to look at the Senator and told him to shut up. Green Man was holding his blaster left-handed. *Detail.* "Take a look at their baggage."

Tan Man—Fi now saw the targets as color-coded—grabbed the old Garqian man by his shoulder and dragged him across the polished tiles a little way from the wall on his backside. The old woman's voice whimpered, terrified. Fi could see now what Gray had meant by baggage: The hostages had small packs strapped to them.

"Six lives are a price worth paying, Jedi," said Gray. "We *will* detonate the charges."

"This wins you no sympathy. Mercy will."

"We don't require sympathy. Just your compliance."

"Let the old couple go, at least."

There was a pause. Fi wasn't sure where Kaim had managed to place the strip-cam, but Gray's shrouded face came closer and Fi saw two pale eyes as if he was looking into them personally.

"Lying Jedi filth! Spy!" Gray hissed, and the sound and image crashed to static and black.

"*Fierfek . . .*" said Atin.

They heard the screams. They weren't only from an old woman. Then there was a thud, and shouting—"Shut up! Shut up, or you die *now*!"—then silence.

Fi looked to the ARC, rifle aimed at the doors: Darman raised the remote detonators in his glove, a mute request for permission to blow the doors.

"Hold fire," said the ARC.

The twin doors began to part and Fi, Atin and Niner had their Deeces trained on the widening gap. He could see the different views through their scopes in his HUD.

"I said *hold*!"

Something tipped and rolled onto the polished marble and the doors sighed shut again. It was Kaim. Fi and Niner edged forward first and the police closed up behind them. Fi wondered how much the hovercams and broadcast droids could see. Could the gang see *them*?

Kaim wasn't moving. Niner put out a cautious hand to pull back the Jedi's robe, and Fi saw a flicker of light and heard Niner catch his breath.

"Booby trap—counting down!"

Fi didn't think.

The police officers were right on top of him, unprotected.

He flung himself flat on Kaim's body, eyes tight shut so he wouldn't see the shattered face, waiting long fractions within fractions of seconds before a shock wave lifted him like a body blow and raw noise filled his helmet. He felt as if he'd been shaken hard in a metal box. For an instant, red light flooded his eyes behind his closed lids.

How long the next moments took he didn't know. But he could hear the ARC shouting, "Droid those cams! Do it! *Now!*"

He could hear yelling, so he wasn't dead. That was something.

Holoflash, 1758: A Huruun Kal group holding Senator Tills has killed a Jedi negotiator. All location cams have been disabled in a news blackout, but we've just witnessed horrific scenes as the Jedi's booby-trapped remains exploded in the terminal. It's thought a member of the elite Republic Commando shielded the blast with his body. Viewers might find the following images distressing.

"What do you use for brains, Fi?" Skirata hissed, supporting Fi's shoulders. "You're a *di'kut.*"

Fi could feel bruises forming everywhere he had places. He sat upright with some difficulty. "Thanks for the sympathy, Sarge. I'm fine."

"You trust that pretty armor a lot more than I would." Skirata suddenly shook him fiercely by the shoulder. "Don't you ever scare me like that again, son. You hear? Let the cops look after themselves."

It hadn't been a big device, just enough to kill or maim a couple of people, but not enough to breach Katarn armor. He'd smothered the blast and the shrapnel that went with it. Fi hadn't been 100 percent sure at the time that the armor would absorb the energy from the blast, and now that the adrenaline had finished coursing through his veins he felt shaky.

The ARC stared down at him, fists on hips. Skirata kept calling him Ordo: Skirata insisted men had names, not numbers, whatever the rules said.

"Nice move," said Ordo.

"Nice skirt." Fi indicated Ordo's battle-scarred belt-spat, shredded at the hem like a flag that had been left too long on its mast. Fi wiped his armor, trying to forget what was smeared on the plastoid-alloy but the smell kept reminding him. "Really suits you. Hand-washable?"

Ordo's expression was hidden behind his visor but his tone wasn't. "It's a *kama,*" he said, all ice.

"Someday, Fi, someone's going to belt you one," Atin muttered. "And it's probably going to be Ordo."

He was right. But Fi didn't know any other way to keep his gut from shaking at times like this. It was how he coped. He was relieved and he was shocked, and now he had to get on with the job. He leaned on his Deece to get to his feet and saw the cams and droids had gone; the illuminated displays in the terminal were black screens and the amber emergency lighting was on.

So Ordo had deployed an EMP device to knock out the holocams, and taken out all the unshielded equipment around them too. *Droiding.* A crazy but necessary move, Fi thought, seeing as it might have triggered whatever explosives the gang had rigged. He linked into Niner's helmet and saw that he was running and rerunning the images of the gang that Kaim had paid for with his life, memorizing the identifying details.

Rugeyan was looking around the terminal hall, chatting on his comlink, the embodiment of pure calculation. "Okay, so we'll have to take the news conferences at the Chamber . . . any more bodies, and they go out via the back . . . I know, it's not good seeing Jedi body parts . . . the grunt was great, right?"

Ordo and Skirata looked at each other as if some common bond had sprung up from nowhere. Fi wondered if they had some comlink of their own: Skirata occasionally slipped something into his ear and removed it again. Ordo cocked his head but Skirata smiled tightly and without humor. He turned to Rugeyan and put a scarred hand on the sleeve of his nice, sharp tunic.

"Son," he said. "I couldn't help noticing that you called my boys grunts. Don't do that again, will you?"

Rugeyan looked down at Skirata as if he'd noticed him for the first time and lowered the comlink. "We want the Senator out now. Nothing else matters."

"I'm glad you pointed that out to me." Fi couldn't see what Skirata did next, but his arm dropped down and suddenly Rugeyan seemed to be taking a *lot* of notice of him. His eyes bulged visibly and a small *uh* noise forced its way past his lips. "Now that I have your attention, may I suggest that you remove yourself from the incident scene and let Captain Ordo and my boys do their jobs?"

Fi was mesmerized. Darman jogged up to the tableau of frozen pain. "Charges laid, Sarge. Ready to go."

Skirata's arm fell back to his side again, and Rugeyan inhaled sharply before brushing down his tunic and striding away with somewhat splayed legs.

"I'll remember that move," said Atin approvingly. "Vau never taught us *anything* like that."

But Vau had certainly taught Atin the exacting procedures for storming a building, Fi knew. He just wondered about Ordo. ARCs weren't team players.

"Fancy a bit of action for a change, Captain?" asked Fi. "Give your Deece a day out?"

"Don't worry, if your luck holds I'll be right in front of you," said Ordo, toneless. "If it doesn't, I'll be *behind* you."

Fi thought about that for a few moments. Then he started wondering again why Nuriin-Ar and his cronies hadn't seized hostages on the transport before it landed; it was an easier location to withstand an assault. The fools were facing certain death. They wouldn't shift the Senate's position. And they had to be stupid if they didn't realize that.

In the end, though, their intelligence levels wouldn't matter. He checked his Deece, rehearsing rapid changes between modes and aware that Ordo kept looking his way.

Holonews Update, 1830: The Haruun Kal government has denied knowledge of Nuriin-Ar, leader of the group that's holding six hostages at Galactic City spaceport. But in an unusually robust statement, the Korunnai ambassador says she "fully understands the group's frustrations" and has urged the Republic to cease interfering in her planet's affairs.

One of the CSF officers brought a tray of caf in flimsi cups and handed Fi one first. A camaraderie had sprung up: Fi rather liked it. The cops actually seemed in awe of what he'd done, and he began to realize that it felt good to be held in that kind of regard.

"No cookies?" said Skirata, and took a cup.

The squad took their helmets off to drink. The officer seemed distracted for a moment, staring at their faces. "I'll see what I can do," he said.

"Don't wait for a tip," said Skirata. Fi smiled to himself.

Obrim and Dovel were observing a few paces away, and the group stared at the hologram of the terminal layout that Ordo projected into the space between them.

"It's an oblong room," said Skirata, and slurped his caf. "No scope for anything clever. It's just going to be a matter of speed, force, and knowing who you're going to drop as soon as you're in there."

"But how are you going to stop them setting off the devices?" asked Dovel.

"By slotting them before they can move," said Niner. "We've done this more than 100 times, and we know how each other thinks. This is probably their first time."

"And their last." Ordo dipped the finger of his glove through the shimmering virtual roof space of the customs hall. "I'll take the roof and keep the hostages still until we get bomb disposal in there to deal with the devices."

"All the hostages?" said Obrim.

"I realize the Senator is a priority."

Dovel chewed his lip thoughtfully, clearly a man who no longer wanted primacy in this incident. Fi thought that was a smart change of heart. If anything went wrong, he knew who would get the blame now.

Ordo got up and tidied his rappel line before fastening it to his belt. "I'll get in position," he said. "And I'm switching to the general comlink channel. We go in at 1915. Darman counts us down, and Obrim's men kill all the lights, okay?"

Dovel's communicator chirped. He answered it and adopted that middle-distance stare that people have when they are trying to concentrate on something that they aren't expecting to hear.

"It's Nuriin-Ar," he said. "He's asking for buckets, food, and water."

"Ah, the power of the need for a 'fresher," said Obrim. "Looks like our hard men are softening."

"Even people who plan to kill engage in displacement activity," said Skirata. "I'll take the stuff in for you."

"I think I should be doing that, Sergeant," said Ordo.

"Yeah, like they'd succumb to your natural charm." Skirata began checking the pockets in his rumpled jacket. He extracted something that looked like a hearing enhancer—no, it *was* a hearing enhancer. Fi had always doubted Skirata's hearing was perfect, and now he knew. "Atin, can you pick up my enhancer's signal? I hate this thing. But it does come in handy."

"It'll do," said Atin, stabbing his finger into a small receiver in his palm. "Are you really deaf?"

"A *bit* deaf. Just like you'd be if you hung around live-fire ranges without a helmet for too long."

"With respect, you'll just add another complication," said Ordo.

Skirata sipped his caf without looking up. "If you mean that my boys will have to worry about shooting me by accident, then it's simple. They won't worry about it. Acceptable losses."

There was a complete silence in all their helmet comlinks for a telling and brief moment: no breath, no swallowing, no lick of the lips. Fi had a sudden mental image so awful that he didn't want to deal with it, not then.

Now it was all down to a well-rehearsed procedure. The charges would detonate, and they would lob in a few flash-bangs so close together that it would feel like the same split second and plunge into reactions so automatic that they wouldn't pause to think what to do next or even know how much time had elapsed.

It was drilled deep, unthinking second nature. Fi longed for the moment instinct and training took him over again.

"I'll give you as many clues as I can, so listen hard," said Skirata. He fidgeted with the enhancer, making the same irritated clicks that Niner had. "And if I'm in the way when you come in, it's too bad, okay? You drop 'em all, straight through me if need be."

"Will do, Sarge," said Fi, and knew he would never do anything of the kind.

Galactic City terminal, 1855.

The doors parted. Fi, standing well back, stared down the scope of the Deece, not planning to take a shot, but ready anyway. Skirata walked forward a few steps.

"Grilled food board," he said, arms held away from his sides, a picture of subservience. "And . . . umm . . . facilities."

Fi could see past him into the enclosed corridor: the hostages were still split into two groups. One of the targets stepped up to Skirata and placed the muzzle of his blaster against his forehead. *Green Man,* Fi thought, and made a mental note of the target's gait. It was a clean shot he couldn't take right then. The sound signal was fuzzy but audible enough.

"Put the buckets down and back off."

Skirata—short, wiry, forgettable, dragging his left leg—looked like a janitor. Fi knew Green wouldn't see what was really there.

"What about the old couple?" said Skirata. "Don't you think they've had enough? Why not let 'em go? Take me instead."

Go on. Go on, let him in . . .

Green paused and then gestured Skirata inside with the blaster. "You can keep them company," he said. "You're too altruistic for a delivery boy. We better search you."

The doors closed. "Stand by," said Niner.

They took up positions either side of the doors, Fi and Niner to the left, Atin and Darman to the right. They could hear Skirata's breathing—remarkably controlled under the circumstances—and the occasional rustle of fabric. They were searching him. The enhancer didn't seem to get their attention; the device was too obvious.

"You okay, missus?" said Skirata's voice. There was a mumbled reply, probably from the elderly Garqi woman. "Lie down. You'll feel better."

"Shut up," said a voice, a new one. *Tan Man,* thought Fi. He'd know that voice the next time he heard it. *You'll get yours. Nothing personal, just business.*

They heard Skirata and the targets again. Fi paused. Every word counted: Skirata was probably risking death or at least a smack in the mouth with a blaster butt to speak at all.

"Here, son, let me have a look at that chrono. . . . wow, that must have cost you something . . . what kind of business you in, then? Where you from? Mayro, eh? What's your name?"

"Quiet."

"Mayro. Never been there . . . you're N'zaet Nir, eh?"

"Shut up." *Tan Man again.*

"Okay, keep your hair on. I'll just sit here with Joz and Cira . . . you okay, sweetheart? Don't worry . . ."

"Shut up." *Thwack.*

There were indistinct sounds of fabric rumpling and occasional breathy sobs in different voices. Fi tried not to think what the *thwack* was. But at least they had a name for the last hostage. It might matter.

He closed his eyes for a second and visualized the layout. Skirata probably had three hostages right next to him, then. That left Senator Till's position unaccounted for as well as his aide. But it was better than nothing.

"Why was he repeating Mayro?" asked Darman. "Where's Mayro?"

Niner's voice filled his skull. "It's Corporate Sector. Ordo, you ready?"

Fi took a deep breath. He activated his helmet spot-lamp and checked the chrono on his forearm plate. When the doors blew and Niner lobbed in the flash-bang—bright and loud enough to stun most species for several vital seconds—he would swing 270 degrees to his left, step in, and aim, ready to take down the first recognizable target he saw. He'd done it time after time.

"Roof team ready," said Ordo. "Darman?"

"Ready." Darman raised his gloved fist. "In three. Two. *Go.*"

Boom.

Light exploded out of the shattered doors and Fi ran into it, Deece raised. Time slowed into a sequence of freeze frames. A man in a green tunic, stunned, squinting against the helmet spot-lamp, shouting "No!" in a voice Fi had memorized as *target,* struggled to raise his blaster, and Fi put a single bolt through his chest. Spot-lamp beams crisscrossed the room. Debris rained down from the ceiling as Ordo crashed down a couple of meters from Fi. Atin dropped Gray with two shots.

A second of utter silence. Then someone in dark brown got up from the floor and Darman and Niner both fired at once.

"Everyone down! Down!" Ordo had his rifle trained on a group of hostages. "Stay still! Republic forces!" And Darman was shouting, "Where's Tan? Where's Tan?"

Fi's lamp swept the wall to his left and he saw a light tan shape and Skirata half across it, transfixed by the beam, yelling, "No, Fi! No!" Fi felt his finger compress the trigger without any intervention from his conscious mind, and time slowed down a hundredfold.

"Fi, no!" Skirata had flung himself across the tan-coated figure. "Hostage, Fi! Hold fire!"

Fi's finger eased back. The silence was sudden and total again, punctuated only by the patter of ceiling panels still falling in chunks on the tiled floor.

I nearly killed him. I nearly killed Skirata.

Ordo, standing over the hostages, suddenly fired his Deece into one of them and yelled at them to stay still. The emergency lighting came on again. Six civilians were frozen in terror.

"Fierfek." said Atin. "I thought he'd shot a hostage for a second."

"Get ordnance disposal in here before these people start going hysterical," said Ordo. "And get the Senator clear first."

There was a man in an expensive suit crumpled on the floor between the other hostages with a blaster beside him.

"He had a weapon," said Ordo. "It's something of a giveaway. Must have swapped coats with our businessman."

Now that all the targets were down, Fi could think only of Skirata's horrified expression in his spot-lamp beam. He fought down an impulse to tell him he was sorry. The old warrior was kneeling in front of the stunned hostages, now making reassuringly cheery comments that everything was going to be fine as long as they *kept very still* just a little longer. They were rigged to explosives and a dead terrorist was still smoking gently in their midst. And yet they kept still, and they kept quiet. People generally did what Skirata told them.

He glanced up at Fi. "Well, not exactly textbook. But dead's dead."

Explosives disposal officers moved in to check the backpacks and the squad moved out. Fi looked at his chrono: The assault had taken less than 30 seconds. He could feel the adrenaline ebbing while his body—which didn't care how trained he was—tackled the aftermath of the massive surge of hormone. His breath rasped hard in his ears as he sat down on a baggage repulsor.

"All clear." The explosives officer came out of the wrecked hallway with an open backpack that rattled as he walked. "And I mean *really* clear. These packs are just full of used comlink parts. Nasty bluff."

Skirata wandered over to Fi and sat down beside him. "We don't like practical jokes like that, do we, lads?" he said. He motioned him to take his helmet off. "Serves the stupid bunch of *di'kute* right."

Obrim stood at the blast-shattered doors, looking bewildered. "Is that it?" he said. "We prat around for more than three hours, and you clear the room in 60 seconds?"

"Twenty," said Fi automatically.

It all looked easy from the outside. It probably would have

looked great to the holocams. Fi could see only that he had come within an ace of doing what he never believed he could. If Skirata hadn't identified the man as a hostage, Fi would have killed both of them with a single round.

Sergeant Kal's nearly a father to this squad. How could I?

He took off his helmet and wiped his palm across his forehead, still unable to shake Skirata's image from his mind.

"You really would have slotted me, wouldn't you?" said the old sergeant hoarsely.

"Sarge, I'm sorry, I—"

"No, you're a good lad." He still seemed able to read Fi's every thought, just as he had in training. "You only did what I taught you to do. What did I say?"

Fi swallowed. "Priority is to drop the bad guys, Sarge."

"Good. I'm proud of you. Sentimentality gets you killed." He tapped Fi's cheek a few times with the flat of his hand. "And matey over there is luckier than he'll ever know, as are we all. They made him change clothes with them for a good reason, I reckon. He's CorSec."

The businessman, N'zaet Nir, was still standing by the wall, examining the scruffy tan jacket and pants as if appalled to find himself in such tatty clothing. He should have been medevaced for a routine checkup by now, but whatever he had said had ensured he was still there, and waiting. He walked up to Obrim.

"I need to leave right now."

"You really should have that checkup, sir."

"But I have an important meeting. I'm a member of CorSec's Direx and it's imperative that I attend."

"Just as well you're in one piece then," said Skirata. "I don't think your government colleagues would have found it amusing if we'd crashed in and shot you by mistake. Especially when the explosives were dummies."

Nir seemed to have forgotten his terror of a few minutes earlier. "No, they would not. We hope to stay out of your disputes with the Separatists. Can I have my suit back now? And who's paying for the damage?"

Fi thought a thank you might have been a nice touch, but he realized he had missed something in the exchange that had made Obrim and Skirata just stare at each other.

Niner walked over to them, followed by Ordo. Neither looked as if anything left them trembling. "What have I missed?"

"It wasn't the Senator," said Obrim. "He wasn't the key hostage.

He was a lure to get us to storm in and kill the real trump card they were holding."

"You want to explain all that, Sarge?"

Skirata raked stubby fingers through his hair. "The Corporate Sector Authority is neutral and the Direx Board is its governing body. They've got serious money and armaments, so you don't want to upset them. So if Fi had shot a Direx member, the political fallout would have been enormous—CorSec might have decided to take sides and throw their money and guns behind the Separatists. Want me to go on?"

"*Fierfek,*" said Fi. But it still didn't feel as close a call as nearly killing Skirata. "That's a new one for the training manual."

"You said it. Heavy-handed Republic overreacts, storms in and kills top CorSec man. Nice stunt, whoever they are."

Obrim shrugged. "Well, you can sleep soundly tonight in the knowledge that you've given Rugeyan a timely public relations coup. Just a shame it wasn't live on RHN . . ."

He trailed off. Ordo had taken off his helmet. For some reason Fi wasn't expecting the ARC to look like them, but of course he did. He looked Fi straight in the eye, but it wasn't like looking in a mirror at all, although it was a striking enough resemblance to reduce Obrim to silence.

"We're not supposed to be in the public eye," said Ordo. "But it doesn't do the Republic's citizens any harm to know what we do." He was staring intently at Fi. "And you, brother, are very mouthy, very annoying, and stupidly brave. I forgive you for the crack about the *kama.* This time, anyway."

Fi didn't feel brave, not right then. He also wondered if smothering the bomb had been any more courageous than Master Kaim's actions. It was pure training, a split-second's decision exactly like Darman's or Atin's—or Ordo's.

And it was another thing Kal Skirata had taught him to do. He remembered that now

Holonews Update, 1930: The siege at Galactic City spaceport has ended with the rescue of Senator Meena Tills and all the remaining hostages. Commando forces stormed a hall in the terminal building and shot dead four terrorists from a group opposed to Republic influence on Haruun Kal. We now have our droid cams back online, and we're going live to the scene—

Rugeyan was as smug as Obrim had predicted. He came back into the terminal hall trailed by journalists and a cloud of fresh hovercams, oozing satisfaction. Obrim stopped them and took him aside, walking him to the knot of commandos and police that was waiting beside the shattered doors.

"Before you strike up the band, you ought to know the explosives were a hoax," said the commander.

Fi watched absolutely nothing cross Rugeyan's face.

"So?"

"Looks like a stunt to get us to go in mob-handed and shoot a member of the CorSec Direx Board, and that has nothing to do with the Senator. We can't be sure who's behind it, so let's think about this before we start crowing."

Rugeyan maintained his blank expression in silence for a few seconds. Then a practiced smile snapped instantly into place. "Commander, those thugs held innocent people and murdered a Jedi Master whose sole concern was the welfare of the hostages. The Senate does *not* tolerate terrorism. We deal with it robustly, and we have shown billions of viewers tonight just what awaits anyone who wants to test our resolve." His smile disappeared like a light going out. "The rest is detail, and that needn't trouble our vigilant media."

He gathered up his smile again and walked back to where the media were waiting.

"Will he remember all that for the cams?" asked Fi.

"He probably talks like that in his sleep," said Obrim. "Anyway, I just want to get home. Unless you boys would like a drink."

Skirata smiled uncomfortably. "We're always on duty, Commander, so we don't get to have a drink. But thanks. You go on home."

Fi couldn't find a joke that would help him right then. He was grateful for the privacy of his helmet.

I really would have fired.

Darman elbowed him in the back, more a playful gesture than one of annoyance. "We missed dinner," he said. "Maybe you can talk the cooks into fixing us something when we get back."

Ordo was listening to his private link, head down. It was a giveaway gesture with ARCs, Fi thought. "CSF transport's here to take us back to barracks," he said, straightening up. "You're shipping out on a new deployment at 0600 tomorrow, Omega."

Skirata jerked his head around for a second, dismay unguarded, and then gave them a smile that didn't quite conceal his anxiety.

"You make sure you get them a decent meal first, Captain." He jabbed a finger in their direction, then appeared to yield to some private thought and gave them all a slap on the back. "No damaging government property, okay? And we'll have that drink one day soon, I promise you."

He winked and pulled up his collar, limping into the crowds outside in the riot of neon and vehicle lights that was Galactic City, and changing before their eyes from time-served commando to anonymous old man as surely as any Gurlanin could shift shape.

"I've never had a proper alcoholic drink," said Atin. "Or a free bowl of *warra* nuts."

"Well, if they're free, *that's* worth staying alive for," said Fi, and they snapped their helmets back into place to become the Republic's ultimate, faceless deterrent once again.

GLOSSARY

A

a (ah) *Mando'a*: but
a'den (AH-den) *Mando'a:* wrath, rage
AA: anti-aircraft
AAA: anti-aircraft artillery
ad (ahd, s.); *ade* (AH-day, pl.) *Mando'a:* child, son, daughter
ad'ika (ah-DEE-kah, s.); *ad'ike* (ah-DEE-kay, pl.) *Mando'a:* child, son, daughter (used affectionately)
adenn (AH-tenn) *Mando'a:* merciless
aliit (ah-LEET) *Mando'a*: family, clan
an (ahn) *Mando'a:* all
ARC: Advanced Reconnaissance Commando
aruetii (ah-roo-AY-tee, s.); *aruetiise* (ah-roo-ay-TEE-say, pl.) *Mando'a:* foreigner, outsider, traitor
atin (ah-TEEN) *Mando'a:* stubborn

B

baatir (BAH-teer, v.) *Mando'a*: to care, to worry about
baay shfat: an obscenity of unknown origin about Hutt
bal (bahl) *Mando'a:* and
Bal kote, darasuum kote, / Jorso'ran kando a tome. / Sa kyr'am Nau tracyn kad, Vode an. (Bahl KOH-day, dah-RA-soom KOH-day, Jor-so-RAHN, KAHN-do ah TOh-may, Sah-kee-RAHM now

trah-SHEEN kahd VOH-day ahn) *Mando'a:* And glory, eternal glory, / We shall bear its weight together. / Forged like the saber in the fires of death, Brothers all. (ancient Mandalorian war chant)

BRB: Big Red Button (emergency hull seal)

buir (boo-EER) *Mando'a:* father

buy'ce (BOO-shay, s.); *buy'cese* (pl.) *Mando'a:* helmet

buy'ce gal (BOO-shay gahl) *Mando'a*: pint of ale (literally, the contents of a helmet)

Buy'ce gal, buy'ce tal / Vebor'ad ures aliit / Mhi draar baat'i meg'-parjii'se / Kote lo'shebs'ul narit (BOO-shay gahl, BOO-shay tahl Vair-BOR-ahd OO-rees AH-leet Mee DRAHR bah-TEE mayg-PAR-jee-SEH Koh-TAY loh SHEBS-ool-NAH-reet) *Mando'a*: A pint of ale, a pint of blood / Buys men without a name / We never care who wins the war / So you can keep your fame (drinking chant of Mandalorian mercenaries)

C

ca (kah) *Mando'a:* night

cannon fodder: soldier (slang)

chakaar (cha-KAR, s.); *chakaare* (cha-KAR-ay, pl.) *Mando'a:* thief, grave robber (general term of abuse)

Cip-Quad: reciprocating quad blaster

CIS: Confederacy of Independent Systems

con: steer a ship

conc (konk): concussion rifle

Coruscanta (KOH-roo-SAN-ta) *Mando'a:* Coruscant

CSF: Coruscant Security Force

cuir (KOO-eer) *Mando'a:* four

cuun (koon) *Mando'a:* our

Cuy'val Dar (koo-EE-vahl dahr) *Mando'a:* those who no longer exist (the term is used for a group of Jango Fett's handpicked clone commando instructors)

cuyir (KOO-yeer, v.) *Mando'a:* to exist, to be

D

dar (dahr) *Mando'a:* no longer

dar'buir (DAHR boo-EER) *Mando'a:* no longer a father

dar'manda (dahr-MAHN-da) *Mando'a:* a state of being "not Mandalorian"; not an outsider, but one who has lost his heritage, and so his identity and soul
darasuum (dah-RAH-soom) *Mando'a:* eternal, forever
Deece: a DC-model rifle (slang)
det: detonator
dha (dah) *Mando'a:* dark
di'kut (dee-KOOT, s.); *di'kute* (dee-KOOT, pl.); *di'kutla* (dee-KOOT-lah, adj.): jerk, moron (impolite)
dinuir (DEE-noo-eer, v.) *Mando'a:* to give
draar (drahr) *Mando'a:* never
dralshy'a (drahl-SHEE-ya) *Mando'a:* stronger, more powerful
droten (DROH-ten) *Mando'a:* people, public

E

e'tad (EH-tad) *Mando'a:* seven
ehn (ayhn) *Mando'a:* three
EM: electromagnetic
EMP (s.); EMPs (pl.): electromagnetic pulse
eniki Huttese: understand
EOD: Explosive Ordnance Disposal (bomb disposal)
ETA: estimated time of arrival

F

flash-bang: stun grenade (slang)

G

GAR: Grand Army of the Republic
gar (gahr, s. & pl.) *Mando'a:* you
Gar ru kyramu kaysh, di'kut: tion'meh kaysh ru jehaati? (Gahr roo keer-AH-moo kaysh, dee-KOOT: tee-ON-mey-kaysh roo je-HAHT-ee) *Mando'a:* You killed him, you moron: what if he was lying?
ge'verd (ge-VAIRD) *Mando'a:* almost a warrior
gihaal (gee-HAAL) *Mando'a:* fish-meal
gra'tua (gra-TOO-ah) *Mando'a:* vengeance

H

HNE: HoloNet News and Entertainment
HQ: headquarters
HUD: heads-up display
hukaat'kama (hu-KAHT-kah-MAH) Mando'a: watch my back, watch my six
hut'uun (hoo-TOON, s.); *hut'uune* (pl.); *hut'uunla* (hoo-TOON-lah, adj.) *Mando'a:* coward

I

IED: improvised explosive device
-ika (EE-kah, s.); *-ike* (EE-kay, pl.) *Mando'a:* suffix for affectionate usage

J

j'hagwa na yoka Huttese: no trouble
jatne (JAT-nay) *Mando'a:* best
jatne'buir (JAT-nay boo-EER) *Mando'a:* best father
jetii (JAY-tee) *Mando'a:* Jedi
jetiise (jay-TEE-say) *Mando'a:* Jedi plural, Republic
jorso'ran (jor-so-RAHN) *Mando'a:* shall bear (archaic)
jurkadir (JOOR-kahd-EER, v.) *Mando'a:* to attack, to threaten, to mess with

K

k'uur (koor) *Mando'a:* hush, be quiet
kad (kahd) *Mando'a*: saber, sword
kama (KAH-ma, s.); *kamas* (KAH-maz, pl.) or *kamase* (kah-MAH-say) *Mando'a:* belt-spat
kando (KAHN-do) *Mando'a*: importance, weight
kandosii (kahn-DOH-see) *Mando'a:* nice one, wicked, well done, classy, noble
kar'tayli ad meg hukaat'kama (kar-TIE-lie ahd mayg hu-KAHT-KA-mah) *Mando'a:* roughly "know who's watching your back"
kar'taylir (kar-TIE-leer, v.) *Mando'a:* to know, to hold in the heart

kaysh (kaysh) *Mando'a:* him, his
ke nu'jurkadir sha Mando'ade (keh NOO-joor-kahd-EER shah Mahn do-AH-day) *Mando'a:* don't mess with Mandalorians
KIA: killed in action
kit: gear, equipment (slang)
kom'rk (KOM-rohk) *Mando'a:* gauntlet
kote (KOH-day, KOH-tay, pl.) *Mando'a:* glory
kyr'am (kee-RAHM) *Mando'a*: death

L

LAAT/c: low-altitude assault transport/cargo
LAAT/i: low-altitude assault transport/infantry
larty: a vessel, LAAT/i
lo (loh) *Mando'a*: into

M

Mando (MAHN-do, s.); *Mando'ade* (Mahn-doh-AH-day, pl.) *Mando'ad:* Mandalorian, son/daughter of Mandalore
Mando'a (Mahn-DOH-ah): Mandalorian-language term for the language itself
meat can: soldier (slang)
meg (mayg) *Mando'a:* which, that
meh (mey) *Mando'a:* if
mhi (mee) *Mando'a:* we
MIA: missing in action
MILINT: military intelligence
Mirdala Mird'ika!; Mando'a: Clever Mird!
MRU: much regret, unable (slang)

N

N'oya'kari gihaal, Buir. (Noy-ah KAR-ee gee-HAAL, boo-EER): I've been hunting fish-meal, Father.
nar dralshy'a (NAR-drahl-SHEE-ya) *Mando'a:* put your back into it, try harder
narir (nah-REER, v.) *Mando'a:* to act, to do
naritir (nah-ree-TEER, v.) *Mando'a:* to place, to put

nau'ur (now-OOR, v.) *Mando'a:* to light up, to illuminate
ner (nair) *Mando'a:* my
ni (nee) *Mando'a:* I, me
ni dinui (NEE DEE-noo) *Mando'a:* I give
ni kar'tayl gar darasuum (nee kar-TILE garh dah-RAH-soom) *Mando'a:* I love you
Niktose (neek-TOH-say, pl.) *Mando'a:* Nikto
nynir (nee-NEER, v.) *Mando'a:* to hit, to strike

O

obs job: observation duty
OCU: Organized Crime Unit
op order: operational order
ops room: operations room
ori; Mando'a: very, exceptionally, extremely
osik (OH-sik) *Mando'a:* dung (impolite)
osik'la (oh-SIK-lah) *Mando'a:* badly wrong, horrible, messed up, screwed up, disgusting
oya (OY-ah) *Mando'a:* let's go hunting, let's roll

P

parjir (par-JEER, v.) *Mando'a:* to win, to be victorious
PIM (s.); PIMs (pl.): Position and Intended Movement (naval term for where a ship is and where it is heading)
PEP: pulsed energy projectile
pod: Kaminoan word for squad
PTC: Perlemian Traffic Control
PWO; Peewo: principal weapons officer

R

rayshe'a (ray-SHEE-ah) *Mando'a:* five
RC (s.); RCs (pl.): Republic Commando
recce (s.); recces (pl.); recce (v.): reconnaissance, to reconnoiter (military)
Red Zero: request for immediate extraction (military)
resol (reh-SOL) *Mando'a:* six

RPC: request the pleasure of your company (slang)
rummage: an examination, a search of a vessel (slang)
RV: rendezvous (slang)

S

sa (sah) *Mando'a:* as, like (comparative)
Sep; Seppie: Separatist
sh'ehn (shayn) *Mando'a:* eight
shabiir (sha-BEER, v.) *Mando'a:* to screw up (impolite)
shabla: impolite emphatic adjective in Mando'a
shag Huttese: slave
sharp: needle (slang)
she'cu (SHAY-koo) *Mando'a:* nine
shebs (shebs, s.); *shebse* (SHEB-say, pl.) *Mando'a:* backside, rear
shiny boy: Republic commando (slang)
slot: kill (slang)
SO: Special Operations
SOCO: scenes-of-crime officer, forensics officer
solus (SOH-loos) *Mando'a:* one
SOP (s.); SOPs (pl.): standard operating procedure
su'cuy (soo-KOO-ee) *Mando'a:* hi

T

t'ad (tahd) *Mando'a:* two
ta'raysh (ta-RAYSH) *Mando'a:* ten
Tagwa, lorda. Huttese: Yes, sir.
takisir (TAH-kees-eer, v.) *Mando'a:* to insult
tal (tahl) *Mando'a:* blood
te (tay) *Mando'a:* the (rare)
tihaar (TEE-har) *Mando'a:* an alcoholic drink; a strong, clear spirit made from fruit
tinny (s.); tinnies (pl.): droid (slang)
tion (TEE-on) *Mando'a:* prefix to indicate a question
tion'meh (tee-ON-mey) *Mando'a:* what if
TIOPS: traffic interdiction operations
TIV: traffic interdiction vessel
tome (TOH-may, pl.) *Mando'a:* together
tracyn (trah-SHEEN) *Mando'a:* fire

Triple Zero: Coruscant (military)
triple-A: anti-aircraft artillery
troch (troch) *Mando'a:* certainly
tsad (sahd) *Mando'a:* alliance, group

U

udesii (oo-DAY-see) *Mando'a:* calm down, take it easy
ures (oo-REES) *Mando'a:* without, lacking
urpghurit: obscenity in an unknown language
usenye (oo-SEN-yay) *Mando'a:* go away (very rude; from the same root as *osik*)
UXB: unexploded bomb

V

vaii (vay) *Mando'a:* where
vaii gar ru'cuyi (VAY gahr roo KOO-yee) *Mando'a:* where have you been
verborir (VAIR-bor-EER, v.) *Mando'a*: to buy, to hire, to contract
verd (vaird, s.); *verda* (VAIR-dah, pl.) *Mando'a:* warrior, warriors (archaic plural)
vod (vohd, s.); *vode* (VOH-day, pl.); *vod'ika* (voh-DEE-kah, affectionate) *Mando'a:* brother, sister, comrade, mate
vor'e (VOHR-ay) *Mando'a:* thanks

W

werda (WAIR-dah) *Mando'a:* shadows (i.e., stealth), archaic plural
wet; wets: organic life-form (slang)
white job: clone trooper (slang)

A former defense correspondent and TV and newspaper journalist, **Karen Traviss** has also worked as a police press officer, an advertising copywriter, and a journalism lecturer. She has served in both the Royal Naval Auxiliary Service and the Territorial Army. Since her graduation from the Clarion East class of 2000, her short stories have appeared in *Asimov's, Realms of Fantasy,* and *On Spec*. Her first novel, *City of Pearl,* was published in 2004 to critical acclaim; her second novel is *Crossing the Line*.